the Kentucky Brothers Trilogy

the KENTUCKY BROTHERS TRILOGY

WANDA E. BRUNSTETTER

Print ISBN 978-1-62029-770-4

eBook Editions:
Adobe Digital Edition (.epub) 978-1-62416-038-7
Kindle and MobiPocket Edition (.prc) 978-1-62416-037-0

All scripture quotations are taken from the King James Version of the Bible.

All German-Dutch words are taken from the *Revised Pennsylvania German Dictionary* found in Lancaster County, Pennsylvania.

This book is a work of fiction. Names, characters, places, and incidents are either products of the author's imagination or used fictitiously. Any similarity to actual people, organizations, and/or events is purely coincidental.

For more information about Wanda E. Brunstetter, please access the author's website at the following Internet address: www.wandabrunstetter.com

Thumbnail design: Faceout Studio, www.faceoutstudio.com

Published by Barbour Publishing, Inc., P.O. Box 719, Uhrichsville, OH 44683, www.barbourbooks.com

Our mission is to publish and distribute inspirational products offering exceptional value and biblical encouragement to the masses.

Printed in the United States of America.

the JOURNEY

Fisher Family Tree

Abraham and Sarah Fisher's Children

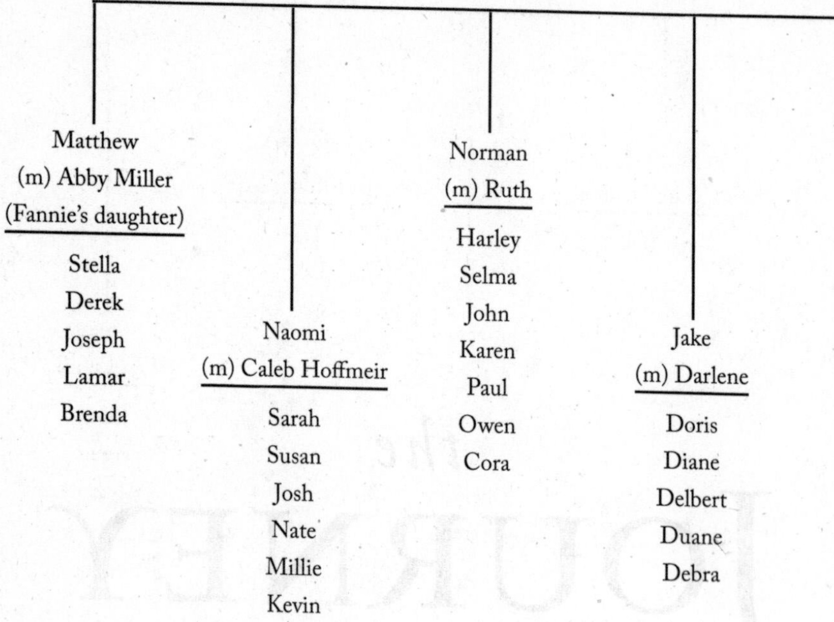

Abraham and Fannie Fisher's Children

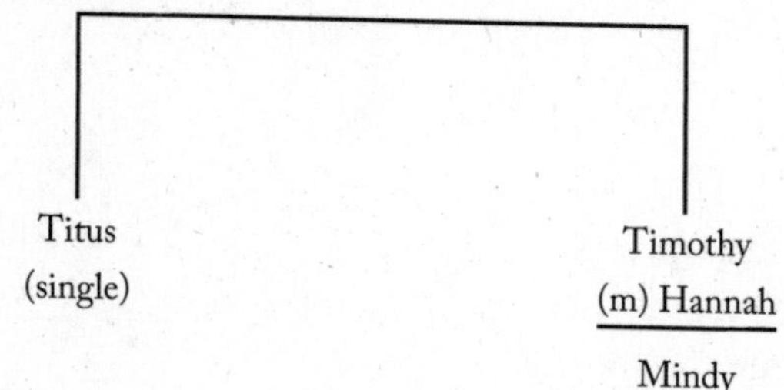

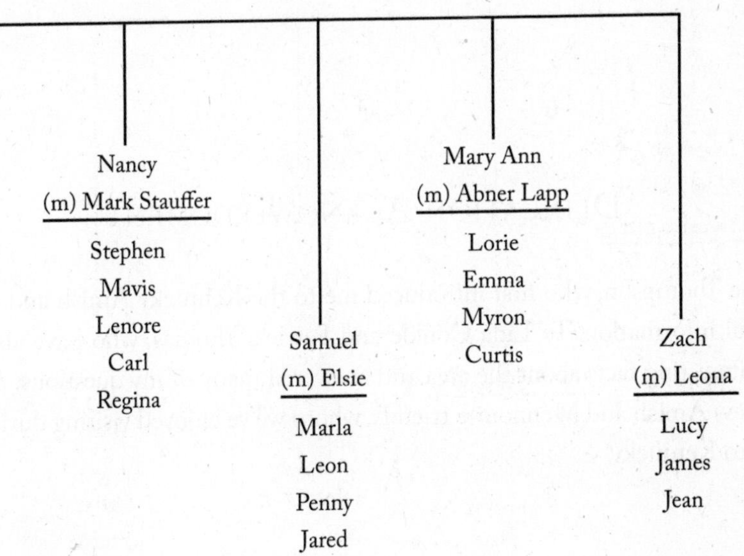

Fannie's Children from her First Marriage

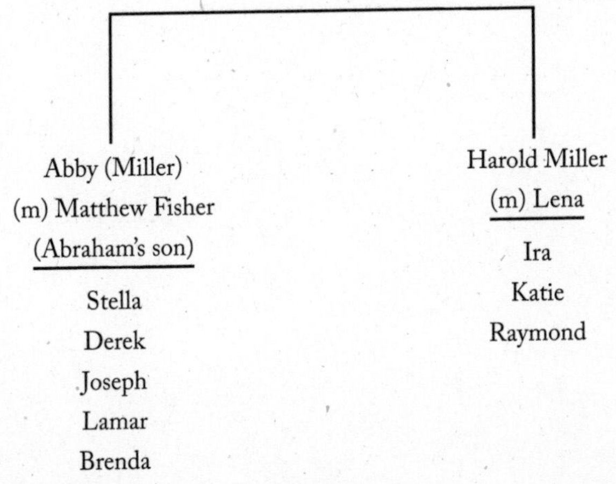

Dedication/Acknowledgment

To Joe Thompson, who first introduced me to the Kentucky Amish and shared helpful information. To Lida Conkle and Patricia Thomas, who have also told me interesting facts about the area and answered many of my questions. And to our new Amish and Mennonite friends, whom we've enjoyed visiting during our trips to Kentucky.

I have learned, in whatsoever state I am, therewith to be content.
Philippians 4:11

Chapter 1

Paradise, Pennsylvania

Titus Fisher liked horses, dogs, and shoofly pie. What he didn't like was a cat that scratched, and a woman he couldn't trust. Today he'd dealt with both.

Gritting his teeth, he grabbed his horse's bridle and led him into the barn, wishing he hadn't gotten out of bed that morning. The day had started on a sour note when Titus had come to the barn to feed the horses and accidentally stepped on one of Mom's cats. Five of the irksome critters lived in the barn, and every one of them liked to bite and scratch. Whiskers, the smallest of the five, was the most aggressive. The crazy cat had been so miffed when Titus stepped on her tail that she'd clawed her way right up his leg, hissing and yowling as she went. When Titus had tried to push Whiskers off, she'd let him have it—leaving a nasty scratch on his leg.

Titus pulled up his pant leg and stared at the wound, still red and swollen. It reminded him of the time when he and his twin brother, Timothy, were six years old and had found a wild cat in the woodpile behind their barn. The mangy critter had bitten Titus's hand, and when the bite became infected, he'd started running a fever. Mom had taken him to the doctor's, where he'd been given a tetanus shot and an antibiotic. Ever since then, he'd had an aversion to cats.

"In my opinion, except for catching mice, cats are pretty much worthless," Titus mumbled as he guided his horse into one of the stalls. When he patted the horse's ebony-colored flanks, the gelding whinnied and flipped his head around to nuzzle Titus's hand. "Not like you, Lightning. You're worth every dollar I paid for you. You're dependable and trustworthy." He grimaced. "Wish I could say the same for Phoebe Stoltzfus."

Titus poured some oats into a bucket, and as his horse ate, he replayed the conversation he'd had with Phoebe on his way home from work that afternoon. . . .

"I'm not ready to join the church yet, and I'm too young to get married." Phoebe flipped the strings of her head covering over her shoulders and blinked her blue eyes. "Why do you have to put so much pressure on me, Titus?"

"I–I'm not," he stammered, "but I've been waiting a long time for you, and I'd thought that when I joined the church two years ago, you'd join, too."

"I wasn't ready then. I was only sixteen and had other things on my mind."

"How well I know that. You were too busy runnin' around with your friends and tryin' out all sorts of worldly things." Titus groaned. "Figured you'd have all that out of your system by now and would be ready to settle down."

She shook her head. "Maybe in a few years I'll be ready."

"You said that two years ago."

"Things have changed." She placed her hand gently on his arm. "My friend Darlene Mast is planning a trip to

Los Angeles, and she's leaving in a few days, so—"

He held up his hand. "Please don't tell me you want to go with her."

"I think it would be fun, and I've always wanted to see the Pacific Ocean." She looked up at him and smiled. "You're full of adventure and like to try new things. Wouldn't you like to see California?"

He shrugged. "Maybe someday, but not right now. What I want is for you to join the church this fall so we can get married."

She shook her head. "I just told you—I'm not ready for that."

"Will you ever be ready?"

"I don't know." She pushed a wisp of soft, auburn hair under her white organdy head covering and turned her gaze away from him. "I—I might not join the church. I might decide to go English."

"Are you kidding?"

"No, I'm not. I don't know if I want to be Amish."

Titus's jaw tightened as the reality of the situation set in. If Phoebe went to California, she might never come back. If she didn't join the church, they couldn't get married. Titus had been in love with Phoebe since he was seventeen years old, but she'd been four years younger than him, and their parents had disapproved. He'd waited patiently until Phoebe turned sixteen. Even then, his folks had been opposed to him courting her because she seemed so unsettled and ran with a wild bunch of kids.

Now Titus, at the age of twenty-two, still wasn't sure he and Phoebe would ever get married. If she did go English, the only way they could marry would be if he broke his vow to the Amish church, which he did not want to do.

"Can we talk about this later?" he asked. "After you've had a chance to think about this some more?"

"There's nothing to think about. I'm going to California." She tipped her head and stared up at him. "If you don't want to come, then I guess it's over between us."

"You can't do this, Phoebe. Are you just going to give up on us like this?"

She shrugged.

"Don't you love me anymore?"

"I–I'm not sure. Maybe we're not meant to be together."

Titus flinched. He felt like he'd been kicked in the stomach by one of his dad's stubborn mules. He had a sinking feeling that once Phoebe left home she'd never come back. All his years of waiting for her had been for nothing.

Titus's horse whinnied and nudged his hand, pulling his thoughts back to the present.

"Stop it, Lightning. I'm not in the mood." Titus kicked at a bale of straw and winced when Lightning whipped his head around and bumped his sore leg.

Lightning whinnied again and stomped his hoof. Then he moved to the other end of his stall and turned his backside toward Titus.

"It's all right, boy. I'm not mad at you." Titus stepped up to the horse and reached out his hand. "I'm upset with Phoebe, that's all."

As though accepting his apology, Lightning nuzzled Titus's neck.

Horses and dogs—that's about all that ever held my interest until Phoebe came along, Titus thought. *If there was only some way to get her out of my system. If I could just tell myself that I don't care anymore.*

the JOURNEY

Pembroke, Kentucky

As Suzanne Yoder stared out the living room window, a sense of discontentment welled in her soul. She enjoyed living in Christian County, especially in the spring when the flowers and trees began to bloom.

I wish I could be outside right now, tilling the garden or even mowing the lawn, she thought with regret. It was too nice to be stuck indoors, yet she knew she needed to work on the quilt she'd started several months ago for her friend Esther Beiler's twenty-fourth birthday, which was less than a month away.

Suzanne's gaze shifted from the garden to the woodshop, where her grandfather and twenty-year-old brother, Nelson, worked. Due to painful arthritis, Grandpa's fingers didn't work well anymore, so he'd recently decided to look for someone else to help Nelson in the shop. Someone younger and more able-bodied. Someone who knew the woodworking trade.

Grandpa wasn't one to sit around or take life easy while others did all the work, but Mom had convinced him that he could still have a hand in the business by ordering supplies, waiting on customers, and keeping the books. Grandpa wasn't happy about it, but at least he wouldn't be sitting on the porch in his rocking chair all day, wishing he could be in the shop.

"I thought you were supposed to be working on Esther's birthday present," Mom said when she joined Suzanne in the living room.

"I was, but my eyes needed a break. I was thinking about going out to the woodshop to see if there's anything I can do to help out."

Mom's dark eyebrows furrowed as she slowly shook her head. "You'll never get that quilt done if you keep procrastinating, and there's no need for you to run out to the woodshop, because I'm sure you and Nelson would only end up in a disagreement. You know how he feels about you hanging around the shop."

Suzanne frowned. No one in the family understood her desire to be in the woodshop, where she could enjoy the distinctive odors of wood being cut, sanded, or stained. It was a shame nobody took her interest in woodworking seriously. Not long ago, Suzanne had borrowed some of Grandpa's tools so she could make a few birdhouses and feeders to put in their yard. She'd never gotten any encouragement in making them, though. She guessed compared to the cabinets, doors, and storage sheds Grandpa and Nelson made, the birdhouses and feeders were insignificant.

Mom touched Suzanne's shoulder. "I'm going to plant some peas and lettuce this afternoon, so if you think you've worked long enough on the quilt today, I could use your help."

Suzanne didn't have to be asked twice. Any chore she could do outdoors would be better than being inside, where it was warm and stuffy. "I'll meet you outside as soon as I put away my quilting supplies," she said.

"That'll be fine." Mom gave Suzanne's arm a light tap and disappeared into the kitchen.

Suzanne glanced out the window once more and sighed as her gaze came to rest on the woodshop. "Guess I won't make it out there today—except to take the men their lunch."

Paradise, Pennsylvania

Titus left the barn and was about to head for the house, when a dark blue pickup rumbled up the driveway. He didn't recognize the vehicle or the young English man with dark curly hair who opened the cab door and stepped out.

"Is this where Zach Fisher lives?" the man asked as he approached Titus.

"Sort of. My dad owns this place, and Zach and his family live in the house behind ours." Titus pointed in that direction.

"Oh, I see. Is Zach at home?"

"Nope, not yet. He's up in Blue Ball, painting the outside of the bowling alley. Probably won't be home till sometime after six."

The man extended his hand. "I'm Allen Walters. I knew Zach when he lived in Puyallup, Washington."

"That was when he thought his name was Jimmy Scott, huh?"

"That's right."

"Zach's my half brother. My twin brother, Timothy, and I were born during the time Zach was missing. He was about six or seven then, I think."

"My mother and the woman Zach thought was his mother became good friends, so Zach and I kind of grew up together."

"Zach's mentioned that," Titus said. "Sure is somethin' the way he was kidnapped when he was a baby and never located his real family until he was twenty-one."

"I really missed Zach after he left Washington, but I'm glad he found his way home." Allen folded his arms and leaned against the side of his truck. "The last time I saw Zach was before he got married, and that was seven years ago. We've kept in touch through letters and phone calls, though."

"Did Zach know you were coming?"

Allen shook his head. "He doesn't know I've moved from Washington State to Kentucky either."

"You're welcome to hang around here until he gets home, because I'm sure he'll be pleased to see you."

"Thanks, I'll do that."

Just then, Titus's mother stepped out of the house and

started across the yard toward them, her slightly plump figure shuffling through the grass.

"This is my mother, Fannie Fisher." Titus motioned to Allen. "Mom, this is Zach's old friend, Allen Walters. He used to live in Washington."

Mom's brown eyes brightened as she shook Allen's hand. "It's nice to finally meet you. Zach's told us a lot about you and your family."

"He's talked to me about his family here, too."

"I explained to Allen that Zach's still at work and said he's welcome to stay here until Zach gets home."

Mom bobbed her head. "Why don't you stay for supper? I'll invite Zach and his family to join us. I think it would be nice for you to meet his wife and children."

"I'd like that," Allen said with an enthusiastic nod.

"If you need a place to spend the night, you're more than welcome to stay here." Mom smiled. "Since Titus is our only son still living at home, we have more than enough room to accommodate guests."

"I appreciate the offer, but I've already reserved a room at a hotel in Bird-in-Hand."

"That's fine, but the offer's open if you change your mind." Mom turned toward the house. "I'd better go back inside and get supper going."

As Mom headed to the house, Titus motioned to a couple of wooden chairs sitting beneath the maple tree on their lawn. "Why don't we take a seat?" he said to Allen. "I'm real interested in hearing why you moved to Kentucky."

Chapter 2

Pembroke, Kentucky

Everything sure looks good," Grandpa said as he seated himself in his chair at the head of the table. "Did you make any part of the meal tonight?" he asked, raising his bushy gray eyebrows as he looked at Suzanne.

"She cut up the cabbage and tomatoes for the coleslaw," Mom said before Suzanne could reply.

"What about the *hinkel*? Who fixed that?" Suzanne's nine-year-old brother, Chad, wearing an expectant expression, pointed to the platter of crispy fried chicken.

"I made the chicken," Mom said.

Chad pushed a hunk of flaming red hair out of his eyes and smacked his lips noisily. "That's *gut* to know, 'cause the last time Suzanne tried to bake a chicken, it came out of the oven chewy like rubber."

"That's because the chicken was old and tough," Suzanne said in her own defense.

The skin around Chad's blue eyes creased as his freckled nose wrinkled. "Wouldn't matter how old the bird was, 'cause you'da done somethin' wrong to it." He touched his jaw. "My mouth was sore the rest of the night after chewin' on that horrible chicken."

Grandpa's pale blue eyes narrowed as he shot the boy a warning look. "That'll be enough. Let's pray so we can eat."

All heads bowed. Suzanne's silent prayer was short and to the point. *Heavenly Father, thank You for this food, and help my family to see that I have other skills that don't involve cooking. Amen.*

Suzanne heard Grandpa rustle his silverware, so she opened her eyes. Everyone else did the same.

"Would ya please pass the macaroni salad?" Suzanne's six-year-old sister, Effie, asked. She had the same red hair and blue eyes as Nelson and Chad, which they'd inherited from their father, who'd died in a farming accident two years ago. Suzanne's hair was more subdued, a combination of her mother's brown hair and her father's red hair.

Suzanne handed Effie the bowl of Mom's zesty macaroni salad, and then she turned to Grandpa and said, "Have you found anyone to work in the woodshop yet?"

He frowned as he shook his nearly bald head. "We'd thought about training Russell, but your uncle Dan needs the boy's help at his dairy, so we've decided to look for someone who already has some woodworking experience."

"There's no need for that," Suzanne was quick to say. "You can hire me."

Her brother Nelson's pale eyebrows lifted high on his forehead. "You're kidding, right?"

"No, I'm not."

"You're not experienced," he said with a shake of his head.

"I've made a few birdhouses and feeders."

"Those are small and don't begin to compare with the finely crafted cabinets, doors, and storage sheds we make in our shop." Nelson motioned to the window facing their yard. "Besides, you've got plenty to do taking care of the vegetables and flowers we grow in our garden and helping Mom in the house."

"But gardening is seasonal, and when I'm in the house for too long, I get bored." Suzanne picked up her napkin and wiped the juice from the chicken on her fingers.

"You wouldn't be bored if you spent more time in the kitchen," Nelson said. "How are you gonna find a husband if you don't learn to cook?"

Suzanne glared at him. "Why does everyone think a woman must marry? I personally don't care if I ever marry."

"You weren't sayin' that last year when you were hopin' James Beiler would start courtin' you," Suzanne's sixteen-year-old brother, Russell, chimed in. He was the only child in the Yoder family who had Mom's brown hair and brown eyes.

Suzanne clenched her fork so tightly that her fingers turned numb. She didn't need the reminder that she'd previously had a crush on Esther's older brother. For a while, it had seemed like James might be interested in her, too, but then he'd started courting Mary Jane Smucker. Last fall they'd gotten married and moved to Lykens, Pennsylvania.

From across the table, Russell squinted his coffee-colored eyes at Suzanne. "I'll bet the reason James dropped you for Mary Jane is 'cause she's such a good cook. About the only thing you can make is soup and sandwiches, and nobody wants that for supper every night."

"That'll be enough," Mom admonished. "Just eat your supper, and leave Suzanne alone."

Chad reached for a drumstick and plopped it on his plate. "Sure am glad Mom knows how to cook."

As much as it hurt to be reminded of her shortcomings, Suzanne knew that her brother was right. Unless she learned to cook, she'd probably never find a man willing to marry her. Well, she wouldn't worry about that until she found a man she was interested in marrying. Right now she needed to concentrate on finding some way to convince Nelson and Grandpa to let her work in their shop.

Until that day comes, she thought, *I'll continue to sneak out to the woodshop when no one's there and see what I can do on my own.*

Paradise, Pennsylvania

"I'm so glad you're here, and I can't wait for you to meet my wife, Leona, and our three kids," Zach said as he, Allen, and Titus made their way across the yard to the picnic tables that had been set up on the lawn.

Allen grinned and draped his arm across Zach's shoulders. "I've wanted to do this for a long time. Just never got around to it until now."

Titus noticed right away the look of happiness on Zach's face. He was obviously pleased to be reunited with his childhood friend.

"So what brings you to our part of the country?" Zach asked, raking his fingers through the sides of his sandy brown hair. "The last time we talked on the phone, you said you were real busy at the carpentry shop in Tacoma and didn't know when you might get away."

Titus was tempted to jump in and share all that Allen had told him that afternoon, but he figured he'd better let Allen do the talking for now.

Allen moved to one of the wooden benches. "Let's sit down. While we're waiting for the rest of your family to show up, I'll tell you the other reason I'm here."

Titus took a seat on one bench, and Allen and Zach sat across from him.

"As you know," Allen began, "after the lumber mill where

I worked in Tacoma shut down, I began working for Todd Foster as a carpenter."

Zach nodded. "That's what Titus does now. He's been working for our brother-in-law, Matthew, for the past year."

"I told him that before you got home," Titus put in.

"Anyway, while I worked for Todd, I built a home that I thought would be for myself. I even acted as my own contractor." Allen leaned his elbows on the table and smiled. "Then before I had a chance to move in, someone offered to buy the house from me. So I sold that home and built several others, which I also ended up selling."

"Is that how you became a full-time general contractor?" Zach questioned.

Allen nodded. "Of course, I had to be licensed and bonded first. Even though I continued to do some of the carpentry on the new homes I built, I hired a paint contractor, an electrician, a plumber, and. . .well, you get the picture."

Zach glanced at Allen's pickup, sitting in the driveway. "The sign on your truck says WALTERS'S CONSTRUCTION, HOPKINSVILLE, KENTUCKY. Is that where you're living now?"

"That's right. After my girlfriend, Sheila, was killed by a drunk driver near the Tacoma mall, I felt like I needed a change."

Zach's eyebrows shot up. "I didn't know about that. I'm sorry, Allen."

"It happened six months ago, and it's my fault for not letting you know. I grieved so hard at first, and then when my cousin Bill, who lives in a small town near Hopkinsville, suggested I move there and start up my business, I jumped at the chance." Allen ran his fingers through his thick curly hair. "I've been working there for the last five months, and since I had some business in Pennsylvania this week, I decided to come see you."

Zach smiled and thumped Allen's shoulder. "I'm real glad you did. I've missed all the times we used to spend together."

"I've missed them, too," Allen said with a nod. "Which is why I'm hoping you might consider the offer I'm about to make."

Zach leaned forward with an expectant look. "What offer's that?"

"I was wondering if you'd like to move to Kentucky and work as a subcontractor for me, painting the houses I build."

Zach clasped his fingers behind his head and squinted his dark brown eyes. "That's an interesting idea, but I was away from my real family for over twenty years when I was living in Washington as Jimmy Scott. There's no way I could move away now and leave them all. Besides, our painting business is doing real well, and I sure couldn't leave Arthur in the lurch."

"I understand, and I'm not trying to pressure you." Allen tapped his fingers along the edge of the table and glanced over at Titus. "I'm also looking for a carpenter who'd be willing to work for one of the Amish men I know in Kentucky. The man has his own woodshop and does quite a bit of my work, but he's got arthritis pretty bad and can't use his hands for woodworking anymore."

"Allen's already talked to me about this, and I said I'd go," Titus spoke up.

"Go where?" Mom asked as she and Dad joined them at the picnic table.

"To Kentucky," Titus replied without hesitation. "Allen knows an Amish man there who needs a carpenter. He phoned the man awhile ago, and when he told him about me, the man said he'd be willing to give me a try."

Deep wrinkles formed across Mom's forehead as her dark eyebrows furrowed. "Why would you want to leave your job here and move to Kentucky?"

"Phoebe and I broke up today."

Mom's brown eyes widened, and her mouth formed an *O*.

"She's going to California with her friend Darlene," Titus explained.

Dad grunted. *"Em Phoebe sei belaudere mehnt net viel."*

"You may think Phoebe's talk doesn't mean very much, but I believe her," Titus said with conviction. "I don't think she's planning to come back, either."

Titus noticed the look of relief on Mom's face. She was obviously glad that Phoebe was leaving.

Dad's steely blue eyes stared intently at Titus. "Just because you and Phoebe broke up doesn't mean you should move to Kentucky."

"I'd like a new start—go someplace where I'm not reminded of Phoebe. I think moving to Kentucky's the best thing for me right now. Allen's agreed to rent a horse trailer so I can take Lightning along. We'll be leaving in the morning."

"You can't be serious!" Mom's voice rose to a high pitch, and her face tightened, making her wrinkles more pronounced.

"Jah, I am," Titus replied.

"What about your job with Matthew?" Zach questioned. "I wonder how he's going to take this news."

"After I made my decision, I called his cell phone and talked to him about it."

"What'd he say?" Dad asked.

"He gave me his blessing and said, since work's been a little slow in his shop lately, he thought he could get along without my help until he can find someone else to take my place."

"You won't make it in Kentucky." Mom shook her head. "You never stick with anything, Titus."

"I stuck with Phoebe—until she dumped me, that is."

"That's true, but sticking with her is nothing to brag about. Phoebe wasn't good for you," Dad said with a scowl.

"Well, I'm hoping Kentucky will be good for me, because I've made up my mind, and that's where I'm planning to go."

Mom planted both hands on her ample hips and whirled around to face Dad. "Abraham, don't just stand there; do something!"

Chapter 3

Hopkinsville, Kentucky

This town isn't as big as some, but I think you'll find everything you need here," Allen told Titus as he pulled his truck into a gas station in Hopkinsville. "There's a hospital, doctors, dentists, chiropractors, restaurants, and plenty of places to shop—including a big Walmart. Most of the Amish who live in the area hire a driver to bring them into town, and I'll make sure you get the names and phone numbers of a couple of people who drive for the Amish."

"I appreciate that." Titus yawned and stretched his arms behind his head. It had been a long drive, and he was tired.

Allen eased his truck up to the pumps and turned off the engine. "As soon as I get some gas, we'll head toward Pembroke, which is where Isaac Yoder's woodshop is located. Once you agreed to come here, I left a message on Isaac's voice mail, letting him know when we'd be leaving, so I'm sure he'll be expecting us soon."

"I hope so. Sure wouldn't want to barge in thinking I have a job and then find out that he didn't know anything about me coming." Titus would never have admitted it to Allen, but he felt nervous about meeting the man he hoped would be his new boss. Starting over in a new place with new people was an adventure, but it was also frightening. What if he messed up? What if Isaac Yoder didn't like his work?

Allen gave the steering wheel a couple of taps. "I've gotten to know Isaac fairly well in the short time I've been here, and I'm guessing that even if he had no idea you were coming, he'd roll out the welcome mat."

Titus chuckled, hoping his nerves wouldn't show. "He sounds like my twin brother, Timothy. He's about as easygoing and friendly as anyone I know."

"After we leave Isaac's place, I'll take you to the trailer I bought as an investment a while back—mostly for the property, though," Allen said. "My real estate agent said the place is fully furnished, but I've only seen the outside, and it's nothing fancy. So I won't charge you much rent, and at least you'll have someplace to live while you're getting settled into your new job and learning your way around."

"Sounds good." A sense of anticipation replaced Titus's nervous thoughts. He'd never been this far from home and realized that this was a good chance to prove his worth to his folks—and to himself.

While Allen pumped the gas, Titus leaned his head back and closed his eyes, letting his thoughts wander. He could still see the pathetic look on Mom's face when he'd said good-bye to her and Dad yesterday morning. She'd pleaded with him not to go, until Dad finally stepped in and told her that they needed to let Titus lead his own life and that he was a grown man and had the right to live wherever he pleased. Mom had tearfully hugged Titus, saying she wished him well, and then she'd said that if things didn't work out for him in Kentucky, he could always come home.

Mom doesn't understand that I need to get away from everything that reminds me of Phoebe, Titus thought. *Even though Phoebe will be in California, if I'd stayed in Pennsylvania I'd see her family, so it would be hard not to think about her. It's better if I make a clean break and start life over here where there are no reminders of the past.*

Titus's stomach growled. He opened his eyes and reached into his backpack, fumbling around for a candy bar. In the process of looking for it, he discovered a note that Phoebe had written him some time ago—when he thought she still loved him.

His stomach tightened. How was he ever going to get her out of his system? He couldn't stop thinking about her, and seeing her love note only made her rejection hurt all the more. He crumpled the note and pushed it into Allen's litter bag.

The truck door opened, and Allen climbed in. "All set!"

"I didn't realize you were done pumping the gas."

"Yep. Ready to meet the man who'll hopefully be your new boss?"

"Uh. . .guess I'm ready as I'll ever be."

"Are you nervous?"

"A little. I've never been this far from home, and starting a new job in a new place is kind of scary," Titus admitted.

Allen nodded. "I'll give you some advice my dad gave me when I left home: 'Those who fear the future are likely to fumble the present.'"

Titus groaned. "I sure don't wanna do that."

"Just do your best and try to keep a positive attitude, and I'm sure everything will work out fine."

"I hope so."

Allen drove out of Hopkinsville and turned left on Highway 68. After they'd gone a few miles, he pointed up ahead. "There's the Jefferson Davis Monument. It's just a couple of roads over to your right."

Titus whistled. "Wow, that building is sure tall!"

"You'll have to go inside the monument sometime and

take a look at the view from up there."

"Think I just might."

"What else would you like to do for fun?" Allen asked.

Titus turned his hands palms up. "Don't really know yet. Maybe some fishing if there's a nearby lake or pond. Oh, and I also like to ride horseback, so hopefully there are some good trails for riding."

"There are several ponds in the area, and I'm sure you can find lots of places to ride your horse. This community doesn't get near as much traffic as Lancaster County, so you can go most anywhere on your horse if you've a mind to."

Titus smiled. "Sounds good to me."

When they reached Pembroke-Fairview Road, Allen turned right. They drove a mile or so, and then he turned onto a dirt road. Titus noticed a sign by the driveway: YODER'S WOODSHOP.

As they continued up the lane, a large white farmhouse came into view. To the left of the house was the woodshop, with another sign above the door. To the right was a huge flower garden with some plants that were just coming into bloom.

As they drew closer, Titus saw a young, auburn-haired woman bent over one of the plants. He took a deep breath, trying to still the pounding of his heart. He couldn't see her face, but from the back, she looked like Phoebe.

Suzanne lifted her head and turned when she heard a vehicle rumble up the driveway. Seeing the sign on the truck, she realized it was Allen Walters. The truck came to a stop, and both doors opened. Allen got out, and so did a young Amish man with dark brown hair whom she'd never seen before.

Grandpa stepped out of the woodshop just then and joined them on the lawn. Curious to know who their visitor was, Suzanne left the garden and hurried into the yard.

"This is Titus Fisher, the young man from Lancaster County, Pennsylvania, I called you about," Allen told Grandpa.

"Glad to meet you." Grandpa shook Titus's hand. Then he looked over at Suzanne and said, "Titus is going to help out in my shop, and if things work out, he'll be hired full-time."

That bit of news didn't set well with Suzanne, but she forced a smile and said, "It's nice to meet you, Titus."

"Same here," he mumbled, staring at Suzanne in a peculiar sort of way. It was almost a look of disgust.

"Titus will be staying in the old trailer I bought awhile back," Allen said.

"Oh, you mean the one Vernon Smucker used to own?" Grandpa asked.

Allen nodded.

"It was sad when the poor man died, because he'd never married and has no family that any of us know about. That old trailer has been sitting empty for quite a spell." Grandpa looked at Allen and slowly shook his head. "I'm surprised you bought the place. Haven't been inside it for a long time, but from what I remember, it was pretty run-down, even when Vernon lived there."

"I bought it as an investment," Allen said. "Figured since there are no homes for rent in the area right now, it'd be a good place for Titus to live."

Grandpa shrugged; then he looked over at Allen's truck and motioned to the horse trailer behind it. "Looks like you've brought a horse with you, huh?"

Allen nodded. "It belongs to Titus."

"I didn't want to leave Lightning behind," Titus explained.

"Didn't you bring a buggy for the horse to pull?" Grandpa asked.

Titus shook his head. "Figured I could ride Lightning to and from work every day."

"That's okay for now," Grandpa said, "but once winter comes, you'll need a buggy."

"I'll get one before then." Titus glanced at Suzanne, and a blotch of red erupted on his cheeks. He cleared his throat and quickly looked away.

Is there something about me he doesn't like? Suzanne wondered.

Just then, Esther Beiler came up the driveway on her scooter. When Esther joined them, Suzanne introduced her to Titus and then added, "This is Titus Fisher. He's from Pennsylvania, and will be working in Grandpa's shop." Suzanne nearly choked on the words. It should be her working for Grandpa, not some stranger who wouldn't even make eye contact with her.

Esther smiled politely, and her milk-chocolate brown eyes shone brightly in the sunlight as she shook Titus's hand. "It's nice to meet you."

"Nice to meet you, too." Titus returned the smile and looked directly at Esther when he spoke. Apparently he found her more favorable to look at than Suzanne. Esther was an attractive young woman—dark brown hair, pretty brown eyes, and a dimpled smile that turned many men's heads. Suzanne felt plain compared to Esther.

"Where in Pennsylvania did you live?" Esther asked.

"Lancaster County, in Paradise. My oldest sister and her husband own a general store there, and several others in my family have businesses there, too."

"My folks lived in Strasburg when I was a baby, but Dad moved our family here before I started school," Esther said.

"Could be my folks and your folks know some of the same people," Titus said.

The sun-dappled leaves of the trees overhead cast a shadow across Esther's pretty face as she nodded. "I wouldn't be surprised."

"You all can get better acquainted some other time." Allen

motioned to the woodshop. "Right now, I think we ought to head in there and meet Suzanne's brother Nelson."

Titus gave Esther another quick smile. "It was nice meeting you." Then he glanced at Suzanne, looked away, and mumbled, "Uh—you, too."

As the men walked away, and the women headed for the porch, Esther whispered, "Titus seems nice, and he's sure good-looking, wouldn't you say?"

Suzanne shrugged. "I suppose so, but he acted kind of odd and would barely look at me."

Esther giggled. "Maybe he saw that smudge of dirt on the end of your *naas*."

Suzanne groaned and swiped her finger over her nose. "So that's what it was. Before you came, I was working in the garden. Guess I must have touched my naas with my dirty finger."

They sat on the porch swing, and Esther glanced at the woodshop. "I hope Titus likes it here enough to stay. We could use more available young men in our area."

"How do you know he's available?"

"You didn't see a beard on his face, did you?"

"No, but that only proves he's not married. It doesn't mean he's not courting someone in Pennsylvania. He could even have plans to be married."

"Are you going to ask?"

Suzanne pushed her feet against the porch to get the swing moving. "No way! If you want to know, you should ask."

Esther grinned, revealing the two deep dimples in her cheeks. "I might, if the opportunity comes up."

"How about now? Why don't you go to the woodshop and see what you can find out?"

Esther halted the swing. "*Ach*, I couldn't do that."

"Why not?"

"He'd think I was too bold. Besides, he and Allen are

talking business with your grandpa and Nelson right now."

"So how are you going to find out what you want to know?"

"I'll ask, but just not in front of anyone." Esther's elbow bumped Suzanne's arm. "Are you interested in him at all?"

"Of course not. I don't even know him."

"Then you wouldn't mind if I took an interest in him?"

"Not at all. I'm sure he'd be more interested in you than he would me, anyway."

"What makes you say that?"

Suzanne held up her index finger. "For one thing, you can cook and I can't."

Esther lifted her gaze toward the porch ceiling. "That's nobody's fault but your own. You're twenty-two years old, and you should have learned to cook by now. If you don't learn soon, you may never find a man."

"I've tried cooking a few things, but Mom has no patience with me in the kitchen. Whenever I mess up she gets frustrated and ends up doing it herself. Why, just last week I tried making some bread." Suzanne groaned. "The crust was so hard, I thought I might have to cut it with a saw."

Esther snickered. "I know you're exaggerating, but if you want to learn how to cook, I'd be happy to teach you."

"Thanks anyway, but there are lots of other things I'd rather be doing. Besides, I'm not interested in finding a man right now."

"Do you think you ever will be?"

Suzanne shrugged. "Maybe someday. . .if I can find one who cooks."

Chapter 4

What did you think of the Yoders?" Allen asked Titus as they headed down the road in his truck again.

"They seem nice enough. I think Nelson and I will get along fine, and hopefully Isaac will be pleased with my work and hire me full-time."

"What'd you think of Nelson's sister Suzanne?"

"I. . .uh. . .can't really say. Didn't talk to her long enough to form an opinion." Titus turned toward the window and spotted several horses grazing in the pasture of an Amish farm. *I came here to forget about Phoebe and start a new life, and what did I find? A woman who looks so much like Phoebe she could be her sister!*

Since Isaac's woodshop was on the same piece of property as the Yoders' home, he'd probably see a lot of Suzanne. Every time he saw her, he'd think of Phoebe, who'd be sitting on some sandy beach in California with nothing on her mind but sunning herself and having lots of fun.

Sure wish I hadn't wasted all those years waiting for her, he thought with regret. *Should have listened to Mom and Dad when they said Phoebe was too young and immature for me. I can't believe I was dumb enough to believe she'd be ready to join the church and marry me when she turned eighteen. She was probably leading me on so I wouldn't court anyone else.*

"Here we are. This is the trailer I was telling you about," Allen said, breaking into Titus's disconcerting thoughts.

Titus stared out the truck window in disbelief. The dilapidated, single-wide trailer had metal siding that was dented in places. Fake-looking shutters hung lopsided at the filthy windows, one of which was obviously cracked. The steps leading to the front door looked slanted, the screen door hung by only one hinge, and the porch sagged like an empty sack of potatoes. If the outside of the trailer was any indication of what the place looked like inside, Titus knew he'd be in for a lot of work to make it habitable.

As though sensing Titus's reservations, Allen offered him a reassuring smile. "Sorry about the condition of the place. Guess the outside needs a little more work than I'd thought. Let's go inside and take a look. Hopefully it's not so bad." He opened the truck door and stepped out. Titus did the same.

As they walked through the tall grass, a crow swooped down from the pine tree overhead, flapping its wings and screeching as though Titus were an intruder. At the moment, that's what he felt like.

"Watch out for that hole," Allen said as Titus stepped onto the porch.

Too late—Titus's foot slipped into the crevice, knocking him off balance. He grabbed the handle on the screen door to keep from falling over and pulled the door right off the hinge. *Oomph!*—he landed on his backside with the screen door on top of him.

Allen picked up the screen and slung it into the yard. "Are you okay?"

Titus clambered to his feet, feeling like a complete fool. "I'm fine. Just never expected that to happen. Guess I should have though; I'm always doing something stupid to embarrass myself."

Allen studied him, then shrugged and opened the front door. "You might want to use the back door until we can get some work done to the porch," he said.

Titus stepped inside and halted. "Ugh! What's that disgusting odor?"

Allen's nose twitched like a rabbit's. "It smells musty in here. I think once we get some windows open and the place airs out, it should be okay."

Oh Lord, what have I gotten myself into? Titus silently moaned. *Maybe I should have listened to Mom and stayed in Pennsylvania. Maybe I'm not capable of making any right decisions.*

—~—

Paradise, Pennsylvania

As Phoebe tossed a few clothes into her suitcase, she thought about Titus and wished he'd been more understanding about her going to California. If he hadn't already joined the church, she was sure he'd have been willing to go with her. Maybe she could get him to change his mind.

Tap. Tap. Tap. "Phoebe, are you in there?"

"Jah, Mom. Come in."

When Phoebe's mother entered the room, she stopped short and stared at Phoebe's suitcase lying on the bed. "I—I was hoping you'd change your mind about going."

Phoebe shook her head. "I'll be leaving this evening after Darlene gets off work."

Mom pursed her lips, and her pale blue eyes narrowed. "If that young woman runs off to California, I doubt her job at the restaurant in Bird-in-Hand will be waiting for her when she gets back, and you might not have a job cleaning house for our neighbors either."

"It doesn't matter. We'll both find other jobs." Phoebe shrugged. "If we come back, that is."

Mom sank onto the edge of Phoebe's bed. "Don't tell me you're thinking of staying in California permanently. I thought you were just going for a short time—to see what it's like on the West Coast."

"I might stay there if I like it." *And even if I don't. Anything to get away from you and Dad always telling me what to do.*

"I guess that means you have no plans to join the Amish church?"

"I don't know yet. I need more time to think about it. I want to enjoy some of the things the English world has to offer. I want to see the Pacific Ocean and walk on the beach."

A few wisps of Mom's faded auburn hair, now streaked with some gray, peeked out from under her covering as she lowered her head. "You've been to a couple of New Jersey beaches with your friends. I don't understand why you think you need to go clear across the country to walk on the beach."

"It's different in California. Darlene's been there once, and she said I would like it."

Mom folded her arms and met Phoebe's gaze. "What about Titus? He's been waiting for you all these years, you know."

Phoebe grunted. "Like you care about that. You and Dad have never liked Titus."

"It's not that we don't like him. We just knew you were too young to think about courtship when he first took an interest in you. Once you turned eighteen, we had no objections to him courting you."

"Well, he shouldn't have been in such a hurry to join the

church. He should have given me more time to decide what I wanted to do." Phoebe closed the lid on her suitcase and zipped it shut. "I don't want to talk about this anymore. I've gotta go."

"But if you're not leaving until this evening, what's the hurry?"

"I'm going over to the Fishers' to see if I can get Titus to change his mind and go to California with us."

—∞—

"You look so *mied*, Mom. Why don't you have a seat while I pour us some tea?" Fannie's daughter, Abby, motioned to the kitchen table.

Fannie pulled out a chair and sighed as she sat down. "You're right. I am tired. Hardly slept at all last night."

Abby poured them both a cup of tea and sat down next to Fannie. "You look awfully sad, too. Are you still *brutzich* over Titus moving to Kentucky?" Abby's dark eyes revealed the depth of her concern.

"I suppose I am fretful," Fannie admitted. "I just can't believe he made such a hasty decision or that Matthew was okay with it. Titus hasn't been working for him very long, and he should have been more considerate about leaving Matthew in the lurch."

"Matthew's fine with Titus's decision, Mom. His business is slow right now, and when it picks up again, he'll hire someone else. Maybe one of Norman's boys will be interested in learning the woodworking trade."

Fannie blew on her tea. "Seems like everything was going along fine one day, and the next day, that English friend of Zach's showed up and whisked my *bu* away."

Abby chuckled. "Titus is hardly a boy."

Fannie sniffed, struggling to hold back the tears threatening to spill over. "Doesn't he care about us anymore?"

"When someone chooses to move away from home, it doesn't mean they don't care about their family. Remember, Mom, you left Ohio and moved here so you could marry Abraham. When you made that decision, I didn't take it personally or think you didn't care about me anymore."

Fannie plucked a napkin from the wicker basket in the center of the table and dabbed at her tears. "I realize that, but I wasn't running from something the way Titus is. Besides, it wasn't long after I moved to Pennsylvania that you came here, too."

"But when you left Ohio, you didn't know I'd eventually move. Only God knew that." Abby took a sip of her tea. "If you're really upset about Titus leaving, maybe you and Abraham should consider moving to Kentucky."

"And leave the rest of our family?" Fannie shook her head vigorously. "Never!"

"You're not living close to Harold and his family," Abby reminded.

"That's different. Your brother didn't move away when I was living in Ohio."

"No, you did." Abby set her cup down and placed her hand on Fannie's arm. "When I first came to Pennsylvania to help when you were pregnant, I never thought I'd move here permanently. It was only to be until after the twins were born and I was sure you could handle things on your own. If my boyfriend, Lester, hadn't died in that horrible fire, trying to save my quilts, I would have gone back to Ohio to marry him as soon as you were able to handle things on your own." Deep wrinkles formed across her forehead. "After Lester died, I saw no reason to stay in Ohio. So in a way, I was doing exactly what Titus has done. I left one place and moved to another in order to get away from unpleasant memories."

Fannie blew her nose on the napkin. "I know you're right, but it's more than just missing Titus that has me so upset."

"What else?"

"I'm worried that since one of my sons has left home, some of the others may decide to leave, too." Fannie nearly choked on the sob rising in her throat. "If more of the family goes, I don't think I could stand it. I really don't."

"As Abraham always says, 'Let's not put the buggy before the horse.' All the men in our family have good jobs here, so it's not likely that any of them will leave Pennsylvania."

"I hope you're right."

A knock sounded on the back door, interrupting their conversation.

"I wonder who that could be." Fannie dabbed at her tears again. "I really don't feel like company today."

"I'll go see." The chair scraped noisily across the linoleum as Abby pushed it aside and stood. "Should I tell whoever it is that you're not up to visitors today?"

Fannie waved a hand. "No, don't do that. It would seem rude. You'd better just invite whoever it is to come in."

Abby left the kitchen and returned moments later with Phoebe Stoltzfus at her side.

Fannie clenched her fingers so tightly that the damp napkin she held began to pull apart. The last person she wanted to see right now was the young woman responsible for her son's decision to move away.

"Is Titus here?" Phoebe asked. "I need to speak to him."

Fannie shook her head. "No, he's—"

"I stopped by Matthew's woodshop but it was closed, so I thought maybe Matthew had gone somewhere with his family and had given Titus the day off."

"Matthew had some errands to run in town, and as you can see, I'm right here," Abby said. "And of course, our *kinner* are in school today." She looked over at Fannie. "Would you like to tell her, or should I?"

"Tell me what?" Phoebe pulled out a chair and sat down.

Fannie's lips compressed as she tapped her fingers along the edge of the table. "Titus is gone—moved to Kentucky—thanks to you."

Phoebe's eyebrows shot up. "Are you serious?"

Fannie gave a nod. "Took all his clothes and even his horse."

"But. . .but I had no idea Titus was planning to leave Pennsylvania. He didn't say a word about it when I talked to him the other day." Phoebe wrinkled her nose, as though some foul odor had permeated the room. "Some people have a lot of nerve!"

"Jah, they sure do." Fannie stared hard at Phoebe. "And I'm looking at such a person right now."

Phoebe's face flamed. "You think it's my fault that Titus moved to Kentucky?"

"That's exactly what I think. He made the decision after you broke up with him and said you were going to California."

"I didn't actually break up with him. I just said—"

"It makes no never mind. Titus is gone, and he left because of you."

Phoebe sat with a shocked expression. Then with a loud *humph*, she jumped up, nearly knocking over her chair, and dashed out the door.

Fannie blew out her breath in exasperation. "I know it's not right to wish the worst for anyone, but I hope that selfish young woman is miserable in California and gets exactly what she deserves!"

Chapter 5

Western Pennsylvania

Phoebe leaned her head against the window in the passenger's side of Darlene's car and closed her eyes. They'd left Lancaster County earlier that evening, after a tearful good-bye from Phoebe's parents. Mom had begged her not to go, and Dad had given her a stern lecture on not becoming caught up in worldly pleasures.

I still can't believe Titus went to Kentucky without telling me, Phoebe thought bitterly. *What's in Kentucky, anyhow? Will Titus find someone else to take my place? Will he end up marrying someone there and stay in Kentucky for good? Should I have listened to him and stayed in Pennsylvania? Should I have agreed to join the church and marry him? But if I'd stayed in Pennsylvania, I might never have had the chance to see California. Besides, I have a lot more living to do before I tie myself down to a husband and kids.*

"I'll bet he doesn't stay in Kentucky even a year," she muttered under her breath.

"What was that?" Darlene asked.

Phoebe's eyes snapped open. "Oh, nothing. I was just thinking out loud."

"Thinking about Titus Fisher, I'll bet." Darlene flipped her blond ponytail over her shoulder. Dressed in a pair of blue jeans and a pink T-shirt, she looked nothing like the plain Amish girl who'd gone to the one-room schoolhouse with Phoebe for eight years.

Phoebe glanced at her own pair of jeans. Mom and Dad had never approved when she'd worn English clothes. They rarely approved of anything she did.

Darlene nudged Phoebe's ribs with her elbow. "Were you thinking about Titus or not?"

"Yes, and I still can't believe he moved to Kentucky."

"Maybe it's for the best."

"What's that supposed to mean?"

"If he'd stayed in Pennsylvania, you might have felt obligated to return home and join the church. This way, you're free to stay in California if you want to."

"I guess you're right." Phoebe yawned. "Sorry. I can hardly stay awake."

"Well, go to sleep then. I'll wake you when I'm ready to stop for the night."

Phoebe closed her eyes and rested her head against the window. She was bound to feel better once they reached Los Angeles.

—ʬ—

Pembroke, Kentucky

When Titus woke up the following morning after a restless night on a lumpy bed, he hurried to get dressed, then made his way to the kitchen. As he passed through the small living room, he stopped and surveyed his surroundings, wondering if he'd been out of his mind for agreeing to stay here. The paneling on the living room walls had been painted an odd shade of yellow; the upholstery on the old rocking chair and sofa was torn; and the only throw rug on the floor was frayed around the edges.

He moved on to the kitchen to check out that tiny room. The hinges on the cabinets were rusty; only one burner on the propane stove worked; the porcelain sink was full of rust stains; the curtains were faded; and several places in the linoleum had been torn, revealing the wooden floor beneath it. Titus had left all the windows open last night, in an effort to air the place out, but he could still smell some mustiness. Obviously nothing had been done to maintain this trailer in a good many years.

Titus opened each of the cupboard doors and groaned. Not a stick of food in the house, of course. Allen had offered to take him shopping last night, but he'd gotten an urgent call from one of his contractors and said he had to rush off. Titus had assured him that he could survive for a while on the snack food he'd brought from home and would get to a store on his own after work today.

Think I'd better eat that granola bar in my backpack, saddle Lightning, and head over to the woodshop, Titus told himself. *It wouldn't be good for me to be late on the first day—especially since I haven't proven myself to Isaac Yoder yet.*

—⁂—

It was almost noon when Suzanne's mother suggested that Suzanne take the sandwiches she'd made out to the woodshop for the men.

"Can't you take them out?" Suzanne asked.

Mom's forehead wrinkled. "You take the men's lunch out to them nearly every day, so why not now?"

"I feel funny around Titus. I don't think he likes me."

"For goodness' sake, Suzanne, he hasn't had a chance to

get to know you, so why would you think he doesn't like you?"

"When he was here yesterday he looked at me in disgust, and then after that he would hardly look at me at all. Esther said it was probably because I had a dirt smudge on my nose, but I think it may have been something more."

"He's probably shy. Give him a chance to get to know you before making assumptions." Mom handed Suzanne the lunch basket. "Now would you please take the men's lunch out to them?"

"Are you sure you won't do it?"

Mom shook her head. "I need to get some baking done, but if you'd rather do the baking, then I'd be happy to take the sandwiches out to the woodshop."

"No way! If I did the baking, nobody would speak to me for the rest of the week because I'm sure I'd ruin whatever I tried to make."

"If you spent more time in the kitchen, you might have learned how to bake by now."

Suzanne didn't say anything in her own defense. She'd had this discussion with Mom before, and apparently Mom didn't realize just how impatient she could be when it came to working in her kitchen. Suzanne figured making excuses to stay out of the kitchen was easier than telling Mom the truth.

"I made enough sandwiches so Titus can have one, too," Mom said. "Unless he went shopping last night, he may not have brought any lunch with him this morning, because I'm sure there was no food in that old trailer."

Suzanne wrinkled her nose. "If there had been, it surely would have been spoiled by now." Lunch basket in one hand, and a jug of lemonade in the other, she turned and hurried out the door.

When Suzanne entered the shop, she found Titus and Nelson sanding some cabinet doors while Grandpa sat at his desk writing something in the ledger.

"I brought your lunch," Suzanne said, placing the wicker basket and lemonade on the desk beside him.

"*Danki.*" Grandpa smiled up at her. "Did you bring enough for Titus, too?"

"Jah." She cast a quick glance in Titus's direction.

"I appreciate that," Titus said, without looking at her. "I haven't had a chance to buy groceries yet, so I didn't bring a lunch with me today."

Suzanne frowned. *He still won't look at me. I wonder why?*

"No need for you to ever bring your lunch to work," Grandpa said. "I'm sure my daughter will be happy to provide your noon meals." He motioned to Suzanne and smiled. "And my helpful granddaughter will bring it out to us whenever she's home."

"What'd you bring today?" Nelson asked, moving across the room toward Suzanne.

"Ham sandwiches, lemonade, and some peanut butter cookies," she replied.

"Did you make the cookies, or did Mom?"

"Mom did."

Nelson's only response was a quick nod.

Suzanne was relieved that neither he nor Grandpa had said anything about her lack of cooking skills. It would be embarrassing to have that announced in front of someone she barely knew.

While the men ate their lunch, Suzanne looked at the set of cabinets Titus and Nelson had been working on. Her fingers ached to pick up a hammer and begin a project of her own. She knew that wouldn't be appreciated, though—especially by Nelson. He'd probably ask her to leave.

In no hurry to return to the house, Suzanne grabbed a broom and started sweeping up the pile of sawdust on the floor. While she swept, she listened to the men's conversation, occasionally peeking at Titus. It didn't take her long to learn that he had a twin brother named Timothy, who'd been married to Hannah almost two years, and that they had a one-year-old daughter, Mindy.

"Your *bruder* must have gotten married when he was pretty young." Nelson thumped Titus's arm. "You don't look like you're much more than twenty years old."

"I'll be twenty-three in October. Mom's always said that Timothy and I have baby faces." Titus's face sobered. "Timothy was twenty when he married Hannah, and she was more than willing to become his wife. But then things always seem to go the way he plans."

"How many other brothers and sisters do you have?" Nelson asked, apparently unaware of Titus's attitude when he'd spoken about his twin.

"Timothy's my only full brother, but we have three half sisters and five half brothers from my *daed's* first marriage. Our *mamm* and her first husband had a girl and a boy several years before Timothy and I were born, so that gives us another half brother and sister. All my siblings are married except for me," Titus added with a frown. At least Suzanne thought it was a frown. Maybe he just had a case of indigestion.

"So your folks were both widowed for some time before you were born?" Grandpa asked.

"Jah."

Nelson whistled. "You have a big family. Ours is small by comparison."

"How many brothers and sisters do you have?" Titus asked.

"Besides Suzanne, there's Russell, Chad, and our little sister, Effie."

"I guess that is small compared to ours." Titus reached for a cookie and took a bite. "Umm. . .this is good." He glanced over at Suzanne, frowned, and then quickly averted his gaze.

Not this again. He's got that look of disgust. Does he think I was listening in on his conversation? Is he irritated that I'm still in the shop? Maybe he thinks like Nelson, that a woman's place is in the house.

When the men finished their lunch, Suzanne set the broom aside and gathered up the sandwich wrappings and empty jug of lemonade; then she put everything in the basket. "I'm going back to the house now," she said to Grandpa. "Is there anything else you'd like me to bring out to you?"

He smiled. "I think we're fine. If we get thirsty we'll drink water from the jug in the ice chest in the back room."

"Okay. See you at suppertime." Suzanne hurried from the shop. At least she'd learned a few things about Titus. She still didn't know whether he had a girlfriend or not.

Of course, she reasoned, *it's not my job to find that out. Esther's the one who's interested in him, and she did say she would ask. I just wonder when she'll do it, and what she'll find out.*

Chapter 6

Paradise, Pennsylvania

As Fannie stood at the kitchen sink, peeling potatoes for supper, her thoughts went to Titus. He'd used Allen's cell phone to let them know he'd made it to Kentucky, but she didn't know how often they might hear from him in the days ahead. She planned to write letters, of course, but knowing Titus, it was doubtful that he'd take the time to write back. Probably would just leave messages on their voice mail from time to time, and she'd never get to speak to him directly.

"What are you thinkin' about?" Abraham asked, touching Fannie's shoulder.

She whirled around. "Ach, you startled me!"

"Sorry."

"How do you know I was thinking about anything?"

He gave her arm a gentle squeeze. " 'Cause I said your name three times, and you just stood there, staring out the window without saying a word."

"I was thinking about Titus and how much I miss him."

"I miss him, too, but we still have the rest of our family living here."

She nodded. "Just doesn't seem the same without one of our special twins."

"The twins are special," Abraham agreed. "Havin' those boys was such a comfort to me after Zach was kidnapped."

"I know they were." Fannie set her potato peeler aside. "Let's sit down so we can be comfortable while we talk."

They sat across from each other at the table. "The twins didn't take the place of my lost son, but they sure filled an empty spot in my heart," Abraham said.

She nodded. "Even though I thought I was too old to have any more *bopplin*, when the twins came along, it was a blessing to me as well."

Abraham smiled. "Remember when Titus and Timothy were teenagers, and how much they liked to joke around?"

"Jah. One of the things they did to irritate each other was to grab the other one's hat and toss it into a tree."

"And remember the time when the boys were fooling around and got too close to a pile of manure?" He reached for the plate of pickles she'd cut up before starting the potatoes and popped one into his mouth. "They ended up with that stinky stuff all over themselves."

Fannie crinkled her nose. "What a stench that was! It took two or three good scrubbings before I had the smell out of their clothes, and I don't know how much soap and water they used to get their bodies smelling good again."

Abraham chuckled. "Another prank those two often pulled was pretending to be each other. 'Course I've always been able to tell 'em apart, because Titus's left eye is a little bit larger than his right eye, whereas the shape of Timothy's eyes is about the same."

"It's the difference in their personalities that's always let me know which twin is which," Fannie said. "Timothy's easygoing and doesn't let much bother him. But Titus has always been impulsive and kind of headstrong."

Abraham gave a nod. "Timothy's a steady worker and has been satisfied to farm with me and work part-time as a painter for Zach. Titus has tried several different jobs and becomes easily distracted."

"Between the two of them, Titus is more immature." Fannie sighed. "Why, that boy couldn't even do his chores without being reminded all the time. I have to wonder how long he'll stick with the new job in Kentucky."

Abraham grabbed another pickle. "I think he'll do okay. Once he starts working, he works hard and does a good job. He just needs to be on his own so he can grow up. I believe Titus might be on a journey to discover himself, and we need to let him find his own way."

"Do you think he'll ever get over Phoebe Stoltzfus?" Fannie asked, going to get the coffeepot from the stove.

"I hope so. Maybe he'll find someone new in Kentucky—someone more mature and settled into the Amish ways—someone who'll make him a good *fraa*."

Fannie frowned. "I'd rather he came back here to find a wife. If he marries a woman from there, he'll probably never move back home."

"I know it's hard for you to see one of our sons move away," Abraham said, as she handed him a cup of coffee. "It's hard for me, too."

Fannie sniffed. "I never thought any of the kinner would decide to leave."

"As much as it hurts to have Titus gone, we need to accept his decision and realize that it's probably for the best."

"Why do you say that?"

"Think about it. If he'd stayed here and kept pursuing Phoebe, she may have hurt him again and again."

"But she's gone to California," Fannie said. "I don't see how she could hurt him from there."

"She'll be back." Abraham grunted and slapped the table with the palm of his hand. "Mark my words, that girl won't last long out there in California among the English."

—w—

Pembroke, Kentucky

"We've put in a good day, but it's time to call it quits," Nelson said, setting his hammer aside.

Titus did the same. "Say, I need to stock up on some food. Can you tell me where the nearest store is located?"

"We do our big shopping at the Walmart in Hopkinsville, but there's an Amish-run store in the area, and they carry most of our basic needs, as well as some bulk foods."

"Where is it?" Titus asked.

"Just off Highway 115—the Pembroke-Fairview Road over near the Fairview Produce Auction. You probably went past the place when Allen brought you here yesterday."

"I don't recall. Just remember seeing the Jefferson Davis Monument."

"The store's not far from there."

Titus grabbed a pen and scribbled the directions on his arm.

Nelson's eyebrows lifted high. "There's no need to mark up your arm with a pen. I'll write it down for you." He quickly scrawled the directions on a tablet and handed it to Titus.

Titus smiled. "Danki."

"How you planning to get to the store?" Isaac questioned.

"Figured I'd ride over on Lightning."

Isaac grunted as he shook his head. "You're gonna need somethin' bigger than the back of your horse to carry groceries home. Why don't you go up to the house and see if Suzanne's free to drive you to the store? Tell her she can take my horse and buggy if she wants."

Titus hesitated near the door. He wasn't sure he wanted Suzanne to take him anywhere. But he guessed Isaac was right—he couldn't carry all the groceries he'd need on the back of Lightning. He grabbed his straw hat from the wall peg near the door, plunked it on his head, and headed out the door. "See you both tomorrow," he called over his shoulder.

When Titus stepped onto the Yoders' back porch, an orange, white, and black calico cat whizzed past his leg. Startled, he jumped back, nearly clipping the critter's tail.

"Go on! Get away! Shoo!"

The cat hissed at Titus, leaped off the porch, and bounded away.

"Stupid *katz*," Titus mumbled as he knocked on the door.

A few seconds went by; then Suzanne opened the door. "Can I help you with something?" she asked, tipping her head.

Seeing her again made Titus's heartbeat pick up speed. He sure wished she didn't remind him so much of Phoebe.

"I. . .uh. . .need to get some food and a few other things, and Nelson said there's a store nearby."

"That would be the Beilers' store. You met Esther Beiler yesterday."

Titus shuffled his feet, feeling more uncomfortable by the second. "Umm. . . your grandpa said I should ask if you'd mind taking me there. Said you could use his horse and buggy."

Suzanne's mother, Verna, stepped out of the house just then. Titus had met her briefly when he left the shop the day before. "I need a few things at the store myself," she said, smiling at Titus. "So Suzanne would be happy to take you to the store."

Suzanne shot her mother a questioning look, but she didn't offer a word of protest.

"You can tie Titus's horse to the back of the buggy, and then when you're done shopping you can drop Titus off at the trailer," Verna said.

"Oh, okay," Suzanne mumbled.

Titus suspected by the slump of Suzanne's shoulders that she wasn't happy about accompanying him to the store. Well, he could understand that because he wasn't thrilled about going with her, either.

—w—

As Suzanne and Titus climbed into Grandpa's buggy, one of Suzanne's cats—a fluffy gray one—leaped in and jumped up on the seat between them.

"Get out of here!" Titus muttered as he pushed the cat out.

Suzanne ground her teeth. He obviously didn't like cats any more than he liked her.

As they headed down the road toward the store, Suzanne tried to make conversation, but that was hard to do when Titus didn't say much in response.

"What's that?" Suzanne asked, when she noticed some writing on Titus's arm.

"What's what?"

"That." She pointed to his arm.

Titus's face colored. "Oh, I. . .uh. . .started writing the directions to the store when your brother told me. . ."

"I can't believe you'd write a note on your arm."

"It's easier than carrying a tablet with me all the time. I've been doing it since I was a kinner." He'd spoken without looking at her again.

Suzanne didn't say what she was thinking, that writing notes on his arm was really strange.

When they arrived at the store, she left Titus to do his shopping while she went after the things Mom needed. She'd just started down the bulk foods aisle when Esther joined her, wearing a frown.

"I thought you weren't interested in Titus."

"I'm not."

"Then what are you doing here with him?"

"He needed to come to the store, and since he doesn't have a buggy, Grandpa volunteered me to take him."

"Oh, I see. Did you find out whether he has a girlfriend or not?"

"No, you said you were going to do that."

"I will, but I need to wait for the right opportunity. I can't just go up to him and say, 'Oh, by the way, I was wondering if you have a girlfriend in Pennsylvania.' "

Suzanne bit back a chuckle. "No, I guess that would seem too bold."

"Why don't you ask him?"

"Why me?"

"Because with him working in the woodshop, you'll see him more often than I will."

"I can't just blurt it out, but if the subject comes up, I'll ask. Does that make you happy?"

Esther's face broke into a wide smile. "I'll be even happier if he's available."

—⁂—

When Titus finished shopping, he found Suzanne talking to her friend. He said a quick hello to Esther and then told Suzanne that he'd gotten everything he needed and was ready to go whenever she was.

"Great. I'll be done soon."

A short time later, Titus and Suzanne paid for their purchases, said good-bye to Esther, and climbed into the buggy. They'd no sooner pulled away from the store, when it started to rain.

"Does it rain much here?" he asked.

"In the spring, mostly, but we can have showers any time."

They talked more about the weather and the kinds of trees and plants that grew in the woods along the road. Titus listened with interest as Suzanne told him that maple, cedar, river birch, willow, and pine trees grew in the area, and that a bush called crape myrtle could grow to be anywhere from fifteen to twenty feet high and six to fifteen feet wide.

"Crape myrtles put on a show all year long," Suzanne said. "Their long-blooming flowers come in pink, red, white, and lavender. In the fall, the leaves turn yellow or red, then drop off to reveal peeling gray and brown bark."

"Seems like you know a lot about flowers and trees," Titus commented, glancing briefly her way. At least he'd been able to make eye contact with Suzanne now that the shock of her looking so much like Phoebe had worn off.

"I enjoy doing almost anything that takes me outdoors, and I also enjoy—" Suzanne pointed to a rabbit skittering into the woods. "Do you like to hunt?"

He nodded. "I've gone deer hunting with my half brothers Jake and Norman a few times."

"I like to hunt and fish," she said, "but Nelson thinks women shouldn't do things like that."

Titus glanced at Suzanne again. She might look like Phoebe, but there were definitely some differences. Phoebe wouldn't go near a hunting rifle, or even a fishing pole. She liked adventure but not the kind that involved tromping through the woods or sitting by a pond for hours, waiting for a fish to bite.

"Do you miss your family?" Suzanne asked, changing the subject.

"I probably will, but I haven't been gone long enough to miss anyone too much yet."

"Not even a girlfriend?"

"Huh?"

"I wondered if you might have a girlfriend back in Pennsylvania."

"I did have one," he mumbled, wishing she hadn't brought the subject up. "But that relationship's over now."

"Oh, I see."

They rode in silence the rest of the way, with the only sounds being the splatter of raindrops against the roof of the buggy and the steady *clip-clop* of the horse's hooves on the road. Titus was glad when Suzanne didn't question him further about Phoebe. It wasn't something he wanted to talk about right now.

When they arrived at the trailer, Titus hopped down from the buggy, untied his horse, and led him to the barn, which wasn't in much better shape than the trailer. Then he returned to the buggy for his groceries. "Danki for the ride," he said, giving Suzanne a nod.

"You're welcome."

As Suzanne's horse and buggy pulled away, Titus hurried into the trailer. When he entered the kitchen, he screeched to a halt. A huge puddle of water sat in the middle of the floor.

Chapter 7

It rained all night, and Titus had trouble sleeping, with the constant *ping, ping, ping* of the water dripping into the pan he'd set on the kitchen floor. No wonder the house smelled so musty. This probably wasn't the first time the roof had leaked. To top it off, he'd discovered some fresh mouse droppings under the kitchen sink and inside a couple of the cupboards. He figured he must have at least one mouse in the house. He'd have to see about getting a couple of traps to take care of that.

Guess I'd better climb up on the roof and see about patching the place where the water's been coming through before I leave for work today, Titus thought as he forced himself to crawl out of bed the next morning. He would have done it last night if it hadn't been raining so hard. So he'd put up with the dripping and spent the evening cleaning out the propane refrigerator, as well as the cupboards, before putting away his groceries. As soon as he got his first paycheck, he planned to hire a driver and go to Hopkinsville to get a new mattress for his bed. If his new job worked out well and he decided to stay in Kentucky permanently, he'd need to find a better place to live, because this trailer wasn't fit for the mice.

—∞—

"I can't believe Allen would expect Titus to live in Vernon Smucker's old trailer," Suzanne said to her mother as they scurried around the kitchen getting breakfast on the table. "I didn't get to see the inside, but if it's anything like what I saw outside, Titus has a lot of work ahead of him to make that place livable."

"I never thought much about it, but you're probably right," Mom said, turning from the stove where she was frying some bacon. "Vernon's trailer has been abandoned for quite a while now, and it's probably not fit for anyone to live in. I think we ought to talk to my daed and Nelson and see about getting a crew of people together for a work frolic soon. The trailer might be livable if a group of us helped fix it up."

"Who are we helping?" Grandpa asked when he and Nelson entered the kitchen.

"Titus," Mom answered. "Suzanne said the trailer he's living in looks pretty bad from the outside, and I'm guessing it's going to need a lot of repairs inside as well. So I was thinking we ought to have a work frolic to help him fix the place up."

"That's a good idea," Nelson said with a nod. "Titus told me yesterday that the place is a mess."

"I'll talk to some folks in our area and see about setting a date for the frolic," Grandpa said. "If we'd known sooner that Allen was bringing someone to work in the woodshop, and that he'd have him stay in Vernon's old place, we could have had the trailer cleaned and repaired before Titus got here."

—∞—

Titus was relieved when he found a ladder, a hammer, some

nails, and a roll of tar paper in the old shed behind the trailer. He would use the tar paper to patch the wooden part of the roof, and when he had the chance to buy some shingles he'd finish the job.

As he set the ladder in place and began to climb, a bird chirped from a nearby tree. "I'm glad someone's in a happy mood this morning," Titus muttered. "I'll bet you wouldn't be singin' so cheerfully if you had to fix a roof."

Titus usually wasn't so negative, but ever since he and Phoebe had broken up, he couldn't seem to find anything cheerful to think about. He needed something positive to focus on—something to get excited about and look forward to.

As the bird continued to sing, Titus stepped onto the roof and glanced around, looking for any low spots where water might be lying. He discovered one area, and was heading in that direction, when—*crack*!—a hunk of wood gave way and his foot went through.

His boot hit something, and he looked down through the hole. "Oh, great. I think I'm standing on the refrigerator!" Titus gritted his teeth and pulled his leg out of the hole. Now he'd have to look for a piece of plywood to repair that hole.

He moved cautiously toward the ladder, wincing from the pain in his calf. He leaned over and pulled up his pant leg. Blood oozed from scratches and a cut.

"Guess I'd better get my leg cleaned up and bandaged before I try to patch this stupid roof," he mumbled. It was a good thing he'd thought to buy a bottle of peroxide and a box of bandages when he'd gone to the store yesterday.

Titus limped his way down the ladder and moved slowly toward the back door. This was not the best way to start out his morning.

What a dummkopp *I am. This is so typical.* He gritted his teeth. *I'll bet this wouldn't have happened to Timothy. He'd have probably seen that rotten board in time to keep from stepping on it. If I hadn't been distracted by that stupid chirping bird, maybe I would've seen it, too.*

Titus shook his negative thoughts aside. He couldn't waste time being angry at himself. He needed to get inside and tend to his leg.

After cleaning the wound, Titus was relieved to see that the cut wasn't too deep and wouldn't require stitches. However, a large bruise was already forming, and it had begun to throb. Well, he couldn't let it stop him from getting the roof patched, so as soon as he'd put a bandage on, he grabbed the hammer from the kitchen counter and limped out the door.

Sometime later, with the roof temporarily patched, Titus saddled Lightning and headed to work.

As he approached the Yoders', he spotted their phone shanty at the end of the driveway. *Since I'm already late, I may as well stop and make a phone call,* he decided.

Titus tied Lightning to a tree and stepped into the shanty; then he took a seat on the folding chair and dialed his twin brother's number. Of course no one answered, because it wasn't likely that anyone from Timothy's family would be in their phone shanty. He left a message on their voice mail, telling Timothy about the condition of the trailer, and asking him to tell their folks he said hello.

When Titus entered the woodshop, he found Nelson sanding a door. "Sorry I'm late," he apologized.

Nelson frowned. "It's a good thing Grandpa's not here right now. He's always believed in starting work on time. He'd probably say, 'No rule of success will work if you don't.'"

"Sorry," Titus mumbled. "I had a rough morning."

"What happened?"

Titus explained about repairing the roof.

"That trailer needs a lot of work." Titus slowly shook his head. "I didn't know the roof was bad until it rained yesterday and left me with a puddle in the middle of the kitchen floor. There's so much work to be done I hardly know where to begin."

"Not to worry," Nelson said. "Grandpa's out right now, spreading the word that the trailer needs repairs, and we're planning to have a work frolic there on Saturday."

"That'd be great." Titus felt relieved. It would be much easier to make the place livable if he didn't have to do it alone. "Is there anything special you'd like me to do today, or should I continue with the cabinets I was working on yesterday?" he asked.

"You can work on the cabinets, and if you're not done when I finish with this door, I'll help you with 'em."

"Okay."

Titus and Nelson worked in silence the rest of the morning. Shortly before noon, Allen showed up. "Thought I'd better come by and see how you're doing," he said, thumping Titus on the back.

Titus groaned. "With the exception of a leaky roof, a scraped-up leg, some problems with mice, and a trailer that needs lots of repairs, I'm doing great."

Allen's thick, dark eyebrows met at the bridge of his nose. "I'd let you bunk in with me, but my house is on the other side of Hopkinsville. With my job taking me all over the place right now, I wouldn't have time to bring you to work every day."

"It's okay. I'm sure the trailer will be fine once it's fixed up."

"My grandpa's out right now, telling folks about the work frolic we're planning for this Saturday," Nelson said.

Allen smiled. "That's good to hear, and I'll be there to help out, too. In fact, I'll go over to the trailer when I leave here and do some measuring so we'll know how much roofing material will be needed."

"That'd be much appreciated," Nelson said. "With your carpentry skills and ours, I'm sure we'll get the job done twice as fast."

"Speaking of carpentry skills, I've just contracted to build a new house on the other side of Hopkinsville, and I'd like you to make the cabinets and doors for it," Allen said.

Nelson nodded enthusiastically. "Sure thing. We're always glad for any work that comes up."

"Great. I'll be by to discuss the details with you as soon as I hear from the homeowners about what type of wood they'd like." Allen turned toward the door. "See you both on Saturday."

~

Suzanne had been working on Esther's quilt most of the morning, but she hadn't accomplished a lot. That was probably because she kept glancing out the window at the birds swooping down from the trees to get a drink of water from one of the birdbaths in their yard. She hated being cooped up in the house on such a warm spring day, but if she didn't work on the quilt, she'd never get it done in time for Esther's birthday.

Suzanne made a few more stitches, glanced out the window again, and was surprised to see Esther walking across the lawn toward the house. Not wanting Esther to see the quilt, she put her needle down and hurried outside.

"I hear there's going to be a work frolic on Saturday to fix up the old trailer where Titus is staying," Esther said when Suzanne joined her on the lawn.

Suzanne could tell from Esther's eager expression that she planned to go to the frolic. "When we found out that the trailer needed lots of repairs, Grandpa decided to schedule the frolic," Suzanne said.

Esther bobbed her head. "He came by our place this morning and told us about it."

"I assume you're planning to go?"

"Oh jah. My folks will have to work at the store on Saturday, but they said I could go to the frolic to help out." Esther smiled. "If I get the chance to speak with Titus alone that day, I may work up the nerve to ask if he has a girlfriend."

"You don't have to do that now," Suzanne said. "I already asked."

Esther's eyes widened. "You—you did?"

"I said I would, remember?"

"Oh, that's right. Guess I didn't figure you'd follow through."

"When I drove him home from the store yesterday, he was talking about his family, so I asked if he had a girlfriend in Pennsylvania."

"What'd he say?"

"He used to have one, but doesn't now."

Esther grinned. "So maybe he might take an interest in me."

"Could be. He's sure not interested in me."

"How do you know?"

"Because he doesn't say much to me, and when he does, he barely makes eye contact."

"Maybe he's shy."

"That's what Mom thinks, but I don't believe so because from what Nelson and Grandpa said at breakfast this morning, Titus had a lot of things to say to them yesterday when they were showing him around the shop."

The back door opened, and Mom stepped onto the porch. "I have lunch ready for the men, and I'd like you to take it out to them," she called to Suzanne.

"Okay."

Esther touched Suzanne's arm. "Mind if I go with you?"

"Suit yourself." She took the basket from Mom and headed for the woodshop, with Esther hurrying along at her side.

When they entered the shop, Suzanne set the basket on Grandpa's desk. "Are you ready for a break? Mom made you some lunch," she said to Nelson, who was sanding a door.

"We're more than ready," he said with a nod.

"Jah, me, too." Titus set the can of stain aside and reached for a rag to wipe his hands. "Things didn't go well for me this morning, and there was no time to make any breakfast," he said without looking at Suzanne.

"What happened?" Esther asked, moving to stand beside him.

He looked right at her, which only confirmed to Suzanne that he liked Esther but was repulsed by her. "My leg got banged up when I fell through the roof, tryin' to fix a hole."

Esther frowned. "That's *baremlich*. You weren't hurt bad, I hope."

"Just a cut, some scratches, and an ugly bruise, but I'll be okay."

"I don't think anyone ought to be living in that old trailer right now," Esther said.

Titus bobbed his head. "I can't argue with that, but the mice sure don't mind, 'cause I've seen evidence of 'em under the sink and in a couple of the lower cupboards."

"What you need is a cat to take care of the mice," Suzanne spoke up. "You can have one of ours if you like."

He shook his head. "Thanks for the offer, but I can take care of the mice by setting some traps."

Suzanne merely shrugged in reply. She couldn't believe he'd rather set traps than let one of her cats keep the mice away.

Maybe it's because I offered him the cat, she thought. *If Esther had offered, I'll bet he would have said yes.*

Suzanne didn't wait around for the men to eat their lunch. Instead, she turned to Esther and said, "I'm going back to the house. Are you coming?"

Esther's gaze went to Titus, then back to Suzanne. "I guess so."

When they stepped outside, Esther plopped her hands against her hips and glared at Suzanne.

"What's wrong?"

"How am I supposed to get Titus interested in me if I can't spend any time with him?"

"No one said you had to leave the shop."

"I wasn't about to stay there and watch Titus and Nelson eat their lunch after you announced that you were leaving." Esther's dark eyebrows drew together. "What's your hurry getting back to the house, anyway?"

Suzanne shrugged. "No hurry. I just didn't feel like watching the men eat. Besides, I'm uncomfortable around Titus. He makes me feel like I'm always wearing *dreck* on my naas."

"You don't have any dirt on your nose today." Esther snickered and touched the end of Suzanne's nose. "Unless he thought one of your little freckles was a speck of dirt."

"That's not funny." Suzanne hurried her steps toward the house. If Mom seriously expected her to bring lunch out to the men every day, Suzanne would just run into the shop, set the basket on the desk, and run back out.

Of course, she reasoned, *if I do that, I'll miss seeing what projects the men are working on, and I can learn a lot from watching. Guess I'll have to take one day at a time and hope Titus becomes a little friendlier once he gets to know me better.*

Chapter 8

Paradise, Pennsylvania

Timothy Fisher had just left the chiropractor's for an adjustment in his lower back, when he decided to stop by Naomi and Caleb's store to say hello before heading home.

"It's good to see you," Naomi said from behind the counter, where she had been reading a copy of one of their Amish newspapers, *The Budget*. It was hard to believe she was forty-seven, because she looked like she was in her thirties. There wasn't a speck of gray in her golden brown hair, and she could still see perfectly without reading glasses, which their younger sister Nancy often wore.

"Good to see you, too. Have you been busy here today?" he asked.

"We sure have, and this is the first chance I've had to take a break." Her cocoa-colored eyes showed no sign of fatigue when she smiled. "Of course, it's springtime, when the tourists start flocking to our area."

His brows furrowed as he leaned on the counter. "I know the tourists are good for business, but I wish they wouldn't stare at us Plain People or snap pictures right in our faces."

Naomi shook her head. "Not every tourist does that, and I think those who stare are probably just curious about our lifestyle and the way we dress."

"I guess you're right, but there are times when I'd like to pack up my family and move someplace where there aren't so many tourists."

"You're not thinking of joining Titus in Kentucky, I hope."

"The idea is kind of tempting, but I don't think Hannah would agree to move. She likes it here, and she and her mamm are really close." He rubbed his fingers along the edge of the counter. "Sometimes I think she and Sally are too close. Hannah goes over there almost every day, and she thinks she has to ask her mamm's advice about everything she does."

Naomi stared down at her paper. Timothy figured she was either bored with the conversation or agreed with him about Hannah being too close to her mother, but was too polite to say so.

"Titus left me a voice mail this morning," he said, changing the subject.

She looked up. "What'd he say?"

"Said he's not happy about the place Allen expects him to rent."

"What's wrong with it?"

"Just about everything, I guess. The roof leaks; the furniture's torn and saggy; the walls need painting; the yard's overgrown with weeds; and the place has *meis*."

Naomi grimaced. "I could put up with a leaky roof and torn furniture, but I can't tolerate mice."

"A few cats would probably take care of his problem, but you know my twin. He hasn't liked cats since we were kinner and that wild cat bit him."

"He ought to be over that by now," she said.

"Titus doesn't get over anything too easily. Why do you

think he moved to Kentucky?"

"He's probably trying to get away from the pain of Phoebe breaking up with him, but moving away from a painful situation isn't always the answer. When I left home many years ago, it was to try and forget the pain of leaving Zach on the picnic table." Naomi sighed. "It didn't do a thing to relieve my guilty conscience, though."

Timothy knew the story well. Even though he and Titus hadn't been born when the kidnapping took place, they'd grown up hearing about how Zach had been taken right out of their yard after Naomi had gone into the house to get cold root beer for a customer. It turned out that the man who'd stolen Zach lived in Puyallup, Washington, and Zach had grown up there, not knowing his real family was Amish and lived in Paradise, Pennsylvania. By the time Zach found out about it and came to Lancaster County in search of his identity, Timothy and Titus were teenagers.

"The past's in the past," Timothy said, smiling at Naomi. "What counts is what we do with today."

She nodded. "I just hope Titus learns that and will make the most of each new day."

Pembroke, Kentucky

Soon after Titus got home from work, he decided to go out to the shed to put the ladder away, as he hadn't taken the time to do it when he'd come down from the roof that morning.

Once he put the ladder back, he went to the barn to see if he could find anything he might use to fix up the place. He spotted a canvas tarp, and when he pulled it back, he was surprised to see an old buggy in need of repairs. He figured with some new wheels, a new windshield, and lots of elbow grease, it would be useable. He pushed the buggy to the middle of the barn. Maybe after the frolic, he'd have time to work on it. Right now, getting the trailer livable was his first priority.

Titus's stomach growled noisily, reminding him that he hadn't eaten since noon. "Guess I'd better get in the house and see about fixing some supper."

He'd just stepped onto the porch when a horse and buggy pulled into the yard. He was surprised to see Suzanne get out and secure her horse to the hitching rail.

"I brought you something," she called.

Curious to see what it was, Titus joined her beside the buggy. He was even more surprised when she reached into the buggy and lifted out the same calico cat he'd seen at the Yoders'.

"This is for you," she said, holding the critter out to him.

Titus took a step back. "What makes you think I want a katz?"

"Her name is Callie, and she'll help keep the mice down."

He shook his head determinedly. "I told you today, I don't need a cat. I'm planning to set some traps for the mice."

"But Callie's a good mouser, and she'll keep you company."

"Don't need any cat company. I've got my horse."

"But horses don't catch mice."

"I appreciate the offer, but I really don't want a cat."

Suzanne's furrowed brows, and the droop of her shoulders, let him know that he'd probably hurt her feelings.

"I appreciate you coming by," Titus said, hoping to ease the tension. "I'll see you tomorrow." He turned and hurried into the house, eager to fix something to eat.

He'd just taken out a loaf of bread and some lunchmeat to make a sandwich when he heard a noise on the porch. He opened the door to step outside, when the calico cat zipped between his legs and darted into the house.

Titus glanced at the hitching rail and saw that Suzanne's horse and buggy were gone. "That's just great!" He gritted his teeth. "I told her no, but she left the stupid katz here anyway. Tomorrow morning I'm taking the critter back to Suzanne, and she'd better not try anything like that again."

Chapter 9

When Titus stepped out his front door the next morning, he nearly tripped over something furry on the porch. He looked down and groaned. The stupid calico cat was curled into a ball, purring loudly.

Before Titus had gone to bed last night, he hadn't seen any sign of Callie, so he'd assumed she'd left and hopefully found her way back to the Yoders'.

"Well, you're going back now." Titus bent down to pick up the cat, but she opened her eyes, let out a piercing howl, and leaped off the porch like she'd been hit with a bolt of lightning. Titus took after the animal in hot pursuit.

Round and round the yard they went, until Titus was panting for breath. Was it any wonder he didn't like cats? They were nothing but trouble.

Callie headed for the porch again, and Titus followed, his jaw set with determination.

Crouched in one corner of the porch, the cat's hair stood on end as she hissed at Titus.

"*Kumme*, kitty. Come here to me now." Titus reached out his hand, and was almost touching the cat, when she swiped the end of his finger with her needle-like claws.

"Yeow!" Titus drew back quickly, and frowned when he saw blood.

The cat continued to hiss as she hunched her back and eyeballed Titus as though daring him to come closer.

Titus stood still a few seconds. He lunged again. This time Callie lunged, too. She sank her teeth into Titus's hand, and he let out another yelp. The cat let go, gave one final hiss, and tore off into the woods.

Titus rushed into the trailer to get a bandage and some antiseptic. It was a cinch that he wasn't going to catch the cat this morning. Maybe he'd scared her badly enough that she wouldn't come back. Hopefully the critter had enough smarts to head for home.

Paradise, Pennsylvania

"Sure wish we'd hear something more from Titus," Fannie said to Abraham as they sat at the kitchen table, eating breakfast. "I went out to the phone shanty and checked our voice mail this morning, but there were no messages from him."

"He called when he got to Kentucky, and he's only been gone a few days," Abraham said. "Give him some time; I'm sure he'll call again soon."

"Maybe we should plan a trip to Kentucky to see him. I'd feel better if I knew what it was like and saw for myself that he was doing okay."

Abraham shook his head. "I don't think Titus would appreciate us checkin' up on him. He needs to make it on his own without our interference. Besides, Timothy and I are in the middle of planting season, and I don't have time to be making any trips." He patted Fannie's arm gently. "You know what your problem is?"

"What?"

"You're too protective of our kinner...especially the twins."

Fannie took a sip of her coffee and was about to say something more on the subject, when the back door swung open and Timothy stepped into the room.

"*Guder mariye*," he said.

"Mornin'," Abraham mumbled around a mouthful of toast.

"Help yourself to a cup of coffee and come join us at the table," Fannie invited.

"Don't mind if I do."

"How's your back doin'?" Abraham asked as Timothy poured himself a cup of coffee and then pulled out a chair at the table and sat down.

"Better. The adjustment Dr. Dan gave me yesterday really helped."

Fannie smiled. "That's good to hear. It's never fun to have a sore back."

"I'll be ready to join you in the field as soon as I've finished my coffee," Abraham said.

"No hurry. Take your time." Timothy looked over at Fannie and smiled. "I thought you might like to know that I had a voice mail message from Titus yesterday."

She perked right up. "Really? What'd it say?"

"He mostly talked about the trailer he's renting from Allen. Said it's a mess and will need a lot of work to make it livable."

Fannie frowned. "Didn't Allen know the place needed work when he suggested Titus move in there? What was he thinking?"

Timothy shrugged. "Beats me. Maybe he didn't know the place was so bad."

"He should have known since he owns the place," Abraham interjected.

"Well, I'm just glad Titus left a message for me, because it's strange having him gone, and I sure do miss him."

Fannie sighed deeply. It didn't seem right that the twins were separated. They'd always been so close. Now that Titus was living two states away, he and Timothy might drift apart.

She directed her gaze toward the window, focusing on two finches eating from the feeder hanging in the maple tree. She thought about how mother birds push their babies out of the nest so they can make it on their own and wondered if Abraham was right. Maybe she was overprotective where her two youngest boys were concerned.

Pembroke, Kentucky

Suzanne had just gone outside to hang some clothes on the line, when Titus rode into the yard on his horse. She found it interesting that he rode horseback, when almost everyone else in their community traveled by horse and buggy. But then, Titus seemed a bit different from the young Amish men she'd grown up around.

She watched as he dismounted and led his horse to the barn. A short time later, he reappeared and strode over to where she stood by the clothesline.

His eyebrows furrowed, and that same look of disgust she'd seen before settled over his face. "Would you mind tellin' me why you left your *dumm* katz at my place when I asked you not to?"

"I didn't, and Callie's not stupid. She jumped out of the buggy when I was driving away, and I figured she'd follow me home."

"Well, she didn't. She made herself at home on my porch, and then when I tried to catch her this morning, so I could bring her back here, this is what I got for my trouble." Titus held up his bandaged finger and frowned.

Suzanne felt concern. "Did Callie bite you?"

"Jah, and then she ran into the woods."

"I can't believe it. Callie never bites."

"Well, she bit me."

"I'm sorry. Does it hurt much?"

"It sure does, and it won't be easy tryin' to work with a sore hand today."

Suzanne was tempted to offer her help in the woodshop but knew Nelson would never agree to that, no matter how much work needed to be done.

"You'd better keep an eye on that bite," she said. "Cats have a lot of bacteria in their mouths, and the wound might get infected."

"I know all about that. It happened to me once when I was a boy." He held up his finger and waved it around. "I put some antiseptic on it, so I'm sure it'll be fine."

Suzanne was about to suggest that Titus go to the clinic and get a tetanus shot, but he started walking away.

"Wait! I wanted to say something else," she called.

He halted and turned to face her. "What?"

When she took a step toward him, her foot slipped on a rock, and she swayed unsteadily.

He reached out to catch her. "You okay?"

Suzanne's face heated with embarrassment. "I–I'm fine. Just lost my balance when my toe hit a rock."

"So what'd you want to say to me?"

"I was just going to say that if Callie shows up at your place again, maybe you should consider keeping her."

His eyebrows shot up. "Are you kidding?"

She shook her head. "She probably bit you because she was scared. If you'd give her a chance, you'd see that she'd not only keep the mice down, but would make a good pet."

He held up his hand again. "Would a good pet do this?"

Before Suzanne could respond, he turned and stomped off toward the shop.

Suzanne clenched her teeth. It seemed like she couldn't say anything right to Titus, and if she wasn't saying something to irritate him, she was doing something stupid to embarrass herself. Maybe the best thing would be to stay as far away from him as possible. But with the work frolic coming up on Saturday, that might be kind of hard to do. Unless she could think of some excuse not to go.

CHAPTER 10

Los Angeles, California

"Don't you just love it here?" Darlene asked Phoebe, as they flopped onto the beach towel she'd placed on the sand.

"It's okay, I guess." Truth was, California wasn't anything like Phoebe had expected, although she'd never admit that to Darlene. Jobs were hard to find, prices were high, and too many people crowded around. But she did like the beach access, and she sure couldn't have had that available to her at home. She also liked the warm sunshine and all the cute guys she'd seen on the beach.

Phoebe had been lucky to find a job at a local ice-cream parlor, but it was boring work, and her wrist hurt when she had to scoop out the hard ice cream to make a cone. Darlene was working as a waitress at a restaurant, which she said paid better tips than her wages. They'd pooled their money to pay rent on a small, one-bedroom apartment, but the place was run-down and not in the best part of town.

While Darlene stretched out on the towel with her eyes closed, Phoebe stared at the waves lapping against the shore, and her thoughts went to home. What were Mom and Dad doing right now? Did they miss her? If she decided to stay in California permanently, would they ever come for a visit? Did she want them to? If they came, they'd no doubt spend the whole time criticizing everything she did and complain about how overcrowded it was. It would probably be best if she didn't encourage them to come.

As a group of young men started a game of volleyball, Phoebe thought about Titus and how many times the two of them had been involved in volleyball games back home. Even when she wasn't one of the players, she'd enjoyed watching from the sidelines.

I'll bet if Titus was here right now, he'd be involved in that game, she thought. *He's always liked volleyball.*

Phoebe scooped up a handful of sand and dumped it on Darlene's bare toes.

Darlene's eyes popped open. "Hey! What'd you do that for?"

"Let's see if we can join that game of volleyball."

Darlene grinned and clambered to her feet. "Good idea. Let's do it!"

Pembroke, Kentucky

When Titus woke up on Saturday to the early morning light, he glanced out his bedroom window and was relieved to see that the sun was shining brightly. Having nice weather would make it easier for those coming to help him work on the trailer.

Titus stepped into the dim hallway, blinked, took a few steps, and stubbed his toe. "Ouch! Guess I should have put my boots away last night, instead of leaving 'em in the hall. If this place was bigger, I'd have more room for things."

He moved on to the bathroom to wash his face, and halted

inside the door. That stupid calico cat was curled into a ball, sleeping in the sink!

He frowned. "How in the world did you get in the house?"

The cat's only response was a quiet *meow*.

Titus had given up trying to return the critter to Suzanne. Every time he'd made an attempt to catch the cat, she'd escaped his grasp. He'd resigned himself to the fact that he was stuck with her, and after seeing the remains of a few mice in the yard, he had to admit, she was a pretty good mouser. He figured as long as she stayed outside he could put up with her, but he wasn't about to invite the mangy critter into his house.

He glared at the cat. "So how'd you get in? I know I didn't leave the front or back door open, and I closed all the windows that don't have screens."

The cat continued to sleep, apparently oblivious to Titus's presence.

Well, he couldn't worry about how she got in right now. What he needed to do was find a way to get her outside without picking her up, because he didn't want to chance getting scratched or bitten again.

Maybe if I throw something over the cat, I can pick her up that way. Titus pulled a bath towel off the hook behind the door, and was ready to drop it over Callie, when she came awake, leaped into the air, and landed on his shoulder.

Her sharp claws dug into his flesh, and he let out a screech. Callie hopped off his shoulder and raced out of the bathroom like her tail was on fire. Titus followed, hollering, "Stupid katz! You're nothing but trouble!"

When he reached the kitchen, where the cat stood, hunched and hissing, he opened the back door, grabbed the broom from the utility closet, and pushed the animal out the door. "Get outside! You don't belong in here!"

Titus slammed the door behind Callie and drew in a deep

breath. If that crazy cat was going to stick around, she'd better learn her place.

He started making a pot of coffee, figuring it wouldn't be long before people began showing up for the work frolic. Beyond the benefit of getting the trailer fixed up, today would give him a chance to meet more of the Amish people who lived in this community.

Titus had just set a bowl of cereal on the table, when he heard a vehicle rumble into the yard. He moved over to the sink and peered out the window in time to see Allen step out of his truck.

Titus opened the back door cautiously, to make sure the stupid cat wasn't waiting for another chance to get inside. Fortunately, she was nowhere in sight.

"Come in for a cup of coffee," he said when Allen stepped onto the porch.

"That sounds good. I need something to wake up this morning."

"You're the first one here," Titus said, leading the way to his cramped kitchen.

Allen glanced around the room and released a low whistle. "I know I saw it the night I brought you here, but it looks even worse than I remember. If I'd known how bad it was, I would have found you somewhere else to stay until we could get the place fixed up."

Titus handed Allen a cup of coffee and motioned for him to take a seat at the table. "If my folks saw where I'm living, Dad would probably say it was the kind of challenge I need, and that it would do me good to rough it for a while. But if Mom saw the way the trailer looks, especially the kitchen, she'd get all worked up and insist that I come right home."

Allen chuckled. "Most mothers are like that where their kids are concerned. They don't want to see them go through any trials or deal with hardships." He blew on his coffee, then took a sip. "When I left Washington to move here, my mother fussed and carried on like I was moving to a foreign country where nobody spoke English and no one had indoor plumbing."

Titus grimaced. "When I first laid eyes on this place, I had my doubts about whether there was indoor plumbing. Figured for sure I'd be stuck using an outhouse and would have to take a bath in a galvanized tub."

"I guess in some parts of the country that's still how it is," Allen said, "but most of the Amish, as well as the Horse and Buggy Mennonites who live around here, have indoor plumbing. Although I do know of a few women in the area who do their laundry in a tub outside."

Titus's eyebrows furrowed as he stared into his coffee. "My mom wouldn't like that, and most of the Amish women I know wouldn't either." His thoughts went to Phoebe. He was sure that she'd never put up with such primitive conditions. She didn't even like using her mother's gas-powered wringer washer, which they kept in the basement. She'd sometimes taken her clothes to one of the local Laundromats in Lancaster County, saying it was easier, and that the clothes came out softer when they'd been dried in an automatic dryer, rather than on a line.

"Why the furrowed brows?" Allen asked Titus.

"I was just thinking about having to wash clothes in a tub outside. Since there's no gas-powered washing machine here in the trailer, I'll probably have to look for a Laundromat someplace nearby."

"There's none close that I know of, but there are a few in Hopkinsville," Allen said. "If you can't get to town often enough to keep clean clothes in your closet, you could always wash them in the bathtub, I guess."

Titus shook his head. "Not if I can help it."

"Then maybe you'd better find yourself a wife who's willing to wash your clothes."

"No way! I'm not interested in marrying anyone right now." He glanced out the window toward the barn. "I am interested in the old buggy I discovered the other day, though."

"What buggy?"

"Found it in the barn, under a tarp. It's in pretty bad shape, so it'll need some work to make it useable, but if you're willing to sell it for a reasonable price, I'd be interested in buying it from you."

Allen looked at Titus like he'd taken leave of his senses. "Why would I want to sell you an old, beat-up buggy?"

"Figured since you own this place, the buggy's yours."

"Legally it is, but I wouldn't think of charging you for the buggy. Especially since you've had to put up with this dump of a house for the last several days." He made a sweeping gesture encompassing the kitchen. "The buggy's yours to do with as you wish."

Titus smiled. "Thanks, I appreciate that."

The *clip-clop* of horses' hooves could be heard coming up the driveway.

"Sounds like the workers are starting to arrive." Allen pushed his chair aside and stood. "Guess I'd better get out there and hand out the supplies I brought with me today. Then I'm gonna roll up my sleeves and get busy with the others so we can make this place livable."

Titus glanced at his bowl of cereal, mostly uneaten and now turned soggy. He guessed he'd better not take the time to eat the rest of it. If the others were about to start working, it wouldn't look right if he didn't make an appearance right away. Besides, he was eager to get started and looked forward to seeing how much they could accomplish in one day.

When Titus stepped outside, he was surprised to see how many Amish men and women had come to help. Allen introduced him to Emmanuel Schwartz, the buggy maker, and Titus asked about getting new wheels and some other things for the buggy he wanted to fix.

"Jah, sure, I've got all kinds of wheels," Emmanuel said with a grin that revealed a couple of missing teeth. "You come by my shop anytime, and I'll let you choose."

"I'll do that as soon as I find the time," Titus said with a nod. He moved on and met the man who owned the lumber mill in the area, an elderly couple who owned a greenhouse, and a widowed woman who ran a bookstore, as well as several other people. It didn't take him long to realize that the folks in this community were friendly and eager to help out.

He was about to grab a hammer and join some of the men who were tearing off his old roof when he spotted Suzanne's friend Esther heading his way.

"Hello, Titus, it's nice to see you," she said.

He gave a nod. "Nice to see you, too."

She smiled, her cheeks turning a light shade of pink. "My folks couldn't be here today, but I came to do some cleaning inside and help feed everyone."

Titus's stomach rumbled at the mention of being fed. He should have gotten up earlier so he'd have had more time to eat a decent breakfast.

"I made some raisin bread, and Rebekah, who owns a bakeshop, brought doughnuts and cinnamon rolls, so whenever anyone needs a break, we'll have everything set up over there." Esther pointed to the tables that had been placed under the maple tree in the middle of the yard, where several women scurried about.

Titus was tempted to head over there, but he knew he really ought to get some work done before he took a break.

As if sensing his dilemma, Esther smiled and said, "Why don't you come over and sample some of my bread now? If you wait too long, it might be gone."

Titus's growling stomach finally won out. "Guess it wouldn't hurt if I had one piece of bread. Might give me more energy to work."

They walked through the tall grass and visited a few minutes while Titus ate, not one, but two pieces of her moist and tasty raisin bread. Esther not only had a pretty face, but she could obviously cook. "This is really good," he said, smacking his lips.

Esther smiled. "I'm glad you like it."

—∞—

When Suzanne climbed down from the buggy behind her mother, she spotted Esther standing under a maple tree, talking to Titus. *I'll bet Esther's happy,* she thought. *She's finally getting to spend a few minutes alone with Titus. Once he finds out what a good cook she is, he'll probably want to court her.*

Mom handed Suzanne a container full of peanut butter cookies. "Would you please take these over to the food table? I'm going inside to see what needs to be done."

"Why don't you take the cookies to the table, and I'll go inside and see what needs to be done?" Suzanne suggested. She really didn't want to be here at all. She'd been hoping she could stay home so she could go out to the woodshop and fiddle around. With Nelson and Grandpa at the work frolic, they'd have been none the wiser. But no, Mom had insisted the whole family come to help out.

"I see Esther over there," Mom said. "Wouldn't you like to visit with her?"

Normally, Suzanne would have enjoyed chatting with Esther, but she didn't want to interrupt the conversation between her friend and Titus.

"Go on now." Mom gave Suzanne a little nudge. "When you and Esther are done visiting, you can come help with whatever needs to be done in the house."

Suzanne hurried across the yard, and as she set the cookies on the table, she heard Titus mention something about finding an old buggy in the barn that he planned to fix up as soon as he found the time. Esther seemed to be hanging on his every word, and Suzanne wasn't about to interrupt.

By this time next year, they'll probably be planning a wedding, Suzanne thought as she leaned against the table. *I, on the other hand, will probably never find a man willing to marry me. Why can't men see that there's more to a woman than a pretty face or the ability to cook? Why can't they be interested in someone who likes to hunt, fish, hike in the woods, or work with wood?*

Suzanne was about to head for the trailer, when Esther touched her arm. "Have you been standing there long?"

"Uh. . .no, not really." Suzanne motioned to the peanut butter cookies. "Just came over to add those to the rest of the baked goods setting out."

"Did you bake them?" Esther asked.

"No, my mamm did." Suzanne hoped Esther wouldn't say anything about her cooking skills—or rather, the lack of them—in front of Titus. From the way he sometimes looked at her, she figured he already thought she was stupid and incapable.

"How are things going with Callie?" Suzanne asked Titus, after he'd helped himself to a cup of coffee. "Since you haven't brought her back to our place, I take it you've decided to keep her?"

"Haven't been able to catch the critter. So I suppose I'll have to let her stay." Titus frowned. "She found her way into the house last night, and I discovered her sleeping in the bathroom sink this morning."

Suzanne bit back a chuckle. "Callie's always liked to sleep in strange places. Even when she was a kitten, I never knew where I might find her."

"I don't care where she sleeps, as long as it's not in the trailer."

"Don't you like cats?" Esther asked.

"Nope, I sure don't."

"How come?"

"They bite and scratch. One nearly took off my finger when I was a kinner, and I've tried to stay away from cats ever since."

"Not all cats bite and scratch," Suzanne said. "And those that do usually have a good reason."

"Humph!" Titus held up his hand. "There was no good reason for your stupid cat to bite me the other day." He set his cup on the table. "I'd better get to work. It was nice talking to you, Esther. Oh, and thanks for that great-tasting raisin bread."

As Titus walked away, Suzanne gritted her teeth. He'd worn a frown on his face throughout most of their conversation, but when he talked to Esther he was all smiles. He was obviously attracted to Esther, and Suzanne had no problem with that. What she didn't understand was what he had against her.

Chapter 11

The air rang with shouts and sounds of carpenters and roofers, the chatter of children, and the laughter of women who'd come to help at the work frolic. By noon, a good many repairs to the trailer had been completed. They had removed the old roof and put on a new one, repaired both front and back screen doors, replaced most of the boards on the porch, cut the overgrown lawn, and weeded quite a bit.

The inside of the trailer looked much better, too. Volunteers had given the home a thorough cleaning, replaced hinges on the broken cabinet doors, re-covered the living room furniture, and brought in a better mattress for Titus's bed. Someone had also given him two sets of sheets, as well as several towels and washcloths. His cupboards and refrigerator had been stocked with plenty of food. Titus was amazed at the generosity of these people, some of whom he hadn't met before.

As he sat at one of the tables on the lawn, enjoying the variety of sandwiches and salads the women served, he decided that he might have made a good decision moving to Kentucky. Things had gone well with his job at the woodshop so far; the trailer, while not in the best condition, was now livable; and he'd made some new friends. He'd show his folks that he was able to make it on his own. He'd show them, as well as the rest of his family, that Timothy wasn't the only one who could succeed.

Titus glanced over at Esther, as she poured him another cup of coffee and smiled. *I know I said I wasn't interested in getting married, but if I were to start courting a woman from Kentucky, and eventually got married, that would let everyone at home know I've settled down and made a life of my own. Of course,* he reasoned, *I'll have to get Phoebe out of my system before I can even think about marriage.*

—∞—

As the noon meal was being served, Suzanne noticed how Esther was conveniently pouring beverages at the table where Titus sat between Nelson and Allen. She'd seen Esther talk to Titus several times during the morning, making it obvious that she was interested in him. If Esther wasn't careful, she might chase him away with her boldness.

Suzanne plunked down on a bench next to her mother. "Sure has turned into a warm day," she commented.

Mom nodded. "I thought you were going to help serve the beverages."

"Esther's doing that."

"She's serving coffee but not lemonade. Since the weather's turned warm, I'm sure some of the men would rather have something cold to drink."

Suzanne shrugged.

"Why don't you carry the jug of lemonade around to the tables and see?"

"All right, but I'd better get a sandwich, before they're all gone." Suzanne plucked a ham sandwich off the platter closest to her and plopped it on her plate. Then she grabbed two of the peanut butter cookies Mom had made, as well as a handful of potato chips. "I'll be back soon," she said, rising from her bench.

Suzanne hurried to the table where the beverages sat and picked up the jug of lemonade. After she'd served the two tables nearest her, she made her way over to the table where Titus sat. "Would anyone like some lemonade?" she asked.

Nelson and Allen both nodded, so she poured some into their cups.

"How about you?" she asked Titus.

"Sure," he replied without making eye contact.

Not this again. Suzanne lifted the jug, and was about to pour some into his cup, when Nelson turned in his seat and bumped her arm.

Whoosh! Lemonade splashed all over the front of Titus's shirt.

"Were you trying to drown me?" Titus sputtered.

"I'm sorry. Nelson bumped my arm, and—"

Before Suzanne could finish her sentence, Titus abruptly got up and headed for the trailer, mumbling something about how clumsy she was.

That's just great, she thought with regret. *At the rate things are going, Titus will never look at me with anything but disgust.*

Chapter 12

For the next two weeks whenever Titus had a free moment, he worked on the old buggy he'd found. He still preferred to ride Lightning to work every day, but when it came to grocery shopping or hauling anything big, having a buggy was a good thing.

As Titus made his way to the kitchen one morning, he felt thankful once again for all the repairs and cleaning that had been done to the trailer. He'd met so many good people the day of the work frolic and again the next day when they'd met for church at the bishop's house.

This coming Saturday would be his day off, and he thought he might like to saddle Lightning and take a ride for a better look around the area. It would be good to do something fun for a change. His new job was working out well, and both Isaac and Nelson seemed to be pleased with Titus's carpentry skills. Unless he messed up and did something stupid, it looked like his position in the woodshop would be permanent.

A knock sounded on the door, and Titus went to see who it was. When he opened it, he was surprised to see Suzanne standing on the porch, holding a flat of primroses.

"I thought you might like to have a little color in your front flower bed," she said. "Even though the weeds are gone, it looks kind of bare."

"I guess it does." He scuffed the toe of his boot along the threshold, not knowing what else to say. By now he ought to be used to seeing Suzanne, since she often came out to the woodshop to sweep the floors or bring them lunch. But each time he saw her, she either said or did something to irritate him. Was it because seeing her still made him think of Phoebe?

"So, is it all right if I plant the flowers?" Suzanne asked.

"Sure." He turned and was about to step back into the house, when she said, "Have I done something to offend you, Titus?"

Titus whirled around and blinked a couple of times. The sunlight brought out the glints of gold in Suzanne's auburn hair. "Wh–what do you mean?" he stuttered.

"You usually don't say more than a few words to me, and when you do, you rarely look right at me."

He forced himself to meet her gaze. "I'm lookin' at you now."

She gave a nod. "I might think you were still irritated about the lemonade bath I gave you the day of the work frolic, but you've acted strangely toward me since the first day we met, and I'd like to know why."

Her piercing blue eyes seemed to bore right through him, and he quickly looked away. "I've forgotten all about the lemonade."

"See, you're doing it again. You're not looking at me when I'm talking to you."

Titus turned his head and looked her right in the eye. "Is that better?"

"Jah."

"Okay," he said, then drew in a quick breath. "You have

done a few things to irritate me, but the real reason it's hard for me to look at you is because you remind me of someone. Someone I'm trying to forget."

"Who?"

"Her name's Phoebe Stoltzfus—the girl I used to court in Pennsylvania." He frowned. "I thought she was going to marry me, but she took off for California with one of her girlfriends instead."

"Is Phoebe Amish?"

He pushed his hands against the doorjamb so hard that his knuckles turned white. "She was raised Amish, but she's never joined the church. Phoebe started running around even before she turned sixteen, and I'm pretty sure she's gonna go English."

"How old is Phoebe now?"

"Eighteen."

"She's still pretty young. Maybe she'll change her mind and return to Pennsylvania and join the church."

"I doubt it. She's been stringing me along since she was thirteen."

Suzanne's eyebrows squeezed together. "You've been interested in the same girl since you were thirteen?"

He shook his head. "I was seventeen when Phoebe was thirteen, and I waited for her until she turned sixteen, so we could start courting." He stabbed the side of the door with the toe of his boot. "For all the good it did me."

"It's no surprise that it didn't work out. She was practically a child when you became interested in her."

"That's what my folks and her folks thought, too. I figure she must be pretty immature even now if she ran off to California without caring at all what I thought."

"Maybe she wasn't the right girl for you."

"Now you sound like my folks. I don't think Mom or Dad

ever liked Phoebe. They tried to discourage me from the very beginning, and so did Phoebe's folks."

"I don't mean to sound like your folks. I just think you might need to find someone who's more mature and settled. Someone like—"

"I might do that if I can find the right woman. I'd like to make sure my job is secure and that I have a home of my own before I think about finding a wife and settling down, though. Need to prove to my family that I can measure up."

"Measure up?"

"To my twin brother, Timothy. He's been doing all the right things since he got out of school. Went to work right away for our older brother Zach; later bought a house with some land he could farm; then found a good woman and got married. He and Hannah have a daughter and another baby on the way." Titus tugged his left earlobe. "Timothy's way ahead of me. I might never get married, much less own a place of my own." He gestured to the trailer. "Might spend the rest of my days rentin' some place like this."

Before Suzanne could respond, Callie leaped onto the porch, darted between Titus's legs, and raced into the kitchen.

Titus grunted. "Stupid critter seems determined to get in. If you had to haul a cat over here, couldn't you at least have picked one that's content to be outside?"

Suzanne frowned. "Callie is usually content to be outside, but if you've been having problems with mice, then I would think you'd want to allow the cat in the house."

"Cats belong outdoors." Titus stepped back inside, grabbed the broom, and chased the cat out the door.

"You don't have to be so mean," Suzanne said with a huff.

"I'm not mean. Just don't want to pick the critter up and take the chance of getting bit again. Besides, a little push with the broom won't hurt her any."

"Maybe not, but I'm sure you scared the poor thing. You'll never make friends with the cat if you chase her around with a broom."

"Who says I want to make friends with the critter?"

Suzanne glared at him. "I don't have time to stand here and debate this with you. Do you want me to plant the flowers I brought or not?"

"Go right ahead." Titus quickly shut the door.

"That man is so rude," Suzanne fumed as she carried the flat of primroses to the flower bed. Obviously Titus didn't know how to care for a cat.

Should I take Callie back? Suzanne glanced around but saw no sign of the cat. After Titus had chased Callie with the broom, she'd disappeared behind the barn. *Maybe when I'm done planting these flowers I'll look for her*, she decided.

Suzanne grabbed the shovel she'd brought along and stabbed it into the hard ground, twisting it angrily. *Callie isn't the only thing Titus doesn't appreciate. He obviously didn't appreciate me bringing over these flowers because he didn't even say thanks. Makes me wonder if his folks taught him anything about manners and how to treat other people. Is it any wonder his girlfriend ran off to California? She was probably tired of his bad attitude. Humph! I think I should speak to Esther about Titus and let her know what he's really like.*

Suzanne had just finished planting the primroses when she heard a pathetic, muffled-sounding *meow*. She glanced to her left and saw Callie rolling in the grass with her head stuck in a soup can.

"Ach, my!" Suzanne jumped up and rushed over to the cat. She tried to pull the can off, but Callie wouldn't hold still. It was going to take two people to free the poor cat—one to hold

Callie and one to pull on the can.

Suzanne hurried across the yard and knocked on the trailer door. Titus pulled the door open a few seconds later. "Are you done planting the flowers?" he asked.

She gave a nod. "But I need your help. Callie has a soup can stuck on her head."

He lifted his shoulders in a brief shrug. "What do you want me to do about it?"

"I want you to help me get the can off."

"If she got it on, she ought to be able to get it off."

"I don't think so, and we can't just leave her like that. Please, Titus, you've got to help me get that can off."

"Oh, all right." Titus stepped off the porch, and Suzanne followed him into the yard, where the pathetic cat was still thrashing about. He bent down, yanked on the can, and it lifted Callie right off the ground. Her claws came out, and he let out a shriek. "Stupid katz clawed a hole in my shirt, and now I think my chest is bleeding!"

"Set the cat down and let me see." Suzanne wasn't sure whom to be more concerned about: Titus, or the poor cat, stuck in a can.

Titus shook his head. "I'm fine. I'll tend to my scratches later." But he did place Callie on the ground.

"Have you got any metal cutters?" she asked. "I think we need some in order to cut the can off Callie's head."

"I think I saw an old pair of tin snips in the barn," he said. "You keep an eye on the cat and make sure she doesn't run away while I go look for 'em."

—∞—

When Titus entered the barn, he found the tin snippers hanging on a nail. He pulled them down, and then slipped on a pair of heavy-duty gloves, as well as a jacket to protect himself.

"Sure don't know why I'm doin' this," he muttered. "I don't even like cats."

When Titus returned to the yard, he found Suzanne squatted down beside Callie, who was squirming around as she pawed frantically at the can that held her captive. "I've got the snippers," he announced. "I'll slip around front and try to cut her free."

Suzanne's eyes narrowed. "You're going to use that old rusty-looking cutter?"

"Sure, why not?"

"It really looks dull. Probably wouldn't cut a stick of butter."

"Well, it's the only pair I could find." Titus knelt on the grass in front of the cat.

"She's scared and might not cooperate with you," Suzanne said. "Maybe I should try and hold her."

Titus shook his head. "We know that's not going to work. She's too upset. Just leave her on the ground, put your hand on her back, and I'll see if I can cut the can off."

As Titus began clipping at the can, the cat flipped her head from side to side.

"Be careful; you might cut Callie's head." The panic in Suzanne's voice let Titus know how worried she was about the cat.

"I'm being as careful as I can, but it would help if she'd just hold still." He gritted his teeth as he continued to cut.

Finally, with one last snip, Callie was free. She shook her head a few times, and growled, crouching low to the ground. Looking up at Titus, she hissed as though threatening him. Then with a high-pitched meow, she darted for the barn.

"Stupid critter," Titus muttered. "She acts like I'm the one who put the can on her head." He stomped on the can and shouted at the cat's retreating form, "Don't play with cans, you ungrateful katz!"

Suzanne stepped in front of Titus and planted both hands on her hips. "If you didn't leave your cans lying around, she wouldn't have gotten herself into such a fix."

"I didn't. Don't know where that can came from. She probably got it out of the garbage." As Titus thought more about the whole situation, it suddenly seemed kind of funny. "Stupid critter put on quite a show for us, didn't she?" he asked with a snicker.

Suzanne glared at him a few seconds; then she looked down at what was left of the can and started to giggle. "She did look pretty silly with her head in that can."

Laughter bubbled in Titus's chest, and he leaned his head back and roared. Soon they were both laughing so hard tears ran down their faces as they held their sides.

Finally, Titus got control of himself and bent to pick up the can. "Sure hope nothin' like that ever happens again. That was downright stressful!"

She gave a nod. "I appreciate the fact that you took the time to free Callie—especially when you don't even like her."

"Couldn't let her spend the rest of her days wearin' a can on her head. Regardless of what you may think, I'm really not mean."

Before Suzanne could respond, he hurried into the trailer and shut the door.

Paradise, Pennsylvania

"Hi, Mom, how's it going?" Samuel asked as he entered the kitchen, where Fannie sat working on a crossword puzzle.

"We're fine here. How are things with you and your family?"

"Everyone's doing well. The older kinner are looking forward to getting out of school at the end of April."

"That's just a few weeks away." Fannie motioned to the stove. "If you have the time, help yourself to a cup of coffee."

"Think I will." Samuel poured himself some coffee and took a seat beside her at the table. "Where's Dad this morning?"

"He had a dental appointment, so he headed to town right after breakfast."

"I'm surprised you could get him to go. Dad's always hated going to the dentist."

"I know, but he lost a filling the other day, and I talked him into going before the tooth started hurting." Fannie took a drink from her cup and filled in the next word on her puzzle.

"Have you heard anything more from Titus?" Samuel asked.

She shook her head. "He left a message for Timothy a few weeks ago, but he's only left one message here, and that was the day he got to Kentucky. I've written to him a few times already, but he hasn't answered any of the letters." She sighed. "Guess he's either too busy or is trying to prove that he's independent and doesn't need me anymore."

Samuel placed his hand over Fannie's. "I'm sure it's not that. Most likely, he's keeping busy."

"I thought I'd feel better about his move if your daed and I went to Kentucky so I could see for myself that Titus is doing okay." Fannie slowly shook her head. "But your daed says he's too busy right now with the spring planting and such."

The back door swung open, and Timothy rushed into the room with one-year-old Mindy in his arms. His face was red and beaded with perspiration.

"What's wrong, Timothy?" Fannie asked. "You look *umgerennt*."

"I am upset. Hannah's outside in the van with our driver and is hurtin' real bad with contractions. She started bleeding awhile ago, too, so we're taking her to the hospital." Timothy moved toward the table. "Hannah's mamm is going with us, so I was wondering if you could keep Mindy while we're gone."

"Of course." Fannie held out her arms, and the child went willingly to her. "Please call as soon as you know something."

"I will." Timothy leaned over and kissed his daughter's forehead; then he turned and hurried out.

Fannie sighed. "I hope Hannah's going to be all right. The *boppli*'s not due for several more months. I sure hope she won't lose it."

CHAPTER 13

Pembroke, Kentucky

As Titus ate breakfast that morning, he thought about Suzanne and how much she resembled Phoebe. He knew it wasn't fair to compare the two women when their personalities weren't the same, but it was hard to look at Suzanne without thinking about Phoebe, which only reminded him of her betrayal. Titus wondered if the ache in his heart would ever heal. He wanted to settle down and get married someday, but would he ever find a woman he loved as much as he had Phoebe?

He added a spoonful of sugar to his coffee and stirred it around. *I'll never find a wife if I don't get a grip on my anger toward Phoebe. And I won't make any points with Isaac if I don't start being kinder to his granddaughter.*

Yesterday, after Suzanne had come into the shop and made a nuisance of herself, he'd stupidly said something to Isaac about his granddaughter being a pest. The elderly man had shaken his arthritic finger as he looked Titus in the eye and said, "Suzanne may be a *pescht* sometimes, but she's my *grossdochder*, and I'd appreciate it if you kept any negative remarks about her to yourself."

A verse from Proverbs 15 that Titus had heard at church last Sunday popped into his head: *"A soft answer turneth away wrath: but grievous words stir up anger."* He knew he'd been unkind to Suzanne several times, and he owed her a thank-you for the flowers she'd planted for him. *If she's still outside, I should probably speak to her before I leave for work,* he decided.

He pushed his chair aside and opened the back door. Suzanne's horse and buggy were gone. "Should have come out here sooner," he mumbled. "Shouldn't have let her leave without saying thanks."

When he got to work, he'd stop by the Yoders' house first and talk to Suzanne.

Titus returned to the kitchen and halted. Callie was perched on the table, lapping milk from his bowl of cereal.

He clapped his hands and shouted, "Get down from there, you stupid katz! I should have left you trapped in that soup can."

Callie leaped off the table and raced outside. That's when Titus realized he hadn't shut the door when he'd gone out to look for Suzanne.

He groaned and set his bowl in the sink. This was not starting out to be a good day. Hopefully things would go better after he'd spoken to Suzanne.

—∞—

When Titus arrived at the Yoders', he put his horse in the corral and went up to the house. Suzanne's mother answered his knock.

"Guder mariye," she said. "If you're looking for Nelson or my daed, they're already out at the shop."

Titus shook his head. "I'd like to speak to Suzanne."

"She's not here. Left right after breakfast. Said she was taking some primroses over to your place to plant. Didn't you see her there?"

He nodded. "She did come by, but she left before I did. Figured she'd be here by now."

"She may have stopped at the Beilers' store on her way home. Said something about needing a few things from there, too."

"Guess I'll have to wait and speak to her later on then."

"Maybe you can talk to her when she brings lunch out to the shop around noon."

"Okay. I'd better get to work now. Sure don't want to be late." Titus turned and sprinted to the shop.

He'd just entered the building, when Nelson rushed up to him and said, "There was a message for you at the phone shanty from your mamm."

"What'd it say?"

"Your sister-in-law's been taken to the hospital."

"Which sister-in-law?"

"I think she said it was Hannah. I didn't erase the message, so you'd better go out and listen to it yourself."

Titus opened the door and raced down the driveway to the phone shanty. Once inside, he took a seat and listened to the message.

"Titus, it's Mom. I wanted you to know that Hannah's in the hospital and may lose the boppli. Timothy left Mindy with us, and he's at the hospital with Hannah. He seemed pretty upset when he was here earlier. Please say a prayer for them, Titus."

Titus dialed his folks' number and was surprised when someone picked up the phone.

"Hello. Who's this?"

"It's Samuel. Is that you, Titus?"

"Jah. What are you doin' in Mom and Dad's phone shanty?"

"I dropped by the house this morning to visit with Mom and was on my way out when I heard the phone ring." There was a pause. "How are you? Is everything going okay with your new job?"

"Other than a few cat scratches on my chest, I'm fine, and so's the job."

"How'd you get the cat scratches?"

"Never mind. It's not important right now." Titus slid his fingers along the edge of the table. "I just listened to a message from Mom. She said Hannah's in the hospital and might lose the baby. Do you have any more information?"

"Not really. I was here when Timothy brought Mindy over. We haven't heard any news yet, but we'll let you know as soon as we do."

"I appreciate that." Titus frowned. "Sure wish there was a phone shanty at the place I'm staying. It'd be easier than having to check messages and make calls from the Yoders'."

"You ought to see about having one put in, or you might consider getting a cell phone."

"You're right; I'll do one or both."

"Is everything else okay?" Samuel asked. "You sound kind of down."

"I'm fine; just tired is all." Titus heard a buggy coming up the driveway and glanced out the open door of the shanty. The rig pulling in belonged to an Amish man Titus hadn't met.

"I'd better get back to the shop. Looks like we've got a customer coming in."

"Okay. Good talking to you, brother. We'll keep you posted."

Titus hung up and said a prayer for Hannah and Timothy. He knew how excited they were about having another child and was sure they'd be very disappointed if she lost the baby.

~

When Suzanne entered the Beilers' store, she found Esther behind the counter, waiting on Mattie Zook, who was married to Enos, one of the ministers in their church.

Suzanne found the items she'd come to get, stepped up to the counter, and waited for Mattie to leave.

"I'm surprised to see you here so early," Esther said when Suzanne placed two spools of thread and a container of straight pins on the counter. "Did you get up with the chickens this morning?"

"No, but I just visited a cocky rooster."

Esther tipped her head. "What are you talking about?"

Suzanne explained about taking the primroses to plant in the flower bed in front of Titus's trailer and how he hadn't even said *thank you*. "If I were you, I'd think twice about a possible relationship with Titus," she added.

"Do you mean because he didn't appreciate the flowers?"

"It's not just that. Titus has recently broken up with his girlfriend back home, who apparently looks like me." Suzanne grimaced. "I'm sure he's not over her yet, so you may as well give up on the idea of him courting you."

Esther's eyebrows squeezed together. "Are you sure the reason you don't want me to have a relationship with Titus isn't because you're interested in him?"

"Of course that's not the reason. I'm not the least bit interested in Titus." Suzanne leaned on the counter and pursed her lips. "Since I remind him of his old girlfriend, I'm sure that's at least one of the reasons I irritate him."

"Did he tell you that?"

"Pretty much."

"That's *lecherich*."

"I agree, but while it might seem ridiculous to us, if Titus is still hurting because of his ex-girlfriend, then I guess looking at me makes him feel even worse."

Esther's forehead puckered. "If he's not over her yet, then I suppose he's probably not interested in beginning a relationship with me. . .unless I can make him forget her."

"I don't think that's a good idea."

"How come?"

"I just told you. He's trying to get over a broken heart. Besides, he hates cats."

Esther slowly shook her head. "Not everyone is crazy about cats the way you are."

"I'm not saying they have to be crazy about cats, but Titus doesn't even like them. When I was there this morning, he chased poor Callie with a broom. Of course, he did help me get a can off her head."

"What?"

Suzanne explained how Titus had cut the can off Callie's head. "Poor Callie was really traumatized, and I'm surprised she's still hanging around his place."

"Maybe she stays because there are so many mice."

Suzanne nodded. "That has to be it. She's certainly not staying because she's treated well. I think I'm going to head over there again and see if I can find her. If I do, I'll take her back to my house where she'll be safe."

Chapter 14

Paradise, Pennsylvania

"I'm so sorry, Hannah," Timothy murmured as he sat beside his wife's bed, holding her limp hand in his. "I know how much you wanted this baby."

Tears welled in her soft brown eyes, and she sniffed a couple of times. "D–didn't you want the boppli, too?"

"Of course I did, but we still have Mindy, and if it's God's will, we'll have another baby sometime."

She pulled her hand away from his and turned her head toward the wall. "I. . .I can't even think about that right now."

"You're right. You just need to rest and get your strength back." He gave her arm a gentle pat. "Why don't you close your eyes and try to get some sleep? I'm going down the hall to phone my folks and let them know we lost the boppli. Your mamm's in the waiting room, and I'll tell her you're resting and that she can come in to see you after you've had a nap."

Hannah only nodded in reply.

Timothy left the room and hurried down the hall, where he found a phone booth outside the waiting room. After he'd called his folks and left a message, he dialed the Yoders' number and left one for Titus as well. He wished his twin was here now so he could talk to him about all this. They'd always been there for each other in the past, and it was hard to have Titus living so far away—especially now, when Timothy needed his support.

He gripped the phone so tightly that his fingers ached. *It's Phoebe's fault Titus isn't here. It was because of her selfishness in running off to California that he decided to leave home. Titus should never have gotten involved with that selfish girl. He should have listened to me and courted Sarah Beechy, who was older and more mature. Of course,* Timothy reasoned, *it's too late for that now. Sarah married Daniel King a year ago, and they're expecting their first baby. What my twin brother needs is to find a mature woman who can cook as well as Mom, is sweet-tempered like our sister Abby, and enjoys the outdoors as much as Titus does.*

Pembroke, Kentucky

When Suzanne pulled her horse and buggy up to the hitching rail in Titus's yard, it didn't take her long to realize that he'd already left for work, because his horse wasn't in the corral, where it had been earlier this morning.

Suzanne climbed down from the buggy and secured Dixie to the rail. Then she headed for the barn, hoping Callie might be there.

When she stepped into the barn, she blinked a couple of times, trying to adjust her eyes to the dimness there. "Here, Callie," she called. "Kumme, kitty. Come."

All was quiet, and there was no sign of the cat. *Maybe she's sleeping in a pile of hay somewhere.*

Suzanne clapped her hands. "Here, kitty, kitty."

Still no response.

Suzanne searched all around the barn, clapping her hands and calling Callie's name, but the cat was nowhere to be found.

Suzanne left the barn and wandered around the yard, continuing to call for the cat. Nothing. Not even a quiet *meow*.

Finally, resigned to the fact that she wasn't going to find the cat today, Suzanne untied Dixie and climbed back in the buggy.

When Suzanne arrived home sometime later, she found Mom outside hanging clothes on the line.

"Do you need my help?" she asked, stepping up to the basket of laundry.

"I appreciate the offer, but I'm almost done." Mom motioned to the paper sack in Suzanne's hands. "I take it you stopped by the store on your way home?"

"Jah. I needed more thread to finish Esther's quilt."

"Are you close to having it done?"

"I'm getting there, and since Esther's birthday is only a week away, I really need to work on the quilt for the rest of today. Unless you need me for something else, that is."

Mom shook her head. "You're free to work on the quilt."

"Okay, great."

"Did Titus like the primroses you took over to his place this morning?" Mom asked.

Suzanne shrugged. "I really don't know. He didn't even say thanks."

"Well, some men don't appreciate flowers that much." Mom smiled, although unexpected tears had gathered in her eyes. "Except for your daed, of course. He enjoyed the beautiful flowers we grow in our garden as much as I do."

Suzanne nodded. "I think you're right, and I sure do miss him."

"Me, too." Mom sniffled, as though trying to hold back her tears. "Last year was hard, losing first my mamm, and then your daed. But for all our sakes, I've tried to focus on the positive."

"You've done a good job of it, too." Suzanne gave Mom a hug. She was thankful they still had Grandpa with them, and hoped he'd live a good many more years.

—∞—

A few minutes before noon, Verna Yoder came out to the shop with lunch for the men.

"Where's Suzanne?" Titus asked when Verna set the basket on Isaac's desk. "She's usually the one who brings lunch out to us."

"Suzanne's in the house, working on a birthday present for her friend Esther."

"Oh, I see. Maybe I'll stop by the house after work today because there's something I need to tell her."

"Would you like me to give Suzanne a message?" Verna asked.

"No, that's okay. What I have to say is best said to her face."

Nelson looked over at Titus with raised brows. "Is there something going on between you and my sister?"

Titus's face heated. " 'Course not. I just need to tell her something, that's all."

"What kind of sandwiches did you bring us?" Isaac asked, as though sensing Titus's discomfort.

"Bologna and cheese." Verna smiled. "There's also a jug of milk and some brownies in the basket."

Titus smacked his lips. "Brownies sound good; I like most anything chocolate."

"You wouldn't like my sister's chocolate pie," Nelson said. "She made it once, and—"

"You should get busy and eat so you can get back to work." Verna gestured to the stack of wood in one corner of the room. "Looks like you've got plenty to do."

"That's a fact," Isaac said with a nod. "Just this morning we got an order for a custom-made storage shed, and also a set of kitchen cabinets. If things keep going like this, I may need to hire another man."

Verna smiled. "I'm glad you're keeping busy. It's better to have too much work than not enough." She moved toward the door. "I need to check the clothes on the line, so I'll leave you three alone to eat."

After the men's silent prayer, Titus grabbed a sandwich and eagerly ate his lunch. Everything tasted good, and he found that he was even hungrier than he'd realized.

They'd just finished eating when an English man who lived in the area entered the shop, also wanting a storage shed.

While Isaac wrote up the man's order, Titus and Nelson started working on a set of cabinets that had been ordered last week. Titus was glad they were busy, because being busy helped take his mind off his concerns for his family back home. He wished he knew how Hannah was doing.

Shortly before quitting time, Verna returned to the shop and told Titus that she'd discovered a message for him on their voice mail.

"Who's it from?" Titus asked.

"Your brother, Timothy, and I think you should go out to the shanty and listen to the message yourself."

It must be bad news about Hannah, Titus thought as he hurried out the door.

When he entered the phone shanty and listened to the message, his suspicions were confirmed. Hannah had lost the baby, and Timothy sounded very upset. He said he didn't know what he could do to comfort Hannah, and asked for Titus to remember them in his prayers.

Titus let his head fall forward into the palms of his hands and said a prayer for them right then. Hearing the grief in his brother's voice made him wonder if he should ask Isaac for some time off so he could go home. But with all the work they had piled up in the shop, he knew that unless it was a real emergency, he probably shouldn't ask for any time off. If only he could call home more often and speak directly to someone, instead of leaving messages all the time.

Titus sat a few more minutes; then he lifted his head, picked up the phone, and dialed Allen's number. He was glad when Allen answered on the second ring.

"Hey, Allen, it's me, Titus. If you're not busy on Saturday, would you be free to come and get me? I want to go to Hopkinsville and see about getting a cell phone."

Chapter 15

Are you sure it's okay for you to have that thing?" Allen asked as he and Titus left the cell phone store on Saturday morning. "I mean, isn't it against your church rules to own a cell phone?"

Titus shrugged. "It's different with every community. Some church districts allow cell phones if you have your own business, but I know of some that won't allow them at all."

"What about this district? Do they allow cell phones?"

"I don't know, but I think I'll keep it to myself for now."

Allen quirked an eyebrow. "You think that's a good idea? Wouldn't want to see you get in trouble with the church."

"I don't want to get in trouble, either, but I need a better way of keeping in touch with my family back home. Since Zach has a cell phone for his business, I'll be able to call him whenever I want. I can even ask Zach to set up a time for me to call Timothy or my folks."

Titus frowned. "Do you know how frustrating it was when I got the message that Timothy's wife had a miscarriage, and I couldn't speak to him directly? Had to leave a message on his voice mail, and that's so impersonal."

"I see your point."

"Are you hungry?" Titus asked as they climbed into Allen's truck. " 'Cause I sure am, and I'd like to treat you to lunch."

"That sounds good to me. Where do you want to eat?"

"I don't know any of the restaurants in town, so you'd better choose."

"All right then, we'll head over to Ryan's Steakhouse and eat ourselves full." Allen grinned. "I learned that expression from Zach after he returned to Pennsylvania to find his roots."

Titus smiled and thumped his stomach. "I'm definitely ready to eat myself full."

—∞—

"I'm finally done with Esther's quilt," Suzanne said when she stepped onto the back porch and found Mom sitting in her chair, shelling fresh peas from their garden.

Mom looked up and smiled. "That's good news. You got it done in plenty of time for Esther's party next Thursday night."

"I draped it over the back of the sofa, in case you'd like to see how it looks."

"I certainly would." Mom set the pan of peas on the porch, rose from her chair, and followed Suzanne to the living room.

"You did a nice job on it," Mom said. "The dahlia pattern looks good with the red and gold material you used."

"I hope Esther likes it."

"I'm sure she'll be very pleased."

Suzanne glanced out the window. "Since I'm done early, I think I'll get my fishing pole and head to the pond for a few hours. If I'm lucky, I might catch a few fish, and we can have them for supper tonight."

"That'd be nice." Mom smiled. "Maybe I'll make a batch of cornbread while you're gone. That always goes good with fish."

Suzanne slipped the quilt into a cardboard box and hurried

out the door. As she stepped onto the porch, she spotted Grandpa sitting in his favorite wicker chair with his eyes closed and his chin resting on his chest. She thought about inviting him to join her at the pond, but didn't want to disturb him, so she stepped quietly off the porch.

As Suzanne approached the barn to get her fishing pole, she nearly bumped into Nelson, who was leading his horse out of the barn.

"What are you up to?" he asked.

"I'm going fishing," Suzanne replied. "What about you?"

"Need to run a few errands. Then I'm heading over to the Rabers' place for supper."

Suzanne smiled. Nelson had been courting Lucy Raber for a few months, so he spent most of his free time over there.

"Did Titus ever get a chance to speak to you?" Nelson asked as he led his horse over to his buggy.

"About what?"

"Don't know, but a few days ago he said he wanted to talk to you about something. Just curious what it was about."

Suzanne's brows furrowed. "The only time I've spoken to Titus this week was on Wednesday morning when I went over to his place with some primroses. I haven't seen him since because I've been busy working on Esther's quilt, and that's also why Mom has brought your lunch out to the shop the last few days."

"I'm guessing Titus probably forgot about talking to you because he has other things on his mind right now."

"What other things?"

"His twin brother's wife had a miscarriage."

Suzanne frowned. "I hadn't heard about that. When did it happen?"

"Sometime Wednesday morning. He seemed real upset about it."

On the way home from Hopkinsville, Titus called Zach. He was relieved when Zach answered right away.

"Hi, Zach, it's me, Titus."

"Hey! It's good hearing from you," Zach said. "How are things going?"

"Okay. I was calling to see if you've heard how Hannah and Timothy are doing."

"Hannah's home from the hospital now, but she's grieving pretty hard over losing the boppli. Timothy's upset, too, but they have the support of both their families, so I'm sure they'll get through it."

"Jah." Titus glanced over at Allen. "Guess who's sitting beside me?"

"Who?"

"Allen. I'm riding in his truck."

"It must be his cell phone you used to call me."

"Actually, I'm talking to you on my own cell phone. Just bought it today."

"Are cell phones allowed in the church district there?" Zach questioned.

"Don't know yet, but I'm hoping they are."

"Shouldn't you have asked someone first, before you bought the phone?"

Titus gritted his teeth. He might have known he'd get a lecture from his older brother. It seemed like he could never do anything without someone in his family questioning him. But then, maybe Zach was right. Buying a cell phone without finding out if it would be allowed was probably a stupid thing to do. However, he'd been desperate to make a more direct contact with his family.

"You still there, Titus?" Zach asked.

"Uh, jah. Just thinking is all."

"I'll be seeing Mom and Dad at church tomorrow. Is there anything you'd like me to tell them?"

"Just say that I'm doing okay and will call and leave them a message soon. Oh, and tell Timothy and Hannah I'm sorry about the boppli, and that I'm praying for them."

"I will. Nice talking to you, Titus. Take care."

Titus clicked off the phone. "It was good talking to Zach, but it made me feel kind of homesick, too," he said to Allen.

"That's understandable. This is your first time living away from your family, so you're bound to miss them." Allen tapped the steering wheel a couple of times. "With me being an only child, it was hard on my folks when I moved away, and it was hard on me at first, too."

"But you're used to it now?"

"Mostly, but that's probably because I keep so busy with my job. When I'm not lining out subcontractors to do the work I've taken on, I'm busy scouting around for land and homes to buy." Allen motioned to a large white house with peeling paint and blue shutters that looked like they were about to fall off. "See that old place?"

"Uh-huh."

"It used to belong to an elderly couple who I understand lived in the area for a long time. Guess the husband died a few years ago, and the wife was put in a nursing home last month. I've been waiting to see if the place comes on the market, because if it does I'm hoping to buy it as another piece of investment property."

"What would you do with it?" Titus asked.

Allen shrugged. "Don't know for sure, but from the outside it looks like it's in pretty bad shape, so I'd either tear it down and build a new house, or I might remodel and sell the place, hoping to make a profit."

Titus studied Allen a few seconds. For a young man just a few years older than him, Allen sure had a lot of drive and determination to succeed. Even more than Timothy, who'd always seemed to know exactly what he wanted.

Not like me, Titus thought. *I'm nearly twenty-three, and I'm still floundering with no real purpose or goals. Is it any wonder my family treats me like a boppli and tells me what to do? If I could only find a way to prove to them that I'm mature and successful in something.*

"Here we are," Allen said, as he pulled his truck into Titus's yard. He motioned to the trailer. "The place sure looks better since we had the work frolic. Are you more comfortable here now?"

Titus nodded. "'Course, I'd like to own a home of my own someday."

"You're welcome to buy this place," Allen said. "I could lease it to you with the option to buy."

Titus lifted one corner of his straw hat and scratched the side of his head. "I'll give that idea some thought." Fact was, he wasn't sure he'd want to buy this old trailer, even though it was a lot more livable now. Still, if he bought it, he'd have a place he could call his own, and eventually he could replace the trailer with a real home.

"Would you like to come in for a cup of coffee?" Titus offered as he opened the truck door.

"I appreciate the offer, but I'd better be on my way. I'm taking a lady friend of mine out to supper tonight, and I don't want to be late."

"Didn't realize you had a girlfriend. Are things serious between you?"

Allen shook his head. "Not really. We're just friends right now, but I guess time will tell."

"Well, have a good evening." Titus lifted his new phone

and grinned. "I'll give you a call on this real soon."

Allen smiled. "Maybe we can go somewhere just for fun some Saturday. I'd like to show you the Jefferson Davis Monument if you're interested."

"That'd be great. Seeing that was one of the things I thought I'd like to do on one of my days off."

"Great. Let's make plans to do it soon."

Titus hopped out of the truck. "See you, Allen."

"Sure thing," Allen called as he got his truck moving.

Titus had just stepped onto the porch when he spotted Callie chomping on the remains of a mouse. He grunted. "You're gettin' fat, ya know that, cat? I think maybe you oughta slow down on the mice you've been eating."

The fat cat ignored him, just kept chomping away.

Titus rolled his eyes and opened the front door. When he stepped into the trailer, a blast of warm air hit him in the face. *This place sure gets stuffy when it's closed up for the day. Think I'll go out to the shed and get that old fishing pole I saw hanging on the wall. Then I'll head to the pond I discovered down the road a piece and cool off.*

Chapter 16

Paradise, Pennsylvania

"I don't know what I can do to help Hannah," Timothy said to his mother, as the two of them sat on her porch, drinking a glass of sweet meadow tea. "She just won't stop talking about how she lost the baby, and now she's beginning to question God."

Mom placed her hand on Timothy's arm. "Would you like me to talk to her about this?"

"You can if you want, but her mamm's already tried, and she got nowhere, so Hannah probably won't listen to you, either."

"It's easy for our faith to waver when things don't go as we'd planned." Mom paused and took a drink of tea. "Since Titus left home, I've found myself questioning God several times, but your daed keeps reminding me that when we suffer disappointments and face difficult trials, that's when we need to pray more and open up the Bible and study God's Word."

Timothy nodded. "I can't force Hannah to do those things, but I can pray for her and share a few verses of scripture."

Mom gave his arm a light tap. "I hope Hannah appreciates what a good husband she has."

Just then, Zach came walking down the driveway, from

the direction of his house. "Thought you'd like to know that I talked to Titus earlier today," he said, stepping onto the porch.

"Did he leave a message on your voice mail?" Mom asked.

"Nope. Spoke to him directly." Zach took a seat in the chair beside Timothy.

"What did Titus have to say?" Mom asked.

"Said he's doing okay, and that he bought a cell phone so he can keep in better touch."

"Are cell phones allowed in the church district there?" Timothy questioned.

Zach shrugged. "Titus said he wasn't sure."

"Knowing my twin, he probably bought the cell phone without asking whether it was allowed or not," Timothy said. "Titus has many good qualities, but he often acts before he thinks."

"He is kind of impulsive," Zach agreed.

Mom nodded. "But he's a good son, and I sure miss him."

"We all do," Timothy agreed, "but I understand his need to move away and make a new start. Maybe the journey he's on will be good for him. Might help him grow into the man God wants him to be."

Pembroke, Kentucky

Suzanne had been fishing for nearly an hour without even a nibble. If the fish didn't start biting soon, she wouldn't have anything to give Mom for supper. She enjoyed the cool shade provided by the nearby trees, but it wasn't worth it if she wasn't getting any fish.

Maybe I need to move to another spot, she decided. *I could try fishing off the small dock that someone built on the other side of the pond.*

Suzanne gathered up her fishing gear, and had just gotten settled on the dock when she spotted Titus heading her way.

A look of surprise registered on his face as he approached her. "Sure didn't expect to see you here," he said, dropping to the dock beside her.

"What kind of a greeting is that?" she mumbled.

Titus looked directly at her. "You don't have to get so huffy. I wasn't tryin' to be rude. Just didn't expect to run into you here at the pond."

With a flick of her wrist, she cast her line into the water. "Didn't you think I knew how to fish?"

"It's not that. I just thought. . . Oh, never mind." Titus turned away. "Seems like I can never say anything right when you're around," he mumbled.

"It seems like I can never say anything right to you, either."

Titus baited his hook and cast his line into the water.

"Nelson mentioned that you'd been looking for me the other day and wanted to tell me something," Suzanne said, changing the subject.

"Uh. . .jah, I did."

"What was it?"

He sat several seconds, staring at her.

"What's wrong? Why are you looking at me that way?"

"I just noticed that your eyes are a darker blue than Phoebe's."

"Phoebe?"

"The girl I told you about the other day. The one who looks like you."

"Oh."

"Her face is a bit thinner than yours, too."

"Are you saying that I'm fat?"

His ears turned pink as he shook his head. "Didn't mean that at all. Just was thinking maybe you don't look as much like

Phoebe as I'd thought."

"So why were you looking for me the other day, and what did you want to say?" she asked.

Titus pulled his straw hat off and fanned his face with the brim. "I wanted to apologize for the way I carried on when I was trying to get the can off your cat's head. Guess I acted pretty immature."

She gave a nod. "Apology accepted."

"I also wanted to thank you for those flowers you planted at my place. They do make the flower bed look nice."

Suzanne smiled. "You're welcome." Maybe Titus did have a nicer side. Maybe it wouldn't be so bad if he and Esther ended up courting.

"Is this a pretty good fishing hole?" he asked, leaning back on his elbows.

"It usually is, but today the fish don't seem to be biting."

"Really? Because I think I have a nibble."

Suzanne watched as Titus reeled in a nice-sized catfish. He took the hook out of the fish's mouth and placed the fish in the plastic bucket he'd brought along.

They sat quietly for several minutes, until Titus reeled in another catfish. "I'm two up on you now," he said with a grin.

"I don't need the reminder." She grimaced. "I've never had such bad luck fishing before. I should have caught several by now."

"What kind of bait are using?"

"Worms. What are you using?"

He held up a worm. "Same as you, only I think mine are fatter."

She snickered. "I doubt the fish are checking for the size of the worms. Guess it's just not my day for fishing, that's all."

"What other things do you like to do for fun?" Titus asked.

"Anything that has to do with being outdoors. Oh, and

I also like to work with—" Suzanne's hand jerked as a fish tugged on her line. "I've got one, and I think it's big!"

When Suzanne reeled in the fish, she was surprised to see that it was bigger than either of the fish Titus had caught so far.

"That's a nice one," Titus said. "I'm impressed."

She smiled, amazed at how well he'd responded to her catching a bigger fish. Maybe he wasn't the kind of man who liked to be ahead of everyone else. Maybe he was nicer than she'd thought.

"What are you doing next Thursday evening?" she asked.

"Probably not much. Why do you ask?"

"I'm planning a surprise birthday party for my friend Esther, and I thought you might like to come."

"That sounds like fun. Where's it gonna be?"

"At my house. Esther just thinks she's coming over for supper, and I'm hoping she'll be surprised when she discovers many of her friends there."

"I don't know Esther well enough to be considered one of her friends," he said. "Do you think she'll mind if I'm included?"

"I'm sure she won't. Esther's always been the friendly type, and I think she's open to making a new friend." *In fact, I know she's open to making you her friend.*

"What time's the party?" he asked.

"Six o'clock."

He pulled a pen from his pocket and wrote the time on his arm. "I'll transfer it to a notebook when I get home," he said when she stared at him.

Suzanne shrugged. *I hope Esther won't mind having a boyfriend who writes notes on his arm.*

Chapter 17

On Thursday evening, Titus headed over to the Yoders' place, using the old, gray, Lancaster-style buggy he'd fixed up. The buggy now had new wheels and battery-operated blinkers. He'd also reupholstered the seats and put new side mirrors on. It wasn't as nice as the buggy he'd had in Pennsylvania, but it would serve for most of his needs.

Titus smiled as he set the box with the birdfeeder he'd made in the back of the buggy. It was modeled after one of the covered bridges back home, and he'd stayed up late last night putting the finishing touches on it. Working with wood was one thing he did well, and he enjoyed it more than painting or any other job he'd done since he was a teenager. Since he didn't know Esther that well, he wasn't sure what her interests were, but he hoped she'd like the feeder.

He'd just stepped into the buggy when his cell phone rang. As soon as he saw Allen's number flash across the screen, he said hello.

"Hey, Titus. How are you doing?"

"Doin' fine. How are things with you?"

"Good. Say, I was wondering if you'd like to see the Jefferson Davis Monument with me this Saturday."

"Sure."

"I'll come by your place in the morning, around ten. Oh, and I'm inviting my friend Connie to go with us, so if there's someone you'd like to ask, feel free."

Titus slid his finger down the side of his nose as he thought about Allen's suggestion. If he went with Allen and his girlfriend, he'd feel like an intruder. If he invited someone to go with him, it'd be more like a double date. But who would he invite? He sure couldn't ask Suzanne. Being with her, on what would seem like a date, would only make him think of Phoebe. He thought about Esther, and wondered if she'd like to see the monument with him.

"You still there, Titus?"

"Uh. . .yeah. . .just thinking about who I might ask."

"There's no pressure. Don't feel like you have to invite anyone."

"Okay, I'll give it some more thought. See you on Saturday."

Titus ended the call and frowned. Why did Allen have to complicate things by inviting his friend?

—∞—

Suzanne was glad all the guests she'd invited for Esther's birthday party had arrived early. This gave Nelson and Russell the chance to see that all the horses were put in the corral and the buggies had been parked behind the barn where they couldn't be seen. Titus had been the last person to arrive, so while they waited for Esther, Suzanne introduced him to some of the young people who'd come from another district in their area.

They'd only been visiting a short time when Russell spotted Esther's horse and buggy pull into the yard. "I'll go out and take care of her horse," he told Suzanne.

"Be sure she doesn't follow you out to the corral," Suzanne called as he headed for the door. "Tell her to come right to the house—that we've got supper ready and are waiting for her."

"Don't worry; I'll make sure she only comes here."

When Russell went out the door, Suzanne put her finger to her lips to let everyone know they needed to remain quiet. Several minutes went by; then the back door squeaked open and clicked shut. A few seconds later, Esther stepped into the room.

"*Hallich gebottsdaag*—Happy birthday!" everyone shouted.

Esther blinked and covered her mouth in surprise. "Ach, my!"

Amid squeals of laughter and everyone talking at once, Esther made her way over to Suzanne and gave her a hug. "You sneaky little thing. I thought you were just having a quiet birthday supper for me."

Suzanne smiled. "I wanted to do something special for you this year."

Tears welled in Esther's milk-chocolate brown eyes. "You're such a good friend. I really was surprised."

"Say, when are we gonna eat?" one of the fellows shouted. "I'm starved!"

"If you men would like to help Nelson and Russell set up tables on the lawn, we womenfolk will bring out the food," Suzanne's mother said.

"Why don't you go outside and relax on the porch until we're ready to eat?" Suzanne nudged Esther toward the door.

Esther hesitated, then took a few steps toward the kitchen. "I don't feel right about not helping."

"Go on now. Just enjoy," Suzanne insisted. Whenever Esther came over for supper, she always scurried around the kitchen, helping serve the food. Suzanne was determined that tonight her friend should just sit and relax.

Esther finally nodded and went out the back door.

A short time later, everyone was seated at the tables. After the silent prayer had been said, Mom passed the platters of food around: chicken fried to a golden brown, creamy macaroni salad with a bit of tangy mustard, pickles, several bags of potato chips, and olives.

"I forgot to bring out the potato salad you made this afternoon," Mom said to Suzanne. "I'll go get it right now."

Mom hurried away and returned a few minutes later with the potato salad, which she set on one of the tables.

Titus plopped a big spoonful of it onto his plate and passed it to Nelson.

"No, thanks," Nelson mumbled around a mouthful of chicken. "Think I'll pass on the potato salad."

"Not me. I've always liked potato salad." Titus shoveled some onto his fork and took a bite. "Yuck!" His face contorted as he looked at Suzanne. "What'd you do, pour a whole bottle of vinegar in there?"

Suzanne's cheeks burned like fire. She knew she shouldn't have made anything for Esther's birthday supper, but Mom had insisted she make the salad, and had even assured her that the recipe was easy to follow.

"It can't be that bad." Esther reached for the potato salad, spooned some onto her plate, and took a bite. Her lips puckered, and her nose wrinkled as she swallowed it down. "Whew. . .that's really strong!"

Suzanne scooped up the bowl and dashed for the house. It was bad enough that she couldn't cook well, but to be embarrassed in front of her friends was mortifying.

When she entered the kitchen, she raced to the garbage can and dumped the potato salad in. Then she grabbed a napkin from the kitchen table to dry her tears and flopped into a chair.

"I'm sorry if we upset you," Esther said, entering the room. "Your potato salad was so strong, it took me by surprise."

Suzanne sniffed. "I. . .I don't know why I even try to cook. I stink at it, that's for sure."

"You don't stink at it. You just need more time in the kitchen, and you need to sample what you make before you serve it. Maybe a bit of sugar would have cut the strong vinegar taste."

"I don't like being in the kitchen. I worry about messing up, not to mention Mom's reaction to it."

"You'll never find a husband if you don't learn to cook. Most men want wives who can fix tasty meals."

Suzanne moaned. "We've been through this before."

"But don't you want to learn to cook so that when you find the man of your dreams you'll be ready for marriage?"

Suzanne folded her arms. "I doubt I'll ever find the man of my dreams. You, on the other hand, have already found someone you're interested in, and once he finds out how well you can cook, I'm sure you'll have him eating out of the palm of your hand."

"Are you talking about Titus?"

"Jah."

"I may be interested in him, but so far, he's shown no interest in me."

"He's here at your party, isn't he? I don't think he would have come if he wasn't interested."

"Maybe he came because he wanted to meet some of the other young people in our area. Or maybe he came for the meal."

"He'll probably never come here for supper again if he thinks I might fix any part of it." Suzanne motioned to the door. "I think we need to get back outside. As soon as everyone's done eating, you can open your gifts. Then we'll have the cake Mom made, which I know will be good."

—෴—

As Titus sat across from Esther, watching her open the gifts, he was filled with a sense of anticipation, wondering if she'd like the birdfeeder he'd made for her. She certainly liked the colorful quilt she'd just opened from Suzanne—even said she planned to save it for her hope chest.

"If Suzanne could cook half as well as she can quilt, she'd probably be married by now," Nelson said with a snicker.

Suzanne shot her brother a look of disdain. Even Nelson's girlfriend, Lucy, didn't appear to be too happy with him.

"You did a nice job on the quilt," Lucy said to Suzanne.

Suzanne smiled, although it appeared to be forced. "Open this one next," she said, pushing the box that held Titus's gift toward Esther.

Esther read the card Titus had taped to the box and smiled sweetly at him. "This is so nice," she said, removing the birdfeeder. "Did you make it, Titus?"

He nodded. "Made it to look like one of the covered bridges we have in Pennsylvania."

Nelson thumped Titus's back. "I'm impressed. Seems like you can make just about anything and do it well."

Titus smiled. It felt good to receive such affirmations. It felt good not to be compared to his twin for a change.

After the cake had been eaten, the young people visited until it was dark; then people started leaving. One of Suzanne's cats leaped into Titus's lap and swiped its sandpapery tongue on his hand. He shooed the cat away and stood. "I'd better go. Thanks for inviting me to the party," he said to Suzanne.

"You're welcome. I'm glad you were able to come."

Titus smiled at Esther. "Would you like me to get your horse?"

"I appreciate the offer," she said, "but Nelson's already gone out to get Ginger, and Russell's volunteered to carry my gifts out to the buggy."

"Okay. I'll walk out with you and hitch your horse to the buggy when he brings her out."

In the light of the full moon, Titus could see Esther's pretty face as she looked up at him and smiled.

They walked across the yard, and when they got to her buggy, he turned to her and said, "Have you ever visited the Jefferson Davis Monument?"

She shook her head. "I've driven by it many times but have never gone inside the gift shop or the monument."

"I'm planning to go there this Saturday with Allen Walters and his girlfriend. I was wondering if you'd like to go along."

Esther nodded eagerly. "That sounds like fun. What time?"

"Allen said he'd pick me up around ten in the morning."

"I'll ask my folks if I can take that day off."

"Great. I'll stop by the store on my way home from work tomorrow evening and see if you'll be free to go or not."

"I'll see you tomorrow then." She flashed him another dimpled smile. "Thanks again for the birdfeeder. I like it a lot."

"You're welcome."

Just then, Nelson showed up with Esther's horse, Ginger, so Titus hitched her horse to the buggy, said good-bye, and went to get Lightning.

—m—

When Titus entered his trailer that evening, he lit a gas lamp and headed down the narrow hallway toward his bedroom. As he approached the bathroom door, he halted. All the toilet paper had been pulled off the spindle and lay shredded on the floor.

He grimaced. "What in the world?"

Meow! Meow!

Titus kicked the toilet paper aside and followed the *meows* coming from his bedroom. When he stepped into the room, he screeched to a stop. At the foot of his bed lay Callie and four tiny kittens!

Chapter 18

As Titus headed to work on Friday morning, he thought about Callie and how she'd chosen his bed as a place to give birth to her kittens. He couldn't leave them there, of course, so he'd found a wooden box and lined it with rags. Then he'd put the cat and her kittens inside and taken the box to the barn. He'd checked on them before breakfast and fed Callie, knowing she needed plenty of nourishment.

"No wonder the cat was getting fat," Titus mumbled as he guided his horse onto the road leading to the Yoders' place. It wasn't that she'd been eating too many mice at all.

He groaned. "Stupid critter came up with a way to get in the house, but hopefully, now that she's had her babies she'll stay put in the barn."

Titus's cell phone vibrated in his pocket, but he was running late and couldn't take the time to stop and answer it now. It would be too hard to hold the cell phone in one hand and control Lightning's reins with the other. He was sure whoever had called would leave a message, so he'd just call them back when he got to work.

Enjoying the early morning breeze and scent of blooming trees along the road, Titus drew in a deep breath and relaxed in the saddle. He'd enjoyed horseback riding ever since he was a boy.

As Titus passed the road leading to the Beilers' store, he thought about Esther and how pleased she'd seemed when he'd invited her to see the monument with him. It might be good to start courting again. Maybe it would help him forget about Phoebe. He still wondered, though, if Phoebe would end up staying in California. It might be best for him if she did. It would be easier than her moving back to Pennsylvania and marrying someone else—maybe even someone he knew.

Feeling a tightness in his throat, Titus forced his thoughts off Phoebe, reminding himself that there was nothing he could do about her decision. He had to concentrate on his life here and hopefully the beginning of a new relationship with Esther.

When Titus arrived at the Yoders', he put Lightning in the corral. He'd just started walking toward the shop when his cell phone vibrated again. He stopped, pulled the phone from his pocket, and said hello.

"Hi, Titus. It's me, Timothy."

"It's good to hear your voice. Was that you who called earlier?"

"Jah. I was gonna leave you a message but decided to try calling again before I did."

"I'm almost at work, so I'm glad you caught me before I went into the woodshop." Titus took a seat in one of the wooden chairs under the maple tree in the Yoders' yard. "How are things going?"

"Not so well." Timothy's voice sounded strained. "Hannah's still not dealing with the miscarriage. She seems to have shut me out. Just sits in the rocking chair with Mindy in her lap, stroking our little girl's face and crying. Hannah's mamm is staying with us for a while, so she's doing all the cooking and cleaning right now."

"I hope things will go better soon."

"Me, too. Mom's tried talking to Hannah, and so has Hannah's mamm, but neither of 'em has gotten very far."

"Maybe you should bring Hannah and Mindy here for a visit. Might be good for all of you to get away for a while."

"We can't do that right now. Dad and I are finishing up planting, and when I'm not helping him, I'm painting for Zach and Arthur. Besides, from what I understand, your place is too small for visitors to stay with you."

"You're right about that. There aren't any hotels close to where I live either. The nearest town with hotels is Hopkinsville."

"It doesn't matter. Even if I could get away right now, I doubt Hannah would come. She's never liked to go very far from home."

"Guess it's a good thing her family lives nearby." Titus glanced up and noticed Isaac heading his way. "I'd better go. The boss is here, and I need to get to work."

"Okay, but keep in touch. Now that you've got a cell phone there's no excuse for not calling."

Titus chuckled. "I'll do my best. I'll talk to you again soon, and I'm still praying for you and Hannah."

"Danki."

Titus had just clicked off the phone and was about to slip it back into his pocket, when Isaac walked up to him wearing a frown. It was the first time he'd seen the elderly man look so stern. "Where'd you get that cell phone?" Isaac asked.

"I. . .uh. . .bought it in Hopkinsville so I could keep in better touch with my family back home."

"Cell phones aren't allowed in our church district." Isaac's bushy gray eyebrows furrowed, making the wrinkles in his forehead more pronounced. "Although I know of a few men who use cell phones anyway, despite what the ministers have decided."

Titus cringed. If cell phones weren't allowed, he'd either have to get rid of his or keep it a secret, which meant he would only be able to use it when other Amish people weren't around. It probably wasn't the right to do, but if others were doing it. . .

"Why aren't you content to use the phone shanty that's on the property where you're staying?" Isaac questioned.

"What phone shanty? I've never seen one anywhere on the property."

"It's out behind the barn a ways, but since the trailer has been sittin' empty for some time, I guess maybe the phone shanty could be covered with an overgrowth of bushes by now."

"I'll have to look for it when I get home this afternoon." *But even if I find it*, Titus thought, *I'm not sure I'll be willing to give up my cell phone.*

—w—

"Looks like my driver's here," Suzanne's mother said, peering out the kitchen window. "I won't be back in time to fix lunch or take it out to the menfolk, because after my dental appointment I have some shopping to do in Hopkinsville, so you'll have to do it."

Suzanne nodded. Since there wasn't much to making sandwiches, she figured she couldn't mess it up too badly. After all, she'd made sandwiches before.

"I'll see you later this afternoon." Mom grabbed her shawl and black outer bonnet, then hurried out the door.

Soon after Mom left, Suzanne went out to the garden to check the bedding plants she'd be taking to the Fairview Produce Auction next week. She noticed Titus talking to

Grandpa, and then the two of them headed for the shop. She wondered if it was hard for Grandpa to go there every day and not be able to do the carpentry work he used to do. Since his fingers didn't have enough strength to hold a piece of wood very long, whenever there was no paperwork to be done, he sat and visited with Nelson and Titus while they worked.

Sure wish they'd let me help out, Suzanne fumed. *If they'd give me a chance, they'd realize that I can do a good job at woodworking, too.*

When Suzanne finished checking the plants, she went out to the barn and fed the cats. As she sat on a bale of straw, watching them eat, her thoughts went to Titus and his dislike of cats. Maybe if Callie stayed at his place long enough, he'd form an attachment to her—or at least build up some toleration.

Suzanne continued to sit, even after the cats had finished their meal and scurried back to whatever place they'd come from. She enjoyed being in the barn, where she could pet the cats, listen to the pigeons coo, and smell the pleasant aroma from the bales of stacked hay.

Her stomach growled noisily, reminding her that it was time for lunch and she needed to go back to the house and make some sandwiches.

When Suzanne entered the kitchen, she found her little sister, Effie, sitting at the table, drawing a picture. "I'm *hungerich*," the girl said, blinking her eyes at Suzanne. "When's Mom comin' home to fix us somethin' to eat?"

"Not for a while, but I'll fix your lunch."

Effie shook her head. "Think I'd better wait for Mom."

"Sandwiches are easy to make," Suzanne said, taking a loaf of bread from the breadbox. "In fact, you can help."

"Can I make peanut butter and jelly?"

"You can make yours that way if you like, but I'm fixing

tuna fish for everyone else."

Effie wrinkled her freckled nose. "Eww. . .I don't like tuna. It stinks like fish."

Suzanne chuckled. "That's because tuna is fish."

"Think I'll stick to peanut butter and jelly."

"That's fine." Suzanne set the jars of peanut butter and jelly on the table beside Effie, along with two slices of bread and a knife. "Here you go. Have fun."

While Effie made her sandwich, Suzanne stood at the counter, mixing the can of tuna fish with mayonnaise and relish, which was the way she'd always liked to eat it. When that was done, she slathered mayonnaise on the pieces of bread, then added the tuna and a hunk of lettuce to each one. Next, she put the sandwiches in plastic wrap, placed them in the lunch basket, and added some of Mom's ginger cookies. Then she grabbed a jug of iced tea and turned toward the door. "I'll be back soon, but if you want to eat while I'm gone, that's fine," she called to Effie over her shoulder. "Oh, and don't forget to pray before you eat."

When Suzanne entered the woodshop, Nelson greeted her with a smile. "What'd Mom make for our lunch today?"

"Mom's in Hopkinsville, so I made tuna fish sandwiches."

"There's no vinegar in them I hope," Titus said with a snicker.

She frowned. "Of course not. But I hope you like mayonnaise and relish."

"Sorry about the vinegar remark," Titus said. "I'm sure the sandwiches will be fine."

Suzanne set the lunch basket on Grandpa's desk. "Where's Grandpa? I saw him come to the shop earlier and figured he'd still be here."

Nelson shook his head. "He was tired and went to the *Daadihaus* to take a nap. Didn't you see him come up?"

"No, but then I've been busy, so he might have gone into his side of the house without me knowing it."

"Grandpa's been really tired lately," Nelson said. "I'm worried about him."

"Is he having more pain than usual?" she asked.

Nelson shrugged. "I don't know, but then he's never been one to complain."

The door to the shop opened just then, and one of their English neighbors stepped in. While Nelson spoke to the man about a storage shed he wanted, Suzanne poured some iced tea into the men's cups and set them beside the sandwiches.

"That was a nice party you had for Esther," Titus said, moving to stand beside Suzanne. "She seemed real surprised, didn't she?"

Suzanne nodded. "I think everyone had a good time."

"I know I did. Plan on having a good time tomorrow morning, too."

"What's happening tomorrow?"

"Esther and I are going with Allen and his friend to see the Jefferson Davis Monument."

"Oh, I didn't realize that."

"Figured maybe Esther had told you."

"I haven't seen Esther since Thursday night." Suzanne moved toward the door. "I hope you and Esther will have a good time," she called over her shoulder.

"I'm sure we will."

As Suzanne headed for the house, her insides felt like a twisted rubber band. She was happy for Esther, since she knew this was what Esther wanted. But she couldn't help feeling a bit envious, wishing someone special would take an interest in her.

—∞—

When Titus got home that evening, he put Lightning away

and then went into the house for a drink of water. He'd just taken a glass down from the cupboard when he heard a familiar *meow*.

"Oh no! Not this again!" He hurried into his bedroom. Sure enough, Callie was curled up at the foot of his bed, with all four of her kittens.

"That's it!" Titus snapped his fingers. "I'm going to find out once and for all how that determined cat's been getting in."

Titus spent the next hour searching every nook and cranny for a hole that led to the outside. He was about to give up when he discovered a small hole in his bedroom closet. He ran out to the barn, found some wood to cover the hole, and hauled Callie and her brood back to the barn. When that was done, he decided to look for the phone shanty Isaac had mentioned earlier today.

Sure enough, it was there. . .several feet behind the barn, hidden under some overgrown vines and thick brush.

Titus figured he ought to wait until morning to clear the growth away from the shanty. Right now, he needed to get inside, because from the looks of the darkening sky, they were in for a good rain.

Chapter 19

When Titus woke up on Saturday morning, he was glad to see that the sun was shining. He hurried to get dressed, then went to the kitchen and fixed himself a bowl of cereal. When he finished with breakfast, he went out to the barn to give Callie some food and was relieved when he found the cat nursing her kittens inside the wooden box. Apparently he'd taken care of the problem of her getting into the house.

He studied the kittens a few minutes. Two were orange, white, and black like their mother, and two were white with black patches. They were kind of cute, but though they might look innocent and sweet right now, they'd soon grow up and would scratch and bite.

Titus left the barn and went around back to take a look at the inside of the phone shanty he'd discovered the evening before. He quickly cleared away the one vine that was still hanging across the front door of the shed. When he opened the door and stepped inside, it was dark and smelled musty. He brushed away several cobwebs that hung from the ceiling.

He left the door open to give more light and to help air out the shanty. Then he picked up the phone sitting on a rickety-looking folding table. There was no dial tone, of course.

Guess I should probably get the phone service connected, Titus thought, *but I'm already paying for my cell phone, so why pay for both?*

A horn honked, and Titus stepped out of the shanty in time to see Allen's truck pull up in front of the barn.

"I'd like you to meet my friend, Connie Myers," Allen said when Titus opened the truck door and climbed into the backseat of the extended cab.

"It's nice to meet you." Titus leaned over the seat and shook Connie's hand. "I'm Titus Fisher."

She smiled. "Yes, I know. Allen's told me about you." Connie's dark hair was cut short in a curly bob, and her eyes were also dark, like well-brewed coffee. She was pretty but wore too much makeup as far as Titus was concerned. Of course, he was used to Amish women, who wore no makeup at all. . .unless, like Phoebe, they liked to experiment with makeup and jewelry during their running-around years.

As Allen headed down the driveway toward the road, Titus tapped him on the shoulder. "Remember when you said I could invite someone to join us?"

"Yeah."

"Well, I invited Esther Beiler, so we'll need to stop by her folks' store to pick her up, if that's okay with you."

"Sure, no problem. I know where their store is, and it's on our way to the monument."

Titus relaxed against the seat and listened to Allen and Connie's conversation. Actually, it was more Connie doing the talking. Titus wondered if there was anything serious going on between them.

When they arrived at the Beilers' store, Titus hopped out of the truck and went inside. He found Esther behind the counter, waiting on a customer.

"I'll just be a minute," she said, smiling at Titus. "My mamm's in the storage room right now, but when she comes back, she'll take my place at the counter, and then I'll be ready to go."

"That's fine." Titus stood off to one side and waited as Esther rang up the English woman's purchases.

Soon, Esther's mother came out of the storage room. "Your daed's going to stock some shelves for a while," she said to Esther. "So I'm ready to take over for you here." Her blue eyes sparkled as she smiled at Titus. "It was nice of you to invite Esther to go with you today. I hope you'll both have a good time."

Titus nodded. "Allen's been to the Jefferson Davis Monument before, and he said it's pretty interesting."

A horn honked from outside, and Titus glanced out the window. "I think Allen's anxious to go," he said to Esther.

"I'm ready." Esther said good-bye to her mother and followed Titus out the door.

Paradise, Pennsylvania

A knock sounded on the back door, and Timothy went to see who it was. He was surprised to find Samuel and his wife, Elsie, on the porch.

"What'd you knock for? Why didn't you just come in like you normally do?" he asked.

"We didn't know if Hannah would be up to company," Samuel said. "So we didn't want to barge right in."

Timothy stepped onto the porch and closed the door behind him. "I'm really worried about Hannah. She still won't say much to me, and she doesn't want to go anywhere or do anything but sit and hold Mindy." He slowly shook his head.

"I'm beginning to wonder if she'll ever be the same."

"Would you like me to talk to her?" Elsie asked. "I had a miscarriage once, so I know how sad she must feel about losing the boppli."

Samuel nodded. "That's right, but God gave us four more kinner after that." He smiled at Elsie. "We're hoping for even more, if it be His will."

When they went inside, they found Hannah sitting in the living room on the sofa, staring at a book she hadn't even opened. The men stood off to one side, while Elsie took a seat beside Hannah. "I know you're sad about losing the boppli," she said, "because I lost one a few years ago, too. But you need to realize that Timothy and Mindy are still here, and they both need you." She touched Hannah's arm. "God knows what He's doing, and if your boppli had lived, he or she might have had some kind of physical problem."

"I. . .I suppose you could be right." Hannah nearly choked on the words.

"The boppli's in heaven now, and that should offer you some comfort," Elsie continued. "Remember, too, that the hardships we experience and the trials we face here on earth will teach us to trust more in God. For the weaker we feel, the harder we'll lean on Him."

Tears welled in Hannah's eyes. "I. . .I know you're right, Elsie, but it's hard not to think about the boppli I lost."

Elsie shook her head. "I understand that, and I'm not at all suggesting you forget about the baby. I just think you need to begin focusing on the family you still have, because they really do need you, Hannah."

"I. . .I suppose so."

Timothy moved over to stand behind Hannah and placed his hands on her shoulders. "We all want to see you getting back to normal."

"I want to get on with life, too." Hannah looked at Elsie and sniffed. "Danki, for coming by and for what you said. I know it's what I needed to hear."

"You're welcome." Elsie took Hannah's hand. "Remember now, I'm here for you, so if you need to talk about this some more, please let me know."

—∞—

Fairview, Kentucky

Titus tipped his head back and whistled. "Wow, that building's even taller than I thought!"

"It's 351 feet high, to be exact. The site marks Jefferson Davis's birthplace, and it rests on a foundation of solid Kentucky limestone," Allen said as they left his truck and approached the monument. "Another interesting fact is that Jefferson Davis was born here on June 3, 1808, and just eight months later, not more than one hundred miles away, Abraham Lincoln was born." He grinned at Connie. "I've become quite interested in history since I moved here."

"Can we go inside?" she asked. "I'll bet there's an awesome view from the top."

"You're right. There is." Allen pointed across the way. "There's the visitor's center, where we can buy tickets to take the elevator to the top of the monument."

"That sounds like fun." Titus's enthusiasm mounted. Just thinking about going inside the monument had him excited. "Don't think I've ever been in a building so high."

Esther's brows furrowed, and she nibbled nervously on her lip. "I. . .uh. . .think I'd rather wait for you down here."

"And miss all the fun?" Titus could hardly believe she wouldn't want to go up with them. "You've got to go up there and have a look around."

She shook her head. "I. . .I can't."

"Why not?'

"I'm afraid of heights."

"Nothing's going to happen to you," Titus said, hoping to offer her some encouragement. "You can hang on to my arm if you're scared."

Her face paled, and she continued to shake her head. "I'm not going up there, Titus. I'll sit on a bench down here or wait for you in the gift shop."

Titus hesitated a minute, wondering if he should stay with her, but he didn't see why he should miss out on the fun because she was afraid of heights. "Okay, whatever," he finally mumbled. What was the point in Esther agreeing to come along if she didn't want to go up in the monument?

"You look umgerennt," Esther said. "Are you upset because I don't want to go up?"

"No, it's okay. Wouldn't want you to go if you're scared." Titus felt like a heel. He didn't want to hurt Esther's feelings or try to force her to do something she was afraid of, but at the same time, he was disappointed.

"Let's head over to the gift shop and see about getting our tickets," Allen said. "We can also look around and see what they might have for sale."

When they entered the gift shop, Allen paid for his and Connie's tickets, and Titus paid for his. Then he turned to Esther and said, "Would you like me to buy something for you to eat or drink while we're up in the monument?"

She glanced at the small chest freezer across the room. "Maybe an ice-cream bar."

"Sure, go ahead and pick out the kind you like."

When they left the gift shop, Esther took a seat on one of the park benches, and the rest of them followed their guide into the elevator that would take them up the monument.

Once at the top, Titus looked down. He was amazed. He could see for miles around—rooftops of houses and barns, treetops, and the highway spread out below. What had looked so big on the ground looked very small.

"This is great!" Titus exclaimed. "Makes me wonder how small we must look in God's eyes when He looks down from heaven."

"Probably like little specks." Allen laughed. "But God knows each of us by name—even the number of hairs on our head."

Connie frowned. "You two aren't going to ruin the day by talking about a bunch of religious stuff, I hope."

"Talking about God shouldn't ruin anyone's day," Allen said. "I started going to Sunday school when I was a boy, and by the time I became a teenager, I'd given my heart to the Lord."

Connie rolled her eyes, as she pulled her fingers through the ends of her curly hair. "Please keep your religious views to yourself, because I'm really not interested."

Allen opened his mouth, like he might say more, but he closed it and pulled a camera from his shirt pocket instead. "Think I'll take a couple of pictures while we're up here. It isn't every day we get to see a sight such as this." He smiled at Titus. "Maybe if I send a few pictures of the area to Zach, he'll decide to pack up his family and move here, too."

Titus shook his head. "I doubt that. Zach seems content to stay in Pennsylvania with the rest of our family. Hopefully, he and the others will come here for a visit sometime, but I don't think any of them will ever leave Lancaster County."

—∞—

Suzanne had spent the morning helping Mom clean house, and by noon she was more than ready for a break.

"Should we make some sandwiches for lunch and eat them outside on the picnic table?" Mom asked.

Suzanne smiled. "That's a good idea. I always enjoy eating outside."

"Would you like to make the sandwiches while I prepare some lemonade?" Mom asked.

"Sure, that's fine."

"Can I help, too?" Effie asked as she skipped into the kitchen. "I think it's fun to squeeze lemons."

Mom smiled and patted Effie's head. "You can squeeze the lemons while I add water and sugar."

While Suzanne started working on the ham and cheese sandwiches, she thought about Titus and the remark he'd made about whether she'd put vinegar on the sandwiches. She knew he'd only been teasing, but it had hurt nonetheless. Still, she couldn't make herself spend time in the kitchen, trying to perfect her skills, when she'd rather be outside doing something else. Besides, with Mom being such a good cook, anything Suzanne ever made would pale by comparison. And since she didn't have a boyfriend and had no hope of marriage, what was the point in learning to cook?

When Suzanne finished the sandwiches, she placed them on a platter and set it on the table. "Is Grandpa in his room?" she asked Mom. "Should I tell him that lunch is ready and we'll be eating in the yard today?"

"I saw him go outside a little bit ago," Mom said. "He said something about a wasp's nest in the barn that needed to be knocked down."

"I'll go out and let him know lunch is ready."

Suzanne left the house and hurried to the barn. When she stepped inside, she didn't see any sign of Grandpa.

"Grandpa, are you in here?" she called.

All she heard was the nicker of the horses from their stalls on the other side of the barn.

Suzanne moved toward the back of the barn, and when she came to a place where a ladder had been set, she halted. There lay Grandpa, facedown on the floor!

Chapter 20

"Kumme, Nelson! *Schnell!*" Suzanne shouted as she hurried from the barn and cupped her hands around her mouth.

Nelson dashed out the back door of the house. "What are you shouting about? Why do you need me to come quickly?"

"It's Grandpa! He's passed out on the barn floor. I. . .I think he must have been trying to climb the ladder and fell." Suzanne's heart pounded, and her voice shook with emotion.

"Where is he?" Nelson asked as he raced into the barn.

"Over there." Suzanne pointed to the spot where Grandpa lay. "I tried to wake him, but he didn't respond."

Nelson tore across the room, and Suzanne followed. "Grandpa, can you hear me?" Nelson felt Grandpa's pulse. "He's alive, so that's a relief." He picked up Grandpa's false teeth. "Looks like these got knocked out of his mouth when he fell."

Suzanne knelt beside Grandpa, gently patting his face. "Wake up, Grandpa. Please, wake up."

Grandpa's eyes fluttered open. "Wh–what happened? How come you two are standin' over me with such worried faces?"

"I found you here, unconscious." Suzanne motioned to the ladder. "Were you trying to climb that to get to the wasp's nest?"

"Jah. Didn't want any of 'em botherin' the horses while they're in their stalls." Grandpa groaned as he tried to sit up. "Think I must've got the wind knocked out of me when I fell, 'cause I hurt all over. Guess that's what I get for thinkin' my shaky old legs could carry me up the ladder."

"I think we'd better call our driver and take you to the hospital in Hopkinsville," Nelson said.

The wrinkles in Grandpa's forehead deepened when he frowned. "What for?"

"To check you over and make sure nothing's broken."

"The only thing broke is my pride," Grandpa muttered. "Seems like I can't do much of anything these days."

"That's not true," Suzanne spoke up. "You're still doing the bookwork in the shop."

"Bookwork's nothin' compared to what I used to do."

Suzanne knew how much Grandpa liked being in the shop, but she also knew it must cause him pain whenever he tried to use his hands.

"We can talk about this later," Nelson said. "Right now we need to make sure you're okay." He slipped his hands around Grandpa's waist, helping him slowly to his feet, while Suzanne gently held on to Grandpa's arm.

Grandpa winced as he tried to stand. "Oh boy. Don't think I'm gonna be able to walk. My right ankle's sore, and it feels like it's swollen. Same holds true for my wrist."

Nelson lowered Grandpa back to the floor. "I'll go inside and get Russell and Chad. Then the three of us will carry you into the house." He looked at Suzanne. "Run down to the phone shanty and call one of our drivers. Let 'em know that we need a ride to the hospital right away."

Allen had just pulled his truck out of the parking lot at the monument site, when Titus's cell phone rang. As soon as he removed it from his trouser's pocket, Esther's eyebrows furrowed.

Ignoring her questioning look, he clicked the TALK button and held the phone up to his ear. "Hello."

"Hi, it's me, Timothy."

"Hey! Guess where I just came from?"

"Where?"

"Went up inside the Jefferson Davis Monument. It's so high you can see for miles around. If you ever come to visit, I'll have to take you there."

"Did you go there alone?"

"Went with Allen and his friend, Connie. Also brought a friend of mine—Esther Beiler."

"I knew it!" Timothy chuckled. "I knew when you moved to Kentucky that you'd find a girlfriend there. What's she like, Titus? Tell me about her."

Titus's face heated. "We're. . .uh. . .we're all just friends." He couldn't say much with Esther sitting right beside him, still wearing a curious expression.

"How are things with you?" Titus asked. "Is Hannah feeling any better?"

"A bit. Samuel and Elsie were here awhile ago, and talking with Elsie seemed to help her some."

"Glad to hear it."

"It's good that you were able to get a cell phone," Timothy said. "Makes it a lot easier to get a hold of you now."

"Jah." Titus glanced at Esther again, but this time, she looked away.

"Guess I'd better let you go. Just wanted to see how you were doing."

"I appreciate you calling. Be sure to tell Mom, Dad, and the rest of the family I said hello."

"I will. Talk to you later."

After Titus put the phone back in his pocket, Esther looked over at him and said, "I didn't realize you had a cell phone. Did you bring it with you from Pennsylvania?"

He shook his head. "Bought it in Hopkinsville so I'd be able to keep in touch with my family back home."

Her forehead wrinkled. "In case you didn't know it, cell phones aren't allowed in our church district. I'm sure our ministers would be upset if they knew you had one."

The disapproving look on Esther's face made Titus wish he'd left his cell phone at home.

"Since there's an old phone shanty behind the trailer, I'll see about getting the phone there connected," Titus said. *I'll just keep the cell phone for emergency purposes and to call home whenever I need to talk directly to someone*, he silently added.

As Esther turned to stare out the window, Titus thought about her fear of heights. It had really put a damper on his day to have her stay below while he went up into the monument. He wasn't really sure that he and Esther were suited for each other but figured he needed to give her a chance. Maybe after a few more dates he'd feel more comfortable with her and discover that they had a few things in common.

Chapter 21

Paradise, Pennsylvania

How's Hannah doing?" Fannie asked when she and Abraham entered Timothy's yard and found him sitting on the porch, with Mindy playing on a blanket nearby.

"She's in our room taking a nap right now, but she's feeling a little better."

"Emotionally or physically?" Fannie asked.

"Both. Samuel and Elsie stopped by yesterday, and Elsie shared a few things with Hannah about the way she felt when she had a miscarriage a few years ago. I think it helped for Hannah to know that someone else understands how she feels." Timothy reached over and patted the top of his daughter's head. "Hannah realizes that Mindy and I both need her, and I think she found comfort when Elsie reminded her that the baby we lost is in heaven."

Fannie nodded and smiled. "I'm glad she's feeling better."

"We wish none of our family ever had to suffer, but unfortunately, everyone must face some trials, Abraham said. "We just need to hold God's hand and let Him lead us through the valleys whenever they come."

"You're right about that," Timothy agreed. "On a different note, I think there's something you both should know."

"What's that?" Fannie asked as she and Abraham took seats on either side of Timothy.

"Titus has a new girlfriend." He grinned.

"Already?" Abraham asked before Fannie could respond. "That son of ours sure does move fast." He nudged Fannie's arm and chuckled. "I think he takes after his daed, at least in that regard."

"It's not funny," Fannie said with a huff. "I don't think it's good that Titus has found someone already."

"Why not?" Timothy asked.

"It's too soon after Phoebe." Fannie frowned. "It's not good to get involved with someone so quickly after breaking up. I think Titus needs to give himself some time to adjust to his new job and surroundings before he starts courting again."

"As I'm sure you recall, we fell in love pretty quickly," Abraham reminded her.

"That was different. We'd both been widowed awhile and weren't on the rebound."

Abraham shrugged. "Maybe Titus needed to find someone right away to help him get over Phoebe."

"You could be right," Timothy put in. "This new girl might be a better fit for Titus, too."

Fannie sighed deeply. "If Titus falls in love with a girl from Kentucky and marries her, he'll never move back home."

Abraham patted her arm affectionately. "Let's not worry about that until the time comes."

Pembroke, Kentucky

"Guess it's time to get my horse and buggy ready. Are you

going to the young people's singing with me?" Nelson asked Suzanne as the two of them sat at the kitchen table with Mom, having a glass of cold apple cider.

She shook her head. "I'd better stay here and help Mom take care of Grandpa."

"I don't need your help," Mom said. "Grandpa's sleeping right now, and the pain medication the doctor prescribed will probably keep him sleeping for several hours."

"Even so, I'd rather stay home." Suzanne took a sip of cider and let it roll around in her mouth before swallowing. It was sweet, yet a bit tart—just the way she liked it. When the apples in their yard ripened in the fall, they'd take them to the Beilers' and make more apple cider, using their press. She always looked forward to that.

Mom tapped Suzanne's shoulder. "You need to get out and have some fun. You'll never find a husband if you don't spend time with other young people your age."

Suzanne's jaw clenched. Not this again. She didn't know why Mom thought she had to get married. They knew several Amish women who'd either never been married or were widowed and had chosen not to marry again. *Of course*, she reminded herself, *if I don't care about getting married, then why do I feel envious when others I know find boyfriends and get married?*

"Suzanne, did you hear what I said?"

"Jah, Mom, I heard."

"Are you going with Nelson to the singing or not?"

Suzanne looked over at Nelson. "Won't you be taking your girlfriend tonight?"

He nodded. "I'll be picking Lucy up on the way to the singing."

"Then I shouldn't go. I'm sure you'd rather spend time with her alone than have your sister sitting in the backseat of your buggy, able to hear every word you're saying."

"Won't bother me any," Nelson said with a shrug. "Besides, maybe there'll be some fellow at the singing who'll ask if he can give you a ride home."

"*Puh*!" Suzanne flapped her hand. "Like that's going to happen."

"It might," Mom put in with a hopeful expression.

"Maybe I don't want a ride home in some fellow's buggy."

"Aw, sure you do," Nelson said with a wink. "Every girl wants to be courted."

"Not me." Suzanne shook her head.

"You're only saying that because you haven't found the right man," Mom said. "Someday, when the time is right, you'll fall in love and get married."

Suzanne figured it was best not to argue. She'd stayed up late last night, waiting for Mom and Nelson to bring Grandpa home from the hospital. Truth was, she was tired and had hoped she could go to bed early. If she went to the singing that wouldn't happen. Still, if she didn't go, she'd have to hear about it from Mom all evening.

Suzanne took another sip of cider and finally nodded. "Okay, I'll go to the singing."

—∞—

"I still can't believe your grandpa was up on a ladder," Esther said to Suzanne after the singing ended and everyone gathered around to visit. "Didn't he know how dangerous that could be? Especially at his age and with his arthritis being so bad."

Suzanne moved closer to Esther on the bench they sat upon. "You're right, he shouldn't have been climbing a ladder, but you know how *schtarrkeppich* my *grossdaadi* can be."

Esther nodded. "Sometimes I think the older people get, the more stubborn they become. My grandma often says that

Grandpa's the most schtarrkeppich man she knows. He's seventy-two years old and still thinks he can keep up with his sons."

"My grossdaadi is the same way," Suzanne said. "Thanks to that fall, Grandpa's right wrist and right ankle are severely sprained, and he has several bruised ribs. Since he's right-handed, he won't be able to do the bookwork at the shop for a while."

"Who'll do it?"

"I told Mom I would. She has enough to do in the house."

"But who's going to sell your bedding plants? Will your mamm have to do that as well?"

"Mom will take care of any customers who come to our place to buy plants, but I'll be responsible for taking the plants to the produce auction."

"Speaking of the auction, Titus and I were over that way when we went to see the Jefferson Davis Monument on Saturday."

"I'd heard you were going. How was it? Did you have a good time?"

"It was interesting to see the monument up close, but I didn't go inside. Only Titus, Allen, and his friend, Connie, took the elevator to the top. I sat on a bench and waited for them below."

"With your fear of heights, I guess you wouldn't have felt comfortable being up so high."

"No, I sure wouldn't." Esther shifted on the bench, and glanced across the room where the young men had gathered. "I think Titus was a little disappointed that I didn't go up, though."

"Did you explain things to him?"

"Jah, but he still seemed disappointed."

"Are you thinking maybe Titus isn't the right one for you?"

Esther shook her head. "It's not that. I just wish we could have done something that we both enjoy."

Suzanne bumped Esther's arm with her elbow. "Here he comes now."

"I just talked to Nelson, and he told me about your grandpa's fall," Titus said, looking down at Suzanne. "I'm sorry to hear it."

"We were glad he wasn't seriously hurt, because at his age it could have been a lot worse." Suzanne sighed and touched her chest. "For some time now, Grandpa has tried to do things he shouldn't do, instead of calling on Nelson or one of the boys. It really scared me when he fell."

"I'd be happy to help out whenever I can," Titus offered.

"That's nice of you."

Esther looked up at Titus and smiled. "Did you enjoy the singing tonight?"

"Sure did."

"Was it like the ones you've attended in Lancaster County?" she asked.

"Pretty much." Titus glanced at Suzanne, wishing she'd go someplace else. He wanted to ask Esther if he could give her a ride home but didn't want to do it in front of Suzanne.

Just then, Ethan Zook, one of the minister's sons, wandered over. Titus held his breath, hoping Ethan wasn't going to ask Esther if he could give her a ride in his buggy. To Titus's relief, Ethan only stopped to ask Suzanne how her grandfather was doing, and then he headed across the room toward a group of young men.

"It's getting chilly," Suzanne said. "Think I'll get my shawl from Nelson's buggy." She gave Esther a quick smile, glanced briefly at Titus, and walked away.

Titus decided that he'd better take advantage of the opportunity while he could, so he leaned close to Esther and whispered, "I'd like to give you a ride home tonight. If you don't already have one, that is."

She gave him another deep-dimpled smile. "I've had no other offers. Even if I had, I can't think of anyone I'd rather ride home with than you."

Titus grinned. "Great. Just let me know when you want to leave."

"I'm ready to go now, if you are," she said sweetly.

"All right then. I'll get my horse and buggy and meet you over by the barn."

Titus hurried out the door and sprinted across the yard, feeling lighthearted and looking forward to the ride to Esther's house. She was a very pretty girl, and he hoped he'd have an opportunity to take her out again so they could get better acquainted.

As they headed down the road a short time later, Esther remained quiet, while Titus tried to think of something to talk about.

"Are you warm enough?" he asked.

"Jah."

"I hope the buggy seat's not too uncomfortable for you. This is an old buggy, and even though I've reupholstered the seats, they're not as padded as I'd like them to be."

"The seat seems fine to me. I'm just enjoying the peacefulness of the evening."

"You're right, it is peaceful. I think the sound of crickets and bullfrogs singing their nightly song makes it seem that way."

"I agree."

"So what do you like to do when you're not working at your folks' store?" he asked.

Before Esther could reply, a noisy *va-room! va-room!*

shattered their peace and quiet. Titus glanced through his side mirror and noticed a single headlight coming up fast behind them. As the vehicle drew closer, he realized it was a motorcycle. It came right up to the back of the buggy; then pulled into the oncoming lane, as though going to pass. Instead of going around, however, the cycle roared alongside the buggy—so close that Titus could have reached out and touched the young man who was driving.

Suddenly, the motorcycle pulled right in front of the buggy, and the driver slammed on his brakes.

Lightning reared up, and the buggy wobbled.

"Whoa! Steady, boy." Titus pulled back on the reins, in an effort to keep control.

The driver of the motorcycle gunned the engine and tore off down the road. Titus's hands turned sweaty and his heart pounded as he continued to try and calm Lightning down.

A few minutes later, the motorcycle reappeared, coming from the opposite direction. When it roared past this time, nearly clipping Titus's buggy, Lightning went wild. He reared up, kicked his back hooves against the front of the buggy, and took off down the road like an angry bull was chasing him.

"Whoa! Whoa!" Titus hollered.

Lightning kept running; the frightened horse was out of control!

Chapter 22

Esther screamed, and Titus's hands shook so badly he could barely hold on to the reins. "Whoa, Lightning! Whoa!"

The buggy vibrated, and Titus wondered if it would hold together under the stress of all the bouncing and shaking around. They hit a bump in the road, and Esther screamed again. "Make him stop, Titus! Make him stop!"

"I'm tryin'," Titus said through clenched teeth. In the five years he'd owned the horse, he'd always been able to get him under control. But then, he'd never had a motorcycle charge after him like this.

When Titus was sure the buggy would flip over, Lightning finally slowed to a sensible trot. Titus glanced in his side mirror and was relieved when he saw no motorcycle headlight. "I think he's gone—must have had enough fun for the night."

Titus guided the horse to the side of the road and handed the reins to Esther. "I'd better get out and make sure this old buggy is okay. Want to check on Lightning, too."

He stepped out of the buggy and examined each of the wheels. Everything looked fine. After Titus had checked his horse over and found him to be okay, he breathed a sigh of relief. *Thank You, Lord.*

"I think that fellow on the motorcycle tried to spook your horse on purpose," Esther said when Titus climbed back in the buggy.

"I believe you're right."

"I don't understand why anyone would do such a thing."

Titus reached for Esther's hand. It felt cold and clammy. "Some people do weird things when they're looking for a thrill, and I'm guessing that fellow thought freaking out my horse was a real kick."

She shivered. "It scares me to think of what might have happened. If the buggy had turned over, we could have been injured or killed."

"But it didn't turn over, and we're fine. I'm thankful the Lord was watching over us and that my horse finally calmed down."

Esther released a lingering sigh. "You're right; we have much to be thankful for."

—∞—

Arriving home from the singing, Suzanne went straight to the house while Nelson put the horse and buggy away.

"How's Grandpa doing?" she asked when she entered the living room, where Mom sat reading a book.

Mom looked up and smiled. "He's doing okay. Was up long enough to eat a bowl of soup, then soon after that, he went back to bed." She patted the sofa. "Come sit and tell me how the singing went tonight."

Suzanne removed her shawl and outer bonnet and placed them on the rocking chair; then she took a seat on the sofa next to Mom. "It went fine. Quite a few young people were there."

"Did anyone special bring you home?"

Suzanne nodded. "Nelson. He's special."

Mom snickered. "I wasn't talking about your bruder. I was hoping some nice young man would have the good sense to ask if he could escort you home from the singing."

"Well, no one did. Esther got an invite, though."

"From who?"

"Titus. He took her to see the Jefferson Davis Monument yesterday, too." Suzanne smiled. "You should have seen the dreamy look on Esther's face when Titus came over to talk with us."

Mom puckered her lips. "I'd rather hoped it would be you Titus took an interest in, not Esther."

Suzanne shook her head. "It's fine with me if he and Esther get together because I have no interest in him at all."

"Why not? He's nice looking, and from what Nelson and your grossdaadi have said, Titus is a hard worker."

"That may be so, but he's not interested in me, nor I in him." Suzanne covered her mouth and yawned. "Think I'll head upstairs to bed."

Mom gave Suzanne's arm a gentle pat. "Sleep well, and I'll see you in the morning."

As Suzanne climbed the steps to her room, she thought more about Titus taking Esther home from the singing, and a feeling of envy washed over her. It wasn't that she'd wanted Titus to give her a ride home; she just wished someone—even someone she didn't care for that much—would have brought her home from the singing. Of course, she wouldn't admit that to anyone. Let everyone think she was content to be an old maid, because that's surely where she was headed.

—ꟺ—

When Titus woke up the following morning, he'd only been

out of bed a short time when his cell phone rang. When he hit the TALK button, he was surprised to hear Mom's voice.

"Hi, Titus. I've been wanting to call ever since I heard you got a cell phone and was hoping I'd catch you before you left for work this morning."

"You caught me all right. I haven't even had breakfast yet." Titus rose from his seat on the bed. "What's up, Mom?"

"I wanted to see how you're doing."

Titus wandered out to the kitchen and turned on the propane-powered stove. He needed a cup of coffee in order to wake up. "I'm good. How are things with you and Dad?"

"We're both fine, but we miss you."

"I miss you and the rest of the family, too."

"Your daed and I stopped by to see Timothy and Hannah yesterday afternoon."

"How are they doing?"

"Better. Hannah's not quite so depressed anymore."

"That's good to hear." Titus moved over to the sink and filled the coffeepot with water. When he glanced out the kitchen window, he spotted Callie slinking across the grass. *Stupid cat. She ought to be in the barn with her kittens. Sure wish I hadn't gotten stuck with her.*

"I hesitate to bring this up," Mom said, "but I spoke with Phoebe's mamm during the meal after church yesterday."

"Oh?" Titus's head started to pound. He hoped Mom wasn't going to lecture him about Phoebe again.

"Arie's been awfully worried since the last time she spoke with Phoebe on the phone."

"How come?"

"Apparently, Phoebe and Darlene are living in a run-down apartment in a bad part of town. Arie's concerned that it might not be safe. Phoebe's also been running around with some English kids, and from what little Phoebe's told Arie, she believes they do some things our church would not approve of."

"There isn't much Arie can do about it, Mom. Moving to California was Phoebe's choice, and she obviously wants to be on her own."

"I know that, but Arie's also worried that Phoebe might never return to Pennsylvania and the Amish way of life."

"She's probably right about that." Titus set the coffeepot on the stove and took a seat at the table to wait for it to perk. He wished Mom didn't feel the need to talk about Phoebe—especially when he was trying so hard to forget her.

"I'm glad Phoebe moved away, because if she'd stayed, she may have dragged you down."

"Why do you say that?"

"I know how easily you were swayed by her, and I'm glad she's finally out of your life."

Titus's fingers tightened around his cell phone. Thinking about Phoebe living in California was bad enough, but did Mom need to mention that he'd been easily swayed by Phoebe? It wasn't as if he'd let her talk him into doing anything bad. Titus's biggest error was in believing Phoebe when she'd promised to join the church and marry him.

"While your daed and I were visiting with Timothy yesterday," Mom continued, "he mentioned that he'd talked to you, and that you're courting a young woman there."

"Her name is Esther, and we're not really—"

"I'm glad you're seeing someone, because I'm sure it's helping you get over Phoebe. But I hope you won't rush into anything. You need to make sure you know this young woman well before you become serious about her."

"Mom, it's not like I'm going to marry Esther. We just went to see the Jefferson Davis Monument on Saturday, and then I took her home from the singing last night."

"Two days in a row? That sounds like you're getting serious to me."

"We're just friends."

"What's Esther like?"

"She has a pretty face and a pleasant personality." He paused, debating about how much he should tell Mom. He didn't want her to think he was getting serious about Esther when he wasn't sure yet how he felt about her. "I'll let you know if we end up getting serious, but right now I need to go. I have to call the phone company. I discovered a shanty out back, and I need to see about them getting the phone in it up and running, and then I need to head to work."

"If you're getting a phone connected in the phone shanty, does that mean you'll be getting rid of your cell phone?"

"I'm not sure. I'll let you know when I decide."

"Okay, son. Take care, and please keep in touch."

"I will, Mom. Bye." Titus clicked off the phone and drew in a deep breath. He wished Mom hadn't mentioned Phoebe. He wished he could forget he'd ever met the beautiful young woman with shiny auburn hair and sparking blue eyes.

—∞—

As Titus entered the woodshop that morning, he discovered Suzanne sitting at her grandfather's desk, going over the books. "How's your grossdaadi doing?" he asked.

"He's in a lot of pain, and since his wrist is sprained quite badly, he won't be able to do the bookwork for a while, so I'll be coming in to get it done."

"I'm sure he appreciates your help."

"I only wish I could do more."

"Is there something I can do to help today?" he asked.

She hesitated a minute and finally nodded. "If you can stay after work for an hour or two, there are several chores you could help Nelson and the boys with."

"Sure, no problem."

"Starting tomorrow, I'll be taking some of our bedding plants to the auction, so that will cut into some of my time around here."

"I've seen the auction building, and I'm hoping I can stop by there sometime."

"I'm sure you'd enjoy it. If you come hungry, there's a place to get food there, too."

He grinned and thumped his stomach. "I'm always eager to find places that serve good food."

Suzanne finished the bookwork, then left the woodshop and went out to the phone shanty to check for messages. Mom's sister Karen, who lived in Michigan, had called saying that she'd be going to the hospital in a few days to have surgery on her back.

Suzanne hurried into the house and gave Mom the message.

Mom turned from her job of doing dishes, and deep wrinkles formed in forehead. "I knew Karen's back was getting worse and figured she might need surgery. I just wasn't counting on it happening so soon. I'd like to go and help out, but with Dad needing more care right now, this isn't a good time for me to be gone." She dried her hands on a dish towel and moved toward Suzanne. "Unless you think you can take over for me while I'm gone."

Suzanne could tell by the look of desperation on Mom's face that she really wanted to be with her sister. But if Mom went away, she'd be responsible for most of the household chores, as well as fixing all the meals. She contemplated things for a few more seconds, then finally nodded. "I'm sure I can manage while you're gone. I just hope no one gets sick from my terrible cooking."

Chapter 23

Suzanne's mother left for Michigan the next day, and for the next few weeks, Suzanne's life was a blur. Besides seeing that Grandpa's needs were met, she'd been going to the produce auction once a week, and out to the woodshop to do the books twice a week. She was also responsible for seeing that her younger sister and brother did their chores every day, not to mention being stuck with the responsibility of preparing all the meals. Since Suzanne didn't know how to cook much of anything very well, she knew they'd been eating a lot of soup and sandwiches.

She had been hoping to spend some time in the woodshop, making birdhouses to sell at the auction, but the only time she could work there without anyone knowing was late at night, and by then she was too exhausted. Even though Titus had been helping with some of the chores, Suzanne had more than she could handle.

Since today was Saturday and the woodshop was closed, it would have been the perfect time to do some work there. Unfortunately, she had to be at the auction the first half of the day, and the last half, she'd spend doing household chores and making sure that Effie cleaned her room.

As Suzanne hurried to make breakfast that morning, her head began to pound. How did Mom manage to get so much done and make it look so easy?

"You look *meid* this morning," Grandpa said as he hobbled into the kitchen, using his cane for support.

She yawned and stretched her arms over her head. "You're right; I'm very tired."

"That's because you're trying to do too much and not getting enough sleep."

"There's much to do, and so little time to do it."

"You don't have to do it all, you know. Some of the bookwork in the shop can wait until your mamm gets home, and I'm sure Russell would be happy to take the bedding plants to the auction for you."

She shook her head. "Russell doesn't know enough about the plants to answer any questions folks might have. Besides, he'll be busy helping at the dairy farm today."

"Oh, that's right." Grandpa took a seat at the table and frowned as he lifted his right arm. "Wish I could do something to help out, but between my sore wrist and ankle, I'm not much good to anyone right now."

"Once your wrist settles down, you should be able to take over the bookwork again." Suzanne handed Grandpa a cup of coffee and poured one for herself.

"I sure miss working with wood." He blew on his coffee and took a sip. "Guess I should be glad Nelson's willing to take over the business for me, because I'd feel even worse if no one in the family wanted to keep the place running. Woodworking's in my blood, and it pleases me to know that it's also in my grandson's blood."

It's in my blood, too, Suzanne thought. *If you'd just give me a chance I'd prove it to you.*

Los Angeles, California

"What was that, Mom?" Phoebe switched her cell phone to the other ear. "I think we have a bad connection, because I can barely hear what you're saying."

"I'm concerned about you and the company you're keeping. Remember, where you go and what you do tells people what you are."

"I already know that, and I don't need any lectures."

"I saw Fannie Fisher the other day. She mentioned that Titus is seeing—"

"Titus saw what?" The phone crackled, making it difficult to hear what Mom was saying.

"He has a—"

More crackling, followed by a buzzing sound.

"Did you say Titus has something?"

"Jah. Titus has a—" Mom's voice faded, and then the phone went dead.

Phoebe groaned. "Stupid cell phone! I'll bet the battery died, and now I'll have to charge it again."

"You'd better quit gabbin' on that phone and get back to work!" Phoebe's boss called to her from the front of the ice-cream store. "There's a line of customers out here, and your break's over!"

Phoebe returned the cell phone to her purse and left the room where the employees took their breaks. She'd have to talk to Mom some other time.

Fairview, Kentucky

"Sure is a warm day, isn't it?" Titus asked Suzanne when he

arrived at the auction and joined her beside the rows of bedding plants she'd brought to sell.

Suzanne nodded. "Summer's almost here, that's for sure."

"Have you sold many flowers so far?"

"I sure have. Things have been real busy here in the parking lot and inside the auction building, as well."

"I'll have to go check it out. Might bid on some lettuce or strawberries." He grinned. "It may surprise you to know this, but I like to cook."

"That is a surprise. Most men I know don't like to be in the kitchen, unless it's to eat something someone else has cooked."

"There are a lot of things I can't make, but one thing I can cook real well is fish."

She blotted her damp forehead with the back of her hand. "I wish I had the time to go fishing again, but with Mom still in Michigan, there's no time for me to do anything fun."

"How much longer will she be gone?" he asked.

"Probably another week or so. Aunt Karen's surgery went well, and she's getting along okay, but Mom wants to stay and help out until my aunt Mary, who lives in Oklahoma, gets there."

Titus's stomach rumbled, and he held his hand against it, hoping she hadn't heard the noise. "You mentioned the other day that there's a place to get a meal here. Where is that, anyway?"

"It's at the end of the auction building, over there." Suzanne pointed to her left and giggled. "From the way your stomach sounds, you probably need to eat something real quick."

He chuckled, although his face heated. "Think I'll go over there and see what they have to eat. Can I bring you something?"

She shook her head. "Thanks anyway, but I brought my lunch from home."

"Okay. Since tomorrow's an in-between Sunday, and there will be no church in our district, guess I'll see you on Monday morning when I come to work."

She gave a nod.

As Titus walked away, he looked back for a minute. The way Suzanne tipped her head as she plucked a dead bloom off one of the mums reminded him of Phoebe. That same old ache settled over him like a heavy blanket of fog, and he quickened his footsteps. Maybe finding something good to eat would take his mind off Phoebe.

~

Pembroke, Kentucky

When Titus got home from the auction that afternoon, he decided to give Zach a call and see how things were going.

He took a seat on the front porch and reached into his pocket for the cell phone. It wasn't there, and it didn't take him long to figure out why. There was a hole in his pants pocket.

"That's just great," Titus muttered. He had no idea where the cell phone had fallen, so he didn't even know where to look. If it had fallen out of his pocket on the way to or from the auction, it had probably been run over by now.

Titus thought about going back to the auction to look for it but figured the place would be closed for the day.

Guess I'll head out to the phone shanty and call Zach from there, he decided. He was glad he'd called the phone company last week and had the phone connected. He'd use that until he found his cell phone or was able to get another one to replace it.

Titus stepped into the phone shanty to make the call, turned on the battery-operated light he'd put there, and was about to pick up the phone, when he noticed something he hadn't seen before. There was a hole in the wall, and as he bent to examine it, he discovered an envelope sticking partway out.

He reached down and gave it a tug. The envelope ripped open and he gasped. There was a wad of money inside—a lot of money!

CHAPTER 24

Paradise, Pennsylvania

I'm glad you stopped by," Naomi said when Samuel entered Hoffmeir's General Store.

"Oh, why's that? Are you in need of some business?" he asked with a grin.

She shook her head and swatted him playfully on the arm. "Can't a *schweschder* just be happy to see her bruder?"

"Of course a sister can be happy to see her brother, and a brother can be happy to see his sister." Samuel gave Naomi's shoulder a playful squeeze, glad that there were no customers in the store right now so they could talk.

"Actually, there's another reason I'm happy to see you here today," she said.

"What's that?"

"Abby and I are planning a surprise party for Mama Fannie's seventieth birthday, and since it's still a few weeks away, we think there's enough time for us to get everything done and make it a special event."

He leaned on the counter. "A surprise party, huh? Think you can pull it off without her finding out about it?"

"I hope so. Even though Mama Fannie's not our real

mamm, she does so many special things for us, and we all love her so much." Naomi smiled. "We want to make her birthday as special as we can."

"Who do you plan to invite?"

"All of her closest friends, and our whole family, of course." She pointed at Samuel. "Now that you know about it, would you help spread the word to a few people for me?"

"Sure. Who would you like me to tell?"

"You can tell our brothers Zach, Timothy, Norman, and Jake. I've already told Nancy and Mary Ann. Abby will tell Matthew and also let her brother and his family know. Hopefully, they'll be able to make the trip from Ohio to help us celebrate." Naomi snapped her fingers. "Oh, and we'll have to let Titus know."

"You think he'll be able to take time off from his new job to come?"

"I'm hoping he can. If we have the party on a Friday evening, he'd just need to miss one day of work. If he takes the bus, he should be able to leave there Thursday after he gets off work, and then go back to Kentucky sometime Saturday. I know Mama Fannie would be thrilled to see him."

"Sounds like you've got it covered. Now the only thing left for us to do is figure out a way to keep her from finding out about the party." Samuel smiled. "Think I'll give Titus a call right away so he can see about getting the time off."

Pembroke, Kentucky

Titus didn't know which problem to deal with first: his lost cell phone or the money he'd just found. He drew in a shaky breath and tried to think. He needed to find the cell phone, because if someone else got a hold of it he could end up having to pay for a bunch of texting charges that weren't his.

He also needed to figure out what to do with the wad of

bills in his hands. He counted them, and they added up to ten thousand dollars. He could do a lot with that much money: buy a new buggy or put a down payment on a place of his own—maybe even toward this place if he decided to buy it from Allen. He needed to think about this. Try to figure out what he should do. Could the old man who used to own this place have put the money in there? Could he have even had that much money? If he did, then why had he been living in a run-down trailer, and why hadn't he put the money in the bank instead of the phone shanty?

Guess the first thing I'd better do is to give Allen a call, Titus decided. *Since he owns this place, I'm sure the money's legally his.*

He reached for the phone and punched in Allen's number. It rang a few times; then his voice mail came on.

"Hi Allen; it's me, Titus. I. . .uh. . .found something in my phone shanty and I need to talk to you about it. I lost my cell phone today, so you can't call me on that. You'd better call my number here and leave a message so I'll know when's a good time to call you again."

When Titus hung up the phone, he decided to try calling his own cell number, hoping someone may have found it and would answer the phone.

Fairview, Kentucky

Suzanne's driver had just pulled into the auction's parking lot at the close of the day, when she heard a phone ring. She looked down and was surprised to see a cell phone on the ground. She hesitated to answer it at first, since she didn't know who it belonged to, but when it continued to ring, she finally bent down and picked it up.

"Hello."

"Who's this?"

"Suzanne Yoder. Who's this?"

"Titus Fisher. Did you find my cell phone, Suzanne?"

Suzanne's mouth opened in surprise. "You. . .you have a cell phone?"

"Jah. It must have fallen out of my pocket. Where'd you find it?"

"It was lying in the auction parking lot. When it rang, I wasn't sure whether to answer or not."

"I'm glad you did, and even more glad that my phone's been found. If you're going to be there awhile I'll come back and pick it up right now."

"Actually, my driver's here, and we're getting ready to leave."

"Why don't you take it home with you, then? I'll come over to get it sometime this evening."

"Uh. . .in case you didn't know it, cell phones aren't allowed in our church district," Suzanne said.

"I've heard that already, but I'm only keeping it for emergency purposes, and to stay in touch with—"

"Our ministers won't be too happy about it if they hear you have a cell phone."

"Are you going to tell them?"

"No, but I think you should. Unless you're planning to get rid of it, of course."

"I don't know. I signed a contract for a whole year, so I'd have to pay a cancellation fee if I discontinue the service."

Suzanne could hear the frustration in Titus's voice, so she decided to drop the subject for now. She'd talk to him more about it when he came over this evening to pick up the phone. "I'd better go," she said. "I need to get home so I can do some chores before I fix supper."

"Okay. See you later then."

Suzanne clicked off the phone and sighed. Didn't Titus care about the rules of their church? Didn't he want to be a member in good standing?

Chapter 25

Pembroke, Kentucky

After supper, Titus went out to the phone shanty to call Allen again and was relieved when Allen answered on the second ring: "Walters's Construction."

"Allen, it's me, Titus. I tried calling you before. Did you get my message?"

"I haven't checked messages this evening. I went over to see Connie, because I needed to tell her that I've decided we shouldn't see each other anymore."

"How come?"

"She's opposed to religious things, and since I haven't been able to get through to her about the importance of a relationship with God, I decided to break things off before *our* relationship had a chance to become serious."

"That's probably a good idea."

"Yeah, but I'll keep praying for Connie. It's not God's will that any should perish, so hopefully, she'll see the light someday." Allen paused. "What'd you call about, anyway?"

"I found something in the phone shanty I think you should know about."

"What's that?"

Titus explained about the money and ended it by saying, "I thought you'd probably want to come over here right away and get it."

Allen released a low whistle. "Wow, that's really something. But I'm not the one who put the money there, so it's not really mine."

"What are you going to do about it?" Titus questioned.

"Guess I'll notify the sheriff and see what he has to say. Could be the money is stolen, and if that's the case, I'll have to turn it over to the sheriff. If not, we can split the money. How's that sound?"

"Sounds good to me."

"Maybe if you're still interested in buying the place instead of renting it, you could use the money as a down payment." Allen paused. "Of course, that depends on what the sheriff has to say."

Titus sat, too stunned to say a word. He'd never expected to find any money, much less have Allen make him such a generous offer. No wonder Allen and Zach had remained good friends since they were kids. A friend like Allen was a friend for life.

"You still there, Titus?"

"Yeah. I'm just thinking about the money."

"If you'd rather use your half for something other than the trailer, that's okay. Just thought you might like to own a place of your own."

"I would, but I won't get my hopes up about that until after you've talked to the sheriff."

"That's good thinking. I'll call you back and let you know as soon as I have some answers. In the meantime, you'd better put the money in a safe place."

"I already have. Oh, and by the way. . .Suzanne found my

cell phone. Guess it fell out of my pocket when I was at the produce auction earlier today. I'm heading over to her place right now to get it."

"Okay, great. After I hear from the sheriff, I'll try calling your cell phone. If I can't get you there, I'll leave a message on your voice mail in the phone shanty."

"Sounds good. Talk to you later, Allen."

Titus hung up the phone and went to saddle Lightning. He still preferred traveling by horseback, but when the weather turned colder this fall, he knew he'd have to start using the buggy more. He was about to mount the horse when Callie zipped out of the barn and started meowing at him.

"Oh great," he muttered. "She wants to be fed." Well, he couldn't let her starve; not when she had babies who were dependent on her. He left Lightning tied at the hitching rail and headed to the barn.

Suzanne had just finished chopping some lettuce and tomatoes when Nelson came into the kitchen. "What are we having for supper tonight?" he asked, peering over her shoulder.

"Haystack. That's one meal I shouldn't be able to mess up."

He chuckled and gave her a pat on the back. "You'll learn how to cook one of these days. . .when the right man comes along to motivate you."

She shrugged. "I doubt that's ever going to happen."

"What about Ethan Zook? I saw him eyeballing you at the singing the other night."

"Right. More to the point, he was eyeballing the food. Ethan's already overweight, and if he's not careful, he'll end up fat like our neighbor, Neil Parker."

"Say, whose phone is that?" Nelson asked, pointing to the cell phone lying on the other end of the counter.

"It belongs to Titus. I found it in the parking lot at the auction this afternoon. Guess it fell out of his pocket. He's coming over here sometime this evening to pick it up." She frowned. "Did you know he had a cell phone?"

Nelson nodded. "I told him it wasn't allowed in our church district and figured he would have gotten rid of it by now."

"I don't think he plans to get rid of it. I think he's going to keep it and hopes that none of our church leaders finds out."

"That's not a good idea, but then it's not our place to tell him what to do."

Suzanne dropped her paring knife and put both hands against her hips. "I wasn't planning to tell Titus what to do. He's clearly got a mind of his own."

Nelson frowned. "Is that how you see Titus, as a know-it-all?"

She nodded.

"I think you're wrong. During the time I've been working with Titus I've had a few insights as to what makes him tick."

"And what would that be?"

"He's insecure and doubts himself. I've seen it in the way he questions his abilities to work with wood. Always has to check with me or Grandpa to make sure things are just right. Even then he sometimes seems doubtful about whether his work is good enough, which is lecherich, because he's a skilled carpenter."

She compressed her lips. "Hmm. . . Guess I haven't spent enough time with Titus to see his insecurities." *Maybe it's because I have too many of my own.*

"He seems to have gained a little more confidence than he had when he first started working for us, but he often compares himself to his twin brother." Nelson turned on the faucet and filled a glass with water. "From some of the things Titus has said, it sounds like his twin is very successful and confident. I'm guessin' that Titus feels inferior to him."

"That's how I feel sometimes when I'm around Esther,"

Suzanne admitted. "She's such a good cook and has so many domestic skills. It's no wonder that Titus and some of the other young men in our district are attracted to her."

"Not all men choose a wife because she can cook," Grandpa said as he limped into the room.

"That may be true, but if it's not because she can cook, then it's probably because she has a pretty face or is easy to talk to." Suzanne grabbed the bowl of lettuce and set it on the table. "That leaves me out, because I'm neither pretty, nor easy to talk to. In fact, most men probably think I'm boring."

"That's just not so. You and I have had plenty of conversations, and you're not the least bit boring." Grandpa pulled out a chair at the table and lowered himself into it. "And as far as you not being pretty enough. . .well, that is lecherich! You're just as nice looking as any of the other young women in our community—even prettier, if you want my opinion."

Suzanne smiled. "You have to say those things because you're my grossdaadi."

"I'd say 'em even if I weren't."

Just then Chad, Russell, and Effie entered the room. "Is supper ready yet?" Chad looked up at Suzanne with an expectant expression. "I'm hungerich."

Suzanne smiled and thumped his shoulder. "Everything but the sour cream's on the table, so if your hands are washed, you can take a seat."

"I washed mine." Effie held out her hands for Suzanne's inspection.

"Me, too," Chad and Russell echoed.

"Then have a seat." Suzanne went to the refrigerator and took out the container of sour cream, as well as some salsa, knowing that the men in her family liked to spice up their haystack a bit. After she'd placed them on the table, she took a seat beside Effie.

All heads bowed for silent prayer; then Suzanne passed around the various items so each person could make their own plate of haystack: cooked ground beef, chopped onions, cut-up tomatoes, shredded lettuce, grated cheese, steamed rice, olives, and broken saltine crackers. When all those things had been passed around, she handed Russell the sour cream. He spooned a good-sized dollop on top of his haystack and took a bite. His eyebrows furrowed and his nose wrinkled. "Yuck! What did ya do to the sour cream? How come it's so sweet?"

"What are you talking about?" Suzanne reached over, spooned out some sour cream, and took a taste. "Eww. . . This isn't sour cream, it's whipping cream. I must have mixed up the containers." She jumped up and removed another container from the refrigerator. "This must be the sour cream."

"If Mom was here, she woulda known the difference between sour cream and whippin' cream," Chad said.

"I know the difference, too. I just took the wrong container from the refrigerator." Suzanne didn't know why she felt the need to defend herself. She'd taken plenty of ribbing from her family about her lack of cooking skills, so she should be used to their comments by now.

"At least you didn't mess up the meal this time," Chad said with a smirk. "Last night the chicken and dumplings you made tasted *baremlich*."

Suzanne's face heated, and she cringed. "I'm sorry. I guess you're right; it was pretty terrible."

"Suzanne's doing the best she can in your mamm's absence." Grandpa pointed his gnarled finger at Chad. "Instead of picking apart what your sister does, you ought to appreciate the fact that she's been willing to pitch in and do so many things for all of us."

"Sorry," Chad mumbled.

"When's Mom comin' home?" Effie wanted to know.

"Whenever Aunt Mary gets there."

"I hope it's not too long," Chad said. "I want her to make some peanut butter cookies."

"We can buy some of those at the bakery," Nelson said. "In fact, I'll pick some up the next time I'm over that way."

Chad smacked his lips. "Sounds good to me."

The conversation around the table shifted to other topics, and when supper was over, Suzanne ran water into the kitchen sink and added the liquid detergent. She was about to start washing the dishes, when her sleek-looking cat, Sampson, leaped onto the counter and stuck his paw into the soapy water.

"You naughty old cat." Suzanne laughed and flicked some water at Sampson, but he just sat there, batting at the sponge in the sink.

Suzanne dried her hands and picked up the cat. "You're cute, but I really don't have the time for this." She opened the back door, and was about to put the cat outside when she spotted Titus riding in on his horse.

She stepped back inside, picked up his cell phone, and met him on the porch. "I'll bet you came for this." She held the phone out to him.

He didn't take the phone; just stood there, shifting his weight from one foot to the other. Was he embarrassed because she'd found out that he owned a cell phone? Was he worried that she might tell one of their ministers about it?

"In case you're worried," she said, "I won't say anything about your phone, but I do think it's wrong for you to have one when you know it's not approved of in this district."

Titus opened his mouth like he was going to say something, when his cell phone rang. She quickly placed it in his hands.

—∞—

Without looking at the screen on his cell phone, Titus clicked the TALK button, thinking it might be Allen. "Hello."

"Hey, Titus, it's me, Samuel."

"Oh, hi. How are things with you?"

"Great. How about you?"

"Fine." Titus struggled with the temptation to tell Samuel about the money he'd found but didn't want to say anything in front of Suzanne. Besides, depending on what the sheriff had to say, he might not get to keep any of the money.

"The reason I'm calling is to tell you about the surprise party we're planning for Mama Fannie two weeks from Friday. We're hoping you can come," Samuel said.

"Of course I'd like to come, but I'll have to talk to Isaac first. I'll call you back tomorrow and let you know, okay?"

"That's fine, and I hope he says yes, because I know how much it would mean to your mamm if you were there. She misses you something awful."

"Okay, I'll see what I can do."

Just as Titus clicked off the phone, Nelson stepped out of the house. "I overheard part of your conversation. What is it you need to talk to my grossdaadi about?"

"My family's planning a surprise party for my mamm's birthday," Titus said. "They'd like me to be there for it, but if I went, it would mean I'd have to miss a day or two from work."

Before Nelson could reply, Isaac limped onto the porch. "I think you ought to go," he said.

"But we're really busy right now," Nelson argued.

Isaac shook his head. "Don't forget what you've been taught since you were a boy. God comes first, and then our family. No job's as important as Titus spending time with his mamm on her birthday, so even if there's a lot of work to do in the shop, it can wait until he gets back."

Titus smiled. "I'll try to plan it so I only miss one day of work."

"Take as much time as you need," Isaac said.

"I appreciate that." Titus turned toward the stairs. "Guess I'd better head for home now. It's starting to get dark."

"Good night then. See you in the morning," Nelson said, ducking into the house.

Titus mounted Lightning and headed down the driveway. He'd only gone a short way, when his cell phone rang again. He halted the horse, pulled the phone from his pocket, and clicked it on. "Hello."

"Titus, it's Allen. I wanted to let you know that I spoke to the sheriff, and he doesn't think the money's been stolen because there have been no reports of any robberies or break-ins around here for quite some time. He's pretty sure the money must have belonged to the old man who used to live there, but since the man's dead and has no living relatives, the sheriff said the money's mine to do with as I choose; although he did suggest that I not spend any of it for a while, just in case some new information develops."

"Wow! I can't believe it."

"I meant what I said earlier. I want you to have half the money."

Titus grinned. This was the best thing that had happened to him since he moved to Kentucky. Tomorrow he would hire a driver to take him to Hopkinsville, where he'd meet up with Allen. After he'd given Allen his share of the money, he'd put his own half in the bank. Titus felt that for the first time in a long time, things were really looking up. Not only was his bank account growing, but he'd be going to Pennsylvania in two weeks for Mom's party. He could hardly wait to see everyone.

Chapter 26

Paradise, Pennsylvania

"I don't see why we have to go out to a restaurant to eat," Fannie complained to Abraham as he helped her into the buggy. "I'd be perfectly happy eating supper at home tonight."

Abraham shook his head. "Not for your seventieth birthday. This is a special day, and you shouldn't have to cook."

"Who says I was planning to cook?" She playfully squeezed his arm. "I thought maybe you might volunteer to do that."

He chuckled. "If I cooked, we'd both be wishin' we'd gone out to eat."

While Abraham went around to the driver's side of the buggy, Fannie reached down, picked up the lightweight robe from the floor, and draped it over her lap. Despite the fact that summer had almost arrived, the evening had turned a bit chilly.

"I wonder what the weather's like in Kentucky right now," Fannie said when Abraham climbed into the buggy and took up the reins.

"I don't know. Most likely hot and humid, same as it's been around here."

"It isn't hot or humid this evening," Fannie said.

"Nope, you're right about that."

"I was hoping Titus might call and wish me a happy birthday, but when I checked our voice mail this afternoon, there were no messages from him." Fannie sighed deeply. "He didn't even send me a card."

Abraham reached over and patted her arm. "I'm sure you'll hear something from him soon."

"I hope so, but I'm not counting on it. We haven't heard from Titus in over a week."

"He's probably been busy."

She sighed again. "You think he'll marry the young woman's he's been seeing and stay in Kentucky for good?"

Abraham shrugged and clucked to the horse to get him moving faster. "Let's just have a good time celebrating your birthday and not worry about Titus right now."

Fannie nodded, but despite her best effort, she couldn't get her thoughts off Titus. She wasn't sure she could accept the idea of any of her children leaving home permanently. *Of course,* she reasoned, *it could be worse. Titus might have run off to explore the English world in California with Phoebe. Poor Arie. How hard it must be, losing her daughter like that. I wonder if Phoebe will ever come home.*

Fannie leaned her head back and closed her eyes as the gentle sway of the buggy nearly lulled her to sleep. She could hardly believe this was her seventieth birthday. Where had the time gone? It seemed like just yesterday that she and Abraham had gotten married.

When the horse whinnied and she felt the buggy turn to the right, she opened her eyes. "What are we doing here?" Fannie asked as Abraham directed the horse and buggy onto the driveway leading to Naomi and Caleb's house. "Are Naomi and Caleb going with us tonight?"

A smile played at the corner of Abraham's lips, but he kept his focus straight ahead.

"Abraham, what's going on?"

No response.

"Abraham, did you hear what I said?"

He gave a slow nod. "They're not actually going out with us. They did ask us to stop by for a few minutes, though. I think they might have a gift for you."

"Oh, I see."

Abraham pulled the buggy up to the hitching rail, secured the horse, and came around to help Fannie down. "Let's use the front door this evening," he said.

She tipped her head back and blinked as she looked up at him. "Now why on earth would we use the front door? We always go in through the back door, and you know it."

His face colored. "Well, it's closer. I mean, the front door's right here."

Fannie slowly shook her head. "I'm not so old that I can't walk around to the back door, you know." She started to head that way, but just then, Naomi stepped out the front door and called, "Happy birthday, Mama Fannie! Come inside a minute; I want to give you something."

Fannie smiled. "We're coming!"

When they entered Naomi's living room, everything was dark. It almost appeared as if no one was at home. Suddenly, a gas lamp was lit and a chorus of voices hollered, "Surprise! Happy birthday!"

Fannie gasped and grabbed hold of Abraham's arm. "You fooled me good on this one."

He laughed. "The reason I didn't want to go around back is because all the buggies are parked out there."

Fannie looked at all the smiling faces that had come to her party: family members and friends alike. She placed her hands against her hot cheeks. "This is just *wunderbaar*, and I was so surprised."

"We have another surprise for you," Naomi said, moving closer to Fannie. She pointed to the kitchen.

Fannie's son Harold; his wife, Lena; and their three children entered the living room.

Tears welled in Fannie's eyes as she stepped forward to greet them. "I can't believe you came all the way from Ohio just for my birthday."

"We wanted to surprise you," Harold said, "and we wouldn't have missed your party for anything."

After Fannie hugged her son and his family, Naomi stepped up to her and said, "There's one more surprise waiting for you in the kitchen."

Just then, the kitchen door swung open, and Titus stepped into the room. "Happy birthday, Mom," he said with a big grin.

"Titus! It's so good to see you!" Fannie's voice caught on a sob as she rushed across the room and gave him a hug. This was, without a doubt, the best birthday she'd had in some time.

The look of delight on Mom's face made Titus even more glad that he'd come home for her party. It felt good to see all his brothers and sisters again, too.

At Naomi's suggestion, everyone moved outdoors, where tables and chairs had been set up in the buggy shed. Several of the women had brought food to share for the meal, and Abby had made a large birthday cake.

"It's sure good to see you," Samuel said, thumping Titus's back. "Since you've been gone, it's been kind of quiet when we have family get-togethers. Some of us even miss all those pranks you used to play."

"If you miss me so much, then you ought to come to

Kentucky for a visit," Titus said.

"I've been thinking about that."

Timothy came up to them, wearing a smile that stretched ear to ear. "I'm sure glad you're here. Seems like old times having the whole family together again." He clasped Titus's shoulder and gave it a squeeze.

"How's it going with you?" Titus asked.

"Okay. Hannah's doing much better now, and it makes me feel good to see her smiling again." Timothy motioned to his wife, who stood across the room, talking to Elsie.

"I'm sure it couldn't have been easy for you either," Titus said.

"No, it wasn't, but Hannah took it much harder."

"Women are more emotional than men," Samuel added, "which means they usually take things harder."

Titus glanced to his left and noticed Phoebe's mother talking to Mom. If Phoebe hadn't gone to California, and the two of them had still been together, she would have probably been here tonight, too. Titus knew Phoebe's mother had been friends with Mom for a good many years, but seeing Arie and Phoebe's dad, Noah, made it difficult not to think about Phoebe and what might have been. Would he ever get her out of his system? Could he forget what she'd done to him? Was he ready to begin a serious relationship with Esther? So many questions raced through his head, but he had answers for none.

—∞—

Pembroke, Kentucky

Shortly after Suzanne entered the Beilers' store, she noticed Esther cleaning some shelves near the back of the building. "*Wie geht's?*" she asked, stepping up to her.

Esther smiled. "I'm doing okay. How about you?"

Suzanne sighed. "I'd be doing better if Mom would come home. It's getting harder to keep up with all the things that are expected of me, and now that Titus is gone, too, we won't have his help with any of our chores for the next few days."

"Is there anything I can do to help?"

Suzanne motioned to the shelves Esther had been cleaning. "I don't see how you can help me when you're busy working here."

"I'm not always busy in the store, and I'd be happy to help you after I get off work." Esther leaned against the shelf. "I could come by your place after I get done at Titus's place this evening."

Suzanne quirked an eyebrow. "How come you've been going over there?"

"To feed his cats. I told him I'd do that while he's in Pennsylvania."

"What do you mean, 'cats'? Callie's the only cat I know Titus has."

"Callie had kittens. Didn't Titus tell you?"

Suzanne shook her head.

"Maybe he forgot. Or maybe he didn't think it was important."

"That's probably more to the point. I'll bet he was upset when Callie had kittens. I'm surprised he didn't haul her and the kittens over to our place."

"You don't like Titus very much, do you?"

"I don't dislike him, but he does irritate me sometimes."

"I think he's really a nice person, and even though we don't seem to have a lot in common, I hope he doesn't decide to stay in Pennsylvania."

"I'm sure he does have his good points, and I doubt he'll stay in Pennsylvania. He seems happy working in the woodshop with Nelson." Suzanne turned aside. "Guess I'd better get what I came for and head home. I'm sure everyone's getting hungry by now, and I need to get something going for supper."

As Suzanne directed her horse and buggy toward home, she thought about Titus and wondered if he was serious about Esther. *I hope I wasn't wrong when I told her that I didn't think Titus would stay in Pennsylvania. Maybe after seeing his family again he'll change his mind about living here.*

Suzanne smiled. *If Titus were to stay in Pennsylvania, Grandpa would have to find someone to take Titus's place in the woodshop. Maybe then I could convince Grandpa to let me work there. I may not be as fast as Titus, but I think I could do most of the things he does, and probably just as well.*

Suzanne's thoughts were halted when she spotted a beige-colored horse running down the road in front of her, with only a lead rope around its neck. The poor thing was lathered up pretty good and acted like it didn't know where it was going.

Suddenly, it turned and trotted along the edge of the road, smacking into the branch of a tree.

A scream tore from Suzanne's throat as the horse then veered to the right and rammed into the side of her buggy.

Chapter 27

Suzanne gripped the reins tighter, guiding Dixie to the left, hoping to get out of the way of the crazy runaway horse. "Easy, Dixie. Easy, girl," she coaxed.

Just then, the horse turned and sped past them again, this time going in the opposite direction. It raced along the center line for a while, then suddenly veered toward the shoulder of the road and darted into the woods.

"Whew!" Suzanne sighed with relief. She was glad the horse was off the road and hoped it would find its way home. "Thank You, Lord," she whispered, "for keeping me and Dixie safe."

Los Angeles, California

"Your cell phone's ringing," Darlene shouted to Phoebe.

"I'm getting ready to take a shower," Phoebe called from the bathroom. "Can you answer it for me?" She didn't want to be bothered with a phone call right now. She'd just gotten home from work and was hot and tired.

A few seconds later, Darlene rapped on the door. "It's your mother. She wants to talk to you."

"Tell her I'll call her back."

"I told her that, but she insists on talking to you now. Said you haven't returned any of her calls for the last two weeks and she's worried about you." Darlene knocked again. "I think you'd better talk to her, Phoebe. It's not right to make your mother worry."

"Oh, all right." Phoebe slipped on her robe and opened the door.

Darlene handed her the phone. "Here you go."

"Hi, Mom. How are you?" Phoebe said as she lifted the phone to her ear.

"I'm fine, but I've been worried about you."

"There's no need to be worried. I'm doing just fine." Phoebe twirled her bathrobe belt around her arm and stared at herself in the mirror. She wished Mom didn't worry so much. She wished Mom and Dad would let her enjoy her independence.

"I've called you several times and left messages, but you never reply. What's going on, Phoebe?" Mom's voice sounded harsh and demanding, making Phoebe feel like a child.

"I've been busy," she muttered.

"Too busy to call your mamm?"

Phoebe gave no reply. Just stepped into the bedroom and flopped onto her bed.

"Your daed and I went to Fannie's surprise birthday party this evening," Mom said.

Phoebe yawned. "That's nice."

"Can you guess who was there?"

"Probably Fannie's family and friends."

"That's right, including Titus."

Phoebe sucked in her breath and bolted upright. "You mean he gave up on his little adventure in Kentucky and moved back to Pennsylvania?"

"No, he just came for the party. He'll be heading back to Kentucky before Monday, no doubt."

"I see."

"I also wanted you to know that Titus has a—"

"I really don't care to hear anything more about Titus, and I was about to take a shower, so I've gotta go. Thanks for calling. Bye, Mom."

Phoebe clicked off the phone and smacked her hand on the edge of the bed. *Why'd Mom find it necessary to tell me about Titus being at Fannie's party? Was she trying to make me wish I hadn't left Pennsylvania so I could have been at the party? Well, whatever the case, it didn't work. Even though things haven't worked out perfectly for me here in California, I'm glad I moved. It's better than having my folks tell me what to do all the time.*

Paradise, Pennsylvania

"I'm so happy you could be here for my party tonight," Mom said as she, Dad, and Titus sat in the living room after they'd come home from Naomi and Caleb's. "I just wish you didn't have to go back to Kentucky so soon."

"I need to be there by Monday evening so I can be at work on Tuesday morning. Isaac Yoder was nice enough to let me have a few days off, but I don't want to take advantage of his generosity." Titus thumped the arm of his chair. "Besides, I've got a cat and a batch of kittens to look after now, not to mention my horse."

Mom snickered. "With your dislike of cats? I can't imagine!"

Titus frowned. "It's not funny. I got stuck with a cat I didn't ask for, and then she had kittens I really don't want."

"Who's watching them while you're gone?" Dad questioned.

"My friend Esther."

"Isn't she the one you took to the Jefferson Davis Monument?" Mom asked.

Titus nodded. "I've taken her for a couple of buggy rides, too."

Dad nudged Mom's arm and grinned. "See, I told you, Fannie. Our son's not only learning some responsibility, but he's got himself a new girlfriend, too. I think moving away from home's been good for him, don't you?"

Deep wrinkles formed across Mom's forehead. "I suppose, but he could have learned to be responsible if he'd stayed right here."

"I don't know about that," Dad said. "Some young people do better when they're out on their own."

A rush of heat shot up the back of Titus's neck. He didn't like it when his folks talked about him like he wasn't in the room. It made him feel like a child.

Titus had thought he might tell Mom and Dad about the money he'd found in the phone shanty, but decided against it, at least for now. If he mentioned it, Mom would probably make a big deal of it, and Dad would tell him how to spend the money.

Titus rose to his feet and turned toward the door leading upstairs.

"Where are you going?" Mom called.

"Think I'll go to bed. It was a long bus ride to get here, and I'm tired."

"So soon? But we haven't had a chance to visit that much." Mom patted the sofa cushion beside her. "Come, take a seat, and tell us about Kentucky."

"We can talk to Titus tomorrow," Dad said. "If he's tired, then we ought to let him go on up to bed."

Mom yawned. "Come to think of it, I'm pretty tired myself. I believe all the excitement of the party took its toll on my old body."

"Mine, too." Dad helped Mom to her feet. "When we get

home from church tomorrow afternoon, we can spend the rest of the day visiting, and Titus can tell us all about Kentucky." He smiled at Titus. "And we want to hear more about your new girlfriend. Maybe you can bring her here to meet us sometime."

"Maybe so. We'll have to see how it goes."

"Is she nice? Has she got the skills it takes to be a good wife?" Mom asked.

Titus's jaw clenched. "I'm not thinking about marriage right now, and I thought we were all going to bed."

"You're right." She gave a small laugh.

Titus leaned down and hugged her; then he hurried up the stairs. He didn't know if he'd ever feel serious enough about Esther to bring her to Pennsylvania, and if he did decide to get married, he hoped Mom wouldn't pressure him to move back home.

Chapter 28

Pembroke, Kentucky

On Monday morning, Suzanne had just started washing the breakfast dishes when she heard a vehicle pull into the yard. She peered out the window and spotted a van parked outside. A few seconds later, Mom stepped out.

Suzanne dropped the sponge into the dishwater, dried her hands on a towel, and hurried out the back door. Grandpa, who'd been sitting on the porch in his favorite chair, smiled at her and said, "Looks like your mamm's finally home."

Suzanne nodded. "I'm ever so glad." She met Mom on the lawn about the same time as Nelson stepped out of the woodshop.

Mom hugged them both. "Did you miss me?"

"Of course," Suzanne said. "It's good to have you home."

"Most definitely." Nelson grabbed Mom's suitcase. "Here, let me carry that for you."

"How's Aunt Karen?" Suzanne asked as they walked toward the house.

"She's getting along fairly well," Mom replied. "Since my sister Mary's helping her now, I felt like I could come home."

She smiled at Suzanne. "How are the kinner? Have they been good for you?"

"I've had no problems with any of them," Suzanne said honestly. "They all pitched in and helped as much as they could."

"That's right." Nelson nodded in agreement. "The only problem Suzanne had was fixing our meals."

Suzanne jabbed her brother in the ribs. "Come on now. My cooking wasn't that bad."

"Never said it was. Just said you had a problem fixing our meals."

"I didn't have any big problems," Suzanne said. "I just kept things simple, which helped a lot."

"Didn't any of the women from our community bring over some meals?" Mom asked as they stepped onto the porch.

"A few were brought in," Grandpa said before Suzanne could respond. "The rest of our meals were mostly soup and sandwiches, and Suzanne did her best." He looked up at her and winked.

Suzanne smiled. Grandpa always tried to see the bright side of things and look past her imperfections.

"How have things been going at the produce auction?" Mom asked Suzanne when they'd entered the house. "Have you sold much?"

"Things have been busy, and many people have stopped to buy our bedding plants and hanging baskets. I'm certain it'll be just as busy in the fall when our mums are ready to sell."

"I'm sure you're right about that." Mom looked over at Nelson. "How are things going for you and Titus in the woodshop?"

"Business is doing well, but Titus has been gone for a few days, so that's put us a bit behind on some orders. He should be back sometime today and will be at work tomorrow morning."

"Where'd he go?" Mom asked, taking a seat in the living room.

"To Pennsylvania for his mamm's surprise birthday party." Nelson motioned to Mom's suitcase. "Want me to take that to your room?"

She nodded. "Then I'll let you get back to work. We can talk more later."

After Nelson left the room, Suzanne took a seat on the sofa beside Mom. "I stopped by the Beilers' store the other night, and Esther informed me that she's been feeding Titus's cat and his horse while he's gone. She also said that Callie has four kittens, which I had no idea about."

Mom's lips compressed. "I find it strange that Titus didn't mention the kittens. Especially since you're the one who took Callie over to his place."

"That's what I thought, too." Suzanne shrugged. "But then, I don't understand a lot of things about Titus."

When Titus got off the special bus that transported Amish and Mennonites from Lancaster, Pennsylvania, to Kentucky he was near the Beilers' store, so he went inside to say hello.

"It's good to see you," Esther said when he joined her near the front counter. "How was the party? Was your mamm surprised?"

Titus nodded. "She sure was. I think me being there was the biggest surprise of all."

"I'll bet it was hard to leave so soon."

"A little bit, but I knew I needed to get back to work, and I was anxious to see Lightning. How's he doing, anyway? He didn't give you any trouble, I hope."

Esther shook her head. "Not a bit. Callie and her babies are fine, too. Those little kittens are sure sweet. I was going to head over there pretty soon and check on them, because I didn't know what time you might get here today." She smiled sweetly at Titus. "Unless you've lined up a driver to pick you up, I'd be happy to give you a ride home."

"I don't have anyone coming for me, so I'd appreciate the ride."

"I'll run in the back room and tell Mom and Dad where I'm going; then I'll go out and get my horse and buggy."

"I can get 'em for you," Titus offered. "Are they around back?"

"Jah. Ginger's in the corral, and the buggy's parked near the shed."

"Okay, I'll meet you out front in a few minutes."

Eager to get home, Titus hurried to get Ginger hitched to the buggy. When he drove it around to the front of the store, Esther was waiting for him.

"Would you like to drive, or would you rather I did?" she asked.

"I don't mind driving."

"Great. Did you get your backpack?" Esther asked as she climbed into the buggy.

"Sure did. Put it in the back of the buggy before you came out of the store." Titus took up the reins and directed the horse onto the road.

"Did your mamm like the little keepsake box you made for her?"

Titus nodded. "She got a lot of other nice gifts, too."

"Do you think your folks will ever come here to visit?" Esther asked. "I'd like to meet them sometime."

Titus chuckled. "If Mom had her way, they'd come for a visit tomorrow. The only trouble is, there's not enough room in the trailer for them to stay with me right now. Maybe someday, if I should decide to buy the place, I can either add on or build something new."

"I didn't realize you were thinking of buying the place from Allen. Do you have enough money for that?"

"Not right now, but I'm saving up for a down payment." Titus considered telling Esther about the money he'd found but decided it was best if he kept it to himself for now.

Their conversation turned to other things—the weather, more about Mom's party, and Callie and her kittens. When they pulled into Titus's yard a short time later, he was surprised to see a beige-colored horse grazing in the pasture next to the trailer.

"Where'd that horse come from?" he asked Esther.

She shrugged. "I have no idea. It wasn't there when I came to feed the animals last night."

"Hmm. . .guess he must belong to one my neighbors. I'll chase him out of the pasture, and hopefully he'll go back to where he belongs." Titus handed the reins to Esther, grabbed his backpack, and climbed down from the buggy. "Danki for the ride home, and also for taking care of the animals for me."

"You're welcome. See you soon, Titus." Esther hesitated a minute, like she wanted to say more, but then she waved and directed her horse toward the road.

Titus stepped into the barn, and seeing that Callie and her kittens were still there, he felt satisfied. At least they hadn't found a way to get into the house.

Next, he went to the stall where Lightning was kept. The horse whinnied and nuzzled Titus's hand. "Did you miss me, boy?" Titus rubbed Lightning behind his soft ears. "I sure missed you."

After a few minutes spent talking to his horse, Titus headed to the trailer. When he entered the living room, he halted and stood there in total disbelief. The cushions from the sofa were on the floor, all of Titus's books had been pulled off the bookshelf and were strewn about. The rocking chair had been turned upside-down, along with the lamp table and lantern, which was now broken.

He dashed into the kitchen for a look around, and discovered that all the cupboard doors hung wide open, and several dishes lay shattered on the floor.

Titus's next stop was his bedroom, where he found that most of his clothes had been pulled out of the closet and scattered on the floor. Even his mattress had been yanked off the bed and overturned. The whole place was in complete disarray!

"Who could have done this, and why?" he grumbled. "Oh, boy! Think I'd better call Allen right away."

Titus pulled out his cell phone to make the call, but soon realized that his battery was dead. He'd have to go out to the phone shanty to make the call.

He hurried outside, and had no more than opened the shanty door when he discovered that someone had been in there, too. The phone cord had been jerked from the wall and thrown on the floor, and several boards had also been ripped from the wall, and even the floor. What a welcome-home present! First a horse grazing in the pasture that didn't belong to him, and now this. What was going on, anyway?

Chapter 29

With heart pounding and head swimming with questions, Titus saddled Lightning and rode out of his yard at a fast pace. When he arrived at the Beilers' a short time later, he quickly tied his horse to the hitching rail and bounded onto the porch. The door opened before he had a chance to knock, and Esther stepped out.

"You look upset," she said. "Is something wrong?"

"There sure is. Someone broke into the trailer while I was gone and made a big mess." He gulped in a couple of deep breaths. "When you came over to feed the animals, did anything look suspicious, or did you see anyone snooping around?"

Esther stood with her mouth slightly open; then she slowly shook her head. "Of course I didn't go inside the trailer, so I don't know how things looked in there. I wonder who would do such a thing."

He shrugged. "I need to use your phone to call Allen. My phone shanty was vandalized, too, and the phone's not working."

"What about your cell phone? Did you get rid of it?"

"No, but I can't use it right now because the battery needs to be charged."

Esther motioned to their phone shanty out back. "Go ahead and use the phone. While you're doing that, I'll go inside and tell Mom and Dad what happened at your place."

Titus hurried out to the shanty and dialed Allen's number. He was relieved when Allen answered right away, and then he quickly explained what had happened.

"What do you think I should do?" Titus questioned. "Do you think the break-in has anything to do with the money I found?"

"I don't know, but I'm going to call the sheriff right now. If you'll wait in the Beilers' phone shanty, I'll call you back and let know what the sheriff wants you to do."

"Okay." Titus hung up the phone. While he waited for Allen's call, he listened to the steady *csst. . .csst. . .csst. . .*of the cicadas as he stared out the open door at a herd of cows grazing in the field across the road. Things had been going along so well until now. What did the break-in mean, and would whoever did it come back?

He popped each of his knuckles and drew in a deep breath, trying to steady his nerves. In all the time he'd lived in Pennsylvania, no one in his family had ever had their home broken into. It was unsettling and made him wonder if things were really as peaceful here in Christian County, Kentucky, as he'd thought them to be. He guessed living in a rural community was no guarantee that a person and their belongings were safe. The world was full of evil, and there was probably no place a person could go where they wouldn't have to worry about crime.

The phone rang sharply, causing Titus to nearly jump out of his chair. He grabbed the receiver on the second ring. "Hello."

"Hi, Titus; it's me, Allen. I talked to the sheriff, and he wants you to head back to the trailer. He and I will meet you there. Don't go inside, though, okay?"

"No, I won't."

When Titus stepped out of the shanty, Esther was waiting for him. "Did you get ahold of Allen?"

"Jah. He called the sheriff, and I'm supposed to meet them both at the trailer."

Her face registered concern. "Do you think that's safe?"

"Don't see why not. I was in the house already, and no one was there."

"Please be careful."

"I will." Titus started walking toward his horse, and Esther followed.

"I was wondering if you'd like to come over here for supper tomorrow evening?" she asked.

"Sure, that'd be nice."

"All right then; we'll see you around six."

"Sounds good." Titus climbed on Lightning's back and rode off.

When he arrived at the trailer, the sheriff was already there. "The place is a mess," Titus said as they entered the living room.

"I see what you mean." The sheriff shook his nearly bald head. "Looks like someone might have been looking for something—maybe that money you found in the phone shanty."

Titus nodded. "I've been thinking that, too."

"I think you ought to stay somewhere else tonight. I'll have some of my men come out, and we'll look for any evidence that might let us know who might have broken into your place."

"Titus can stay with me tonight, and then I'll take him to

work tomorrow morning," Allen said as he entered the trailer. He halted just inside the door. "Wow, they really did a number on the place, didn't they?"

Titus grimaced. "The sheriff thinks whoever did this may have been looking for the money I found in the phone shanty."

Allen nodded. "He's probably right."

"Do you think they'll come back?" Titus asked the sheriff.

"I doubt it, but if they do, I want you to notify me right away."

"Guess you'd better grab whatever you need for the night so we can get going," Allen said. He looked over at Titus. "I haven't had supper yet, and I'm sure you haven't either, so we can stop at one of the restaurants in Hopkinsville before we go to my house."

"That's fine, but I need to feed my horse before we go, and also the cat in the barn. She's nursing a batch of kittens so I need to make sure she's fed."

"Sure, no problem."

When the sheriff left, and Titus had gathered up the clothes he needed, he went out to the barn. After he'd put Lightning away and fed the animals, he noticed that the horse he'd seen in his pasture was still there.

"I don't know who that horse belongs to," Titus told Allen, "but I'm thinking we ought to capture the critter and put him in the barn for the night so he doesn't wander off."

Allen gave a nod. "I'm willing to try if you are."

Titus got a rope from the barn, and then he and Allen headed for the pasture. It took a couple of tries, but Titus finally managed to get the rope around the horse's neck.

"Look there," Allen said, pointing to the horse's flanks. "He has a number painted on his flanks, which makes me wonder if he came from the horse auction near here."

"It's too late to do anything about it tonight," Titus said. "We can call and check on it in the morning."

Allen nodded. "Hopefully before tomorrow's over, we'll have some answers about the horse, as well as the break-ins."

Chapter 30

Suzanne had just started hanging out some wash on Tuesday morning, when Allen's truck pulled into the yard. She was surprised to see Titus step out of the passenger's side and follow Allen into the woodshop. Titus almost always rode his horse to work, and it seemed odd that Allen had given him a ride.

Curious to know what was going on, Suzanne finished hanging the laundry and headed for the shop. When she entered the building, she heard Titus telling Nelson about a beige-colored horse he'd found in his pasture when he arrived home from Pennsylvania last night. From the description he gave, it sounded like the same horse that had rammed her buggy.

She stepped between Titus and Allen. "I had a close encounter with a runaway horse the other day. It rammed into my buggy and ran wildly down the road."

"Were you or your horse and buggy hurt?" Titus asked with a look of concern.

"No, thankfully not, but it did shake me up a bit."

"I can imagine."

"I'm wondering if it was the same horse that ended up at your place."

"Could be," Titus said with a nod. "There's a number painted on the horse's flanks, so Allen put in a call this morning to see if the horse might have been one that was sold at the auction."

"What'd you find out?" Suzanne asked.

"Nothing yet. I'm waiting to hear back," Allen said.

Just then Allen's cell phone rang. "Maybe that's the guy from the auction now. Think I'll take the call outside." Allen pulled his cell phone from his pocket and stepped out the door.

"How was your trip to Pennsylvania?" Suzanne asked Titus. "Was your mamm surprised?"

"She sure was—especially about me being there."

"It's good that you were able to go."

"Jah, but what I came back to made me wish I hadn't gone."

"You mean finding a stray horse in your pasture?"

He shook his head. "That was only part of it. What really upset me was—"

"That was the sheriff," Allen said when he returned to the shop.

"What'd he say?" Titus asked.

Allen frowned. "Guess they didn't find any helpful evidence, but he thinks it would be best if neither of us spends any of the money you found until the sheriff is sure it's not stolen. He also said that you can return home now, but he wants you to let him know if you see or hear anything suspicious."

"What's this about you finding money at your place?" Nelson asked before Suzanne could voice the question.

Suzanne felt a ripple of apprehension zip up her spine as Titus told how he'd found an envelope full of money in his phone shanty, and how the shanty, as well as the trailer, had been broken into and ransacked while he'd been in Pennsylvania. It had been some time since they'd had any break-ins in the area, and the last time it had happened, the whole community had been on edge for many weeks afterward.

"The sheriff thinks someone out of the area may have stolen the money Titus found, and then hidden it in the phone shanty because they were on the run," Allen said.

"But why would they break into the trailer?" Suzanne asked.

"Because the money's not in the phone shanty anymore," Titus spoke up. "Allen and I split the money, and we put it in the bank before I left for Pennsylvania. If the person who put the money in the phone shanty went looking there and couldn't find it, they might have thought the money was in the trailer."

Allen's cell phone rang again.

"Maybe that's the sheriff calling back," Nelson said.

Allen glanced at the phone and shook his head. "It's the guy from the horse auction."

Everyone got quiet while Allen took the call. When he clicked off the phone, he turned to Titus and said, "We were right. The horse was sold at the auction, and it got away before its new owner could get it loaded into the horse trailer. The man's been notified, and he'll be going over to your place this evening to get the horse."

"I hope he gets there before six," Titus said. "I'm supposed to go over to the Beilers' for supper this evening."

I'll bet Esther's happy about that, Suzanne thought.

"I'm sure it'll be okay if he comes while you're gone," Allen said. "He knows what the horse looks like, and I told him you'd put it in the barn."

"Guess that'll be fine then," Titus said. "Since Lightning will be with me, I won't have to worry about the man taking the wrong horse."

the JOURNEY

—∞—

Paradise, Pennsylvania

"Guder mariye, Mom. I decided to stop by on my way to work to see if you and Dad have heard anything from Titus since he returned to Kentucky," Zach said as he entered the kitchen, where Fannie sat at the table, drinking a cup of tea.

"He called and left us a message when he got off the bus."

"Have you heard anything since then?"

Fannie shook her head. "But he's only been back a day, so I don't expect we'll hear from him again anytime soon. Why do you ask?"

Zach pulled out a chair and took a seat at the table. "Allen called me last night. The trailer where Titus has been staying got broken into while he was gone, so Titus spent last night at Allen's."

Fannie's eyes widened. "That's baremlich! Why didn't Titus let us know about this?"

"Maybe he knew Allen had called me and figured I'd give you the message." Zach shrugged. "Or maybe Titus decided not to say anything because he didn't want to worry you."

Fannie gripped the handle of her teacup so tightly she feared it might break, so she quickly set it back down. "He's right; I'm very worried. If this had happened when Titus was at home, he could have been hurt."

"You're right, but God was looking out for Titus because he was here with us and not in the trailer."

"Have the police been called? Did they catch the person who broke in?" Fannie picked up her teacup again and took a sip, hoping it would help calm her down.

"Allen said he called the sheriff, and the sheriff thinks the person who broke in may have been looking for the money

Titus found in his phone shanty."

Fannie nearly choked on the tea in her mouth. "What money? What's this all about, Zach?"

Zach ran his fingers down the side of his face. "I'm not really sure, Mom. Allen just said Titus had found some money, and that they suspect it may have been stolen. If that's the case, then whoever stole the money and hid it in Titus's phone shanty might have come looking for it while he was gone."

A jolt of fear coursed through Fannie's body. She pushed her chair aside and hurried across the room.

"Where are you going?" Zach called when she reached the door.

"Out to the field to speak with your daed. He needs to have a talk with Titus and convince him to come home where he belongs."

—ꝏ—

Pembroke, Kentucky

When Titus finished work for the day, Nelson asked if he needed a ride home.

"Guess I do," Titus replied. "Since I rode here with Allen this morning, and my horse is in the barn at my place, I figured I'd have to walk home this afternoon."

"There's no need for that," Nelson said. "I heard Suzanne tell Mom that she's planning to take some of her hanging baskets over to the greenhouse. Guess all the ones they had there have sold, so they need more. Since the greenhouse is on the way to your place, I'm sure Suzanne wouldn't mind giving you a ride home."

"Okay, I'll go up to the house and ask her now. See you tomorrow morning." Titus headed out the door.

He found Suzanne out by the barn, putting a hanging

basket full of petunias into the back of her buggy. "Do you want some help?" he called.

She smiled. "I appreciate the offer, but this is the last one I need to load."

"Nelson mentioned that you'll be going over to the greenhouse, and since it's on the way to my place, I was wondering if you'd mind giving me a ride home."

Suzanne shook her head. "I don't mind. In fact I'm ready to go right now."

"That's great." Titus climbed into the passenger's side of the buggy.

When Suzanne took her seat on the driver's side, he smiled and said, "I appreciate this. I don't mind walking, but I'm tired and still have to clean up the mess in my trailer."

"I'd stay and help, but I need to get these flowers delivered to the greenhouse before they close for the day."

"That's okay," Titus said. "I'll be going over to the Beilers' for supper this evening, and Esther said she'd come over after we eat and help me clean up the place."

"Oh okay." Suzanne glanced at Titus, then quickly looked away. "Uh. . .did you see your ex-girlfriend when you were in Pennsylvania?"

He shook his head. "As far as I know, Phoebe's still in California."

"Oh. I thought maybe she came home for your mamm's party."

"Nope. Just her folks were there."

"Oh, I see."

They rode in silence the rest of the way, and when they arrived at Titus's place, Suzanne halted her horse at the hitching rail. "Mind if I take a look at the horse you found?"

"Nope. Don't mind at all. If his owner hasn't come for him yet, he'll be in the barn where I put him last night."

Titus led the way to the stall where the horse lay sleeping.

"That's the same horse that was running wild on the road," Suzanne said. "I was worried about it getting hit or causing an accident, so I'm glad he found his way to your place where he's been kept safe."

Titus started walking toward the barn door, knowing Suzanne was in a hurry to go. As they both stepped out of the barn, a truck pulling a horse trailer entered the yard. A middle-aged man wearing a cowboy hat got out. "I understand you found my horse," he said, approaching Titus.

Titus nodded. "He's in the barn. I'll get him for you."

"I appreciate you taking care of him for me," the man said. "How much do I owe for your trouble?"

"You don't owe me anything." Titus motioned to Suzanne. "I can't speak for her, though. It was her buggy your horse ran into the other night."

The man turned to Suzanne. "If your buggy was damaged I'd be happy to pay for the repairs."

She shook her head. "There was no damage. It scared me; that's all."

"All right then. Guess I'll get my horse loaded into the trailer and head out. Thanks again for all you've done."

Titus smiled. "You're welcome."

"I understand that Callie had some *busslin*," Suzanne said after the man left with his horse.

"That's right; she had four kittens to be exact," Titus said.

"How come you never mentioned it to me?" she asked.

"Thought I had."

"No. I heard about it from Esther."

"Guess I must have forgot."

"Can I see them?"

"Sure. They're in a box near the back of the barn. Let's go take a look."

Titus led the way, and when they came to the box, Suzanne leaned over and stroked the top of Callie's head. "You have some cute little busslin," she murmured.

"Did you know she was pregnant when you gave her to me?" Titus asked.

Her forehead wrinkled as she looked up at him. " 'Course not. This is just as big a surprise to me as it must have been to you. Besides, you've had the cat for a while now, so she may have found a mate since she's been living here."

Titus frowned. "Don't know what I'm gonna do with the kittens once they're weaned, 'cause I sure don't need five cats hanging around."

"They'd help keep the mice down."

"Maybe so, but I still don't care much for cats, and I don't need five of 'em here, making trouble all the time."

"I'm sure you'll be able to find them good homes." Suzanne picked up one of the kittens and held it close to her face. "It's so soft and cuddly. Makes me wish one of our cats would have a batch of kittens soon."

"You can have one of these if you like."

"Maybe, but I may wait and see if Frisky has any kittens this year first." She moved toward the barn door. "I'd better go, or the greenhouse will be closed by the time I get there. When you see Esther this evening, tell her I said hello," Suzanne called as she hurried out to her buggy.

"I will."

When Suzanne climbed into her buggy and headed down the driveway, Titus turned toward the trailer. *Guess I'd better head inside and get a few things picked up so I can take a shower and get over to the Beilers' by six.*

He hurried inside, and had just finished cleaning up some of the things in his bedroom, when he heard footsteps on the back porch. Thinking Suzanne must have come back, he went to answer the door. Two middle-aged men—one heavyset with thinning blond hair, and the other shorter and stocky with thick, wavy brown hair—forced their way into the trailer.

"We want to know where our money is," the shorter man said, pointing a gun at Titus. "It was in the phone shanty out back, but when we came here lookin' for it, we discovered that it was gone. Have you seen it?"

Titus gulped in a quick breath as he took a step back. "It… it was there, but I took it out."

The other man stepped forward and grabbed Titus by his shirt collar. "You'd better tell us where it is, or you won't live to see tomorrow."

Chapter 31

Paradise, Pennsylvania

Fannie raced into the field, frantically waving her hands. "Abraham, stop what you're doing! We need to talk!"

Abraham climbed down from the hay mower and cupped his hands around his mouth. "What's that you're sayin'?"

She motioned for him to come over.

"What's wrong?" Abraham asked as he stepped up to the fence. "You look umgerennt."

"I'm very upset. Zach just came by and said he'd talked to Allen, and Titus found some money, and. . .and his place was broken into, and I'm worried that—"

Abraham held up his hand. "Slow down, Fannie. You're talking so fast I can barely understand what you're saying."

Fannie took a deep breath and started over. "Sometime before Titus came here for my birthday party, he found some money in his phone shanty. Then while he was here, someone broke into the trailer and made a big mess." She reached over the fence and clutched Abraham's arm. "The sheriff's been contacted, but I don't think it's safe for our son to be there anymore. You need to call Titus and talk him into moving back home!"

"Calm down, Fannie," Abraham said. "I'm not going to do that."

"Why not?"

"Because Titus wouldn't appreciate us treating him like a boppli. Besides, if the sheriff's been notified, then he's probably investigating things."

"That might be so, but Titus could still be in danger."

Abraham rubbed the bridge of his nose and squinted. "You may be right, but you know what, Fannie?"

"What?"

"The way things are goin' in our world today, none of us is ever really safe. We could be hit by a car when we're ridin' in our buggy; we could be struck by lightning while we're out in the fields; we could be—"

"Okay, okay, I get your point, but that doesn't mean I'm not worried about Titus."

"Don't waste your time on worry, Fannie. Pray. Pray that God will keep Titus safe, and that the sheriff will find the person who broke into the trailer."

Pembroke, Kentucky

"Now where's that money?" The shorter of the two men glared at Titus, his beady blue eyes unwavering as he pointed his stubby finger at Titus's chest.

"It. . .it's not here in the trailer." Titus's face heated, and a trickle of sweat rolled down his forehead. He couldn't believe this was happening to him.

"Where is it, then?" The heavyset man slammed Titus against the door. Searing pain shot from his head all the way down his back.

"It. . .it's in the bank."

The man growled and punched Titus in the stomach, causing him to double over. "You'd better not be lyin' to me."

"I'm not."

The other man stepped forward and shoved Titus against the small table beside the sofa.

Titus wobbled but managed to keep his balance. *Dear Lord*, he prayed, *help me know what to do.*

"That money belongs to us," the bigger man said. "You've got no right to it!"

Titus knew he needed some help, and he needed it quickly. He groped in his pocket, feeling for his cell phone. It wasn't there. *What'd I do with it? Could I have left it at work today?*

The sound of buggy wheels crunching on the gravel drifted in through the window, so Titus edged closer to the window to look out. *Oh no. It's Suzanne. What's she doing back here?*

"What are ya lookin' at, kid?" the shorter man asked.

Titus jerked his head. "Uh. . .nothing."

The other man grabbed Titus by his suspenders, nearly lifting him off the floor. "Let's go. You're takin' us to the bank, and you're gonna get our money right now!"

Titus didn't think he had the nerve to walk into the bank with these men and withdraw the money, but he figured he didn't have any other choice. He just wished Suzanne wasn't out in the yard. He didn't want her involved in this; she could be in danger.

He jerked the door open and called, "Get out of here, Suzanne! Schnell!"

"Now what'd ya do that for, you stupid kid?"

Titus felt a sharp blow to the back of his head; then his world went dark.

—~—

It didn't take Suzanne long to realize that Titus was in trouble.

The heavyset man who'd hit Titus was obviously an intruder. Could he be the same person who'd broken into the trailer while Titus was in Pennsylvania? Could this have something to do with the money Titus had found?

With heart pounding and hands sweating so badly she could barely hold on to the reins, Suzanne got her horse and buggy moving quickly and raced out of the yard. She wanted to stay and see if Titus was okay, but first she needed to get to a phone and call for help. Since the Beilers' place was the closest, that's where she would go.

When she arrived a short time later, she raced to the house and pounded on the door.

Esther answered Suzanne's knock, and she quickly told her friend what had happened.

"Ach, my!" Esther exclaimed. "Now I know why Titus is late for supper. We were beginning to wonder if he'd forgotten." She clasped Suzanne's arm. "We'd better run out to the phone shanty and call the sheriff right now."

When they returned to the house a short time later, Suzanne explained to Esther's folks all that had happened. "I'm worried about Titus," she said. "I'm going back to his place to see if he's okay."

"I'm going with you," Esther put in.

Esther's father, Henry, shook his head firmly. "I cannot allow that, girls. The man who hit Titus is obviously dangerous. We need to let the sheriff handle this."

Suzanne knew Henry was right, but she felt almost sick thinking about what had happened to Titus and wondering if he'd been seriously hurt. She paced back and forth on the Beilers' front porch until she heard sirens heading in the direction of Titus's place and knew it must be the sheriff.

With no thought for her safety, Suzanne darted down the porch steps, untied her horse from the hitching rail, and climbed into her buggy. Taking up the reins, she directed Dixie onto the road.

When she arrived at Titus's place, she saw that the sheriff and several of his men had the trailer surrounded and were calling for those inside to come out.

When there was no response, two of the sheriff's deputies cautiously entered the house.

Suzanne held her breath and waited to see what would happen.

Several minutes went by; then one of the deputies stepped out of the trailer. "There's no one inside except Titus, and he's lying on the floor with his head bleeding. You'd better call for an ambulance right away," he called to the sheriff.

Suzanne's heart pounded as she leaped from the buggy. *Dear Lord, please don't let Titus be dead.*

Chapter 32

Suzanne picked up a magazine and thumbed through a couple of pages. She'd been sitting in the hospital waiting room for the last hour, waiting to hear how Titus was doing. Knowing he'd need someone to go to the hospital with him, after the sheriff had called for the ambulance, she'd put her horse in Titus's barn and ridden with Titus.

Someone touched Suzanne's shoulder. She jumped up from the chair and whirled around, surprised to see Esther and her parents.

"We came as soon as we got your phone message," Esther said. "How's Titus?"

Suzanne shrugged. "I haven't heard anything yet, and I'm really worried. What if he's—" Her voice caught on the sob rising in her throat.

"You took a chance going over to his place when I told you not to," Henry said. "You could also be in the examining room right now; not just Titus."

"I. . .I couldn't help it. I needed to know whether he was all right."

"Why'd you go over there in the first place?" Dinah asked.

"I was on my way home from the greenhouse and decided to stop and see if I could help him clean up the mess in the trailer." Suzanne drew in a shaky breath. "I hope Titus will be okay."

Esther reached for Suzanne's hand and gave her fingers a gentle squeeze. "We just need to keep the faith and pray for him."

"Who were those men, and why'd they want to hurt Titus?" Henry asked.

"I'm not sure, but from what I heard the sheriff say while we were waiting for the ambulance, I think it has something to do with the money Titus found in his phone shanty." Suzanne paused for a breath. "By the time the sheriff got to Titus's place, the men were gone. They'd just run off and left Titus bleeding on the living room floor."

Dinah's eyes widened. "If those men aren't caught, they might come back or try to hurt someone else."

"Not to worry," Allen said, stepping into the waiting room. "I just spoke with the sheriff, and the men have been caught. They were found hiding in the woods." He looked down at Suzanne and smiled. "Thanks for letting me know about Titus. How's he doing, do you know?"

She shook her head. "I haven't heard a thing since they took him in."

"I'm going up to the nurse's station and see what I can find out, and then I'm going to phone Titus's brother Zach so he can let his folks and the rest of the family know. I'll be back soon." Allen paused and pulled a cell phone from his pocket. "This belongs to Titus. He left it in my truck this morning. Too bad he didn't have it with him when those men showed up at the trailer. He might have been able to call for help." He turned and hurried from the room.

Suzanne sucked in another deep breath and tried to relax. If she felt this bad about Titus, she could only imagine how Esther must feel.

"Do you think Titus's folks will come here when they get the news?" Esther asked her mother.

Dinah nodded. "I'd travel any distance if one of my kinner had been hurt."

"It would be nice to meet Titus's folks," Esther said, "but not under these conditions."

Suzanne shuddered. She couldn't imagine how horrible it would be for his parents if they traveled all this way only to be told that their son was dead.

Stop thinking negative thoughts, she scolded herself. *Pray, and thank God in advance for Titus's healing.*

Paradise, Pennsylvania

Fannie had just sat down on the sofa beside Abraham, hoping to read awhile before going to bed, when the door flew open and Zach rushed into the room, his eyes wide and his face glistening with sweat.

"What's wrong? You look umgerennt. Has something happened?" Abraham asked.

"I am upset. Something pretty terrible has happened." Zach paced the floor for several seconds; then he finally took a seat in the rocking chair across from them and drew in a couple of deep breaths. "I don't want to frighten you, but I just had a phone call from Allen, letting me know that Titus is in the hospital in Hopkinsville."

Fannie dropped her book and sat up straight. "What's happened? Why's Titus in the hospital?"

Zach explained all that he'd heard, and ended by saying,

"Allen spoke with one of the nurses, but she wasn't able to give him any information about Titus's condition."

Fannie jumped up. "This wouldn't have happened if he hadn't moved!" She trembled as she turned to face Abraham. "We have to go to Kentucky!"

Abraham nodded grimly. "You're right. We'll leave right away."

Hopkinsville, Kentucky

Titus moaned and opened his eyes. A middle-aged woman wearing a white uniform stood beside his bed. "Wh–where am I?"

"You're in the hospital." She placed her hand gently on his shoulder. "You have a concussion and a pretty deep gash on the back of your head. You'll have to stay in the hospital a few days for observation."

He moaned again. "No wonder my head hurts so much."

"There's a young man out in the hall who says he's your friend. Would you like to see him?"

"Sure."

The nurse left the room, and Allen entered a few seconds later. A deep frown etched his forehead as he moved toward Titus's bed. "I'm really sorry about this. I should never have let you go home alone."

"It's not your fault. You had no idea the men who ransacked the trailer would come back."

"I've talked to the sheriff, so I know the men have been caught, but I have no idea what happened before the sheriff came. Do you feel up to filling me in?"

"The men have been caught?"

Allen nodded. "After one of them slugged you on the head,

they took off. But the sheriff's deputies caught them hiding in the woods behind your place. They're in jail now, and the sheriff will be questioning them about the money they hid." Allen took a seat in one of the chairs beside Titus's bed. "It's a good thing we haven't spent any of that money, because I'm sure now that it was stolen."

Titus tried to sit up, but it hurt too much, so he lay there with his eyes closed, trying to remember all that had happened. "Everything seems kind of hazy, but I remember getting ready to go to Esther's for supper, and then..." He paused and rubbed his forehead. "Then two men showed up and demanded that I tell 'em where the money was."

"What'd you say?"

"Said it was in the bank." Titus grimaced, as the details became clearer. "One of them shoved me real hard, and the other one said I'd have to take 'em to the bank and get the money. Then I heard a horse and buggy pull into the yard, and when I saw that it was Suzanne, I shouted a warning to her. That must have been when I got hit on the head, because I don't remember anything after that." His eyes snapped open. "Where's Suzanne? Is she okay?"

"She's fine. She and Esther, as well as Esther's folks, are in the waiting room." Allen glanced toward the door. "I think Suzanne was really worried about you, because the sheriff told me that she insisted on riding to the hospital with you in the ambulance."

"Tell her I said thanks."

"If you'd like to tell her yourself, I'll go ask her to come in."

"Maybe later. I'm tired and my head hurts too much to talk anymore right now."

"Okay. I'll leave you alone to rest." Allen stood. "Oh, I forgot to mention. I phoned Zach and asked him to let your family know what happened. I'm sure your folks will hire a driver and come to Kentucky right away."

Titus moaned. "That's just great. If Mom sees me in the hospital, she'll insist that I move back home. Well, I won't do it. Kentucky's my home now, and I'm stayin' put."

CHAPTER 33

Fannie's heart pounded as she and Abraham hurried down the hall toward Titus's hospital room. They'd hired a driver to bring them to Kentucky, and it had taken them over twelve hours to get here. She was not only tired and stiff from riding in the van so long, but she was also apprehensive about what they'd learn when they saw Titus.

"Don't look so glum," Abraham said, as they approached the door. "From what we were told, Titus's injuries aren't life threatening."

"I know, and I'm grateful for that, but it upsets me to know he was hurt by those men, and I shudder to think of how much worse it could have been."

He nodded. "We have much to be thankful for, because the Lord was surely watching out for our son."

Fannie paused at the door, and tears gathered in her eyes. She blinked several times, to keep them from spilling over. "Are you going to help me convince Titus to come back home with us once he's well enough to travel?"

Abraham shrugged. "Let's not talk about that right now.

Let's put on a happy face and say hello to our son."

—∞—

When the door to Titus's room opened and his folks stepped in, he blinked a couple of times. "Mom. Dad. I figured you'd come."

Mom moved quickly to the side of his bed, and Dad followed. "How badly are you hurt?" Dad asked.

"I have a concussion and a gash on the back of my head, but I'll live. 'Course, I have a chunk of hair missing now because they had to shave it in order to stitch up the wound. Guess I'll have to wear my hat all the time until my hair grows back." Titus forced himself to smile. He figured he'd better make light of the situation so Mom wouldn't be too upset.

"Tell us what happened," Dad said as he and Mom seated themselves in the chairs beside Titus's bed.

Titus explained all that had transpired, being careful not to make it sound as frightening as it actually had been.

Mom's eyebrows drew together as she reached for Titus's hand. "You need to move back home. It's not safe for you here."

"The men have been caught, and there's no reason for me to move back."

"Oh, but I think—"

Dr. Osmond entered the room.

"These are my parents," Titus said, motioning to Mom and Dad. "They came here from Pennsylvania because they were worried about me."

"And well they should be." The doctor moved closer to Titus's bed. "I'm going to release you to go home, but only if you promise to take it easy for the next several days."

"Oh he will," Mom spoke up, "because we're going to be there to make sure that he does."

"That's right," Dad said with a nod. "We'll go home with

him and stay until he's well enough to manage on his own."

Titus appreciated the fact that his folks had come, but he was worried about what they would think when they saw the trailer. It was bad enough that the place was so cramped; now thanks to the men who'd broken in, everything was a mess.

Pembroke, Kentucky

"This place is a disaster," Suzanne said to Esther as they worked together to get things cleaned up in Titus's trailer.

Esther wrinkled her nose. "I can't believe those horrible men did this, can you?"

Suzanne shook her head. "What I really can't believe is that they hurt Titus. He did nothing but try to warn me that they were here."

Esther stared at Suzanne. "You like him, don't you?"

"Who?"

"Titus. Who else are we talking about?"

Suzanne focused on sweeping the floor and said nothing.

"I saw how worried you were about Titus the night we were at the hospital."

"Of course I was worried. Titus was hurt, and I didn't know how badly."

Esther set the broken dish she'd been holding on the kitchen table and stepped in front of Suzanne. "Do you like him or not?"

Suzanne looked up. "Titus and I have had our share of differences, but as I've gotten to know him better, I've come to realize that he's really a caring person. Even the way he cared for that runaway horse let me know what type of person he was." Suzanne dropped her gaze to the floor. "I do like him, but only as a friend."

"Would you like to be more than friends? Do you wish you were being courted by him?"

"I know how much you care for Titus, and I wouldn't think of trying to come between you."

"I was interested in Titus at first, but after spending some time with him, I've recognized that we'll probably never be serious about each other."

"Why not?" Suzanne asked, fixing her gaze on Esther.

"We don't have much in common, and he's really not my type. So if you're interested in him, you have my blessing." Esther bent to pick up another piece of broken glass and tossed it in the garbage.

"Are you sure about that?"

Esther nodded. "I don't think he's serious about me, either."

"Well, even if I were interested in Titus, he'd never be interested in me," Suzanne muttered.

"How do you know?"

"Because I look like his ex-girlfriend. Besides, I can't cook, and what man wants a woman who can't cook?"

"I've told you before that I'd be happy to teach you."

"I guess it would be easier to learn from you than Mom." Suzanne sighed deeply. "When it comes to cooking, I've always felt like a failure next to her."

Esther slipped her arm around Suzanne's waist. "You're not a failure. I'm sure you can learn to cook, and if you let me teach you, I'll try to be very patient."

"We'll see." Suzanne glanced out the window. "A van just pulled in. Looks like Titus and his folks are here now."

"Oh great. We're not done cleaning the kitchen yet."

"At least we got the rest of the house picked up, and it shouldn't take us long to finish in here." Suzanne motioned to the few broken dishes that were still on the floor.

"Let's go meet Titus's parents and see how he's doing, and

then we'll finish cleaning in here," Esther said.

They hurried from the room, and Suzanne opened the back door just as Titus and his parents stepped onto the porch.

"I'm surprised to see you both here," Titus said when they'd entered the house.

"We heard you might be coming home today, so we came over to clean up the house before you arrived," Esther replied.

"That was nice of you." Titus motioned to his parents. "These are my folks, Abraham and Fannie. Mom, Dad, meet Esther and Suzanne."

Fannie and Abraham shook hands with Esther first, saying it was nice to meet her. Fannie acted a little cool toward Esther, though. When she shook Suzanne's hand, she stared at her strangely. Suzanne wondered if there was something about her that Titus's mother didn't like. Could it be because she reminded her of Titus's ex-girlfriend?

"It was nice of you both to clean up the place," Fannie said, directing her comment to Suzanne, "but now that I'm here, I can take over the job."

Suzanne glanced at Esther, wondering if she felt Fannie's coolness.

Esther merely smiled and said, "We're almost done. We just have a few more dishes to pick up in the kitchen."

"Oh, I see. I guess you can do that while we get Titus settled in his room." Fannie glanced around. "This place is so small. Does it even have a bedroom?"

"It's at the back of the trailer, but I'm not going to bed." Titus motioned to the sofa in the living room. "Why don't we have a seat so we can visit awhile?"

Sensing Fannie's hesitation, Suzanne said, "I think Esther and I had better finish cleaning the kitchen, and then we'll be on our way." She smiled at Titus. "You look much better than when I saw you in the hospital. How are you feeling today?"

"My head still hurts, but I'm doing okay."

"Remember now, the doctor said you'll have to take it easy for several days." Fannie put her hand on Titus's shoulder. "That's why your daed and I will be staying to help out and see that you behave yourself."

Titus's face colored, obviously embarrassed by his mother's comment making it seem as if he were a child.

"I guess we'd better get back to work. It was nice meeting you." Suzanne smiled at Titus's parents.

"Nice meeting you, too." Abraham returned her smile, but Fannie only nodded before taking a seat on the sofa beside Titus.

Suzanne moved toward the kitchen. "Are you coming, Esther?"

"Of course." Esther followed Suzanne into the kitchen.

"For whatever reason, Titus's mamm doesn't like me," Suzanne whispered to Esther.

"What makes you think that?"

"Didn't you see the strange way she looked at me? She didn't want to visit with us either."

"She acted kind of cool toward me, too, but I think she's just concerned about Titus and probably thought visiting might make him tired."

"Maybe so." Suzanne pushed the garbage can into the center of the room and started picking up the rest of the broken dishes as fast as she could.

—∞—

Shortly after Esther and Suzanne left, Mom turned to Titus and said, "No wonder you like it here and don't want to leave."

"What do you mean?" Titus asked.

"That young woman with auburn hair reminds you of Phoebe, doesn't she?"

Titus nodded. "She did at first, but since I've gotten to know her—"

"You're staying in Kentucky because of her, not the other young woman, am I right?"

" 'Course not. Suzanne and I aren't even courting. It's Esther I've gone out with a couple of times, but I'm not really serious about her, either."

"Then why don't you come home?" Mom asked.

"Because I want to start a new life here. I like it in Kentucky, and there's nothing for me in Pennsylvania anymore."

"Your family's there."

"I realize that, and as much as I miss everyone, I need to make it on my own without anyone in the family telling me what to do or how to do it."

"Titus is right," Dad put in. "He needs to make his own way, just like I did when I was his age."

Mom sat with her arms folded, staring straight ahead. After several minutes, she turned to Titus and said, "I have no objections to you making it on your own, but I think you could do that just as well if you were at home."

Titus's jaw clenched. He was too tired to argue, but before Mom and Dad left for home, he'd try to make Mom understand that he wasn't going back to Pennsylvania, and that no matter what she said, he planned to make Kentucky his permanent home.

Chapter 34

You two can have my bed tonight, and I'll sleep on the sofa in the living room," Titus told his folks after they'd finished eating a late lunch.

"This place is much too small for even one person to be living in," Mom said. "After looking around, I've discovered a lot of things you need."

"Like what?"

She picked up a piece of paper and a pen she'd found in a kitchen drawer. "I'm going to make a list for you. Let's see now. . .pie pans, a spice rack, rolling pin, mixing bowls, and—"

Titus held up his hand. "I'm not planning to do any baking, Mom, so you don't need to get carried away with that list you're making."

Her forehead creased. "I just thought—"

"In fact, there's really no need for you to make a list at all, because I'm getting along fine with the things I have now."

Mom opened her mouth like she might argue the point, but the rumble of a truck pulling into the yard interrupted their conversation.

"Looks like Allen's here," Titus said, going to the window to look out.

When Allen entered the trailer moments later, they all took seats in the living room.

"I came by to see how you're feeling." Allen clasped Titus's shoulder and gave it a squeeze.

"Other than my head still hurting, I'm doing okay," Titus replied. "Just glad to be out of the hospital and back here again."

Allen smiled. "I also wanted to let you know what I learned today from the sheriff about the money you found."

Titus's interest was piqued. "I'm anxious for you to fill me in."

"We'd like to hear it, too," Dad said.

Allen leaned forward, resting his elbows on his knees. "About a month before Titus came to Kentucky, two men broke into an elderly couple's home in Tennessee and stole their money."

Mom's eyes widened. "What in the world would an elderly couple be doing with that much money in their house?"

"I don't know, but I guess one of the men—Harry's his name—used to do yard work for the couple. When he found out they had a large sum of cash in the house, he and his buddy, Marvin, tied the old folks up and took their money. The two men were on the run, looking for a remote area to hide out, when they saw a sheriff's car and got scared. Then, finding what appeared to be an abandoned trailer, they hid the money in the phone shanty here, and took off, planning to come back to get it when they felt it was safe.

"While Titus was in Pennsylvania, the men returned to the phone shanty to get the money. When it wasn't there, they broke into the trailer and searched for it. Of course they didn't find it there, but they soon realized that someone was now living in the trailer, so they came back shortly after Titus arrived home from Pennsylvania. Of course, we all know what happened after that."

"The money will have to be returned to the couple," Titus was quick to say.

Allen nodded. "That's right, but there's a reward of a thousand dollars for finding the money, so that will be yours."

Titus shook his head. "Now that I know what happened, I can't take that old couple's money. It wouldn't be right."

"I think it would hurt their feelings if you don't accept it. They're very grateful and want you to have the reward."

"Oh, all right," Titus finally agreed.

Mom looked over at Allen and frowned. "I can't believe you'd expect Titus to rent this place from you. It's in horrible shape and hardly fit for a person to live in."

"I feel bad about that," Allen said, "but when I bought the place, I didn't realize it was as run-down as it was. Just bought it for the property as an investment."

"You should have seen it before some of the folks in our community came and helped me clean and do some repairs," Titus said. "It looks much better now. Or at least it did before those men broke in."

Mom wrinkled her nose. "I can't imagine it looking much worse than it does now."

"Well it did, believe me." Titus motioned to the sofa. "All the furniture was worn out, but some of the women covered it with slipcovers."

"Tell her about the hole in the roof and how you fell through, trying to put a patch on it so it wouldn't leak," Allen said.

Deep wrinkles formed in Mom's forehead. "Were you hurt, Titus?"

"Just scratched up my legs a bit. Nothing serious." *Sure wish Allen hadn't brought that up.*

"But you could have been seriously hurt, and I think—"

Allen rose to his feet. "I need to get going. Please let me know if you need anything."

Titus smiled. "I will."

"I'll be by again soon to check on you."

"Thanks, I appreciate that."

Allen told Titus's folks good-bye, and headed out the door.

Soon after he left, Titus heard a desperate-sounding *meow* on the porch. "That must be Callie. She has four kittens to feed, so she's probably hungry and waiting to be fed."

"Tell me where you keep the cat food, and I'll feed her," Mom said.

"Her food's in the barn on a shelf near the box where she has her babies."

"I'm sure I can find it." Mom hurried out the door.

Titus was glad for a few minutes alone to talk to Dad. It seemed like Dad hadn't been able to get in more than a few words with Mom talking so much.

"I wish Mom wouldn't hover over me all the time," Titus complained. "She treats me like I'm still a little boy. Doesn't she realize I'm a grown man now, and I want to live my own life without being told what to do?"

"Don't let your mamm upset you," Dad said. "As I'm sure you know, she's had a hard enough time dealing with you moving from home. Finding out that this place had been broken into and that you'd been hurt didn't help things any."

"Sure hope the whole time you're here she won't hover over me and try to convince me to move back home."

"If she does, I'll put a stop to it," Dad said. He gave Titus's arm a light tap. "I think the fact that you and Timothy are our youngest kinner, coupled with her having had you in midlife, has caused her to worry more about both of you."

"Worrying won't change anything. She needs to give me a

chance to prove myself."

Dad gave a nod. "I agree. Be patient, and give her a little more time to adjust to the idea that you're out on your own."

"So what do you think of the little bit of Kentucky you've seen so far?" Titus asked.

"It's nice. Not nearly so congested with people and cars as what we have in Lancaster County."

"That's one of the things I like about it here," Titus said. "That, and the fact that there are lots of places to hunt, fish, and ride my horse. There's also good, fertile land that can be bought for much less than what you'd pay back home."

"Are you thinkin' of buying some land?"

Titus nodded. "Think I might buy this place from Allen. The trailer isn't much, but there's some acreage with it that could be farmed—if I ever decide to do any farming, that is."

"I'm guessin' Timothy would be interested in farming here, but knowing how close Hannah is to her mamm, I doubt he'd ever move."

"I know what you mean."

"Do you have it in your mind to stay in Kentucky, even if all your family remains in Pennsylvania?" Dad asked.

"That's my plan now, but I guess it could change if things don't work out for me here."

"You mean with your job?"

"That, and whether I'm able to buy this place or not."

"Do you need a loan? Because if you do, I'd be happy to—"

"I appreciate the offer, Dad, but I really want to do this on my own. I'm making pretty good money working for Isaac Yoder, and Allen's offered to let me lease this place with the option to buy."

"That's great." Dad gave Titus's arm another light tap. "Remember now, if you change your mind or need anything, just let me know."

—∞—

When Suzanne entered the woodshop that afternoon, she found Nelson on his knees, sanding some cabinet doors. She stood several seconds, breathing deeply of the aromas in the shop. Most people would have turned up their nose at wood being sanded and cut, but not her. She loved everything about being here, and her fingers itched to create something beautiful from the pieces of wood stacked in one corner of the room.

"Did you need something?" Nelson asked, looking up at her with a curious expression.

"Just came out to see if you needed some help. I'm sure with Titus not being able to work right now you must be getting behind on things."

"You're right, I am. I was going to ask Russell to sand these while I cut some wood, but he's busy mowing the lawn."

"I can do the sanding for you," she said.

He quirked an eyebrow. "You sure about that? It can get awful dusty, and it'll wear your fingernails down."

"I don't care about that. My nails are already worn down from all the gardening I do." She held her hands out to him. "I'd really like to help."

"All right then; here you go." He handed her a piece of sandpaper. "Now make sure you sand with the grain of the wood and not across the grain."

She frowned. "I know how to sand, Nelson. I've watched you and Grandpa do it many times. And don't forget about the birdfeeders I've made."

"A birdfeeder doesn't have to be perfect, but cabinets do." Nelson motioned to the row of cabinets sitting across the room. "Those are being done for a lawyer who lives in Hopkinsville. His wife's real picky, so every cabinet door needs to be done very well."

Irritation welled in Suzanne. Nelson obviously doubted her ability to do a good job. Well, she'd show him how well she could sand! If she did a good enough job, maybe he'd let her do something more than sand a few doors.

Chapter 35

On Saturday morning, Titus's folks got ready to head for home. Mom turned tearful eyes on Titus and said, "Please, come for a visit whenever you can."

"I'll try, but with me being off work for the past week I'm sure Nelson's behind on things, and I probably won't be able to get away for some time."

"Maybe you can come home for Thanksgiving or Christmas," Dad said.

Mom bobbed her head. "It wouldn't be the same without you."

"I'll have to wait and see how it goes." Titus peered out the living room window. "Looks like your driver's here."

Mom gave Titus a hug. "Take care of yourself, and call as often as you can so we'll know how you're doing."

"I will." Titus hugged Dad, too. "Have a safe trip, and tell the rest of the family I said hello."

Mom gave Titus one final hug; then she and Dad went out the door.

Titus stood on the porch as he watched his folks get into their driver's van. When the vehicle disappeared, he went inside and stretched out on the sofa with a sigh of relief. He appreciated them staying until he felt better, and he knew he'd miss Mom's good cooking. What he wouldn't miss was her hovering and constant badgering him about moving home.

He closed his eyes and rested awhile, then finally decided he ought to go over to the Beilers' store and talk to Esther. When Titus entered the store, he found Esther standing on a ladder, dusting some empty shelves.

"It's good to see you. How are you feeling?" Esther asked after she climbed down.

"The back of my head's still a little tender, but otherwise, I'm doing okay. I plan to go back to work on Monday."

"Are you sure you're up to that?" she asked with a look of concern.

"Jah. I've sat around letting my mamm wait on me long enough."

"How much longer will your folks be staying?"

"They left this morning."

"Oh, I see."

Titus leaned on the edge of the counter. "I heard there's going to be another singing tomorrow evening. I was wondering if you'd like to go with me."

Esther's face flushed, and she quickly averted his gaze. "I. . . uh. . .don't think I'll be going to the singing."

"How come?"

"I'd rather not go this time, that's all."

Titus stroked his chin. *What's going on? It seems strange that Esther's acting so disinterested, when not long ago she was practically flirting with me.*

"Are you sure you don't want to go?"

"I'm positive."

Titus figured it was best not to press the issue, so he said good-bye to Esther and left the store.

Think I'll ride over to the produce auction and see what's going on there, he decided. *I'm not in a hurry to go home and sit by myself for the rest of the day, anyway.*

—∾—

Fairview, Kentucky

Suzanne had just sold four hanging baskets to one of her English neighbors when she spotted Titus heading her way. Her heart skipped a beat. She wished there was something she could do to make him notice her without being obvious. Maybe if she learned to cook as well as Esther did, Titus would see her in a different light.

"Are you feeling better?" Suzanne asked when he joined her by the flowers.

He nodded. "My folks left today, and I plan to be back at work on Monday morning."

"I'm sure Nelson will be glad to hear that." Suzanne figured that, with Titus returning to work and Grandpa taking over most of the bookwork again, Nelson probably wouldn't want her hanging around the shop anymore. She'd have to sneak out there after dark and work on some project of her own, the way she'd done several times in the past.

Titus motioned to the few hanging baskets she had left. "Looks like business is going well for you today."

"It has. In fact, I've been so busy since I got here that I haven't had a chance to buy myself any lunch."

"Would you like me to go inside and get something for you?" Titus offered.

Suzanne smiled. "I'd appreciate that."

"What would you like?"

"A hot dog, a bottle of water, and a bag of chips would be fine." She moved toward her cash box. "Let me give you some money."

Titus shook his head. "That's okay. I'll get it. Think I'll buy myself a hot dog, too."

"Feel free to eat your lunch inside before you bring mine out to me," she said. "Other than the folding chair I brought, there's really nowhere to sit. Besides, it's warm out today, so you'd probably be more comfortable eating at one of the picnic tables inside."

"I'm not worried about the heat or a place to sit, but I'll be back soon with your lunch." Titus hurried away.

When he returned a short time later, he had two hot dogs, a bag of chips, and two bottles of water. "Since you don't have any customers right now, why don't we take a seat in there to eat our lunch?" He motioned to his buggy, parked a short distance away.

She hesitated at first, wondering if she should leave her plants for that long. "I guess I can keep an eye out for customers from there," she finally said.

They took seats in his buggy, and when Titus closed his eyes to offer a silent prayer, she poked his arm and said, "Aren't you going to take off your hat?"

He frowned. "There's still a bald spot on the back of my head, and I'm sparing you the misery of looking at it."

"I'm sure it doesn't look that bad."

"Oh, yeah?" Titus jerked off his hat and turned his head so she could see the back of it.

Suzanne suppressed a giggle. He did look pretty silly with a hunk of hair missing.

"You're not saying anything." Titus turned around so he was facing her again. "It looks baremlich, doesn't it?"

"It's not terrible, but I can see why you might want to keep your hat on. Someone could think you'd faced the mirror the wrong way when you shaved this morning."

Titus's lips twitched, and then he leaned his head back and

roared. "I like your sense of humor, Suzanne. In fact, the more time I spend with you, the more I like you."

She felt the heat of a blush cover her cheeks, but oh, it was nice to hear him say such a thing. "I. . .uh. . .like you, too," she murmured without looking at him. She was afraid if she did, he might be able to tell just how much she actually did care for him.

"Guess we'd better pray now so we can eat," Titus said.

They closed their eyes, and after their prayer, Titus told Suzanne the details about the money he'd found and about getting a reward.

"That's great. What are you going to do with it?" she asked.

"I'll probably put it in the bank."

"That sure was a frightening ordeal you went through," Suzanne said as they began to eat.

"It was, and when you showed up at my place, I was afraid for you, too."

A flush of heat cascaded over Suzanne's cheeks once more. It made her feel good to know he'd been concerned about her. Of course, he'd probably have hollered a warning to anyone who'd showed up that day.

"Did you hear that there's going to be another singing on Sunday evening?" she asked.

He drank some of his water and nodded. "I asked Esther if she'd like me to pick her up, but she said she wasn't planning to go."

"Oh? Did she say why?"

"Nope. Just said she wasn't going this time." He blotted his lips with the paper wrapped around the hot dog.

"Will you go to the singing anyway?"

He shook his head. "Probably not. Think I'll stay home and rest."

"Oh, I see." Suzanne hoped the disappointment she felt

didn't show on her face. If neither Esther nor Titus would be at the singing, she guessed she wouldn't go either.

—ɯ—

Los Angeles, California

"I'll be going home at the end of the month," Darlene told Phoebe as they headed down the beach toward the concession stand.

Phoebe halted and whirled around to face her friend. "You never mentioned going home for a visit. Is something special going on?"

Darlene shook her head. "I'm not going for a visit. I'm tired of living here, and I'm going home to stay."

Phoebe frowned. "I thought you liked California. It was your idea to come here, you know."

"I realize that, but I've changed my mind. I miss my family, and living in the English world isn't as exciting as I thought it would be."

Irritation welled in Phoebe's soul. "How am I supposed to pay the rent on our apartment if you're gone?"

"I figured you'd probably go back to Pennsylvania, too."

Phoebe shook her head vigorously. "There's nothing for me there anymore."

"What about your folks and the rest of the family?"

"If I moved back home, they'd be after me to join the church."

"Would joining the church be so bad? At one time, you said you were going to join, remember?"

"Of course I remember, but that was when Titus and I were courting. It's over between us, and he's living in Kentucky." Phoebe started walking again, a little faster this time. "You can go back to the Plain life if you want to, but I'm staying here!"

Chapter 36

Pembroke, Kentucky

On Monday morning when Titus entered the woodshop, he hesitated inside the door. It felt good to be back; he'd missed working in the shop, but he was surprised to find Isaac, going over the books. He was even more surprised to see Suzanne crouched on the floor with a piece of sandpaper in her hand, working on a cabinet door.

"Looks like I've been replaced," he said, kneeling beside her.

She shook her head. "Not a chance. I've only been helping out with some sanding because Nelson was getting behind."

"Ah, I see." Titus still couldn't get over how easy Suzanne had been to talk to at the produce auction the other day. When he was with Esther, he had to think of things to say. Since he and Esther didn't have much in common, it was difficult to make conversation.

Pushing his thoughts aside, Titus turned to Nelson and said, "I'd have been back here sooner, but the doctor said I couldn't start working again until today."

Nelson, who'd been staining some of the cabinets, slowly shook his head. "It's not a problem. We got along okay, although it's good to have you back in the shop."

"That's right," Isaac put in, "and I'm happy to be back at my desk again."

"Now that you're both working here again, Suzanne's help won't be needed, and she'll have more time to do other things," Nelson added.

Suzanne abruptly stood. "I guess if I'm not needed here I'll head up to the house!" Without waiting for anyone's response, she tossed the piece of sandpaper down and rushed out of the shop.

Nelson looked at Titus and shrugged. "What can I say? My sister's been acting kind of strange here of late. But then to me, she's always seemed a bit strange."

Titus couldn't help but notice how upset Suzanne had looked when Nelson said her help was no longer needed. He wondered if she'd rather be sanding wood than doing household chores.

He bent to inspect the cabinet door she'd been sanding and was surprised to see what a top-notch job she'd done. It almost seemed like she'd had experience sanding.

—∞—

Paradise, Pennsylvania

"Aren't you going to do the breakfast dishes?" Abraham asked when Fannie remained at the kitchen table after breakfast was over. "You've always washed the dishes right away."

"I'm really tired today. I'll do them later."

Abraham frowned. "If you'd go to sleep at night instead of lying awake, worrying about Titus, you'd have the energy you need to get things done during the day." He motioned to the kitchen floor. "Looks like this hasn't been swept for a few days, and I'm gettin' low on clean shirts, so I'd appreciate it if you'd wash some clothes today."

Fannie yawned. "I'm planning to."

"Better not wait too long. I read in the paper that rain's in the forecast."

"Okay." She yawned again and poured them both a cup of coffee.

"Ever since we got home from Kentucky, you've done nothing but worry and fret." He touched her shoulder. "You can worry yourself silly about Titus, but it won't change a thing. Just give your worries to God, and let Him take care of our son."

She gave a slow nod. "I know you're right, but it's hard for me not to think about what those men did to him. With Titus living so far away, I struggle not to be anxious."

"I know, but it's not healthy to worry the way you've been doing. You ought to be more like Abby. *Sie druwwelt sich wehe nix.*"

"What do you mean she doesn't worry herself about anything? Everyone worries about something, Abraham."

"That may be so, but from what I can tell, she worries less than most, and she doesn't let things affect her the way you've done lately." He glanced at the battery-operated clock on the wall across the room. "I'd better get out to the fields, or Timothy will wonder what's happened to me."

"Okay. Don't work too hard, and have a good day."

Soon after Abraham left, Abby stopped by. "You look so tired, Mom," she said. "Haven't you been sleeping well?"

Fannie shook her head. "I've been worried about Titus, and it's hard for me to relax. Every time I close my eyes, I see him lying in that hospital bed with a bandage on his head."

Abby poured herself some coffee and took a seat in the chair beside Fannie. "Can I give you some advice that someone gave me once when I was worrying about things?"

"Sure."

"When going to bed at night you should empty the pockets of your mind, because if you go to sleep with worries, it'll drain your energy through the night."

"How am I supposed to empty the pockets of worry from my mind?" Fannie questioned.

"Simply say to yourself, 'I'm putting these worries into God's hands,' and then close your eyes and go to sleep."

"I wish it were that simple." Fannie took a sip of coffee.

"It can be simple if you remember what God says about worry." Abby smiled. "In Matthew 6:34 it says: 'Take therefore no thought for the morrow: for the morrow shall take thought for the things of itself.' And Psalm 55:22 says, 'Cast thy burden upon the Lord, and he shall sustain thee.' " She touched Fannie's arm and gave it a tender squeeze. "You need to do that, Mom. Hide God's Word in your heart and dwell on it until you fall asleep at night."

The tension Fannie had felt earlier began to disappear. "I know you're right, and I appreciate those reminders from God's Word. I do need to remember that our Father's in control, and that He's watching over Titus, as well as the rest of our family."

"Did you enjoy your time in Kentucky with Titus?" Abby asked.

"I certainly did. Just wish we could've stayed longer. I still miss him, you know."

"I'm sure he misses you, too, but it's good that he's making a life of his own and is enjoying his job there, don't you think?"

"Jah. It seems like Titus is becoming more responsible, too—more like Timothy in that regard."

"I just can't get over how much those two still look alike," Abby said, taking their conversation in a different direction. "Why, I'll never forget the time when the twins were bopplin and I got them mixed up while I was giving them a bath. I ended up bathing the same boppli twice."

"Their personalities are different, though, and that makes it easy for most people to tell them apart."

"I remember once when we got the brilliant idea to tie a ribbon around Titus's ankle so we'd know it was him. That worked fine until I forgot to remove the ribbon when I bathed him. Of course it got soggy and fell off." Abby snickered. "Then there was the time that Leona, being just a young girl herself, came over to see the twins and suggested we put a blotch of green paint on Titus's toe. That worked fine for a while, until the paint wore off."

Fannie laughed so hard that tears rolled down her cheeks. It felt good to find a little humor in something. She'd been much too serious lately. "It's a good thing only one of our twins has moved to Kentucky, because I doubt that anyone there would be able to tell them apart."

Pembroke, Kentucky

Suzanne's mother had gone to an all-day quilting bee, so it was Suzanne's job to make lunch for the men today. Along with the sandwiches and hard-boiled eggs she planned to take out to them, she thought it would be nice to make some butterscotch pudding for their dessert. She'd use a box of the instant kind, figuring it wouldn't be too hard to make.

Following the directions on the box, she took out a metal bowl, the eggbeater, and some milk. Carefully, she measured the milk into the bowl and added the package of pudding.

Her nose twitched. "Yum. This sure smells good. I love the aroma of butterscotch."

When Suzanne placed the beater inside and started turning the handle, the bowl slid across the counter, and some of the pudding splashed out.

"This isn't working out so well," she mumbled, blotting the counter with some paper towels. She'd seen Mom use the eggbeater before, and the bowl had never slid around for her like that.

Suzanne pushed the bowl against her waist and started beating again. *Whoosh!*—the bowl slipped off the counter and fell on the floor, spilling pudding on her dress, down the cabinet, and onto the floor, where it seeped under the cabinet.

"That's just great," she fumed. Not only was the pudding ruined, but she'd have to clean the floor and would need to change her dress.

Suzanne wet the mop under the faucet and started with the floor. When that chore was done, she went up to her room to change.

Several minutes later, she returned to the kitchen, put the sandwiches in a plastic container, took the eggs she'd boiled earlier from the refrigerator, and grabbed a handful of cookies Mom had made yesterday. Then she placed everything in the lunch basket, picked up a jug of iced tea, and headed out the door.

When Suzanne entered the woodshop, Grandpa tipped his head and stared at her strangely. "Weren't you wearing a green dress earlier?"

"You're right. I was."

"Mind if I ask why you're wearing a blue dress now?"

"I had a little accident in the kitchen."

"Why am I not surprised?" Nelson said, rolling his eyes.

"Here's your lunch!" Suzanne placed the basket and jug of iced tea on the workbench with a huff.

"What'd you bring us?" Titus asked.

"Ham and cheese sandwiches, hard-boiled eggs, and chocolate chip cookies."

He grinned. "Sounds good."

Suzanne waited until the men had said their silent prayer. She was about to leave, when Titus picked up an egg and cracked it on his forehead. *Whoosh!*—runny egg spilled out of the shell, ran down his face, and dripped onto his shirt.

"Oh no!" Suzanne grabbed the roll of paper towels near the sink and handed it to Titus. "I'm so sorry."

Nelson slapped his leg and chuckled. "I've heard that raw eggs are supposed to be good for a person's hair, so maybe that runny egg will grow the missing hair back on your head," he said to Titus.

Titus mumbled something under his breath as he wiped the egg off his face; then he turned to Suzanne and said, "Did you give us raw eggs on purpose?"

"No, of course not. I really thought they were hard-boiled. I must have grabbed raw eggs by mistake, thinking they were the ones I'd boiled earlier."

"What made you crack that egg on your forehead?" Nelson asked. "Were you just *abweise*?"

"I was not showing off. I've always cracked eggs that way." Titus looked at Suzanne. "At least the ones I don't think are raw."

Suzanne was so embarrassed, she just wanted to hide. *I'll never get Titus's attention in a positive way if I keep messing up and making myself look bad in his eyes.*

Without waiting for the men to finish their lunch, she turned and rushed out the door.

Chapter 37

Los Angeles, California

Phoebe frowned as she stared at her meager breakfast—an overripe banana and a glass of water. It had been four weeks since Darlene had gone home, and Phoebe had been forced to take a second job during the evening at a convenience store in order to pay the rent on the apartment she'd shared with Darlene. The cost of living was much higher in California than it had been back home, and Phoebe's money was so tight that she'd had to cut back on everything and barely had enough to eat. Another frustration was that she didn't have any free time to do fun things such as going to the beach, shopping, or out to lunch. The few friends she'd made while living here all had steady boyfriends, so they couldn't be bothered with her anymore.

It was probably for the best. With two part-time jobs, she barely had enough time to sleep, let alone socialize or do anything fun.

Phoebe stared at the calendar on the kitchen wall and grimaced. It was hard to believe, but she'd been away from home over four months already. When she'd first come to

California, she'd expected her life to be easy and carefree, but things were getting more difficult every day.

She pushed away from the table and grunted as she tossed the banana peel at the garbage can and missed. "I don't care how bad it gets," she muttered. "I'm not about to admit defeat and go home!"

Paradise, Pennsylvania

Fannie had just taken some throw rugs outside to hang on the line, when she spotted Arie Stoltzfus's horse and buggy coming up the lane. Except for the Sundays when they went to church, Fannie hadn't seen much of Arie lately. She wondered if Arie had been busy or was just keeping to herself.

"Wie geht's?" Fannie asked when Arie joined her under the clothesline.

"I've been better." From the slump of Arie's shoulders and her furrowed brows, Fannie knew Arie must be upset about something.

"What's wrong?" Fannie asked, feeling concern for her friend.

"I'm worried about Phoebe."

Fannie finished draping the rugs over the line and motioned to the house. "Let's go inside where it's cooler and you can tell me about it. The humidity today is so bad it hurts."

Once inside, they took seats at the kitchen table, and Fannie poured glasses of iced tea. "Are you still upset because Phoebe moved to California?" she asked.

Arie nodded slowly. "But I'm even more upset now because Phoebe's friend Darlene has come home—without Phoebe."

"Oh, I didn't realize that."

Arie took a sip of iced tea and blotted her lips on a napkin.

"This is so refreshing. Danki."

"You're welcome."

Arie sighed as she set the glass on the table. "Not only did my daughter choose to stay in California, but now she's living alone. To make matters worse, she won't answer any of my phone calls, and I can hardly sleep because I'm so worried about her." The dark circles beneath her eyes confirmed that she hadn't been sleeping well. "Short of a miracle, I don't think Phoebe will ever return to Pennsylvania and the Plain life."

"I know it's hard to have her living in another state," Fannie said. "It's been hard for me to accept Titus moving to Kentucky."

"It's different for you," Arie said. "Your son's joined the church and has settled down. My daughter's still going through her running-around years and may never return home and join the church."

Fannie placed her hand over Arie's. "You need to keep the faith and pray that God will touch Phoebe's heart and she'll decide to come home." Fannie couldn't believe she was saying such a thing. The truth was, she'd been glad when Phoebe left—at least until Titus had decided to leave, too. If Phoebe had stayed in Pennsylvania and joined the church, Titus would never have left home.

"It's not so easy to keep the faith," Arie said. "Especially when Phoebe won't answer my calls."

"You and your family weren't living here at the time," Fannie said, "but back when Naomi was a young woman dealing with the guilt of leaving her baby brother on the picnic table when he was kidnapped, she left home for a while, too."

"Where'd she go?"

"Went to Oregon with her English friend Ginny. Abraham was so upset about it, he almost made himself sick. But God answered our prayers and brought Naomi home. You'd never know such a thing had happened now, because she's happy and content and such a good *mudder* to her kinner."

"Oh, I pray that will be the case for Phoebe someday."

Fannie placed her hand on Arie's arm and shared some of the scriptures Abby had previously mentioned to her.

Arie sniffed and swiped at the tears trickling down her cheeks. "I appreciate the reminder and know that I do need to trust the Lord where my daughter's concerned. From now on, I'll try to remember to trust God more and put Phoebe into His hands."

—∞—

Pembroke, Kentucky

Titus had just finished breakfast and was getting ready to leave for work, when a knock sounded on the back door. He hurried across the room to answer it, and was surprised to see Bishop King standing on the porch.

"Can I come in?" the bishop asked.

"Well, I. . .uh. . .was about to leave for work."

"It's important, and I won't take much of your time."

"Of course. Come in." Titus led the way to the kitchen and motioned for the bishop to take a seat at the table.

When the bishop sat down, Titus seated himself in the chair opposite him.

Bishop King cleared his throat a few times, while stroking his full gray beard. "It's come to my attention that you own a cell phone. Is it true?"

Titus nodded slowly. "I use it mostly to keep in touch with my family in Pennsylvania. My brother Zach has a cell phone because of his painting business, so it's easier for me to get ahold of him now, rather than having to leave messages on his or my folks' voice mail."

The bishop tapped his fingers on the table and looked at Titus with furrowed brows. "Cell phones are not allowed in this district. Figured someone would have told you that by now."

A trickle of sweat rolled down Titus's forehead, and he wiped it away. "I did hear that, but I was hoping you might make an exception in my case, since it's hard for me to get ahold of my family."

The bishop shook his head sternly. "There are no exceptions to the rule. You'll have to get rid of the cell phone if you expect to remain a member in good standing."

"But I signed a yearlong contract, and—"

"That's too bad, but I can't allow you to have a cell phone and expect others in our district to adhere to the 'no cell phone' rule."

"I suppose not." Titus drew in a deep breath and sighed. "I don't want to do anything to jeopardize my standing in the church, so I'll stop using the cell phone and pay the fee to disconnect the service."

The bishop smiled and gave a nod. "Maybe you can set up a certain time to call your family each week. That's what many others do, you know."

"Okay, I'll do whatever you say."

"This bread is sure good, Mom." Chad reached for a slice of banana bread, sniffed it, and then popped it into his mouth. "Mmm. . .it tastes even better than it smells." He smacked his lips noisily.

"Duh net so laut schmatze!" Mom scolded. "You're old enough to know better than to make such a noise when you eat."

"Sorry," the boy mumbled.

"When you become a daed someday, you'll need to set a

better example for your kinner," Grandpa said.

Chad slowly nodded. Suzanne figured becoming a dad was probably the last thing on her brother's young mind.

"This *is* tasty bread," Effie said after she'd eaten a piece. "Danki for makin' it, Mom."

Mom shook her head and motioned to Suzanne. "She's the one who deserves the thanks."

Nelson's eyebrows lifted high on his forehead as he stared at Suzanne with a look of disbelief. "You made the bread?

She nodded. "For the last several weeks, I've been going over to Esther's for cooking lessons."

"Well, that would explain it," Nelson said. "Esther's a really good cook."

"That's true," Mom agreed, "and she has a lot more patience in the kitchen than I do, which is why I'm sure I haven't been able to teach you much, Suzanne."

Grandpa took a piece of banana bread and slathered it with butter. "My daughter has a lot of good qualities, but she does tend to be a bit picky about things—especially when it comes to what goes on in her kitchen."

Mom frowned, but then a smile played at the corner of her lips. "I'm not picky. I just like things done in an orderly fashion. I'll also admit that for me, it's usually easier to do things myself than to wait for someone else to do them. It's a fault I need to work on."

"And I haven't been the best student," Suzanne said. "That's mostly because there are so many other things I'd rather do than spend time in the kitchen."

"Then why the change now?" Grandpa asked.

Suzanne wasn't about to blurt out that she'd decided to learn how to cook so she could impress Titus. That would be embarrassing and no doubt bring on some teasing from her siblings.

"So, how come you've been learnin' to cook?" Russell asked, poking Suzanne's arm.

"I just decided it was time; that's all."

"I'll bet she's interested in some fellow and knows she'll need to be able to cook if she's gonna get him to marry her." Nelson winked at Suzanne.

"Who's the fellow?" Effie questioned. "And when are ya gettin' married?"

Suzanne's face heated, and she stared at the table, hoping no one would realize how embarrassed she was. "There is no fellow, and I'm not getting married anytime soon—maybe never." *But I wish I was*, she mentally added.

Chapter 38

For the rest of summer, and into the fall, Suzanne continued to take cooking lessons from Esther and practice what she'd learned on her family. She was getting better at cooking, and even her baking skills had improved. Unfortunately, she hadn't had the chance to let Titus sample anything she'd made, because he and Nelson had been installing some cabinets and doing the trim work on the inside of a new house in Hopkinsville, which took them away from the shop every day. While they were gone, Grandpa continued to do the bookwork and usually spent a few hours every day in the shop to greet any customers who came in.

This morning, Mom had accompanied Grandpa to his doctor's appointment in town, which meant nobody was in the shop. That gave Suzanne the perfect opportunity to sneak out there and work on a project of her own that she'd begun a few weeks ago when no one else was around.

Suzanne entered the shop and lit the gas lamps. Then she pulled out the bedside table she'd started working on from the back of the storage closet, where she'd hidden it under a tarp.

She hummed as she began sanding the legs. The wood felt smooth beneath her fingers, and she didn't even mind the bits of sawdust that blew up to her nose. This was where she belonged—where she felt comfortable and at peace. Even though she'd learned to cook fairly well, she doubted that she'd ever feel this content baking a pie or roasting a chicken. If only her desire to work with wood could be accepted by the men in the family. If she just could make them see how much she loved spending time out here.

Suzanne reached for another piece of sandpaper, and in so doing, knocked a jar of nails off the shelf. The jar broke as soon as it hit the floor, and nails flew everywhere.

"Oh great," she mumbled. "Now I have to waste my time picking all that up."

She bent down, picked up a piece of broken glass, and let out a yelp. Her finger was bleeding, and the cut looked pretty deep and had begun to throb. But a close examination convinced her it wouldn't require stitches.

Suzanne left her work and opened the desk drawer where Nelson kept some bandages. The box was empty. *Guess I'd better go up to the house for a bandage and some antiseptic.*

She grabbed a paper towel from the holder near the sink and wrapped it around her finger. Then she pushed the table back into the storage closet, threw the tarp over it, and hurried from the shop.

—m—

Titus and Nelson had finished working at the house in Hopkinsville a little earlier than expected, so they decided to stop at the shop and see if any orders had come in during their absence.

"There's no paperwork on the desk," Nelson said, "but look there." He pointed to some broken glass on the floor. "Looks like Grandpa must have busted a jar sometime today. I'd better get the broom and dustpan from the storage room and sweep it up before one of us gets a hunk of glass stuck in the bottom of our shoe."

"I'll get it," Titus said.

He opened the door to the storage closet and was about to remove the broom, when he noticed what looked like a table leg sticking out from under a canvas tarp. He pulled the cloth back. Sure enough, it was a small wooden table, but it wasn't quite finished. It appeared to be partially sanded but no stain had been added.

Titus bent down and studied the table. It had been finely crafted, with perfectly shaped corners and a small drawer in the front. He was about to drop the canvas back in place when he noticed a bloodstain on one of the table legs.

"Did you make that little table?" Titus asked Nelson when he returned with the broom and dustpan.

"What table's that?"

"The one in the storage closet. It looks like a bedside table."

Nelson shook his head. "Never knew there was a table in there. I wonder if Grandpa made it when he's been out here doing the books. I'll have to ask him about it."

Titus began sweeping up the glass and had just finished when Suzanne entered the shop, wearing a bandage on her finger. *Could she have been here working today? Might she have made the table? No, that's ridiculous. If she could do woodworking that well, Isaac or Nelson would have put her to work in the shop by now.*

"I'm surprised to see you two here so early," Suzanne said. "I figured you'd be working late again."

"We did all we could for the day and decided to come back here to see if any orders had come in," Nelson said.

She glanced at the floor, but said nothing about the broken glass. Maybe she didn't know about it. Maybe she'd cut her finger on something in the house, barn, or outside while doing some chore.

Suzanne looked at Titus and smiled. "If you have no other plans for this evening, we'd like you to stay for supper."

Titus smiled. "I have no plans, and I'd be happy to stay." Truth was, he was tired and hungry and didn't feel like going home to an empty house and fixing himself something to eat—especially not tonight on his birthday, which he hadn't mentioned to anyone. He didn't want them to feel obligated to help him celebrate. If he were still living at home, Mom would have done something special for his and Timothy's birthday. When Titus got home, he planned to call and leave a birthday message on Timothy's voice mail.

A short time later, when Titus entered the kitchen with Nelson, he sniffed the air. Suzanne's mother was a good cook, so he looked forward to the meal. "Something sure smells good in here," he told Verna, who stood near the stove. "What'd you make for supper?"

"Not a thing," Verna said. "I was in Hopkinsville most of the day with my daed. Suzanne fixed the meal."

Remembering some things Nelson had said about his sister's cooking, Titus wondered what kind of a meal he was in for this evening. Well, as hungry as he was, he'd eat almost anything.

—∞—

As they ate the chicken and dumplings Suzanne had prepared, she couldn't help but notice that Titus seemed to be enjoying himself. He'd had two helpings already, which meant he was either very hungry or liked what he'd eaten.

"How are things coming along with your job at that house in Hopkinsville?" Grandpa asked Nelson.

"Real well. If things keep going as they have, we should be done with all the trim work and doors by the end of the week."

"That's good to hear," Grandpa said, "because the last few days, I've taken a few orders for Christmas gifts."

"Here it is fall already, and I can't believe Christmas is only two and a half months away," Verna said. "It seems like the days just fly by anymore. I don't even know where summer went."

"That's 'cause everyone's been so busy," Russell chimed in.

"You're right about that," his mother agreed.

"This is sure a good meal," Titus said around a mouthful of dumpling. "I'm glad I decided to stay. To tell you the truth, I wasn't looking forward to spending the evening alone either."

Suzanne smiled. "I'm glad you're enjoying it, and I hope you'll like the pie I made for dessert."

His eyebrows lifted. "What kind of pie?"

"Lemon shoofly. It was one of Grandma's favorite pies to bake."

"I've never heard of lemon shoofly," Titus said. "Is it anything like the traditional Lancaster County wet-bottom shoofly pie?"

"It's similar, but we think it's even better," Mom interjected. "The pie has molasses in it, but the addition of lemon juice tones down the molasses a bit."

Titus smiled. "If it's half as good as regular shoofly pie, then I'm anxious to try it."

After everyone had finished eating, Suzanne brought out the pie. "Here you go." She placed the pie, decorated with twenty-three lit candles, on the table in front of Titus.

He blinked a couple of times and looked up at her with a curious expression. "What are the candles for?"

"Happy birthday," she said with a grin.

"How'd you know today was my birthday?"

"Your mamm left a message on our voice mail for you this morning. She said she'd tried to call your phone but got a busy signal, so figuring we'd give you the message, she called here to wish you a happy birthday."

"I'll bet I left the door to the phone shanty open by accident last night. One of the cats probably got in and knocked the receiver off the hook," Titus said.

Suzanne pointed to the pie. "You'd better blow out your candles before they melt all over the pie."

Titus leaned forward and blew the candles out in one big breath. Then Suzanne cut a generous slice and handed the plate to him.

He quickly forked a piece into his mouth. "Umm. . . This is really good. I'll have to get the recipe from you and pass it on to my mamm."

Suzanne sighed with relief. Titus had enjoyed everything she'd fixed for supper this evening, and she was glad they'd been able to help him celebrate his birthday. It had to be hard to be away from family on any special occasion.

After everyone finished their pie and the final prayer had been said, the children went to their rooms, while Grandpa and Nelson retired to the living room for a game of checkers.

"If you're not in a hurry to go home, why don't you stick around awhile and play the winner?" Grandpa said to Titus.

"I appreciate the offer, but I think I'll help Suzanne do the dishes, and then I'd better head for home."

"You like to do the dishes?" Nelson looked at Titus like he'd taken leave of his senses.

"Didn't say I liked to do 'em," Titus replied. "Just said I'd help. Figured it's the least I can do to say thanks to Suzanne for the good meal and for making my birthday special."

Nelson shrugged. "Suit yourself."

"If you two are going to do the dishes, then I guess I'll find a book and read for a while," Verna said.

After everyone else left the room, Suzanne filled the sink

with warm water and added some liquid detergent, while Titus finished bringing the dirty dishes over to the sink. "Would you mind washing while I dry?" she asked Titus. "I cut my finger today, and since I'm wearing a bandage, I don't want it to fall off in the dishwater."

"No problem; I don't mind washing."

Suzanne took out a clean dishcloth and waited for him to wash a few of the dishes and put them into the drainer before she started drying.

"So how'd you cut your finger?" he asked as he sloshed the dishrag over one of the plates.

Suzanne's face heated with embarrassment. How would Titus react if she told him how she'd cut it? Would he think, the way Nelson did, that a woman's place was in the kitchen, not in the shop working with wood?

Instead of answering Titus's question, Suzanne quickly changed the subject, telling him about the young people's gathering that would be held at the Beilers' home on Sunday evening.

"There will be hot dogs and marshmallows to roast around the bonfire," she said. "And plenty of hot apple cider."

He smacked his lips. "Sounds good to me."

"Do you think you might go?"

"Probably. How about you?"

"I'd like to, but Mom doesn't like me to take the horse and buggy out by myself after dark."

"Won't Nelson be going?"

"I'm sure he will, but he'll be taking his *aldi*, and I don't want to intrude." Suzanne stacked the clean plates and set them in the cupboard.

"I'd be happy to give you a ride there and back," Titus said.

She smiled and nodded. "I'll look forward to going."

Chapter 39

I'm going outside to enjoy this beautiful autumn weather while I wait for Titus to pick me up," Suzanne told her mother on Sunday evening.

Mom smiled. "It's nice that he's taking you to the young people's gathering. He's obviously interested in you."

Suzanne shook her head. "I think he was just being nice when he offered to take me. Titus and Nelson have become good friends, and he probably figured Nelson needed the chance to be alone with Lucy."

"I don't know about that. I saw the way Titus looked at you when he was here for supper the other night. I really do think he has courtship on his mind."

"I know he's not seeing Esther anymore," Suzanne said, "but Titus and I have had our differences since he moved here, so I'm not sure he'll ever see me as someone he'd want to court."

"Things weren't always good between me and your daed before we started courting, but once he realized I was a woman, and not the little girl he'd gone to school with, he changed his mind real quick."

"This is just one ride. I doubt it means anything more to Titus," Suzanne said as she went out the door.

When Suzanne stepped onto the porch, a gentle breeze caressed her face. The cooler weather they'd been having felt good. She glanced into the yard and spotted a squirrel poking its head in and out of a pile of brush, while two of her cats chased each other across the lawn.

She directed her gaze to the field where they grew their colorful mums. As much as she enjoyed tending the flowers, it was nothing compared to working with wood.

She thought about the table she'd hidden in the woodshop storage closet and wondered what she should do when it was finished. Should she keep it, sell it, or give it away? The table might make a nice Christmas present for Mom.

Suzanne's thoughts halted when she heard the *clip-clop* of horse's hooves. Titus was here. It was time to go.

Titus didn't know why, but he felt nervous with Suzanne sitting on the buggy seat beside him. He'd spent time with her before, but never like this on what felt like a date. As Titus guided his horse and buggy down the road, he wondered if he'd made a mistake offering Suzanne a ride tonight. Would she, and probably some others, think they were courting? Did he want to court her? If tonight went well, should he ask her out again?

"I've been wondering about something," he said, looking over at her.

"What's that?"

"I noticed that you were wearing a bandage the other night, and when I asked about it, you changed the subject."

"Oh, that." She turned her head away from him. "I. . .uh. . . cut my finger on a piece of glass."

"In the woodshop?"

"Jah. I knocked over a jar of nails, and it fell on the floor and broke."

"Did you touch something with your bloody finger after that?"

"I touched a lot of things. Why do you ask?"

"I found a small table in the storage closet, with a bloodstain on one of the legs. Figured whoever had cut themselves must have touched the table leg."

Suzanne sat several seconds, without saying a word. She looked over at him and said, "I'm the one who made the table."

He blinked a couple of times. "Are you serious?"

She gave a nod. "I've made some other things, too."

"Like what?"

"Birdhouses and feeders. The table was the first piece of furniture I've made."

"Why was it in the storage closet under a tarp?"

"I didn't want Nelson to see it."

"How come?"

"He thinks a woman's place is in the kitchen." She sighed. "He doesn't realize how much I enjoy working with wood."

His brows furrowed. "It is unusual. I mean, I've never known a woman carpenter before. At least not any Amish women."

"Guess I'm an exception to the rule."

Titus wasn't sure what to think of this. Suzanne was a mystery to him. One day she couldn't cook at all, and the next day she'd made a real tasty meal. One day she was sanding cabinet doors in the woodshop, and the next day she'd made a table—and not a bad-looking one at that.

Suzanne may look similar to Phoebe, he thought, *but she's nothing like her at all. She's got spunk, but she doesn't show off. She's already joined the church, so she's settled and not likely to leave the faith. Maybe I should pursue a relationship with her. I'd better think this over some more.*

They drove the rest of the way in silence. The only sounds were the *creak-creak* of the buggy wheels and the steady *clippety-clop* of Lightning's hooves against the pavement. Titus figured the silence was better, because at the moment, he couldn't think of anything else to say.

When they arrived at the Beilers', Suzanne went to speak with Esther, while Titus put his horse in the corral.

"I was surprised when I saw Titus's horse and buggy come in, and then you stepped down," Esther said to Suzanne. "I'll bet you're happy that he asked you to come with him tonight."

"Shh. Don't make an issue of it," Suzanne whispered. "I think he was only being nice when he offered to take me to and from the singing."

Esther leaned close to Suzanne's ear. "Has he had a chance to taste anything you've cooked since I've been giving you lessons?"

"He ate supper with us the other night and said he liked my chicken and dumplings, as well as the lemon shoofly pie I made in honor of his birthday."

"I didn't know it was his birthday."

"Until I listened to a voice mail message for him from his mamm, I didn't know it either."

"Well, if he enjoyed the meal you prepared, then I think there may be some hope for the two of you."

"I'd like to think so, but I'm not getting my hopes up." Suzanne motioned to the barn, where several young people were heading. "Looks like the singing's about to begin. Guess we'd better head in there, too."

Suzanne and Esther followed the others into the barn, and soon everyone found seats. They sang for over an hour, as their voices lifted in harmony and echoed off the barn walls. Then everyone moved outside to the bonfire Esther's father had started. Suzanne enjoyed the warmth of the fire, and even the smoky smell didn't bother her. She'd always loved sitting around a fire, especially on a chilly fall evening such as this. She gazed up at the three-quarter moon above, wishing Titus would join her at the bonfire, but he took a seat beside Ethan Zook instead and didn't even look Suzanne's way.

I'm sure by telling Titus I like to work with wood I probably ruined any chances I might have with him, she thought. *He probably thinks, like Nelson, that a woman's place is in the kitchen.*

"Are you going to have a hot dog?" Esther asked.

Suzanne shook her head. "I'm not hungry right now."

"At least have some hot cider then. My daed made it, and it's really good."

"Okay." Suzanne was on her way to the refreshment table when a gust of wind came up, and several dust devils whirled in the distance. As the wind increased, it grew so strong that it blew the paper plates and cups right off the table.

"Grab the tablecloth, or everything will go!" someone hollered.

Just then, another gust came up, this one a little stronger than the last, carrying debris from the yard that was quickly caught up in the air. Most of the young people started running for the barn, and someone quickly put the bonfire out so that sparks wouldn't fly. The corral gate flew open, and suddenly all the horses were out, running all around the yard.

Titus and some of the other young men chased after the horses.

"You'd better watch out," Ethan shouted as he raced past Titus. "I think the cover on the Beilers' manure pit just blew off."

Titus stepped back, and—*splat*—he stepped right into the pit.

Chapter 40

When Titus woke up the next morning, he was relieved he could no longer smell the putrid odor of manure on his body. He couldn't believe he'd fallen into the Beilers' manure pit while trying to chase down the runaway horses. The pit was only a few feet deep, but when he'd stepped into it, he'd lost his footing and ended up flat on his back.

The stench had been horrible, and he'd held his breath, unable to bear the despicable odor, while Esther's dad hosed him off with water so cold it made his teeth chatter. That hadn't helped much, other than to get most of the manure off his clothes, and he'd taken a lot of ribbing from some of the fellows. Even Suzanne had giggled when she'd seen him standing there, sopping wet. It was kind of funny, now that he thought about it, but at the time, he'd been pretty miffed.

While some of the young men had continued to round up the horses, Titus had gone into the Beilers' house and taken a warm shower. Then Esther's mother had given him a shirt and some trousers that had belonged to Esther's older brother, Dan, who was married and no longer lived at home. Even after the shower, Titus had been able to smell the sickening manure aroma.

It reminded him of the time when he and Timothy were boys and had fallen into a pile of manure when they'd been fooling around. They'd gotten in big trouble with Mom for it, too.

Not wishing to subject Suzanne to sitting beside his smelly body, Titus had asked Ethan Zook to take her home. Then Titus had headed to his place and taken another long shower with plenty of soap and shampoo. It sure wasn't the way he'd intended the evening to go. He'd hoped that on the way home he might talk to Suzanne more about woodworking and see if she'd like him to put in a good word with Nelson about it.

Guess I'd better not say anything to him until I've spoken to Suzanne, he decided as he left his bedroom and headed to the kitchen to fix breakfast. *She might not want me to say anything to Nelson about the table she'd made.*

—ᴥ—

Paradise, Pennsylvania

Samuel had just entered the kitchen when Elsie, who was stirring a kettle of oatmeal, motioned for him to come over. "I've something to tell you," she said.

"What's up?"

"I was going to tell you this last night, but you came home from work late and fell asleep before I had a chance to say anything."

"Tell me what?"

"I went to see the doctor yesterday. What I've suspected is true. I'm going to have another boppli, and it'll be born next spring."

Samuel slipped his arm around Elsie's waist and pulled her to his side. "That's real good news. Have you told anyone else yet?"

She shook her head. "I wanted to tell you first, and then our kinner and both sides of our family."

He smiled. "Think I'll stop by my folks' on the way to work this morning and give them the good news."

Elsie sighed and leaned her head on his shoulder. "I'm hoping we have another boy this time. Then Jared will have someone to play with who's closer to his age."

"That would be nice, but I'll be happy whether God chooses to give us a boy or a girl. The main thing is that the baby's born healthy."

"I agree." Elsie removed the kettle from the stove. "The oatmeal's ready now, so if you'll call the kinner to the table, we can eat and give them our news."

Pembroke, Kentucky

As Suzanne helped Mom with breakfast, she thought about how things had gone last night. Not only had the unexpected wind put a stop to their young people's gathering, but Titus hadn't even brought her home. Of course, he'd used the excuse that he smelled bad when he'd told her that he'd arranged for Ethan to give her a ride, but she wondered if the real reason had something to do with her telling him about the table she'd made.

He'll probably blab to Nelson or Grandpa about what I've been doing, she thought as she placed a plate of buttermilk pancakes on the table. *Maybe I ought to tell them myself and get it over with. But if I do that, they might not let me go out to the shop anymore.* Suzanne got the pot of coffee from the stove. *Or maybe Titus was upset because I laughed when he fell in the manure pit. But then, some of the others laughed, too.*

"Everything's ready now," Mom said, placing a platter of bacon on the table. "Would you please call everyone in for breakfast?" she asked Suzanne.

"Sure."

Suzanne felt a nip in the air as she stepped onto the porch

and rang the bell so those who were outside doing their chores would know breakfast was ready. When she stepped back inside, she cupped her hands around her mouth, and called for Effie to come downstairs to eat.

A short time later, everyone gathered around the kitchen table. After the silent prayer, Mom passed the platters of bacon and pancakes.

Grandpa sniffed deeply. "Ah, I do love the smell of maple-cured bacon." He forked a couple of pancakes onto his plate and poured syrup over the top. "Who made these?" he asked after he'd taken his first bite.

"Suzanne did, while I cooked the bacon," Mom replied.

Grandpa looked over at Suzanne and smiled. "Good job! For a young woman who's always disliked being in the kitchen, you're turnin' into a pretty fine cook." He winked at her. "I've got a hunch it won't be long until you find yourself a husband."

The heat of a blush warmed Suzanne's cheeks. She was pleased that Grandpa liked the pancakes but worried that he might suspect she was interested in Titus. She certainly didn't want him to know that she'd asked Esther to give her cooking lessons in the hope of gaining Titus's approval.

"Say, Grandpa," Nelson said after he'd taken a drink of milk, "do you know anything about the table inside the storage closet in the woodshop?"

Grandpa shook his head. "I saw it there, too. Thought maybe you'd made it."

"Nope, it wasn't me."

"Must have been Titus, then. I'll ask him about it when he shows up at the woodshop this morning."

Feeling a sense of panic, Suzanne balled her napkin tightly into her hands and blurted out, "There's no need for you to ask Titus because I'm the one who made the table."

Everyone turned to look at her, eyes wide and mouths hanging open.

Chapter 41

Suzanne held her breath as she waited for the family's response to her confession. What if she wasn't allowed to go in the woodshop anymore? She didn't think she could deal with that—didn't think she could ever stop making wooden things. And it would be unfair if she was asked to give it up.

Grandpa was the first to speak. "I'm not really surprised by this, Suzanne. We all know you've made a few birdfeeders, and I've known for some time that you'd rather be out in the woodshop than doing anything in the house."

"That's true," Suzanne said in a voice barely above a whisper.

"How would you like to help out in the shop during our busier times?" Grandpa asked. "With Christmas sneaking up on us, I'm sure we'll be getting a lot more orders."

"I'd like that very much." Tears welled in Suzanne's eyes. She could hardly believe he'd actually invited her to work in the shop—and it would be doing more than bookwork or sweeping the floor. This was too good to be true.

Nelson looked at Grandpa with a grim expression. "You

can't be serious. Suzanne will only be in the way, and I thought you agreed with me that her place is in the house, doing womanly things."

Suzanne slapped her hand on the table, jostling her silverware. "That's lecherich, and it's old-fashioned thinking! Just because I'm a woman doesn't mean I can't do some things a man's capable of doing."

"I agree with Suzanne," Mom put in. "When your daed was alive and had the dairy farm, I used to help him a lot."

"That was different. Milking cows isn't anything like woodworking, and it's not nearly as dangerous," Nelson said.

"It can be dangerous," Russell spoke up. "I remember the time Dad got kicked by one of the cows and it broke his leg."

"That's still not as dangerous as working with wood." Nelson pointed to Suzanne. "You could cut your hand, smash your finger, or any number of things."

"I'll be careful," Suzanne asserted. "Accidents can happen in the kitchen or even out in the garden."

Nelson gave a nod. "That may be true, but only if you're not careful, and you were obviously not careful when you cut your hand on the piece of glass the other day."

"I was careful. I just—"

Grandpa clapped his hands. "That's enough! Since the shop is still mine, it's up to me to do the hiring and firing. I say Suzanne can help out whenever it's needed." He reached for another pancake. "Now let's finish our breakfast so we can get to work."

—∞—

Titus had just finished eating breakfast when he heard a vehicle pull into the yard. He glanced out the kitchen window and saw Allen getting out of his truck.

"It's good to see you," Titus said after he'd invited Allen

into the kitchen. "Would you like a cup of coffee?"

"Guess I could have one, but I can't stay long. Just came to give you some good news." He pulled an envelope out of his jacket pocket and handed it to Titus. "It's the reward money you have coming."

"I'd almost forgotten about that." Titus smiled. "I'll put the money in the bank the next time I go to town. May as well let it draw some interest."

"I have some other good news as well."

"What's that?"

"I've been given the opportunity to buy a used, but very nice, double-wide manufactured home. I'd like to move the old trailer out of here and have the new home brought in." Allen took a sip of coffee from the cup Titus had just handed him.

"A newer place would be nice," Titus said, "but I guess that would mean I'd owe you more money every month for rent."

Allen shook his head. "I'll charge you the same as you're paying now, and then if you're still interested in buying the place, you can start making your payments count toward the purchase price."

Titus sat for a few minutes, mulling things over. Finally, he gave a slow nod. "That's what I'd like to do."

"Great. I'll get the papers drawn up and bring them over to you sometime later this week. Within the next couple of weeks, you ought to have a new place to call home."

Titus grinned. "I can't wait for that."

Allen drank the last of his coffee and stood. "I'd better get going. A man who lives in Cadiz wants me to give him a bid on remodeling part of his house."

After Allen left, Titus glanced at the clock. He still had half an hour before he needed to leave for work, so he decided to go out to the phone shanty and call Zach. "Hey, Zach, it's me," Titus said after he'd made the call.

"It's good hearing from you, Titus. How are things?"

"Other than me stepping into a manure pit last night, everything's fine and dandy."

"How'd that happen?"

Titus related the story.

Zach chuckled. "Guess it could have been worse."

"I suppose."

"You didn't have your cell phone in your pocket when you fell in, I hope."

Titus grimaced. "No, but I won't be using it anymore."

"How come?"

Titus explained about giving up the cell phone, and finished by saying, "After the bishop confronted me, I knew it wouldn't be right to keep using the phone."

"I think you've made the right decision," Zach said. "If you had your own business and were away from home a lot, you'd probably need a cell phone. Under the circumstances, I'm sure you can get by using the one in your phone shanty."

"I guess."

A fly buzzed overhead, and Titus swatted at it. He'd be glad when the weather turned colder and there weren't so many bugs to contend with. If Samuel were here, he'd probably have caught the pesky fly in his hand. He'd always been real good at bug catching.

"Say, I heard some good news this morning when Samuel came to work."

"What's that?"

"Elsie's expecting another boppli, and Samuel's sure excited about it."

"That's great. Tell him I said congratulations."

"I will. I'd let you tell him yourself, but he's up on a ladder, painting the trim on a house we need to get finished before colder weather sets in."

"That's okay. You can give him my message. Oh, and I have some good news of my own to share."

"What is it?"

"Allen was here awhile ago, and he's getting me a better place to live—a used manufactured home—to replace the old trailer I'm living in now."

"That should give you more room."

"It will, but the best part is I'm going to apply the rent I'm paying him toward the purchase of the double-wide, as well as the property here."

"That must mean you're definitely planning to stay in Kentucky."

"Jah. I like it here, and I enjoy working in the Yoders' woodshop."

The fly landed on the table beside the phone, and Titus smacked it with the palm of his hand. One less buzzing insect to irritate him.

"Think you'll ever settle down and get married?"

"I don't know. Maybe. Esther and I aren't seeing each other anymore, but I've begun to care for Suzanne. So if things work out between us, I might eventually think about marriage."

"Sounds like you're making some mature decisions. Mom and Dad will be pleased."

"They may be pleased that I'm finally growing up, but probably not so pleased about me buying this place and staying here. I know Mom's still hoping I'll move back home."

"From what Leona's heard from Abby, Mom's doing better with all that. I think she's finally come to realize that you have to make a life of your own, even if it means being away from the family."

Titus smiled. "Guess I won't really understand the way Mom feels until I get married and have some kinner of my own."

"That's true enough. Since Leona and I had Lucy, James, and Jean, I see things differently than I did before they were born."

"Say, Zach, before we hang up, I've been wondering about something."

"What's that?"

"Do you still keep in touch with the man who kidnapped you and let you think he was your father?"

"Sure. We call each other every few weeks. In fact, Jim and his wife, Holly, are planning to come here for a visit sometime next year."

"So you don't hold a grudge against him for what he did?"

"Not anymore. I forgave Jim a long time ago." There was a pause. "Why do you ask?"

Titus ran his fingers through his hair. "I've been thinking about Phoebe lately."

"What about her?"

"I've been nursing a grudge against her long enough. Fact is, if I had Phoebe's address, I'd write her a letter so she'd know I've forgiven her for hurting me like she did."

"You could always ask Mom to get Phoebe's address. From what I understand, Mom and Arie are still friends, so I'm sure Arie would give Mom the address for you."

Titus gnawed on his lower lip. "I'm not so sure about that. Mom and Dad disapproved of my relationship with Phoebe. If I ask Mom to get Phoebe's address, she might think I want to get back with Phoebe."

"Just tell her you don't want it for that reason. Tell her what you told me—that you only want to let Phoebe know you've forgiven her."

"I'll give it some thought, but please don't say anything to Mom about this. If I decide to ask for Phoebe's address, the request should come from me."

"No problem, I won't say a word."

"Thanks." Titus pulled out his pocket watch. "I'd better go, or I'll be late for work. Tell the family I said hello, and don't forget to let everyone know not to call my cell phone number anymore."

"I'll do that. Take care, Titus."

Titus hung up the phone and sprinted for the barn. He needed to feed Callie and her kittens, get Lightning saddled, and head to work. When he got there, he hoped he'd have the chance to speak to Suzanne, because he needed to apologize for not taking her home from the young people's gathering.

Chapter 42

When Titus entered the Yoders' yard, he was disappointed not to see Suzanne outside. She was often in the garden or hanging clothes on the line, but not today. He was tempted to go up to the house and ask to speak to her, but he was already late and didn't think he should take the time to stop. Maybe he'd see her at lunchtime or after work. He hoped so.

Titus put Lightning in the corral and hurried toward the shop. When he opened the door, he found Nelson and Isaac in what appeared to be a heated discussion. They stopped talking as soon as they saw him, and he wondered what could be going on. He'd never heard the two of them say an unkind word to each other. Maybe Nelson had been getting after Isaac for trying to do too much.

"Sorry I'm late," Titus said. "Allen stopped by this morning, and then I made a quick phone call before I left home, and I'm afraid it set me behind."

Isaac flapped his hand. "It's fine. You're here now; that's all that matters."

"This wasn't a good day to be late," Nelson mumbled.

"We've got a lot of work that needs to be done, and since Grandpa and I have an errand to run at noon, that'll leave you in the shop alone."

"No problem,"Titus said. "I'm sure I can work on whatever needs to be done and wait on any customers who might come in."

"If things get real busy and you need some help, just run up to the house and get Suzanne," Isaac said.

"Sure, and while she's here, maybe she can make a table or two." The sarcasm in Nelson's voice was unmistakable. Apparently he knew about the table Suzanne had hidden in the storage room. Maybe she'd felt guilty about it and had told him the truth.

It's not my place to say anything, Titus decided. *If Suzanne told Nelson about the table she made, she might not have said anything to Isaac. Even if she did, it's best if I don't let on that I know. It might not set well with Nelson or Isaac if they learn that I was the first person Suzanne told.*

—ᴥ—

"Would you like me to take lunch out to the men now?" Suzanne asked her mother after they finished making some tuna fish sandwiches with zucchini relish.

"I'd appreciate that," Mom said. "I still need to wash another load of clothes."

"No problem. I think I'll put some of my banana bread in the lunch basket, too. They can have that for dessert."

"That's fine. Oh, and don't forget the jug of apple cider in the refrigerator. I'm glad we were able to use the Beilers' cider press to make more, because I opened the only jar left from last season."

Suzanne put everything together and headed out the door. When she entered the woodshop, she discovered that Nelson and Grandpa weren't there and Titus was working alone.

"I brought lunch out for the three of you," she said to Titus, "but it appears that you're the only one here right now."

He looked up from staining a door and nodded. "Nelson and your grandpa had an errand to run and left me in charge of the shop until they get back."

Suzanne frowned. *I wonder why they didn't call me out to help. Maybe Grandpa didn't think they were busy enough for my help today. Or maybe Nelson talked him out of letting me work in the shop.*

Titus motioned to the basket she'd placed on Grandpa's desk. "If you made enough food for three of us, why don't you stay and join me for lunch? I sure can't eat it all by myself."

"Thanks, I think I will." Suzanne took everything out of the basket. Then after Titus washed up at the sink, they took seats on either side of the desk and said their silent prayers.

"I made tuna fish mixed with relish again," she said, handing him a sandwich.

He grinned at her. "That sounds good."

They ate their sandwiches in silence; then Titus leaned forward and looked intently at Suzanne.

"What's wrong?" she asked. "Have I got tuna fish on my face?"

He shook his head. "I was just thinking what pretty eyes you have. They're darker and bluer than I thought."

She felt the heat of a blush spread across her cheeks. "Danki."

"I hope you weren't upset with me for not taking you home last night. With the way I smelled, I didn't think you'd want to sit in the closed-in buggy, holding your nose all the way home."

She chuckled. "You did smell pretty bad."

Titus sniffed his arm and snickered. "It took two more

showers after I got home, but I think I finally got the smell off. I washed my clothes, too, but my shoes are ruined." He shook his head. "Still can't believe how I fell into that manure pit."

"It was awfully dark, and you couldn't see where you were going."

"That's the truth. Sure hope nothing like that ever happens to me again."

"I guess the only thing worse than falling into a manure pit would be getting sprayed by a skunk."

He wrinkled his nose. "That happened to me and Timothy once. We were heading outside to feed the chickens and ran into a couple of skunks in the yard. Before we knew what happened, they let us have it." He waved his hand in front of his nose. "That smell was horrible! It took a whole lot of soap and a good dousing with tomato juice before Mom would even let us in the house."

She laughed. "I guess there are some things from our childhood we'll never forget."

"You're right about that." Titus smiled. "I got some good news this morning that made me almost forget about the manure bath."

"What news?"

"I'll be getting a double-wide manufactured home soon. Allen's having it brought in and will be taking the old trailer out."

"That is good news. The trailer is still in pretty sad shape, and it'll be nice for you to have something better to live in."

He nodded. "Especially since I'm planning to buy the place and stay where I am."

"I'm glad you're staying." She handed him the loaf of banana bread. "Would you like some of this?"

He took a slice and chomped it down. "Your lemon shoofly pie was really good, but so is this. You ought to take some of the banana bread to the produce auction on Saturday. I'm sure folks would buy it when they stop to look at your colorful mums."

"That's a thought. Maybe I will take some banana bread."

He winked at her, and another wave of heat washed over Suzanne. Was Titus flirting with her, or was he just in a jovial mood?

"I thought you might like to know that this morning I told my family about the table I made," she said, changing the subject.

"What'd they say?"

"Mom and Grandpa seemed to understand my desire to work with wood, but Nelson wasn't supportive at all. He got pretty upset when Grandpa said I could help in the shop during busier times. I think he's still convinced that a woman's place is in the house, slaving over a hot stove or scrubbing floors." Suzanne took a piece of banana bread for herself. "If you want my opinion, I think my twenty-year-old brother is more old-fashioned than my seventy-four-year-old grandfather."

"I guess age isn't always a factor when it comes to being old-fashioned." Titus smiled. "I'm glad you'll be working in the shop. If there's anything you need help with, just let me know."

"I appreciate that, and I'm glad to know you don't disapprove."

"Not at all. I think everyone ought to have the right to do what they like best."

"By the way," Suzanne said, "I was wondering what you plan to do with Callie's kittens now that they're fully weaned and getting so big."

"Guess I'd better run an ad in the local paper or put a sign out by the road." Titus reached for another piece of bread. "While I can't say that I've become a cat lover, I have learned to tolerate Callie. But that doesn't mean I want a whole passel of cats hanging around."

"I'm sure if you advertise you'll be able to find them all good homes."

Titus swiped a napkin over his mouth and studied her intently again.

"Now what's wrong?"

"Nothin'. I was just wondering if you'd like to—"

The shop door opened, and Bishop King stepped in. "I need to order some new kitchen cabinets," he said, looking at Titus. "Can you have them done in time for my wife's birthday next month?"

"I think so," Titus said with a nod. "Let's go to the back of the shop, and you can pick out the wood you'd like."

Titus would be busy with the bishop for a while, so Suzanne gathered up the leftovers from lunch and headed to the house. She couldn't help wondering what Titus had been about to say before the bishop came in.

After work, Titus hoped to speak to Suzanne again, but Verna informed him that Suzanne had gone to the Beilers' store. So Titus headed for home, hoping he'd have a chance to speak with her tomorrow, for he still had one question he wanted to ask.

When Titus arrived home, he took care of Lightning, then headed to the phone shanty to call his folks. He was surprised when Mom answered.

"Titus, is that you?"

"Jah. I was going to leave you a message and was surprised when you answered the phone."

"I just came out to the phone shanty to check for messages and heard the phone ring. Did you have a nice birthday? Did you get our card and phone message?"

"I sure did." Titus picked up the pen lying beside the phone and drew a doodle of a cat on the tablet. "Suzanne made my birthday special, too."

"Oh?"

"She invited me to supper and baked a real good pie." He snickered. "Even served it with birthday candles."

"Suzanne's the young woman who looks like Phoebe, right?"

"Jah, but she's really nothing like her. In fact—"

"Your daed and I had another surprise today," Mom interrupted.

"What's that?"

"Samuel dropped by this morning and told us that Elsie's expecting another boppli."

"I already know, and it's good news."

"Did Samuel call you?"

"No, I talked to Zach. He said Samuel had given him the news when he got to work this morning."

"Oh, I see. So how are things going with you?"

"Pretty good. Allen came by this morning, and he's bringing in a used manufactured home to replace the old trailer."

"That's good to hear," Mom said. "I wasn't too impressed with the one you're living in now."

"I haven't been impressed with it either." Titus chose not to mention that he planned to buy the new place. He figured he'd tell Mom about it later. If he mentioned it now, she might become upset and start going on about how she didn't want him living in Kentucky.

They talked about other things for a while, and then Titus finally told Mom the reason he'd called. "I was wondering if you could do me a favor."

"Sure. What do you need?"

"I was wondering if you'd speak to Arie Stoltzfus and get

Phoebe's address for me."

There was dead silence on the other end of the line.

"Mom, did you hear what I said?"

"I heard. I just can't believe you'd ask me that. I thought you moved to Kentucky to get away from everything that reminds you of Phoebe. Now you want to contact her? What's happened, Titus? Are you hoping to get back with her? Are you going to try and convince her to move to Kentucky and marry you?"

"'Course not. It's over between me and Phoebe. I just want to write and let her know that there are no hard feelings and that I've forgiven her for hurting me the way she did."

"Is that all?"

"Jah."

"Well, if that's the case, I'll speak to Arie sometime this week and ask for Phoebe's address."

"Danki, Mom. I appreciate it."

"As soon as I get the address, I'll call and leave the information on your voice mail."

"Okay, Mom. Tell everyone I said hello."

When Titus hung up the phone, he sat a few minutes, wondering if Mom would really ask Arie for Phoebe's address. If so, would Arie give it to her? If she did, what should he write to Phoebe, and what, if anything, would be her response?

Chapter 43

Paradise, Pennsylvania

Fannie stared at the phone, trying to figure out what she should do. She'd told Titus that she'd get Phoebe's address for him, and she wanted to believe what he'd said, but the fear of them getting back together plagued her so much, she wasn't sure she could follow through with what she'd promised. Maybe if she let it go awhile, Titus would forget the whole idea.

That wouldn't be right, she told herself. *I said I'd do it, so I need to keep my word, and I need to believe that Titus was telling the truth when he said he wasn't trying to get back with Phoebe.*

With a sigh of resignation, Fannie picked up the phone and dialed the Stoltzfuses' number. It rang several times; then their voice mail came on. Fannie left a message, asking Arie for Phoebe's address, and then she hung up the phone. "There, that's done. Now I can get on with the rest of my day."

—∞—

Pembroke, Kentucky

Maybe I should have asked Mom to get Phoebe's phone number instead of her address, Titus thought after he'd hung up the phone. He shook his head. *No, a letter's probably the best way to contact her. Don't think I could deal with hearing her voice on the phone. It might make me start missing her again, and I sure don't need that.*

Titus left the phone shanty and headed for the house. Callie met him on the back porch, with all four of her brood meowing and looking up at him pathetically. He really should have gotten rid of them by now, but he'd been too busy to run an ad in the paper. He'd have to do that soon, because he didn't want to keep five cats around.

"I know you're hungry," Titus said as Callie brushed her tail against his legs. "Okay, follow me, and I'll get you all some food."

Think I might keep one of Callie's kittens so she has some company, he decided. *I'll take the rest of the cats with me to the produce auction this Saturday and see if I can find them good homes.*

When Titus stepped back outside, he leaned against the barn and inhaled deeply. Fall was definitely in the air; he could smell the leaves that had fallen from the trees in his yard and were starting to decay on the ground. He felt a crisp autumn breeze and heard the chattering of squirrels in a nearby tree. He loved this rural area, where there wasn't much traffic and tourists were few and far between.

He glanced at the old trailer he'd called home for the last six months and smiled. In two more weeks, he'd have a new home; only this one had the potential of being his own. That gave him a sense of belonging like never before.

Think I'll go for a walk before I head inside to fix something for supper, he decided.

—∞—

As Suzanne headed home from the Beilers' store late that afternoon, she heard the sound of dogs barking in the distance.

Her horse must have heard it too, for the mare whinnied and started to run. Suzanne pulled back slightly on the reins. "Whoa, girl. Not so fast."

To her relief, the barking stopped, and her horse slowed to an easy trot. When she neared the road leading to Titus's place, she was tempted to stop. But what reason would she give for her visit? She didn't want to appear to be pursuing him. If Titus was interested in her, chasing after him would probably turn him away.

"I don't know why I'm thinking such thoughts," she muttered. "Just because Titus has been nicer to me lately, and took me to the young people's gathering the other night doesn't mean he's interested in me."

Suzanne relaxed her grip on the reins and tried to focus on other things. The trees lining the road had lost most of their leaves, and there was a distinctive aroma of fall in the air. Soon Thanksgiving, then Christmas would be here, and there'd probably be plenty of snow on the ground.

Her thoughts turned to Titus again, wondering if he would go to Pennsylvania to spend the holidays with his family. It seemed logical that he would, but if he decided to stay here, she'd ask Mom if they could invite Titus to join them for Thanksgiving and Christmas dinners.

Suzanne's musings were halted when her horse whinnied again and started limping. *Oh great. I'll bet she's thrown a shoe.*

Suzanne brought the horse and buggy to a stop and climbed down to check the horse's hooves. Sure enough, Dixie had lost her left front shoe.

Suzanne hoped if she took it slow and easy that they'd be able to make it home okay. She was about to climb back in the buggy, when a pack of six dogs in various sizes darted out of the woods, snarling, yipping, and growling.

Suzanne hurried for the buggy, but as she was about to put

her foot inside, the horse bolted and took off down the road, pulling the buggy behind.

Suzanne chased after it, hollering, "Whoa, Dixie! Whoa!"

The horse kept running, and the pack of dogs headed straight for Suzanne!

Suzanne's chest heaved as she drew in a deep breath and released a primal scream. "Dear Lord, please help me!"

Chapter 44

Titus slowed his steps and listened. He thought he'd heard the shrill yapping of dogs. Sure enough, there it was again, followed by a woman's scream.

He stepped out of the woods and hurried toward the sound. "Oh no!" he gasped when he saw several mangy-looking dogs chasing Suzanne down the road behind her horse and buggy.

"Hey!" Titus shouted, waving his hands. "Get away from her, you mangy *hund*!" He glanced around, looking for something to use to ward off the dogs, and was relieved when he spotted a limb that had fallen from a nearby tree. He bent to pick it up and also grabbed a couple of rocks, which he quickly hurled at the dogs.

The dogs barked continuously as they turned away from Suzanne and headed for Titus.

"Run to your buggy, schnell!" Titus shouted, noticing that Suzanne's horse had stopped running and was now standing along the shoulder of the road.

As Suzanne ran to the safety of her buggy, Titus wielded the limb, smacking first one dog and then another. They snarled and yapped, snapping at him, and tearing his pant leg with their sharp teeth. He kicked at one dog and sent it running into the woods.

One of the other dogs turned toward Suzanne's horse and buggy again, but Titus smacked it in the rump, and it took off for the woods, along with three of the others. Just one dog was left, the biggest and meanest-looking one of the pack. Baring its teeth, it lunged for Titus's leg.

Titus hated to hurt any animal, but this could be a life-or-death situation. A pack of wild animals could take a man down, and Titus felt as if he was fighting for his survival. With what seemed like superhuman strength, he charged at the animal with the tree limb, wielding it back and forth as he shouted for the dog to go. One more quick swing with the hunk of wood, and the critter went whimpering into the woods to join his crazed companions.

Titus stood for several terrifying moments, waiting to see if the dogs would return.

When the dogs' barking and yapping faded into the distance, he hurried to Suzanne's buggy and climbed in beside her. Seeing that Suzanne was trembling and sobbing, he pulled her into his arms.

"It's okay. The dogs are gone," he said, gently patting her back.

She continued to sob, wetting the front of his shirt with her tears.

"Look at me now," he whispered. "The dogs are gone, and you're okay."

Tears glistened in her eyes as she looked at him. "Danki for coming to my rescue. I. . .I don't know what I would have done if you hadn't showed up when you did."

"What were you doing out of your buggy?" he asked.

"My horse threw a shoe. I got out to check on her, but

then those horrible hund came charging out of the woods." Suzanne's chin trembled. "I was never so scared in my life."

Titus tipped her chin up with his thumb and gazed at her pretty face. Every instinct, every fiber of his being, made him want to kiss her. But he figured that wouldn't be appropriate, and he didn't want to scare her off. So instead of kissing Suzanne, he pulled slowly away and reached for her hand.

"You're not hurt, are you?" Suzanne asked.

"No, I'm fine." Titus pulled up his pant leg. "It's torn, and there's a welt on my ankle, but thankfully none of the dogs drew blood."

"I couldn't believe it when those hund came charging after me like that." Suzanne's voice quavered, even though she felt much calmer than she had a few moments earlier. The whole ordeal had left her feeling drained. "I had no idea a pack of wild dogs was running around here."

Titus frowned. "When dogs are abandoned, they sometimes form packs. Without proper feeding and care they can become wild and will go after anything that moves. I'm going to notify the local Humane Society and see if they can trap those dogs before they end up hurting someone."

A cool breeze blew into the buggy, and Suzanne shivered. "It scares me to think some child might fall prey to any of those ferocious animals."

Titus looked over at her with obvious concern. "If you're too upset to drive, I'd better take you home."

She shook her head. "After my horse threw a shoe, she started limping. Then when the dogs showed up and started chasing her, she ran like there was no tomorrow. I'm afraid if I try to take her the rest of the way home, she might become lame."

"She won't if we go slow and easy, but I think it might be best if we take her to my place. It's closer, and you can leave Dixie there until you're able to get someone to come out and give her new shoes. As soon as we get the horse settled in my barn, I'll drive you home in my rig," he said.

"That's nice of you." She managed a smile, despite the fact that her eyes still stung with tears. "I've already been gone longer than I'd planned, and I need to get home and help Mom with supper."

"Where were you coming from?" he asked.

"I'd been to the Beilers' store."

Titus gave Suzanne's fingers a gentle squeeze. "During lunch today when our conversation was interrupted by the customer, I was about to ask you a question."

"What were you going to ask?"

"I was wondering if you'd like to visit the Jefferson Davis Monument with me on Saturday. I really liked it when I went before, and I thought it would be fun to see it again before the bad weather sets in."

"Saturday's the day of the produce auction, remember?"

"I was thinking we could go to the monument in the afternoon, after things wind down at the auction."

Hope welled in Suzanne's soul. Titus was asking her to go out with him. That must mean he was interested in pursuing a relationship with her.

He nudged her gently with his elbow. "So what do you say? Would you like to see the monument with me?"

"Jah, I would." *You have no idea how much I would.*

Chapter 45

Fairview, Kentucky

Titus had arrived at the auction early on Saturday morning, bringing with him a pet carrier he'd borrowed from Suzanne so he could transport three of Callie's kittens. To his relief, by noon he'd found homes for all of them. It made him feel less guilty about getting rid of the cats, knowing they'd all have good homes. It had done his heart good when he'd seen the look of joy on the face of the little girl who had taken the smallest of the three cats and told her mother how happy she was that she'd come to the auction.

After he'd given the last cat away, Titus stepped into the auction building, where many Amish and English folks had gathered.

"Do I hear fifteen?" the auctioneer hollered as he pointed to a basket full of squash and pumpkins. "Fifteen. . . fifteen. . .yep!"

Titus stayed and watched awhile as various produce items were auctioned off. Then he glanced out the door at the parking lot and noticed Ethan heading toward Suzanne's table, which was full of baked goods. A feeling of jealousy coursed through him, wondering if he had a rival. Maybe he shouldn't have been so hasty when he'd asked Ethan to take Suzanne home last Sunday night. Maybe it would have been better if he'd taken her home himself, even though he'd smelled like putrid manure.

Think I'll head over there now and see if I can tell if anything's going on between those two, he decided.

—∞—

"Heard you had some good banana bread over here," Ethan said, stepping up to the table where Suzanne stood. "Thought I'd better buy some now, before it's all gone."

She smiled. "It has been selling quite well. Almost as well as my potted mums." She motioned to one of the loaves of bread. "How many would you like?"

"Have you got any I could sample?"

"Sure." She handed him a napkin and cut a slice from the loaf she'd been using for samples.

Ethan wasted no time eating it, and when he was done he said, "That was sure good. Think I'll take two loaves."

Suzanne put the bread in a paper sack and handed it to him.

He grinned at her. "If I'd known you had such good banana bread, I'd have been over here sooner."

She smiled. "I'm glad you like it."

Ethan gave her the money and then leaned on the table. "Say, I was wondering if you'd like to go to the next singing with me. Heard there's gonna be another one in a few weeks."

Suzanne glanced to her left and noticed Titus heading her way. "Well, I. . .uh. . .don't know. I might already have a ride."

"With who?"

"I'll have to let you know later, Ethan. I have to keep working here for the next hour, so I really can't talk about this right now."

"Oh, okay." As Ethan walked away, Suzanne couldn't help feeling a bit irritated that he'd never paid her much attention until he'd tasted her banana bread. Was food the only way to a man's heart? Was the fact that she was learning to cook the reason for Titus's sudden interest in her, too, or did he see her for the person she really was?

"Looks like you've done well selling your banana bread today," Titus said when he joined Suzanne by the table.

"It has gone fast." She smiled at him. "Maybe I'll bake more and bring it out to the woodshop for lunch sometime next week."

"That'd be nice." He moved a little closer. "Are you still planning to go to the monument with me this afternoon?"

"Of course."

"Good. We can leave as soon as you're ready."

"I'll probably have to stay here for another hour or so, but after the auction winds down, I'll be free to go."

"Okay." He started to move away but turned back around. "Oh, thought you might like to know that I brought three of Callie's overgrown kittens here today and found homes for all of 'em."

"That's good news. Was Callie upset when you took them away this morning?"

"Not really. I think keeping one cat as a companion for her was a good idea because when I headed out, she and Buttons were sleeping side by side on the porch."

"Buttons?"

He nodded. "I decided to call him that because the little black spot on his head looks like a button."

She smiled. It was good to see the way Titus had learned to like—or at least tolerate—cats.

Just then another customer showed up, looking to buy a pot of mums.

"I'd better let you go," Titus said. "I'll be back to pick you up in an hour."

—∞—

Paradise, Pennsylvania

Fannie stepped into the phone shanty to check for messages, and was disappointed to find none. She thought it was strange that she hadn't heard anything back from Arie yet.

Maybe Arie hasn't responded to my message because she doesn't want me to have Phoebe's address, Fannie thought. *Maybe she thinks I want the address for myself and that I might write something to Phoebe that will cause her never to come back.*

Fannie left the shanty and headed up to the house. When she stepped inside, she found Abraham in the utility room, taking off his dusty work boots.

"Why the worried frown?" he asked, touching the wrinkles in her forehead.

"I just checked our voice mail for messages and can't figure out why Arie hasn't responded to me about Phoebe's address."

"There's a good reason for that," he said, removing his straw hat and placing it on one of the wall pegs. "Arie and Noah aren't home right now. They went to Michigan for her niece's wedding and won't be back until sometime next week."

"Oh, I see." Fannie smiled with relief. "Hopefully, I'll hear something back from her as soon as she gets home."

—∞—

Fairview, Kentucky

When Titus and Suzanne stepped off the elevator at the top of the Jefferson Davis Monument, she gasped. "This is wunderbaar! If I'd known you could see so far, I would have come up here sooner."

"I can't believe you've lived here since you were a girl and have never visited the monument," Titus said.

She laughed lightly and shrugged. "I guess that's how it is with most folks. They travel to other places to see things instead of visiting places close to home."

Titus nodded. "I remember when Harold, my mamm's son from her first marriage, came to Lancaster to visit for the first time. He was anxious to see all the sights in our area—some things we'd never seen ourselves until we went there with him and his family."

She smiled as she peered out the viewing window. "I'm glad you invited me to come here, because it's certainly worth seeing."

Titus was pleased that Suzanne had been willing to go up to the top with him. She obviously wasn't afraid of heights the way Esther was.

"Should we go down now and take a look inside the museum?" he asked. "There are some interesting displays about how the monument was made."

"Sure, I'd like to see that."

They went back down in the elevator, and when they stepped outside, Titus took Suzanne's hand and led the way to the museum. After they'd seen everything there, he bought them both an ice-cream bar.

"This has been fun," Suzanne said as they headed to his buggy a short time later. "I'm glad you invited me."

"I'm glad you came. Oh, there's something I forgot to tell you," Titus said as he helped Suzanne into the buggy.

"What's that?"

"I called the Humane Society, and the man I spoke to said they've had several other calls from people in our area who've seen the wild dogs. They sent someone out to patrol the area and managed to capture the dogs."

"That's a relief."

"It sure is." Titus gathered up the reins. "Guess it's time for me to get you home."

"Would you like to have supper with us again? Knowing Mom, I'm sure there will be plenty of food."

"I'd be happy to stay." Titus smiled. If things kept going this way, he and Suzanne would be officially courting soon. Maybe by this time next year, she might even be his wife.

Chapter 46

For the next two weeks, Titus saw Suzanne as often as he could. She'd begun working in the woodshop a few days a week, which gave them more time to visit. To makes things even nicer, Titus had been invited to the Yoders' for supper several more times, and he'd taken Suzanne to the last singing they'd had.

Today, the old trailer would be taken away, which meant Titus would need a place to stay for a few days until the new manufactured home was hauled in and set up. Verna Yoder had invited him to stay at their house and share a room with Russell, which meant he wouldn't have far to go to work each day.

Titus was glad it was Saturday and he didn't have to work in the woodshop, because he still had some packing to do before Allen and the crew he'd hired to move the trailer showed up. Most of Titus's things would be stored in the barn until he moved into the new house, so he'd take only the clothes he needed while he stayed with the Yoders. He planned to take his horse and buggy to the Yoders' later in the day and would come back to his home every evening to check on things and feed Callie and Buttons. Titus had come to appreciate the cats for keeping the mice down, and he had to admit it was kind of fun to watch the two cats play.

As he headed to the kitchen to pack a few more boxes, he thought about the other night, when he and Suzanne had been sitting on her porch, drinking hot apple cider and eating popcorn. Samson, one of Suzanne's cats, had joined them, sitting at Titus's feet, begging to be fed.

Titus chuckled as he remembered how comical it had looked when a piece of popcorn fell on the porch and Samson started batting at it. Then, when the popcorn got stuck on the cat's claw and he'd tried to shake it off, Suzanne and Titus had a good laugh.

Titus smiled as he bent to close up a box of dishes. Except for when he'd been with Phoebe, he couldn't remember having such a good time with any woman the way he did when he was with Suzanne.

He grimaced. *I can't believe Mom still hasn't been able to get Phoebe's address for me.* The last time he'd talked to Mom, she'd said Phoebe's folks had gone to Michigan for a wedding, but surely they must be back by now. At this rate, he'd never get a letter written to Phoebe.

—∞—

As Suzanne headed down the driveway to get the mail that morning, she heard a loud *meow*. She turned and saw Samson, following in her footsteps. This was not unusual for the cat, because ever since he'd been a kitten he'd liked to go for walks with Suzanne.

Suzanne's thoughts went to Titus, and how, when he'd first moved to Kentucky he'd made it clear that he had no fondness for cats.

She chuckled to herself. *I think Callie coming to live with him and giving birth to those kittens changed all that.* Sometimes when people were around someone long enough, they'd begin to see them in a different light. That had certainly been true of Suzanne and the way she felt about Titus. When he'd first come to work in the woodshop, she could barely tolerate him. Of course, she was sure the feeling had been mutual.

Since she and Titus had become better acquainted, she'd quickly discovered how much they had in common, and now saw him in a completely different light. What she'd previously seen as arrogance, she now realized was his way of disguising his feelings of inadequacy. Thankfully, he seemed more sure of himself now, as did she.

She'd come to realize more fully that Titus had a caring attitude toward others. He'd proven that when he'd helped out while Grandpa was recuperating from his fall. Even the way Titus had taken care of Callie and her brood was proof that he cared.

Suzanne looked forward to the time Titus would be staying at their house while he waited for his new home to be set up. She realized that since she and Titus had started courting, she been happier than she ever thought possible. All this time she'd been saying she didn't need a boyfriend and didn't care about getting married, but now that seemed to be all she could think about.

By the time Suzanne reached the mailbox, she'd convinced herself that Titus was the perfect man for her. She just hoped the feeling was mutual.

—ꝏ—

Paradise, Pennsylvania

When Fannie entered Naomi and Caleb's store, she spotted

Arie talking with Naomi at the front counter. She waited until Naomi had rung up Arie's purchases and placed them in a paper sack; then she stepped up to Arie and said, "It's good to see you. I heard you went to Michigan for your niece's wedding."

"That's right."

"How long have you been back?"

"We got home a week ago," Arie said, avoiding eye contact.

"Did you get the message I left on your voice mail?"

"Jah." Arie's cheeks turned pink as she dropped her gaze to the floor.

"Then why haven't you responded?"

"Let's go outside." Arie motioned to the door. "I'd rather not discuss this in here."

Fannie glanced at Naomi and noticed a look of concern on her face. "I'll be back to do my shopping after I speak with Arie," she said.

Naomi nodded. "Of course. Take your time."

Fannie followed Arie out the door and around back to the hitching rail where Arie's horse and buggy were parked. She waited until Arie had put the paper sack in the buggy, then touched Arie's arm and said, "If you got my message and have been home a week already, how come you haven't replied by now?"

Arie's eyebrows furrowed. "Why would you need my daughter's address? Are you planning to write her because you're still upset that she jilted your son?"

Fannie shook her head vigorously. "Of course not. Titus asked me to get the address for him."

"Titus did? Whatever for? Is he hoping Phoebe will come back to him?"

"I'm sure that's not what he has in mind. He just wants to set things right—to apologize for the ill feelings he's had toward Phoebe and to let her know that he's forgiven her for hurting him the way she did."

Arie sucked in her lower lip and her eyes narrowed. "Is that all there is to it?"

"Jah."

"All right then, I'll give you Phoebe's address, but I won't guarantee she'll answer his letter. For the last several months, she hasn't responded to my phone calls or any of the letters I've written." Arie sighed deeply, and tears welled in her eyes. "Unless God performs a miracle and changes Phoebe's heart, I'm afraid Noah and I will never see or hear from our daughter again."

Los Angeles, California

Phoebe's stomach growled as she hurried down the street toward the ice-cream shop. She'd forgotten to set her alarm and had woken up late, so she hadn't taken the time to eat breakfast. Not that there was much in her apartment to eat, anyway. She had cereal but no milk, bread but no butter, and coffee but no sugar to sweeten it. If she didn't get more hours at her evening job soon, she didn't know what she would do. Between Phoebe's two part-time jobs, she was barely making enough to pay the rent and buy a few groceries. In order to save money, she'd started riding an old bike she'd bought at a pawn shop. It was cheaper than taking the bus to and from work and whenever she went shopping. It didn't matter that the basket on the bike didn't hold a lot, because she couldn't afford to buy much, anyway.

When Phoebe entered the ice-cream shop she knew immediately that she was in trouble because her boss, Toby, stood behind the counter with his arms folded, glaring at her.

"You're late," he growled, nodding at the clock on the far wall. "What's your excuse this time, Phoebe?"

"I. . .uh. . .forgot to set my alarm, and—"

"You've used that line before, and it's gettin' kind of old." Toby pointed to the freezer where the ice cream was kept. "As if your tardiness isn't bad enough, the container of strawberry ice cream was nearly full at the beginning of your shift yesterday, and now it's almost empty. What have you got to say about that?"

She dropped her gaze to the floor. "I. . .uh. . .sold a lot of ice cream yesterday."

"Did everyone buy strawberry?"

"Well, no, but—"

"You think I don't know what's been going on behind my back, or when I'm not here in the shop?"

She gave no reply.

"You've been helping yourself to the ice cream whenever you want, haven't you?"

A lump formed in Phoebe's throat as she nodded slowly. "I. . .I was hungry."

"What's the matter? Have you been forgetting to pack a lunch, just like you've forgotten to set your alarm?"

She shook her head. "I don't have much money, and I—"

"So you think it's okay to steal from me?" His steely blue eyes seemed to bore right through her. "I thought you Amish folks were honest and upright."

A feeling of shame washed over Phoebe. While she no longer dressed in Amish clothes, she'd told Toby when he'd first hired her that she'd grown up in an Amish home in Pennsylvania. She guessed he thought that meant she would set a good example. He was probably right—she should have—but he wasn't the one doing without for lack of money. He didn't have to work two jobs to make ends meet, either.

"I know I just got paid yesterday, but that money's gone already, so I'll pay you back for the ice cream I ate when I get my next paycheck."

Toby shook his head. "There won't be a next paycheck for you, young lady. I've had enough of your deceitful ways." He pointed to the door. "You'd better turn around and head out now, because as of this minute, you're fired!"

Phoebe stood a few seconds, letting his words sink in; then she whirled around and dashed out the door. With only one part-time job, she wouldn't have enough money to pay the rent, much less get food. "What am I going to do now?" she wailed.

Chapter 47

Pembroke, Kentucky

When Titus woke up Saturday morning two weeks later, he looked around in amazement. He'd moved into his new house two days ago, and liked it a lot. No more squeaky drawers in the kitchen, bumping into the wall when he got out of bed, or dealing with leaky faucets or a toilet that overflowed. The manufactured home had been well cared for by its previous owners and had plenty of room. It had three bedrooms, one and a half baths, a full-sized kitchen, living room, dining room, and even a utility room where Titus's new gas-powered wringer washer sat. It was nice not to have to haul his clothes to the Laundromat anymore.

Guess I should call my folks and let them know I'm settled into my new home, Titus thought after he'd gone to the kitchen and poured himself some coffee. *Come to think of it, I haven't been out to the phone shanty to check messages since I moved in here. Guess I may as well do that now.*

He added a spoonful of sugar to his coffee, picked up the mug, and headed out the door.

When he entered the dimly lit shanty, he turned on the

battery-operated lantern, making it easier to see. The light on the phone was blinking, so he knew he had at least one message.

Titus took a seat at the table, punched the button to listen to the messages, and leaned back in his chair.

The first message was from Allen, reminding Titus that he'd be coming by later this afternoon to check things over on the house. He said he wanted to make sure everything was working right and that he'd picked up a used bedroom set he thought Titus could use if he had any overnight guests. Allen also said he'd be bringing the paperwork for Titus to sign in order to purchase the house and land.

He smiled. *Now that's good news. Sure wish I'd had the manufactured home with an extra bedroom when Mom and Dad were here. Maybe Mom would have felt better about me living here if she'd seen this place instead of the old trailer.*

Titus listened to the next message. It was from Mom, saying she'd spoken to Arie Stoltzfus and that she'd gotten Phoebe's address for him.

He picked up the pen lying beside the phone and started to jot down the information on his arm, but changed his mind and used the tablet instead. It was time to grow up and act more mature.

Titus stared at Phoebe's address, and his thoughts took him on a journey to the past, remembering how things used to be between him and Phoebe. . . .

"Sure wish I didn't have to sneak over here like this in order to see you," Titus said as he and Phoebe hid in the shadows behind her father's barn. "It's not fair that our folks won't let us court until you turn sixteen."

Phoebe moved closer until her arm was brushing his. "We can court without them knowing, just like we're doing now."

"Puh! This ain't courtin'," he mumbled. "I want to take you out for rides in my buggy, bring you home from singings, take you on picnics and to volleyball games, and come calling at your house."

"We only have another year to wait, and then we can begin officially courting," she whispered. "In the meantime, we can keep meeting each other like this, and our folks will never have to know."

"I'd wait forever for you, Phoebe." He lowered his head and kissed her.

Titus blinked a couple of times as his mind snapped back to the present. The past was in the past, and he must look to the future now—a future that would perhaps include Suzanne as his wife someday living here in his new Kentucky home.

Titus clicked off the lantern, tore the sheet of paper with Phoebe's address from the notepad, and stepped out of the shanty. He'd go back to the house, fix himself something for breakfast, and write Phoebe a letter. Then, knowing he'd done the right thing, he could put his focus fully on the future.

When a sandpapery tongue swiped Suzanne's arm, her eyes popped open. "Samson, what are you doing on my bed, you big, bad cat?"

Samson nuzzled her hand with his nose and purred. Suzanne snuggled him close, enjoying the feel of the cat's soft, sleek fur.

She turned her head toward the window, remembering that she'd left it partially open last night—apparently wide enough for the cat to get in. "You need to go back outside now," she said.

Pushing the covers aside, she slid out of bed, opened the

window fully, and set Samson on the branch of the maple tree growing outside her bedroom window. He'd used the tree as a way into the house a few times before, so she knew he'd have no problem finding his way to the ground.

Suzanne hurried to get dressed, and when she stepped into the kitchen a short time later, the pleasant aroma of hickory-smoked bacon greeted her, making her mouth water in anticipation.

"Guder mariye," Mom said, turning from her job at the stove long enough to smile at Suzanne. "You look tired. Didn't you sleep well last night?"

"I slept okay once I fell asleep," Suzanne replied. "Just had a hard time turning off my thoughts."

"Thoughts about what?"

Suzanne's face heated. She wasn't about to admit that she'd been thinking about Titus. "Just things, that's all."

"You sure it was 'things' and not someone special?"

Suzanne shrugged in reply.

The bacon sizzled and spattered as Mom flipped it over in the pan. "You don't have to hide it from me, Suzanne. I fell in love once, and I know the signs."

"I do care for Titus," she whispered, hoping no one else in the family could hear their conversation. "I'm just not certain he cares for me."

Mom swatted the air with her spatula. "You're kidding, right?"

Suzanne shook her head.

"During the time he was staying with us, I saw the expression on his face whenever the two of you were in the same room." Mom smiled. "It was the same look your daed had on his face when we were courting."

"What look was that?" Nelson asked when he and Grandpa entered the room.

"The look of love." Mom smiled and pointed the spatula in Nelson's direction. "The same look I've seen on your face whenever you're with your aldi."

Nelson shrugged. "I won't deny it. I do care for Lucy, but I'm not sure it's love I actually feel. Right now, I only see her as a good friend."

"If you're not in love with the girl, you shouldn't be leading her on." Grandpa ambled across the room and took a seat at the table. "You've been courting Lucy for some time now, and she's likely thinkin' she'll be gettin' a marriage proposal soon."

Nelson's eyes widened. "You really think so?"

Grandpa gave a nod. "Would you like my advice, son?"

"Sure."

"If you're not in love with Lucy and don't see her as a potential wife, then you ought to break things off with her now, before she gets hurt."

"I'll give it some thought," Nelson mumbled, his face turning red.

Suzanne was glad the focus of the conversation wasn't on her anymore, but she felt sorry for Nelson, who looked awfully befuddled. Suzanne had thought he and Lucy were getting serious. She couldn't believe how wrong she'd been.

Suzanne glanced at the chair Titus had occupied while he'd been staying with them and winced. *Maybe him courting me doesn't mean anything, either. Maybe he's just spending time with me because he needs a friend.* A lump formed in her throat, and she swallowed hard in an effort to push it down. *Maybe he'll never say he loves me or that he wants me to be his wife.*

Los Angeles, California

Phoebe had been sitting at the table going over the want

ads for the last half hour when she heard a loud knock. She tiptoed from the kitchen and looked out the peephole in her apartment door.

Oh no, it's Mr. Higgins. I'll bet he's here to collect the rent I owe for this month. She held her breath when he knocked again.

"Phoebe Stoltzfus, are you in there?"

Go away. Go away. If I wanted to talk to you, I'd open the door.

Three more knocks, then all was quiet. Phoebe breathed a sigh of relief. She couldn't answer the door, because she didn't have enough money to pay the rent, and without another part-time job, she would never have enough.

Satisfied that she'd escaped a confrontation with her landlord, Phoebe returned to the kitchen. As she moved toward the sink to get a glass of water, her gaze came to rest on the unopened letter lying on the counter. It had arrived two days ago—another letter from Mom, no doubt pleading with Phoebe to come home and join the church.

"Well, I won't do it," Phoebe muttered with a determined set of her jaw. "I'm not going back there. No, never!"

Chapter 48

Hopkinsville, Kentucky

As Suzanne sat across from Titus at a table in Ryan's Steak House, she couldn't help but smile. They'd both needed some things at Walmart, so after the woodshop had closed for the day, they'd hired a driver to take them to Hopkinsville. Since they were hungry by the time they got there, they decided to eat supper before they went shopping. Their driver had told them he had a few errands to run and would pick them up in an hour.

Suzanne never tired of spending time with Titus. In fact, the more time she spent with him, the more her heart ached to be his wife. She just wished he'd give some indication as to how he felt about her.

"I can't believe it's November already," Titus said, halting her thoughts. "Seems like just yesterday that I moved into my new place."

"Time has passed quickly," she agreed. "Thanksgiving's only a few weeks away, and then Christmas will be upon us."

He cut another piece of his juicy steak. "Any idea what you might like for Christmas?"

A proposal from you...or a declaration of love, she told herself.

"I. . .uh. . .don't really know."

"I'd thought about making you something in the woodshop—something you could put in your hope chest, but with you workin' there part-time now, it's hard to make anything without you knowing about it."

Hope welled in Suzanne's soul. He wanted to make her a gift for Christmas, and he'd mentioned it being for her hope chest. Did that mean he had marriage on his mind, or was it just wishful thinking?

"To tell you the truth, I don't even have a hope chest," she said, reaching for the salt shaker and adding some to her mixed green salad.

His eyebrows lifted. "How come?"

"I've never had a serious boyfriend and figured I'd probably never get married, so I didn't see a need to store up things for a hope chest."

"What about me? Don't you consider me your boyfriend? After all, we've gone several places together, and I'm always over at your house it seems."

A wave of heat washed over her face as she slowly nodded. "Jah, that's true."

He grinned and gave her a wink. "I'm glad we got that settled."

Suzanne's hopes for the future soared. While Titus still hadn't said he loved her, and there'd been no mention of marriage, the fact that he'd affirmed that he was her boyfriend, made her think it was just a matter of time until he said the three words she longed to hear most: *I love you.*

—∞—

Paradise, Pennsylvania

"It was nice of you to invite us for supper this evening,"

Elsie told Hannah.

Samuel bobbed his head. "The fried chicken tastes real good."

Hannah smiled. "I'm glad you like it. My mamm gave me the recipe."

Timothy swiped his napkin across his face. "My fraa's a good cook. There's no doubt about it."

"Is that why you married me?" Hannah asked with raised eyebrows. "Because I can cook?"

" 'Course not." He winked at her and reached over to pat their daughter's head. "I knew you'd give me beautiful kinner, like this little *maedel*."

Hannah wrinkled her nose. "You're just like your twin bruder. . .a big *bloge*."

Timothy chuckled. "And that's why you married me—because you like to be teased."

She rolled her eyes and forked another piece of chicken onto his plate. "I think you'd better eat. It'll keep you out of trouble."

Samuel, being the more serious type, wasn't sure how to take the banter between Timothy and Hannah. Could there be an underlying power struggle going on, or were they just teasing each other?

"Have you heard anything from Titus lately?" Samuel asked.

Timothy nodded. "Last time we talked, he said he's all settled into his new home and liking it a lot. Fact is, he seems to like pretty much everything about living in Kentucky. . . including his new aldi, Suzanne."

"Uncle Titus has a girlfriend?" Samuel's eight-year-old daughter, Marla, questioned.

"So it would seem," Timothy replied.

"I'll bet Phoebe Stoltzfus wouldn't like that if she knew," Marla said.

"Well, she doesn't know, because she's living in California." Hannah frowned. "That girl was never anything but trouble for Titus. I don't see what he ever saw in her."

Samuel didn't think this was an appropriate conversation for his children, so he quickly changed the subject again. "I've been thinking about making a trip to Kentucky to see Titus." He looked over at Elsie and smiled. "Don't you think that would be fun?"

She reached for her glass of water and took a drink. "I don't know, Samuel. Given the nausea and fatigue I've been having with this pregnancy, I'm not really up to a trip anywhere right now. Maybe we could go sometime next year, after the boppli's born and old enough to travel."

Samuel nodded. "That makes good sense."

Timothy looked over at Hannah and said, "Maybe we should go with 'em. It would be a fun trip for Mindy."

"There's nothing for me or Mindy in Kentucky," Hannah said sharply.

"How do you know?" Timothy asked. "You've never been there."

She gave a decisive nod. "That's right, and I don't want to go there, either!"

Los Angeles, California

Phoebe yawned and stretched one arm over her head. She'd just returned home from her job at the convenience store and was exhausted. They'd had a lot of customers this evening: some demanding and impatient, and some—like the two bikers who'd showed up shortly before her shift ended—who'd given her a hard time because she wouldn't go out with them.

Whatever happened to her dream of starting a new,

exciting life in California? Why was nothing going right for her anymore? The only reason she was still in this apartment was because Charlene, one of her coworkers, had loaned her enough money to cover this month's rent. Phoebe still hadn't found a second job, and she knew she couldn't keep borrowing money forever. If something didn't go her way soon, she'd have no other choice but to move back home.

She flopped down on the shabby brown sofa and thumbed through the mail she'd picked up before she'd headed upstairs to her apartment. There were two advertising flyers, an electric bill she wouldn't be able to pay, and two letters. The first one was from Mom, so she tossed it on the coffee table. When she saw the return address on the second letter, her mouth went dry. It was from Titus, in Kentucky.

Phoebe's fingers trembled as she tore the letter open and read it silently:

Dear Phoebe,

This letter is long overdue, but it's taken me some time to come to the place where I could forgive you for walking out on me. I realize now that I've been hurting myself by hanging on to the bitterness I felt when you broke up with me. God has changed my heart and shown me many things about myself, as well as others, since I moved to Kentucky. I'm a different person—more confident and mature. I'm even buying my own place—a manufactured home on several acres of land.

I also want to ask your forgiveness for anything I may have said or done to hurt you in the past. I still don't understand why you'd want to leave the Amish faith and go English, but that's your choice, and it's not my place to say what's right or wrong for you.

I hope things are going well for you in California and

that you've found happiness in whatever you're doing. I wish you all God's best.

Most sincerely,
Titus

Tears welled in Phoebe's eyes and coursed down her cheeks. Titus was obviously happy in Kentucky. She was miserable here in California. Titus had forgiven her and wished her God's best. She was bitter and angry toward God, as well as everyone else.

Phoebe wasn't sure when all that bitterness had begun, but she thought it may have started when she was thirteen and her folks had forbidden her to see Titus.

She sat for several minutes, mulling things over; then she gathered up Titus's letter and hurried into her bedroom to pack. God must be blessing her already, because she knew exactly what she needed to do. By this time tomorrow, she'd be on a bus headed for Kentucky.

Chapter 49

Pembroke, Kentucky

Suzanne took a seat on the sofa, prepared to embroider the pillowcases she'd made the other day. Even though she didn't have a cedar chest to put the things in, she'd decided that in case Titus should ever propose, she ought to have some things ready for marriage. She would put them in a cardboard box for now.

"What's that you're working on?" Mom asked when she came into the living room and took a seat in the rocking chair across from Suzanne.

"I'm doing some embroidery work on the pillowcases I made."

"For your hope chest?"

"Jah."

Mom smiled. "I'm glad to see that you're taking an interest in more domestic things now and have begun making some things you can use when you get married."

"*If* I get married," Suzanne corrected. "Titus hasn't asked me yet, and he may never ask."

"I think he will. Just give him time. From some of the

things you've told me, I assume that he was hurt badly by his ex-girlfriend when she ran off to California. He might be taking his time before he gets serious again."

"I realize that, but I hope he won't take too much time. I'm not getting any younger, you know."

Mom leaned her head back and laughed. "For goodness' sake, Suzanne; you're only twenty-two. It's not like you're *en alt* maedel."

"I'll turn twenty-three in January, and I feel like an old maid. Many women my age are already married and starting their families by now." Suzanne threaded her needle and stuck it into the cotton material.

Mom started the rocking chair moving, causing it to squeak against the wooden floor. "Esther's a few years older than you. Do you think she's an old maid?"

"I guess not, but she's had several boyfriends. I wouldn't be surprised if she finds someone who wants to marry her soon."

"You need to have patience. And whatever you do, don't say or do anything to make Titus think you're trying to push him. Men want to do the wooing, and we women need to be smart enough to at least let them think they're in control of the situation." Mom stopped rocking and leaned forward in her chair. "Just be yourself, and take an interest in the things Titus likes. Eventually he'll come to his senses and realize he can't live another minute without asking you to be his fraa."

Just then, Effie shuffled into the room, looking a bit under the weather. "Look," she said, holding her arm out to Mom. "I've got itchy spots here and on my tummy, too."

Mom studied Effie's arm and then felt her forehead. "You're running a fever, that's for sure. From the appearance of these bumps, I'd say you've come down with a case of *wasserpareble.*"

Effie's eyes widened. "Chickenpox?"

"That's what it looks like to me. Have the pox been going around at school?" Mom asked.

Effie shrugged. "Maybe so. Sarah Beth's been out of school all week, and Brian and his sister Peggy weren't there today, so I guess they might have wasserpareble."

Suzanne groaned. "You'd better stay away from me then, because I've never had the chickenpox, and I sure don't need them now."

Tennessee

Phoebe stared out the bus window, trying to concentrate on the passing scenery so she wouldn't worry about how things would go when she saw Titus. What if he wasn't happy to see her? What if he asked her to leave?

He won't do that. I'm sure he won't, Phoebe told herself. *He said in his letter that he's forgiven me for breaking up with him, and I know how much he cared about me even when I was only thirteen.*

Phoebe put her head against the seat and closed her eyes. Her body felt stiff, and she was tired of sitting on crowded buses with people she didn't know. She'd gotten on the first bus at the Greyhound station in Los Angeles two days ago at seven fifteen in the evening, had made two transfers, and would arrive in Clarksville, Tennessee, by seven fifteen this evening. That was the Greyhound bus station closest to Pembroke, Kentucky, where Titus lived.

When she got to Clarksville, she would get a taxi to take her to Titus's place. It would probably be expensive, but she thought she had enough money. The bus ticket had cost her $209, but she'd started out with $300, which she'd borrowed from Charlene, so she should have enough to pay the taxi driver. She'd promised to send Charlene the money she owed for the bus ticket, as well as the rent she'd paid on her apartment. Unless she found a job, however, she probably wouldn't be able to make good on her word until after she and Titus got married.

Of course, she reminded herself, *the only way Titus will agree to marry me is if I'm willing to join the Amish church. He made that clear after he joined the church himself.* She leaned toward the window, trying to find a comfortable position, more anxious than ever to get off the bus.

I've tried living in the English world by myself, and it didn't work out very well, so I think I'm ready to go back to living the Plain way of life. I just don't want to go home and join the church there, because I'm sure Mom will try to make me feel guilty for leaving home, and Dad will probably lay out a bunch of rules, the way he did when I lived there before. Well, I'm not going back to Pennsylvania. I'm going to start a new life in Kentucky with Titus.

Pembroke, Kentucky

Titus had gone out to the barn right after he'd done the supper dishes so he could continue working on the hope chest he planned to give Suzanne for Christmas. Since he wanted it to be a surprise, he knew better than to work on it in the Yoders' woodshop. Suzanne spent a lot of time out there these days even when she wasn't helping them work. Sometimes it was to bring the men their lunch, and sometimes just to sit and watch. When she wasn't in the shop, she was in the kitchen, perfecting her baking skills. Titus always looked forward to sampling what she'd made and was impressed with how well she'd learned to cook.

He'd just started sanding the hope chest when he heard a car pull into the yard. It didn't sound like Allen's truck, so he figured it must be one of his English neighbors.

He set the sandpaper aside and headed for the barn door. When he stepped outside, he was surprised to see a taxi parked in his driveway.

When the back door of the cab opened, and a young woman with shiny auburn hair hanging down her back, stepped out, Titus froze. It was Phoebe Stoltzfus! He'd have recognized her anywhere, even without her Amish clothes. The question was, why had she come?

Chapter 50

Phoebe, wh–what are you doing here?" Titus stammered as a trickle of sweat rolled down his forehead. He couldn't believe she was standing in front of him. It felt like he was in the middle of a dream.

Phoebe gave him a dimpled smile—the same smile that used to make his heart feel like melting butter. "I came to see you," she said ever so sweetly.

"How'd you know where I live?"

She tipped her head slightly and snickered. "Your address was on the letter you sent me."

"Oh, that's right." Titus felt like a gibbering idiot. Having Phoebe show up out of the blue had taken him completely by surprise.

"Things didn't work out for me in California, so after I got your letter, I decided to catch a bus and come here to see you."

He shifted from one foot to the other, as his heart began to pound. Seeing Phoebe again had stirred up emotions he thought he'd managed to bury. "I. . .uh. . .guess you'll be heading to Pennsylvania from here?"

"Why would I go there?"

"To see your folks, of course."

She shook her head. "I came to be with you. I want us to start over again."

Titus swallowed hard. "Phoebe, I—"

"So this is your place?" She motioned to the manufactured home behind them.

He nodded, not trusting his voice. The longer she stood there smiling at him, the harder it was to think or even breathe.

"It looks nice. Can I see the inside?"

"I guess so." Titus didn't know what else to do—especially since her taxi had already gone.

When they entered the house, he gave her a quick tour, the whole time feeling as if he were dreaming and unable to wake up. When he'd sent her that letter, he'd never imagined she would come here to see him.

"This is perfect," Phoebe said. "There's lots of space, and even a guest room where I can stay."

He shook his head hard, as reality set in. "Huh-uh. No way! You can't stay here."

"Why not?"

"It wouldn't be right, and you know it, Phoebe."

"But I have no place else to go."

"I'll call my driver and have him take you to a hotel in Hopkinsville."

She frowned, causing tiny wrinkles to form across her forehead. "I can't stay at a hotel, Titus."

"Why not?"

"I have no money for that. I had to borrow money from a friend to pay for my bus ticket here, and I used what I had left to pay for the cab."

Titus didn't know what to do. He felt sorry for Phoebe, just like he had when she was a teenager and used to complain that her dad was too strict. After thinking things over a few minutes, he finally said, "Guess I could take you over to the Beilers' place and see if you can stay with them tonight."

"Who are the Beilers?"

"They're part of my church district, and they own a general store in the area. They only have one daughter still living at home, so I'm sure they must have an extra room."

Phoebe's lower lip protruded in a pout, the way it often had when they'd been courting and she hadn't gotten her way. "Are you sure I can't stay here with you?"

"Of course I'm sure, and I'm surprised you'd even ask."

Her face colored to a deep pink, and she quickly averted his gaze. "You're right, Titus. I don't know what I was thinking."

Titus picked up her suitcase and opened the door. "I'll get my horse and buggy ready, and then we can head over to the Beilers' and see if they'd mind putting you up for the night."

"Do we need to go there right now? We have a lot of catching up to do, so can't we sit here and visit awhile?"

"We can talk on the way over there." Titus hurried out the door, eager to get away from Phoebe so he could think. Being in her presence made him feel befuddled and disoriented, like he'd lost his ability to think or see things clearly.

When he entered the barn to get Lightning, he glanced at the hope chest and winced. What would Suzanne say when she found out that Phoebe was here? How would this turn of events affect his and Suzanne's relationship?

—∞—

"It feels strange to be riding in a buggy again," Phoebe said as she slid a little closer to Titus on the seat.

"I guess it would. What's it been now. . .nine months since you left for California?"

"I went there the first part of March, so it's been eight months."

He glanced at her, and his gaze came to rest on her faded blue jeans. "I guess you threw away all your Amish clothes, huh?"

She nodded and released a lingering sigh. "I wish I still had them now."

He offered no reply.

"Things were great when Darlene and I first got to California. We shared an apartment and both had jobs. Then all of a sudden she decided to move back home, which left me in the lurch."

"How so?"

"The rent on the apartment was too much for me to pay with the money I earned at the ice-cream store where I worked during the day. So I had to get an evening job working at a convenience store." Phoebe grimaced. "Even with two jobs, it was a struggle for me to pay the rent, utilities, cell phone, and also buy food. I paid the fee to end the cell phone agreement, cut way back on groceries, and starting riding an old bike so I wouldn't have to scrape money together for bus fare." She glanced over at Titus to gauge his reaction, but he kept his focus straight ahead and said nothing.

"One day I was late getting to work at the ice-cream store," she continued. "My boss was really upset and fired me."

Still no response from Titus. Was he even listening to what she was saying, or didn't he care?

She reached over and placed her hand on his knee. "Did you hear what I said?"

"Jah. Just thinking is all, and you're makin' it hard, so please take your hand off my knee."

Her chin trembled as she pulled her hand aside. Titus seemed so distant, as though he wished she hadn't come. "You can't imagine how hard it's been for me," she said, struggling not to give in to her tears. "With only one job, I couldn't make ends meet, and the way things were going, I would have been kicked out of my apartment soon and ended up on the street, begging for money and food."

"Sorry to hear you've been through so much. With things being so bad, I'm surprised you didn't return home."

She shook her head and swallowed against the lump clogging her throat. "I told you before. I can't go back there. Mom would say, 'I told you so,' and Dad would lay down a bunch of rules."

He turned his head and looked at her with a grim expression. "So you came here because you were out of money and had no place else to go?"

She placed her hand cautiously on his arm, hoping he wouldn't ask her to move it, and was relieved when he didn't. "That's not how it was, Titus. When I got your letter, it made me miss what we used to have. I realized that I still cared for you, so I came here, hoping you'd take me back."

No response. Just a blank look on Titus's face. Did he believe her? Did he still have feelings for her? Surely he couldn't have forgotten what they'd once shared.

"I'd like to stay in Kentucky and see about joining the church," she said.

"That's. . .uh. . .not a good idea."

"How come?"

"It's different here, and there'd be a lot of adjustments for you to make."

"I'm good at adapting. I did plenty of that while I was in California." Phoebe leaned close to his ear. "I know I'll have to prove myself, and I hope you'll give me a chance."

He glanced at her, and then looked quickly away. "It's not that simple, Phoebe. You see, I have a—"

She squeezed his arm tenderly. "Remember how much fun

we used to have when we were courting?"

"Jah, but—"

"Remember how you always said you'd never love anyone but me?"

"I did say that, but now I'm—"

"Please don't send me away," she pleaded. "I just can't go home, and I really want to be here with you."

When Titus gave no reply, a sense of desperation welled in Phoebe's soul. Didn't he want her anymore?

A few minutes later, Titus guided his horse and buggy off the road and turned up a driveway. "This is the Beilers' place," he said. "I think it's best if you wait in the buggy while I speak to them."

"Okay," Phoebe said with a nod. Oh, she hoped they would let her stay.

Titus hopped down, secured his horse to the hitching rail, and sprinted for the house.

Phoebe leaned back in the seat and drew in a deep breath to help calm her nerves. She knew she'd taken Titus by surprise, showing up the way she had, and even though he was obviously confused right now, she felt sure that after they spent some time together, everything would work out. She'd make sure it did.

Chapter 51

As Titus lay in bed that night, staring into the darkness, he replayed the events of the evening. He'd explained Phoebe's appearance to the Beilers the best that he could, and they'd graciously agreed to let her stay with them until she figured out what she was going to do. Then he'd said good-bye to Phoebe and hurried back home, feeling the need to be alone so he could think things through.

"What I wish Phoebe would do is go home," he mumbled. "If she stays here, it'll wreck things between me and Suzanne, and I might even weaken and take Phoebe back."

Titus turned onto his side and punched his pillow a couple of times, trying to find a comfortable position. Was it possible that Phoebe had been telling the truth about wanting to live in Kentucky and join the Amish church? Did she still have feelings for him, as she'd said, or was she just in need of a place to stay?

Do I still care for her? Titus asked himself. *Could I have only thought I was falling in love with Suzanne because she looks similar to Phoebe?*

If that were true, and he really didn't love Suzanne, then

he needed to know it now before he asked her to marry him.

I need wisdom in knowing what to do, Lord, Titus silently prayed. *Things were going along fine until Phoebe showed up. I thought I had my future planned out, and I figured Suzanne would be a part of it. I'm not sure about anything right now. Please show me what I should do.*

Titus tossed and turned for another hour until he finally made a decision. Tomorrow morning, before he went to the woodshop, he'd stop at the Yoders' house and speak to Suzanne. He didn't want her finding out about Phoebe from Esther or anyone else in her family. He needed to tell her himself.

When Phoebe awoke the following morning, she felt disoriented and out of place. With a feeling of panic, she sat up and glanced around the room. "Where am I?" she murmured. This was certainly not her apartment in California.

At the foot of the bed sat a cedar chest, with the pair of jeans she'd been wearing last night, draped over it. Across the room stood a dresser, desk, and a wooden chair. The only window in the room was covered with a dark green shade.

Her gaze came to rest on her suitcase, lying opened on the floor underneath the window. Suddenly, things came into focus.

Oh that's right. I'm at the Beilers' house. I'm staying in what used to be their oldest son's bedroom.

Still stiff and a bit sore from sitting on the bus so many hours, Phoebe pulled the covers back, clambered out of bed, and reached around to rub the knot that had formed in her lower back. She shivered as she plodded across the cold wooden floor in her bare feet. It sure was chilly here in November. Nothing like the warm balmy weather in southern California.

She slipped into her blue jeans and T-shirt, ran a brush

through her hair, and hurried down the stairs, following the welcoming aroma of freshly perked coffee coming from the kitchen.

"Good morning," she said to Esther, who stood at the cupboard, cracking eggs into a bowl.

"Morning," Esther mumbled in a voice barely above a whisper.

Esther's mother, Dinah, turned from where she stood at the stove and smiled. "Good morning, Phoebe. Did you sleep well?"

Phoebe gave a nod. "I didn't sleep much on the bus ride here, so a good night's rest in a real bed was what I needed."

Dinah motioned to Phoebe's jeans. "If you're going to church with us this morning, then you'll need something else to wear. Esther can loan you one of her dresses, since you look to be about the same size."

"I'd appreciate that." Phoebe glanced over at Esther, but Esther ignored her and started stirring the eggs she'd cracked into the bowl.

"Esther," Dinah said, "why don't you take Phoebe upstairs and see what you have that might fit her while I finish breakfast?"

Esther nodded and set the bowl aside, but her pinched expression let Phoebe know she wasn't too happy about it.

Phoebe followed her quickly out of the room.

"Why'd you really come here?" Esther asked when they entered her bedroom. "Was it to cause trouble for Titus?"

Phoebe shook her head. "Of course not. I came because I care about him."

"I see." Esther went to her closet and took out a plain, dark dress. "You can try this on and see if it fits." She handed the dress to Phoebe and turned to stare out her bedroom window.

"Well, what do you think?" Phoebe asked after she'd put on the dress.

"It looks a little short, but I guess you can let the hem down a few inches."

Phoebe stared down at the dress. "I don't think it's too short."

"That's probably because you're used to seeing the dresses English women wear, which, of course, are much shorter than any of ours."

Phoebe moved over to the dresser and picked up the hand mirror that had been lying there. "Guess I'd better pin up my hair and put a covering on. Have you got an extra one I can wear?"

Esther opened her top dresser drawer and pulled out a white organdy head covering that she handed to Phoebe. "You can wear this today."

"After church is over, I'll probably go home with Titus," Phoebe said, "because we need to talk—to make some plans."

Esther tipped her head. "What kind of plans?"

"Plans for our future. He asked me to marry him once, and now I'm ready to say yes."

Esther's face blanched, and she blinked a couple of times. "You're kidding, right?"

"No, I'm completely serious. I told Titus on the way over here last night that I want to stay in Kentucky and join the Amish church. Once I'm a member, we can be married."

"You really think he's going to marry you after you walked out on him?"

"He told you about that?"

Esther nodded. "It's taken Titus a long time to get over you, and now that he has a serious girlfriend, do you think you can just show up here and expect him to welcome you back like nothing ever happened?"

Phoebe's jaw dropped. "What did you say?"

"I said, do you think you can just—"

Phoebe held up her hand. "No, the part about Titus having a girlfriend."

"Her name's Suzanne, and she's a good friend of mine." Esther took a seat on the edge of her bed and folded her arms. "At first Titus and Suzanne didn't get along so well. I think it was because she reminded him of you."

"In what way?"

"She has the same color hair and eyes as you."

"So what are you saying—that Titus hated me so much that he hated her?"

Esther shook her head. "Hate's a very strong word, Phoebe. Titus is a good Christian, and I don't think he has it in his heart to hate anyone. I think he was so crushed by what you'd done to him that seeing Suzanne, who resembles you in some ways, kept his wounds open for a time."

Phoebe stood as though glued to the floor, not sure what to say. If Titus had a girlfriend, why hadn't he told her so last night?

"There was a time when I thought Titus and I might become a couple," Esther said. "We'd even gone a few places together, but we both realized that we didn't have much in common."

"Oh, I get it now. You want Titus for yourself, so you're trying to make me think he's in love with someone else."

Esther shook her head vigorously. "That's ridiculous. Titus and I are only friends, but Suzanne cares deeply for him, and I'm quite sure he feels the same way about her."

"We'll have to wait and see about that." Phoebe whirled around and started for the door.

"Where are you going?"

"Downstairs. Your mom's probably got breakfast ready by now, and I'm half starved!"

—∞—

Suzanne squinted against the ray of light invading her room and groaned. Her head pounded, and her throat ached something awful. She hoped she wasn't sick. Pushing the covers aside, she forced herself out of bed.

Shuffling across the room in her bare feet, she stopped in front of her dresser and looked in the mirror. "Oh no," she gasped when she discovered several blistery spots on her face. She looked at her arms. More spots. "Not the wasserpareble!" she moaned.

She needed to let Mom know she was sick and wouldn't be going to church today, so she slipped on her robe and made her way down the stairs. She found Mom in the kitchen, mixing a container of orange juice.

"I'm sick. I've come down with the chickenpox," Suzanne said, touching one of the spots on her face.

Mom's lips compressed as she slowly shook her head. "I'd hoped you were immune to them, but it looks like I was wrong. You'd better go back to your room and get into bed. I'll get a tray and bring yours and Effie's breakfast up to you soon."

"I can't afford to be sick right now," Suzanne said with a moan. "With Christmas coming, we've been getting lots of orders in the woodshop, and my help is needed there."

Mom patted Suzanne's arm gently. "They got along before you started helping, and they'll get along without your help until you're feeling better. Wasserpareble is harder on adults than children, so you'll need to get lots of rest, drink plenty of liquids, and whatever you do, no matter how much the pox might itch, don't scratch them."

A knock sounded on the back door. "Whoever that is, you'd better not let them in unless they've had chickenpox," Suzanne said as she hurried up the stairs to her room.

Titus knocked on the door a second time. A few seconds later, Verna opened the door. "Titus, I'm surprised to see you here this morning. Shouldn't you be at home, getting ready for church?"

"I got up early, hoping I could speak to Suzanne."

"She's upstairs in her room. Both she and Effie are sick with the wasserpareble, so unless you've had them, you'd better not come in."

"Timothy and I both got 'em when we were eight years old, and I've got a few scars where I scratched to prove it." Titus leaned against the doorjamb and pulled in a deep breath, still trying to deal with the tension he'd felt ever since Phoebe had arrived. "If Suzanne's feeling up to it, I really need to talk to her about something."

"I'll go upstairs and see." Verna turned, leaving Titus alone on the porch. When she returned several minutes later, she shook her head and said, "Suzanne isn't feeling up to company right now, and I think she's also embarrassed about her spots."

"She shouldn't be embarrassed in front of me."

"Maybe in a day or two she'll feel well enough to visit with you. Would you like me to give her a message?"

"Uh—no. Guess it can wait until she's feeling better."

"You're welcome to join us for breakfast."

"I appreciate the invite, but I had a bowl of cereal before I left home."

"All right then. I'll see you at the Zooks' for church." Verna smiled and closed the door.

Titus headed for his horse, a heavy weight resting on his shoulders. He needed to tell Suzanne about Phoebe, but maybe it was best that he hadn't been able to do that today. He also needed to speak to Phoebe again. They'd left too much unresolved last night.

Chapter 52

Paradise, Pennsylvania

"How are you feeling these days?" Fannie asked Elsie Sunday afternoon as they sat in her living room with some other women after church. "Is your morning sickness any better?"

"A little," Elsie replied, "but I'm awfully tired most of the time." She rested her hands against her stomach. "Can't remember feeling this way when I was carrying any of my other four."

"It's different with each one," Naomi spoke up. "At least that's how it's been for me."

Abby, who sat on the other side of Naomi, bobbed her head. "With Stella and Brenda, I had no morning sickness at all, but with Lamar, Derek, and Joseph, I sure did."

Elsie smiled. "Guess all bopplin are different when we're carrying them, just like after they're born."

Everyone nodded in agreement.

"Mind if I join you?" Arie asked when she entered the room.

"Not at all. Have a seat." Fannie patted the sofa cushion next to her, and Arie sat down.

"How are things with you?" Fannie asked. "You look meid today."

"I am tired." Arie stifled a yawn. "I haven't been sleeping well for some time, and after the message we discovered on our voice mail in the phone shanty last night, I hardly got any sleep at all."

"Was it bad news?" Abby asked before Fannie could form the question.

"I'm not sure." Arie placed her hands in her lap and clenched her fingers together. "The message was from a young woman named Charlene, who said she was a coworker of Phoebe's. Apparently, Phoebe recently borrowed some money from this woman, and now something's come up and Charlene needs Phoebe to pay her back."

"Is she expecting you to pay the money Phoebe owes?" Fannie asked.

Arie shook her head. "I don't think so. She thought Phoebe would be here and asked that she call her right away."

"But Phoebe's in California, isn't she?" Elsie questioned.

"That's what we thought, but since Phoebe moved to California, she hasn't kept in good touch with us." Arie's chin quivered, and she blinked, as if trying to hold back her tears. "I phoned Charlene back, and when I told her that we hadn't heard anything from Phoebe in several months, she said Phoebe had told her that she needed some money for a bus ticket to Kentucky so she could see a friend."

Fannie sucked in her breath. "Titus?"

Arie gave a nod. "I would assume so."

Fannie's heart began to pound. If Phoebe went to Kentucky and contacted Titus, they might end up together again. Titus was just beginning to make a new life for himself, and if Phoebe influenced him as she had in the past, he might lose his way.

"Charlene said she figured Phoebe would return to Pennsylvania after visiting with her friend in Kentucky." Arie looked over at Fannie, as though struck with a new realization. "Has Titus called you lately? Has he said anything about Phoebe?"

Fannie, trying not to let on about the concerns she felt, shrugged and said, "The last time I spoke to Titus, he made no mention of Phoebe."

"Maybe he didn't know she was coming," Naomi interjected. "Maybe Phoebe decided to go there and surprise him."

A knot formed in Fannie's stomach. Could Phoebe be in Kentucky right now? If so, how would it affect Titus's future?

—m—

Pembroke, Kentucky

Phoebe didn't know how she'd managed to sit through the three-hour church service that had been held in the buggy shed of a family named Zook. It wasn't the backless wooden benches or even the length of the service that bothered her, though, for she'd become used to that from growing up in an Amish family. What bothered Phoebe the most were the curious stares in her direction. She'd been introduced to a few people before the service began, but most of the others probably wondered who she was, and maybe why the dress she wore was a few inches shorter than those of all the other women who were present.

When the service was over and lunch had been served, Phoebe wandered around, looking for Titus. She was pleased when she spotted him over by the barn, talking to a young man who looked to be about his age. She waited until there was a lull in the men's conversation; then she asked if she could speak to Titus alone.

He started walking toward the area where all the buggies were parked, and then turned to face her. "What's up?"

She glanced around to make sure no one could hear their conversation. "Esther told me that you have a girlfriend. Is it true?"

He nodded.

"How come you made no mention of it last night?"

"I tried to a couple of times, but you kept interrupting me."

"Is she here today?"

He shook his head. "She's at home, sick with the chickenpox."

"Esther said your girlfriend looks like me. Is that also true?"

"She has auburn hair and blue eyes."

Phoebe tapped her foot and gave a slow nod. "Hmm. That's interesting."

"What do you mean?"

"You must still have feelings for me if you picked someone to court who looks like me."

A splash of color erupted on Titus's clean-shaven cheeks. "I didn't care for Suzanne at first because she reminded me of you. Every time I looked at her, I thought of you, and how much you'd hurt me."

"And now?"

"Now it's different. I've gotten to know Suzanne and have discovered that she and I have a lot in common."

"Are you planning to marry her?"

"I don't know; maybe." He sighed. "I've been thinking about it."

Phoebe's hand trembled as she placed it on Titus's arm. "What about me? Won't you give me another chance?"

He shrugged and dropped his gaze to the ground.

She stepped in front of him and looked up so he'd have to see her face. "I told you last night I want to join the Amish church and live here with you. Doesn't that count for anything?"

A muscle on the side of his neck quivered. "I thought I knew what I wanted and was sure I had my future planned out. Now that you're here I'm so *verhuddelt*."

"Spend some time with me, and I promise you won't be confused anymore. Give me a chance to prove myself, and you'll see that you feel the same way about me as you did before."

"Oh, you mean before you left for California and broke my heart?" His tone was clipped, and she could see the hurt on his face.

"Jah, before I left for California." She took a step closer. "Before our folks made so many rules that finally came between us."

Titus swallowed hard and wiped his sweaty forehead with the back of his hand. Being this close to Phoebe, hearing her promising words, made him feel more confused than ever. If only she hadn't run off to California. If she'd just settled down and joined the church while they were both living in Pennsylvania, they'd be married by now—maybe even starting a family. Was it too late for them? And what about Suzanne? Were his feelings for her real, or had he only imagined them, transferring what he'd felt for Phoebe to Suzanne?

"Have you met many people here today?" he asked, feeling the need to change the subject.

Phoebe shook her head. "Just a few. Esther and her mother introduced me to a couple of women before church, and then I met a few more after the noon meal. One of them was Verna Yoder. Is she related to the woman you've been courting?"

Titus's heart raced like a herd of stampeding horses. If Esther and Dinah had introduced Verna to Phoebe, did Verna know Phoebe was his ex-girlfriend from Pennsylvania? If she did, then she'd no doubt tell Suzanne. He couldn't let that happen. He had to make sure he told her himself.

"I've got to get my horse," Titus said, moving away from Phoebe.

"You're leaving already?"

"Jah. There's someplace I need to go."

"Where?"

"I need to speak to Suzanne." Titus hurried off before Phoebe could respond.

—∞—

When Titus arrived at the Yoders' he stood on the porch and prayed for wisdom to know the right words before he knocked on the door.

Isaac opened the door. "Ah, Titus, it's good to see you. You must have taken a detour on your way home from church today."

Titus nodded. "I came to see Suzanne. Is she feeling any better?"

Isaac shook his head. "Not much. Still feverish and dealing with a sore throat. Both she and Effie are covered with spots."

"Since Verna was at church today, I guess you stayed home to look after your granddaughters?"

Isaac grinned. "That's right. Can't do as much as I want to these days, but I'm still able to check on them and see that they get plenty of water and calamine lotion."

Titus smiled, although he had to force it, for the butterflies in his stomach made him feel nauseous. "I really need to speak to Suzanne."

"I'll go see if she's willing." Isaac turned away, leaving Titus on the porch. He returned several minutes later. "She's sleeping, and I didn't want to disturb her."

"Oh, I see."

"Is there a message I can give Suzanne when she wakes up?" Isaac asked.

Titus slid the toe of his boot across the wooden boards on the porch, as he struggled with what to do. Finally, in desperation, he whispered, "I need Suzanne to know that my ex-girlfriend from Pennsylvania is here."

"What's that?" Isaac cupped his hand around his ear. "With you whispering like that I couldn't make out what you said."

Titus motioned for Isaac to step onto the porch. He didn't want to risk waking Suzanne and having her overhear what he'd said. He really wished he could say this to her face so he could explain things to her.

Isaac grabbed his jacket from a wall peg near the door and stepped onto the porch. Then he took a seat in one of the wicker chairs, and Titus seated himself in the chair beside him.

"Now what's this you want to tell Suzanne?" Isaac asked.

Titus repeated what he'd said before about Phoebe showing up, and was just about to say that she'd taken him by surprise, when his horse whinnied loudly.

Titus looked at the hitching rail, and was shocked to see Phoebe climb down from his buggy.

"What in the world?" He leaped off the porch and raced across the yard. "What's going on?" he shouted at Phoebe. "What were you doing in my buggy, and how come I didn't know you were there?"

Phoebe's chin trembled as she looked up at him with tears in her eyes. "When you said you were going to see your girlfriend, I decided I'd better come, too. Since I knew you'd never agree to that, when you went to get your horse, I hid in the back of your buggy."

Irritation welled in Titus, and his hands shook as he held his arms tightly against his sides. "You had no right to do that, Phoebe! What were you thinking?"

Phoebe's tears trickled onto her cheeks, and she started to sob. "Pl–please don't yell. It—it upsets me when you yell."

Titus felt remorse. He'd always been putty in Phoebe's hands whenever she'd turned on the tears. He put his hand on her back and patted it gently. "I'm sorry for yelling, but you had no right to come here uninvited. I needed to speak to Suzanne alone and explain about you being here before she hears it from someone else."

Phoebe sniffed and swiped at her tears. "I thought we could do that together. I thought if Suzanne met me and saw how much you and I care for each other, she'd understand."

Titus stood there, too numb to say a word. Apparently nothing he'd said to Phoebe so far had sunk in. "I'm not sure if I care about you anymore," he said firmly. "To tell you the truth, I'm not sure about anything right now."

—

Roused from her sleep by loud voices, Suzanne forced herself out of bed. Was someone in the yard hollering, or had she been dreaming?

She padded across the room, lifted the shade at her window, and looked down. Her breath caught in her throat, and she grabbed the windowsill for support. Titus stood beside his buggy, and a young woman was next to him—a woman Suzanne didn't recognize but who looked familiar.

Despite the weakness she felt, Suzanne forced herself to get dressed and make her way downstairs. When she peered out the kitchen window, she could see the woman's face. *Oh my. . .she looks a lot like me.*

Suzanne went to the utility room and slipped into a jacket; then she stepped outside. She barely took notice of Grandpa, who stood on the porch, slowly shaking his head. All Suzanne could think about was getting to Titus's buggy and finding out who the woman beside him was.

"Wh–what's going on here?" Suzanne asked when she stepped up to Titus.

His cheeks turned red, and he looked at Suzanne with a kind of desperation. "Uh, Suzanne, this is Phoebe Stoltzfus. She arrived from California last night."

Phoebe nodded. "That's right. I spent the night at your friend Esther's."

Suzanne's vision blurred, and she swayed unsteadily. Then everything faded, and she toppled to the ground.

Chapter 53

Titus stood with Isaac, staring down at Suzanne as she reclined on the living room sofa. After she'd fainted, Titus had carried her into the house; then Isaac had put a cold washcloth on her forehead and patted her cheeks. She'd come to fairly quickly but hadn't said a word to either of them since she'd regained consciousness.

"Are you okay?" Titus asked, taking a seat on one end of the sofa near Suzanne's feet. "It gave us a scare when you fainted like that."

"I'm fine," she mumbled.

"Here, drink some of this." Isaac offered Suzanne some water.

She reached for the glass, sat up, and took a sip.

"Would someone bring me some more ginger ale?" a young voice called from upstairs. Titus realized it was Effie.

"Jah, sure. I'll be right up." Isaac excused himself and left the room.

Titus was on the verge of saying something to Suzanne, when she spoke.

"Why didn't you tell me that Phoebe was coming to see you?"

"I didn't know. She just showed up unexpectedly."

"How'd she know where you live?"

"She got my address from a letter I'd written her."

Tears welled in Suzanne's eyes, and she blinked several times, as though trying to keep them from spilling over. "I didn't realize you'd been writing to her all this time. If I'd known I never would have—"

"I haven't stayed in touch with Phoebe," Titus interrupted, his frustration mounting. "It was just one letter, to let her know that—"

"To let her know that you're still in love with her and want her back?"

Titus shook his head determinedly. "No, no. It wasn't like that. I wrote Phoebe to say I'd forgiven her for what she'd done and that I wanted her to know I wished her God's best."

"But you must have given her some encouragement or she wouldn't have come to Kentucky."

He shook his head again. "I didn't offer any encouragement, and I never mentioned the idea of her coming here."

Suzanne lifted both hands in the air. "Well, she must have gotten the idea from somewhere. In all the time you've been living here, she never came to see you before, so why now?"

Titus ground his teeth together. This wasn't going well. "I just told you, when Phoebe got my letter, she decided to come."

"Do you still love her?"

Suzanne's direct question and her furrowed brows made Titus begin to sweat. "No. I don't know. Maybe."

"I figured as much." Suzanne looked away. "She's waiting outside for you, so you'd better go."

"Please look at me, Suzanne." Titus reached over and touched her chin, turning her head to face him. "I'm worried about you. You fainted when you found out who Phoebe was, and I know you were very upset."

"I fainted because I'm weak and sick from the wasserpareble."

"Maybe that was part of it, but I think the shock of seeing Phoebe was too much for you."

She dropped her gaze and stared at the glass, clasped firmly in her hands.

Titus shifted on the sofa, feeling the tension between them. Tension that hadn't been there until Phoebe came on the scene and interrupted his life. "I'd like to stay so we can talk about this some more."

"What's there to talk about? You're not sure whether you're still in love with Phoebe, which means you're obviously not sure about us. Until you are sure, I don't think there's anything left to say." Tears slipped out of Suzanne's eyes and splashed onto her pale cheeks.

Titus wanted to hold Suzanne and reassure her that nothing had changed between them, but she was obviously too upset to talk about this, and right now, he was too confused. He sat for a moment, then rose from his seat and headed across the room. He was almost to the door when he turned and said, "I need some time to think and pray about this. When things become clear, and I come here to talk to you again, I hope you'll listen."

She didn't look at him and gave no reply.

Titus whirled around and went out the door. He hoped he would find the answers he sought before it was too late.

—∞—

Paradise, Pennsylvania

As Fannie and Abraham sat in their living room that evening, drinking hot cider, Fannie told him about the news Arie had shared.

"I wonder if Phoebe really did go to Kentucky," she said. "And if so, has she found Titus by now?"

Abraham set his mug down and drew his fingers through the end of his beard. "Guess we won't know that until we hear something from him. I'm sure if she showed up, he'd tell us. Don't you agree?"

"I don't know. He knows we never approved of Phoebe, so if they are back together, he might try to hide it as long as he can."

"It won't do any good to worry about it tonight," Abraham said. "We'll just have to wait until we hear from Titus."

"I'm not going to wait on Titus." Fannie pursed her lips. "Tomorrow morning, I'm going out to the phone shanty and call him. When his voice mail picks up, I'll leave a message and set a time for tomorrow evening that he can call when I'll be waiting in the shanty by the phone."

"Do whatever you want, but if you say too much on the subject of Phoebe, you could push Titus away." Abraham drank the remainder of his cider, set his empty mug on the table beside his chair, and stood. "I'm tired. Think I'll go to bed. Are you coming, Fannie?"

"In a bit. I want to sit here by the fire awhile."

When Abraham left the room, Fannie picked up her Bible, which had been lying on the coffee table. She turned to a place she'd marked with a ribbon and read James 1:5, which she'd underlined some time ago: "If any of you lack wisdom, let him ask of God, that giveth to all men liberally, and upbraideth not; and it shall be given him."

Fannie shut the Bible and closed her eyes. *Heavenly Father: Give me wisdom to say the right words when I speak to Titus, and may Your will be done concerning our son's future.*

Pembroke, Kentucky

"I don't see why I have to go back to the Beilers' place right now," Phoebe said as Titus directed his horse and buggy in that direction. "I think we need to talk."

"What good is talking when you don't listen? You've always wanted to have everything your own way."

"That's not true," she said, hoping he would see the sincerity on her face.

"Jah, it is, and you know it."

"Is it wrong because I want you? Is that what you're saying?"

"You say you want me now, but you've said that before—when we were courting. Then you changed your mind and took off for California. Now you're here, and I think it might be only because you have no money and believe you have no other place to go. I'm not convinced you came here because you love me."

"I did come because I love you. Why won't you believe me?" Phoebe's voice sounded desperate even to her own ears. Well, she couldn't help it; she was desperate. Desperate to make Titus understand, and desperate to win him back.

"It's hard to believe someone who's told so many lies," he said, turning his head away from her.

"I wasn't really lying before. I was just confused."

"So you broke up with me and left Pennsylvania because you were confused?"

"That's right. I've been confused and angry with my folks for a long time—ever since they first tried to come between us."

He glanced back at her and slowly shook his head. "If that's your only excuse, then it's a poor one at best. My folks weren't in favor of me courting you either—not even after you'd turned sixteen. But do you see me staying angry at them?"

"I don't know how you feel toward your folks. I only know that I've always felt like I could do nothing right as far as Mom and Dad were concerned, and it makes me angry that they've never wanted me to have any fun."

Titus shook the reins to get his horse moving faster.

She clasped his arm. "Are you going to give me another chance or not?"

"I don't know. I need time to think and pray about it."

"How much time?"

"Don't know that either."

"Until you decide, I'll stay at the Beilers' and wait. Dinah said I could stay there for as long as I like."

"You can do whatever you want, but it may be a while before I make a decision." Titus paused and turned to look at her again. "When I do decide, it might not be what you're hoping to hear."

Her heart sank with a feeling of dread. If only she could say or do something to get through to him.

He guided his horse and buggy off the road and onto the Beilers' driveway. "Here we are."

"Are you coming in?" Phoebe asked when he pulled up in front of the house instead of by the hitching rail.

He shook his head. "Good-bye, Phoebe."

She sat a few seconds. Unable to speak around the lump in her throat, she stepped out of the buggy and sprinted for the house. She was fearful that she might lose Titus to Suzanne and didn't know what she could do about it. Should she keep trying to win him back, or should she go home and face Mom and Dad? But if she went home, how would she get there? She'd used the money she'd borrowed from Charlene and didn't even have enough left for a bus ticket.

I just can't go home, she told herself. *I have to stay here and make Titus see that he loves me, and that we're meant to be together.*

Chapter 54

On Monday evening, Titus went out to the phone shanty to check for messages. He found one from Mom, asking him to call her at seven o'clock that night. He pulled out his pocket watch. It was five minutes to seven now, so if he stayed in the shanty, he could make the call soon.

While Titus waited, he checked for other messages. Allen had called, saying he was sorry he hadn't been around lately but he'd had a job to oversee in Trigg County and would be over to see Titus as soon as the job was complete.

Titus glanced at his pocket watch again. It was time to call Mom. When he dialed the number it rang just once, and then Mom's voice came on. "Hello."

"Hi, Mom, it's Titus."

"It's good to hear from you, son. I take it you got my message?"

"I did. That's why I'm calling."

There was a pause. Then Mom said, "Is. . .uh. . .Phoebe there?"

"Jah. She got here last week."

Mom groaned. "Oh, dear, I was afraid of that. What's going on, Titus? Why's Phoebe there? Were you in contact with her the whole time she was in California? Are the two of you back together?"

"Please, slow down, Mom. I can only answer one question at a time."

"Then start with my second question. Why is Phoebe in Kentucky?"

"She was down on her luck and didn't have any money. I believe she panicked, thinking she might have to go home."

"Would home be so bad? I don't see why everyone thinks they have to leave home."

Titus tapped his fingers along the edge of the table. *Not this again. Is Mom going to start up about me leaving home?*

"From what Arie said, one of Phoebe's friends loaned her some money for a bus ticket to Kentucky. Did you know she was coming?"

"I had no idea. I was taken completely by surprise when she showed up at my house."

"Have you kept in touch with Phoebe since she went to California?"

"'Course not. The first and only time I've written to Phoebe was to let her know that I'd forgiven her."

"Did you say anything in the letter that might make her think you wanted her to come there?"

"No, I did not." Titus opened the shanty door to let some cool autumn air in, but quickly shut it again when Callie tried to get in. He didn't appreciate being quizzed like this. He wondered if Mom thought he was lying to her.

"Where's Phoebe staying? I hope not with you."

Titus gripped the edge of the table so hard that his knuckles turned white. Why did Mom have to assume the worst? Didn't she think he knew right from wrong?

"Titus, did you hear what I said?"

"Jah, Mom, I heard. Phoebe is not staying here. She's at the Beilers' place."

"Will she be staying there for good? Are you two getting back together?"

"You're asking too many questions, Mom, and I don't have the answers."

"What do you mean?"

"I mean that I don't know how long Phoebe will be staying, and I'm trying to make a decision about whether I want to give her another chance."

"What? After all that girl has done—stomping on your heart and telling so many lies? I can't believe you'd even consider getting back with her."

"Phoebe says she wants to stay here and join the Amish church. She says she still loves me."

"Do you love her?"

"No. Maybe. I'm not sure. I'm verhuddelt right now."

"I don't understand why you're confused. What about Suzanne? You mentioned some time ago that the two of you were courting."

"We have been, and I thought I was falling in love with her and that she might even be my wife someday."

"Until Phoebe came along, right? Just like always, I'll bet she smiled sweetly and told you a bunch of lies. She probably said those things because she's desperate and thinks she has no other place to go. I don't mean to be judgmental, Titus, but if Phoebe broke your heart once she'll probably do it again."

"You might be right," Titus admitted, "but it's my decision to make, and that's why I'm going to take this week to pray about it and read God's Word for direction. Whatever decision I make, I want it to be God's will for me."

"That's good thinking," Mom said in a more accepting

tone. "I'm glad you're seeking God's will in this, and I'm sure your daed will be, too."

"Did you think I wouldn't seek God's will?" Titus didn't mean to sound defensive, but he'd always felt like he had to prove his worth to his folks, as well as others.

"I just thought—"

"I'm not the immature boy who left home in the spring. I've grown a lot since then, and I'm putting my trust in God these days."

"I'm glad to hear it, and I'll be praying for you as you make your decision."

"I appreciate that."

"I'd better let you go now," Mom said. "Besides, I need to call Arie and let her know that Phoebe's in Kentucky and that I'll keep her posted if I hear anything else."

"Okay, Mom. I'll talk to you soon." Titus hung up the phone and headed straight for the house. He had a lot more thinking and praying to do throughout the rest of this week. One thing he'd already decided was that he wouldn't see either Phoebe or Suzanne until he'd reached a decision. He didn't want to be influenced by anything either of them might say. He would go to work every day and spend his evenings praying and reading God's Word, as he sought the right answers.

For the rest of that week, Titus prayed and meditated as often as he could. On Saturday morning, he took his Bible and went out to the barn, where he could listen to the nicker of his horse and smell the aroma of freshly stacked hay as he spent time communing with God.

Seeking wisdom and a sense of peace, he took a seat on a wooden crate, leaned against the barn wall, and opened his Bible. Philippians 4:11 caught his attention: "I have learned, in whatsoever state I am, therewith to be content."

He pondered that awhile, realizing that he'd been more content since he'd moved to Kentucky than he'd ever been in Pennsylvania. Maybe it was because he was out on his own—away from the pressure of his family to measure up and be more like Timothy. Maybe it was because in this part of Kentucky, life was slower and more peaceful than it had been in Lancaster County. Or maybe it was because he'd gotten to know Suzanne and her wonderful family.

He turned to the book of Proverbs and read verse 30 of chapter 31: "Favour is deceitful, and beauty is vain: but a woman that feareth the Lord, she shall be praised."

Titus compared first Phoebe, and then Suzanne to the description of the woman in the scripture he'd read. Phoebe was beautiful on the outside, and so was Suzanne. But Phoebe's inner beauty was sorely lacking, whereas Suzanne's inner beauty was clearly evident in the things she said and did. As Titus recalled, Phoebe had never feared the Lord or tried to please Him. She hadn't even wanted to join the church, choosing rather to do her own thing and seek worldly pleasures. Suzanne, on the other hand, was a member in good standing in her Amish community, and her Christian attitude and helpfulness toward her family had been obvious to Titus from the beginning—even when he'd shied away from her because she'd reminded him of Phoebe.

For the past week, while Titus had been at work, he hadn't been able to get his mind off Suzanne. He'd seen the shawl she'd left hanging on a wall peg, and caught the sweet smell of the lilac soap she used as he walked by. Whenever Verna had brought lunch out to the men, Titus thought of Suzanne and asked how she was doing. He and Suzanne had become good friends over the last few months, but had he transferred his feelings for Phoebe to Suzanne, or did he care for Suzanne because of the woman she was? Did he still have feelings for Phoebe, or had they died when she'd gone to California?

Meow! Meow!

Titus looked down. Callie brushed his pant leg and looked up as though begging him to pet her.

Setting his Bible aside, he leaned over and scooped the cat into his arms. A few months ago, he'd never have done that. He'd have been afraid of getting scratched or bitten. But Callie had proven him wrong about cats. She was not only a good mouser but had become a good pet, too.

"It just goes to show that a body can be as wrong about a cat as they can about a person," he said, running his fingers through Callie's soft fur.

The cat answered with a *meow*. Then Buttons showed up and got in on the act. Titus petted both cats for a while and then closed his eyes and whispered a prayer. "Thank You, Lord, for giving me a sense of peace about what I should do."

All that week, Phoebe had moped around the Beilers' place, thinking about Titus and wondering what she could do to make him see that she was the right woman for him. She didn't like the fact that he hadn't come over to see her all week. How was she supposed to win him back if they didn't spend time together?

By Saturday, Phoebe was out of patience. Since the Beilers were at their store working and wouldn't have a clue what she was up to, she decided to use one of their horses and buggies to drive over to Titus's place.

She'd just put on a jacket and had opened the back door, when she spotted Titus riding in on his horse. She shut the door behind her and ran out to greet him. "I'm so happy to see you," she said as he tied his horse to the hitching rail. "I was getting ready to come over to your place right now."

His brows furrowed. "I thought I'd made it clear that I didn't want to see you until I'd had time to pray and make up my mind."

"I couldn't wait any longer." She moved closer to him. "Have you made up your mind?"

He nodded. "After much prayer, Bible reading, and thinking things through, it's come clear to me that I'm not in love with you, and that what we used to have wasn't a relationship that would last a lifetime."

Phoebe frowned. This was not the response she'd hoped for. "Titus, I don't think you're—"

He held up his hand. "Please, hear me out."

She compressed her lips and waited for him to continue.

"When I first came to Kentucky, I was all mixed up—full of anger and bitterness toward you and struggling with self-doubts about my ability to make a life of my own or do anything right. But I was finally able to move forward with my life."

His jaw quivered slightly. "I believe the Lord has chosen Suzanne for me, and I think the best thing for you to do is go home and work things out with your folks. I'd be happy to give you the money you'll need for the bus ticket to Pennsylvania."

Phoebe shook her head as anger boiled in her chest. "No, thanks. I'm not going back there!"

"Is it because you're afraid to face your folks and admit that things didn't work out as you'd planned?"

She shrugged.

"Since things didn't work out for you in California, did you ever think that God might be nudging you to go home?"

"How do you know He didn't want me to come here? How do you know He doesn't want us to be together?"

Titus touched his chest. "I don't feel a sense of peace or joy when I'm with you anymore. If you're honest with yourself, I don't think you feel any peace or joy with me, either."

Titus's words stung like icy cold raindrops on a windy day. "So you're not going to give us another chance?" she asked, unable to admit defeat.

"No. It's over between us."

She wrinkled her nose. "You're not thinking straight, Titus, and you'll be sorry for this someday."

He slowly shook his head. "The only thing I might be sorry about is that I didn't come to my senses sooner."

Tears stung Phoebe's eyes, and she started to sob.

Titus hated to hurt Phoebe's feelings, but he saw no other way. He just wished he'd seen her for who she was when they both lived in Pennsylvania. She'd never really loved him; he was sure of that now. She'd only cared about her own needs.

Being selfish and self-centered was not the way a Christian should act. Their church taught that a follower of Christ should be humble, not full of pride; obedient to God's Word, not rebellious; kind, not mean-spirited; and always thinking of others, not oneself. Phoebe had never shown any of the Christian attributes. Titus didn't know why he hadn't seen it when they were younger, other than the fact that he'd been blinded by Phoebe's good looks and flirtatious ways.

Suzanne, on the other hand, was everything he really wanted in a woman. She was kindhearted, smart, humble, full of fun, and he was sure she loved the Lord. If she'd have him, he was going to ask her to be his wife.

"I've got to go now, Phoebe. Think about my offer to give you the bus fare home, and let me know if you change your mind." He turned toward his horse.

"Wait a minute! Where are you going?"

Titus said nothing but climbed on Lightning's back and rode away.

—ꟺ—

"How are you feeling today?" Mom asked when Suzanne entered the kitchen.

"A little better." Suzanne went to the cupboard and removed a glass. "But I'd feel even better if I'd hear something from Titus."

"He was in the woodshop every day this week. You could have gone out and talked to him."

Suzanne filled her glass with water and took a drink. "I thought about that, and I could have asked Nelson or Grandpa if Titus had said anything to them about me or Phoebe, but I decided against it. Whatever Titus decides, it'll be better if I hear it from him when he's ready."

Mom moved away from the stove and put her arm around Suzanne. "If you and Titus are meant to be together, things will work out. If he chooses Phoebe, then he wasn't the man God wanted for you."

Suzanne blinked against tears threatening to spill over. "If he chooses her and they stay here in Kentucky, I don't think I could bear it. Every time I'd see them together, my heart would break in two."

"I know it'll be hard, but God will give you the strength to deal with things if it happens that way." Mom smiled. "In Isaiah 66:13 it says that God comforts us like a mother comforts her children."

Suzanne didn't respond. Instead she started setting the table. If Titus ended up marrying Phoebe, she'd accept it as God's will, but she wouldn't stay here. She'd have to find someplace else to live.

Chapter 55

After Titus left, Phoebe stormed into the house, dropped to the sofa, and covered her face with her hands. She couldn't believe he had turned her away. When they'd been courting, he'd promised that he'd always love her, but apparently he'd lied. If she couldn't make him see that she'd be better for him than Suzanne, then she had come here for nothing. She'd have been better off in California, living on the street.

Hot tears rolled down Phoebe's cheeks. It was hard not to feel sorry for herself when her whole life was messed up and nothing had turned out the way she'd hoped. Why was it that things went so well for some people, and for others, nothing seemed to work out?

The back door opened and banged shut. Phoebe pulled her hands away from her face and quickly dried her tears on the front of her apron.

"What's wrong, Phoebe?" Esther asked, as she entered the room. "Have you been crying?"

Phoebe nodded slowly and nearly gulped on the sob rising in her throat. "Titus came by this morning. I. . .I told him that

I love him, but he said he doesn't love me anymore. He thinks he belongs with Suzanne." She sniffed deeply and reached for a tissue from the box on the table beside the sofa. "I can't believe he'd choose her over me. I've known him a lot longer than she has, and the whole time he and I were courting, he kept saying he wanted to marry me and would never love anyone else."

Esther sat down beside Phoebe and reached out to touch her trembling shoulder. "I don't think you really love him. I think you've been using him because you need a place to belong, and he's the person you thought you could turn to in your hour of need."

Phoebe sat with her head down and shoulders slumped. She knew Esther was right but couldn't admit it, not even to herself.

"You need to get your life straight, and in order to do that, you have to give your heart fully to the Lord," Esther said.

"I told Titus that I'd join the Amish church. Isn't that good enough?"

"No, it's not. Being Amish is our way of life, but joining the church is giving your heart to the Lord. You must see yourself as a sinner who needs to be saved, and then joining the church will be your confession of faith." Esther reached for the Bible lying on the table beside the box of tissues. She opened it and said to Phoebe, "Romans 3:23 reads, 'For all have sinned, and come short of the glory of God.'"

Phoebe's tears spilled over onto her dress. "I. . .I know I've done many wrong things in my life, and I wouldn't blame God if He didn't forgive me."

"But you *can* find forgiveness," Esther said, gently patting Phoebe's back. "In 1 John 1:9 it tells us, 'If we confess our sins, he is faithful and just to forgive us our sins, and to cleanse us from all unrighteousness.'"

"I've heard that verse before when I've gone to church with

my family. I just never took it to heart." Phoebe gulped on another sob. "I. . .I want to seek forgiveness and turn my life over to Christ right now."

—∞—

Eager to speak to Suzanne, Titus got Lightning moving at a fast trot. He'd already wasted enough time trying to reason with Phoebe when he should have been at the Yoders', opening his heart to Suzanne. If only, from the beginning, he hadn't been taken in by Phoebe's beguiling ways.

But then, if I hadn't courted Phoebe, and she hadn't run off to California, I wouldn't have come to Kentucky or met Suzanne, he reasoned.

Titus urged Lightning on until the Yoders' house came into view. Then, guiding the horse up the driveway, he stopped in front of the hitching rail. He'd just stepped down from the saddle when Nelson came out of the woodshop and motioned for him to come inside.

Titus secured Lightning and headed up the driveway.

"Are you working here today?" he asked when he entered the shop and found Nelson sitting at his grandfather's desk.

"Jah. I don't normally work on Saturdays, but since Grandpa went shopping with Mom today, I thought I'd take a look at the books and see how we're doing, and then maybe do some sanding on those." He motioned to a set of cupboard doors leaning against the far wall.

"If you needed my help, I could have come to work today." Titus leaned on one end of the desk.

"That's okay. With all you've had on your mind this week, I figured you needed the day off."

"You're right about that. I've been doing a lot of thinking and praying all week."

"Have you reached a decision?"

Titus nodded. He'd shared his frustration and confusion about Phoebe with both Nelson and Isaac this week and knew they'd been praying for him. "I'd like to tell you what I've decided, but I think it's only fair that I discuss it with Suzanne first."

"That makes good sense." Nelson pointed to the ledger. "Don't mean to change the subject, but we have a lot of orders stacking up. I hope we can get them all done before Christmas."

"I think between you, me, and Suzanne working here in the shop we'll be able to get everything done."

Nelson scratched his head. "I'm afraid I haven't been fair to my sister. I've come to realize that she's happy working with wood, and I apologized to her last night. Said I shouldn't have been so narrow-minded about her wanting to do a job I'd thought was only for a man."

"I'll bet she was pleased to hear you say that."

"Jah. Even gave me a hug."

Titus smiled.

"So what'd you come here for?" Nelson asked. "Was it to speak to Suzanne?"

Titus nodded.

"She's up at the house, so go right ahead. She might be resting on the sofa, but you can go in."

"I will. See you later, Nelson." Titus hurried out the door.

He'd only made it halfway to the house when Suzanne's little sister, Effie, came running out of the barn. "Kumme! Schnell!" she hollered, waving her hands. "Something's wrong with Fluffy!"

Titus knew Fluffy was one of Suzanne's favorite cats, so he took off on a run behind Effie. When he entered the barn, he followed her to the stack of hay on the far side of the room. "Where's Fluffy?" he asked.

Effie pointed a trembling finger toward the first stack of hay. "She's behind there."

Titus hurried across the room and peered behind the bales of hay. What he saw made him cringe. Poor Fluffy had managed to get herself tangled in a piece of baling twine that had apparently come loose from the hay. The twine was wrapped around the cat's body so tightly that all she could do was roll pathetically from side to side.

There would have been a day when Titus would have hesitated to pick up the cat for fear of getting scratched, but he didn't think twice about helping Fluffy now.

He scooped the cat into his arms and took a seat on a bale of hay. Then he proceeded to untangle the twine, being careful not to frighten the poor critter any more than she was.

"Don't hurt her. Don't hurt my sister's katz." Effie stood beside him, eyes wide and mouth hanging slightly open.

"I won't hurt the cat. I'm only trying to help her." Titus grimaced. "If Fluffy would hold still, it would make things a lot easier."

"I'll pet her head and talk softly to her," Effie said. "Maybe that'll calm her down."

Titus nodded. "That's a good idea. Keep petting her until I get the twine off."

It took some time to accomplish the task, but Titus kept at it until he'd untangled the mess and Fluffy was free. "Here you go," he said, handing the cat to Effie. "That was quite an ordeal, so maybe you ought to get her some water and see if she wants to drink."

Effie said thank you, and holding the cat to her chest, she skipped to the other side of the barn.

Titus rolled the piece of twine into a ball and put it up on a shelf so none of the other cats would end up in a mess like Fluffy had been.

Eager to get to the house and speak with Suzanne, Titus rushed out of the barn. He'd only taken a few steps, when a horse and buggy pulled into the yard. He waited to see who was driving, and was shocked when Phoebe climbed down and secured the horse to the hitching rail next to Lightning.

"Not this again," he mumbled. "What are you doing here, Phoebe?"

"I needed to talk to you, and since I figured you were going to see Suzanne, I borrowed one of the Beilers' horses and buggies and came here."

"I thought I'd made clear the way I feel when I talked to you earlier."

"You did, but I need to tell you what happened after you left."

Titus crossed his arms and tapped his foot impatiently. "What happened?"

"After talking to Esther awhile and listening to her quote some verses of scripture, I realized what a terrible person I've been, and I—I gave my heart to the Lord." She smiled. "From now on, I want to start living for Him."

"Are you saying that to impress me, in the hope that I'll reconsider and take you back, or is this for real?"

"I'm not trying to impress you or get you back. I really did confess my sins and ask the Lord to take control of my life."

"If that's true, then I'm glad for you, but it doesn't change anything between us, Phoebe."

"I understand that, and I didn't come to stir up trouble. I came to say that I'm sorry for everything I've said or done to hurt you. No matter how bad things were for me in California, I shouldn't have come to Kentucky uninvited." She paused and flicked her tongue over her lips. "But I'm really glad I did, for if I hadn't come here, I might never have found a personal relationship with the Lord." She stepped toward him and smiled. It seemed like a genuine smile. "I know what I need to do now."

"What's that?"

"I need to go home and make things right with Mom and Dad. So if your offer to give me money for a bus ticket is still open, then I'll gladly accept it with much appreciation."

Titus could hardly believe Phoebe had found the Lord, but her attitude did seem to have changed, and he was more than happy to give her the money she needed in order to go home. He reached into his pocket and handed her several bills. "I wish you all the best."

"I wish the best for you, too." Phoebe slipped her arms around his waist and gave him a hug. "Thanks for the money. I appreciate it a lot."

Hearing voices outside, Suzanne went to the living room window and peered out. She gasped, shocked by what she saw. Titus and Phoebe stood in the front yard, hugging each other!

"Guess that's all I need to know," Suzanne muttered as she turned away from the window with a heavy heart. Titus and Phoebe were obviously back together. But did he have to hug her right here on their property where Suzanne could see? Was he deliberately trying to hurt her?

Tears coursed down Suzanne's cheeks, and she did nothing to wipe them away. *I was a fool for letting myself fall in love with Titus. He only pretended to like me because I reminded him of her.*

She'd just taken a seat on the sofa, when she heard the back door open. A few seconds later, Titus entered the room.

Suzanne leaped off the sofa and rushed toward the stairs, unwilling to hear what she was sure he was going to tell her.

"Where are you going?" he called.

"Upstairs to my room."

"Please, don't go. We need to talk. I want to tell you what I've decided about Phoebe."

She whirled around to face him. "I already know what you've decided. I saw the two of you outside, hugging."

"It's not what it seems." He moved toward her, and she took a step back.

"How is it then?

"Phoebe came over because she figured I'd be here talking to you—telling you what I'd decided."

"That you love her?"

"No, it's not that at all." Titus motioned to the sofa. "Let's sit down so I can explain things."

Suzanne seated herself on one end, and he sat beside her. "Phoebe came over here to tell me that she's confessed her sins and has found a personal relationship with the Lord," he said, looking at her intently.

"Did she think that would make you see her in a different light and take her back?"

"No, she wanted to apologize for all the things she's done to hurt me, and when she said she wanted to go home to Pennsylvania, I offered to give her the money for a bus ticket. She was grateful and hugged me, that's all."

"I see."

Titus took hold of Suzanne's hand and gave her fingers a gentle squeeze. "I've spent this past week thinking, praying, reading my Bible, and seeking God's will for my life." He smiled at her in such a sweet way that her heart nearly melted. "It's you I love, Suzanne, and if you're willing, I'd like you to marry me sometime next year."

Suzanne blinked. "Are you sure about this? You're not just saying it because you feel sorry for me?"

He shook his head. "I've never been surer of anything in my life. I was verhuddelt when Phoebe first showed up at my place, but my head's clear now, and I realize that the love I thought I'd felt for Phoebe was nothing more than infatuation.

I think I only wanted her because she was a challenge and her rebellious spirit excited me. Now that I've matured and am walking closer to the Lord, I want a woman I can trust—someone who thinks of others, not just herself."

"Do you think I'm that woman?" she dared to ask.

"I know you are." Titus leaned toward her and lowered his head so their lips were almost touching. "Is it all right if I kiss you, Suzanne?"

She nodded. He pulled her close and gently kissed her lips. When their lips parted, he whispered, "I'm so thankful God brought me to Kentucky, and even more thankful He brought you into my life." Then he kissed her again.

—∞—

That evening, as Phoebe stepped onto the bus, she thought about the things she'd learned during her brief stay in Kentucky. She realized what a selfish person she'd been and realized she needed time to grow and learn how to live her life for the Lord instead of herself. She also needed to seek God's will about His choice for a husband for her. As Esther's mother had said to her before she'd gotten on the bus, "Fulfillment doesn't come from marrying someone, but in a relationship with the Lord."

Phoebe took a seat and closed her eyes. *Help me, Lord, to remember all that I've learned, and when I see Mom and Dad, I pray that they won't criticize or lecture me for leaving, but will welcome me home instead.*

—∞—

When Titus returned home, after spending the evening at Suzanne's, he went out to the phone shanty to call his folks and leave a message, letting them know that Phoebe was on her way home, and that he and Suzanne were together as a couple.

He was about to make the call when he decided to check his messages first. He discovered one from Mom.

"Something horrible has happened, and we need you to come home right away. Elsie was carrying a basket of dirty laundry down the basement stairs, and she tripped over something and fell." There was a pause, and then Mom started crying. "When Elsie hit the bottom of the stairs, she broke her neck." Another pause. "She's dead, Titus. Elsie and the boppli she was carrying are both dead. The funeral will be in three days, and we hope you'll be there."

Titus sat, too numb to move. All the joy he'd felt over his relationship with Suzanne had been replaced with a deep ache in his heart for his half brother Samuel. Phoebe wouldn't be the only one heading home this week. Titus would be going now, too, only he'd be arriving for a funeral.

When the numbness wore off enough for Titus to think, he picked up the phone and called his folks' number. Then he left a message letting them know that Phoebe was on her way home to her folks, and that'd he be there for Elsie's funeral and would leave as soon as he could secure a ride.

Chapter 56

Paradise, Pennsylvania

When the bus stopped at the station in Lancaster on Monday morning, Phoebe picked up her purse and the book she'd brought along to read and stepped off the bus. She'd just gotten her suitcase from the compartment on the side of the bus, when someone called her name.

She looked to the right, and her heart started to pound. Mom and Dad were heading her way, waving their hands.

"Mom, Dad, what are you doing here?" she asked as they hurried toward her.

"We hired a driver and came to pick you up," Dad said.

"How'd you know I was coming?"

"Fannie told us. She'd gotten a message from Titus."

Mom threw her arms around Phoebe and gave her such a forceful squeeze that it nearly took Phoebe's breath away. When Dad hugged her, too, Phoebe knew without a doubt that her folks were as glad to see her as she was to see them. She felt like the prodigal son in the Bible, returning home after his rebellion, to welcoming arms.

Phoebe explained that she'd come home to stay, had

sought God's forgiveness for her sins, and was ready to take classes so she could join the Amish church.

"I'm so glad to hear that," Mom said tearfully.

"What about Titus? Will he be staying in Kentucky?" Dad asked.

Phoebe nodded. "I ruined things between us when I ran off to California, and now he's found someone else."

Mom put her arm around Phoebe's waist as they walked toward their driver's van. "It obviously wasn't God's will for you and Titus to be together."

"That's right," Dad agreed. "Someday when the time is right, you'll find someone else."

Phoebe didn't answer but kept walking.

"Did you hear about Samuel's Elsie?" Mom asked Phoebe when they reached the van.

"Samuel Fisher?"

"Jah. Elsie was killed on Saturday when she tripped while carrying laundry down the basement stairs. She fell to the bottom of the stairs and broke her neck. Both she and the boppli she was carrying died."

Phoebe gasped. "That's baremlich!"

"You're right, it's a terrible thing," Dad said as they all climbed into the van. "Poor Samuel is not only grieving for his wife and unborn baby, but now he has four kinner to raise by himself."

"Titus must not have known about this when he gave me money for my bus fare home," Phoebe said. "I wonder if he'll come for the funeral."

"Oh I'm sure of it," Mom said. "What brother wouldn't want to be there when someone in his family dies?"

Phoebe's heart went out to Samuel and to all the Fisher family. She knew the days ahead would be difficult for them. It was a good thing they had each other to lean on for strength.

Most importantly, they had the Lord.

She reached over and took Mom's hand. She was thankful that she'd finally seen the light and come home. Families needed each other. She knew that now without a doubt.

—∞—

Pembroke, Kentucky

"Are you sure you're feeling up to going to Pennsylvania with me?" Titus asked as he and Suzanne climbed into Allen's truck.

"Of course I'm sure," she said, offering him what she hoped was a reassuring smile. "It's been a few weeks since I came down with the wasserpareble, and since my pox marks are mostly gone, or at least crusted over, I'm no longer contagious. If I was, I wouldn't have agreed to come. I'm glad I'm going, though, because I not only want to be there for you, but I'm also anxious to meet the rest of your family."

"I appreciate you coming with me more than you know, and I appreciate Nelson and Isaac letting us both have the time off." Titus looked over at Allen, who sat in the driver's seat. "I'm thankful for your willingness to take us to Pennsylvania, too."

"Wouldn't have it any other way," Allen said as he started the engine. "Besides seeing that you make it home in time for the funeral, I want to be there for my good friend Zach. Want him to know he has my support."

"I'm sure Zach will appreciate that," Titus said. "I think everyone in our family's going to need a lot of support, Samuel most of all. I can't imagine how he must feel right now."

Suzanne thought about the emotional turmoil she and her family had been through when Grandma and Dad had died just a few months apart. They'd needed all the support they could get, and if it hadn't been for family and friends, she didn't think they could have survived the ordeal.

"We may as well relax and try to get some sleep," Titus said, "because it's a long drive between here and Pennsylvania." He chuckled and motioned to Allen. "Except for you, of course. You need to keep your eyes open and on the road."

Allen laughed, and Suzanne smiled. It amazed her that Titus could say something humorous, even though inside he must be hurting.

No wonder I love him so much, she thought as she leaned her head against his shoulder and closed her eyes. *I can't wait for our journey to Pennsylvania to end so I can meet the rest of his wonderful family.*

Even though Titus had been the one to suggest it, he couldn't sleep. He had too much on his mind.

He looked over at Suzanne, sleeping peacefully with her head on his shoulder. He felt blessed to have found such a special, caring woman.

When Titus first left Pennsylvania for Kentucky, he'd been on a journey to find himself. He'd not only discovered who he was and what he could do well, but he'd learned a lot more. He'd drawn closer to God on this journey, made several new friends he could count on, and had found a woman who loved him unconditionally.

Now a new journey stretched before him. He and Suzanne were traveling together to his home to comfort those in mourning and offer Samuel support and hope. Although the road might be difficult at times, Titus was confident he and Suzanne would make the journey together. Not only did they have each other, but God would never leave them.

Suzanne's Lemon Shoofly Pie

Ingredients for crumb topping:
1½ cups flour
½ cup white sugar
½ cup shortening or butter, softened
½ teaspoon baking soda

Ingredients for pie filling:
1 egg
Zest of 2 lemons
Juice of 2 lemons, strained
2 tablespoons flour
½ cup white sugar
½ cup molasses
¾ cup boiling water

1 unbaked pie shell

Preheat oven to 350 degrees.

Combine all ingredients for crumb topping and work together until they form a crumb-like mixture.

Stir together all filling ingredients until well blended and pour into unbaked pie shell. Sprinkle crumb topping evenly across pie filling. Bake for 45 to 60 minutes.

the HEALING

Dedication/Acknowledgment

To Irene Miller, one of my very special Amish friends.

[God] healeth the broken in heart,
and bindeth up their wounds.
Psalm 147:3

Chapter 1

Paradise, Pennsylvania

"*Alles is fix un faddich.*" Bishop Jacob Weaver clasped Samuel Fisher's shoulder and gave it a squeeze.

Samuel, who stood on his front porch with a few others from his community, gripped the railing so tightly his fingers ached. The last few days, and even now, he'd felt as if he were walking through a thick fog, barely able to hear what anyone had said to him. Yet the truth of the bishop's words—that all was completely done—slammed into Samuel with the force of a tornado. Overcome with emotion, he could barely manage a nod. They had just returned from the cemetery where they'd buried Elsie, his wife of ten years. He wasn't sure how he'd made it through the last couple of days, much less the funeral and graveside service, but frankly, he was too tired and too numb to care. Somehow, he was now expected to carry on without her, and that thought was overwhelming.

Samuel's mind hadn't rested since that awful day when he'd found his wife at the foot of the stairs. Over and over he kept asking himself, *How do I go on? How can I survive without my Elsie?* With his feelings so raw, he couldn't imagine where to begin. Constant thoughts and plaguing questions drained every bit of his energy.

Samuel realized he wasn't the first person to go through something like this, but even knowing that, all he felt was despair. The misery was more than he could bear. Well, he couldn't do it! The thought of caring for his and Elsie's four children and going to work every day was too much to think about. But if he didn't work, who would buy food and pay their bills?

And if he stayed home from work and wallowed in self-pity, he'd only be reminded of Elsie. Everywhere he looked, he would see her face: in the kitchen, where she'd prepared their meals; in the yard, where she'd worked among the flowers; in their bedroom, where she would take down her hair at night and allow him to brush her long, silky tresses as they discussed the day's events and all their plans for the future—a future that would no longer include his beloved Elsie.

"I'll let you visit with your family now, but please remember, you can call on me or any of the ministers in our church if you need anything. Oh, and no matter how sad you feel, take the time to read God's Word and pray, because being alone with God is the only way you will find the strength to press on." The elderly bishop, who'd been a friend of the family for a good many years, gave Samuel's shoulder another firm squeeze and walked away, leaving Samuel to his disturbing thoughts.

Was it only last week that he and Elsie had discussed the approach of Thanksgiving and the huge meal they planned to have? They'd smiled and laughed as they'd reminisced about last year's holiday with their children and several of Samuel's family members sitting around the table. Elsie had commented on how she loved to watch the children's eyes grow big as saucers when the mouth-watering turkey, almost overflowing the platter, had been set in the middle of the table. All the laughter and chatter while they'd enjoyed the holiday feast was a special time for them as a family. Abruptly, those holidays and everything else Samuel and Elsie had shared had come to a halt. How quickly things could change.

In an attempt to force his thoughts aside, Samuel stared into the yard. A cold wind had scattered the fallen leaves all about. The trees were bare and empty—just like Samuel's heart. He knew that some men who'd been widowed married within the first year of their wife's death, but Samuel was certain he would never marry again, for how could anyone fill the horrible void left by Elsie's untimely death?

He caught sight of his children playing in the yard with some other children as though nothing had happened. Of course, the little ones didn't understand that Elsie was never coming back, but he was sure eight-year-old Marla and six-year-old Leon did. So how could they frolic about as if they hadn't just witnessed their mother's coffin being lowered into the ground? Surely, they must miss her as much as Samuel did. Maybe the only way they could deal with it was to run and play, trying to block it all out. Samuel wished he could find a way to block out the pain.

He looked away and sank into a nearby chair with a groan. *Nothing will ever be the same. I'll never be able to laugh with the children again. No more catching flies for their entertainment. No more walks in the woods, holding Elsie's hand. No more anything that used to be fun.*

Samuel closed his eyes, and a vision of Elsie's twisted body lying at the bottom of the stairs came uninvited into his head. Would he ever be able to get that image out of his mind? Would he ever know peace again?

Marla and Leon had seen their mother fall that day, and when Samuel rushed into the house after hearing their screams, he'd found them close to her body, sobbing and pleading with her to open her eyes. The two youngest children—four-year-old Penny and two-year-old Jared—he'd discovered in the kitchen, hiding behind the stove. Even before the paramedics arrived, Samuel had known Elsie was dead. He'd found no pulse, and she wasn't breathing. Later, Samuel learned that Elsie had suffered a broken neck from the fall, as well as severe internal injuries. Their unborn baby, still underdeveloped in his mother's womb, had also perished.

"Samuel, you shouldn't be sitting out here in the cold by yourself."

Samuel's eyes snapped open. When he looked up and saw his older sister, Naomi, looking down at him with concern, he mumbled, "Didn't realize I was alone, and I'm too numb to feel the cold."

Naomi seated herself in the chair beside him. "I feel your pain, Samuel. I truly do."

Samuel stared straight ahead. "How can you feel my pain? Your husband's still alive, and you've never lost a child—not even one who wasn't fully formed."

"I realize that, but I hurt with you, and I want to help ease your pain."

"There's nothing you can do."

She reached for his hand and gave his fingers a gentle squeeze. He could see the depth of Naomi's concern in her ebony-colored eyes. "God loves you, Samuel, and so do I."

"If God loves me, He wouldn't have taken Elsie away from me and the *kinner*," Samuel whispered, as the bitter taste of bile rose in his throat.

"Zach was unfairly taken from our family when he was a

boppli, but it didn't mean God no longer loved us."

"That was different. Zach didn't die; he was kidnapped." Samuel pointed to the front door, where Zach and the rest of their family had gathered inside after the funeral dinner. "Zach came back to us. Elsie's gone from this earth forever."

"Her body's gone, but she was a Christian in every sense of the word, and I'm certain that her spirit lives on in heaven," Naomi said softly. "Someday you'll see her again."

"*Someday* could be a long time from now." Samuel swallowed hard, fighting to keep his emotions under control. "I wish it had been me who'd died. Why didn't God take me instead of Elsie?"

"You mustn't say such things. Your kinner need you now more than ever."

Samuel lowered his gaze to the porch floor. "They needed their *mamm*, and I can't take care of them without her."

"You don't have to, Samuel. God will see you through this. With the help of your family and friends, you'll make it."

Samuel rose to his feet, trying hard not to let the fear and loneliness he felt at the very core of his soul overtake him. "I can't talk about this right now. I need to be alone." Taking the porch steps two at a time, he hurried into the yard. He was halfway to the barn when his older brother, Norman, stepped up to him. "Are you okay, Samuel?"

"How can I be okay when Elsie's gone?" Just saying those words were hard enough, making him wish it was all just a horrible dream.

Norman's brown eyes became glassy as he put his hand on Samuel's shoulder and gave it a reassuring squeeze. "You have to accept her death as God's will. It's the only way you'll get through this."

Samuel's face heated, despite the chilly air. "What would

you know about it? Your *frau*'s not dead!" He shrugged Norman's hand away and stormed across the yard. It was easy for Norman to say such words when he'd never experienced the pain of losing his wife. Yet Samuel knew that his brother meant well, and if the tables were turned, he'd probably have tried to offer comfort to him in much the same way.

As Samuel moved on, he heard his brothers Jake and Titus, who stood outside the barn, talking about the upcoming Thanksgiving holiday.

"I wish I could stay and join you for the holiday," Titus said, "but we have a lot of orders that need to be filled in the woodshop before Christmas, so Suzanne, Allen, and I will have to head back to Kentucky tomorrow morning."

"It's good you could come for the funeral," Jake said. "I'm sure it made it easier for Samuel to have his whole family here."

My whole family's not here. Elsie was my family, and she's not here. Samuel's fingers clenched as he hurried his steps. When he entered the barn moments later, he was greeted by the soft nicker of the horses in their stalls. He dropped to a seat on a bale of straw and stared vacantly at Elsie's horse, Dolly, standing in one of the stalls, her head hanging over the gate. Did the mare know Elsie was gone? Did she miss her, too? He'd have to sell the horse now. If he kept the mare, he'd think of Elsie and be reminded that she would never hitch Dolly to the buggy again. Every waking hour, his thoughts were like a roller coaster, reflecting back over the ten years they'd been married. He wasn't ready to let go—he wanted to think about nothing but the memories they'd made together. But then his thinking would jump ahead, trying to imagine his life without Elsie. It was too much, too hard to grasp. For the last three days, he'd been falling into a fitful sleep at night, and finally, when he succumbed to exhaustion, it would be dawn.

Mornings, he found, were the worst: his mind came to full alert, yet he still felt fatigued when he forced himself out of bed. He'd pace the floor, a million questions swimming in his head, wondering, *Where do I go from here? Will I always feel this restless and unsure?*

Halting his thoughts, Samuel noticed several pieces of hay falling through cracks in the loft above and was reminded of all the chores he had to catch up on. His pitchfork lay on the floor, where he'd dropped it the day he'd heard his children's screams that their mamm had fallen down the stairs.

A cat sprang down from the loft, and Samuel jumped. Purring softly, it rubbed its side against Samuel's legs. Elsie loved their cats, and they knew it. "Here, kitty, kitty" was all she had to yell, and the critters would come running, knowing their bowls had been filled. To Samuel, they were just plain old barn cats, good for only one thing—to keep the mice down. Elsie, though, loved all the farm animals and had a special way with them.

The barn door squeaked open and then clicked shut. Samuel looked up and saw Titus step inside. "I saw you come in here," Titus said. "I wanted to talk to you alone and thought this might be a good time."

"What'd you want to say?" Samuel asked. Truly, he just wanted to sit by himself for a spell, without interruption, but he didn't want to be rude—especially when his brother had come all the way from Kentucky to attend Elsie's funeral.

Titus took a seat on the bale of straw next to Samuel. "I'm real sorry about Elsie. It was a shock to hear that she'd died, and I know you and the kinner are really going to miss her." His dark brown eyes looked as sorrowful as the somber expression on his face.

Samuel, not trusting his voice, could only nod.

They sat for several minutes in silence until Titus spoke again. "If you ever feel the need for a change, I want you to know that you'd be welcome in Kentucky. I'd be pleased to have you stay with me for as long as you want."

"Me moving from here won't bring Elsie back." Samuel knew he sounded bitter, but he couldn't help it.

" 'Course not, but it would give you a new start. Maybe that's what you need." Titus leaned closer to Samuel. "Moving to Kentucky helped my wounded heart to heal after Phoebe and I broke up."

Samuel shrugged. "I'll give it some thought, but right now I just need to be alone." He couldn't imagine how moving to Kentucky could help his broken heart. Besides, his situation wasn't anything like Titus's.

"Okay, I'll head back to the house now, but remember, brother, I love you." Titus gave Samuel's arm a light tap and slipped quietly from the barn.

Dolly whinnied, and Samuel's vision blurred from the tears burning his eyes. *Oh, Elsie, I'll never love anyone but you. Sweet Elsie, I'll always miss you.* He lowered his head into his hands and let the tears flow freely.

Pembroke, Kentucky

As Esther Beiler stood beside her mother at the counter near the front of their store, she sensed that something was wrong. Mom had been acting kind of strange all morning, as though a heavy burden lay on her heart. Esther had been tempted to ask what was wrong but figured if Mom wanted to talk about it, she would. Besides, they'd been busy with customers all morning.

"How long does Dad plan to be in Hopkinsville today?" Esther asked as she reached for a tablet and pen to start a list of supplies they needed for the store.

"Just long enough to run a few errands." Mom's dark brown eyes looked lifeless, as though she hadn't been getting enough sleep, and Esther couldn't help but notice the dark circles beneath her eyes.

The bell above the front door jingled, and Verna Yoder entered the store. "Brr. . ." she said, stepping up to the counter. "It's downright cold out there today. Bet it won't be long until we see some snow."

"I hope not." Mom shook her head. "I'm just not ready for *windere* yet."

"Well, like it or not, Dinah, winter's on the way. I can feel it in my bones." Verna rubbed her hands briskly over her arms, hidden beneath her black woolen shawl.

"Have you heard anything from Suzanne since she and Titus left for Pennsylvania?" Esther asked, curious to know when her best friend might be coming home.

Verna gave a nod. "She called when they first got there, and then I discovered another message from her this afternoon."

"How are things going for Samuel and his family?" Mom asked.

"Not so well," Verna replied. "Suzanne said Samuel's taking his wife's death pretty hard, which of course is to be expected. The poor man didn't even want to talk to most of the folks who'd come to the house after Elsie's funeral. Suzanne said Titus was going to suggest that Samuel and his kinner move here."

"What? After just losing his fraa?" Mom clicked her tongue noisily. "I'm surprised Titus would even suggest such a thing."

"I'm sure he meant well," Esther was quick to say. "He probably thought it would be good for Samuel to get a new start—go someplace where there aren't so many painful memories." Esther didn't know why she felt the need to defend Titus. It wasn't like he was her boyfriend or anything. The short time they'd courted after Titus had first moved to Kentucky hadn't amounted to anything more than friendship. Now he planned to marry Suzanne, which made Esther happy, because she knew Suzanne and Titus were very much in love and seemed well-suited for each other.

"I think it might be good for Titus's brother to move to Kentucky," Verna said. "Look how well Titus has done here. Everyone can see how happy he and my daughter are when they're together."

"You do have a point," Mom said. "Guess we'll just have to see whether Samuel accepts Titus's invitation, and if he does, only time will tell how well it will go."

Verna smiled. "Well, I'd best get what I came here for." She turned and headed down the aisle where the cleaning supplies were kept.

Sometime later after Verna had left the store, Mom turned to Esther and said, "There's something I need to tell you."

"What is it?" Esther questioned.

"I spoke with Dan's wife this morning." Deep wrinkles formed across Mom's forehead. "Dan and Sarah have put off telling us for as long as they could, but she admitted to me that your brother's been having some health problems lately, and after numerous tests, they've learned that the reason for his unusual symptoms is because he has multiple sclerosis."

Esther gasped. "That's *baremlich*!"

"I agree. In some cases it can be a terrible thing, and from what I understand, the symptoms are often quite different for most people. Because Dan is so fatigued and suffering from such a loss of balance, he won't be able to keep his stands going at the two farmer's markets in Lancaster County." Mom drew in a quick breath. "So after talking with your *daed* about this, we've decided to sell the store and move to Strasburg so we can help out."

Esther's mouth dropped open. "After all these years of living here, you're moving back to Pennsylvania?"

Mom nodded. "Dan and Sarah need our help, and since we've had experience running our store, we ought to be able to handle the stands Dan has at Green Dragon and Root's Farmer's Market. Being in Pennsylvania will also put us closer to your brother James and his family, since their home in Lykens is only a few hours from Dan's."

Esther leaned heavily against the counter, feeling the need for support. It was bad enough that her older brother was ill, but if Mom and Dad sold the store and moved back to Pennsylvania, would they expect her to go with them?

Chapter 2

As Esther began washing the breakfast dishes, she glanced at the calendar on the wall to her right. It didn't seem possible, but Thanksgiving was over and Christmas was less than a month away.

It will be a difficult Christmas for our family this year, she thought. *For Dan and Sarah because Dan's health is failing; for Mom, Dad, and me because we're all worried about Dan and because giving up the store will be hard for my folks; and for me, too, since I'll no longer have a job.*

Tears welled in Esther's eyes and dribbled onto her cheeks. She'd never been one to give in to self-pity, but then she'd never felt so burdened.

A knock on the back door brought Esther's thoughts to a halt. When she opened it, she was pleased to see her friend Suzanne Yoder.

"Brr. . . It's sure cold this morning," Suzanne said as she stepped into the house and removed her black outer bonnet.

"I think winter's on its way." Esther led the way to the

warm and cozy kitchen.

"Maybe we'll have a white Christmas." Suzanne's blue eyes twinkled, and a wisp of her pretty auburn hair peeked out from under her white head covering. It was in sharp contrast to Esther's dark hair.

Esther handed Suzanne a cup of tea. "Maybe this will warm you up."

"*Danki*." Suzanne set the cup on the table, removed her black woolen shawl, and took a seat. "I haven't talked to you for a while. How are things going?"

"Not so well. Mom talked to my sister-in-law Sarah last week, and we learned that Dan has MS. Due to his loss of balance and extreme fatigue, he's not able to work like he did before, so my folks are planning to move to Strasburg to help out."

Suzanne's eyebrows furrowed. "I'm sorry to hear that—sorry about Dan, and sorry to hear that you'll be moving."

Esther shook her head. "I'm not going with them."

"They're leaving you to run the store by yourself?"

"No, they're selling it to Aaron and Nettie Martin, the Mennonite couple who moved here last month. I'll be staying here at the house, but I'll have to find some other job to support myself."

"Are your folks okay with that? I would think they'd want you to move with them."

"They do want that, but when I explained that I want to stay here with my friends in the place I love, they finally agreed." Esther sighed. "Now I just need to find a job."

Suzanne took a sip of tea. "Maybe Ethan Zook will marry you, and then you won't have to worry about finding a job."

Esther's eyebrows shot up. "Ethan Zook? Why would you think he'd be interested in marrying me?"

"You're a good cook, and he likes to eat, so—"

Esther held up her hand. "I'm not the least bit interested in Ethan, and I doubt he sees me as anything more than a friend."

"Let him taste some of your delicious boyfriend cookies, and I bet he'll be down on his knees, proposing marriage."

Esther giggled. "You're such a kidder."

"I'm glad you're staying. I'd miss you terribly if you moved away." Suzanne gave Esther a hug. "I'll keep my ears open about any jobs in the area, and of course I'll be praying."

"I appreciate that."

They sat quietly for a while, sipping their tea and nibbling on some banana bread Esther had made the night before. It was good to sit and be quiet with her friend. They'd always been there for each other, in good times and bad.

"What's new in your life?" Esther asked after they'd finished their refreshments. "Have you and Titus made any definite plans for the future?"

Suzanne's cheeks flushed as she gave a slow nod. "We've only told our immediate families so far, but we're planning to be married next fall."

"That's real good news. You two are perfect for each other, and I'm sure you'll have many happy years as husband and wife."

"I hope so. As you well know, our relationship got off to a rocky start when Titus first moved to Kentucky."

"That was only because you reminded him of his ex-girlfriend."

Suzanne nodded. "When Phoebe came here and tried to win Titus back, I thought I'd lost him forever."

"But he chose you over her, and soon he'll be your husband."

"*Jah.* I can hardly wait."

"Will you continue to work at the woodshop with Titus

and Nelson after you're married?" Esther asked.

"We haven't discussed it, but I hope so. I love working with wood, and I'd miss being in the shop."

"You and Titus will work things out. Will he be going home to Pennsylvania for Christmas?" Esther asked.

Suzanne shook her head. "We're very busy in the woodshop right now, and since it's only been a few weeks since we were there for his sister-in-law's funeral, Titus will be staying here for Christmas."

Esther smiled. "I'm sure you don't mind that he'll be staying."

"I am looking forward to having Titus over to our house for Christmas, but I know his family will miss him." Suzanne sighed. "I'm sure he'd like to be there for his brother, because from what Titus has told me, Samuel's still going through a really hard time."

"That's understandable."

"Titus is concerned because Samuel won't answer any of his phone calls. He knows from talking with his folks that Samuel's extremely depressed."

"I've never lost anyone that close to me, but I'm sure it's going to take some time," Esther said, wondering if she'd be able to cope with something as painful as losing a loved one. She thought about Dan and hoped he wouldn't lose his battle with MS.

"It was terribly hard on Mom and the rest of the family when my daed died," Suzanne said. "And when we lost Grandma, that was very difficult, too."

Esther wished no one ever had to die, but she knew that dying was a part of living, and for a Christian who had accepted Christ as their Savior, death meant leaving this world and spending an eternity in the presence of the Lord. She prayed that when the time came, those beliefs would give her strength and carry her through the days when she would need it most.

Paradise, Pennsylvania

Samuel moved slowly through the cemetery, weaving in and out among the plots until he came to Elsie's simple headstone. His throat constricted as he knelt on the cold ground beside it.

"Elsie May Fisher," he murmured, reaching out to touch the inscription on the headstone. "Loving wife and mother."

A gust of chilly wind blew, stirring up the dried leaves scattered around and whipping Samuel's straw hat from his head. He shivered and grabbed for it before it spun away. Winter was just around the corner, and soon it would be Christmas.

Hot tears pushed against his eyelids, and he blinked several times in an attempt to force them back. Thanksgiving had gone by in a blur, and Samuel didn't think he could deal with Christmas this year. He couldn't stand the thought of going to the kids' school Christmas program, knowing Elsie wouldn't be with him to watch Marla and Leon say their parts. Samuel felt as if his life had come to a screeching halt the day he'd lost his wife. He knew it was wrong to wish that he was dead, but he couldn't help it because that was still exactly how he felt.

He lifted his gaze to the sky and blinked against the snowflakes that had begun to fall. *Why, God? Why'd You have to take Elsie from us? Don't You know how much the kinner need her? Don't You care that my heart is breaking? How will I get through this? How do I go on?* Over and over, he kept asking the questions, hoping, praying his pleas would be heard.

No response. Nothing but the eerie sound of the wind

whipping through the trees outside the cemetery fence.

He shivered again but knew it had nothing to do with the frosty air that engulfed him. The chill he felt was from his grief—a chill that went all the way to his heart, to the very core of his being.

Feeling the cold all the way to his bones and trembling badly, Samuel finally stood and made his way out of the cemetery. From there, he wandered aimlessly down the road, until he came to his folks' house. Samuel and the kids had been staying with his father and stepmother, Mama Fannie, ever since Elsie died. Samuel couldn't stand being alone in his house, and he couldn't deal with caring for the children. How could he, when he could barely care for himself?

He remembered how the other night, he'd stuck his head into the room Penny and Marla shared and seen them both kneeling on the floor by their bed with their hands folded. They'd obviously been praying. Were they asking God to give them their mother back?

Puh! Now that would take a real miracle, he thought bitterly. But God didn't give people miracles like that anymore. Just Lazarus and God's Son, Jesus—those were the only two people he knew about that had ever been raised from the dead. No, Elsie wasn't coming back, and he and the children somehow had to learn to live with that fact.

The stairs leading to his folks' back porch steps creaked as Samuel plodded slowly up them. When he entered the house, he heard voices coming from the kitchen.

"I'm worried about Samuel," Mama Fannie said. "I know he misses Elsie, but he's grieving so hard he can barely function. If it weren't for the fact that he's staying with us, I doubt he'd eat anything at all."

"I know you're concerned, Fannie, but try not to worry,"

Dad said. "It's going to take some time for Samuel to come to grips with Elsie's death. He'll come around eventually; you'll see."

"I hope so, because losing their mamm has been hard on the kinner, and if their daed remains in such a state much longer, they might think they've lost him, too."

Samuel's boots clomped noisily across the hardwood floor as he stormed into the kitchen. "My kinner are not going to lose me, and I'd appreciate it if you'd stop talking about me behind my back!" These days his guard was always up, feeling defensive about nearly everything. It seemed to be the only way he could protect his emotions and not allow his feelings to control him.

Mama Fannie blinked her dark eyes as she lifted her chin. "We're just concerned about you, son."

"Well, you don't have to be. I'm fine, and so are my kinner. Or at least we will be once we've moved."

"Moved where?" Dad asked, giving his beard, sprinkled generously with gray, a quick tug.

"To Kentucky."

Mama Fannie's eyebrows shot up. "What?"

"I've decided that if I'm ever going to move on with my life I need to get away from here so I can leave all the painful memories behind."

Mama Fannie jumped up and clutched the sleeve of Samuel's jacket. "You're not thinking straight right now. You need to give yourself more time to heal."

"I don't need more time. I need to get away—make a fresh start someplace else."

The wrinkles in Mama Fannie's forehead deepened, and when tears welled in her eyes, she covered her face with her hands. "I can't stand the thought of losing another one of my boys to Kentucky. Please, Samuel, won't you give this more thought?"

Samuel stood there, shaking his head.

"I've been taking care of your kinner since Elsie died, and if you take them to Kentucky, I'll miss them so much. Besides, they don't know anyone there and won't have the support of family and friends."

"They'll know Titus," Dad put in. "I'm sure they'll make friends with others in the community there, too."

"That's right," Samuel agreed. "And don't try to talk me out of it because I've made up my mind." He hated talking so severely to the dear woman who'd become his mother when he was a young boy, but being in the protective shell he'd put himself in, he couldn't let his shield of defenses down—not to anyone—not even his family.

Mama Fannie lifted her face and sniffed deeply. "Wh–when do you plan to leave?"

"We'll head for Kentucky after the first of the year. In the meantime, I'll get in touch with Titus and let him know we're coming. Hopefully, he or his contractor friend, Allen Walters, will be able to help me find a job."

"Shouldn't you at least wait until spring?" Mama Fannie persisted. "Traveling in the dead of winter could be dangerous. Besides, I've heard it said that when someone loses a mate they shouldn't make any major changes for at least six months. And in my opinion, it would be better to wait a whole year," she added with a decisive nod.

Making no further comment on the subject, Samuel moved quickly toward the door.

"Where are you going?" Mama Fannie called.

"Out to the phone shanty to call Titus." Samuel hurried away before she could say anything more, and at the same time, feeling terrible that he'd spoken so sternly to his folks.

Chapter 3

I still wish you weren't going," Mama Fannie said as Samuel and his children sat at the kitchen table having breakfast on the second day of January. "I wish you'd reconsider and stay here with your family."

Samuel's jaw clenched so tightly that his teeth hurt. Mama Fannie's constant badgering about moving to Kentucky was beginning to get on his nerves. Didn't she understand that he needed to get away? All his sisters and brothers and their families had come for supper last night so they could say good-bye. They'd shed lots of tears, but at least none of them had given him a hard time about moving.

"Samuel, did you hear what I said?" Mama Fannie reached over and touched his arm.

"Jah, I heard, but I'm not going to change my mind, so you may as well stop badgering me about it."

"Samuel's right," Dad said before she could respond. "He's a grown man, and he has every right to do what he feels is best for him and his children."

Mama Fannie looked up at Samuel and scrunched her nose. "How can moving to Kentucky be best for any of you? How can leaving your family here and moving two states away be a good thing?"

"Because I say it is!" It was so easy to say; he only hoped he could convince himself to believe it. This decision hadn't come easy, but he didn't know what else to do. He couldn't stand to stay here anymore—couldn't deal with anything that reminded him of Elsie.

"*Daadi*, please don't yell at Grandma." Marla began to cry, and then the younger ones, Leon, Penny, and Jared, followed suit.

Samuel felt like covering his ears. "*Es dutt mie leed*—I am sorry," he mumbled, looking first at Mama Fannie and then his children. "Now hurry up and eat your breakfast, kids, because our driver will be here soon."

"Grandma, will you and Grandpa come visit us in Kentucky?" Marla asked, swiping at the tears trickling down her cheeks.

"Of course we will," Dad was quick to say. "Maybe in the spring when the weather's better. And for sure when Titus and Suzanne are married in the fall."

Mama Fannie smiled, although there was no sparkle in her eyes. "I'm sure you'll be coming back here for visits, too."

"Can we come back to Pennsylvania for my birthday?" Marla asked, looking at Samuel with a hopeful expression.

He shook his head. "Your birthday's next month. That's too soon for us to be goin' anywhere."

"How come?"

"Because the weather will be bad, and hopefully I'll be busy working."

"The weather's bad now," Mama Fannie reminded. "And

you don't even have a job yet."

Samuel's defenses rose once again. "I'll find something to do; you'll see."

"Since Zach's friend Allen is a general contractor, I'll bet he can find you some painting jobs," Dad said.

"Puh!" Mama Fannie dismissed the idea. "Who's going to want their house painted in the dead of winter?"

"Some folks want the inside of their houses painted," Samuel said. "Besides, we won't have many expenses because we'll be staying with Titus—at least until my house here sells and I can find a place there to buy or rent."

"At the very least, I'm sure you can find some odd jobs to do. You've always been pretty handy with things." Dad thumped Samuel's back.

A horn honked outside, and Samuel jumped up and rushed to the window. "Our driver's here. Get your coats on kids, and then say good-bye to your *grossdaadi* and *grossmudder* so we can head out."

Marla started to cry again, and so did the others, including Mama Fannie, whose sobs were the loudest of all.

Unable to deal with any of it, Samuel grabbed his jacket from the back of the chair and hurried out the door. He figured Dad would get Mama Fannie and the kids under control, and then they could get on the road. For many reasons, he was unyielding in his decision to move to Kentucky. The most crucial, though, was for his children. He was sure he could be a better father to them there—where he wouldn't be thinking of Elsie all the time.

He paused a moment to look out across the land—a land he and Elsie had lovingly tended together. Like the hawk perched high on a branch overlooking the field, Samuel felt very much alone.

the Healing

Pembroke, Kentucky

"Look at that." Esther pointed out the kitchen window. "Isn't that a sight to behold?"

"What is it?" Mom asked, while sponging off the table.

"Five does are in the yard, and they're playing in the snow like a bunch of frisky puppies."

Mom dropped the sponge and stepped up to the window beside Esther. "*Ach!* They're so cute!"

Esther smiled as she watched the deer kicking up their feet, looking like young fillies that had just found their legs.

"If you're done washing the dishes now, would you mind going to the store for me?" Mom asked. "I've made a list, and I need several things."

"Which store?" Esther asked. "The one we used to own or one of the stores in Hopkinsville?"

"Oh no, I don't expect you to hire a driver and go clear into town. The things I need can be bought at our old store."

"Okay." Esther turned away from the window, reluctant to leave behind the peaceful feeling she felt whenever she watched nature's antics. Those moments were cherished, and time seemed to stand still when she gazed out at the beautiful scenery surrounding them. She never forgot how truly blessed she was to have entertainment like that right outside their door. If only the distraction could delay her trip to the family business she'd grown to love. Truth was, she dreaded the thought of stepping into their old store and seeing someone else running it almost as much as she dreaded Mom and Dad leaving for Pennsylvania tomorrow morning. But now that the store was under new ownership, there was no reason for them to stay, because Dan's condition was worsening, and he needed them more than ever.

"Here's my list." Mom handed a piece of paper to Esther. "Take your time getting there. With all the snow on the ground, the roads might be slippery, so you'll need to be careful."

"I will." Esther slipped into her woolen jacket, put her black outer bonnet on her head, and went out the door. She figured Mom would probably worry about her even more after they moved and she was living on her own here at the house. But she'd be fine; she'd show herself, as well as them, how well she could manage on her own.

Esther stepped onto the porch and paused to watch the deer that had now moved out into the pasture. Grazing on what corn they could find after the harvest, they looked in her direction, watchful, yet undisturbed, as she made her way to the barn to harness her horse, Ginger.

When Esther pulled her horse and buggy up to the store's hitching rail sometime later, more than a few negative thoughts raced through her head. What if the new owners weren't as friendly to the people in their community as Mom and Dad had been? What if they decided to raise their prices and people couldn't afford to shop there anymore? What if they didn't keep the store adequately stocked, the way Mom and Dad had always done?

Shaking her disturbing thoughts aside, Esther entered the store, but when she saw Aaron and Nettie Martin behind the front counter, while their two oldest daughters, Roseanna and Lucinda, kept busy stocking shelves, she almost felt sick. It didn't seem right that someone else was running the store where she and her folks had worked so many years. It didn't seem right that one of her brothers was having severe health problems either.

Esther gave herself a mental pep talk. Her folks' help was needed—not only at Dan's place, but also at his two stands, where he sold soft pretzels, popcorn, and homemade candy. And for Esther. . . Well, she'd been working at the store most of her young adult life, so maybe it was time for a change. Now if she could only find a job that paid well and was something she truly enjoyed.

Esther had just gone down the aisle were the vitamins were kept when she noticed Titus Fisher come into the store.

"I figured you'd be hard at work in the woodshop by now," she said as he approached her.

"I'm heading in that direction but wanted to come by here first and pick up a few things. My brother Samuel and his kinner are moving here and should arrive within the next day or so. Of course, that all depends on how well the weather cooperates," he added. "If they have to deal with lots of icy roads, it could slow them down—especially the trailer that's hauling Samuel's horse, not to mention the truck with the buggy and other things in it," he added.

"When I last spoke with Suzanne, she said Samuel might be moving here, but I didn't think he'd be coming so soon," Esther said. "Why doesn't he wait until spring when the weather is better?"

"I think he's anxious to leave Pennsylvania and the painful memories of losing his wife."

"I guess that's understandable, but what will he do for a job?"

"Samuel's a good painter, and he also has some carpentry skills, so until he can find some paint jobs, he may be helping Nelson, me, and Suzanne in the woodshop. As soon as we have enough work for another person, that is."

"I see. Where will he and his kinner stay?" she asked.

"With me for now. . .until Samuel's able to either buy or build a place of his own. He's put his home in Pennsylvania up for sale, but until it sells he won't be able to afford to buy another place here."

"It's a good thing you have that nice double-wide manufactured home now, because there certainly wouldn't have been room for all of them in the dingy old trailer you used to rent from Allen."

"That's for sure. That place was so small there was barely room for me, let alone a family of five." Titus smiled. "Hopefully by the time Suzanne and I are married, Samuel will have his own place, but if he doesn't, then I guess we'll just have to make do."

Esther didn't say anything, but she wondered how everything would work out. Having Samuel and his kids living there could affect Titus and Suzanne's relationship—especially if Samuel's family wasn't able to move out before Titus and Suzanne got married.

Guess it's not my concern, Esther told herself as she looked over Mom's list and continued the shopping. *I'd better just concentrate on my own problems right now.*

CHAPTER 4

Portland, Oregon

Bonnie Taylor sat at her kitchen table, staring at the telephone. She'd just had a call from a lawyer in Hopkinsville, Kentucky, letting her know that her grandmother had died and left everything to her—including the old house that had been sitting empty since Grandma had gone to a nursing home several months ago.

Neither Bonnie nor her widowed father had gone to Kentucky to see Grandma after she'd gone to the nursing home. Bonnie's excuse was that she'd been working long hours for an advertising agency in Portland and couldn't get away. Dad had no excuse at all, other than the grudge he'd held against his folks ever since Bonnie could remember, which was why the few trips they'd made as a family to Kentucky while Mom was still alive had been brief. Bonnie was sure Dad had only agreed to go to make Mom happy, because she'd often said it was important for Bonnie, their only child, to get to know her grandparents on her father's side. Bonnie had never understood what the problem between Dad and his folks was about. She'd broached the subject with him once and had been told that it was none of her business and not to bring it up again.

Tears welled in Bonnie's eyes. At Mom's insistence, and despite Dad's disapproval, Bonnie had spent a week with Grandpa and Grandma almost every summer until Mom had died of a brain tumor shortly after Bonnie turned thirteen. Grandma and Grandpa had always been kind, and she'd enjoyed being with them. They'd taken her to church, where she'd learned about God, but she'd never mentioned it to Dad because after Mom died he'd become bitter and wouldn't let Bonnie visit his parents anymore. When Grandma sent Bonnie a Bible for her birthday that year, Dad threw it out and shouted some things Bonnie didn't care to repeat. Life had been terrible for Bonnie after that, and then two years before she'd graduated from high school, she'd made the biggest mistake of her life. But that was in the past, and she wouldn't allow herself to think about it right now.

Once Bonnie got her diploma and realized that she needed a fresh start, she'd taken some classes at the community college in Portland. When she landed the job at the advertising agency where she presently worked, she'd moved out on her own. Soon after that, she'd begun attending a church near her apartment, but she'd never taken an active part in any of the activities the church offered for people her age. Instead of socializing, she'd immersed herself in her job. It was better that way, she'd decided.

Bonnie's mind snapped back to the issue at hand. Grandma was dead, and she really needed to go to Kentucky—not only to attend Grandma's funeral, but also to sort through her things and decide what to do with them. Then there was the house; it would need to be sold.

Bonnie had some vacation time coming, so she'd use that to go to Kentucky for Grandma's funeral and then get the house put on the market. Hopefully, Dad would set whatever problems he'd had with his parents aside and go with her.

Paradise, Pennsylvania

Fannie entered the store her husband had given to his daughter Naomi and her husband, Caleb, several years ago.

"It's good to see you," Naomi said. "You must need something badly to have braved the cold weather and icy roads today."

"The roads weren't so bad, and I do need a few things," Fannie said. "However, the main reason I came by was to see if you've heard anything from Samuel."

Naomi shook her head. "Have you, Mama Fannie?"

"No, and I'm getting worried. It's been two whole days since they left, and I would think they'd have gotten there by now."

"If the roads between here and Kentucky are icy, then they've probably gone slow." Naomi smiled, although her ebony-colored eyes showed a bit of concern. "I'm sure we'll hear something soon."

"I hope so." Fannie leaned on the counter. "How are things with you and your family? Is everyone doing okay?"

"With the exception of Caleb, everyone's fine," Naomi said.

"What's wrong with him?"

"He has a really bad cold, and last night when he coughed and bent over at the same time, his back spasmed." Naomi winced, as though she could almost feel her husband's pain.

"He's hurting real bad so he stayed home to rest today."

"Has he been to see the chiropractor?"

"No. Said he figured it would get better on its own in a few days."

Fannie grunted. "Men. They can be so *schtarrkeppich* sometimes."

"That's for sure, and my husband is probably the most stubborn man of all."

The door jingled, and Timothy's wife, Hannah, entered the store with her pretty little blond-haired daughter, Mindy, who was two. Since Hannah's hair was brown, and so was Timothy's, Mindy took after Hannah's mother, whose nearly gray hair had originally been blond.

"*Wie geht's?*" Fannie asked.

"We're fine," Hannah replied. "How are you doing?"

"I'd be better if I'd hear something from Samuel."

Hannah rolled her eyes. "I still can't believe he moved to Kentucky. First Titus, and now Samuel. I sure hope Timothy doesn't get any ideas about moving there."

"That would be baremlich," Fannie said. "I don't think I could stand losing three of my boys and their families to Kentucky."

"I think you're worried for nothing," Naomi put in. "I'm sure Timothy has no plans to move."

Hannah wrinkled her nose. "He'd better not because I like it here in Pennsylvania, and I'd never agree to move to Kentucky."

Fannie was certainly relieved to hear that. "Think I'll say hello to Abby while I'm here," she said, moving toward the back of the store where the quilt shop was located. "Is she working today?"

"Jah," Naomi said. "She came in early this morning."

Fannie said good-bye to Hannah and hurried into the adjoining room, anxious to visit a few minutes with her daughter.

Pembroke, Kentucky

"According to the directions your brother sent us, we must be close to his place now," Samuel's driver, Stan Haman, said as he turned his van onto Pembroke Road.

"It's right here." Samuel motioned to his right where he saw a mailbox with Titus's name and address on it. "We finally made it," he said, turning in his seat to look at the kids.

The children stared wide eyed out the window.

When they pulled into the driveway covered with several inches of snow, a double-wide manufactured home came into view.

Stan had no sooner stopped the van, when Titus came out of the house, waving and smiling from ear to ear.

Samuel hopped out of the van and met Titus in the yard. After the long drive from Pennsylvania, it felt good to stretch his legs.

"It's great seeing you." Titus gave Samuel a hug. "Did you have a good trip?"

"It was slow because of the snow, and the kinner were fussy," Samuel said, "but we made it safely at least."

Titus opened the back door of the van, and the children scrambled out, squealing and running around in the snow. Their black Lab, Lucky, followed, barking and bounding at their heels.

"Guess I'd better get my horse, Socks, out of the trailer," Samuel said, shaking out more kinks in his legs as he walked to the back of the van where the trailer was hitched. "Do you have an empty stall for him in your barn?"

Titus nodded. "There's plenty of room, and I'm sure my horse, Lightning, will be glad for the company."

Sometime later, when everything had been unloaded and Samuel's driver had gone, Titus escorted everyone into the house and showed them around.

"I only have three bedrooms here," he said, "so the boys will have to share a room with you, and the girls can have the third bedroom."

"Guess that's how it'll have to be then," Samuel said as they walked down the narrow hall and looked into each room. He hoped it wouldn't be long before he could get a place of their own, but by living here, they'd not only have a roof over their heads, but he'd have Titus's help with the kids—at least in the evenings when Titus wasn't working. The question was who would watch them during the day once Samuel found a job?

Guess there's a lot of things I didn't think about before I decided to move, he thought as he watched the children play with two cats they'd discovered in the barn and brought into the house. *Sure hope I didn't make a mistake by coming here. Maybe I should have prayed about the move. But then, God doesn't seem to be listening to me lately, so what would have been the use?*

Samuel knew he shouldn't let his thoughts go in that direction. They were here now, and as time went on, hopefully things would start falling into place. He'd just need to give it some time.

Chapter 5

"Have you called Mom and Dad yet?" Titus asked Samuel as they sat at the table, drinking coffee while the kids took the cats back to the barn.

"I suppose I should do that now. If I don't call them soon, Mama Fannie will probably leave a string of messages on your voice mail."

"She already has." Titus smiled. "You know how Mom tends to worry. Nearly hounded me to death when I first moved to Kentucky."

Samuel grunted as he forced himself to stand. He was bone-tired despite the fact that he hadn't done much all day other than to haul their things into the house and put his horse in the barn. He hadn't brought any of his household items or furniture along because he knew he wouldn't have a place to put them right now. Besides, when he'd put his house up for sale, he'd advertised it as fully furnished. He didn't want any of the furniture he and Elsie had chosen when they'd first gotten married. It would just be one more reminder that she was gone. So all he'd brought to Kentucky were his and the kids' clothes, some of his tools, his horse and buggy, a box of toys for the kids, their troublesome dog, and a few personal things that had belonged to Elsie. He'd asked his sister Mary Ann to put Elsie's things in a box because he hadn't had the strength or the courage to sort through them. He knew he'd have to do it at some point, but not yet. Right now, he wasn't even able to look at Elsie's things.

"You okay?" Titus asked, bringing Samuel's thoughts to a halt.

"Jah, sure. Why do you ask?"

"You said you were going out to the phone shanty to call Mom and Dad, but you've been standing there several minutes now, staring at the door."

"I was thinking," Samuel mumbled.

"About what you're gonna say to Mom and Dad?"

Samuel shook his head. "That's easy enough. I'm just going to tell 'em we got here okay. I was thinking about other things." He hurried out the door before Titus had a chance to question him further. He didn't want to talk about his feelings, and he hoped Titus wouldn't pry. He wanted the chance to start over and needed to concentrate on finding a way to earn a decent living so he could provide for his kids, because he wasn't about to let Titus support them very long.

Samuel stepped behind the barn to the phone shanty Titus had shown him earlier. After he'd made a call to his folks and left a message, he dialed his brother Zach's cell phone.

"Hey, Zach, it's me, Samuel," he said, when Zach's voice mail came on. "Just wanted you to know that we made it to Titus's okay. Talk to you soon."

Samuel hung up the phone and trudged back through the slippery, wet snow toward the house. He was sort of glad he merely had to leave a message for his parents and brother.

Right now, holding a conversation and answering a lot of questions would have drained him even more.

He'd only made it halfway there, when the two cats the kids had been playing with earlier darted out of the barn, followed by Lucky, who was hot on their heels. Hissing and meowing, the cats ran up the nearest tree. Lucky slid across the snow after them, bounced against the tree, and toppled over. He didn't stay down long though. He leaped to his feet and started barking frantically as he pawed at the trunk of the tree.

Samuel's son, Leon, dashed across the yard hollering at the dog, "*Kumme*, Lucky!" He slapped the side of his leg a couple of times. "Come to me now!"

The dog kept barking as he crouched in front of the tree, looking up at the cats huddled together on a branch high above.

"I was gonna play with the *katze* till Lucky came along and scared the life outa 'em," Leon grumbled.

Samuel bent down and grabbed Lucky's collar, but the dog growled and bared his teeth.

"Knock it off!" Samuel shouted. "You know better than that. Now come with me, you *dummkopp hund*."

"Lucky ain't stupid, Daadi. He's a very *schmaert* dog," Leon said, lifting his chin to look up at Samuel.

"He's not too smart when he doesn't do what he's told." Samuel pulled Lucky to his feet and continued slipping and sliding in the direction of the barn. He was almost there, when a horse and buggy rolled into the yard. He recognized Suzanne when she climbed down from the buggy, but he didn't know the young, dark-haired woman with her.

When Esther stepped out of Suzanne's buggy, she noticed a tall Amish man with light brown hair peeking out from under his dark blue stocking cap. He held onto the collar of a black Lab, thrashing about, kicking up snow with its back feet.

"That's Titus's brother, Samuel," Suzanne said to Esther. "I'd introduce you, but he seems a little busy right now."

Obviously struggling to gain control over the dog, Samuel leaned to the right, then to the left. With a sudden jerk, the dog pulled free, and Samuel fell, facedown in the snow. He came up, red-faced and hollering, "You dummkopp hund! I should have left you in Pennsylvania to fend for yourself!"

It was a comical sight, and Esther struggled not to laugh. She could tell by the way Suzanne's face was contorted that she thought it was funny, too.

The young boy with sandy brown hair who stood nearby wasn't laughing. He looked up at Samuel and said in a pathetic little voice, "Daadi, please don't yell at Lucky. He just wants to be free to run."

"Well, he's not gonna be free. I'm puttin' him away in the barn so he can't terrorize those cats anymore!"

"Don't think he means to hurt the katze," the child said. "Think he just wants to play with 'em."

Ignoring the boy's comment, Samuel chased after the dog, grabbed hold of its collar, and pulled the struggling animal to the barn.

Feeling the need to comfort the boy, who appeared to be on the verge of tears, Esther knelt in the snow beside him. "My name's Esther. What's yours?"

"Leon." The child dropped his gaze to the ground. Was he shy or just upset about the dog and not wanting to let on?

"How old are you, Leon?" Esther asked.

"Six. I'm in the first grade at school."

"Is Lucky your dog?"

Leon lifted his head and looked right at Esther. "Nope.

He liked our mamm the best, but after she went to heaven, he started hangin' around my daed." Tears welled in Leon's brown eyes, and he sniffed a couple of times. " 'Course Daadi don't like Lucky much. He don't like much of anything since *Mammi* died."

Esther's heart went out to the boy. She was sure that he wasn't just upset about the dog. He missed his mother and didn't understand the reason for his dad's behavior.

A few minutes later, Samuel reappeared—without the dog.

"It's good to see you, Samuel," Suzanne said, shaking his hand. "How was your trip?"

"It went okay."

Suzanne motioned to Esther. "This is my friend Esther Beiler. We were on our way to the bakery but decided to stop here first and see if Titus wanted us to pick something up for him."

Samuel barely glanced at Esther. Then with a quick, "Nice to meet you," he tromped off toward the house.

"Maybe we picked a bad time to come," Esther whispered to Suzanne.

Suzanne shrugged. "We're here now, and I want to see Titus, so let's go inside." She looked down at Leon and held out her hand. "You'd better come with us. It's too cold to be out here in the snow."

When they stepped into the living room, Esther was surprised to see Titus sitting on the couch with two young girls, one with blond hair and one with brown hair, on either side of him. In his lap he held a small, blond-haired boy wearing diapers and a white T-shirt. Titus looked perfectly comfortable with the children.

He'll make a good father someday, Esther thought, *and Suzanne will be a good mother.*

"Did anything unusual happen outside?" Titus asked, looking at Suzanne. "When Samuel came in a few minutes ago, covered in snow, he tromped off to his room like he was really upset."

Suzanne explained what had transpired with the dog and went on to say how angry Samuel had gotten.

"My *bruder's* going through a rough time right now, so we'll need to be patient with him," Titus said.

Suzanne touched Leon's shoulder as she nodded at the three children sitting with Titus. "We need to help his kinner adjust to their new surroundings, too."

"Jah." Titus looked at Esther. "Would you like to meet my nieces and nephews?"

She smiled. "I met Leon outside, but of course I'd like to meet his brother and sisters, too."

"This is Marla." Titus motioned to the girl on his left. "She's eight years old, and here on my right is Penny. She's four. Now this little guy here is Jared, and he's two," he said, placing his hand on the boy's blond head.

Esther knelt on the floor in front of the couch, smiling up at the children. "*Mei naame* is Esther."

The children nodded as they stared at her with curious expressions.

Esther stayed like that for several seconds then rose to her feet. Samuel's children were obviously not comfortable around her yet. She'd always loved children and hoped she'd have the chance to get to know these four in the days ahead. But for now, not wanting to overwhelm them, the simple introduction would suffice.

Chapter 6

During Bonnie's first two days in Kentucky, she'd stayed at a hotel in Hopkinsville. The first day she had attended her grandmother's funeral—alone, without her father because he'd refused to come here for his own mother's funeral. The service had been held at the small church in Fairview where Grandma and Grandpa had attended. There wasn't a large crowd, since many of Grandma and Grandpa's friends were old and had passed on, but the people who had come seemed nice and offered Bonnie their heartfelt sympathies at her grandmother's passing.

The second day, Bonnie had met with Grandma's lawyer, Michael Givens, to go over the will and some other important papers. She still couldn't believe Grandma had left her the house, as well as all her money. It really should have gone to Dad, but when she'd called him the other day, he'd said he wanted nothing that was his folks, including their money—nothing at all. Mr. Givens had reminded Bonnie that since her father was Grandma and Grandpa's only child and was estranged from his parents, she should accept what had been left to her and be grateful.

This morning, Bonnie had driven out to her grandparents' home in the small town of Pembroke, where she'd been going through cupboards and closets and putting some things in boxes. It was a monumental job, but if she was going to get the place ready to sell, it had to be done. It was difficult sorting through these things—especially Grandma's, as she'd been the last one living in this cozy old house. In the dresser drawers, Bonnie had found an abundance of cotton hankies with lace edges, several sweaters and slippers Grandma had obviously knitted, two flannel nightgowns, and some of Grandma's lingerie.

As Bonnie sat on the edge of the bed in Grandma's room, which was on the main floor of the rambling old house, her fingers trailed over a pair of light blue knitted slippers. Grandma had taught her how to knit during a summer visit when Bonnie was twelve. She'd also helped Bonnie sew an apron, which she'd worn when she helped Grandma bake some cookies. Those were happy memories, and Bonnie wished she could relive them.

The rumble of a vehicle interrupted Bonnie's musings. She went to the window facing the front yard and looked out. A dark blue truck was parked in the driveway, next to the small red car she'd rented when she'd flown into Nashville. A young man with dark curly hair stepped out and trudged through the snow up to the house.

Bonnie left the room and hurried to the door before he had a chance to knock.

"Hi. I'm Allen Walters," the man said. "I was driving by and noticed a car parked in the driveway so I decided to stop."

Bonnie tensed and folded her arms. "If you're selling

something, I'm really not interested."

He shook his head. "I'm not a salesman. I'm a general contractor, and I understand that the woman who used to live here passed away recently, so I was wondering if the place might be up for sale."

Bonnie relaxed a bit. She might be able to sell the place quicker than she'd thought. She smiled and extended her hand. "I'm Bonnie Taylor, and this house belonged to my grandparents, Andy and Margaret Taylor. I live in Portland, Oregon, but when I found out that Grandma had died, I came here for the funeral. Today I've been going through her things, trying to decide what I should get rid of and what I might want to keep."

"Did your grandmother leave the house to you?" he questioned.

Bonnie nodded.

"Are you going to sell it?"

"That's the plan." She hugged her arms around her chest, feeling the cold air penetrate her skin. "So if you bought the house, would it be for you?"

He shook his head. "I already have a house in Hopkinsville. However, I'm still interested in buying this place."

"How come?"

"I often buy homes that need fixing up. Then after I renovate them, I turn around and sell them again."

"In other words, you make a profit?"

Allen nodded, reached into his jacket pocket, and handed Bonnie his business card. "Give me a call once you've decided how much you want for the place."

"Okay."

As Allen walked away and Bonnie shut the door, a feeling of nostalgia washed over her. She didn't know why, but she was suddenly having second thoughts about selling the house. But if she didn't put Grandma and Grandpa's place on the market, what would she do with it?

She moved toward the fireplace to warm up and took a seat on the floor near the hearth. Looking about, despite the fact that the house was in dire need of repairs, it had a certain appeal and quaint-looking charm. The solid oak cupboards in the kitchen, with matching table and chairs; the spacious dining room with a built-in hutch; a roomy living room with a cozy window bench near the window; a simple, but beautiful, stained-glass window above the front door—this homey place reminded her of a quaint bed-and-breakfast she'd stayed in once along the Oregon coast. She'd been relaxed and comfortable there and hadn't wanted to leave.

I wonder what Grandma would think if I turned her house into a bed-and-breakfast. There are no hotels nearby—the closest ones are in Hopkinsville. If I opened a B&B, it would give folks visiting this area a nice place to stay. Bonnie rubbed her hands together in front of the fire as she contemplated the idea. *But then, if I did that, I'd either have to hire someone to run the place or move here and run it myself.*

She stared at the flames lapping against the logs in the fireplace as she continued to ponder things. *I'm really not that happy living in Oregon anyway, so if I quit my job and moved to Kentucky, it would be a new beginning for me. I have fond memories here, and it would certainly be an adventure.*

—~—

Samuel flopped onto the sofa in Titus's living room with a groan. He hadn't slept well last night, and it had been all he could do to hitch his horse to the buggy this morning and take Marla and Leon to school. As soon as he'd dropped them off, he'd come right back, prepared to spend the day resting. He knew he couldn't lounge around forever though. Once he found someone who'd be willing to watch his kids, he'd look for a job.

"Can Jared and me go outside and play?" Penny asked, tugging on Samuel's shirtsleeve.

Samuel shook his head. "You can play in here."

She thrust out her bottom lip in a pout. "We wanna play in the *schnee*."

"I said no. It's cold outside, and you don't need to play in the snow."

"But there's nothin' to do in here. Uncle Titus don't have no toys for kids to play with."

"The toys we brought with us when we moved are in one of the boxes in my room." Samuel rose from his seat. "Let's go see."

Samuel headed for the bedroom, with Penny and Jared trudging after him. He looked through a couple of boxes that had been stacked along one wall, but the kids' toys weren't in any of them—just their clothes. When he opened another box, his breath caught in his throat. It was full of Elsie's things.

"What's this?" Penny asked, pulling a soft yellow baby blanket from the box. It was one Elsie had made for the baby she'd lost when she'd fallen down the stairs.

Samuel grabbed the blanket from Penny and clutched it to his chest. "It's nothing. Just a blanket, that's all."

She reached out her hand. "Can I have it, Daadi?"

"No!" he said a bit too harshly. Then, gaining control of his emotions, he put the blanket back in the box.

To Samuel's relief, he found another box marked KIDS' TOYS. Picking up the box, he hauled it out to the living room, set it on the floor, and opened the flaps. While the kids played with their toys, he would lie on the sofa and take a nap. Sleeping was the only way he could deal with his pain and escape from the raw emotions that still consumed him every waking moment and even in his dreams.

As Esther headed in her buggy down the road toward Titus's house, she thought about Samuel's children and wondered how they were doing. She'd done some baking this morning and had decided to take a batch of cookies to the kids.

Sometime later, Esther pulled her horse and buggy into Titus's yard and was surprised to see little Penny and Jared rolling around in the snow with only lightweight jackets and no mittens or boots.

"What are you two doing out here in the cold?" Esther asked after she'd tied her horse to the hitching rail.

"We're makin' snow angels," Penny said, standing up and pointing to her latest impression.

Looking around at all the imprints, Esther could see that the children had been quite busy. The urge to plop down and relive that special childhood memory was hard to resist, but right now she wanted to take the cookies inside and speak to Samuel about his two youngest children.

"Where's your daed?" Esther couldn't imagine him letting them play out here by themselves. Especially little Jared, who was hardly more than a baby. What if he'd wandered off?

"Daadi's in there." Penny pointed to the house.

With the container of cookies tucked under one arm, Esther took the children's hands, and they trudged through the snow to the house, where she knocked on the door. When no one answered, she turned the knob and went in. Samuel lay asleep on the sofa. She didn't know whether to wake him or tiptoe to the kitchen and leave the cookies. Before she had the chance to decide, Samuel sat up with a start.

"Wh–what's going on? What are you doing here?" he mumbled, barely looking at her.

"I brought some cookies for your kinner," she explained. "When I got here, I was surprised to see the little ones playing in the snow by themselves, wearing only thin jackets and no boots or mittens."

"What?" He jumped up and glared at his children. "What were you two doing out there? I told you not to go outside!"

Penny and Jared turned red-faced and looked guilty. Crystals of snow slowly melted from their hair.

"Would you two like some peanut butter cookies?" Esther pointed to the container she held. "I made them this morning."

The children's eyes lit right up. "Can we have some *kichlin*?" Penny asked, looking up at her father.

"I should say no, since you disobeyed me and went outside, but if you promise to behave yourselves, you can have some cookies," he said. "Go to your rooms first and take off your jackets and wet shoes before you go to the kitchen."

"Okay."

Penny grabbed her little brother's hand, and they hurried down the hall.

Esther felt a bit awkward, standing there holding the cookies, so she looked at Samuel and said, "Should I put these in the kitchen?"

"Jah, sure," he mumbled without looking at her.

I wonder who'll watch Samuel's kids once he gets a job, Esther thought as she headed to the kitchen. *I hope he's not foolish enough to leave them home by themselves.*

Chapter 7

"Hey, Titus! How's it going?" Allen asked when he stepped into the woodshop where Titus knelt on the floor, sanding a cabinet door.

Titus looked up and smiled. "Pretty good. How are things with you?"

"Not bad." Allen looked at Suzanne's brother, Nelson. "How's business overall? Have you been keeping busy here at the shop, or do you need more outside jobs?"

"We can use all the work we can get right now." Nelson, who was just a few years younger than Suzanne, pushed his red hair off his freckled forehead and frowned. "Things were real busy before Christmas, but they've slowed down a lot since then. Suzanne's not even working here in the shop this week."

"That's too bad. Things have been a little slower for me, too, but hopefully work will pick up in the spring." Allen smiled. "When it does, I'm sure I'll have a lot more jobs for you."

"I hope so." Titus swiped a hand across his sweaty forehead. "With five more people living in my house right now, I need to keep working steady."

"Hasn't Samuel found a job yet?" Allen asked.

Titus shook his head. "He's been here two weeks already, and as far as I know, he hasn't really been looking."

"How come?"

"Says he doesn't have anyone to watch the kids, but I'm sure if he finds a job we can find someone willing to watch them," Titus replied.

"I understand he's done some painting for Zach."

"That's right. He also has some carpentry skills, and we'd hoped to hire him to help out here, but as I said before, we don't have much work right now."

"If I hear of anything, I'll be sure to let him know." Allen turned toward the door. "Guess I'd better get going. I've got several errands I need to run yet today."

Two weeks ago, Bonnie had returned from Portland, where she'd put in her resignation at the advertising agency, told her landlord she was moving, and packed up her things. She'd also told her dad good-bye, which of course, hadn't gone well at all. Even though he'd tried to dissuade her, she'd returned to Kentucky and spent the last few days cleaning and organizing more things in her grandparents' home. Some things she'd tossed out, some had gone to a charity organization in Hopkinsville, and some—like dishes, glassware, and linens—she would put to good use. Even with everything she'd done, there were more closets and cupboards she hadn't gone through—not to mention all the stuff in the attic.

Bonnie had also applied for a business license and taken care of some other necessary paperwork involving opening her new business, but there were still some major repairs that would have to be done to the place before she could even think about advertising or opening for business. She'd also have to hire someone to help at the B&B—cleaning the guest rooms and hopefully helping her prepare the food she would serve for breakfast every morning.

"So much to do," she muttered as she made her way to the kitchen to clean out a few more cupboards. "Sure hope I haven't bitten off more than I can chew."

She found one of Grandma's aprons in the pantry and slipped it on. *Oh Grandma, I miss you and wish I'd come to visit while you were in the nursing home. Were you lonely there? Did you think no one cared?*

Bonnie remembered the day of Grandma's funeral when one of the women who'd attended the service had mentioned that she'd gone to the nursing home to visit Grandma at least once a week. *I'm thankful Grandma's friend was there for her, even though I wish now it had been me. So many regrets. Why do I always look back and wish I could do things differently? Why can't I make wise decisions at the right time, and do things I won't later regret?*

Knowing she couldn't undo the past, Bonnie resolved to keep a positive attitude and stay busy for the rest of the day. She'd just taken a sponge and some cleanser from under the kitchen sink when she heard a vehicle pull into the yard. She peered out the window and noticed a pickup truck parked in the driveway. When a young man with curly dark hair, wearing a baseball cap, got out, she realized it was the same man who'd stopped by two weeks ago, asking about buying the house.

Bonnie slipped into her sweater, hurried to the door, and opened it just as he stepped onto the porch.

"Good morning," he said. "Remember me?"

She nodded. "Allen Walters, right?"

"That's correct." Allen offered her a wide smile, revealing two deep dimples. "I was in the area and thought I'd stop by and see what you've decided about selling this place."

She leaned against the doorjamb. "I've actually decided not to sell."

"Really? I'm surprised. This place is so big, and unless you have a large family then—"

"I'm not married. It'll just be me living here—at least until I get the place ready to open for business."

He tipped his head. "What kind of business?"

"I've decided to turn my grandparents' home into a bed-and-breakfast."

"Are you sure that's a good idea? I mean, this place is old, and from what I can tell, it needs a whole lot of work."

"I realize that, but it's roomy and has lots of charm. Besides, from what I've seen, there aren't a lot of places for visitors to stay in the area unless they go to a hotel in Hopkinsville."

"You do have a point, but bringing this place up to code would involve quite a bit of money and time."

"I quit my job in Oregon, so I have the time. Between what I have in my savings and the money my grandparents left me, I should be able to live comfortably for a while and also pay for any necessary repairs that need to be done." She folded her arms. "Since you're a contractor, would you be interested in doing the work for me?"

"I might be able to do some things, but I couldn't do everything because before I came here this morning I got a call about remodeling a house not far from where I live, and I'll have to start on that right away." Allen gave the brim of his baseball cap a tug. "Come to think of it, I do know someone who's a qualified painter, and he's also done some carpentry work. He's a widowed Amish man with four kids. He's new to the area and needs a job right now. His name is Samuel Fisher, and he's living with his brother whose home is not too far from here."

"That sounds like a good possibility. From what I understand, the Amish are really hard workers."

"You're right about that. Any of them I've ever known do quality work. Would you like me to bring Samuel by so you can talk to him?"

She nodded. "I'd appreciate that very much."

—∞—

Realizing it was time to fix Penny and Jared some lunch, Samuel forced himself to head out to the kitchen, where he fumbled around in the propane-operated refrigerator, searching for something the kids would eat. Penny liked most things, but Jared was picky.

He finally decided on peanut butter and jelly sandwiches, knowing both kids liked that. He'd just gotten the kids seated at the table when a knock sounded on the door.

"I wonder who that could be." Samuel ambled over to the door, and when he opened it, he was surprised to see Allen Walters standing on the porch. He'd met Allen when he'd brought Titus and Suzanne to Pennsylvania for Elsie's funeral, but Samuel hadn't said more than a few words to him. Of course, he'd been so consumed with his grief, he hadn't said much to anyone that day. Even now, he found it hard to make conversation. He just wanted to be left alone.

"Hi, Samuel. How are you doing?" Allen asked as he brushed some fresh-fallen snow off his jacket.

"Gettin' by," Samuel mumbled.

"Any leads on a job yet?"

Samuel shook his head. " 'Course I haven't looked that

hard, since I have no one to watch my kids." He glanced over his shoulder and frowned when he noticed that Jared had a blob of strawberry jam stuck to his chin and some sticky peanut butter on the front of his shirt.

"I was wondering if you'd be interested in doing a remodeling job at a house not far from here. The young woman who lives there is planning to turn the place into a bed-and-breakfast."

Samuel knew he needed a job—he couldn't lie around here forever, sponging off Titus. "I am interested in the job," he said, "but as I said, I'll need to find someone to watch my kids while I'm at work."

"I think I know someone who'd be perfect for the job," Allen said. "If it's all right with you, I'll head over to her place now and talk to her about it."

Samuel gave a nod. He hoped whoever Allen had in mind was good with kids, because Jared could be a handful at times.

Chapter 8

The following morning while the kids finished their breakfast, Titus and Samuel sat on the sofa in the living room, drinking coffee and visiting before Titus left for work.

"Sure hope this snow goes away soon," Titus said with a frown. "Makes me wish I was in Sarasota, Florida, right now."

Samuel winced at the mention of Sarasota. Elsie had always wanted to visit there, and Samuel had promised to take her and the kids someday, but of course, it hadn't happened. So many regrets. So many wishes that never came true.

Titus nudged Samuel's elbow. "Did I say something wrong? You look *umgerennt*."

Samuel shook his head, keeping his regrets to himself. "It's nothing. I'm not upset."

Someone knocked on the front door, and Titus rose from his seat. When he returned, Allen was with him.

Allen smiled at Samuel and said, "I've got good news. I found someone to watch your kids, so as soon as she gets here, I can take you over to the Taylor place so you can speak to the owner about what she needs to have done. If she hires you, then you can begin right away, since the kids will have a sitter."

Samuel sat a few seconds, letting it all soak in. He hadn't expected Allen would find him a job, much a less a sitter. But this was the chance he needed, so he couldn't turn it down. "Sure," he said with a nod. "That sounds good."

Titus thumped Samuel's arm. "I knew God would provide a job for you."

"I don't have the job yet." Samuel shrugged, not wanting to get too excited about it. He'd had too many disappointments already. "I have to speak with the owner first and see what she needs done. Maybe it's something I'm not qualified to do. Or maybe she's interviewing other people and will hire one of them."

"Don't sell yourself short," Allen said. "I'm sure you're more than qualified, and as far as I know, Bonnie hasn't interviewed anyone else. In fact, she asked if I knew of someone who could do the work, and my first thought was you."

"Even so, that doesn't mean she'll hire me. And there may be things I might not be able to do." Samuel wouldn't give in to the mounting hope of this job, fearing it would be snatched away from him before he had the chance to even meet the woman.

"You sound like me when I first moved to Kentucky," Titus interjected. "I didn't have much confidence in myself and was always afraid I'd mess up."

Samuel knew his brother was right. Since Elsie had died, he didn't feel like he could do much of anything right—especially where his kids were concerned.

Another knock sounded on the door. "I'll get it." Titus hurried out of the room. When he returned, Esther Beiler was with him.

"If you came to get the container you brought the cookies in the other day, it's in the kitchen." Samuel stood. "I'll get it for you."

Esther shook her head. "I'm not here for my container. I came to watch your kinner while you go with Allen to see about a possible job."

"Oh, I see." Samuel knew from what Titus had told him about Esther that she wasn't married and lived alone because her folks had moved to Pennsylvania. Since she was single, he didn't know how much experience she'd had with children. He'd give her a chance, but if it didn't work out, he hoped he could find someone else.

—∞—

Bonnie had just stepped outside to feed a stray cat that had been hanging around the place the last couple of days, when she saw Allen's pickup pull into the yard. She waited on the porch, watching as Allen and a tall Amish man got out of the truck and sloshed their way through the wet snow to the house.

"I'd like you to meet Samuel Fisher," Allen said to Bonnie when the men joined her on the porch. He gestured to Samuel, then to Bonnie. "Samuel, this is Bonnie Taylor, and this old house that needs fixing used to belong to her grandparents."

Bonnie smiled and shook Samuel's hand, noting the strength in his handshake. She also noticed that he barely made eye contact with her. Was he shy, wary of strangers, or just an unfriendly sort of person?

"Come in out of the cold," Bonnie said. "I'll show you what I think needs to be done inside."

Allen motioned to the broken railing on the porch and the peeling paint on the side of the house. "Looks like there's a lot to be done out here as well."

"You're right about that," Bonnie said as the men followed her into the house. "Let's start in the kitchen." She led the way and pointed out all the things she felt needed fixing: walls to be painted, stained and torn linoleum to be replaced, an electric stove with only two burners that worked, and the need for a second oven.

"I can do the painting no problem, because I did a lot of it when I lived in Pennsylvania and worked for my older brother," Samuel said. "I can also replace the linoleum, but the stove and oven will involve electrical hookups, which I know nothing about."

"No problem," Allen said. "I can talk to Adam Jarvis, the electrician who does most of my work, and see if he can take care of any electrical problems for you."

Bonnie smiled. "I'd appreciate that."

"What else needs to be done in the house?" Samuel asked, looking around.

"Well, there are six large bedrooms here, a living room, dining room, and two full bathrooms. As near as I can tell, every one of them needs some kind of updating or repairs. That should keep you busy throughout the rest of winter, and then this spring, when the weather improves, you can start on the outside of the house."

Samuel leaned against the kitchen counter and gave her a nod. "I'm willing to do whatever I can."

"Great!" Bonnie clapped her hands and then motioned to the kitchen table. "Let's have a seat, and we'll talk about your wages."

—∞—

Esther smiled as she watched Jared and Penny sitting on the

living room floor, each holding one of Titus's cats. The one Penny held was Callie, an orange, black, and white calico. The cat in Jared's lap had white hair with a black spot on his head. That cat Titus had named Buttons. Esther figured the cats would be in for a challenge with the feisty black Lab she'd seen out in the yard. The dog obviously belonged to Samuel, because Titus only had cats.

Jared got up off the floor, set Buttons on the sofa, and climbed up beside him.

"I don't think your uncle Titus allows the cats to be on the furniture," Esther said in German-Dutch, so that Jared, who hadn't learned English yet, would understand. "Please put the cat on the floor."

Jared just sat there, stroking the cat's head, as though he hadn't heard a word she'd said.

"Jared, did you understand me?"

The boy gave no reply, nor did he make any effort to put the cat on the floor.

"His thinker ain't workin' so well today," Penny said. "Fact is, he don't do much of anything he's told—not since Mammi died anyways. I think he misses her, same as me."

Esther's heart went out to Penny and Jared. No doubt the two older children missed their mother as well. After all, she'd only been gone a little over two months. Poor little Jared wasn't much more than a baby, and what child of his age didn't need his mother's nurturing?

"Why don't we all go into the kitchen and have a snack?" Esther suggested.

Penny jumped up, raced to the front door, and put the calico cat outside. Jared climbed down from the sofa and put his cat outside as well. Then both children followed Esther into the kitchen. Penny climbed onto a chair, and Esther picked Jared up and lifted him into his high chair. Then she gave them each a glass of milk, some crackers, and a few apple slices.

The kids were just finishing their snack when the back door opened and Allen stepped in. "I came by to tell you that Samuel's going to start working for Bonnie right away—that is if you're free to stay here with the kids for the rest of the day."

Esther nodded. Now she'd just need to think of something to keep Penny and Jared occupied for the next several hours.

Chapter 9

By the time Bonnie dropped Samuel off at Titus's, after he'd worked at her place most of the day, he was exhausted. It was a good kind of exhaustion though—the kind that comes from working so hard that your muscles ache—the kind that keeps a person so busy there's no time to think or dwell on the past. Besides securing a position that would give him a steady income for the next few months, putting in a good day's work helped take his mind off Elsie and how much he missed her. Sleeping and working. . .those were the only times when he felt free of his pain and despair. Well, if working was what it took, then he'd keep busy doing something from now on.

Samuel was almost to the house when he decided to give Zach a call. He hadn't talked to anyone from home in several days and wanted to let them know he'd found a job.

He crunched his way through the snow, and when he entered the dilapidated-looking shanty, he flipped on the battery-operated light sitting beside the phone.

He could see his breath in there, and the small wooden

structure seemed even colder than it was outside, so he wasted no time in making the call. When Zach answered, Samuel told him about Bonnie Taylor and the work he'd be doing at her house, and how it would eventually be turned into a bed-and-breakfast.

"That's good news about the job," Zach said. "Finding work during the winter months is sometimes hard to do."

"Bonnie said she'll have work for me in the spring, too. She wants the outside of the house painted and also any necessary repairs that will need to be done. Plus, there's an old guest house on the property she wants me to fix up. Your friend, Allen, will do some of the carpentry work when he's able to fit it into his schedule, and one of the electricians he knows will do all the electrical work."

"When does she plan to open the B&B?"

"Hopefully by late spring, but not until all the repairs and remodeling have been done. The place is pretty run down right now and needs a lot of work, so it could take longer than planned, I suppose."

Woof! Woof! Samuel's black Lab bounded in through the open door and flopped a wet, snowy paw on Samuel's knee, obviously wanting his attention.

"Get down, Lucky," he grumbled. "Guess that's what I get for not shutting the door."

"What's up with the dog?" Zach asked.

"He's just making a nuisance of himself, like usual." Automatically, Samuel scratched behind the dog's ears as Lucky leaned in closer for more. Lucky used to love it whenever Elsie petted him. He'd been her dog from the time he was a pup, and it had been comical to watch the mutt follow her all over the place.

"How are the kids adjusting to the move?" Zach asked.

"Do they like it there?"

"I guess they're okay with it." Truth was, Samuel hadn't bothered to ask any of them if they liked their new home or not. Even if they didn't like it that much, they were kids, and kids adjusted to things easier than adults. They seemed to have adjusted to their mother's absence, because they rarely mentioned her name. But then of course, Samuel didn't talk about Elsie either. It was better that way. Better to deal with the agony of losing her in silence.

"Guess I'd better let you go," Zach said. "It's probably cold out there in the phone shed."

"They call 'em shanties here, and you're right. It is pretty cold."

"I'll let the rest of the family know about your new job," Zach said.

"Okay. Talk to you later then."

Samuel hung up the phone, but before he could stand, Lucky whimpered and flopped his other paw on Samuel's knee. Samuel knew the dog missed Elsie and wanted more of his attention, but he didn't feel like it right now. He just wanted to get into the house, where it was warm. So he pushed Lucky away, stepped out of the shanty, and sloshed his way through the snow. These days even their family pet seemed like a nuisance—and at times like now, he was the biggest nuisance of all.

When Samuel entered the house and stepped into the living room, he halted. Esther was seated in the rocking chair, with Jared asleep in her arms. A wisp of Esther's dark hair had escaped her head covering and lay across her slightly pink cheek. She looked so content holding Jared like that.

A lump formed in his throat. Seeing Esther with Jared made him think of Elsie, and how she used to rock Jared to sleep each night. It didn't seem right that someone else should be holding his little boy. It didn't seem right that Elsie wasn't here to care for him and the other children.

Samuel took a step, and the floor creaked beneath his feet.

Suddenly, Esther's eyes snapped open. "Oh, you're home!" She glanced at the battery-operated clock on the far wall. "I—I didn't realize it was getting so late."

"Guess you wouldn't, since you've been sleeping."

"I must have dozed off after Jared fell asleep in my arms." Esther looked down at the rosy-cheeked boy and smiled. "He's sure a cute little guy."

Samuel just removed his hat and jacket and draped them over a chair.

"How'd it go today?" Esther asked.

"Fine. I'll be going over there every day until the work's all done. Can you keep watchin' the kids for me? I'll pay you a fair wage of course."

"I'd be happy to watch them. I enjoyed myself today, and I think the kinner and I got along quite well."

"Where's Penny?" he asked, glancing around the room.

"She's in her bedroom with Buttons."

Barely looking at Esther, Samuel scratched the side of his head. "Buttons?"

"One of Titus's cats has a mark on its head that looks like a black button."

Samuel raised his eyebrows, as irritation set in. "I hope that cat's not on the bed, because Penny knows her mamm doesn't approve of pets on the furniture. I—I mean, when Elsie was alive, she didn't approve." Embarrassed and angry, Samuel whirled around and headed down the hall toward the room Penny shared with Marla.

~

Seeing the angry look on Samuel's face, Esther was afraid Penny might be in trouble with her father. She wished there was something she could do to intercede on the child's behalf.

It's probably best if I don't say anything, she decided. *Samuel might not appreciate my interference with the discipline of his children.*

A few minutes later, Penny appeared, red-faced and sniffling as she carried Buttons to the front door and put him outside.

"Would you like a cookie?" Esther asked after Penny had closed the door.

Penny nodded soberly. "Okay."

Esther rose from her seat and placed Jared on the sofa. Taking Penny's hand, she went to the kitchen.

Penny took a seat at the table while Esther got out the cookie jar. She'd just placed two cookies on a napkin in front of Penny when Samuel stepped into the room.

"What's goin' on?" he questioned.

"I'm giving Penny a little snack." Esther motioned to the cookies. "Would you like some?"

He frowned as he shook his head. "She shouldn't be eating anything now either. We'll be having supper soon, and too many cookies will spoil her appetite."

"Oh, I didn't realize you'd be starting supper so soon. Your two oldest children aren't home from school yet."

Samuel slapped the side of his head. "Oh, great! I forgot about picking them up. I should have asked Bonnie if she'd mind stopping by the schoolhouse before she dropped me off here." He looked at Esther, then dropped his gaze, the way he'd done when she'd first met him. "Can you stay awhile longer—while I go get the kinner?"

"Certainly."

Samuel started for the door, but turned back around and pointed his finger at Penny. "No cookies for you! You need to learn to follow the rules."

Esther flinched as the door slammed behind Samuel. If she hadn't known that he was still grieving for his wife, she'd have thought he wasn't a nice man. Hopefully after he'd worked through his grief, he would be kinder to his children, although since the kids were grieving, too, Esther thought Samuel should be more tolerant and kind. But she chose to keep her opinion to herself.

—∞—

Bonnie stared out the kitchen window in awe. The shadows from the fence outlining her grandparents' property made incredible patterns on the glistening snow in the front yard. It made her wish she was a child again and could go outside and romp in the snow. She remembered when she and her parents had come here for Christmas one year, and she and Grandpa had made a snowman together. It had been so much fun. But then it was always more fun to do something like that when you had someone to share it with. She wished her dad, who had always seemed to be working when she was a child, had spent more time with her.

I suppose I could go outside and make my own snowman, she thought, *but it's so cold out there now, and I really should fix something for supper. When Samuel comes tomorrow, maybe I'll suggest that he bring his children over here on Saturday. We can all build a snowman, and afterward I'll fix them hot chocolate with marshmallows.* That's what Bonnie's grandma had fixed her and Grandpa when they'd come in from the snow, and it had added to the special memory of the day.

Bonnie turned away from the window, opened the pantry door, and took out a jar of spaghetti sauce and a package of angel-hair noodles. She'd just placed them on the cupboard, when she heard a dog barking in the backyard.

She opened the door to see what was going on, and a shaggy-looking, brown-and-white terrier of sorts bounded onto the porch. She'd never seen a dog quite like him before and figured he was probably a mixed breed.

"Shoo! Go on now!" Bonnie waved her hand, took a step forward, and tripped on a loose board.

"Oh!" She grabbed the handle of the screen door just in time to keep from falling on her face. Here was another job that couldn't wait until spring. She'd ask Samuel to fix it first thing tomorrow morning.

Bonnie turned her gaze on the dog again. It had plopped down on the porch and was lying there with its nose between its paws and a forlorn look in its cocoa-colored eyes. The poor thing looked unkempt and underfed. Could it be a stray someone had abandoned? Or maybe it had gotten away from its owner and become lost. Bonnie didn't want to take the dog in—especially if it belonged to someone else. Besides, she already had a stray cat to feed.

She stepped back into the house and shut the door, certain that the dog would get tired of lying there and hopefully would go back to wherever he'd come from.

Bonnie opened the jar of spaghetti sauce and got it heating on the stove; then she took out a kettle to cook the noodles in and set it in the sink. When she turned on the faucet to fill the kettle with water, she heard the dog again.

Woof! Woof! Woof! The loud barking was followed by scratching at the door.

With an exasperated groan, and determined to send the dog on its way, Bonnie turned off the water and opened the back door. When she stepped onto the porch, being careful to avoid the loose board, the dog leaped up and put both paws on her knees.

She looked down at her jeans and grimaced. They were wet!

She leaned over, picked up the dog, and tromped down the steps. Then she set him in the snow. "Go home!" she said, pointing to the road.

The dog just sat there, looking up at her with such forlorn-looking eyes. With his tail swishing against the snow, he stayed put, watching as if patiently waiting for Bonnie to change her mind.

Bonnie tried again. "Go home!" She clapped her hands and stomped her feet a few times—partly to get the dog moving, and partly to keep herself warm. She'd been foolish to come out here without a jacket.

Despite more coaxing, clapping, and pointing to the road, the dog wouldn't budge.

"Suit yourself," she said with a shake of her head. "If you want to sit out here in the cold snow, that's up to you." With all there was to do around the house, as much as she'd like to, she couldn't let herself get attached to a dog, because dogs needed a lot of care.

Bonnie turned and hurried back into the warmth of the house. When she stepped into the kitchen, she let out a shriek. Water was all over the kitchen floor!

"Now how could that have happened?" she fumed, instantly forgetting about her four-legged visitor. "I know I turned off the water before I went outside."

It didn't take long for Bonnie to realize that there was water seeping out from under the sink. "Ugh!" She slipped off her shoes and socks, and then waded through the water in her bare feet. When she opened the cupboard door beneath the sink and leaned over, she knew immediately what the problem was. A rusty-looking pipe had sprung a leak. "That's just great," she said with a moan.

Bonnie reached in and closed the shut-off valve, thankful that it wasn't stuck, because she had no idea where any of Grandpa's tools might be. Even if she had known where they were, she wasn't sure she'd know how to use them. Since she wouldn't be able to use the kitchen sink until the pipe was repaired, she'd have to use the sink in the bathroom. Now that was convenient!

Once the water was off, she sloshed her way back across the wet room, grabbed a mop from the utility porch, and started sopping up the water. This was just one more thing she'd have to ask Samuel to do. At this rate, she would never get the place ready to open as a bed-and-breakfast this spring.

She groaned. "I wonder what else will go wrong."

Chapter 10

Samuel shook the reins and clucked to his horse to get him moving quickly down the road. He was on his way to Bonnie's with the kids, and they'd all been chattering away like a bunch of magpies ever since they left Titus's place. They were obviously excited about going to Bonnie's, but Samuel couldn't help feeling irritated by their exuberance. It was as if they didn't miss their mother anymore. Could they have forgotten her so quickly?

I wonder why I let Bonnie talk me into bringing the kids over today, he thought with regret. *The last thing I want to do is build a snowman. Think I'll just let the kids play in the snow while I do some work on Bonnie's place.*

Samuel thought about some of the things he'd done there this past week. He'd put a new pipe under her kitchen sink, repaired several loose spindles on the banister leading upstairs, stripped some wallpaper in the kitchen and then painted the walls, replaced all the loose boards on the porch, and hauled some boxes up to the attic for Bonnie. The house was old, and it seemed like there was no end to the work that needed to be done. He figured he might not to have to look for any outside paint jobs until late spring or early summer because he'd probably be working for Bonnie that long.

"Daadi, Leon keeps pokin' me!" Penny shouted, bringing Samuel's thoughts to a halt. "Would ya make him stop?"

"Knock it off, Leon," Samuel called over his shoulder, "or you won't be making a snowman when we get to Bonnie's. You'll be in the house, workin' with me."

"But she started it," the boy complained. "She's hoggin' the seat."

"Huh-uh. He's the one hoggin' the seat," Penny retorted.

Samuel gritted his teeth. He didn't have the patience to deal with this right now. If only Elsie were here, she'd know what to do to quiet the kids and make them stop arguing.

"Stop pinchin' me!" Penny's piercing squeal sounded like a baby pig that had been cheated out of its mother's milk.

"I didn't pinch ya," Leon countered. "Jared's the one who pinched you, and that's the truth."

All was silent for a few seconds; then Jared started to cry. Samuel figured Penny had probably pinched him.

"If you three don't stop it, you're gonna be in trouble," Marla, who sat in the front of the buggy beside Samuel, said in her most grown-up voice.

"Ya can't tell us what to do, Marla." Leon said.

"Daadi, Leon just leaned over the seat and poked my shoulder," Marla tattled.

"Knock it off!" Samuel hollered at the top of his lungs. "If I hear one more peep out of any of you, I'll turn this horse and buggy around and head back to Titus's place. Is that clear?"

Except for a few sniffles, all was quiet.

I'm starting to sound like an angry, mean man, Samuel thought as he clenched the reins tighter. *But these petty little issues between the kids are really getting on my nerves.*

—ﾛ—

Bonnie glanced out the kitchen window, wondering if Samuel and his children would be here soon. She looked forward to meeting them and hoped they were looking forward to making a snowman today.

She thought this would be a good chance for Samuel to relax and have a good time. He seemed so sullen and kept to himself much of the time. With the exception of discussing the repairs that needed to be done, they'd had very little conversation.

A whimper pulled Bonnie's thoughts aside and she looked down. The stray terrier she'd found earlier in the week cocked his head and looked up at her pathetically. She'd asked around the neighborhood and hadn't been able to find the dog's owner, so she'd finally weakened and taken him in. After all, she couldn't leave the poor pooch outside in the cold, nor could she stand the thought of the dog going hungry. She'd ended up giving him a bath and trimming his matted hair. The little fellow was really quite cute once all that dirt was gone. She'd even named the mutt Cody, which she certainly wouldn't have done if she hadn't decided to keep him.

"What's the matter, Cody?" Bonnie asked, reaching down to pet the dog's silky head. "Do you want to go out, or are you just looking for some attention?"

Cody whimpered and nuzzled her hand.

Bonnie continued to pet the dog a few more minutes; then she went to the front door to see if he wanted to go out. When she opened it, she caught sight of Samuel's horse and buggy heading up the driveway.

Woof! Woof! Cody raced out to greet them.

Bonnie grabbed her coat and stocking cap, slipped into her boots and gloves, and hurried outside. As soon as Samuel pulled the horse up to the hitching rail, his four children clambered out of the buggy and started frolicking in the snow. Bonnie waited on the porch until Samuel and the children walked up to the house.

"This is Marla, Penny, Leon, and Jared," Samuel said, motioning to each of the children.

Bonnie smiled. "My name's Bonnie Taylor, and I'm glad you could come over to play in the snow today."

The children stared up at her without saying a word.

Samuel nudged the oldest girl. "Say hello to Bonnie."

"Hello," she said in a voice barely above a whisper. The other children echoed her greeting.

"It's nice to meet you, and now I'm wondering—is everyone ready to help me make a snowman?" Bonnie asked.

All heads nodded. All except for Samuel's, that is. He was staring at the front of the house where the paint was peeling in several places.

"You're going to help us build the snowman, aren't you?" Bonnie stepped up to Samuel.

He shook his head. "Thought I'd get some more work done inside while you and the kids are out here playing in the snow."

"Are you sure you want to work today? You've worked hard all week, and I think you should take the day off."

He shook his head. "There's a lot to be done here, and the sooner I get it finished, the sooner you can open your bed-and-breakfast."

"Okay." Bonnie figured he wasn't going to change his mind, so she bent down, scooped up a clump of snow, and formed it into a ball. "Come on, kids, let's get that snowman started!"

Yip! Yip! Cody raced around the yard, running circles around the children. Then he leaped up and grabbed the edge of Marla's scarf.

"Hey! Come back with that!" Marla dashed after the dog, waving her hands, and Leon did the same.

Woof! Woof! Woof! Cody circled the yard a few times, dragging the scarf through the snow.

Bonnie clapped her hands and shouted, "Cody, drop that scarf!"

When the dog didn't listen, she joined Marla and Leon in the chase. She knew they'd all be exhausted by the end of this day.

—∞—

As Esther's horse and buggy approached Titus's house, she was filled with a sense of excitement. Since Samuel paid his children so little attention, she'd decided to see if the kids wanted to help her build a snowman today. That was something she hadn't done in several years, so it should be fun for her as well.

When Esther pulled into Titus's yard, she spotted him out by the barn. He waved and then secured her horse, Ginger, to the hitching rail.

"What brings you by here this morning?" he asked when she climbed down from the buggy.

"I came to see if Samuel's kinner would like to help me make a snowman."

"That's too bad, because they're not here right now."

"Where'd they go?"

"Samuel took 'em over to Bonnie Taylor's. They're gonna make a snowman over there."

"Oh, I see." Esther couldn't help but feel disappointed.

She'd really been looking forward to spending time with the children today.

"Say, I have an idea," Titus said. "Why don't you go over to the Taylor place and join them? Do you know where the house is located?"

She nodded. "Margaret Taylor used to come into our store sometimes, and when her husband, Andy, was ill, I made a delivery to their house a few times."

"Well, good. You'll know how to get there then."

"I wouldn't want to intrude." Esther felt a bit awkward and tried to hide her disappointment.

Titus shook his head. "I'm sure Bonnie wouldn't mind, and I know the kinner would be glad to see you."

"I'd be glad to see them, too."

"So if you're going, would you mind taking Penny's mittens? She forgot them this morning."

"I'd be happy to take them to her." Esther was glad for a legitimate excuse to show up at Bonnie's. That way it wouldn't look like she was trying to interrupt the fun Bonnie had planned for the kids.

—∞—

When Esther arrived at the Taylor place sometime later, she spotted Samuel's children out in the snowy front yard. Marla and Jared were rolling a good-sized snowball, although the little guy seemed to be more of a hindrance than a help. Leon and Penny, with the help of a young woman with curly blond hair peeking out from under her stocking cap, rolled another.

"Hello," Esther said as she approached the group. "It looks like you have a good start on a snowman."

The kids stopped rolling their snowballs long enough to tell Esther hello, and the woman held out her mittened hand.

"I'm Bonnie Taylor. Are you one of my neighbors?"

"I'm Esther Beiler," she said as she shook Bonnie's hand. "My folks used to own the general store in the area, and your grandparents shopped there sometimes." She gestured to the children. "I've been watching Samuel's kids while he's working for you, and when I stopped by there this morning, Titus said Samuel had brought the kids over here."

"That's right." Bonnie offered her a friendly smile. "We're building a snowman."

Esther held up the mittens she'd brought along. "Titus gave me these and said they were Penny's."

"It was nice of you to bring them by," Bonnie said. "When they got here, and Penny realized she'd left her mittens at home, I gave her a pair of mine, but as you can see, they're much too big for her small hands."

Esther handed the mittens to Penny, and the child smiled appreciatively.

"Where's your daed?" Esther asked.

Penny pointed to the house. "He's in there, workin'."

"Oh, I see. I figured he'd be out here helping you build the snowman."

"Nope," Leon chimed in. "Our daadi's always workin' now."

"Workin' or sleepin'," Marla interjected. "He hardly talks to us anymore, and when he does, he usually yells."

Esther glanced at Bonnie and noticed the concern showing in her dark brown eyes. Was she worried about Samuel, too?

"I tried to talk him into playing in the snow with us, but he insisted on working today," Bonnie said.

"That's 'cause he don't like bein' with us no more," Leon said with a tone of sadness in his voice.

Esther's heart clenched, and Bonnie gave the boy's shoulder a squeeze. "I'm sure that's not the case. I think your daddy just likes to keep busy."

Leon silently started rolling his snowball again.

"Would you like to join us?" Bonnie asked Esther. "I think Marla and Jared could use some help."

"I'd be glad to help out." Esther felt an immediate connection with Bonnie and hoped she would have the chance to get to know her better.

As they worked on the snowman, Bonnie told Esther about her plans to open a bed-and-breakfast. "Of course," she added, "once the place is ready to go, I'm not sure what I'll do about fixing my guests their breakfast." She wrinkled her nose. "I get by in the kitchen, but I'm definitely not the world's best cook, and I don't think my guests would be satisfied with cold cereal and toast every morning."

"Last year I taught my friend, Suzanne, how to cook, and she's doing real well on her own. I'd be happy to give you some pointers as well."

Bonnie smiled. "That'd be great."

"Whenever you're ready, just let me know. I could come over some Saturday or in the evenings after I'm done watching Samuel's kids."

"When you mentioned that your folks had a store in the area, I thought you might be working there."

Esther shook her head. "They sold the store not long ago and moved to Pennsylvania to help my brother, because he has MS and can't manage on his own anymore."

"I'm sorry to hear that. I know a young woman in Oregon who has MS, and she's really struggling with it."

"Dan's doctor bills are mounting up already, so besides the fact that I enjoy being with Samuel's children, some of the money I earn watching them will be sent to my brother to help with his medical expenses."

"Doesn't he have any health insurance?"

"No. We Amish don't believe in buying health insurance. We take care of our own."

"Oh, I see. I guess there's a lot about the Amish I don't know. Maybe while you're teaching me to improve my cooking skills, you can enlighten me about the Amish who live in this community. After all, if we're going to be neighbors, it would be helpful if I understood the people living around me."

Esther smiled. "I'd be happy to answer any questions you might have."

"I appreciate that, and I'll be happy to pay you for helping me learn my way around the kitchen." Bonnie stopped rolling her snowball and let the kids take over. "In fact, once the B&B is up and running, would you be interested in coming to work for me here?"

"That's a tempting offer, but if Samuel finds another job after he's done working for you, I'll probably still be watching his children."

"Maybe you could come over here in the late afternoons or early evenings to clean the guest rooms and help with the preparation of the food I'll be serving my guests for breakfast the next day."

"I'm sure I could manage, but I'll have to get permission from my folks first," Esther replied. "Some Amish families in our church district don't approve of their daughters working in English people's homes. And even if they do say it's okay for me to work for you, I won't be allowed to listen to the radio or watch any TV."

"That's fine," Bonnie said. "I don't watch much TV myself."

Esther smiled. "While I'm waiting for Mom and Dad's answer, if there's anything you need my help with right away, I could probably do that."

"Actually, there is. I'm still going through my grandparents' things, so you could help me with that, as well as some of the cleaning I still haven't done."

"That sounds good to me." Esther felt sure God had provided more work for her, and she looked forward to calling Mom and Dad and hopefully beginning a second job soon.

She smiled to herself. All those concerns in the beginning—wondering what she would do after her parents left and how she would earn money—were now being lifted because everything seemed to be working out well.

Chapter 11

Esther was relieved when she received permission from her folks to work for Bonnie, with only a caution about not using anything in the house for worldly pleasures. Esther didn't think she'd have a problem with that because she was content to do without modern things.

So for the next two weeks, Esther went over to Bonnie's every day after Samuel got home from work. She enjoyed spending time with Bonnie, as she was doing now, and was impressed at how quickly they had become friends. Not that Bonnie would replace Esther's friendship with Suzanne—she was sure nothing could ever come between them.

Esther glanced at Bonnie, who stood at the kitchen counter kneading bread dough. "You're doing well, but be careful not to work the dough too much," she said. "My mother taught me when the dough feels elastic and quits sticking to your fingers, then it's ready and time to let rise."

Bonnie smiled. "I can't tell you how much I appreciate you teaching me how to do this. It'll be so nice to offer my B&B

guests homemade bread every morning."

"In the spring, when the rhubarb in your grandma's garden patch ripens, maybe we can make some rhubarb jam."

"I remember Grandma serving that on toast when I was a girl and came here to visit. It was so good." Bonnie smacked her lips. "She made strawberry-rhubarb pie, too."

"Then there must be some strawberry plants hidden under all that snow in the garden."

Bonnie nodded. "I believe there are."

The rumble of a vehicle interrupted their conversation. "It's Allen," Bonnie said, peering out the window. She smiled. "I'm so thankful he introduced me to Samuel."

The smile on Bonnie's face when she mentioned Samuel's name made Esther wonder if Bonnie might have a personal interest in him.

Surely not, she told herself as Bonnie went to the door to let Allen in. *Bonnie's English and Samuel's Amish, so I'm sure she wouldn't be romantically interested in him. She probably just appreciates all the work he's doing for her. I shouldn't let my imagination get carried away like I sometimes did when I was a child.*

"Sorry it's taken me so long to get over here," Allen said when Bonnie opened the door. "I got busy all of a sudden with work I hadn't expected."

"It's okay," Bonnie said. "Nothing I've needed you to do has been critical, and Samuel's been a big help to me in so many ways."

"Hi, Esther," Allen said when he and Bonnie entered the kitchen. "I wondered if that was your buggy I saw parked outside."

Esther smiled. "I came over to help Bonnie do some baking."

"I'm not much of a baker," Bonnie said, "so I appreciate Esther's lessons."

Allen sniffed the air. "I can tell. Is that fresh bread I smell right now?"

"Yes, it sure is." Bonnie motioned to the loaf of bread she'd already baked. "If you're still here when it's cooled, maybe you'd like a piece."

"That'd be nice. There's nothing quite like eating fresh bread." Allen looked over at Esther and said, "I've had some of the good-tasting breads and cookies you taught Suzanne to make, so I'm sure that whatever you and Bonnie make will be real good, too." He grinned and gave her a wink. "I must say, though, there's no better smell wafting through a house than bread baking in the oven."

Esther's face heated. Was Allen flirting with her? *Of course not, silly. There goes my wild imagination again.*

Samuel stepped into Titus's phone shanty with a feeling of dread. He'd received a voice mail from Mama Fannie a few days ago asking him to call at 9:00 a.m. on Saturday morning, when she would be in the phone shed. Since he knew Mama Fannie had disapproved of him moving to Kentucky, he figured he might be in for a lecture on how foolish he'd been for leaving Pennsylvania.

"Guess I may as well get this over with," he mumbled as he dialed the number.

"Hi, Mama Fannie. It's me, Samuel," he said when she answered her phone.

"It's good to hear from you. How are you and the kinner doing?"

"Okay."

"I talked to Zach the other day, and he said you've been working for an English woman in the area."

"That's right. Her name's Bonnie Taylor, and she's planning to open a bed-and-breakfast in the spring."

There was a pause, and then Mama Fannie said, "How old is she?"

"Beats me. I've never asked."

"You must have some idea how old she is. Is she older than me?"

"I'd say she's probably in her late twenties or early thirties."

"Is she married?"

"Nope." Samuel put his hand to his forehead. He already knew where this conversation was headed.

Another pause. "Do you think it's a good idea for you to be alone with her all day?"

Samuel felt his defenses rise. "You have nothing to worry about, Mama Fannie. Bonnie's a nice woman, and most of the time she's not even around when I'm working. She's often out shopping or working in some other part of the house."

"Can't you take one of the kinner with you when you're over there? That way no one can say anything about you being alone with a woman."

"As you know, my two older ones are in school all day, and I'm not about to bring the younger ones to work with me." Samuel grunted. "They'd only get in the way."

"But don't you think—"

"I hate to cut this short, but there are some things I need to get done yet today, so I'd better go," Samuel said, cutting her off in mid-sentence.

"Oh. I see."

Samuel knew from the tone of her voice that he'd hurt her feelings, so he quickly added, "It's been good talking to you,

Mama Fannie. Tell Dad and the rest of the family I said hello."

"Okay. Tell your kinner I said hello, too. Oh, and tell Marla I'll be mailing her birthday card out to her soon."

"I will. Bye." Samuel quickly hung up the phone. If Mama Fannie was going to badger him about working for Bonnie, he might make fewer calls home. He knew her intentions were good, but sometimes she didn't know when to quit. He didn't remember her being this way when he was young and figured it might have something to do with her age. Their bishop said once that the older a person got, the more they worried about things.

Paradise, Pennsylvania

When Timothy arrived home after helping Zach and his crew paint the inside of a grocery store, he was disappointed that he didn't find Hannah in the kitchen. He was tired and hungry and hoped she'd have supper waiting for him. Painting all day was hard work, but the money he earned paid the bills and kept him busy during the winter months when he wasn't able to farm.

He was about to head down the hall to see if she was in the living room when he spotted a note on the kitchen table. It was from Hannah and said that she'd taken Mindy and gone to her folks' house to help her mother clean and do some baking. She also said there was a container of vegetable soup in the refrigerator that Timothy could heat for his supper.

He frowned. It seemed like Hannah's mother was more important than him. But then that was really nothing new. Hannah was tied to her mother's apron strings and thought she had to be over there nearly every day. When Hannah wasn't at her folks', her mother was over at their place. It was getting old, and Timothy was tired of it.

He draped his jacket over the back of a chair and took a kettle and a bowl out of the cupboard. He'd just started heating the soup when the back door opened and his mother entered the house.

"I'm surprised to see you, Mom. What are you doing here at this time of the day?" he asked.

Her forehead wrinkled. "Is that any way to greet your mamm?"

"Sorry. I just figured you'd be at home having supper right now."

"We already ate, and when your daed fell asleep in his recliner, I decided to come over here and talk to you about something." She glanced at the single bowl he'd set on the table. "Where's the rest of your family? It looks like you're planning to eat alone."

He nodded. "Hannah and Mindy are at her folks' house."

Mom's lips compressed. "Again? She seems to go there a lot."

Timothy merely shrugged and said, "What'd you want to talk to me about?"

"Not what, but whom. Samuel, to be exact."

"What about him?"

"Did you know that he's been working for an English woman who's planning to open a bed-and-breakfast this spring?"

"Jah, I heard about that. From what Samuel said, Bonnie Taylor's a very nice woman."

"Well when I spoke with Samuel on the phone earlier today, I told him that I didn't think it was a good idea for him to be alone with this woman, and he got defensive."

"Can you blame him, Mom?"

"What's that supposed to mean?"

Timothy could see by his mother's pinched expression that he'd hurt her feelings. "I just think you to need to remember that your boys are grown men now, and we have the right to make our own choices—even if what we decide doesn't go along with your thinking."

"I don't mean to be overbearing," she said sincerely. "I'm just concerned."

"I know your intentions are good, but I'm sure there's nothing to be worried about where Samuel's concerned. I think you ought to concentrate on keeping Dad happy."

Her eyes narrowed. "What do you mean? Has your daed told you he's unhappy?"

"No, no, of course not. I just meant that Dad should be your primary concern, not your grown children."

"Are you saying I shouldn't be concerned about my kinner?"

"I'm not saying that at all, but I think you worry too much." Timothy wished they could start this conversation over. Every word he said seemed to make Mom more agitated.

"I probably do worry too much," she admitted, "but I can't seem to help it. I just want what's best for everyone."

"God doesn't want us to worry, Mom. You've told all of your kinner that at one time or another."

"You're right, I have, and I'll try not to worry or interfere." Mom gave Timothy a hug. "I love you, son."

"I love you, too."

She smiled and turned toward the door. "Guess I'd better head for home now, before your daed wakes up and misses me. If you talk to Samuel anytime soon, please don't mention that I spoke to you about him working for that English woman," she requested as she went out the door.

"I won't say a thing," he called to her retreating form.

As Timothy continued to heat his soup, he thought about his conversation with Mom and hoped she would be careful not to pester Samuel about working for the English woman. Samuel wore his emotions on his sleeve since Elsie died, and if Mom wasn't careful, she might push him away. Could Mom's constant pressuring be one of the reasons Samuel had moved to Kentucky, or was it simply because he needed a fresh start?

Wish I could start over someplace new, Timothy thought. *If Hannah wasn't so dependent on her mother, I might think about moving to Kentucky, too.*

Chapter 12

Pembroke, Kentucky

Esther smiled to herself as she guided her horse and buggy down the road toward Titus's house. It was the first Saturday in February, and she had plans to meet Suzanne and take Samuel's kids sledding. Esther had enjoyed sledding since she was a girl and used to race her older brothers, James and Dan, down the hill behind their house. Besides, a day of sledding meant she wouldn't have to be alone. It was quiet and lonely in the house since Mom and Dad had moved to Pennsylvania. She missed them both so much. At times she found herself wishing she'd moved there with them, but if she had, she wouldn't have met Samuel's children. Spending time with them had filled a void in her life that she hadn't even realized was there. The children seemed to need her—especially since Samuel paid so little attention to them.

Esther thought about the other day when she'd been holding Jared in her lap as she visited with Penny, who sat on the floor playing with her doll. Both children were equally sweet, each in a different way. Even though Jared could be a bit rambunctious at times, he always obeyed, as did Samuel's other children. Esther had noticed that they weren't nearly as obedient with their father, but maybe that was because he ignored them so much of the time. Could they be using their disobedience as a way to get his attention? She knew Samuel was still grieving over his wife's death, but she wished he would wake up and realize all that he was missing by ignoring the children and being so harsh when he was with them.

When Esther had seen Titus the other day, he'd agreed to go sledding with them and said he'd try to talk Samuel into joining them, too. From what she'd observed and what the children had told her, Samuel did nothing for fun. He was either working or sleeping. That meant when Titus got home from work each day, he not only had the responsibility of doing the cooking and cleaning, but he had to keep an eye on Samuel's children. Esther wondered how things would be once Samuel had a place of his own.

If he ever gets a place of his own, she thought. *What if Samuel plans to stay with Titus indefinitely? Poor Suzanne might end up with a ready-made family. Would that mean she'd have to quit working with Titus and Nelson at the woodshop in order to care for the kinner, or will Samuel want me to continue caring for them?*

Esther's horse snorted, pulling her thoughts aside. Ginger seemed to like the snow, prancing along with her head held high, blowing what looked like steam from her nostrils.

It is beautiful, Esther thought as she noticed the trees along the road, heaving with snow, bending down to touch the glistening ground. Seeing the beauty God had created made Esther feel closer to Him.

Ginger whinnied a greeting as they passed another horse and buggy, and Esther waved when she saw it was Ethan Zook, one of their minister's sons. Ethan waved in response and tipped his hat in her direction. Apparently he'd left his buggy outside last night and hadn't taken the time to clean the snow off this morning, for it was covered with white.

Esther knew that some folks saw the snowflakes piling up into drifts across the road as a nuisance, but she saw the beauty in it. The frosty cold clung tightly to the earth now, but in another month spring would be here and all signs of snow would most likely be gone. *Spring*, she thought wistfully. *Even in the oldest folks, it brings out a burst of youthful energy. I think just about everyone loves the feeling of freedom after being cooped up during the cold winter months.*

Lost in thought, Esther smiled at what spring would bring when it arrived in all its glory. She could almost hear the bubbling sounds as streams flowed from the melting snow and the birds singing joyfully as they migrated home. Oh how she welcomed spring's unfolding splendor and the warmth in the breeze. But for now, she was content to enjoy the moment of this winter's solace.

Esther breathed in the scent of pine, heavier in the air from branches recently broken with the weight of ice and snow. Overhead, a hawk's shrill cry was joined by the crows announcing their protest.

When she pulled into Titus's yard a short time later, she noticed Suzanne's buggy parked outside the barn.

She climbed down from her own buggy and was about to unhitch the horse when Titus stepped out of the barn. "I'll put Ginger away for you," he said, joining her beside the horse.

"Danki." She motioned to the back of the buggy. "I brought three sleds with me, so while you take care of my horse, I'll get them out of the buggy. Oh, do you know if Suzanne brought any sleds we can use?"

Titus shrugged. "I'm not sure. She's in the house right now, helping the kinner get into their boots."

"Is Samuel going with us today?"

Titus turned his hands palm up. "I don't know. I asked, but he never said. You can ask him, too, if you like."

"I might do that." Esther hurried to the back of the buggy, took out the sleds, and leaned them against the side of the barn. Then she trudged her way through the drifts up to the house.

When she stepped inside, she was greeted by four exuberant children wearing boots, heavy jackets, stocking caps, and mittens. All except for Penny, who only wore one mitten.

"I can't find my *fauschthensching*," Penny said, holding up her hand.

Esther chuckled. "It's right here." She reached around behind the child and lifted the mitten that dangled down her back from under her hat.

Penny squinted. "Now how'd that get there?"

Everyone laughed. Everyone but Samuel, who sat slouched on the sofa, looking like he was half asleep.

"Are you going sledding with us?" Esther asked.

He shook his head.

"What do you plan to do all day?" Titus asked when he entered the house.

"Ich daed yuscht so lieb gear nix duh," Samuel said.

Esther looked at Suzanne and slowly shook her head. She couldn't believe Samuel had said he would just as soon do nothing, when he could spend the morning having fun with his children. Was he really that depressed?

"Please come with us, Daadi," Leon pleaded. "You never do nothin' fun with us since Mammi died."

"Ich fiehl saddle schlect heit." Samuel stood and ambled out of the room.

Titus turned to Suzanne. "Since my bruder has just told the kids that he feels out of sorts, I think I'd better forget about sledding and stay home with him today."

"Oh." Suzanne's look of disappointment, as she dipped her head, was as clear as the sorrowful expression on Leon's face. Esther's heart ached for her friend. Suzanne had obviously counted on Titus joining them. Esther felt bad for Samuel's children, too. Didn't Samuel realize that going sledding with the children might lift his spirits? He'd never recover from his loss if he didn't do anything fun. Esther remembered that after Suzanne's dad died, their whole family grieved, but when her Grandpa suggested they all go fishing one afternoon, there had been a change in Suzanne's mother, who seemed more positive about life after that, which in turn, caused everyone else in their family to become more joyous.

"Sorry about the change of plans," Titus said, looking sincerely at Suzanne, "but as long as Samuel's still having bouts of depression, I wouldn't feel right about leaving him here alone."

"I understand that, but I wish. . ." Suzanne's voice trailed off, and then, turning away from Titus, she motioned toward the door. "Come on, kids; let's go sledding."

Tap! Tap! Tap!

"Samuel, can I come in?"

Samuel rolled over on his side so that he faced the wall. He didn't want to talk to Titus right now. He just wanted to be left alone.

Tap! Tap! Tap!

Samuel figured if he didn't respond, the tapping would only continue. So he pulled himself to a sitting position and called, "Come in."

The door opened and Titus stepped into the room. "You know, you're not doing yourself or the kinner any good by pulling away like you have," he said, taking a seat on the edge of the bed.

"I'm not pulling away."

"Jah, you are. You won't join the kinner in anything they do that's fun, and—"

Samuel leaped to his feet and started pacing. "I can't do anything fun! I'm miserable without Elsie. Not that I'd expect you to understand." He stopped pacing and whirled around to face Titus. "You've never lost a mate, and you have no idea how empty I feel without Elsie. The pain is unbearable. It's like my heart has been torn in two."

"I know you're hurting, and you're right, I don't understand, but Mom and Dad do. As you well know, they both lost their first mates, and I'm sure it wasn't easy for either of them." Titus stepped up to Samuel and placed his hand on his shoulder. "Maybe someday, when the time is right, you'll find someone else, the way our folks did."

White hot anger boiled in Samuel's chest as he glared at his brother, hoping he would get the point. "I am never getting married again. Don't you get it? No one could ever take Elsie's place in my heart!"

Titus blinked and held up his hand. "Of course not. You don't have to get so riled. I just meant—"

"I don't want to talk about this anymore. I need to be alone." Samuel grabbed his jacket and stormed out of the room. "Why can't everyone just leave me alone and quit telling me how I'm supposed to feel?" he mumbled under his breath.

—∞—

"Sorry I forgot to bring my sled," Suzanne said as she and

Esther trudged through the snow behind the children and Lucky, their exuberant Lab.

"That's okay. We can manage with the three I brought." Esther smiled. "I think this is going to be a fun day for all of us, don't you?"

Suzanne exhaled, releasing a sigh. "I suppose."

"Are you disappointed because Titus didn't come with us?"

"Jah, but I understand why he felt the need to stay with his bruder."

"Do you think Samuel will ever get over his wife's death?" Esther asked, knowing everyone dealt with grief in their own way, at their own pace.

"I hope so, but I think it'll take some time, just as it did for my mamm when my daed died. From what Titus has told me, Elsie was the love of Samuel's life, and the two of them were really looking forward to having another child, so losing the boppli she carried made it that much harder for Samuel."

"I'm sure it did. I just hate to see him looking so sad."

"I know, but until he's able to come to grips with his loss, there isn't much any of us can do but pray for him and offer support."

They walked in silence for a while; then Esther said, "I don't think Samuel likes me."

"How come?"

"He doesn't say much whenever I'm around, and when he does, he won't look at me."

"Titus was like that with me when he first moved to Kentucky," Suzanne said. "It really bothered me, too."

"But that was because you reminded him of his ex-girlfriend, Phoebe."

Suzanne nodded. "I was so relieved when he chose me over her."

"Have you heard anything about how she's doing since she went back to Pennsylvania?"

"From the few things Titus's mamm has told him, I gather that Phoebe's getting along pretty well and has even decided to join the church."

"Is she being courted by anyone there?"

Suzanne shrugged. "I don't think so, but I don't know for sure. Titus doesn't talk about her much anymore, and I'm glad. When Phoebe showed up here out of the blue, it was hard for me, and I felt insecure about my relationship with Titus."

"But things are okay between you now, aren't they?"

"For the moment, they are. If Samuel doesn't mess them up, that is."

"What do you mean?"

"Samuel's always around, and I miss not having the quality time Titus and I used to have together." Suzanne bumped Esther's arm with her elbow. "Speaking of Samuel, if you think he doesn't like you, then maybe you should ask him why."

Esther shook her head. "I don't think that's a good idea."

"Why not?"

"Samuel's hard to figure out, and I don't want to say or do anything that might make him angry at me. I enjoy watching the kinner and wouldn't want to lose my job."

"I don't think you have to worry about that. Samuel needs someone to watch them while he's working, and since you're so good with the kinner, he'd be foolish to let you go."

Esther was about to comment, when Penny stopped walking, turned toward Esther and Suzanne, and pointed upward. "Look there—some *gens*!"

Esther leaned her head back. Sure enough, there was a flock of honking geese cutting across the sky. "Looks like spring can't be too far off now." She smiled. "They're heading back north."

"And look over there." Suzanne pointed to her left. A small doe pranced into the empty cornfield, now covered with snow.

"Ach, how cute!" Penny watched the doe a minute, then she hurried on.

After they'd gone a bit farther, Marla handed her sled rope to Leon and joined Esther and Suzanne. "I'm hopin' I get a sled of my own for my *gebottsdaag*," she said.

"When is your birthday?" Esther asked.

"I'll be nine years old next Saturday. Daadi hasn't said a thing about it, though, so I'll bet he forgot." Marla frowned deeply and scrunched up her nose. "He don't remember much of anything anymore."

Esther gave the girl's shoulder a gentle squeeze. "I'm sure he won't forget something as important as your birthday."

Marla shrugged. "We'll see."

As they continued on, Esther determined in her heart that she would do something special for Marla's birthday. That way, if Samuel should forget, the child wouldn't be quite so disappointed.

"Since we only have three sleds, we'll have to take turns," Suzanne said when they came to the top of a hill that looked perfect for sledding.

"Me first! Me first!" Leon shouted, hopping up and down. He raced for one of the sleds and took off down the hill before Esther had a chance to respond. Barking and nipping at the back of the sled, Lucky followed.

Marla grabbed another sled and went right behind him. "Look out, Leon—here I come!"

"Penny's kind of little to manage the sled by herself," Esther said to Suzanne, "so maybe I should ride down the hill with her."

"That's a good idea," Suzanne agreed. "When one of the

others gets back with their sled, I'll take Jared for a ride with me."

Esther seated herself on the sled, situated Penny in front of her, and pushed off with her feet.

"Whee. . . This is *schpass*!" Penny hollered.

"Jah, it's a whole lot of fun." Esther giggled as they gathered speed and the snow sprayed back in their faces. The faster they went, the more she laughed, enjoying the memory of her youth when life was so simple and carefree.

When they reached the bottom of the hill, Lucky was there, ready to slurp Penny's cheek.

Penny giggled as she turned her head. "Get away, Lucky! You're gettin' my face all wet."

Woof! Woof! The dog wagged his tail, and with one final slurp, he dashed up the hill behind the others.

They went up and down the hill several more times, with Esther taking turns with Suzanne as they gave Penny and Jared rides on the sled.

"I wanna ride by myself now." Before anyone could stop her, Penny grabbed hold of the sled Marla had been using and took off down the hill in a flash. Lucky raced ahead of her, barking excitedly and zigzagging through the snow.

"Penny, look out!" Esther shouted.

It was too late. Lucky bumped the sled, and Penny screamed as her hat flew off. The sled flipped over, and Penny landed at the base of a tree with a horrible *thud*!

Chapter 13

Esther raced down the hill and dropped to her knees beside Penny, who was laying facedown in the snow. Lucky stood over her, whimpering.

Esther pushed the dog aside and quickly turned Penny over. "Ach, my!" she gasped when she saw blood oozing out of a gash in the little girl's forehead.

Penny's eyes opened and she looked up at Esther with a blank stare. "Wh–what happened?"

"You flew off the sled." Esther removed the scarf she wore around her neck and wrapped it around Penny's forehead to stop the bleeding.

"Is she okay?" Suzanne asked, kneeling on the snow beside Penny. Marla and Leon had joined them now, too, wearing worried expressions.

"There's a nasty-looking cut on her forehead. I think she either hit the runner of the sled or the tree." Esther felt deep concern, but she tried to remain calm for the children's sake, as she didn't want to frighten them. "She could have a concussion, and I'm sure she's going to need stitches," she whispered to Suzanne. "We need to get her back to the house right away."

"Let's put her on the sled, and I'll pull it to the house. That'll be quicker and easier than one of us trying to carry her," Suzanne said.

Once they got Penny situated on the sled, Esther carried Jared, while Marla and Leon pulled the other two sleds, and they headed as quickly as possible for the house.

"Sure wish we didn't have to quit sleddin'," Leon complained as they trudged along.

"We can't sled no more, dummkopp. Penny's been hurt." Marla's chin quivered. "You don't want her to die, like Mammi did, do ya?"

"I ain't no dunce, and Penny ain't gonna die," the boy shot back.

"She might. Mammi died when she fell down the *schteeg*."

Leon's face turned white as the snow beneath their feet. "Ya really think so?"

"Your sister is not going to die," Esther was quick to say. "She'll be fine once we get her cleaned up and see if she'll need to go to the doctor for stitches."

Marla gave a nod, but Leon didn't look one bit convinced. It was obvious that the pain of losing his mother was still very real. Esther wished there was something she could do to bring healing to Samuel's children. Samuel, too, for that matter, but she didn't think he'd ever let her get close enough to offer comfort. He didn't seem to let anyone get close to him—not even his children or Titus.

Esther had a tender heart toward those who were hurting. She'd been like that since she was a child. She remembered once when her brother James had broken his arm after falling from a tree in their yard. She'd felt his pain as if it were her own. Then there was the time her dog, Rascal, had gotten hit by a car. When they'd brought Rascal home from the vet's, she'd stayed by his side for hours on end.

"We're almost there," Suzanne said, pointing to the house as it came into view. "I think I see Samuel out by the barn."

—∞—

When Samuel spotted Suzanne pulling Penny on a sled, he knew something was wrong. They hadn't been gone very long, and he was sure the kids wouldn't have agreed to quit sledding so soon.

As the group drew closer, he noticed that Penny had a scarf wrapped around her forehead, and both Suzanne and Esther wore looks of concern.

"*Was is letz do?*" he asked, dropping to his knees beside the sled.

"Penny fell off the sled and cut her forehead on either the runner or a tree," Suzanne replied, explaining what was wrong.

"Wasn't anyone watching her?"

Esther stepped forward. "We were, but she jumped on the sled and took off down the hill, and then before we hardly realized what had happened, Lucky darted in front of the sled and Penny flew off."

"I ought to get rid of that good-for-nothing mutt!" Samuel's hand shook as he removed the scarf from Penny's head. There was a fairly deep gash on her forehead, and he knew immediately it was going to need stitches. "I'll take you into the house where it's warm, and then I'm going to call a driver so we can go to the hospital in Hopkinsville, where you can be seen by a doctor."

He scooped Penny into his arms and hurried into the house. When he placed her on the sofa and took a seat beside her, everyone gathered around, exchanging concerned glances.

"What's going on?" Titus asked, stepping out of the kitchen. He halted when he looked at Penny. "What happened to her?"

Samuel repeated what Suzanne had told him about the accident, and then he added, "They weren't watching the kinner close enough. I shouldn't have let 'em go sledding."

"Don't blame Esther or Suzanne," Titus said. "It sounds like Lucky was the cause of the accident, and I'm sure he didn't run into the sled on purpose."

Samuel grunted. "I realize that, but it wouldn't have happened if they'd been watching Penny closer. She's too young to ride on the sled alone." He stood. "I'm going out to the phone shanty to call one of your drivers so I can take Penny to the emergency room at the hospital." Samuel turned and rushed out the door.

He was almost to the phone shanty when Allen's truck pulled into the yard. Allen waved at Samuel and called, "I was at Bonnie's doing some work for her and decided to stop by here on my way home to see how everyone's doing."

Samuel raced over to Allen. "Penny cut her head on the sled, and I need someone to take us to the hospital. Would you be able to do that?"

Allen hopped out of the truck. "Of course I can."

"Thank you," Samuel said, relieved that Allen had shown up when he did. "I'll get Penny and meet you in the truck."

Esther glanced at the clock on the wall in Titus's kitchen, where she and Suzanne had begun making lunch while Titus kept the children entertained in the living room. "Samuel and Penny have been gone two hours already. I wonder what's taking so long."

Suzanne shrugged. "Maybe they had to wait awhile in the emergency room. This time of the year, more people seem to get sick."

Esther frowned. "I'm afraid Samuel thinks I'm not a responsible person. I'd be really disappointed if he won't let me watch his kinner anymore because of this."

"I don't think you have to worry about that. Samuel was just upset when he saw the gash on Penny's forehead, and he needed someone to blame." Suzanne placed a loaf of bread on the counter. "One good thing came from Penny's accident though."

"What's that?"

"Samuel pulled out of his depression long enough to focus on something other than his own pain."

"I suppose that's true, but it's too bad it took Penny getting hurt to get his attention."

"Is lunch ready yet?" Titus asked, poking his head into the room. "The kinner say they're feeling *hungerich*." He thumped his stomach. "To tell you the truth, I'm kind of hungry myself."

Suzanne laughed. "You're always hungry, so what else is new?"

"Guess you're right about that," he said with a grin, and they all laughed even harder when his stomach let out a growl of protest.

"We'll call you as soon as we have everything on the table," Suzanne said after their laughter died down.

When Titus returned to the living room, Esther and Suzanne finished making tuna fish sandwiches. They'd just called everyone to eat when Samuel returned home with Penny. Allen was with them.

"How's Penny?" Esther asked before anyone else could voice the question.

"She doesn't have a concussion, but she did need several

stitches." Samuel pointed to the bandage on Penny's forehead. "She was a brave little *maedel.*"

"They gave me a lollipop," Penny said with a nod. "So I didn't cry no more after that."

Esther was relieved to hear that Penny was okay. She left her chair and bent to give the sweet little girl a hug; then she motioned to the table. "We were just about to eat some lunch, so why don't you both take a seat and join us?"

"No thanks. I'm not hungry." Samuel barely glanced at Esther before hurrying out of the room, but Penny didn't hesitate to find a chair.

Esther grimaced as she gripped the edge of her apron. *He's obviously upset, and I'm sure he still blames me for Penny's accident. Everything had been going so well, and the kinner were having some much-needed fun this morning. Now I wish we'd never gone sledding.*

CHAPTER 14

Don't forget about the birthday supper I'm fixing for Marla tomorrow evening," Esther said as she and Bonnie sat at the kitchen table, having a cup of tea in Bonnie's kitchen.

"Thanks for the reminder," Bonnie said, watching the steam rise from her cup. "I've been so busy with things around here all week that I'd almost forgotten about the birthday supper. I'll have to go shopping tomorrow morning and see what I can find to give Marla for a present." She lifted her teacup and took a drink. "Do you know what she might like?"

Esther blotted her lips with a napkin. "I'm giving Marla a drawing tablet and some colored pencils. Suzanne said she'd bought a couple of puzzles, and I think Titus is giving her a sled, which I know she really wants. I'm not sure what, if anything, Samuel will give her."

"I'll need to get her something different than the others, then. Any suggestions at all?" Bonnie asked.

"She might like a doll or a game."

Bonnie gave a nod. "I'll drive to Hopkinsville in the

morning and see what I can find."

"The party's a surprise, so I haven't said anything about it to any of Samuel's kids, because they'd probably tell Marla."

"I assume Samuel knows though."

"I hope so. Titus was supposed to tell him." Esther's furrowed brows showed her obvious concern. "Samuel seems to be living in a world of his own most of the time, so it's hard to say whether he'll remember his daughter's birthday or not."

"I think the grief he feels over his wife's death has taken a toll on him." Bonnie finished her tea and set the cup down. "I can understand that, because when my mother died from a brain tumor, my father sank into depression, and I don't think he's ever fully recovered. I believe he may have felt guilty because they argued so much when she was alive."

"I'm sorry about your mother." Esther placed her hand on Bonnie's arm and gave it a couple of soft pats. "It must have been hard on you to lose your mother, too."

Bonnie gave a slow nod. "I was only thirteen, and it was rough going through my teen years with only a father who barely knew I was alive. At least Samuel has the support of Titus, as well as his family in Pennsylvania. My dad's an only child, and he really had no one after Mom died; although I'm sure my grandparents would have offered him support if he'd let them." She pushed away from the table and stood. "That's enough talk about death for one day. Shall we get started on my baking lesson?"

"I'm ready if you are." Esther stood, too. "Would you like to make Marla's birthday cake?"

Bonnie nibbled on her bottom lip as she contemplated the idea. "I'd better not. It would probably turn out to be a flop."

Esther went to the cupboard and took down a sack of flour. "I don't think it will be a flop, and you'll never learn to bake a cake unless you try."

Bonnie smiled. "With your help, I'll give it a try."

The following evening as Esther set the table in Titus's kitchen, she hummed softly. The chicken and potatoes baking in the oven were almost done; a tossed green salad was chilling in the refrigerator, along with some cut-up pickles and carrots sticks; and a kettle of creamed corn simmered on the stove. Marla and Leon had been home from school for about an hour, and as soon as Suzanne, Titus, Bonnie, and Samuel got here, they could eat.

"Somethin' smells really good in here." Marla sniffed the air as she entered the kitchen. "How come you're cookin' supper, Esther? Uncle Titus usually does that."

"I thought your uncle deserved a little break tonight," Esther replied.

"How come you're puttin' so many plates on the table?"

Esther smiled, watching the youngster's expression. "Because I'm staying for supper, and a few others are coming to join us."

"Who's coming?" Marla questioned.

"Bonnie Taylor and Suzanne."

"Are they comin' because it's my birthday?"

"Jah."

The little girl's eyes lit up, and her face broke into a wide smile. "I got a couple of cards in the mail yesterday, but I didn't think anyone was gonna do anything special for my birthday. Last year Mammi made a chocolate cake with vanilla icing, and all my cousins came over for my birthday." Her face sobered. "Since Mammi's gone and we've moved here, I guess there won't be no more parties like that anymore."

Esther's heart clenched. One minute Marla had seemed so happy, and the next minute her joy had turned to sorrow. Samuel wasn't the only one who missed Elsie. His children were still grieving, and he was too immersed in his own pain to see theirs.

"I know you must miss your mamm a lot, and I'm sure it's been hard for you to move away from all your family and friends in Pennsylvania." Esther bent down and gave Marla a hug. "I know I can't take the place of your *mudder*, but I would like to be your friend, and I want to make your birthday a special one."

Tears welled in Marla's eyes, and she sniffed a couple of times. "Danki, Esther."

The back door opened just then, and Titus entered the kitchen, along with Suzanne.

"Umm. . . Something smells real good in here," Titus said, sniffing the air. Then he leaned over and gave Marla a hug. "Happy birthday, Marla."

She grinned up at him, all tears forgotten. "Did Daadi come with you?"

Titus shook his head. "But I told him about your birthday supper, so I'm sure he'll be here soon."

Just then, a knock sounded on the back door.

"Come in," Titus said, looking to see who it was.

A few seconds later, Bonnie stepped into the room, carrying a box with Marla's birthday cake inside. With Esther's help, she'd made a chocolate cake with vanilla icing, and they'd decorated it with little heart-shaped candies, since tomorrow would be Valentine's Day.

Marla seemed excited when she saw the cake and ran into the other room to get her brothers and sister. After everyone had made over the cake awhile, Esther mentioned to Suzanne that supper was ready, and she wondered if they should eat or wait for Samuel.

"I say we eat," Titus said before Suzanne could respond. "The kinner are hungry, and there's no point in making 'em wait or letting this fine meal be ruined trying to keep it warm for Samuel. He can eat when he gets here."

Esther didn't feel right about having supper without Samuel, but Titus was right: the children needed to eat. So with the help of Suzanne and Bonnie, the food was quickly put on the table and everyone took their seats. They were almost finished with the meal when the back door opened and Samuel stepped into the kitchen.

"What's goin' on?" he asked, looking at the table as everyone watched him.

"We're eating supper." Titus's tone sounded a bit miffed as he motioned to the platter, where only a few pieces of chicken were left. "And you're late."

"Uh—well—the paint job I was working on today took longer than I expected. Then my driver was late pickin' me up," Samuel mumbled as he set his lunch pail on the counter. "Besides, I didn't realize we were having company for supper."

Esther was about to say something, but Suzanne spoke first. "We're celebrating Marla's birthday tonight. Titus said he told you about it."

Samuel's face turned bright red as he looked at Marla with a guilty expression. "Happy birthday."

She smiled, although it didn't quite reach her eyes. Did she realize that her father had obviously forgotten about her birthday supper? It was certainly evident to Esther.

"We're just about done here," Esther said, "but there's still some food left, so if you'd like to take a seat at the table, we'll wait until you're done eating before we cut the birthday cake."

"No, that's okay. Go ahead and serve the cake. I'm not that hungry anyway."

"You're gonna have a piece of birthday cake, aren't you, Daadi?" Marla asked, turning to her father with a look of anticipation.

"Jah, sure." Samuel took a seat and leaned his elbows on the table. He looked tired and a bit befuddled. Esther was even more sure that he'd forgotten today was Marla's birthday.

"Bonnie made this beautiful cake," Esther said, placing it on the table in front of Marla.

Bonnie smiled. "I couldn't have done it without Esther's help, and I hope it tastes as good as it looks."

"Esther's a great teacher, so I'm sure the cake will be delicious," Suzanne said.

All heads bobbed in agreement. Everyone's but Samuel's, that is. He sat staring at the empty plate in front of him as though in deep thought.

"Now for the candles," Esther said, placing nine candles in the center of the cake. Then Titus lit a match to light the candles, and everyone sang "Happy Birthday" while Marla beamed from ear to ear. When the singing ended, she closed her eyes and blew out the candles with one big breath.

"Did ya make a wish?" Leon asked his sister.

"I did, but it's a secret, and I can't tell ya what it is or it won't come true."

"You can't get what you want from blowin' out birthday candles and makin' a wish," Samuel mumbled. "If you could, I'd bake a cake myself and put a hundred candles on it."

The room got deathly quiet, as all eyes became fixed on Samuel.

He lifted his shoulders in a quick shrug. "I'm just saying. . . I don't believe in wishes."

Marla's chin trembled, and so did Penny's. Esther figured if she didn't do something quick, she'd have a couple of crying girls on her hands.

"Let's cut the cake now so we can taste how good it is," she said, taking a knife from the kitchen drawer. "Suzanne, would you get us some dessert plates?"

Suzanne hurried over to the cupboard and took out enough plates for everyone at the table. Then, as Esther cut the cake and handed each one a piece, Suzanne served up scoops of vanilla ice cream.

"Umm. . . This cake is *appeditlich*," Titus said, smacking his lips.

All heads bobbed again—even Samuel's this time. "It is delicious, and you did a good job making it," he said, looking at Bonnie with a grateful expression.

Bonnie smiled. "Thank you, Samuel."

Esther couldn't help but notice how comfortable Samuel seemed to be around Bonnie. Not like when he was with her—stiff, as though he could hardly stand to look at her.

Esther mulled things over as she ate her cake. *Why would an Amish man be more comfortable around an English woman than he is with an Amish woman? Is there something he finds more appealing about Bonnie than me?* Esther picked up her glass of water and took a drink, forcing her troubling thoughts aside. This evening, she needed to keep her focus on Marla and on making her birthday special.

When everyone finished their cake and ice cream, Suzanne gave Marla her gift.

"Danki. I like it," Marla said after she'd opened a box with two puzzles in it. Then Titus presented Marla with a sled, which he said Suzanne had helped him pick out. Marla seemed quite happy with that gift as well.

Next, Esther handed Marla the present she'd bought. When Marla opened it and removed the drawing tablet and colored pencils, she fairly beamed. "Danki, Esther! Now I can draw a whole bunch of pictures."

Esther smiled. She was pleased that she'd given Marla something she liked.

"Now it's my turn." Bonnie pushed away from the table and returned with the beautifully wrapped gift she'd brought into the house before supper. "I hope you like this," she said, handing it to Marla.

Marla quickly tore off the pink tissue paper and gave Bonnie a happy smile when she pulled out a cute little doll dressed in Amish clothes. "Danki. I really like it. I like everything I got." She turned and looked expectantly at her father, as though waiting to see if he had a gift for her, too.

Esther held her breath, wondering what Samuel would do.

Samuel, feeling guilty and stupid for forgetting his daughter's birthday, didn't know what to say or do. Truth was, he didn't have anything to give Marla. *Elsie would never have forgotten one of our kinner's birthdays,* he thought. *What's wrong with me?*

Suddenly, an idea flashed into his head. There was that box in his room with Elsie's things that he hadn't gone through yet. "I'll be right back," he said, rising from his chair.

"Where ya goin'?" Penny called as he started out of the room.

"To get your sister's present."

Samuel hurried to his room, pulled the box away from the wall, and flipped open the flaps. After a bit of searching, he located one of Elsie's favorite teacups. Thinking Marla might like to have something that belonged to her mother, he returned to the kitchen and gave it her. "This was one of your mamm's favorite *kopplin*," he said.

Marla smiled and lifted the delicate china cup to her lips, as though pretending to drink from it. "Danki, Daadi. Knowin' this was Mammi's makes it my best gift of all."

"Let me see it." Penny reached across Jared, and he turned his head sharply, bumping Marla's arm and knocking the cup out of her hand. It landed on the floor, shattering into several pieces.

Marla gasped and burst into tears.

"Now look what you did!" Samuel pointed at Penny. "You not only took away your sister's birthday present, but you broke your mamm's favorite cup!"

Hands shaking, and forehead beaded with sweat, Samuel stormed out of the house.

Chapter 15

"I'd better go talk to Marla and Penny," Esther said after the two girls had gone tearfully to their room. "This was not a good way for Marla's party to end, and I'm sure she and Penny both could use a bit of comforting right now."

"I'll stay here and clean up the broken cup," Suzanne said.

"I'll clear the table and do the dishes," Bonnie spoke up.

Titus pushed his chair away from the table. "Think I'd better go outside and have a talk with my bruder. No doubt, he could use a bit of comforting, too."

Esther glanced at the boys. Leon sat with his head down, staring at his half-eaten piece of cake. His father's outburst had no doubt upset him. Little Jared, however, seemed unaffected by the whole ordeal. Wearing a grin on his chocolate-smudged face, he sat in his high chair happily eating the piece of birthday cake Esther had given him before Samuel stormed out of the house.

Esther gave Leon's shoulder a tender squeeze. "Would you like some more ice cream?"

He shook his head. "I ain't hungry no more. Think I'll get ready for bed." He leaped off his chair and hurried out of the room.

Esther sighed. Three upset children, and one angry father. What a terrible way for the evening to end. She wished now that she hadn't even planned a party for Marla. But if she hadn't made the effort, there probably wouldn't have been a party at all.

Esther left the kitchen and hurried down the hall to the bedroom the girls shared. She found them both curled up on the bed, crying as though their little hearts had been broken.

"It's all right," she said, taking a seat on the bed beside them and gently patting their backs. "Don't cry."

Penny sat up and hiccupped on a sob. "Daadi's m–mad at me. He thinks I—I broke the kopplin on purpose."

Marla sat up and leaned against Esther. "He don't love us no more."

Esther slipped her arms around both girls' waists, drawing them closer to her. "It was just an accident, and neither of you is to blame. I'm sure once your daed calms down he'll realize that." Esther hoped she was right, and she prayed that when Titus spoke to Samuel, he'd make him understand that it was just an accident.

—m—

Samuel paced back and forth in the barn for a while; then he plopped down on a bale of straw. He'd been stupid to give Marla one of Elsie's cups. She was still a little girl and didn't know how to take care of such a delicate thing.

But of course, he reminded himself, *it wasn't really Marla's fault she dropped the cup. If Penny hadn't reached across Jared, and if Jared hadn't turned his head, he wouldn't have bumped Marla's arm and she wouldn't have let go of the cup. I realize now that none of my kinner are old enough to be anywhere near such a delicate cup.*

Samuel leaned forward and let his head fall into the palms of his hands. He should have left all of Elsie's things with Mama Fannie for safekeeping. Then when the girls were old enough, he could have let them choose whatever they wanted.

"I'm so stupid," he muttered. "Seems like I always make bad decisions, especially where my kinner are concerned."

A cold, wet nose brushed against Samuel's hand, and when he lifted his head, he saw Lucky at his side.

"Go away!" Samuel pushed the dog away. "I don't want to be bothered with you right now."

The dog whimpered and dropped his head onto Samuel's knee, looking up at him with understanding eyes. Did the critter realize Samuel needed some comfort, or was Lucky simply in need of attention? He figured it was probably a bit of both.

With a groan of resignation, he patted the dog's head. After all, the poor critter had done nothing wrong. Truth was, sitting here petting Lucky's silky head felt kind of nice. It was a good way to relieve some of his stress. Maybe he ought to pay the dog more attention from now on instead of always hollering at him to get out of the way or go lie down. In spite of everything, he knew Lucky had to get used to his new surroundings, just like the rest of them. The only thing left that was familiar to the poor dog was Samuel and the kids.

Lost in thought, Samuel sat for several minutes, scratching behind Lucky's ears, until the barn door opened and Titus stepped in. *Oh, great. I hope he didn't come out here to lecture me.*

"You okay?" Titus asked, taking a seat on the bale of straw beside Samuel.

Samuel motioned to Lucky. "I wasn't until the mutt came

and offered me some comfort. After sitting here petting him awhile, I've calmed down a bit."

"You were pretty upset in there." Titus reached over and put his hand on Samuel's arm. "What happened with the teacup was just an accident, you know."

Samuel nodded. "I probably overreacted, but I wanted to give Marla something special that belonged to her mamm, and I'd hoped it would mean as much to her as it did to me."

"I'm sure it did. Didn't you see the way her eyes lit up when you handed her the kopplin?"

"Jah. She's probably just as disappointed as I am that it broke."

"I know she is. She and Penny both ran crying to their bedroom after you yelled and stormed out of the house. I'm sure they both feel responsible for the cup being broken."

"Guess I'll need to apologize to the both of them, and then I should find something else to give Marla." Samuel gently pushed Lucky aside and stood.

"Where are you going?"

"To the house, to talk to the girls."

"Can it wait awhile? Esther's in with 'em right now."

Samuel frowned, as irritation welled in his chest. "They're my kinner, not hers. It ought to be me talking to them, don't you think?" More annoyed with himself that he'd forgotten his daughter's birthday and the fact that he'd been pushing everyone close to him further and further away, even their beloved pooch, had made Samuel feel more agitated when he'd heard that Esther was comforting the girls. Then again, why shouldn't they be comforted by her? In their own little ways, all four of his children had tried reaching out to him, but instead of giving comfort to the children as a dad should, Samuel had once again reacted harshly. His children were trying to go on with life the best they could without their mother—why couldn't he?

"I do think you need to talk to them, but right now what they need is a woman's gentle touch." Titus motioned for Samuel to take a seat. "And I think you and I need to talk."

"About what?"

"Sit down, and I'll tell you what's on my mind."

Samuel wasn't used to having his younger brother tell him what to do, and it kind of irked him. But since he was beholden to Titus for allowing him and the children to stay with him, he figured he'd better at least listen when Titus said he wanted to talk.

He returned to the bale of straw and leaned his head against the wall behind him, figuring he was probably in for a long lecture about what a rotten father he was. Well, he felt like a rotten father, so he might as well admit it.

"I forgot it was Marla's birthday today, and I gave her the cup so she wouldn't know I'd forgotten," Samuel said.

"I figured as much." Titus pulled a piece of straw from the bale of hay he sat upon and stuck it between his teeth. "I wanted to suggest that unless you can find something of Elsie's that's not breakable, you probably should wait until Marla's older to give her more of Elsie's things."

"I've already come to that conclusion." Samuel groaned and slapped the side of his head. "I'm not a good daed anymore."

"You are a good dad," Titus said. "You're just dealing with your own grief, and I don't think you realize how much your kinner are hurting."

"They don't act like it. They carry on like they don't even miss their mamm."

"Do you remember what it was like when you lost your real mother?"

"Jah, I do."

"How old were you when she died?"

Samuel shrugged. "I was pretty young—maybe seven or eight, and I missed her a lot—especially at first, but I kept it pretty much to myself."

"How'd Dad deal with it?"

"He didn't talk much about Mama—at least not to me. Things didn't get a whole lot better till he met Mama Fannie and they decided to get married."

"Maybe you ought to think of getting married again."

Samuel's face heated, and his whole body tensed. "I've told you before—I'll never love anyone the way I did Elsie, so I won't be gettin' married again!"

CHAPTER 16

Paradise, Pennsylvania

On a Friday morning in the middle of March, Timothy knew the minute he stepped into his parents' house that his mother had been doing some baking. The delicious aroma of ginger and cinnamon wafted up to his nose, causing his mouth to water.

"Is that gingerbread I smell?" he asked when he entered the kitchen and found Mom bent over the oven door.

She whirled around, nearly dropping the pan in her hands. "Ach, Timothy! You shouldn't sneak up on me like that!"

"I wasn't sneakin'," he said with a grin. "I'm surprised my noisy boots didn't alert you to the fact that someone was coming."

"I did hear some clomping but thought it was your daed."

"Nope. After we came in from the fields, Dad went out to the barn to feed the horses." Timothy sniffed deeply and pointed to the pan she held. "That looks like gingerbread."

"You're right; it is." She placed a cooling rack on the counter and set the pan of bread on top of it. "Would you like some after it cools?"

He smacked his lips. "Sounds good to me."

"Are you and your daed done for the day, or just taking a break?" Mom asked.

"We're finished. The ground's too wet to get much plowing done. Guess that's to be expected when spring finally comes." He went to the cupboard, took out a glass, and filled it with water. "Mind if I ask you a question, Mom?"

She motioned to one of the chairs at the table. "Have a seat and ask away."

Timothy set his glass down on the table and seated himself. "Do you think it's normal for a married woman to spend more time with her mother than she does her husband?"

"I assume you're talking about Hannah?" Mom asked, taking a seat across from him.

He gave a nod. "As I've told you before, it seems like every time I turn around, Hannah's either over at her mamm's or her mamm's at our place."

"She and Sally do seem to be very close."

"Jah, but you and Abby are close, and she's not over here all the time."

"That's true. Abby's husband and children come first, and if I thought she was spending more time with me than them, I'd say something about it."

Timothy grunted. "I doubt Hannah's mamm would ever say anything to Hannah about her not spending enough time with me. Fact is, I think Sally would have preferred that Hannah stay single and livin' at her parents' home for the rest of her life."

Mom waved away the idea with her hand. "I don't think it's that bad, son."

"Maybe that was a bit of an exaggeration, but I think

Hannah and her mamm are too close, and I wish there was some way I could stop it."

"Have you tried talking to Hannah about the situation?"

"Many times, and she always gets defensive. Even said I was selfish and wanted her all to myself." He took a drink of water and frowned. "I just want to know that the woman I married would rather be with me than anyone else. If Dad didn't need my help farming this place, I'd consider selling our home and moving my wife and daughter to Kentucky."

Mom's eyes widened as she drew in a sharp breath.

"Oh, don't worry," he was quick to say. "Hannah would pitch a fit if I even mentioned the idea."

"Can't say as I'd blame her for that." Mom's eyebrows drew together so they nearly met at the bridge of her nose. "Don't forget, your daed and I visited Titus in Kentucky last year, and I didn't see anything there that would make me want to move."

"Land's cheaper, and it's less populated in Christian County than here. Titus has said so many times."

"Jah, well, just because your twin likes it there doesn't mean you would." Mom leaned forward with her elbows on the table and looked at him intently, the way she had when he was a boy about to receive a stern lecture for something he'd done wrong. "If you think things are bad between you and Hannah now, just move her two states away from her mamm and see what happens."

"I didn't say I was planning to move. Just said I'd consider it if Dad didn't need me here. 'Course, I'd have to talk Hannah into it first, which would be nigh unto impossible."

Mom pursed her lips, causing the wrinkles around her mouth to become more pronounced. "I don't think it's right for Hannah to spend so much time with Sally that she's begun to ignore you, but if it's affecting your marriage, then you'd better have a talk with Jacob Weaver or one of our other ministers. Running from one's problems is not a good idea."

Timothy nodded, but didn't say anything. Truth was, he didn't think his mother would be any happier about them moving to Kentucky than Hannah's mother would be. Well, she didn't have to worry, because short of a miracle, Hannah would never agree to move anywhere that was more than five miles from her folks. What he needed to do was figure out some way to get Hannah paying more attention to him and less to her mother.

Pembroke, Kentucky

"Would you like to have supper with us this evening?" Suzanne asked Titus as the two of them worked on a set of new cabinets one of their neighbors had recently ordered.

"Sorry, but I can't," he said, reaching for another piece of sandpaper. "I need to fix supper for Samuel and the kinner."

Suzanne's frown was so intense that deep lines were etched in her forehead. She looked downright miffed. "You've got to be kidding. Surely Samuel can fix supper for his family."

Titus shrugged. "He probably could if he set his mind to it, but it's all I can do to get him to eat a decent meal, let alone cook anything."

"I know you're concerned about your bruder, but you can't do everything for him. Since Samuel and his kinner moved here, we hardly see each other anymore."

"That's not true." Titus gestured to the cabinets they'd been sanding. "We see each other here at work almost every day."

Her nose wrinkled, like some foul odor had permeated the room. "That's not the same as spending time together doing something fun. Thanks to Samuel, you haven't taken me anywhere or come over for supper even once."

"I'm sorry about that, but it won't always be this way. Once Samuel works through his grief, I won't feel like I have to be there for him all the time."

"What if he never gets over Elsie's death?"

"I'm sure he will. He just needs a little more time." Titus started sanding again. "I talked with Allen the other day, and he's going to ask Samuel to paint a couple of rental houses he recently bought in Hopkinsville. So if Samuel keeps busy, I'm sure that'll help with his depression."

"I thought he was painting the outside of Bonnie's Bed-and-Breakfast."

"He has started on that, but he can't work on it when it's raining. The painting he'll do for Allen will be inside work." Titus stopped sanding and reached over to touch Suzanne's arm. "Are you *missvergunnisch* of the time I spend with Samuel?"

She looked at him intently. "I'm not envious, but I am afraid that because of him, we might never get married."

"That's *lecherich*. Samuel won't stop us from getting married this fall."

"It's not ridiculous. Samuel's been here over two months already, and he's made no effort to find a place of his own."

"His house in Pennsylvania hasn't sold yet, and even if it had, I doubt he could handle raising the kinner on his own."

Suzanne's cheeks flushed a bright pink. "There's no way I can think of moving into your house and starting a family of our own if Samuel and his kinner are still living there. Your place isn't big enough for that, and I'm sure it would eventually cause tension in our marriage."

Titus knew Suzanne was right. After the last couple of

conversations he'd had with his twin, he knew Timothy and Hannah's marriage was full of tension. He didn't want to start his marriage out with differences between him and Suzanne, but he couldn't push Samuel and his kids out of the house either.

"I'll have a talk with Samuel about looking for a place of his own as soon as I feel he's ready," he said.

"What if he's not ready before fall?"

Titus took Suzanne's hand and gave it a gentle squeeze. "Let's pray that he is."

CHAPTER 17

Esther's stomach growled as she stepped into the kitchen, devoid of any pleasant smells. Even though Mom and Dad had been gone for two months, it still seemed strange not to have Mom here fixing breakfast in the mornings. She and Mom had always been close. Not an unhealthy kind of close, where she couldn't do anything without asking her mother first. No, she and Mom had a special bond—an understanding of one another's needs. Whenever Esther had been afraid as a child, Mom had always been there to calm her fears. When she'd had trouble making a decision, she'd gone to Mom for advice.

It wasn't easy to do that now, since Mom and Dad lived two states away. Of course, she could always write Mom a letter or leave her a message on Dan's voice mail. But it wasn't the same as sitting down with a cup of tea and having a good heart-to-heart conversation.

Knowing she needed to set her thoughts aside and fix something for breakfast so she could get over to Titus's to watch the children, Esther heated some water for tea, fixed herself a plate of scrambled eggs, and paired it with a slice of the delicious raisin bread Suzanne's mother had given her last night.

When she took a seat at the table and bowed her head, the first thing she prayed about was her brother.

Dear Lord, please help the doctors find something that will make Dan feel better. Help him find new ways to do things. If he has to begin using a wheelchair, help the transition to be easy. Help Sarah and their kinner to accept the changes and be an encouragement to Dan.

Be with my brother James and his family at their home in Lykens, and of course bless and be with Mom and Dad.

Help Samuel through his struggle with grief, and I pray that I may be a blessing to his kinner today. Help me know what to do to help them through their grief. Amen.

—⁂—

"That looks really good, Samuel," Bonnie said when she'd finished spading her garden plot and joined Samuel on the side of the house where he'd been painting.

Samuel gave a nod and stopped painting long enough to move the ladder to a different spot.

"I'm glad I chose a pale yellow for the color."

"Jah, it looks pretty good," he said.

"Jah, means yes, doesn't it?"

"That's right."

"Esther's been explaining some things to me about the Amish way of life, and I'm hoping to learn some Pennsylvania-Dutch words. She's already taught me a few, but if you're willing, I'd be happy if you'd teach me some, too."

"Why would you want to learn Pennsylvania-Dutch?"

"Since so many of my neighbors are Amish, I thought it

would be a good idea if I was able to understand some of their words."

Samuel picked up his paint brush. "We do speak English, you know."

"Of course, but when my Amish neighbors are talking among themselves, they usually speak their own language."

"So you want to know what they're saying?"

She chuckled. "Jah. That way I can be sure they're not talking about me."

He smiled. At least it felt like a smile. He hadn't found anything to smile about in such a long time he wasn't sure he knew how to smile anymore. "You seem like a nice person, Bonnie. I can't imagine anyone saying anything negative about you."

Bonnie's cheeks flamed. "That's kind of you, but I'm no saint. I'm sure there a few things about me that some folks might not like."

"Sure don't know what it'd be. You've been nothing but kind to me."

"Well, that's because you're such a nice man."

Samuel felt kind of embarrassed by that comment and wasn't quite sure how to respond, so he just shrugged and said, "Guess I'd better get back to work or this house will never get painted."

Paradise, Pennsylvania

"How come you're home so early today?" Hannah asked when Timothy entered the kitchen and found her fixing a sandwich for Mindy. "I figured you and your daed would be working in the fields until late now that the weather's improved."

"We've been pushing the horses hard all morning, so we're giving them a rest," Timothy said. "Thought I'd grab an early lunch while I'm here."

"Oh, I see. Would you like me to fix you a sandwich?"

"That'd be nice." Timothy leaned over and kissed the top of Mindy's head; then he looked back at Hannah. "I'm surprised to see you here."

Her brows furrowed. "Where else would I be?"

"Figured you'd probably be over at your mamm's. That's where you seem to spend all your time these days."

"That's *narrisch*, Timothy. I'm not over at Mom's all the time."

He moved over to the sink to wash his hands. "Jah, you are, and my comment may seem foolish to you, but it's not to me."

"What's that supposed to mean?" Hannah placed Mindy's sandwich on the tray of her high chair and poured her a glass of milk.

"When we got married, I figured I'd come first and then any kinner we had." He glanced back at Mindy, now eagerly eating her sandwich.

Hannah plopped her hands against her slender hips and stared up at him innocently. "I've always put you and Mindy first."

"Oh really? Is that why I've come home so many times and discovered that you were over at your mamm's?" He shook his head. "I hardly ever get to visit with my wife anymore, and I'm gettin' mighty sick of it." Timothy's voice grew louder, and Mindy's eyes widened as she looked up at him fearfully.

"It's okay," he said, gently patting her plump little arm. "Daadi's not mad at you."

"No, he's mad at me," Hannah mumbled, turning her back to him.

Timothy took hold of his wife's arm and turned her to face him. "I think we need to talk."

"Not if you're going to yell." Hannah motioned to Mindy. "I don't want to upset her."

"Let's go in the living room," he suggested.

She hesitated but finally nodded.

After they'd both taken a seat on the sofa, Timothy turned to Hannah and said, "I think we should move."

Her mouth dropped open. "What?"

"I think we should move."

"Where?"

"To Kentucky."

She shook her head vigorously with a determined set of her jaw.

"We need a new start."

Hannah's eyes filled with tears. "It's because of my mamm, isn't it? You want to move to Kentucky to keep me away from her."

Timothy wasn't sure what to say. He didn't want Hannah to think he disliked her mother, but he needed her to understand that her place was with him.

"Will you give up the notion of moving to Kentucky if I agree to stay home more?" she asked tearfully.

Timothy flinched. He hated it when Hannah cried. It always made him feel guilty—like he'd done something wrong. "Even if you stayed home more, your mamm would end up over here," he said, keeping his voice down.

"No, she wouldn't. I'll ask her not to."

"Oh, great. Then she'll think it's my fault and that I'm trying to come between the two of you. As it is, I'm not sure she likes me all that well anyhow."

"That's not true. Both of my parents like you just fine. And

Mom won't think you're trying to come between us."

"How do you know that?"

"Because I'll tell her it was my idea—that I've come to realize that I need to spend more time with you, and that she needs to be with Dad more." Hannah clutched Timothy's shirtsleeve. "Please don't make us move. We wouldn't be happy in Kentucky; I know we wouldn't."

"Maybe you're right," Timothy said. "It would be hard to start over in a new place."

A look of relief spread across her face as she bobbed her head. "That's right. Look what a hard time Samuel's having. He's no better off now than he was when he lived here."

"I guess you have a point." Timothy pulled Hannah into his arms. "If you're willing to give me more of your time and put my needs ahead of your mamm's, then I'll forget about moving."

She smiled up at him sweetly, and his heart nearly melted. "Danki, Timothy. You won't be sorry; you'll see."

Chapter 18

Pembroke, Kentucky

Esther was pleased when she stepped into the phone shanty and discovered a message from her mother, asking her to call.

She reached for the phone, dialed Dan's number, and was surprised when Mom answered the phone.

"Mom! It's so good to hear your voice. I got your message but never expected you'd be near the phone when I returned your call. I figured I'd have to leave a message for you."

"I just came out to the phone shanty to make a call, and the phone rang as soon as I stepped inside. It's so good to hear from you, Esther."

"It's good hearing from you, too."

"How are things going?" Mom asked. "I've been concerned because I haven't heard from you in several days, so that's why I left a message."

"Everything's fine. I'm keeping busy with my two jobs. Oh, and Samuel finished painting the outside of the B&B yesterday, so Bonnie will be opening for business soon—hopefully within the next week or two."

"Does that mean you'll be working there more?" Mom asked.

"I believe so. Bonnie mentioned the idea of me moving into the guest house on her property so I could be closer and help her fix breakfast for her guests every morning."

"But if you did that, our house would be sitting empty, and that might make it easy for someone to break in and steal things."

"I hadn't thought of that. So I'll just keep getting up early and going over there to help with breakfast whenever she needs me to."

"I'm glad you're keeping busy, Esther."

"How's Dan doing?" Esther asked, while watching with fascination as a spider created an intricate web in the corner of the shanty.

"About the same. The new medication he's taking is helping some, but I think he may have to start using a wheelchair soon, because he's still struggling with extreme fatigue and is very wobbly on his feet. Your daed's keeping busy at the two farmer's markets where Dan has his stands, and I've been helping him some there whenever I can."

They talked awhile longer, catching up on things, until Esther glanced at the battery-operated clock sitting on the phone table and realized what time it was. "I'm sorry, Mom, but I'm going to have to hang up now. It's time for me to go over to Titus's to watch the kinner. Allen lined up some paint jobs for Samuel, and I need to get there before his driver picks him up."

"Okay, I'll let you go," Mom said. "Take care, and do keep in touch so we know how you're doing."

"You do the same. I miss you and Dad, and it's been good talking to you. Bye, Mom."

When Esther hung up the phone, she hurried to the barn to get her horse. She had taken the buggy out of the shed before coming to the phone shanty, so all she had to do was hitch Ginger to the buggy. She looked forward to spending another day with Samuel's children because she was becoming more and more attached to them—especially Penny and Jared, who were with her most of the day. Caring for them gave her a taste of what it would be like if she had children of her own.

"I wonder if I'll ever fall in love and get married," she murmured as she stepped into Ginger's stall.

The horse whinnied and nuzzled Esther's hand.

"What do you think, Ginger?" Esther asked, patting the gentle mare's flanks. "Will any man ever ask me to marry him?"

With a shake of her mane, and a little nicker, Ginger answered, as if telling Esther not to worry.

Bonnie had just taken a seat on the window bench in front of the dining room window to have a second cup of coffee, when a knock sounded on the front door. She set her cup down and went to see who it was.

When Bonnie opened the door, she was surprised to see a young Amish boy wearing a bedraggled-looking straw hat standing on the porch, holding a fat red hen. When she'd first heard the knock, she'd thought it might be Allen, as he'd stopped by to say hello to her several times in the last few weeks. But since she hadn't heard a vehicle pull in before the knock sounded on her door, she'd quickly dismissed that idea.

Bonnie had never seen the young boy who stood staring up at her now, but then there were a lot of Amish in the area she hadn't met yet. "May I help you?" she asked.

"Ya need any chickens? We've got more just like her in

our coop at home, and ya can have as many as ya like for a fair price."

"I don't know what I'd do with even one chicken," she said.

"Ya raise 'em for the eggs. . .and for eatin', of course." The boy tipped his head back and grinned up at Bonnie. "Ya got a husband I can talk to 'bout this?"

Bonnie shook her head. "I live here alone. This was my grandparents' house, and it'll soon be turned into a bed-and-breakfast." She gestured to the sign Samuel had put up on the front of the house that read: BONNIE'S BED-AND-BREAKFAST.

The boy glanced at the sign then back at Bonnie. "How many beds have ya got for sale, and are ya chargin' folks to eat breakfast here, too?"

She bit back a chuckle. "I don't sell beds. I'll be renting rooms to people who need a place to stay when they're visiting this area, and I will also feed them breakfast."

"What about supper? Ya gonna feed 'em supper, too?"

"No, just breakfast."

"Don't ya think folks oughta have some supper? They'll get awful hungry if all they get is breakfast every day."

Bonnie was sure the boy didn't understand the concept of a bed-and-breakfast. He was young and probably quite innocent to the things of the modern world. "I might consider offering supper to my guests sometime in the future, but for now, I'll only be serving breakfast."

"If ya had some chickens, you'd have plenty of eggs to fix for breakfast." He looked down at the chicken he held and grinned.

Bonnie mulled the idea over a few seconds and finally said, "How many chickens do you have for sale, and how much would you charge me for them?"

"We've got fifteen hens we could sell ya for three dollars

each, and we'll throw in a rooster for free, 'cause you're gonna need them eggs fertilized if you're plannin' to raise more chickens. If ya say yes, I'll run home and tell my dad; then he'll haul the chickens over to ya after he takes me to school."

"That's fine." Bonnie smiled, tickled by the young boy's salesmanship. "What's your name, anyway?"

"Amos Bontrager. What's yours?"

"I'm Bonnie Taylor, and you know what I think, Amos?"

"What's that?"

"I think you're a pretty good little salesman."

Amos shook his head. "Naw, you're just a good customer." He turned and bounded down the stairs.

"What in the world have I gotten myself into?" Bonnie muttered as she returned to the house. "I don't know the first thing about raising chickens, but I guess that's about to change."

"I hope you're in the mood for oatmeal this morning, because that's what I fixed," Titus said, placing a bowl on the table in front of Samuel. He gestured to the children, already gathered around the table. "As you can see, they're waiting to eat."

"Oatmeal's fine," Samuel said with a shrug. "It really doesn't matter to me."

"I don't like *hawwermehl*," Leon complained when Titus placed several more bowls on the table. "Makes me think I'm eatin' horse food."

"Oatmeal's not horse food." Marla poked her brother's arm. "Just eat it and be thankful."

"Nobody's eating anything until we've prayed." Titus gave Penny and Jared their bowls; then he pulled out his chair at the head of the table and took a seat.

All heads bowed, and when their time of silent prayer was over, Titus picked up the container of brown sugar and handed it to Leon. "If you put some of this on the oatmeal, it'll taste just fine."

The boy scowled. "Nothin' can make horse food taste fine."

"It's not horse food," Marla insisted.

"Jah, it is."

"No, it's not."

"If Leon's not eatin' horse food, then neither am I," Penny said with a shake of her head.

Marla's face turned red. "It's not horse food!"

Leon bobbed his head. "Uh-huh."

"You like Esther's hawwermehl kichlin, don't ya?"

"Jah, but that's different."

"No, it's not. Oatmeal cookies have brown sugar and raisins in 'em, same as what ya can put on oatmeal cereal."

"It's not the same, and I don't like hawwermehl cereal!"

"That's enough!" Samuel slammed his fist down on the table so hard that his glass of milk toppled over.

Jared let out a piercing howl, and Samuel thought his head might explode.

Titus jumped up, grabbed a dishtowel, and quickly mopped up the mess. "It's okay, Jared," he said. "There's nothing to cry about."

Jared continued to howl, and Samuel wanted to scream. It seemed like he could never say or do anything right where the kids were concerned, and all their fussing really got on his nerves.

I wish it had been me who'd died, instead of Elsie, he thought. *She was always better with the kids than me.* He grimaced, as another thought popped into his head. *But if I had died, then*

Elsie would have had the responsibility of trying to raise and support them by herself. Dear Lord, why couldn't You have let Elsie live? How can I can accept her death as Your will? Will I ever feel at peace and happy again?

Chapter 19

Esther took a seat on the sofa in Titus's living room and reached into the satchel she'd brought with her. Penny and Jared were both taking naps, so this was a good time to write a few thoughts in her journal.

As much as I miss Mom and Dad, she wrote, *I'm glad I stayed here in Kentucky. This is home to me, and I enjoy coming over here each day to care for Samuel's kinner. With each passing day I've become more and more attached. When school's out near the end of April, I'll become better acquainted with Marla and Leon. I just wish I could get to know. . .*

Esther paused and lifted her pen. Did she dare write everything that was on her heart?

It's all right, she told herself. *No one but me will ever see what I've written in my journal. No one but me will know my deepest thoughts.*

I have the strangest feeling whenever I'm around Samuel, she continued to write. *I know he's hurting, and it's as though I can almost feel his pain. I want to reach out to him, but I'm not sure how. He keeps his distance and will barely look at me whenever we speak. Yet he doesn't seem that way with Bonnie. He's always willing to help or answer any of her questions.*

A sense of anxiety clutched Esther's heart. Maybe what she'd imagined before wasn't so crazy. Samuel might actually have a personal interest in Bonnie, and she could be interested in him as well. The other day, Bonnie had told Esther that Samuel had taught her some Pennsylvania-Dutch words, and she'd also made some comment about how comfortable she felt when she was around Samuel.

Why would Bonnie ask him to teach her some of our words when she had already asked me? Esther wondered. *Is the reason Bonnie wants to learn our language so she can understand what we're saying, or is she thinking of leaving her modern, English world and—*

"Mammi! Mammi!" Penny's shrill voice echoed down the hallway.

Esther slipped the journal into her satchel and hurried toward the bedroom Penny shared with Marla. She found the little girl curled up on her bed, sobbing.

"What's wrong?" Esther asked, leaning over the bed and gathering the child into her arms.

"I—I miss my mamm." Penny's shoulders shook, and she turned her face toward the wall.

Esther took a seat on the bed. "I know you do," she said softly. "I'm sure your sister and brothers miss her, too."

Penny sniffled. "I–I'm afraid I might forget her." She sat

up and rubbed her eyes. "Sure don't wanna forget my mamm."

"Of course not, and if you talk about your mamm, it will keep her memory alive in your heart." Esther patted Penny's back, hoping to offer the comfort she needed. "You can talk to me about your mamm anytime you like."

"Danki, Esther." Penny leaned against Esther's shoulder with a sigh. "I like you a lot."

"I like you, too," Esther murmured.

"Will you be my new mamm?"

Esther's throat tightened as she slipped her arm around Penny's waist. "I can't be your mamm, sweet girl, but I will be your friend."

—∞—

Bonnie had just picked up her laundry basket and was about to head to the basement, when she heard the whinny of a horse outside. She put the basket on the floor and went to the kitchen window to look out. A horse pulling an open wagon was coming up the driveway. She didn't recognize the Amish man driving the rig, but when she saw several wooden crates in the back of the wagon, she knew it must be Amos Bontrager's father bringing her chickens.

Bonnie slipped into a sweater and hurried out the door.

"You must be Amos's father," she said, when the man halted the horse and climbed down from the wagon.

He gave a nod. "My name's Harley Bontrager. Where do you want the chickens?"

Bonnie gulped. Until this minute, she hadn't realized she didn't have any place for chickens. "Umm. . . Let me see." She glanced around the yard. She couldn't put them in the garage; they'd make a mess and probably hop all over her car. She couldn't let them run free, because she was sure they'd never stay in the yard. Then, too, if she was going to run a B&B, her guests wouldn't want chickens running all over the place, leaving their droppings. *Oh dear, what was I thinking when I agreed to buy these chickens?*

Her gaze came to rest on the storage shed, where Grandpa had kept his lawnmower and yard tools. It wasn't a large structure, but she was sure it was big enough to temporarily house sixteen chickens.

"We can put them in there for now." She gestured to the shed. "I'll have to take out the mower and other tools first though."

Harley tipped his head, and his pale blue eyes seemed to be sizing her up. He probably thought she was a city slicker who didn't have a clue how to raise chickens. Well, it was true; she didn't. But she'd let Amos talk her into buying the chickens so she'd have fresh eggs, and now that the critters were here, she felt obligated to take them.

"Can you wait a few minutes while I clear out the shed?" she asked Harley.

"Sure. I'll help you clear it out, and then I'll need to be on my way. I have to get back to plowin' my fields soon before it starts raining."

Bonnie glanced up. There wasn't a cloud in the sky, but maybe Harley knew something about the weather that she didn't. Or maybe he was just anxious to be on his way.

"I appreciate your help," she said, hurrying toward the shed.

"Where do you want me to put everything?" Harley asked when she opened the shed door.

"I guess we can put them in the garage for now, but I'll have to pull my car out first."

One thing always leads to another, she thought, as she hurried toward the garage. *I have to clear out the shed to make room for chickens and clear out the garage to make room for the yard tools. What next?*

By the time Bonnie had moved her car out of the garage, Harley had the lawnmower, several shovels, a pair of hedge clippers, and two rakes out of the shed. While he put them in the garage, Bonnie went into the shed to see what else needed to go. She figured she'd better remove several clay pots that sat on a shelf. She'd heard that chickens liked to roost, so they might get up on the shelf, and she wouldn't want the pots to get broken because she might want to fill them with flowers and set them out on the front porch for a bit of color.

After she'd hauled the pots to the garage, she returned to the shed, where Harley was gathering more tools. When they'd gotten everything out, she turned to him and said, "I guess you can bring the chickens in now."

"Have you got any nesting boxes?" he asked.

"What are those?"

"Small wooden boxes where the hens can lay their eggs."

"There are some boxes in the attic. I suppose I can use those."

"You'll also need some chicken feeders, watering trays, cracked corn, and laying mash."

She sighed. "Oh my, I am unprepared. I sure hadn't figured on all of that."

"You can't expect chickens to survive if you don't feed and water 'em. And if you want plenty of eggs, you'll need to give 'em some laying mash." Harley's dark eyebrows drew together. "You sure you wanna do this?"

Bonnie thought about the desperate look she'd seen on Amos's face this morning and knew she couldn't say no. She had a hunch that the Bontragers needed money, and even though they weren't charging her a lot for the chickens, she wanted to help out.

"I know it seems that I didn't think things through very well, but I haven't changed my mind," she said, more determined than ever. "So let's get those chickens unloaded, and I'll pay you for them."

After Bonnie got her laundry started, she would head to Hopkinsville and see about getting the things she'd need for the chickens. She also thought she'd better buy a book that would tell her everything she needed to know about raising chickens. Then later, she'd drop by Samuel's and see if he would be willing to build her a chicken coop. It was a cinch she needed one, and soon.

Chapter 20

A cold foot pushed against Samuel's side, jolting him awake. "How many times have I told you to stay on your own side of the bed?" he grumbled as Leon looked at him with sleepy eyes.

"Sorry, Daadi," the boy mumbled. "Don't know where I am in the bed when I'm sleepin'."

Samuel couldn't dispute that fact. He'd found the boy on the floor a few times since he'd begun sharing a room with him and Jared. He glanced at the other side of the room, where Jared lay sleeping on a cot. Bunking in with two active boys wasn't the best arrangement—for him or them. But what else could he do? His house in Pennsylvania still hadn't sold, he wasn't making enough money yet to build or buy a home, and there was nothing for rent in the area right now. Besides, if he moved out on his own, he'd have to deal with the kids by himself, not to mention cleaning, cooking, and doing whatever other chores needed to be done. Right now, the thought of him and the children being on their own seemed overwhelming to Samuel.

He looked at the battery-operated clock on the table by his bed and realized it was only 5:00 a.m. The kids didn't usually get up for school until six.

"I'm awake now, so I may as well get up." Samuel poked Leon's arm. "You, too, since you're the one who woke me."

Leon yawned. "I'm sleepy."

"That's because you've been thrashin' around all night." Samuel pulled the covers aside. "Now climb out of bed and get dressed. You've got chores to do."

Leon clambered out of bed and plodded over to the window. Lifting the shade, he said, "It's still dark outside, and it's Saturday, so there's no school. Can't I sleep awhile longer?"

"No." Samuel put on a shirt, slipped into his pants, and pulled his black suspenders over his shoulders. How could he have forgotten that today was Saturday?

"I'm hungerich," Leon complained. "Can I wait to do my chores till we've had breakfast?"

"No!" Samuel didn't know why, but every word the boy said made him more irritated. He couldn't remember feeling so impatient with the kids when Elsie was alive. He wasn't so forgetful then either.

"Should I wake Jared?" Leon asked.

"You'd better not. If you wake him now, he'll be cranky and out of sorts all day." The last thing Samuel wanted was another issue to cope with. He might not know much about caring for the kids on his own, but he knew that his two-year-old boy needed eight to ten hours of sleep at night, plus at least one nap during the day, or he was impossible to deal with. At least for Samuel, he was. Elsie never seemed to have a problem with Jared. He also knew that Jared was a heavy sleeper, and even loud voices in the room didn't wake him. You had to shake the boy's arm and practically shout in his ear to get him awake.

'Course Jared wasn't like that with Elsie. All she had to do was pick him up and carry him across the room, and he woke right up—in a pleasant mood, too. Not like with me; he usually cries whenever I hold him. Guess that's because I don't have Elsie's gentle touch.

Samuel jammed his feet into his boots. *Stop thinking about Elsie. You need to find something to do to keep your mind busy.*

He turned to face Leon, who was still standing in front of the window. "I asked you to get dressed!" Didn't the boy do anything he was told?

Leon's chin quivered. *"Ich bin mied wie en hund."*

"I don't care if you are tired as a dog. You woke me out of a sound sleep, and since I'm getting up, you are, too."

"But, Daadi..."

"Don't argue with me. Just do as you're told."

"You're a *schtinker*," the boy said defiantly.

Samuel stomped across the room and grabbed Leon's arm roughly. "So you think I'm a mean person, do you? Well, I'll show you how mean I can be." He lifted the boy off his feet, flopped him facedown on the bed, and gave his backside a couple of well-placed swats.

He didn't think he'd hit the boy that hard, but Leon let out a yelp that could have woke the soundest sleeper. In fact, it did. Jared sat straight up and started howling like a wounded heifer.

Unable to deal with it, Samuel rushed out of the room. He'd be heading over to Bonnie's after breakfast to build her a chicken coop, and he could hardly wait to get there. He was glad Titus didn't have to work on Saturdays and would be here to watch the kids, because right now, he didn't have the patience to deal with even one of his kids, let alone all four!

—~—

Bonnie was surprised when she looked out the kitchen window

and saw Samuel's horse and buggy pull into the yard. It was only 7:00 a.m. She hadn't expected him until nine, which is when he said he'd be over.

She set her coffee cup on the counter and stepped outside onto the porch. Despite the early morning chill, there wasn't a cloud in the sky, and no wind at all. It looked like the promise of a beautiful spring day.

"Guder mariye," Bonnie said, joining Samuel near the garage, where he'd tied his horse to the hitching rail he'd constructed several weeks ago. "Did I say 'good morning' right?"

Samuel gave a nod. "Good morning to you, too. Hope it's okay that I came early," he said, without offering an explanation.

"It's fine. I've been up since five. For some reason, I couldn't sleep."

"I can relate to that," he muttered. "I was up early, too."

Cock-a-doodle-do! Cock-a-doodle-do!

Bonnie grimaced. "That noisy rooster's probably the reason I woke up at the crack of dawn."

Making no comment about the rooster, Samuel moved to the back of his buggy and removed a box of tools. Having grown up on a farm, he was probably used to many strange animal sounds. "Where do you want me to build the chicken coop?" he asked.

Bonnie studied the expansive yard a few minutes. "I don't want it too close to the house. It might turn guests away if they can smell the chickens."

"I'd think about getting rid of the rooster if I was you," Samuel mumbled. "Some folks might not appreciate getting woke early in the morning by an irritating rooster."

Bonnie could see by Samuel's sour expression that he was agitated about something, and she was fairly certain it had nothing to do with roosters. She was tempted to ask but figured if he wanted to talk about it, he would.

"Guess I'll keep the rooster for a while and see how it goes," she said. "If any of my guests complain, then I may need to get rid of him though."

Samuel nodded at the box of tools he held. "So where do you want the coop?"

"How about there?" Bonnie pointed to a patch of ground several feet behind the garage. "That should be far enough from the house that my guests won't have to deal with the chicken smells."

"Okay. How big do you want the coop to be?"

"I hadn't thought about that. How big do you think it needs to be?"

"I'd say an eight-by-twelve chicken coop ought to be big enough," he said as he started walking toward the area she'd suggested.

Bonnie followed, and when they got there, he set the tool box on the ground and turned to face her. "I'm guessin' you'd like an outside run for the chickens, too?"

"I suppose that would be a good idea. I can't keep them cooped up all the time, and I certainly don't want them running all over the place."

He tipped his head and stared at her strangely. "I've been wondering. . . Have you ever had chickens before?"

"No, and it shows, doesn't it?" She grinned. "Truth be told, the only experience I've had with chickens are the ones fried golden brown." Bonnie hoped her comment might bring a chuckle from Samuel, but he never even cracked a smile.

"Where's the lumber you want me to use?" he asked. "When you called and left a message for me the other day you said you'd ordered some wood for the coop."

"I did. The Amish man who owns the lumber mill in the area had it delivered for me yesterday. It's piled up on the other side of the garage."

"Okay. I'll cut the pieces I need then start hauling 'em over." Samuel started walking in that direction.

"I'll be in the house. Esther's coming over soon to help me do some more cleaning before I open for business," Bonnie called. "If you need anything, just let me know."

Okay now, she thought as she hurried along. *That's one more thing taken care of. Let's see what I can get into next.*

As Bonnie neared the front door, she stopped and traced her finger on the porch table, leaving a streak of pollen dust. She sneezed. "Yep. Spring is definitely in the air."

Chapter 21

When Esther pulled into Bonnie's yard, she saw Samuel's horse and buggy parked at the hitching rail. He'd no doubt come to build a chicken coop, as Bonnie had mentioned he was going to do when she'd spoken to Esther yesterday.

When she stepped down from the buggy and heard a steady—*Bam! Bam! Bam!*—she knew for certain that was why Samuel had come.

Curious to see how things were going, Esther made sure her horse was secure and headed around the garage. In a clearing several feet away, she saw Samuel hard at work.

"Looks like you have a good start on the chicken coop," she said, stepping up to him.

"It's comin' along," he mumbled without making eye contact.

"How big is it going to be?"

"Eight by twelve feet." Still, he wouldn't look at her.

Bam! Bam! Bam! He hammered another piece of wood to the frame.

She figured she probably wasn't going to get much more out of him, so she turned and headed for the house. She wished he'd be a little more sociable.

Esther found Bonnie in the kitchen, scouring the kitchen sink. "Looks like you're hard at work," she said, removing her black outer bonnet and placing it on one end of the counter.

Bonnie pushed a strand of her curly blond hair away from her face. "Seems like there's always something to do around here." She nodded toward the window. "Now that I've got chickens, it means even more work for me. Lately, I find myself asking, 'What was I thinking?'"

"You could have said no when that little boy came by with his chicken and sales pitch."

"I know, but he was so cute, and I figured his folks probably needed the extra money."

Esther smiled. "You have a tender heart, Bonnie."

A blotch of red erupted on Bonnie's cheeks. "I just care about people. My grandma used to say that if a person loves God, they'll love His people."

"That's what I believe, too, and it's what the Bible teaches." Esther made a sweeping gesture of the room. "Now, what would you like me to do today?"

"With all the renovations that have been done, there's dust everywhere," Bonnie said. "So it would be good if you dusted the living room, dining room, and the banister on the stairs."

"Sure, I can do that." Esther found the dust rag and some furniture polish in the utility room, and then she quickly set to work.

She started in the living room first, and when all the dust had been cleared away from the furniture, window ledges, and fireplace mantle, she moved on to the dining room. Finished with that, she went up the stairs and was about to start working her way down, cleaning the banister rungs, when she heard Samuel come into the house.

"I came for a drink of water," she heard him say to Bonnie when he entered the kitchen.

"Would you rather have a glass of iced tea?" Bonnie asked.

"That sounds good."

"Have a seat, and I'll fix you a sandwich to go with your tea," Bonnie said. "When Esther finishes up with what she's doing, I'll fix her one, too."

"I appreciate the offer, but you don't have to do that."

"It's no trouble. You've been working hard all morning, and I'm sure you're hungry by now."

"Guess I am at that."

Esther tried not to eavesdrop, but their voices floated out of the kitchen and up the stairs. So while she continued to dust and unavoidably listened, she wondered once more why Samuel was so talkative to Bonnie but would barely say more than a few words to her.

"When you first got here this morning, you seemed kind of down," Bonnie said. "I wasn't going to bring it up, but I've been wondering if there might be something wrong."

"Actually, there is. I had a little trouble at home this morning with Leon," Samuel said. "When I told him to get dressed and do his chores, he smarted off to me, so I gave him a spanking."

"Oh, I see."

"I don't normally lose my temper so easily, but it irked me when he said I was a mean person." Samuel groaned deeply. "Guess I *was* mean to him, and now I feel like a bad father."

Esther grimaced. *Poor Leon must have been upset when Samuel spanked him. But the boy shouldn't have said what he did. Even so, I've seen how short Samuel can be with the kinner.*

Maybe he overreacted, the way he did the night Marla dropped her mother's cup. She was pleased when she'd learned that Samuel had apologized for that and had bought Marla several new books for her birthday present, but he obviously had a long way to go if he was going to establish a loving relationship with his children.

"You're not a bad father because you disciplined your son," Bonnie said. "Besides, kids usually get over things quickly and don't hold grudges the way some adults do. Well, most kids, anyway," she added.

"That may be, but I plan to apologize to Leon as soon as I get home."

"When I was little and my dad got mad at me, he never said he was sorry for anything he said or did."

Esther could hear the hurt in Bonnie's voice. No wonder she'd decided to leave Oregon and move here.

Samuel and Bonnie continued to talk for a while, as Bonnie shared with him some details about her childhood. She'd told Esther a few things during the times they'd spent working together, but not nearly as much as she was sharing with Samuel right now. Apparently Bonnie's father had been very harsh. . .especially after his wife died.

"It's hard to live in the same house with someone when there's a lot of stress and undercurrent going on," Bonnie said.

"I know what you mean." Samuel paused. "There's been a lot of tension at Titus's house these days—between me and the kids and between me and Titus."

Esther thought about a conversation she'd had with Suzanne the other day, remembering how upset Suzanne was because Titus spent all his free time with Samuel and the kids instead of her. Esther figured the solution to the problem would be for Samuel to find a place of his own. If things didn't get better soon, she was afraid Suzanne might break her engagement to Titus.

—⁂—

"I can't believe you're stuck watching Samuel's kids again," Suzanne said when she dropped by Titus's house that afternoon and he said that he couldn't go shopping with her because Samuel was over at Bonnie's, building a chicken coop.

Titus put his finger to his lips. "Be careful what you say. The kinner are playing in their rooms. All except for Leon, that is. He went outside some time ago. Did you see him in the yard?"

Suzanne shook her head. "Couldn't Esther watch the kinner today?"

"Nope. She was supposed to go over to Bonnie's to help her clean."

Suzanne folded her arms and tapped her foot impatiently. "Are we ever going to start courting again?"

"Sure. Just as soon as Samuel finds a place of his own."

"When's that going to be?"

Titus shrugged.

"Have you asked him yet?"

"Well no, but. . ."

"What happens if he gets too comfortable with these living arrangements? He'll never move out if you don't ask, and you promised you would."

"I will when I think he's ready. Once Samuel's home in Pennsylvania sells he'll have enough money to start looking for a place of his own."

"With the economy what it is, his house may never sell, and I doubt he'll ever start looking for a place of his own here. Not unless you say something to him."

Titus's teeth snapped together with a *click*. "What do you want me to do. . .throw my own bruder out of my house?"

"Of course not, but. . . Oh, never mind." Suzanne's shoulders slumped as she turned and opened the front door.

"Where are you going?" he asked, stepping onto the porch behind her.

"Shopping. Alone!" Suzanne hurried off, leaving Titus there, shaking his head. *She doesn't understand. If she's not going to be more understanding, then maybe she's not the right woman for me.*

Before Titus went into the house, he decided to go outside to see if Leon was ready to come in for lunch. When he didn't see any sign of the boy, he stepped into the barn to look there. It was dark and quiet. The horses were in the pasture, so it made sense that he didn't hear them, but if Leon was in here playing, there ought to be some sign of him.

Titus cupped his hand around his mouth. "Leon! Are you in here?"

No response.

"Are you hungry for lunch?"

Still no reply.

Thinking the boy might be hiding somewhere, Titus looked around the barn, checking in every nook and cranny. When he'd searched in all the obvious places, he left the barn and walked around the yard again, calling Leon's name. There was no sign of Leon at all.

The hair on the back of Titus's neck prickled. What if Leon had wandered off by himself? With the exception of walking to and from school now that the weather was warmer, the boy didn't know the area that well.

Titus dashed down the driveway and looked up and down the road. No sign of Leon there either.

He raced back to the house and spotted Marla in the living room, sitting on the sofa, reading a book to Penny and Jared. "Have you seen Leon?" Titus asked.

Marla shook her head, but Penny nodded.

"When did you see him?"

"He came in the house awhile ago. Said he had to get somethin'. After that he went outside and never came back."

A shiver of fear shot up Titus's spine. *If Leon doesn't show up soon, I don't know what I'm going to tell Samuel when he gets home.*

Chapter 22

When Suzanne got home from Titus's, she hurried to put her horse away and then went straight to the house. She was still upset about the argument she'd had with Titus and hoped her mother was home so she could tell her about it.

She found Mom in the kitchen, cutting up pieces of chicken.

Mom turned and smiled. "I've got the chicken almost ready to go in the oven, so supper should be ready in about an hour. Did Titus come home with you?"

Suzanne shook her head.

"Is he coming over later then?"

"No. He's watching Samuel's kinner again while Samuel builds a chicken coop for Bonnie Taylor." Suzanne dropped into a seat at the table. "I'm sure Samuel will be home by suppertime, but I guess Titus figures he needs to be there to cook the meal."

"Doesn't Samuel know how to cook?"

Suzanne shrugged. "He probably could if he set his mind

to it, but why would he want to when Titus is there to do it all for him?"

Mom placed the chicken in a baking pan and put it in the oven. After she'd washed and dried her hands, she poured them some tea and took a seat beside Suzanne. "You're upset with Titus again. I can see it on your face and hear it in your voice. Did you two have an argument about Samuel?"

"Jah. It seems like all we do anymore is argue." Suzanne blinked as tears pricked the back of her eyes. "I—I don't think we're going to be married this fall. I think he loves his bruder more than he does me."

Mom placed her hand on Suzanne's arm. "I don't think Titus loves Samuel more than you. He loves him in a different way and no doubt feels a sense of responsibility to be there for Samuel and his kinner, because he knows they're still grieving."

"I understand that, but Titus isn't helping Samuel by doing everything for him or being there all the time. If something doesn't change for the better soon, I'm going to break up with him."

"Ach, Suzanne! You can't mean that."

Suzanne reached for a napkin and blew her nose. "I want things to be the way they were before Samuel and his family moved to Kentucky. I want to go places with Titus and have him come here to visit and share meals with us like he used to do."

Mom took a sip of her tea. "Have you tried talking to him about this—let him know how you feel?"

"Of course I have. That's why we keep arguing. Every time I express my feelings, Titus gets upset and says I need to be more understanding." Suzanne paused and drew in a deep breath. She was so upset her hands had begun to shake. "I do feel sorry for Samuel, and I know losing Elsie couldn't be easy for him, but he shouldn't expect Titus to sacrifice his own life to care for him and his kinner."

"Have you prayed about this matter?" Mom asked. "Have you asked God to give you more patience and understanding?"

Suzanne hung her head in shame. "I have prayed, but my prayers have always been that Samuel will find a place of his own and that Titus and I can begin courting again." She blotted the tears streaming down her face. "I—I guess I do need more patience and understanding. Guess I'm not setting a very good Christian example."

Mom lifted Suzanne's chin and looked like she was about to say something, when Grandpa entered the room.

"Where's Titus?" he asked. "I thought he'd be joining us for supper this evening."

"I invited him, but he said he couldn't come because he had to watch Samuel's kinner." Suzanne felt her cheeks to see if all the tears were gone. She hoped Grandpa wouldn't know she'd been crying.

"He must not be watching 'em too well because when I was on the way home from visiting the bishop just now, I saw Samuel's boy, Leon, getting into someone's car."

"Whose car was it?" Mom asked.

Grandpa shrugged. "Beats me. I've never seen it before. Thought at first it might be someone Titus knows, but the more I think about it, the more concern I feel."

Alarm rose in Suzanne's chest. She was sure Titus would never allow any of the children to go off in a car without him or Samuel accompanying them—much less with a stranger.

"Do you know the make or color of the car?" Suzanne asked.

He squinted and rubbed the bridge of his nose. "The car was kind of a silver gray. It was one of those little compact cars, but I don't know the make, and I didn't take notice of the license plate number either."

"Did you get a look at the driver?" Mom questioned.

"Not a good one. Just saw the back of his head. I think his hair was blond, and he wore a baseball cap."

As fear gripped Suzanne, she pushed her chair quickly aside and stood. "I'm going back over to Titus's. He needs to know about this!"

—∞—

"Where's Bonnie?" Samuel asked, poking his head into the living room, where Esther was cleaning the brick on the front of the fireplace.

"Upstairs. Do you need me to get her?"

He shook his head. "That's all right. Just wanted to tell her I'm done with the coop and am heading home now."

"Okay. I'll let her know." Esther was tempted to mention what she'd heard Samuel and Bonnie talking about earlier, but didn't want him to think she'd been eavesdropping. Besides, he might not want to talk to her about the problem he'd had with Leon this morning, although he sure hadn't minded discussing it with Bonnie.

Samuel hesitated, like he wanted to say something more, but then he turned and headed out the door.

Esther's stomach growled noisily, and she glanced at the clock on the mantle. No wonder she was hungry. It was almost five o'clock. She should head home soon and start supper, but the thought of eating alone held no appeal.

"Was that Samuel's voice I heard?" Bonnie asked when she came downstairs a few minutes later.

"Yes, he wanted me to tell you that he'd finished the chicken coop and was going home."

"Oh, good. Would you like to go outside with me and take a look at it?"

"Sure." Esther put her cleaning supplies aside and followed Bonnie out the door.

As they approached the new chicken coop, Esther heard the chickens clucking. "Sounds like they're in there already," she said to Bonnie. "Samuel must have transferred them from the shed to the new coop before he left."

Bonnie opened the door, and as they stepped inside, they were greeted by a cackling hen that managed to slip between her legs. "Shut the door, quick, before she gets out! She might be hard to catch."

Esther complied, and in so doing, she spotted a straw hat on the floor. "Looks like Samuel left this behind," she said, bending to pick it up. "I'll drop it off to him on my way home. Speaking of which, I should probably be heading out soon."

Bonnie smiled. "No problem. You've done enough for today. I wouldn't be this far along with all the cleaning if it weren't for you."

As Samuel headed for Titus's place, he rehearsed what he was going to say to Leon. The boy needed to know he was loved but that he couldn't talk disrespectfully to his father—or any other adult, for that matter.

First off, I need to apologize for being so harsh, Samuel reminded himself. *I should never have lost my temper like that with him this morning.*

When Samuel guided his horse and buggy into Titus's yard a short time later, he saw Titus step out of the phone shanty.

"I've got some bad news," Titus said, joining Samuel beside his buggy.

"What's wrong?"

"Leon is missing."

"Wh–what do you mean?"

"He disappeared. I've searched everywhere for him—in the house, in the barn, all around the yard. He's nowhere to be found."

Samuel leaped out of the buggy. "He's got to be somewhere. Have you checked with the neighbors?"

Titus nodded. "I've made several phone calls, but no one's seen Leon."

"I'm going down the road to look and call for him. He might be hiding in the woods."

Clippety-clop! Clippety-clop! A horse and buggy pulled into the yard. It was Esther.

"You left this at Bonnie's," she said, leaning out the buggy and holding Samuel's straw hat out to him.

"Just leave it somewhere," Samuel said, barely looking at her. "I'm heading out to look for Leon."

"Isn't he here?" she asked.

Titus stepped forward and explained the situation.

She gasped. "I hope he's okay."

"Esther, could you stay with the kinner so I can go with Samuel to look for Leon?" Titus asked.

"Sure, no problem. I'd be happy to stay. I can fix the kinner their supper, too."

Just then, Suzanne's horse and buggy pulled in. She jumped out quickly and dashed up to Samuel. "Is Leon here?"

Samuel shook his head.

"He's missing," Titus said. "I've looked all over for him. Samuel and I are going to search along the road and in the woods if need be."

She drew in a quick breath. "I hate to tell you this, but my grandpa just told us that he saw Leon getting into someone's car."

"Whose car?" Samuel asked.

"He didn't recognize it, and he didn't get a good look at the man who was driving the vehicle either."

Samuel's heart pounded like a herd of stampeding horses as he broke out in a cold sweat. "I'm sure Leon wouldn't have gotten into the man's car unless he'd been forced." He squeezed his fingers into the palms of his hands until they dug into his flesh. "I think my boy's been kidnapped, and I'm the one to blame."

Chapter 23

What'd the sheriff have to say?" Titus asked when Samuel stepped out of the phone shanty.

"He said they'd be searching for Leon, and that we should also keep looking. He wanted me to give him a picture of Leon, but I told him I didn't have any." Samuel frowned. "Sure wish I did though."

"You gave him a good description of Leon, didn't you?" Titus asked.

"Of course, but I'm not sure how much it'll help." Samuel moaned deeply. "I can't believe my boy's been kidnapped. Makes me think about how everyone in my family felt when Zach was snatched from our yard."

Titus placed his hand on Samuel's shoulder and gave it a squeeze. "We don't know for sure that Leon's been kidnapped."

"Suzanne said her grandpa saw Leon get into a stranger's car. I've warned my kinner many times not to go anywhere with someone they don't know, so I'm sure Leon didn't get into the car willingly." Samuel drew in a quick breath and released it with another moan. "I was pretty young when Zach was taken, but I can still remember how upset everyone was, and Naomi blamed herself for it. She felt like everyone else blamed her, too." He rubbed his forehead, where sweat had beaded up, feeling more anxious by the minute. "I can understand that now, because I blame myself for Leon being taken."

"It's not your fault. You had no way of knowing someone would come along and coax the boy into their car."

"What makes you think he was coaxed? Maybe Leon was forced." Samuel clenched his fingers as he held his arms tightly against his sides in an effort to keep from shaking. "Either way, I'm the one to blame. If I hadn't gotten angry with him this morning, he wouldn't have taken off."

"He might not have taken off. He may have just gone outside to play."

Samuel wrung his hands as he shook his head. "I don't think so. If he'd been playing, he wouldn't have been out by the road; he'd have been in the yard or barn."

"You're upset and need to calm down. I think you ought to go in the house and be with your kinner while we wait for the sheriff."

"Of course I'm upset. You'd be upset, too, if you had a son who'd gone missing." Samuel glared at Titus. "And I'd appreciate it if you'd stop tellin' me what to do. I'm going to get my horse buggy so I can look for Leon by myself." Samuel hurried away. *Lord, help me. I'd never be able to live with myself if anything happens to my boy.*

"I'm glad we're both here right now," Esther told Suzanne as they scurried around Titus's kitchen getting supper ready. "Not only do the kinner need to be fed, but someone needs to be here to watch them while Samuel's out looking for Leon and Titus is in the shanty making phone calls."

"Titus will probably be awhile calling his family back home, and I'm sure they'll be quite upset when they hear the news," Suzanne said. "I just hope Leon is found soon and that he hasn't been harmed. Titus and Timothy weren't born during the time of their brother Zach's kidnapping, but from what Titus has been told, the whole family was in a terrible turmoil after Zach disappeared. It took twenty years for him to be reunited with them. Can you imagine that?"

"That's baremlich. Sure hope things turn out better for Leon. Samuel's suffered enough over the loss of his wife and unborn baby. I can't imagine how he'd deal with losing Leon, too."

"Let's not think about that." Suzanne took out a loaf of bread and stacked several slices on a plate. "We need to think positively and pray for Leon."

Esther nodded. "I have been praying, and will continue to do so until he's found."

The back door swung open just then, and Titus stepped into the kitchen, looking very upset.

"Did you get a hold of your family in Pennsylvania?" Suzanne asked.

He nodded soberly. "They took it pretty hard—especially Dad. I think it brought back memories of when Zach was taken."

"I figured it might," Suzanne said.

"Then when I hung up from talking to Dad, the sheriff called."

"What'd the sheriff say?" From the grim expression on Titus's face, Esther feared it wasn't good news.

He leaned against the wall as though needing it for

support. "Some English fellow came into his office awhile ago and said he'd seen a young Amish boy walking along the side of the road. Since the boy was alone and appeared to be crying, the man stopped to see if he was okay."

"Was it Leon?" Suzanne questioned.

"From the description the man gave the sheriff, I'd say it was." Titus moved over to the table and took a seat. "Anyway, the man tried to get the boy to give him his name, but he wouldn't. When he asked where the boy lived, he said Pennsylvania."

"Why would Leon say something like that?" Esther asked.

Titus shrugged. "Maybe because he's from Pennsylvania."

"Or maybe he was trying to get to Pennsylvania," Suzanne put in.

Esther drew in a sharp breath. "Could Leon have been running away from home?"

"That's a definite possibility. I heard some raised voices this morning, and Samuel told me awhile ago that he'd lost his temper with Leon." Titus pinched the bridge of his nose. "Anyhow, thinking the boy was lost, the man decided to take him to the sheriff's office."

Hope welled in Esther's chest. "Is Leon with the sheriff now?"

Titus shook his head. "As the man neared Hopkinsville, he realized that he was almost out of gas. So he stopped at a station just inside the city limits, and while he was pumping the gas, the boy hopped out of the car and took off down the street."

"Did the man catch up with him?" Esther asked, hoping against hope that he had.

"Afraid not. Leon must have hidden somewhere, because the man lost sight of him real quick." Titus continued to rub his nose. "So the man went on to the sheriff's office and reported the incident, and the sheriff called here because the description of the boy fit Leon."

"If Leon's somewhere in Hopkinsville, surely he'll be found," Esther said, again feeling hopeful.

"I hope so." Titus frowned. "Trouble is, there are so many places he could hide."

"At least we know he hasn't been kidnapped, and I'm sure he'll be found." Suzanne's voice sounded optimistic, but the look of doubt on her face cancelled it out.

Esther moved over to the table to stand beside Titus. "You don't suppose Leon will try to get to Pennsylvania."

Titus shook his head. "I don't see how he could. He's only six years old and wouldn't even know where to catch a bus. Besides, he has no money."

"Jah, he does," Marla said, entering the room. "Penny said she saw Leon with Daadi's wallet earlier. Guess Daadi must have forgot to take it with him today."

Esther gasped, and Suzanne's mouth dropped open.

Titus pushed his chair back and stood. "I'd better go out to the phone shanty and leave a message for my folks again. They need to know about this latest information, just in case Leon somehow ends up in Pennsylvania. Sure wish Samuel would get back so I can fill him in on all this."

"I don't understand why Samuel went out looking for Leon," Suzanne said. "He had to know that if someone picked Leon up in a car, there was no way he could catch up to them in his horse and buggy. Especially after so much time has gone by since Grandpa saw Leon."

"My bruder's no dummkopp. He's just concerned about his son and is desperate to get him back." Titus shot Suzanne a look of irritation then rushed out the door.

Suzanne groaned and thumped her head. "Oh, great. He's mad at me again."

Esther put her arm around Suzanne's waist, hoping to offer some comfort. "I'm sure he didn't mean to be so sharp. He's obviously worried about Leon, and Samuel, too. Everything will work out as soon as the boy is found."

"*If* he's found," Marla said. "What if my bruder never comes home?"

Chapter 24

Samuel hated to give up his search, but it was dark and he couldn't see much of anything. Discouraged, yet trying to remain hopeful that Titus might have heard something from the sheriff by now, he turned his horse and buggy in the direction of Titus's house. He couldn't shake the nagging fear that he might never see his son again, and he couldn't stop blaming himself.

Dear Lord, he silently prayed, *please take care of my boy, and bring him safely back to us. If You'll grant me this one request, I promise I'll be a better daed from now on.*

When Samuel stepped into the house a short time later, he found Titus sitting in the living room by himself.

"Where is everyone?" he asked.

"Suzanne and Esther were exhausted, so I told 'em to go home, and the kinner are all in bed," Titus said.

"I went a long ways up the highway and stopped at every house I saw," Samuel said. "No one has seen Leon or the car he was riding in." He sank into the rocking chair and leaned his head back. He, too, was exhausted. "Have you heard anything from the sheriff?"

"He said Leon wasn't kidnapped. The man who picked him up thought he was lost so he decided to take him to the sheriff's."

"Is he here? Did the sheriff bring my boy home?" Samuel leaped out of the chair, feeling truly hopeful for the first time since he'd learned that Leon was gone.

"No, he's not here. When the man stopped for gas, Leon hopped out of the car and ran."

"Where is he now?"

Titus shrugged. "We don't know. The man lost sight of him, but the sheriff and his deputies are out searching for Leon. I'm sure it's only a matter of time before he's found."

Samuel's shoulders drooped as he glanced at the clock on the far wall. It was almost ten. The later it got, the worse he felt. Leon had to be frightened out there by himself.

Samuel began to pace—praying, thinking, and praying some more.

"You're not doing yourself any good by doing that," Titus said. "We just need to pray."

Samuel's jaw clenched as he whirled around. "I've been praying. Not that it's gonna do any good. God sure didn't answer my prayers when I asked Him to keep Elsie and our unborn boppli safe from harm, now did He?"

"God's ways are not our ways."

Samuel dropped into the rocking chair again and let his head fall forward into his hands. There wasn't much else he could do for Leon right now except pray, so even if he had lost faith in receiving an answer to his prayers, he closed his eyes and continued to plead with God.

Heavenly Father, Esther silently prayed as she knelt on the floor beside her bed, *please be with Leon tonight. He must be so scared out there all alone. Help the sheriff, or someone else, to find Leon and bring him safely home.*

When Esther's prayer ended, she stood and moved over to the window. It had started raining, and she shivered as she listened to the splattering raindrops hitting the window. It was a chilly spring night—too cold and wet for a little boy to be out on his own.

I wonder if Samuel gave up his search and came home. If I feel this bad about Leon, I can only imagine how terrible Samuel must feel.

Esther folded her arms across her chest. She knew Samuel loved his children, even though he often ignored them. Perhaps the pain of losing his wife had caused Samuel to pull so far into himself that he'd forgotten that his children missed their mother and needed their father. During the time Esther had spent taking care of them, she'd seen how needy they were—especially little Jared, who often called her "mammi." The poor little fellow still sucked his thumb and had a hard time falling asleep unless he was rocked. Not that Esther minded rocking him. She enjoyed holding Jared on her lap and stroking his soft skin. His hair smelled so good after a bath, and his warm, steady breathing nearly lulled her to sleep. She enjoyed everything about caring for Samuel's children, and the more she was with them, the more she longed to become a mother.

Heavenly Father, she prayed once more, *please, please keep Leon safe.*

—∞—

Paradise, Pennsylvania

The sound of heavy footsteps woke Fannie from a restless sleep. In the darkness of the room, lit only by the glow of the moon shining through their bedroom window, she could see her husband's silhouette.

"Abraham, what are you doing up?" she whispered.

"I'm standing by the window."

"I can see that, but why?"

"I couldn't sleep. I'm worried about Samuel and think we ought to go to Kentucky to be with him."

Fannie slipped out of bed and made her way across the room to stand beside Abraham. He was in the middle of planting season and never would have considered going anywhere unless it was an emergency. "I'm worried about Samuel and Leon, too," she said, "but when Titus called to tell us about Leon, he said we should wait until tomorrow to make a decision about going there. By morning, we may have received word that Leon's been found."

"Maybe some stranger will find the boy and take him away. Maybe our family will have to suffer through yet another kidnapping."

Fannie could hear the fear and desperation in Abraham's voice. Even after all these years, the pain of having his own son kidnapped had truly never left him. It was as if Leon's disappearance had stirred up all the old hurts and doubts from the past.

She slipped her arm around his waist. "We must trust God, Abraham. He knows where our grandson is, and if it's His will, then Leon will be found."

"And if it's not?"

"Try not to think about that," she said. "Let's keep our thoughts positive and pray for the best. If we don't have some good news by tomorrow morning, we'll call our driver and head to Kentucky."

Abraham grunted. "Let's hope we're not too late."

Chapter 25

Pembroke, Kentucky

A knock sounded on the front door, causing Bonnie to jump. She'd been lying on the sofa, reading a book, and hadn't expected any company this late at night.

She rose from the sofa and padded across the room in her bare feet. Peeking out the little window near the top of the door, she was surprised to see Allen standing on the porch. Quickly, she opened the door.

"I hope I'm not disturbing you," he said. "I went by Titus's place, but it looked dark, so I figured they'd probably all gone to bed. Then when I came by here and saw a light in your window, I decided to see if you'd heard the news about Samuel's boy."

Bonnie nodded. "Esther stopped on her way home from Titus's this evening and told me Leon was missing, but I haven't heard anything since then. Have you?"

He shook his head. "I can only imagine how Samuel must feel."

"I know, and I've been praying for him, as well as Leon."

"Me, too."

"Would you like to come in for a cup of coffee or some hot chocolate?" she asked.

"Hot chocolate sounds good. I could use a little pick-me-up before I head home."

Bonnie led the way, and Allen followed her into the kitchen.

"Have a seat," she said, motioning to the table. "I'll heat some water for the hot chocolate. All I have is the instant kind, but with a couple of marshmallows on top, maybe you won't know the difference."

He chuckled.

"What's so funny?"

"I was just thinking about how Samuel's brother Zach and I used to get into his mother's cupboards when we were kids. One of our favorite things to snack on was marshmallows. We'd eat 'em till our stomachs were nearly bloated."

She smiled and tossed the bag of marshmallows on the table in front of him. "Here you go. Take as many as you like."

"I've got better sense than to eat the whole bag, but I will have one while we're waiting for the water to heat." Allen opened the bag, reached inside, and popped a marshmallow into his mouth. "Yum. It's been too long since I've had one of these."

Bonnie took two mugs down from the cupboard and emptied a package of hot chocolate mix into each. When the teakettle whistled, she poured the hot water in and stirred it well. The delicious aroma of chocolate wafted up to her nose as she handed Allen a mug.

"I assume since you knew Samuel's brother when you were a child, you must have grown up in Pennsylvania," Bonnie said, taking a seat across from him.

Allen shook his head. "I grew up in Washington State. So did Zach."

She tipped her head in question.

"It's a long story, but to give you the shortened version, Zach was kidnapped when he was a year old, and the man who took him lived in Washington. Zach grew up thinking his name was Jimmy, and that Jim and Linda Scott were his parents."

Bonnie's eyes widened. "That's terrible! No one in their right mind would steal a baby from his family. How did Zach end up back in Pennsylvania?"

Allen added a marshmallow to his hot chocolate and stirred it around. "After Linda died from cancer, the truth came out, so Jimmy, who was twenty-one at the time, went to Pennsylvania in search of his real family."

"Did he find them right away?"

"Nope. He didn't even know their names, so he had no idea where to look. I believe it was God's divine intervention that brought the pieces of the puzzle together for Zach. In the end, the bishop in their church district identified him by a birthmark on his neck."

Bonnie leaned back in her chair. "That's the most incredible story I've ever heard! Someone should write a book or make a movie about it."

"Yeah, it probably would make a good story." Allen's forehead wrinkled. "I missed Zach after he moved to Pennsylvania, but I knew he was where God wanted him to be, and he seems very content to be Amish."

"You've mentioned God twice now. Do you have a personal relationship with Him?"

He nodded. "I accepted Christ as my Savior when I was a boy, and Zach did, too."

"So do you have a church home?"

"Yeah. I attend a great Bible-preaching church in

Hopkinsville. How about you? Have you found a church to attend since you moved here?"

She nodded. "I've been going to the church my grandma attended in Fairview. The people there are nice, and I enjoy the sermons, as well as the music."

"Have you gone to church most of your life?" he questioned.

"No, not really. My mother took me a few times when she was still alive, but it wasn't until I was seventeen that I found the Lord," Bonnie said. "I went to church with a friend of mine, and when the pastor talked about the need to seek God's forgiveness for our sins, it was as though he was speaking directly to me, because I felt so terribly guilty."

He leaned forward and stared at her intently. "I know we've all sinned and need God's forgiveness, but I can't imagine that a woman as nice as you would have anything to feel terribly guilty about."

She dropped her gaze to the table, unable to share the details of her shameful past with him. Instead, she changed the subject. "After my mother died, my dad became bitter and angry. I was worried at first that he was going to drink himself to death and I'd become an orphan, but then he got control of his drinking and became a workaholic instead." She lifted her gaze and picked up her mug. "Dad and I had never been very close, but after he started working long hours at the bank he manages, we drifted even further apart." Tears sprang to her eyes, and she blinked to keep them from falling onto her cheeks. "To make things worse, he's had a grudge against his parents for many years, so when Grandma died, he wouldn't even come here with me to attend her funeral."

"Sounds like what your dad needs is the Lord."

She nodded. "I've been praying for that since I accepted Christ, but Dad's so stubborn and thinks he can do everything in his own strength. He won't even go to church, much less talk with me about spiritual things."

"Well, don't give up praying," Allen said. "In 2 Peter 3:9, God's Word tells us that it's not His will that any should perish, so maybe God will bring someone into your dad's life or cause something to happen that will open his eyes and give him peace."

Yes, Bonnie thought, *and I hope that someday God will give me a sense of peace.*

Samuel's eyes snapped open, and he glanced at the clock on the far wall. It was almost midnight. Apparently he'd dozed off. He looked over at Titus, sprawled out on the sofa with his eyes closed. He'd obviously fallen asleep, too.

I wish we'd hear something from the sheriff, Samuel thought. *I wish God would answer my prayers.*

Tap! Tap! Tap!

Someone was at the front door. What if it was the sheriff and he'd brought bad news?

Samuel rose to his feet and hurried to the door. Good or bad, he had to know.

When he opened it, relief flooded his soul. There stood the sheriff with a tired and very guilty-looking Leon at his side.

"Oh, thank the Lord!" Samuel scooped the boy into his arms and hugged him tightly. "Where was he? Where'd you find my son?" he asked the sheriff.

Before the sheriff could respond, Titus woke up and joined them. "Praises to God, our prayers have been answered!" He put his hand on Leon's head. "I'm going out to the phone shanty and leave another message for the family in Pennsylvania, letting them know you've been found." He slipped past them and hurried out the door.

Samuel turned to the sheriff and asked again, "Where'd you find my son?"

"Inside Walmart. One of the employees found him in the men's room about an hour ago," the sheriff replied. "The man called me, and I went there right away. After questioning the boy, his story was pretty much the same as what the man who'd picked him up in his car earlier today told me."

"What were you doing at Walmart?" Samuel asked as he seated Leon on the sofa.

The boy dropped his gaze to the floor. "I—I was hungerich and *vergelschdere*. Figured I could find somethin' to eat in the store. When I got there, I had to go to the bathroom."

"Well, if you were hungry and scared, you should have told someone you were lost and needed to go home. What possessed you to run off like that?" Samuel's voice shook with all the emotion he felt.

Leon's chin trembled. "I—I thought you didn't love me no more. I was gonna head on back to Pennsylvania."

"Pennsylvania's a long ways off, and you would have gotten lost for sure. You should have known better than to try something like that, and you ought to know I still love you."

Leon's eyes filled with tears that quickly spilled onto his cheeks. "I'm sorry, Daadi. You're always hollerin', and after you gave me a *bletsching* this mornin', I figured you'd be better off without me around." He sniffed and leaned his head against Samuel. "I'm sorry for spoutin' off and callin' you a schtinker. Guess I deserved to be punished."

Guilt as heavy as a load of hay weighed in on Samuel. "I'm the one who should be sorry, son." Choking with emotion, he pulled Leon into his arms. "I've been hurting so much since your mamm died, and because of my grief, I haven't been a good daed to you, Jared, or your sisters. With God's help, I promise to do better from now on."

Chapter 26

Has there been any word on Leon?" Suzanne asked when she arrived at Titus's house on Sunday morning and found him standing on the porch, looking out into the yard.

"Jah. An employee at the Walmart in Hopkinsville found Leon in the men's room last night."

"That's sure good news. What was he doing there, anyway?"

Titus gave Suzanne the details on Leon's adventure, and ended by saying, "It was close to midnight when the sheriff brought him home."

"I'm sure Samuel was very relieved."

"We all were." Titus shuffled his feet a few times. "There's something I need to say to you, and I think I'd better say it before we go to church this morning."

"What's that?"

"I'm sorry for the disagreement we had yesterday. You were right. I've been neglecting you lately, and I'll try to do better from now on." Titus took a step toward her. "Am I forgiven?"

Suzanne nodded. "I'm sorry for my part in the argument

as well. I should be more understanding of Samuel's situation, because I know he is relying on you and really has no other place to go right now."

"What do you think about me hiring a driver so we can go to Ryan's Steakhouse in Hopkinsville for supper one evening?"

"That'd be nice. When did you want to go?"

"How about this coming Saturday? We can go in a little early and do some shopping and then eat supper around five."

"What about Samuel and the kinner? If we're having supper at the steakhouse, who'll fix their supper at home?"

"Samuel's planning to take them to the pond near my place this Saturday so they can do some fishing and have a picnic supper."

"Won't he expect you to fix the food for their picnic?" she asked.

"Nope. Samuel said he's gonna ask Esther to fix the meal."

"Oh. Well he won't be sorry about that, because Esther's a wonderful good cook. If it weren't for her teaching me how to cook, I wouldn't have agreed to marry you this fall."

His forehead wrinkled as he stared at her with a look of confusion. "Is the only reason you said yes to my proposal because you know how to cook?"

She swatted his arm playfully. "Of course not, silly. I said yes because I love you and want to be your wife, but if I hadn't learned to cook, I wouldn't make a good wife, and you deserve to be fed well after we're married."

Titus moved closer and put his arms around her waist. "I'd marry you even if you didn't know how to boil water and I had to do all the cooking myself."

Since no one else was outside and could witness their display of affection, Suzanne melted into his embrace, thankful that everything was all right between them again.

—∞—

Paradise, Pennsylvania

"Our prayers have been answered," Abraham said when he entered the kitchen where Fannie stood at the stove, stirring a kettle of oatmeal.

She whirled around. "Was there a message about Leon?"

A wide smile stretched across his bearded face. "Titus left a message saying the boy's been found and is back with Samuel again."

Fannie crossed both hands over her chest and looked upward with gratitude. "Thank You, Lord!"

"It's not good that he ran away, but it's a relief to know he wasn't kidnapped." Abraham slowly shook his head. "I'd never want anyone to go through the misery I went through after Zach was stolen. There were times when the pain was almost unbearable. I always wondered where he was and whether he was okay or not. Until he came home to us, I was never completely at peace."

Fannie gave Abraham a hug. "I know what a terrible time that was for you. I, too, am relieved that Leon's been found." She pulled back slightly. "Where was he, anyway?"

Abraham told Fannie everything Titus had said. "I'm sure the boy was pretty scared out there on his own."

Fannie clucked her tongue. "Things must be really bad between Samuel and Leon if he was so upset that he decided to run away."

Abraham's face sobered. "Titus said Leon had been trying to come here."

"What?" Fannie's mouth opened wide. "How did he think he was going to get here?"

Abraham shrugged his broad shoulders. "From what Titus said, Leon had Samuel's wallet, and I believe he thought he could either catch a bus or hire a driver to bring him here."

Fannie sank into a seat at the table. "I think Samuel ought to move back to Pennsylvania so we can help with the kinner like we did before."

"That's not the answer, Fannie. What the kinner need is Samuel's attention. Those kids suffered a great loss when their mamm died, and they need their daed now more than ever." Abraham joined her at the table. "From what Titus said in a previous phone conversation, Samuel's been so immersed in his own pain that he hasn't paid much attention to the needs of his kinner. He even blamed Suzanne and her friend Esther when Penny got hurt on the sled awhile back."

"Which is exactly why he needs to be living closer to us—so he can be sure they're getting the proper attention."

"He'll be fine, Fannie. This thing with Leon really gave him a scare, and Titus said that Samuel's planning to spend more time with the kinner from now on. Fact is, he's taking them fishing and on a picnic this Saturday."

"That's good, but it's just one day of fun. The kinner need someone with them all the time—someone who'll give them every bit of the love that they need."

"They have Esther to care for them," he reminded.

Fannie brushed his words aside. "That's not the same as having someone in their family with them. Besides, if Esther's doing such a good job, then why'd Leon run away?"

"I told you before. He was upset with Samuel, and Esther wasn't even watching the kinner that day; Titus was in charge of them."

Before Fannie could comment, the back door opened and Timothy entered the kitchen. "Since it's our in-between

Sunday and there's no church in our district today, Hannah and I thought we'd visit at her brother's church," he said, looking at Abraham. "Just wondered if you and Mom would like to go with us."

"Not today," Abraham said. "Your mamm and I didn't get much sleep last night on account of Samuel's Leon."

Timothy's eyebrows drew together. "What's wrong with Leon? Is he sick?"

"He went missing yesterday," Abraham replied. "We left a message on your voice mail last evening. Didn't you get it?"

Timothy scratched his head. "I haven't checked for messages since yesterday morning." He took the cup of coffee Fannie offered him. "Danki, Mom."

"You're welcome."

"So tell me about Leon. Is he still missing?"

Abraham shook his head. "Thank the good Lord, Leon is back where he belongs, and I think things are going to be better between him and his daed from now on."

"Well, I think we ought to plan another trip to Kentucky soon, even though our grandson is home safe and sound," Fannie said. "I want to see for myself if things are any better."

Abraham shook his head. "Timothy and I are too busy planting the fields for me to go anywhere right now."

"But you were all set to go when you first heard Leon was missing."

"That was different. It was an emergency."

She frowned. "If you won't go to Kentucky now, then how are we supposed to help Samuel with the kinner?"

"We can pray for them." Abraham gave Fannie's arm a gentle pat.

—∞—

Pembroke, Kentucky

Anxious to know if there had been any word on Leon, Esther decided to stop by Titus's place before going to church. She figured if Leon hadn't been found, everyone would be in a state of grief—especially Samuel, who she knew blamed himself for Leon's disappearance. If only there was something she could do to make Samuel and the children feel better, but she realized that no one in Samuel's family would ever feel better until Leon had been found.

Esther stepped onto Titus's porch, and was about to knock, when the door opened and Samuel appeared.

"Esther, I—I didn't know you were here." His face turned red, and he looked a bit befuddled.

"I came by on my way to church to see if there's been any word on Leon."

Samuel smiled widely. It was the first time Esther had seen him smile like that—at least when he'd been looking at her. "The sheriff brought Leon home last night."

Esther appreciated the way Samuel's appearance changed when he allowed himself to smile. "Where was he?" she asked.

"At Walmart." Samuel gave Esther the details of Leon's disappearance. "I'm ever so thankful my boy's okay. Don't know what I'd do if I lost another member of my family right now."

Esther reached out her hand to offer comfort, but when he stepped back, she quickly pulled it away. "I'm glad Leon's okay," she murmured.

He gave a slow nod. "Me, too."

"Will you be going to church today?" she asked.

"Jah. Wouldn't feel right about staying home. Especially

after God answered my prayers and brought Leon home."

She smiled. "I understand. It was an answer to all our prayers."

"The whole ordeal left me pretty shook up, and it's made me realize that I need to spend more time with my kinner." Samuel folded his arms and leaned against the door. "I've decided to take the kinner on a picnic supper at the pond this Saturday, and while we're there we'll do a little fishing."

"That sounds like fun. I'm sure you will all enjoy the day."

Samuel shifted his weight slightly. "Say, I. . .uh. . .was wondering. I'm not much of a cook, so would you be willing to fix us something we could take along to eat?"

"You want me to make your picnic supper?"

"Jah, if you don't mind."

"I'd be happy to do that, Samuel." Esther smiled. She figured if Samuel was asking her to fix the food for the picnic supper, he probably meant for her to go along. She hoped so, anyway, because a picnic with Samuel and his children would certainly be fun.

Chapter 27

On Saturday afternoon, Esther arrived at Titus's house, filled with anticipation. She'd fixed a nice picnic supper for Samuel and his children—fried chicken, potato salad, baked beans, dill pickles, and carrot sticks. For dessert she'd made a pan of brownies and two dozen of her favorite boyfriend cookies. Knowing how much Samuel's children yearned to spend time with him, she figured they were probably looking forward to today even more than she was.

Esther reached into the back of her buggy to get the box of food she'd prepared just as Titus stepped out of the barn.

"Need some help?" he asked.

"I'd appreciate it."

He sniffed the box. "Whatever's in here sure smells *gut*."

"Samuel asked me to fix the food for their picnic, and I hope they'll all think it's good. You're a pretty good cook yourself," she added. "I'm surprised he didn't ask you to make the picnic supper."

"I'm taking Suzanne out for supper this evening, so that's

why he didn't ask me." Titus picked up the box and started walking toward the house. Esther followed.

"I'm glad you and Suzanne are going out," she said. "It's been awhile since the two of you went anywhere alone."

He nodded. "After what happened with Leon, I think Samuel plans to spend more time with the kinner and keep his focus on them instead of allowing himself to be so consumed with grief over losing Elsie."

"I'm glad to hear he wants to spend more time with the kinner. I've tried to give them lots of attention, but it's not the same as spending time with their daed." Esther smiled. "I'm also glad things are better between you and Suzanne. I've been worried about you two."

"No need to worry," he said. "I think everything with us is back on track."

Esther opened the door for Titus, and when they entered the house, Titus took the box of food to the kitchen. Esther found Samuel sitting on the living room sofa, with all four of his children gathered around.

"Wie geht's?" she asked.

Samuel looked up. "We're doing good now that Leon's back home. Everyone's looking forward to going to the pond today."

The children bobbed their heads in agreement.

"I brought the food for your picnic supper," she said.

Samuel smiled. "We appreciate that."

Penny looked up at her father. "Is Esther goin' with us, Daadi?"

Samuel's face turned bright pink. "Well, I. . .uh. . .thought it would be good for us to spend some time alone together."

Esther placed her hand on Penny's shoulder. "I'll be with you on Monday." She hoped the disappointment she felt about not being included in their plans didn't show on her face.

"Is everyone ready to go?" Samuel asked, thumping Leon's shoulder.

The children all nodded and climbed down from the sofa.

"All right, let's get the food Esther prepared, grab our fishing poles, and we'll head for the pond." Samuel stood and turned to Esther. "I sure do appreciate your being willing to fix the picnic supper and also for allowing me to spend some time alone with my kinner."

Esther managed a weak smile. It was the best she could do to hide her disappointment. "I hope you have fun and catch lots of fish." She followed them out the door and watched as they scrambled into Samuel's buggy. It was good to see the children so happy today, and she hoped they'd have a good time at the pond. She was glad to see Samuel take an interest in the children, too. She'd seen a different side of him since Leon had run away—a softer, more sensitive side. Truth was, Esther had begun to have feelings for Samuel that she could no longer deny. Of course, she'd never admit that to anyone, because she was sure Samuel had no interest in her other than as someone to watch his children—and fix their picnic supper.

As Samuel's rig pulled onto the road, Esther started walking toward her horse and buggy. She was almost there when Titus came out of the house and called out to her. "Have you got a minute? There's something I'd like to talk to you about."

"Sure." Esther stopped walking and waited until Titus joined her. "What's up?"

He ran his finger down the side of his nose, looking a bit unsure of himself. "I'm. . .uh. . .not quite sure how to say this, but I'd like to hear your thoughts on something."

"What's that?"

"As much as I enjoy having Samuel and the kinner living with me, I'm afraid if they're still here by the time Suzanne and I are wed, it will put a strain on our marriage. Even though things are better between Suzanne and me now, I don't think she'd be happy sharing a home with my bruder and his four active kinner."

"You're probably right, but if Samuel isn't able to buy a place by then, I'm sure Suzanne will learn to deal with it."

"Maybe so, but. . ." Titus kicked at a stone beneath his feet. "The thing is. . . I was wondering. . ."

"Is there something you think I can do to help Suzanne adjust to the idea that she might have to share her home with Samuel and the kinner?" Esther questioned.

"No, but I was wondering if your folks might be interested in renting their place to Samuel."

Esther's eyebrows lifted. "How could they do that? I'm living there, remember?"

"I was thinking since you're working at the B&B, maybe you could stay there."

"Bonnie mentioned the idea of me living in the little guest house on her property, but I'd have to get Mom and Dad's permission to do that. I'd also have to ask if they'd mind renting their place to Samuel."

"Well, let me know what they say, and if they're agreeable to the idea, we can mention it to Samuel." Titus started to turn toward the house, but then he stopped and motioned to a fishing pole leaning against the barn. "Oh, oh. Looks like Samuel forgot one of their poles."

"I'll be going near the pond on my way home," Esther said. "So unless you have some objections, I'll take the fishing pole along and give it to him."

"That'd be great. Danki, Esther."

—∞—

"Be careful not to get too close," Samuel warned Jared, who was edging near the water. "Marla, keep an eye on your bruder, please."

"Okay, Daadi." She turned to smile at Samuel, and then she darted after her little brother.

Samuel took a seat on the blanket he'd spread on the ground and leaned back on his elbows. The warm spring sun shining down on his face felt so good, and for the first time since Elsie died he allowed himself to fully relax.

"Daadi, aren't ya gonna fish with us?" Leon asked, bumping Samuel's arm.

"I'll fish in a minute, son. I want to sit here awhile and enjoy this nice spring day."

Leon took a seat beside him while Penny went off to play with Marla and Jared. "I wish Mammi could be here with us," the boy said. "I sure do miss her."

Samuel's throat constricted. "I miss her, too, but I'm glad I have you and your brother and sisters."

Leon gave a nod. "Jah."

They sat quietly together, watching as the girls and Jared pitched rocks into the pond. The birds in the nearby trees chirped happily while the bullfrogs sang their deep-throated chorus, but the peacefulness of the moment was interrupted by a noisy vehicle pulling in.

Samuel turned his head and was surprised to see Bonnie climb out of her car. Frolicking at her side was her little mixed-breed terrier, Cody.

Marla, Penny, and Jared rushed excitedly toward the dog, but Leon remained on the blanket with Samuel.

"Wie geht's?" Bonnie called, waving at Samuel.

"Doin' pretty good. How about you?"

"Just fine. I've been wanting to check out this pond for a while but haven't taken the time until now." When Bonnie took a seat on the blanket beside Samuel, Leon gave her a strange look, but she didn't seem to notice.

"I'm surprised to see you here," she said to Samuel. "I thought you might have a paint job to do somewhere today."

He shook his head. "I wanted to spend the day with my kinner."

"Kinner means children, right?"

"Jah."

"Are ya learnin' the *Deitch*?" Leon asked.

She laughed. "Well, I'm trying to anyway. Your daed's taught me a few Pennsylvania-Dutch words."

"How come?" the boy asked.

"Because she asked me to," Samuel replied.

Leon looked at Bonnie and squinted. "Why do ya wanna learn Amish words?"

Samuel gave Leon's arm a light tap. "How come you ask so many questions? Are you writing a book?"

Leon shook his head. " 'Course not. I'd never be able to think up enough words to write a whole book."

Samuel lifted Leon's straw hat from his head and ruffled his light brown hair. "Why don't you join the others for a while? I'll call you when it's time to eat."

"I thought we was gonna fish."

"We will. After we've eaten."

Leon shrugged and shuffled off toward his brother and sisters, who were kept busy chasing after Bonnie's dog.

Bonnie looked over at Samuel and smiled. "I was glad when I heard that Leon had been found. I'm sure you must have been very worried about him."

"I was, and Leon's disappearance opened my eyes to the fact that I need to spend more time with my kinner."

"Like you're doing today?"

"Jah. We came here to do a little fishing and enjoy a picnic supper." Not wishing to appear rude, he motioned to the cooler he'd brought along, full of beverages and the food that needed to be kept cold, as well as the box of picnic food Esther had prepared that didn't need cooling. "If you don't have other plans for supper, you're welcome to eat with us 'cause there's more than enough food."

"That'd be nice. I really wasn't looking forward to going home and eating by myself."

"Should we call the kinner and eat now?" he asked.

"I'm ready to eat whenever you are."

—∞—

When Esther pulled her horse and buggy into the clearing near the pond, she was surprised to see Bonnie's car parked next to the tree where Samuel's horse and buggy had been tied.

She stepped out of the buggy, tied Ginger to another tree, and reached inside the buggy to get the fishing pole. As she headed across the clearing toward the pond, she saw Samuel, his children, and Bonnie sitting on a blanket together. Her heart felt like it had plummeted all the way to her toes. They were eating the food that she'd prepared!

"It's nice to see you." Bonnie smiled up at Esther. "Would you like to join us?"

Esther shook her head. "I just came to bring this." She held the fishing pole out to Samuel. "It was left by the barn."

"Guess I forgot it. Danki, Esther," Samuel said.

Esther gave a nod then turned toward her buggy.

"Are you sure you won't join us?" Bonnie called.

"No thanks. I'd better get home."

As Esther climbed into her buggy, a lump formed in her throat. Samuel was obviously interested in Bonnie, or he wouldn't have invited her to join them for supper. What hurt the most was the fact that he'd asked Esther to fix the picnic supper when he'd planned to invite Bonnie to join them all along.

Chapter 28

As Esther sat at the desk in her room one Saturday evening, writing in her journal, she felt as if a heavy weight rested on her shoulders. Ever since Titus had suggested she rent her house to Samuel, her mind had been swirling with unanswered questions. She'd been praying about it, too, but was still unsure what to do. It would be hard to leave the roomy home she'd lived in since she was a young girl and move into the small guest house on Bonnie's property.

Of course, Esther reasoned, *if Mom and Dad agreed to rent their house to Samuel, that would mean more money coming in to help with Dan's medical expenses.*

As Esther's thoughts shifted gears, she wrote in her journal:

I'm confused about so many things. Even though Bonnie later explained that Samuel hadn't invited her to join them at the pond until she'd shown up there with her dog, it hurt my feelings.

I'm concerned that there might be something besides

friendship between them. Is it my imagination, and am I the only one who sees it? Would Bonnie be willing to give up modern things and join the Amish faith? Could Samuel give up his plain way of life to go English?

Knowing she needed to focus on something else, Esther glanced at the calendar on her bedroom wall. Monday would be her twenty-fourth birthday, and so far she hadn't received even one card in the mail—not even from Mom and Dad. Had everyone forgotten about her birthday? Mom and Dad had a good excuse, she supposed, because they were so busy helping out at Dan's. Last year Suzanne had given Esther a surprise party and invited all their friends. This year, her birthday would probably go right on by, unnoticed. She thought about the birthday supper she'd made for Marla and how Samuel had forgotten his daughter's birthday. Maybe this was the year for forgotten birthdays.

Tears slipped out of Esther's eyes, dribbling down her cheeks, and she sniffed and wiped them away. *I'm just feeling sorry for myself. I'm sad because I have feelings for Samuel and he doesn't even see me. I'm also struggling with the idea of moving out of my home. But if I don't ask Mom and Dad about letting Samuel rent their house, then Suzanne and Titus's relationship will be affected when they get married. I really need to talk to Mom and Dad soon.*

—∞—

On Monday morning, before Esther headed to Titus's to watch Samuel's children, she spotted the mail carrier in front of their box. As soon as he pulled his vehicle away, she hurried down the driveway to get the mail. She was pleased to find a birthday card from her folks, as well as one from both of her brothers. At least her family had remembered her birthday, which made her feel much better.

She rushed back to the house and took a seat at the kitchen table so she could read the letter Mom had enclosed with the card. Things were about the same with Dan, and Dad was keeping busier than ever at the two farmer's markets. Mom ended the note by asking when Esther might be able to come for a visit.

I need to call Mom and Dad right now, Esther decided.

"Are you sure you have time to help me with this today?" Samuel asked Allen as they started painting the inside of a two-story home in Fairview.

"I have some extra time this morning, so it's not a problem. Besides, the Carsons want the job done by the end of the week, and since Frank, the other fellow who does painting for me, is tied up with another job right now, I figured I'd help you here today." Allen dipped his brush into the can of off-white paint. "Painting's not my specialty, but I think I know enough about it to do a fairly decent job."

"I'm sure you do. Would you rather paint the stairwell or the dining room?" Samuel asked.

Allen shrugged. "It doesn't matter to me, but since you're a better and faster painter, maybe you should tackle the dining room."

"Okay."

As Samuel and Allen worked, they visited about the warm spring weather they'd been having.

"It was just starting to turn warm when I took my kids to the pond for a picnic a few weeks ago," Samuel said.

"I never did ask you about that. Was it fun?"

"It was a good day, and Bonnie was there, too. After we ate, she tried her hand at fishing."

"Oh, really?" Allen took a step back, and the next thing Samuel knew, the poor fellow was bouncing down the stairs on his backside. He hit the bottom with a sickening *thunk*!

Samuel dropped his paintbrush and rushed forward. "Allen, are you all right?"

"Oh, my aching back! I don't think I can move," Allen groaned.

Samuel grabbed Allen's cell phone from his shirt pocket and dialed 911.

Chapter 29

"Sorry I'm so late," Samuel said to Esther when he arrived home from work that afternoon. "Allen fell down the stairs while we were painting that house in Fairview, and now he's in the hospital."

Esther's eyes widened. "Oh my! Was he seriously hurt?"

"He's not critical, but his back is sure sore and spasmed up."

Esther frowned. "That's awful. Is he going to be all right?"

"I think so, but it'll take some time. They gave him something for the pain and swelling, and I think they may put him in traction for a while."

"That's too bad." Esther slowly shook her head. "Allen won't be able to work for a while I guess."

"No, he sure won't. I'll have to finish the paint job we were working on by myself, which means I might be late getting home for the rest of this week. Will that affect your job at Bonnie's Bed-and-Breakfast?"

"I don't think so. As long as I go over there sometime every evening to help Bonnie get things ready for her guests the next morning, it doesn't matter what time I get there." She shrugged. "Besides, I only have to go when she has guests."

"Well, good." Samuel removed his straw hat and set it on the small table by the sofa. "It's sure quiet in here. Where are the kinner?"

"They're out in the barn, playing with the katze."

"Guess I'll wander out there and say hello." He moved toward the door. "You're free to go now, Esther."

She hesitated a minute, then nodded. "I'll see you tomorrow, Samuel."

"I'm sorry I'm late," Esther said when she arrived at Bonnie's that evening. "Samuel got home later than usual because Allen got hurt today."

Bonnie's forehead wrinkled in a worried frown. "What happened to Allen?"

Esther explained what Samuel had told her. "I can't imagine how much pain Allen must be in," she said.

Bonnie grimaced. "A back injury can be painful all right. Does Samuel know how long Allen will be in the hospital?"

"I guess it all depends on how long it takes for his back to heal."

"From what I've observed, Allen probably won't make a good patient."

"What makes you think that?" Esther asked.

"He seems to be a workaholic, and workaholics don't like to be laid up very long." Bonnie pointed to herself. "I tend to be like that, too."

Esther smiled. Bonnie was a hard worker, but she'd never thought of her as a workaholic.

"I have two couples arriving later this evening," Bonnie

said. "So are you ready to help me whip up a tasty breakfast casserole I can serve them tomorrow morning?"

"I'm ready if you are."

They headed for the kitchen, and as they prepared the vegetables and meat that would go into the casserole, Esther mentioned that she'd spoken to her folks about renting their home to Samuel, and they'd agreed. "That is, if you're still willing to let me stay in your guest house," she quickly added.

"That would be fine with me." Bonnie smiled. "And if you stayed there, you'd be close to the house here, which would make it easier for you to help me prepare breakfast for my guests and get the rooms serviced."

"Would it be possible to remove the wiring in the guest house so I could live in it without breaking any of our church rules?"

"I don't think that would be a problem at all. I can speak to Allen's electrician about it. The guest house is pretty small, but with some elbow grease I think we could make it quite livable."

"That'd be great," Esther said. "I'll talk to Samuel soon about the possibility of him renting my folks' house."

A knock sounded on the door just then.

"That must be one of my guests." Bonnie hurried into the living room to answer the door. She returned a few minutes later with Suzanne at her side.

"You're not one of the B&B guests," Esther said when Suzanne set a paper sack on the table.

Suzanne chuckled. "No, I'm sure not. I came over to give you this." She reached into the paper sack and handed Esther a wrapped present. "*Hallich gebottsdaag.*"

Esther smiled. "I didn't think you remembered that today was my birthday."

"Of course I remembered. I could never forget my best friend's birthday." Suzanne gave Esther a hug.

Esther unwrapped the present and was surprised when she discovered a leather journal inside the box.

"I know you have one already," Suzanne said, "but you write in it so much, I figured you'd probably be needing a new one soon."

Esther smiled. "You're right about that."

"There's also a Walmart gift certificate in there."

Esther reached into the box again and pulled the certificate out. It was for twenty-five dollars. "Danki, Suzanne. I'm sure I can put this to good use."

Bonnie stepped forward then. "Happy birthday, Esther. If I'd known today was your birthday I'd have baked you a cake or taken you out somewhere special to eat."

"It's okay," Esther said. "I don't need a cake or supper out. I'm just happy to be here with good friends like the both of you."

Chapter 30

"Any word on Allen?" Esther asked the following morning when she entered Titus's house and found Samuel in the living room putting on his work boots.

He shook his head. "But Titus and I have a driver coming to pick us up soon so we can go to the hospital to see Allen."

"You're going this morning?"

"Jah. Figured we'd go before we started work for the day, because with the job I'm on I'll probably be working late, and then Titus can watch the kinner this evening while you're at the B&B, helping Bonnie."

Titus entered the living room just then. "With all the practice I'm getting watching my nieces and nephews, I ought to be pretty good at bein' a daed by the time Suzanne and I have kinner."

Esther nodded and smiled. Then she looked at Samuel and said, "There's something I'd like to discuss with you."

"What's that?" he asked.

"I've been thinking about moving out of my house and

staying in the guest house on Bonnie's property."

"Why would you want to do that?"

"For one thing, there's just one of me roaming around in that big old house, and I think the place would be better for someone with a family. I thought maybe you and the kinner would like to live there. I've already spoken to my folks about it, and they're fine with the idea. The rent they would charge wouldn't be too much either."

Samuel scratched the side of his head. "Well, I don't know. . . ."

"It sounds like a good idea to me," Titus chimed in. "I think it'd be better for you and the kinner than staying here with me where there's not nearly as much room."

Samuel's forehead wrinkled. "Are you trying to get rid of me, Titus?"

" 'Course not, but wouldn't you like to have a place of your own?"

"It wouldn't be mine," Samuel said with a shake of his head. "I'd only be renting the house, remember?" He looked over at Esther and frowned. "Did you come up with this idea for my benefit or yours?"

"Wh–what do you mean?" she stammered.

"Figured maybe you needed the rent money. Am I not paying you enough to watch the kinner?"

She shook her head. "That's not it. I just thought. . ."

"And why would you want to stay in that little guest house when you can have a big house all to yourself?"

"I've only been sleeping at home. Quite often I eat supper with Bonnie, and then I go home, only to sleep, feed my horse, and do a few chores. If you and the kinner were living in my folks' house, I could come over there to watch them and make sure the house is clean, and I can even see that your laundry is done."

"That's a lot more work than you're doin' right now," Samuel said. "You're gonna wear yourself out if you're not careful."

Esther looked at Titus, hoping he'd speak on her behalf. To her relief he did.

"I really do think it's a good idea, Samuel, and I don't think Esther will have any more work than she does now. Maybe less, since she won't have to come over here every day and keep this place clean, too."

A horn honked, and Samuel went to the window. "Our driver's here. We'd better go."

"Will you at least give the idea of renting Esther's folks' house some thought?" Titus asked.

Samuel nodded and hurried out the door.

"It'll work out; you'll see," Titus said to Esther before he followed Samuel outside.

Esther hoped she hadn't made a mistake suggesting that Samuel rent the house. He was obviously not too thrilled about the idea.

She turned toward the kitchen to start breakfast for the children and was surprised to see Leon already sitting at the table with a bowl of cold cereal.

"How long have you been up?" Esther asked.

"Got up when Daadi did." He shoveled a spoonful of cereal into his mouth. "We sleep in the same room, and once he starts movin' around, I wake up."

"I'll bet you'd like to have a room of your own, wouldn't you?" she asked.

He bobbed his head. "Used to have one when we lived in Pennsylvania."

Maybe I should have mentioned to Samuel that my house has five bedrooms, she thought. *That might have given him more incentive to move there.*

"I'm hungerich," Penny said when she and Jared bounced into the kitchen a few minutes later. "What's for breakfast?"

Esther motioned to Leon. "Your bruder's having cold cereal. Would you like that, too, or should I fix you an egg?"

"I want *pannekuche*!" Penny announced.

Esther smiled. "I think that's a good idea. In fact, I didn't have much for breakfast this morning, so I might have a couple of pancakes, too."

Marla entered the room just then, yawning and rubbing her eyes.

"Would you like to help me make some pannekuche?" Esther asked.

Marla grinned and rubbed her stomach. "I sure would! Our mamm used to make pannekuche, and they were real good."

I wonder what it would be like if I were these children's mother, Esther thought as she went to the cupboard to get out the flour and other dry ingredients. *I wonder how it would be if I were Samuel's wife.*

"Did ya hear what I said?" Marla tugged on Esther's apron, pushing her foolish thoughts aside. Marrying Samuel and becoming these children's mother were nothing but silly dreams.

Soon after Bonnie's B&B guests left the house to do some touring of the area, she decided to head for Hopkinsville and see how Allen was doing. By going early in the day, she would have time to do some shopping and get back to the B&B before her guests returned this afternoon.

As Bonnie pulled her car out of the driveway and headed in the direction of Hopkinsville, she thought about the pot of pansies she'd put in the backseat and wondered if Allen would like them. He'd worked hard helping Samuel get the repairs and remodeling done on the B&B, so going to see him and taking a little get-well gift was the least she could do. Allen seemed like a nice man who cared about others and wanted the best for everyone. It was too bad he'd injured his back. She was sure he was anxious to start working again. If she were in his place, she certainly would be.

It seemed odd that a man as attractive as Allen wasn't married. As far as Bonnie knew, he didn't even have a girlfriend. If he did, he'd never mentioned it, although they'd talked about lots of other things when he'd been helping remodel her grandparents' house.

Of course, she reasoned, *I never said anything to him about why I'm still single. Would someone like Allen show an interest in me if he knew what I'd done in the past? Would I even want him to?*

She gave the steering wheel a tap. *The best thing I can do is just concentrate on my new business and forget about love and marriage, because I decided a long time ago that I would never get married.*

—~~~—

Hopkinsville, Kentucky

"How are you feeling this morning?" Samuel asked when he and Titus entered Allen's room.

Allen groaned. It was nice to see his friends, but he wasn't sure they'd enjoy his company much. He'd been irritable ever since the accident happened—partly from the pain, but mostly because he didn't like being laid up. "I've been better," he mumbled.

"Any idea how long you'll have to be here?" Titus asked.

"Nope, but since I'm in no shape to go home yet, I may as well accept the fact that I'm here, albeit against my will."

Samuel took a seat in one of the chairs beside Allen's bed, and Titus sat in the other chair. "Is there anything we can do for you?" Titus asked.

"Not unless you can figure out a way to take charge of all the jobs I've got going right now." Allen winced as a spasm of pain shot through his back. "I should have been watching what I was doing yesterday. Just one false step, and wham!" He winced again. "Don't know what I'll do if I can't get back to working soon."

"I'll do whatever I can to help out, but what about one of the English fellows you have working for you?" Samuel asked. "Can't one of 'em take over till you're back on your feet?"

"Maybe Ron. I called him last night, and he said he'd come here sometime today to talk about it."

"If there's anything I can do, let me know, too," Titus added.

"Thanks, I appreciate both of your offers."

The door to Allen's room opened just then, and Bonnie entered. "How are you feeling?" she asked, stepping up to Allen's bed.

"I've been better, but I guess I'll live."

"I was sorry to hear about your accident." She lifted the pot of pansies she held. "I thought maybe these might cheer you up a bit, and they'll certainly add some color to the room."

"Thanks. That was nice of you." Allen motioned to his bedside table. "You can put them over there."

Bonnie set the pansies on the table, and Samuel offered her his chair.

"I assume Esther's watching the kinner today," she said, taking a seat and directing her question to Samuel.

He nodded. "She got there a few minutes before our driver showed up."

Bonnie looked back at Allen and said, "Any idea how long you'll be in the hospital?"

"My muscles are really in spasm, so I'll probably be here a few more days." He frowned. "I'm not sure how well I'll do on my own after they let me out of here though. With all this pain, I can barely think, let alone fend for myself."

"Do you know someone you could ask to come in and help out?" she questioned.

"I think my mom might come. I had one of the nurses call her and Dad after I got settled in here yesterday, so I wouldn't be surprised if they don't catch the next plane out so Mom can take care of me."

Bonnie nodded affirmatively. "It would be good if you had the help."

"I do need help," Allen said. "What I don't need is my mom hovering over me and telling me what to do, which I'm sure is exactly what she will do."

Chapter 31

Allen rolled onto his side, trying to find a comfortable position on the sofa. It had been a week since he'd come home from the hospital, and his mother had been hovering over him the whole time the way she'd done when he was a boy. Dad had gone home three days ago, saying he needed to get back to work.

Allen thought about the time last year when Titus's folks had come to see him after he'd been hit by two men who'd broken into his house. Titus had complained that his mother hovered over him too much while they were there to help out. Allen guessed maybe that's what most mothers did when their kids—even the grown ones—became sick or got hurt.

"I'm going out for a while to do some shopping," Allen's mother said when she entered the living room. "Do you need me to do anything before I go?"

Allen shook his head.

"Would you like a cup of tea?"

"No, Mom. You ought to know that I don't drink tea."

"Of course I do, but this is iced tea, and since it's such a warm day, I thought it might be refreshing."

"No thanks." He nodded at the half-empty bottle of water on the coffee table. "I'm fine with that."

Mom pushed a wisp of graying blond hair away from her face and smiled. "You know what I think you really need, Allen?"

"What's that?"

"You need a wife to take care of you."

Not this again. How many times had she pestered him about finding a good Christian woman and settling down? Did she really think that would make him find a wife any sooner?

He forced a smile. "You know I have nothing against marriage, but I haven't found the right woman yet."

"You're not still grieving over Sheila's death, are you?"

"No, Mom." Truth was, Allen had pined for his girlfriend long after she'd been hit by a car and killed. But he'd come to grips with it and was ready to get married, if and when he fell in love again.

Mom's forehead wrinkled. "You're not interested in that Amish woman you told us about, I hope."

"You mean, Esther?"

She gave a quick nod.

"If I was interested in her, would you have any objections?" he asked.

"From what you've said about her, she seems like a very nice young woman, but I can't imagine you leaving your way of life to join the Amish faith. I wouldn't think she'd want to leave her faith to become part of the English world either."

"No, I don't suppose she would."

"Then you won't pursue a serious relationship with her?"

"There's no need to worry about that. Esther and I are just friends."

"What about the woman who runs the B&B? When she stopped by here the other day, she seemed quite friendly, and she's very pretty, too."

"Bonnie and I are just friends, same as me and Esther." Allen pulled himself to a sitting position and gritted his teeth. His back still hurt whenever he moved the wrong way, but it felt stiff if he didn't get up and walk around once in a while.

Mom rushed forward with a look of concern. "Do you need some of your pain medicine?"

He shook his head. "I thought you were going shopping."

"I am. Just want to be sure you're okay before I leave."

"I'm fine. If I need anything, I can get it myself." Allen offered her what he hoped was a reassuring smile and motioned to the front door.

"Okay, I'm going." She gave him a quick peck on the cheek. "I'll see you later then."

When Mom went out the door, Allen made a trip to the kitchen to refill his water bottle and then returned to the sofa. It wasn't that he didn't appreciate all his mother had done for him. He probably couldn't have gotten through this past week if it hadn't been for her. But he was anxious to get better so she could go home to Dad and he could get his life back as it had been before the accident.

Pembroke, Kentucky

"There's a *fliege* in the house." Penny pointed at the buzzing horsefly circling the kitchen. "Can you get it, Daadi?"

"It's not bothering anyone. Just eat your breakfast," Samuel mumbled after he'd spooned some cold cereal into his mouth. They'd moved into Esther's house a few days ago, and he was having a hard time coping with things by himself. He hadn't realized how much he'd relied on Titus until they'd moved out on their own.

"If ya don't get the fliege, it might land in my cereal," Penny complained.

"If you're that worried about it, then get the fly swatter and take care of the critter yourself," Samuel said.

"You're the bug master," Leon said. "If anyone can get that nasty old fliege, it's you, Daadi."

Samuel grunted. He knew he was good at catching bugs, but did that mean he had to catch every spider and fly that came along? He had better things to do than catch a pesky old fly this morning.

Bzz. . . Bzz. . . Bzz. . . The fly buzzed noisily over Samuel's head, and then it swooped down, almost landing in his bowl of cereal. "All right, that does it!" Samuel dropped his spoon to the table, reached out, and scooped the fly into his hand.

The children clapped. "You got that old fliege!" Penny shouted. "Are ya gonna take it outside?"

"That's exactly what I'm going to do." Samuel pushed away from the table and headed for the door. He smiled to himself. It felt kind of nice hearing his children cheering him on and clapping with delight just from him catching a fly, rather than looking at him and wondering when he was going to yell next.

Opening the door, he held his head a bit higher, and when he stepped onto the porch, he spotted Esther's horse and buggy coming down the lane. She was here early today.

As soon as Esther turned up the lane to her house she spotted

Samuel on the porch. Her heartbeat picked up speed the way it always did whenever she saw him. The more her heart ached to be with him, the more convinced she was that they'd never be together, for Samuel still hadn't shown her the least bit of interest—at least not in a romantic sort of way. She figured the only way she and Samuel would ever be together was in her dreams. Could it be that she was only attracted to him because of his children, or was it the look of hurt she still sometimes saw on Samuel's face that drew her to him?

No, she told herself, *my attraction to Samuel goes much deeper than that. I've noticed a gentleness and deep sense of devotion to his kinner that I didn't see when he first moved here. He's a hard worker, too, who takes his responsibility for his family seriously. He's also quite nice looking and more mature than so many of the young men in our church district who like to show off and fool around while trying to get a girl's attention.*

She thought about Ethan Zook, who'd wanted to bring her home from the last young people's singing. Esther had turned him down, saying she'd brought her own horse and buggy. She was glad she'd had that as an excuse. While Ethan was a nice enough fellow, she wasn't the least bit interested in him, and they had nothing in common. Ethan didn't like dogs or cats, and as far as she could tell, his primary interest was in food—mostly how much and how often he could eat the food.

Bringing her thoughts to a halt, Esther pulled her horse and buggy up to the hitching rail and climbed down. When she joined Samuel on the porch, she smiled and said, "Are you headed to work already, or am I late today?"

He shook his head. "You're not late, and I'm not headed to work yet either. Just came out here to dispose of a pesky old fliege." He opened his hand and released a big, black horsefly into the air.

"What were you doing with a fly in your hand?" Esther asked in surprise.

"Caught it with my bare hand. Been catchin' flies that way ever since I was a boy."

Esther's eyes widened. "I've never known anyone who could capture a fly like that."

He grinned. "My boy Leon calls me the bug master. Guess that makes me the bug master from Lancaster."

She giggled. It was nice to see Samuel smiling and making a joke. "Have you heard how Allen's doing?" she asked.

"I talked to him yesterday. Said he's getting along fairly well, but I think he's impatient and anxious to get back to work."

"Is his mother still there with him?"

Samuel nodded. "He said he appreciates her help, but she's beginning to get on his nerves because she fusses about everything and won't let him do a thing for himself."

"She's no doubt concerned that he'll do too much."

"You're probably right. I remember once when my back went out, Elsie fussed over me like I was an invalid." Samuel's face sobered, and he dropped his gaze to the porch. "I'd give anything to have her here, fussing over me right now."

Impulsively, Esther reached out and touched his arm. "I'm sorry for your loss, Samuel."

He just turned and opened the door.

As they entered the house, a feeling of nostalgia washed over Esther. It seemed strange to have someone else living in the home she'd grown up in, and it seemed equally strange to come over here to watch Samuel's children after spending the night in the little guest house at Bonnie's. She knew it was foolish to daydream about impossible things, but she secretly wished she and Samuel were married and that they lived here, raising his children together. But of course, that was nothing but a silly dream—just like it was crazy that her legs were still shaking after touching Samuel's arm.

Chapter 32

As spring turned to summer, Esther developed a routine. Up early in the morning to help Bonnie serve breakfast to her guests, head over to her house to watch Samuel's children, then back to the B&B when Samuel got home from work.

Since this was Saturday and all of Bonnie's guests had just checked out, Esther and Bonnie decided to visit some yard sales.

"Every June there's a forty-mile stretch of yard sales along one of the highways in the area," Esther told Bonnie as they climbed into Bonnie's car. "Lots of Amish people hire drivers so they can go to as many yard sales as possible, looking for the best bargains."

"Everyone likes a bargain." Bonnie chuckled. "Me most of all."

"Are you looking for anything in particular?" Esther asked.

"Not really, but I'm sure I'll know what I want when I see it." Bonnie glanced over at Esther. "What will you be looking for today?"

Esther shrugged. "I don't really know. Maybe something

for Samuel's children. They don't have a lot of toys. In fact, I found Jared playing with a can full of rocks the other day."

Bonnie's dark eyebrows shot up. "Surely Samuel's not so poor that he can't afford to buy his kids a few toys."

"They do have some, but I think they get bored playing with the same toys all the time."

"I'm sure they'll appreciate whatever you might buy for them, but you know kids are funny. Back home, I knew a family that gave their children every toy imaginable. Their mother would find it so amusing when her kids asked to play with some of her pots and pans instead of the new toys. She'd laugh and tell me how the pots and pans would entertain them for hours at a time. So who knows, maybe Jared was really having fun with that can of rocks."

After they'd both had a good laugh, they rode in silence for a while. Bonnie concentrated on the road while Esther enjoyed the beauty of a lovely summer day. "How can one look around and not see all the wonderful things God created for our enjoyment?" she said after they'd passed a farmhouse with a garden full of colorful flowers.

"I don't know," Bonnie replied. "God is everywhere—in the sun, moon, and stars. His artistic hand can be seen in every changing season, too."

"Which season do you like best?" Esther questioned.

"I think summer, when everything is in full bloom. I love watching the hummingbirds flit from one flower to the next. How about you?"

"I like summer, too, but autumn is my favorite time of the year, when the leaves are changing colors and the weather's begun to cool. There's so much beauty to take in. It's like a vibrant quilt blanketing the trees."

"That's a descriptive way of saying it, Esther," Bonnie said.

"You certainly do have a way with words."

Esther smiled. "Or sometimes I think of it as God taking a paintbrush to create a beautiful masterpiece."

"Yes, that's right." Bonnie pointed to her left. "Oh, there's a yard sale at that house. Should we stop now or check it out on the way back?"

"Let's stop now. If we wait until later, all the good stuff might be gone."

"You do have a point." Bonnie turned into the driveway and parked the car. When they hurried across the lawn, Esther noticed several tables full of various items, and on the grass sat furniture and decorator items for the yard.

"Oh good, I see some Christmas decorations." Bonnie rushed to one of the tables and scooped up a box of colored lights, a couple of large red bows, and a fake snowman with an odd-looking nose. "These will look great when I decorate the B&B for Christmas this year. I hope I get some guests over the holidays to enjoy the decorations."

"Will your dad be coming for Christmas?"

"I doubt he'll ever come here." Bonnie moved toward the woman who was taking the money. "Guess I'd better pay for these and put them in the car. Did you see anything you want to buy?"

Esther shook her head. "I don't think so, but I'll continue looking while you pay for the decorations."

As Bonnie walked away, Esther offered a silent prayer on her friend's behalf. She couldn't imagine how it would feel to be shut out of her parents' life like that, and it was obvious by the way Bonnie so quickly changed the subject that it hurt to talk about it.

—m—

"Where's Jared?" Samuel asked after he'd finished giving Leon a haircut. "I need to cut his hair next."

"He's in our room, hidin' under the bed."

Samuel's forehead wrinkled. "What's he doing there?"

"Guess he don't want his hair cut."

"Well, he's beginning to look like a shaggy dog, and it's way past time for a haircut." Samuel left the kitchen and tromped up the stairs to the bedroom Jared and Leon shared. Leon had wanted his own room, but Samuel felt better about having Jared in with his brother. He was too young to be alone yet, and Samuel was glad when Leon agreed to the arrangement.

It was nice living in a house where there were enough bedrooms so Samuel could have his own room. With the girls sharing a room and the boys sharing a room, there were still two more bedrooms he could use when any of his family from Pennsylvania came for a visit, which he hoped would be soon, because he really did miss them. He was sure most of his family would come for Titus's wedding in the fall, if not before, so that was something to look forward to.

When Samuel entered the boys' bedroom, he knelt on the floor and peered under the bed. Sure enough, there lay Jared. "Kumme. Come out," he said.

Jared said nothing; he just started to cry.

Samuel reached under the bed and touched Jared's arm. "*Haar schneide*—haircut," he said in a much softer voice.

Jared still wouldn't budge. "Esther," he said with a whimper. "I want Esther."

Samuel frowned. If Esther were here, would Jared be willing to let her cut his hair? Probably so, since he clung to her whenever he could. Samuel had to admit, Esther was real good with the kids. She was a capable young woman, a real good cook, and she was pretty to look at, too.

Shaking his thoughts aside, he decided to try a new

approach and promised Jared that if he let him cut his hair, he could have some of the cookies Esther had baked when she'd been here yesterday.

When Jared finally crawled out, Samuel picked the boy up and carried him downstairs to the kitchen. Then he set him on a wooden stool, draped a towel around his shoulders, and picked up the scissors.

For the first few minutes everything went fine, but when Penny dashed into the room saying Lucky was chasing a bird, Jared whipped his head around.

Snip!

"Oh no," Samuel groaned. He'd taken a hunk out of Jared's hair that he hadn't meant to. He made a few more snips, trying to even it up, but with little success. "I can't glue it back on, so I guess we'll just have to live with it till it grows out." He sent Jared into the other room while he went to wash clothes.

Downstairs in the basement, Samuel fumbled with the washer but couldn't get it started. "What on earth is wrong with this thing," he grumbled. This was turning into a frustrating day!

"How come the washer's not goin'?" Marla asked when she joined him in the basement a few minutes later.

"Beats me. I can't get the crazy thing to work."

"It won't start till ya turn on the gas," she said, pointing to the valve.

Samuel frowned, feeling pretty dumb. He should have known to check for that.

"I'll bet if Esther was here she woulda known what to do," Marla said. "Esther seems to know everything about runnin' a house."

Samuel couldn't argue with that, but Esther wasn't here now, and he had to learn to do some things by himself.

—∞—

"Whew! I can't believe how long we've been gone or how much we bought today," Bonnie said when she and Esther returned to the B&B that afternoon.

"We did find some pretty good bargains." Esther placed a large paper sack on the table. It held the toys she'd bought for Samuel's children: two dolls—one for Marla and one for Penny; a set of building blocks for Jared; and a baseball, glove, and bat for Leon.

"Guess I'd better haul the box of Christmas decorations I bought up to the attic," Bonnie said. "Then I'll need to go outside and feed the chickens. I've gotta keep my hens happy so they'll continue laying eggs. My guests seem to enjoy having fresh omelets for breakfast, and so do I." She chuckled. "No one's complained about the rooster crowing yet either."

"That's good. Personally, I enjoy the crow of a rooster greeting me in the morning."

Bonnie smiled. "Same here."

"Would you like me to put the decorations away while you're outside?" Esther asked.

"I appreciate the offer, but you look tired. In fact, I'm concerned that you've been doing too much these days."

"What do you mean?"

"I'm wondering if it's become too much for you to keep working two jobs."

Esther shook her head. "I enjoy what I'm doing here and at Samuel's, too. Besides, going over to my old house during the weekdays is closer to the B&B then it is to Titus's place, so it's been working out real well for me. Since I've been sending some of the money I make to my folks to help with my brother's medical expenses, I really need the income from both jobs."

"I understand, but if things get to be too much, you can always bring the kids over to the B&B for part of the day and they can play outside while you do the cleaning."

"I'll think about it, but right now, I'm going to take these decorations up to the attic for you." Esther picked up the box and carried it upstairs.

When she entered the attic, her foot bumped the door. *Bam!*—it slammed shut.

She set the box on the floor, grabbed the door handle, and gave it a yank, but the door wouldn't budge.

Feeling a little bit desperate, Esther pounded on the door and hollered for help, but there was no response. Of course not—Bonnie was outside feeding the chickens.

Don't panic, Esther told herself. *Bonnie will come in soon, and then she'll hear me calling and open the attic door. I just need to relax and stay calm.*

Whoosh! Something flew past Esther's head. She thought it was a bird at first, but when it swooped past her again, she realized it wasn't a bird at all—it was a bat!

Chapter 33

Esther dropped to her knees and tried not to panic. While one of her biggest fears was high places, at the moment, being trapped in the attic with a bat seemed much worse.

I need to get out of here now! Several minutes went by, and Esther pounded on the door. "Help! I'm trapped in the attic with a bat!"

No response. Where was Bonnie? Surely she couldn't still be out feeding the chickens.

The bat made another pass over her head, and Esther screamed. If she didn't get out of here soon, she didn't know what she would do.

She thought about Samuel and the way he'd caught that fly the other day. If only catching a bat could be as simple. Not that she'd have the courage to do it of course. She might be brave enough to whack the bat though—if she could find something suitable to use.

Esther glanced around the attic but didn't see anything that would make a good club. *I wish I had that baseball bat*

I got for Leon with me right now, she thought. *Maybe there's something in one of the boxes up here I can use.*

She crawled over to the box closest to her and was about to open the flaps, when the bat swooped in front of her face, brushing her nose with the tip of its wing. She screamed and covered her head with her hands. Being trapped in the attic was definitely worse than her fear of heights!

Bonnie's stomach rumbled as she entered the house. It was past time to fix supper. *I think I'll fix some spaghetti tonight,* she decided. *That's one of my favorite meals, and it appeals to me right now.*

She checked in the pantry for some tomato sauce, but seeing none there, she decided to go to the basement, where she kept her excess canned goods as well as the strawberry-rhubarb jam she and Esther had made this spring.

She opened the basement door and turned on the light, then carefully descended the stairs. Heading toward the shelves where the canned goods were kept, she spotted an old pie cupboard in one corner of the basement. She'd been meaning to take a closer look at it for some time, thinking that if it was in good enough condition she would put it to good use in the kitchen.

Think I'll take a minute and check it over right now, she decided.

Bonnie knelt on the floor beside the cupboard. The outside appeared to be in pretty fair shape. Just a little bit of sanding and a coat of varnish and it should be good as new.

She opened the cupboard doors, and when she looked inside, she was surprised to see a stack of old newspapers. "I think Grandma must have saved just about everything," she said with a chuckle. She pulled out the newspapers and was even more surprised when an envelope fell to the floor. She soon realized that it was a letter addressed to her dad.

Bonnie slipped the envelope into the pocket of her jeans, took three cans of tomato sauce from the shelf, and then headed upstairs.

Back in the kitchen, she placed the sauce on the counter and took the letter from her pocket. She noticed that the postmark on it was older than she was, and the envelope was still sealed shut. *I wonder who it's from and if Dad even knew about this letter.*

She stared at the letter several seconds then tore it open and read it silently.

Dear Ken,

When you told me that you and your folks were moving to Kentucky, I wanted to tell you that I'd been secretly going out with Dave, but I didn't have the nerve to say it to your face. So I hope you'll forgive me, but I decided the best way to tell you was to send this letter instead of saying it to your face before you moved. I hope you'll be happy living in Kentucky, and I'm sure someone as nice as you will find another girlfriend who'll care as much about you as I do Dave.

Wishing you all the best,
Trisha

Bonnie sat staring at the letter. *Trisha must have been Dad's girlfriend before he and his folks moved to Kentucky. Obviously Dad didn't know about Trisha's letter, since it's never been opened. I wonder what he would say about this now. Did Trisha write to Dad again, or was this the only time? Should I tell Dad about the letter or pretend I never saw it? Would he even care after all these years?*

Unsure of what she should do, Bonnie placed the letter on the counter and flipped the radio on to her favorite Christian station. When a song of worship and praise came on, she turned up the volume and sang along: "I will give you all my worship. I will give you all my praise. You alone I long to worship; You alone are worthy of my praise."

By the time the song was over, Bonnie had the water boiling for the spaghetti and was about to put it in the kettle, when the lights flickered then went out. She groped around in the top drawer below the counter and was relieved when she found the flashlight. Then she made her way slowly to the living room and discovered that the lights were out there, too. Since it was a calm evening with no wind or rain, she figured someone in the area must have run into a pole and knocked the power out.

Remembering that Esther had gone up to the attic with the box of Christmas decorations, and seeing no sign of her now, Bonnie called Esther's name as she swung the flashlight around the room.

No response. Could Esther still be in the attic, or had she gone out to the guest house?

Bam! Bam! Bam!

Bonnie tipped her head and listened. The sound seemed to be coming from upstairs. She returned to the kitchen, turned off the stove since there was no power, and went up to investigate. When she reached the top of the stairs, the pounding grew louder, and she heard Esther's voice calling for help.

Bonnie rushed to the attic door and turned the knob. Nothing happened. It appeared to be locked. "Esther, are you in there?"

"Yes, and the light blew out so now I'm in the dark with—"

"The lights are out throughout the house. I think someone may have hit a pole." Bonnie grabbed the doorknob and pulled again, but it still wouldn't budge. "The door must be locked from the inside. Try to open it, Esther."

"I have tried, but there's no button to unlock it, and if there's a key somewhere, I can't find it in the dark."

Bonnie grimaced. If there was a key to the attic door, she didn't know about it, and if the door was locked, short of taking it off the hinges, she had no idea how to get it open. The job would require more strength and expertise than her limited handywoman skills. Besides, with it being so dark, she'd never be able to see well enough to do anything constructive. What she needed right now was a man's help.

"Hang on, Esther," she called through the door. "I'm going to get you some help."

Samuel and the kids had just finished supper when someone knocked on the back door. He opened it and was surprised to see Bonnie on the porch holding a flashlight.

"Esther's locked in the attic and our power is out," she said breathlessly. "Can you come help me get her out?"

Samuel glanced over at his children sitting at the kitchen table. "I'd like to help, but I'm not comfortable leaving my kids here alone."

"I'll stay with them while you're gone," Bonnie offered.

Samuel hesitated a minute and finally nodded. "They're almost done eating supper, so if you'll make sure they clear the table and that the dishes get done, I'd appreciate it."

"Sure, no problem."

"Hopefully I won't be gone too long." Samuel grabbed his straw hat and hurried out the door.

—∞—

Whoosh! The bat swooped past Esther's head once more. It was so close that she could hear the flutter of its wings. *Dear Lord, don't let it touch me again.*

As Esther's fear escalated, she crouched closer to the floor.

Sometime later, Esther heard footsteps clomping up the stairs. She figured Bonnie had probably gone for one of her English neighbors—maybe Harold Reece who lived down the road.

The doorknob rattled; then everything got quiet. Esther leaned against the door. She hoped whoever was out there hadn't given up, because she didn't think she could stand being trapped in here with that bat much longer.

Esther heard some banging, which gave her a ray of hope. Suddenly the door came off, and she fell into a pair of strong arms. As a beam of light hit the man's face, Esther looked up. "Samuel?"

Chapter 34

Samuel, I—I didn't know that was you." Esther stammered. "Danki for getting me out of that attic."

He gave a nod, thinking how cute she looked as her cheeks turned a pinkish hue. Then he berated himself for having such a thought. Thankfully, she didn't know what he'd been thinking. "Bonnie came over to get me. She stayed at the house with my kinner so I could come over here."

"Th–there's a bat in the attic," Esther rasped. Her covering was askew, and she quickly pushed it back in place.

"A baseball bat?"

She shook her head "No, a bat that flies—and swoops—and. . ."

Seeing how shaken Esther was, Samuel suggested she go downstairs while he tried to capture the bat.

She looked up at him, eyes wide and wrinkles in her forehead. "Are—are you sure?"

"Jah. Go on down."

She hesitated but finally nodded. "Be careful, Samuel.

Capturing a bat isn't the same as catching a fly."

"I'll be fine," he assured her.

As Esther started carefully down the stairs, Samuel stepped into the attic and hit the light switch, relieved when it came on. It would be much harder to try and capture the bat with only the light from his flashlight.

Whoosh! The bat flew right over his head.

Samuel ducked. Gathering his wits, he grabbed an old sweater he spotted draped across a wooden trunk, and then he began a merry chase after the bat. After several foiled attempts, he finally captured the creature inside the sweater and hurried down the stairs.

"Got it trapped in this sweater!" he said to Esther, who stood shivering in the living room near the fireplace.

"Wh–what are you going to do with it?" she asked in a shaky voice.

"I'll take the critter outside and let it go." Samuel stepped onto the porch, opened the sweater, and gave it a shake.

When he returned to the living room, Esther pointed to the sweater and squealed. "It–it's still there!"

Samuel looked down. Sure enough, the bat was clinging upside-down to the sweater. He'd thought the bat had let go, but with it being so dark outside, he must not have seen it.

He rushed back outside and gave it another good shake. This time he saw the bat flap its wings and fly off into the night.

"Good riddance," Samuel mumbled as he headed back to the house. "You've caused enough trouble for one night."

—∞—

Just as Samuel stepped into the B&B, the telephone rang. Esther hurried into the kitchen to answer it. "Bonnie's

Bed-and-Breakfast," she said when she picked up the receiver.

"Is this Bonnie Taylor?" a woman's voice asked on the other end of the line.

"No, this is Esther Beiler. I work for Bonnie, but she's not here right now. May I take a message?"

"I'm a nurse at a hospital in Portland, Oregon. I need to speak to Bonnie because her father's been admitted here after being involved in a car accident."

Esther's eyebrows squeezed together. "I'm sorry to hear that. Is he seriously hurt?"

"I can only discuss that with Bonnie. Can you please have her call me as soon as she returns home?"

Esther wrote down the number the nurse gave her and promised to give Bonnie the message. When she hung up, she returned to the living room and told Samuel about the phone call.

"That's too bad. I'd better get back to the house right away and let Bonnie know." Samuel said a hurried good-bye and rushed out the door.

—∞—

When Samuel entered his house with a worried expression, Bonnie felt immediate concern. "Were you able to get Esther out of the attic? Is she okay?"

He gave a nod. "She's fine, but while I was there, Esther got a phone call from a hospital in Oregon. It seems your dad's been in a car accident."

Bonnie gasped. "How bad is it?"

"I don't know. The nurse wouldn't give Esther any details. Just said you should call as soon as you got home."

Bonnie grabbed her purse and flashlight and then hurried out to her car.

When she arrived at the B&B a short time later, Esther gave her the phone message, and Bonnie called the hospital. When she hung up the phone, she turned to Esther and said, "My dad's injuries aren't life-threatening, but he broke several bones. I need to go to Oregon right away."

Esther nodded. "Of course."

Bonnie clasped Esther's arm. "Would you be willing to run the B&B while I'm gone?"

Esther's eyes widened. "Can't you close it until you get back?"

Bonnie shook her head. "Several people are scheduled to arrive in the next couple of weeks, and I wouldn't feel right about cancelling their reservations."

"I'd be happy to do it," Esther said, "but it might be difficult since I'm supposed to go to Samuel's every day to watch his children."

"Maybe Samuel can bring the kids to the B&B in the mornings before he leaves for work, and you can watch them here. Since it's summer now and the weather's so nice, the kids would probably be happy to play outside most of the day."

Esther nodded. "If Samuel's agreeable to the arrangement, then I'm willing to do it."

Bonnie gave Esther a hug. "I appreciate it so much. Now I need to get a plane ticket and find someone to drive me to the airport in Nashville."

Chapter 35

Portland, Oregon

As Bonnie parked her rental car in the hospital parking lot, her heart started to pound. What if Dad didn't want to see her? When she'd returned to Oregon after Grandma's funeral and told him she'd decided to quit her job and move to Kentucky in order to open a bed-and-breakfast, he'd said that if she was going to do something that foolish, she may as well not bother to ever come home again.

Did he mean it? she wondered. *Will he ask me to leave?*

Things had been strained between her and Dad since Mom had died, and she'd probably made them worse by moving to Kentucky. But she liked it there and appreciated Esther, Samuel, and Allen, who'd become her friends.

She was pleased that Esther had been willing to handle things at the B&B while she was gone. Allen had taken her to the airport in Nashville, and Samuel had even agreed to come over every day and feed her chickens when he dropped the kids off for Esther to watch. That was surely proof of their friendship.

Bonnie turned off the car's engine and whispered a prayer.

"Lord, give me the strength to face my dad, and help him to be receptive to my visit."

When Bonnie entered the hospital and spoke to the nurse in charge on her dad's floor, she was again told that the accident had left him with a broken leg, a broken arm, several broken ribs, and lots of nasty bruises.

"In order for him to be released, he'll need to have some help," the nurse told Bonnie. "His arm and leg will both be in a cast for at least six weeks."

Bonnie drew in a deep breath as she leaned against the nurse's station. She could take Dad back to Kentucky, but in his condition, she knew he wouldn't be up for that. Besides, as much as he hated it there, she was sure he'd never agree to go.

The nurse stepped out from behind her desk. "Would you like me to show you to his room now?"

"Yes, please."

Bonnie followed the nurse down the hall, and when she entered her father's room, she found him asleep.

"I'll just sit beside his bed until he wakes up," she whispered.

The nurse nodded and slipped quietly from the room.

Bonnie took a seat in the chair and winced when she saw the purple bruises on her father's swollen face. There was a cast on his left arm, and on his right leg, too. If not for the pain medicine the nurse said they'd been giving him, he'd no doubt be in a whole lot of pain.

Sometime later, Dad opened his eyes. He looked over at Bonnie and blinked a couple of times. "Wh–what are you doing here?"

"I came as soon as I heard you'd been in an accident."

"What for? You don't care about me," he said, looking straight at her.

She placed her hand on his shoulder. "That's not true, Dad. I love you very much."

"Humph! If you loved me, you wouldn't have run off to Kentucky."

"I went there for Grandma's funeral." *And you should have gone, too,* she silently added.

He turned his head toward the opposite wall. "You didn't have to stay."

"I like it there, Dad. Turning Grandma and Grandpa's house into a bed-and-breakfast has been a challenge, but it's also quite rewarding."

"Humph!"

"The nurse said you're going to need some help after you're released from the hospital."

"I can manage."

She shook her head. "You'll be wearing your casts for at least six weeks."

"Yeah, thanks to the stupid driver who broadsided my car! That guy clearly wasn't watching where he was going."

"Is there anyone you'd like to ask about coming to stay with you during your convalescence?"

"Nope, and I'm not goin' to no convalescent center either."

"Then I guess you're stuck with me, because I'm not going back to Kentucky until you're able to manage on your own. Are you okay with me staying?"

"I guess so. What other choice do I have?"

She bit back a smile. He wasn't as tough as he liked her to believe. Now she just needed to give Esther a call to see how things were going and ask if Esther thought she could handle running the B&B for the next six weeks. She'd do that as soon as she visited with Dad awhile.

the HEALING

Pembroke, Kentucky

Esther had just finished polishing the hardwood floor in the downstairs hallway of the B&B when Marla, who was outside playing, hollered something. Esther whirled around, slipped on the floor, and dropped to her knees, bending her toe back. Today had not started out on a good note. First she'd cut her finger on a sharp edge while dusting the china hutch, then she'd gotten a splinter in her hand from the broom when she'd been trying to get some cobwebs off the outside of the house. Now she had a sore knee and a sore toe and needed to go outside and see what Marla was hollering about. This whole arrangement of watching Samuel's kids at the B&B and trying to handle reservations as well as guest accommodations was a bit more than she could handle. But she had promised Bonnie she would do it, so she'd manage somehow until Bonnie returned, which she hoped wouldn't be too long from now.

Esther started for the back door, but the telephone rang, so she dashed into the kitchen to answer it.

"Bonnie's Bed-and-Breakfast."

"Hi, Esther. It's me, Bonnie. How are things going there?"

Esther glanced at the kitchen door, where Leon now stood, holding a chicken. "Everything's fine. How's your dad?"

"He's pretty banged up and will need some help until his arm and leg have healed—probably six weeks."

"That's too bad. Does he have someone there to take care of him?"

"No, not really." There was a pause. "I said I'd stay to help out. Do you think you could manage that long without me?"

Esther glanced at Leon again, who had taken a seat in

a chair at the kitchen table and held the chicken in his lap. "Umm. . . Yes, I'm sure I can manage. Feel free to stay as long as you need to."

"Oh, thank you, Esther. I really appreciate your willingness to take over for me, and I'll pay you extra for doing this."

"Helping others is what friends are supposed to do." Esther snapped her fingers to get Leon's attention, and then motioned for him to take the chicken outside. Leon frowned but did what she asked.

Esther had no more than hung up the phone, when Marla dashed into the kitchen. "Penny's up a tree, and she can't get down! I yelled before and tried to tell you she was goin' up, but you never came outside when I called."

"Why is Penny up a tree?" Esther questioned.

"She wanted to get Bonnie's fluffy gray cat down."

Esther moaned. *What more can go wrong?*

Chapter 36

"Stay in here and keep an eye on Jared," Esther instructed Marla. "He's in the living room playing with the blocks I got for him awhile back."

Marla hurried off to the living room, and Esther rushed out the back door. As much as she feared high places, she couldn't leave Penny stuck in the tree. She thought about sending Marla or Leon up after their sister but didn't think either of them was strong enough to help Penny down. Besides, they might lose their balance and fall. The last thing she needed was for another one of Samuel's children to get hurt.

Of course, I might get hurt, too, she reasoned. *And then what would I do?*

Esther tipped her head back and looked up at Penny, crouched on a branch high in the tree, with the gray cat perched on the branch next to her. "I'm going to get a ladder to get you down. Sit very still, okay?"

Penny gave a nod. "Hurry. I'm *vergelschdert.*"

"Try not to be frightened." Esther said in what she hoped

was a voice of reassurance. Truth was she was probably as scared as Penny right now.

She headed to the barn and spotted Leon prancing around the yard with the chicken he'd brought into the house. "Please put that *hinkel* away and come steady the ladder for me," she said to the boy.

Leon hurried off toward the chicken coop while Esther went to the barn. Once she had the ladder in place and was sure Leon had a grip on the legs, she ascended it slowly. *First a bat in the attic that about scared me to death, and now this. How many other fears must I deal with? Help me, Lord,* she prayed. *Still my racing heart and help me not to be afraid.*

By the time Esther reached the branch where Penny sat, the fluffy gray cat had leaped to the ground.

"Slip your arms around my neck and wrap your legs around my waist," Esther told Penny.

The frightened girl's chin trembled. "I–I'm vergelschdert."

"I know, dear one. I'm scared, too," Esther admitted, "but we can do this. God will help us. You'll see." *Please, Lord, please help us.*

She thought about Philippians 4:13: *"I can do all things through Christ which strengtheneth me,"* and it bolstered her faith.

Penny did as Esther had instructed, and once Esther was sure the child had a good grip on her, she slowly and carefully descended the ladder. When she reached the bottom, she set Penny on the ground. "Please don't ever do anything like that again."

"Are. . .are you gonna punish me?"

"No. I think you've learned a lesson today." Esther gave Penny a hug, which helped her as well, because her arms and legs were shaking.

Tears dribbling down her cheeks, Penny nodded. "Jah, and I—I won't ever do that again." She pointed at the cat scampering through the grass. "He wouldn't come down when I called, and then when I went up the tree, he jumped down."

"You're a dummkopp, Penny," Leon said, stepping away from the ladder. "I told ya not to go up in that tree."

"I'm not a dummkopp. You're the dummkopp," Penny said tearfully.

Leon wrinkled his nose. "Am not!"

"Are so!"

Penny shook her finger at him. "Am not!"

Esther held up her hand. "That's enough. Neither one of you is stupid."

She motioned to the ladder. "While I put this away, I want the two of you to go into the house. When I come inside, we'll have something cold to drink."

The children scampered off while Esther picked up the ladder and headed for the barn. She longed to be a wife and mother, but after a day like today, she wasn't sure she was cut out for it. At least she didn't have any B&B guests checking in today.

Inside the barn, Esther was greeted by Bonnie's yappy little dog as it wagged its tail and bumped her leg with its cold, wet nose. "Not now, Cody," she said, pushing the dog away with her hand. "I don't have time to play."

Woof! Woof! Cody wiggled and continued to wag his tail.

"I said, not now." Esther pushed past the dog, put the ladder away, and hurried into the house. When she stepped into the kitchen, she halted. Marla sat at the table, reading Esther's journal! Esther had been writing it in earlier and had foolishly left it on the counter, never thinking anyone might read it.

Esther scooped up the journal and slipped it into a drawer. She hoped Marla hadn't read anything she'd written about Samuel. "It's not polite to read someone's private thoughts," she told Marla. "You should have asked me first."

The girl's face reddened. "S–sorry. I didn't know it was yours till I started reading."

Esther placed her hand on Marla's shoulder. "Next time you see something you're curious about, please ask before you touch it."

"I will."

"Where's Jared?" Esther asked.

"Sleepin' on the living room floor."

Esther was tempted to move him to the sofa or Bonnie's downstairs bedroom but figured he might wake up if she did. Besides, the floor was carpeted, and he was probably comfortable or he wouldn't have fallen asleep there.

"Have Penny and Leon come inside yet?" she asked Marla.

Marla shook her head. "Did you get Penny out of the tree?"

"I did, and the cat came down on its own. I told Penny and Leon to come inside so we could all have a snack, but I guess if they're not in the house, then they didn't listen too well."

"A snack sounds good 'cause I'm hungerich," Marla said. Apparently she didn't care whether her brother and sister had come into the house or not.

"I'll fix some cheese, crackers, and lemonade as soon as your brother and sister come in. Why don't you go outside and see what's taking them so long?"

"Okay." Marla left her seat and hurried out the door.

Esther stepped into the living room to check on Jared. He was fast asleep on the floor, sucking his thumb and holding in his other hand one of the blocks Esther had found at the yard sale.

She smiled as she gazed at the child. What a precious little boy. How sad that he would grow up never knowing his mother. She wondered if Samuel would ever remarry, and if he did, would the children accept his wife as their new mother? Would they accept her if she was the woman Samuel chose to marry?

Esther shook her head. *I shouldn't allow myself to even think such thoughts. Especially when Samuel has given no indication that he has any interest in me. I'm still worried that he might be interested in Bonnie, but I don't have the nerve to ask.*

She moved back to the kitchen and had just taken a brick of cheese from the refrigerator when the back door swung open and Marla stepped into the room, followed by Leon and Penny.

"I found these two in the chicken coop," Marla announced. "They were lookin' for eggs."

"Did you find any?" Esther asked, directing her question to Leon.

Leon shook his head. "Nope, and I was hopin' there'd be some green ones today."

"Maybe tomorrow." Esther motioned to the bathroom down the hall. "If you three will go wash your hands, I'll get our snack ready to eat."

The children didn't have to be asked twice. They rushed out of the kitchen, tickling each other and giggling all the way.

By the time they returned, Esther had a plate of crackers and cheese on the table and was pouring the lemonade she'd made earlier.

"Can we go outside on the porch to eat our snack?" Leon asked. "That way we can watch for Daadi."

"I suppose that will be all right," Esther said. "I'll leave the door open so I can hear if Jared wakes up."

Esther handed the crackers to Marla and the plate full of cheese to Leon and told them to go outside and wait for her on the porch.

The children filed out of the house, and Esther came behind him with a tray that held the pitcher of lemonade and glasses. They'd just seated themselves around the table on the porch, when Samuel's horse and buggy pulled into the yard.

"Daadi's here!" Leon leaped off the porch and raced across the lawn. Penny and Marla followed. It did Esther's heart good to see the children so excited about seeing their father.

She watched as Samuel tied his horse to the hitching rail and headed to the house with the children. He walked with an easy gait and seemed to be more relaxed than usual. It was good to see him pick Penny up and laugh as he swung her onto his shoulders. When he'd first come to Kentucky, he hardly looked at the kids. Now it seemed he couldn't get enough of them. *Maybe the pain of losing his wife is lessening,* Esther thought. *Maybe Samuel's heart is finally healing.*

When Samuel and the children stepped onto the porch, Marla pointed to the table. "Esther fixed us a snack, Daadi. Will you sit with us and eat some, too?"

Samuel looked at Esther, as though seeking her approval.

She smiled and said, "There's plenty, and you're more than welcome to join us."

Samuel put Penny in a chair and took the seat beside Esther. "How'd things go here today?" he asked.

"Esther rescued me from a tree," Penny said before Esther could respond.

Samuel squinted at Penny. "What were you doing in a tree?"

"She went up after a dumb old *katz,*" Leon spoke up. "I told her not to, but she wouldn't listen."

Marla looked at Esther and smiled. "Even though Esther's afraid of high places, she was brave and climbed the ladder to get Penny down."

Esther's face heated. Marla must have read the part in her journal where she'd mentioned being afraid of heights. If she'd read that, what else might the girl have read?

Making no comment on Esther's fear of heights, Samuel looked at Penny and frowned. "You ought to know better than to climb into a tree. If you'd fallen, you could have been hurt." He looked over at Esther. "I appreciate you going up after her, and I'm sorry for the trouble she caused."

"It was no trouble," Esther said. "I'm just glad she wasn't hurt."

"The katz's okay, too, Daadi." Penny grinned widely. "He leaped outa that old tree and landed right on his feet."

"Just like I told ya he'd do," Leon said with a smirk. "You shoulda listened to me."

Fearful that the children might start an argument, Esther quickly handed each of them a glass of lemonade, along with some crackers and cheese. Then she passed the plate to Samuel and gave him some lemonade, too.

He took a drink and smacked his lips. "Umm. . . This sure hits the spot on a warm day such as this. Danki, Esther."

"You're welcome."

"Esther's a real good cook," Marla said. She reached for a cracker and put a piece of cheese on top. "Tell Daadi about the raisin bread you made this mornin', Esther. He likes raisin bread a lot."

"There's still some left, if you'd like a piece," Esther offered.

Samuel shook his head. "I appreciate the offer, but cheese and crackers is plenty for me right now."

"I can send some home with you," Esther said. "Maybe

you'd like it for breakfast tomorrow morning."

"That'd be nice." Samuel took another drink of lemonade. "Have you heard anything from Bonnie today?"

"Jah." Esther repeated all that Bonnie had told her when she'd called and ended it by saying, "So she'll be gone at least six weeks, and I'll be in charge of things here until she returns."

Samuel's eyebrows furrowed. "That will mean a lot of extra work for you. Maybe I should try to find someone else to watch the kinner till Bonnie gets back. That way you won't have so much to do."

"I'm sure I can manage." No way was Esther going to tell Samuel about the terrible day she'd had. If he thought she couldn't manage everything she was responsible for right now, he might look for someone to replace her. Esther loved being with Samuel's kids and didn't want to give that up, no matter how tired she was or how badly things might go on some days.

Marla placed both hands on her father's cheeks. "Please don't get no one else to watch us, Daadi. We don't want anyone but Esther."

Penny and Leon nodded in agreement.

"All right," Samuel said, looking at Esther. "But you must let me know if things get to be too much for you."

He turned back to look at the kids. "You must behave yourselves and help Esther whenever you can. And no more climbing trees, is that understood?"

All heads bobbed in agreement.

Esther smiled. *If I can prove to Samuel how capable I am, maybe he'll take an interest in me. Maybe someday he'll smile at me the way he does Bonnie.*

Chapter 37

For the next two weeks Esther kept busy watching Samuel's children and running the B&B. As she developed a routine, things seemed to get easier. The best part was that Samuel had agreed to go on a picnic supper with her and the children this evening. Esther really looked forward to that. She glanced at the clock on the kitchen wall. *He should be here soon.*

The back door flew open, and Leon rushed into the room, carrying a wicker basket. "Look what I found," he announced. "There was six eggs, and every one of 'em is green!"

Esther smiled at his exuberance. "Let's get them washed, and then we'll put them in the refrigerator."

"Can we boil some eggs and take 'em to eat with the other things you're fixin' for our picnic supper?" he asked.

She nodded. "Would you like plain boiled eggs, or should I make deviled eggs?"

Leon's blue eyes squinted as he looked up at Esther with a quizzical expression. "Don't want no eggs made by the devil."

Esther bit back a chuckle. "Deviled eggs aren't made by the devil, Leon."

"Then how come they're called 'deviled eggs?'"

"The fact that the eggs are seasoned with spice is what gives them the name 'deviled' eggs," Esther said as she took some eggs from the refrigerator that had already been boiled.

Leon just shrugged and placed the basket of eggs he'd gathered on the table.

Esther figured he hadn't really understood her explanation.

Just then Marla bounded into the room. "There's a car in the driveway, and some English folks are walkin' up to the house."

Esther glanced at the calendar and groaned. In her excitement over the picnic supper, she'd forgotten about the guests who were supposed to arrive this afternoon. Well, at least she didn't have to feed them anything until morning. She'd get them checked in, show them to their room, and then return to the kitchen to finish putting things together for their picnic.

"Could you go check on Penny and Jared while I tend to the guests?" Esther asked Marla.

"Jah, sure." Marla dashed out of the room, and Esther went to the door. When she opened it, a strong wind hit her full in the face, and then she noticed it had begun to rain. She hoped it wouldn't last, or they might have to cancel their picnic supper.

By the time Esther had the guests settled into their room and had returned to the kitchen, the rain was coming down harder.

"How we gonna go on a picnic when it's rainin' like this?" Leon frowned. "We'll get soakin' wet."

"We can eat in the house," Marla said when she entered

the room with Jared and Penny. She looked at Esther. "Isn't that right?"

Esther nodded. "I don't see why not. We can have an indoor picnic right here in the kitchen."

Leon wrinkled his nose. "It won't be as much fun if we hafta eat in here. Me and Daadi was gonna do some fishin' if we went to the pond."

"We can go there some other time," Esther said. "That is, if your daed's willing to go," she quickly added.

"I'm sure he will be," Marla said. "Daadi likes to fish."

"He likes it when someone else does the cookin', too," Penny added.

Esther smiled. If she couldn't get through to Samuel any other way, maybe her cooking skills would reach him.

Samuel grimaced as he guided his horse and buggy down the road toward the bed-and-breakfast. Shortly before he'd gotten off work today, he'd developed a headache. He could usually tell when he got one of these headaches that rain was on the way—his sinuses started to plug up on him, and the headache followed. He'd been right, because it was not only raining like crazy, but his head felt like someone had been smacking it with a hammer all day.

When Samuel had arrived home from work, he'd taken some aspirin before showering and changing his clothes, but the headache hadn't let up. Now, thanks to the rain beating down, he was having a hard time seeing out the front window of the buggy. He hoped the kids were ready to go when he got there, because he was anxious to get back home. Due to the nasty weather, he knew they wouldn't be having a picnic supper this evening and was sure the kids would be disappointed, same as him. He'd begun to realize why his kids liked Esther so much. She was sweet, even-tempered, and real smart, too. And she cared about them as if they were her own. He'd been fortunate to have found someone like her to oversee the children when he was at work.

Samuel's stomach rumbled noisily, and he pressed his hand against it. "Sure wish I didn't have to fix supper tonight," he mumbled, taking his thoughts in a different direction. It wasn't easy working all day and then going home and having to cook a meal—especially when he wasn't that great of a cook. *Maybe we'll just settle for sandwiches,* he decided.

When Samuel pulled into Bonnie's yard, he was greeted by her yappy little dog. "Don't you have the good sense to get in out of the rain?" Samuel muttered when Cody started running back and forth, barking at his horse and leaping into the air like he was half crazy. The mutt sure had a lot of energy, and he liked to bark at nearly everything he saw. Samuel was surprised Bonnie didn't get rid of the dog. For that matter, he wondered what had possessed her to even take the stray in. Well, he guessed it was none of his business. He had enough to deal with when it came to Lucky.

Samuel climbed out of his buggy and hollered at Cody to get in the barn. It took several more times of him ordering the dog to go, but when the critter finally did as he was told, Samuel secured his horse to the hitching rail and hurried across the yard.

"Daadi, guess what?" Marla said excitedly when Samuel entered the house.

He bent down to give her a hug. "What?"

"Since it's raining, Esther said we could have our picnic supper in the kitchen."

"Is that a fact?"

She bobbed her head. "Please say we can stay, Daadi, 'cause she's fixed lots of good food, and I'm hungerich."

Samuel smiled despite his throbbing headache. "I guess we'd better stay then, 'cause I wouldn't want any of my kinner to starve to death, and I'm sure that whatever Esther's fixed for supper will be a whole lot better than the cold sandwiches I was going to make if we went home and ate."

"I get sick of sandwiches, so I'm glad we're not goin' home to eat." Marla tugged on Samuel's hand. "Esther's got everything ready now. Let's go in the kitchen so we can eat."

—~~—

Esther smiled when Samuel entered the room holding Marla's hand, and she was pleased to see that Marla was smiling, too. "Since it's raining, I thought we could have our picnic in here." She motioned to the table, which was fully set.

He gave a nod. "So I've been told."

Everyone took their seats, and after the silent prayer had been said, Esther passed the food around. There was chicken, fried golden brown; tangy potato salad; carrot and celery sticks; savory, maple-flavored baked beans; and spicy deviled eggs. She'd even thought to cover the table with a red-and-white-checkered tablecloth, so it seemed more like they were having a picnic. It did her heart good to see the children's smiling faces. This might not be the picnic they'd planned, but at least they were all together, and she was glad Samuel had agreed to stay. She hoped they'd have time after the meal to sit and visit while the children played.

Esther had just taken a bite of chicken when the telephone rang. She excused herself and took the portable phone that was usually in Bonnie's kitchen into the hall so she wouldn't disturb the conversation going on at the table. When she realized it was someone wanting to make a reservation at the B&B, she took a seat at the desk near the front door and wrote down the information in the reservation book.

Esther hung up the phone several minutes later and was about to return to the kitchen, when the phone rang again. "Bonnie's Bed-and-Breakfast."

"Esther, is that you?"

Esther recognized her mother's voice and she smiled. "Jah, Mom, it's me."

"How are you doing? Are you still running the bed-and-breakfast by yourself, or is Bonnie back from Oregon now?" Mom asked.

"I'm still on my own. Bonnie will probably be gone another four weeks," Esther replied.

"Are you managing okay by yourself? You're not tempted to watch TV, I hope."

"No TV, and I'm getting along fine and keeping busy." Esther wasn't about to tell Mom all the trouble she'd had since Bonnie had left. Mom would be concerned, and she didn't need one more thing to worry about.

"How's Dan doing?" Esther asked.

"I'm sorry to say he's no better. He still tires easily, and he's using a wheelchair most of the time now."

"That's too bad. I'm sure he appreciates you and Dad being there."

"Jah. I know both Dan and Sarah are real glad we came to help out."

They talked awhile longer; then remembering her guests in the kitchen, Esther explained that she needed to go. She'd no more than hung up the phone, when the middle-aged couple who'd checked into the B&B earlier came down the stairs asking for directions to one of the restaurants in Hopkinsville.

By the time Esther finished talking to them and returned to the kitchen, Samuel and the kids were done eating.

"I'm sorry for taking so long," Esther apologized. "But I'm glad you went ahead and ate without me."

"It was very good." Samuel pushed back his chair. "I hate to eat and run, but I think we need to get home."

Marla's brows puckered. "Do we hafta go? We haven't had dessert yet, and I wanted to stay and visit with Esther awhile."

"Maybe some other time," Samuel said. "I've been fighting a sinus headache for the last several hours, and I need to go home and lie down."

"I'm sorry to hear you're not feeling well," Esther said. "Would you like some aspirin or willow bark capsules?"

He shook his head. "I took a couple of aspirin before coming here, but it hasn't helped. Think I just need to lie down awhile."

"Of course. I understand, and I'll just send the strawberry-rhubarb pie I made for dessert home with you." Esther was disappointed that she'd have to eat a cold supper by herself, but she felt bad about Samuel's headache. *So much for a fun evening with Samuel and the kids,* she thought with regret. The way things were going, it didn't look like she and Samuel would ever have a chance to really sit and visit.

Chapter 38

When Esther woke up the following morning, she felt disoriented. It had rained most of the night, and the constant *Ping! Ping! Ping!* against the window in the guest house bedroom had kept her awake for several hours. Some of the time it had rained so hard that she thought the roof might cave in.

She'd also been unable to sleep because she'd been thinking about Samuel and wondering how he was doing. When he and the children had left after supper, he'd looked exhausted. She knew that even though he had a headache, he'd have to do his evening chores and see that the children were put to bed. What Samuel needed was a wife who could help raise his children, but then Samuel might have other thoughts about that. Some widowed Amish men she knew had found another wife within the first six months, and they didn't even have any children. To be widowed and trying to raise four children by himself had to be very difficult for Samuel. Of course, he did have her and also Titus to help with the children, but if he had a wife. . .

Now don't let your thoughts take you where they shouldn't go, Esther told herself as she climbed out of bed. It was dark in the room, so she lit the gas lamp and then ambled over to the window and lifted the shade. The rain had stopped, and the sun shone brightly, spilling its warmth into the room. Since today was Saturday, and she wouldn't have Samuel's children to watch, maybe she could get some gardening done. Of course, the first thing on her agenda was to walk over to the B&B and fix breakfast for her guests, who would no doubt be up pretty soon.

Esther turned toward the dresser, picked up the hand mirror, and frowned. There were dark circles beneath her eyes—an indication that she looked as tired as she felt this morning. It hadn't been easy taking charge of things while Bonnie was gone. Esther knew Bonnie was where she needed to be right now, but she'd be glad when she came back and took over again.

What if she doesn't come back? Esther thought. *Maybe Bonnie will decide that her father needs her to stay there with him, and she'll sell the B&B. Then I'd have no place to stay, because it wouldn't be right to ask Samuel and the kinner to move out of Mom and Dad's house. If they moved back with Titus, it would cause problems between him and Suzanne again, and they might end up not getting married.* She splashed some cold water on her face from the basin she kept on the dresser, trying to clear her mind of the troubling thoughts. *It's best if I don't worry about this. I just need to trust that Bonnie will come back. I need to trust God to work everything out.*

Shortly after Esther cleaned up the kitchen, her two B&B guests, a middle-aged couple from Tennessee, headed out to do some shopping and sightseeing.

Esther stepped outside with a plastic container for the produce she planned to pick and was halfway to the garden when Allen's truck pulled in.

"I was in the neighborhood and decided to drop by and see how you're doing," he said when he got out of his vehicle and joined her on the grass.

"I'm doing okay." Esther pointed to the garden. "I was just getting ready to pick some green beans and tomatoes."

"Do you need some help with that?"

"Is your back healed well enough to be working in the garden?"

He gave a nod. "My mom went back home last week, and I'm good as new. She never would have left if I wasn't doing better."

"I'm glad to hear your back's not hurting anymore. Falling down the steps like that, your injuries could have been even worse." Esther thought of Samuel's wife, who had died because she'd broken her neck when she'd fallen down the steps in their home. Allen was fortunate that his back hadn't been injured seriously enough to leave him with any permanent disability.

"Since I have some free time this morning, I may as well help you," Allen said.

"I appreciate that." She handed him the plastic container. "You can use this and start on the beans if you like, while I go get another container for the tomatoes."

As Allen headed for the garden, Esther went to the house. When she returned a few minutes later, she found Allen kneeling beside a clump of beans.

"Have you heard anything more from Bonnie? Do you know when she'll be back?" he asked, looking up with a hopeful expression. Was Allen concerned about Bonnie or just making polite conversation?

"She called a few days ago." Esther moved toward a row of tomatoes. "Said her dad's getting along pretty well, but it'll be awhile before he's out of his casts."

"I imagine he'll need some physical therapy after the casts come off."

"I hadn't even thought about that." Esther picked a couple of ripe cherry tomatoes and placed them in her container. "I guess that means Bonnie might stay in Oregon longer than six weeks."

"That will probably depend on whether her dad can manage on his own when the casts come off." Allen wiped the perspiration from his forehead. "Whew! Sure is a hot, humid day. And look at the birds drinking from the birdbath over there." He pointed across the yard. "I'll bet they're feeling about as hot as I am right now."

"Are you thirsty? I could run back to the house and get you some water," Esther offered.

"Not right now. I haven't picked enough beans to earn a break yet."

She chuckled. "A quick drink of water wouldn't be much of a break."

"It would be if I drank it and then plopped down in that." He motioned to the hammock suspended between two maple trees in the front yard.

She smiled. "It does look inviting."

"It's been a long time since I kicked back and rested in a hammock."

"Do you have a hammock at your place?"

He shook his head. "But my folks had one when I was a boy."

"Well, feel free to take a nap in the hammock after you're done picking the beans."

He grinned. "I might just take you up on that."

For the next hour, they worked in silence, until each of them had their containers full. Then they carried them up to the house and Esther poured two glasses of lemonade and fixed a plate of cookies. "Should we take our snack outside?" she asked.

"Sounds good to me. My mother always says everything tastes better when it's eaten outside."

Esther smiled. "I think she might be right about that."

They sat in the chairs on the porch, and Allen took a drink from his glass. "This lemonade is sure good, Esther, and it does hit the spot."

"Yes, I agree." Esther handed him the plate of cookies. "Would you like to try one of these?"

"Thanks." He grabbed a cookie and took a bite. "Umm. . . This is really good. I've never tasted anything like it before. What kind of cookie is it?"

"They're called boyfriend cookies, and the ingredients include butter, whole wheat and soy flour, sugar, vanilla, and eggs. Oh, and there's also oatmeal, salted peanuts, and carob chips in the recipe."

He wiggled his eyebrows playfully. "Not only real tasty, but they're a healthy kind of cookie."

She gave a nod. "Boyfriend cookies are one of my all-time favorites."

"How come they're called boyfriend cookies?"

"I don't really know for sure. I guess maybe it's because they're good enough for a girl to serve her boyfriend when he comes to call."

"Speaking of boyfriends. . . Do you have a boyfriend, Esther?" he asked.

She shook her head. *No, but I wish I did.*

"That's odd. I would think a pretty girl like you, who's also a great cook with a pleasant personality, would have a string of suitors just waiting in line to court her."

Esther's face heated. She wasn't used to receiving such compliments—especially from an attractive English man like Allen.

"Sorry if I embarrassed you," Allen said. "I'm just surprised that you don't have a boyfriend, because you certainly have all the attributes most men would like if they're looking for a wife."

Esther stared out into the yard, thinking about Ethan Zook and knowing how he appreciated her cooking abilities and would no doubt start courting her tomorrow if she showed him the least bit of interest. But she wanted a man who would appreciate her for more than her cooking skills. She wanted someone who thought she was fun to be with and liked her personality. The man she wanted was Samuel, but he didn't seem to notice any of her attributes.

As Esther and Allen sat in pleasant camaraderie, they continued to visit. Allen told Esther about a new house he'd been contracted to build over in Trigg County. "It's going to be a big one," he said. "Over four thousand square feet."

"Will Samuel be doing the painting on that one?" she asked, curious to know if he'd be keeping busy, which would allow her to continue watching the children.

"I think he will." Allen set his empty glass on the table. "Samuel was a big help to me when I was recuperating. He worked extra hard and helped out wherever he could, and if he's willing to do the painting on the house, then as far as I'm concerned, he's got the job."

"Samuel seems to like keeping busy," Esther said. She remembered Bonnie saying she thought Allen was a workaholic. Well, from what she'd observed, Samuel was one, too. But that was good in many ways. It allowed him to earn a living so he could support his children, and it meant Esther would continue to be employed by Samuel. At least she hoped she would. She'd be very disappointed if he ever found someone else to watch the kids.

"You're right about Samuel," Allen said. "With four kids to feed and clothe, he needs a good income." He set his empty glass on the table and stood. "Now that I've had a little snack, I think I'll take you up on that offer to relax in the hammock. . . unless you'd like to lay claim to it first."

"You go right ahead," Esther said. "I'm going inside to wash the produce we picked. Then I'll probably sit outside and listen to the birds awhile. When they sing, I like to think they're serenading me."

"All right then, if I fall asleep, wake me in an hour. I really should bid on a couple of jobs before this day is out."

Esther watched as Allen settled himself in the hammock. He looked so relaxed and at peace with the world. If Allen really was a workaholic, as Bonnie had said, then he probably didn't take much time for himself. She could relate to that, because here of late she hadn't been able to take much time for herself either, but she didn't really mind. She liked keeping busy.

—m—

Portland, Oregon

"Never thought I'd admit this, but it's been nice having you here." Bonnie's dad gave her a half-smile from across the breakfast table. "I appreciate you coming to take care of me. Sure couldn't have managed without you these weeks."

She reached over and placed her hand over his. "I love you, Dad, and I'm glad I could be here to help out."

He lowered his gaze to the table. "Don't know how you can love me. I haven't been the best dad." He pulled his fingers through the sides of his thinning brown hair. "It's hard for me to deal with the fact that you chose to move to Kentucky—especially when you knew how things were between me and my folks."

"Whatever the problem was between you and Grandpa and Grandma, you need to forgive them, Dad. Holding a grudge will only make you sick, and if you're not willing to forgive your parents, then God won't forgive you."

He blinked a couple of times. "Forgive me for what? I'm not the one who forced their only child to leave his friends in Oregon and move all the way to Kentucky, where he hated it."

"I can't understand why you'd hate Kentucky. I think it's beautiful there." Bonnie reached for her cup of coffee and took a drink. "Besides, from what you've told me before, you were only seventeen when your folks left Oregon. I'm sure you made other friends after you moved."

"I did make a few, but I was in my senior year of high school when we moved, and it was hard to start over again. It was even harder to leave my girlfriend, Trisha, because we planned to get married after we graduated from school and found a job." Deep wrinkles formed across Dad's forehead. "After I moved, she found another boyfriend and ended up marrying him instead of me."

Hearing the name Trisha caused Bonnie to remember the letter she'd found in Grandma's pie cupboard. She'd brought the letter along, planning to give it to Dad, but in all the busyness of caring for him, she'd forgotten about it until now.

"I'll be right back, Dad. I have something I think you need

to see." Bonnie rose from her seat and went to get her purse in the other room. When she returned, she handed him the letter. "I found this in an old pie cupboard down in Grandma's basement. It was stuck in the middle of some newspapers."

Dad's brows furrowed as he stared at the envelope. "Was it open when you found it?"

She shook her head. "Since I wasn't sure what it was, I went ahead and opened it. Sorry. I didn't mean to be snoopy."

Dad pulled the letter from the envelope, and as he read Trisha's message, his eyes turned glassy. He sat silently for a while before he spoke, as though letting what he'd read sink in. "I—I had no idea Trisha was planning to break up with me even before I moved. If she'd only had the nerve to say so, I'd have probably been glad I was moving. All those years I spent mad at my folks were for nothing." He thumped the side of his head. "What a waste of time, and now it's too late. I can't bring Mom and Pop back, and I can't tell them how sorry I am for giving them such a hard time. I had a chip on my shoulder, and we argued about everything because I thought they were too strict. As soon as I graduated from high school, I joined the army. Then later, I came back here. By then, Trisha was already married, of course, and soon after that, I met your mom."

"Did you love Mom?" Bonnie dared to ask. "Or did you marry her on the rebound?"

"Yes, I did love her, but I guess in my mind, she was second choice." He grimaced. "As you well know, your mom and I argued a lot. She never understood why I didn't want to visit my folks, and when she insisted on taking you there so you could get to know your grandparents, it caused even more friction between us."

"I'm sorry you disapproved, but I wouldn't have wanted

to grow up never knowing your parents—especially since Mom's parents were no longer living by the time I was born. Grandma and Grandpa Taylor may have been a little strict and old-fashioned in some ways, but they were good people."

"Yeah, you're right. I guess your mom did a good thing by taking you to visit them in Kentucky, even sometimes when I refused to go along. I just wish you weren't living there now. I miss you, Bonnie."

"I miss you, too, and you're always welcome to visit me there. Of course, I'll come here for visits whenever I can, too."

He gave a nod. "I'll look forward to that."

"You know, Dad, since I've been living in Kentucky, I've gotten to know several Amish families there. They're family-oriented, and they've taught me a lot about putting God first and then the needs of family and friends."

"Guess that's something I've never really done," he said with a tone of regret. "I sure didn't put your needs first after your mother died, and when I forced you to give up your baby, I thought you might hate me for the rest of your life."

She shook her head as tears gathered in her eyes. "After I became a Christian, I forgave you for that. And looking back on it now, I'm sure that you did what you thought was right."

"Would you pray with me, Bonnie?" he asked as his own eyes filled with tears. "I need to ask God to forgive me for the ill feelings I harbored toward my folks, and I need His forgiveness for all the times I yelled at your mom." He took Bonnie's hand and gave her fingers a gentle squeeze. "I'm sorry for everything I've ever done to hurt you as well."

Bonnie swallowed around the lump in her throat. "I forgive you, Dad. Now let's pray so you can seek God's forgiveness and find a peace in your heart that only He can give."

Pembroke, Kentucky

Samuel had just dropped the kids off at the Zooks' home so they could play with Ethan Zook's younger siblings and was heading over to the B&B to pick up Marla's sneakers, which she'd left there last night. It seemed like his oldest daughter had become forgetful lately. This was the second time in less than a week that she'd left something at the B&B. He was beginning to wonder if she was doing it on purpose so he'd have to go after her forgotten items.

But why would she do that? he reasoned. *She sure can't enjoy watching me inconvenience myself.*

When Samuel pulled into Bonnie's yard sometime later, he was surprised to see Allen sleeping in the hammock. He was even more surprised to see Esther sitting on a blanket near the hammock, with a glass in her hand. They looked very cozy.

I wonder why Allen's here and why he's sleeping in the hammock. Could there be something going on between Esther and Allen? Samuel frowned. Come to think of it, while he and Allen had worked together a few times, Allen had mentioned that he thought Esther was very nice and would make a good wife for some lucky man. Could he have been talking about himself?

Samuel had never admitted it until now, but in the last few weeks, he'd begun to realize that his heart was beginning to heal. He still missed Elsie, of course, but the raw ache he'd felt for the first several months after her death had finally faded, and he felt like he might be ready to open his heart to love again. He'd even thought Esther might be the one. But if

Esther was interested in Allen, then there was no hope for the two of them. Should he make his feelings known or keep quiet and see what happened between Esther and Allen? If Allen wanted Esther, then he'd most likely expect her to leave the Amish faith, because Samuel was sure Allen would never give up his modern way of life to become Amish. Or would he?

Chapter 39

The tail of Samuel's horse switched back and forth, letting Samuel know the impatient animal was tired of standing in the driveway.

"Okay. Okay." Samuel pulled up to the hitching rail, climbed out of his buggy, and secured his horse. "Be good now, Socks," he said, patting the horse's flanks. "I won't be gone long."

Samuel sprinted across the lawn and stopped in front of the blanket where Esther sat. "Sorry to disturb you," he said, "but I came to get Marla's sneakers. She told me this morning that she forgot to bring 'em home when I picked the kinner up last night."

Esther nodded. "They played in the sprinkler yesterday, and their shoes got wet, so we set them on the back porch to dry. I spotted the sneakers this morning and realized that Marla was the only one who didn't take hers home."

Samuel grunted. "That's because she's become so *vergesslich* lately."

"She's not the only one who's forgetful," Esther said. "I got so relaxed sitting here in the sun that I forgot about the rest of the produce I'd planned to pick in the garden today." She glanced over at Allen, who appeared to be asleep. "I think this warm weather made him drowsy, too."

Samuel was tempted to ask why Allen was in the hammock and not working today, but he figured it was none of his business—although he was quite curious.

Esther rose to her feet. "I'll get Marla's shoes now. Would you like me to bring you a glass of lemonade or some iced tea?"

Samuel shook his head. "I appreciate the offer, but I should get back to the house. The kinner are over at the Zooks', playing with their youngest kinner, so I'm going to use this time by myself to get the laundry and a few other things done."

She nodded with a look of understanding. "I'll be right back."

When Esther went to the house, Samuel seated himself on the blanket where she'd been sitting. He'd only been there a few minutes when Allen's eyes snapped open. As he swung his legs over the hammock and sat up, he looked at Samuel and blinked. "Wh–where's Esther, and how long have you been here?"

"Esther's in the house, getting Marla's sneakers, and I got here a few minutes ago. I'm surprised you didn't hear my horse and buggy pull in," Samuel said. "For that matter, with Esther and me standing just a few feet from the hammock, I'm surprised you didn't wake up sooner."

Allen yawned and stretched his arms over his head. "Guess I was more tired than I thought, 'cause I never heard a thing."

"How's the pain in your back?" Samuel asked, instead of posing the question uppermost on his mind.

"Much better. In fact, I'm feeling so good that I picked

some beans from Bonnie's garden. Esther's had a heavy load since Bonnie went to Oregon to take care of her dad, and I figured she could use a little extra help."

"Oh, I see." Samuel leaned back on his elbows and studied Allen. He was a successful businessman, nice looking, and seemed to be real smart about a lot of things. He was sure Allen could have any woman he wanted. The question was—did he want Esther?

"How come you're looking at me so strangely?" Allen asked. "Have I got dirt on my face or something?"

Samuel's face heated. "There's no dirt on your face, but I do have a question I'd like to ask."

"What's that?"

"Are you interested in Esther?"

Allen tipped his head. "Interested in what way?"

Samuel scrubbed his hand down the side of his face. "Are you planning to court her?"

Allen's jaw dropped, and he nearly jumped out of the hammock. "Now what made you ask something like that?"

"Well, you're always saying what a good cook she is, and you've mentioned a few times that she'd make a good wife. So I figured. . ."

Allen grinned and thumped Samuel's back. "A good wife for you, my friend, not for me. It doesn't take a genius to see that you care for her. Every time I've seen the two of you together, it's written all over your face."

Samuel sat, dumbfounded. He couldn't believe how wrong he'd been. But even if Allen was out of the picture, there was still Ethan Zook to be concerned about. Samuel had noticed Ethan hanging around Esther after their last church service, and he'd seen Ethan talking to Esther several other times, too. Samuel was afraid if he didn't move fast he might lose Esther.

But if he moved too fast, he might scare her away. Besides, what would his family back home think about him choosing another wife so soon? It hadn't even been a year since Elsie died.

"So what do you have to say?" Allen thumped Samuel's back again. "Are you in love with Esther or not?"

"I—I do care for her," Samuel admitted, "but I'm afraid it might be too soon for me to make a commitment to another woman. Besides, I don't know if Esther has feelings for me."

"Well, if the look I've seen on her face whenever you're around is any indication, then I'd say she definitely has feelings for you."

"You really think so?"

"If I was a betting man, I'd place a large bet on it. And if I was you, I'd take action soon, because any woman as sweet, pretty, and capable as Esther is bound to turn some fellow's head, and I think that fellow ought to be you."

Samuel pondered that a few seconds, then nodded. "I'll give it some serious thought."

Allen grinned. "Glad to hear it. Well, I have a couple of jobs I need to bid, so I'd better head out. Do think about what I said." He thumped Samuel's back one more time and headed for his truck.

As Allen's rig pulled out, Samuel glanced up at the house, wondering what was taking Esther so long. Just at that moment, she stepped out the door and headed his way, carrying Marla's shoes.

"I'm sorry for taking so long," Esther said, "but I got a phone call from someone wanting to make a reservation at the B&B, and it took awhile to discuss the details."

"No problem. I was visiting with Allen."

She glanced at the spot where Allen's truck had been

parked. "I see that he's gone."

"Jah. Said he had some jobs to bid."

"That's right. He mentioned it earlier, before he took his nap." Esther handed Marla's shoes to Samuel. "Guess I'd better get back to work in the garden, or it'll never get done." She smiled. "I'll see you and the kinner at church tomorrow."

Feeling as if he had a wad of sticky chewing gum in his mouth, all Samuel could do was nod. He wanted to ask if Esther would join him and the kids for supper this evening, but the words seemed to be stuck in his mouth.

Esther started walking toward the garden, and he moved in the direction of his horse and buggy. Maybe some other time would be better to ask Esther out.

Samuel had just untied his horse from the hitching rail, when Bonnie's dog darted out of the barn, barking and nipping at the horse's heels. Socks whinnied and kicked up his back feet, just missing the terrier's head. Not to be dissuaded, Cody kept barking and nipping at Socks's tail. Samuel tried to calm the horse, but the more the dog carried on, the more agitated Socks became.

"Cody, come here!" Esther clapped her hands as she raced across the yard. She was almost to the buggy, when Samuel's horse whipped his head around and knocked her to the ground.

Samuel gasped and raced to Esther's side.

Chapter 40

I'm fine, Samuel," Esther said after Samuel had carried her into the house and placed her gently on the sofa.

"Are you sure?" The deep wrinkles in Samuel's forehead let Esther know he was truly concerned.

"Yes, I'm fine. Nothing's broken, and the only thing hurt was my pride when I ended up face-down in the dirt."

He knelt on the floor beside her, and as he pushed a wayward piece of her hair back under the black scarf she wore as a head covering, a pained expression crossed his face. "It scared me real bad when my horse knocked you down. You should have stayed back, Esther. With those crazy animals carrying on like that, you could have been seriously hurt."

Esther was surprised at Samuel's concern and tenderness toward her. Was she imagining it, or was it possible that he cared about her in the same way as she did him? Oh, how she wished it were true. She'd give anything if. . .

"Esther, I—" Samuel looked away, as though unable to make eye contact with her.

"What is it, Samuel? What were you going to say?"

He lifted his gaze and said in a near whisper, "I've been thinking that it might be time for me to start courting again."

"You—you have?" Esther's heart hammered in her chest, and her mouth went dry as she waited for his answer.

"Jah, and I. . .uh. . .am planning to take the kinner out to supper in Hopkinsville this evening, and. . .well, I was wondering if you'd like to go along."

Esther smiled. Even though having the children with them certainly wouldn't be considered a real date, Samuel had asked her to go with them, and she was grateful for that. *He must not have feelings for Bonnie, after all. It really was my silly imagination.*

"I'd be happy to go out to supper with you this evening," she murmured, fighting back tears of joy.

He grinned. "That's good. Jah, that's a very good thing. I think the kinner will be happy about this 'cause they really do like you, Esther."

"I like them, too." *And you as well,* Esther silently added. *In fact, I'm sure I'm in love with you.* Esther knew that Samuel probably wasn't ready to make such a confession yet, but maybe in time he would come to love her, too.

They sat for several seconds, looking at each other and smiling, until loud barking, followed by a shrill—*Yipe*! *Yipe!*—pulled their gazes apart.

Samuel leaped to his feet and raced out the door.

Esther clambered off the sofa and quickly followed him across the yard, where Cody lay on the ground near Socks, whining.

"Ach! Looks like the dog's been hurt!" Samuel knelt beside Cody and did a quick examination. "I'm almost sure the poor critter has a broken leg. I'm guessin' Socks must have kicked him pretty hard." He grimaced. "Guess I'd better forget about doing any laundry today and call for a driver, 'cause I think we'd better take this poor little dog to the vet's."

—∞—

Elkton, Kentucky

When Esther and Samuel entered the vet's office, she was surprised to see Suzanne sitting in the waiting room. "What are you doing here?" she and Suzanne both asked at the same time.

"I brought Samson in to have him neutered yesterday, and I'm here to pick him up." Suzanne looked at Samuel, who was holding Cody. "Isn't that Bonnie's little terrier?"

He gave a nod. "He was nipping at my horse and ended up getting kicked. I'm pretty sure his leg is broken."

"Oh, that's a shame." Suzanne looked at Esther. "Does Bonnie know about this?"

Esther shook her head. "I'll call her once I know something definite."

Samuel walked up to the receptionist's desk, and after she told him to bring the dog back to the examining room, he turned to Esther and said, "Why don't you wait here and visit with Suzanne while I take Cody in?"

"Okay." Esther was thankful Samuel was willing to do that, because she didn't relish the idea of watching while the doctor examined Cody. It hurt her to see anyone in pain—even an animal.

Suzanne motioned to the chair beside her. "Why don't you take a seat?"

Once Esther was seated, she told Suzanne how she'd been knocked to the ground by Samuel's horse and how Samuel had carried her into the house. "He had such a look of concern on his face," she said. "He even invited me to join him and his kinner for supper in Hopkinsville this evening."

"I knew it!" Suzanne's face broke into a wide smile. "And I'll have to say this—it's about time."

"You knew Samuel was going to invite me to join them for supper?"

"No, but I knew he'd get around to inviting you somewhere soon."

"How'd you know that?"

"I've seen the way Samuel looks at you whenever he thinks you're not looking. He's come to care for you, Esther. I'm sure of it." Suzanne squeezed Esther's hand. "I think the two of you are perfect for each other, and I believe Samuel realizes that, too."

"I hope you're right," Esther said, "but I guess I won't really know unless he asks me to go someplace with him again." It was strange, but she'd never seen Samuel look at her in a special way. Usually when he was around, he looked the other way. But he had invited her out and seemed real happy about it, so maybe he did have strong feelings for her.

"Why wait for Samuel to ask you to go someplace else? Why don't you invite Samuel and the kinner over to the B&B for supper sometime soon?"

"I had them over not long ago when it rained and we couldn't go on a picnic, but if I ask them again, Samuel might think I'm being pushy, and I sure don't want that."

"I doubt that he would think that. Besides, what man in his right mind would turn down one of your delicious meals?"

"So you think I should try to win Samuel's heart with my cooking?"

"I think you've already won his heart." Suzanne chuckled. "But a little taste of your cooking from time to time wouldn't hurt either."

"Do you think Samuel's really ready to start courting again?" Esther asked, needing some reassurance. "I mean, do you think his heart has healed enough after losing his wife that he might actually consider marriage again?"

"I believe it has, but from what I know of Samuel, I don't think he'll rush into anything."

"No, and I wouldn't want him to."

"I have some news of my own," Suzanne said. "Titus and I have decided on the second Thursday in October as the date we'll get married."

"That's *wunderbaar*. Do both of your families know?"

"Mine know, and Titus was supposed to call his folks and give them the news this morning." Suzanne touched Esther's arm. "I'd like you to be one of my attendants at the wedding."

Esther smiled and nodded. "I'd be honored."

"Maybe by next fall it'll be you and Samuel getting married," Suzanne said, gently nudging Esther's arm.

Before Esther could reply, Samuel entered the waiting room, this time without Cody.

"What'd the doctor say?" Esther asked, rising from her seat.

"Said the dog's leg is definitely broken, and it's a bad break, so he'll have to do surgery on it." Samuel slowly shook his head. "Guess Cody will have to stay here at the vet's for a few days."

Esther frowned. "Oh dear. I sure dread telling Bonnie this news."

Paradise, Pennsylvania

"How are things going with you and Hannah these days?"

Fannie asked Timothy when he and Abraham took a break from the fields and came to the house for lunch.

"They're a little better." Timothy reached for another piece of bread and slathered it with peanut butter. "I've been trying to do more things to help Hannah at home, and I've taken her and Mindy on a couple of picnics so far this summer."

"Is she still going over to her mamm's every day?" Abraham questioned.

"Nope. She goes over about once a week, and I'm okay with that."

Fannie smiled. "I'm glad to hear it."

Timothy nodded. "I just hope it lasts."

"As long as you keep working on your marriage, I'm sure things will only get better," Fannie said. "Oh, and by the way, while you two were out working in the fields this morning, I checked our phone messages, and there was one from Titus."

"What's new with him?" Abraham asked as he reached for the platter full of lunchmeat and cheese.

"He and Suzanne have set a date for their wedding. It'll be on the second Thursday of October."

"Did you tell him we'd all be there to witness their marriage?" Timothy asked.

She nodded. "I can't wait to see Titus again as well as Samuel and his kinner."

"Same here," Timothy agreed. "It'll not only be good to see everyone, but I'm anxious to see what Kentucky's like."

Fannie frowned. "I didn't see anything special about it when we were there last year."

Abraham bumped her arm with his elbow. "But Titus and Samuel seem to like Kentucky, so maybe they see something that you might have missed."

"Jah, maybe so." With a shiver of apprehension, Fannie

sent up a silent prayer: *I know Timothy said he'd never move because of Hannah, but please, Lord, don't let him change his mind and take his family from here.*

Chapter 41

Pembroke, Kentucky

Esther hummed as she cleaned up the kitchen. Things were going so well in her life these days, she felt like pinching herself. During the last few weeks, she'd gone out to supper with Samuel and his children in Hopkinsville, they'd all gone fishing together twice, and she'd shared another picnic supper with Samuel and the children—this time at the pond. Tonight, Samuel and the children would be coming to the B&B for supper again, and she could hardly wait. While Samuel hadn't actually said he loved her, or was thinking of getting married again, the time they'd spent together so far had been quite pleasant, and he'd been very attentive to her needs. The children, of course, seemed to enjoy having Esther around, so she was fairly certain they would accept the idea of her marrying their father, should Samuel ever propose.

I shouldn't get my hopes up, Esther thought as she grabbed a sponge and began wiping the table. *As much as I desire to become Samuel's wife and the mother of his children, it might never happen. And if that's how it goes, then as much as it will hurt, I'll need to accept it as God's will.*

As she rinsed the sponge, Esther turned her thoughts to other things. Bonnie had called last night, saying her father was much better and that she'd be returning to Kentucky. In fact, her plane would arrive in Nashville late this afternoon, and she'd contacted Allen about picking her up.

If they get here in time for supper, maybe Allen would like to join us, Esther thought. She hadn't seen him since the day he'd helped her pick beans, but Samuel had mentioned that Allen had been really busy with work, so she figured that was probably why he hadn't dropped by again.

A knock sounded on the back door, and Esther dried her hands and went to answer it. She was surprised to see Ethan Zook on the porch.

"Guder mariye," he said with a grin. "The locust are rattling from the trees pretty good, and it looks like it's gonna be another hot one today, jah?"

Esther nodded. "It was hot yesterday and didn't cool down much during the night, so it'll probably be hot and sticky the whole day."

Ethan's boots scraped noisily against the porch as he shuffled his feet a few times. "The reason I came by is. . . Well, I'm goin' to the Walmart store in Hopkinsville this afternoon and wondered if you'd like to go along." He shuffled his feet a few more times. "Thought maybe after we're done shoppin' we could eat supper at whichever restaurant you choose."

"I appreciate your asking," Esther said, "but I have other plans for this evening."

Ethan dropped his gaze to the porch. "Sorry to hear that. I was hopin' you'd be free to go with me."

"Maybe some other time," Esther said, although she didn't know why. She had no interest in going anywhere with Ethan, and since it appeared that she and Samuel were courting, she probably should have told Ethan that she'd been seeing Samuel instead of letting him believe she might be available to go out with him some other time. But if she'd told him that, he may have repeated it to someone else, and if Samuel heard it and didn't really have courting on his mind, it could be quite embarrassing—for both her and Samuel.

Esther was about to tell Ethan good-bye, when he leaned close to the door and sniffed deeply. "Have ya done any baking lately? I sure enjoyed that banana bread you gave my mamm awhile back." He smacked his lips noisily. "That was real tasty and moist."

Esther forced a smile. "I'm glad you liked it, but I haven't made any more banana bread since I gave the loaf to your mamm. The only baking I've done is just basic bread and some cinnamon rolls for the guests who've stayed here at the bed-and-breakfast."

Ethan's rather plain, hazel-colored eyes brightened, and he patted his portly stomach. "You wouldn't happen to have any cinnamon rolls now, would ya? I'm kinda partial to those, too."

She shook her head, trying her best not to let her annoyance show. She just wished Ethan would go. "The last of the cinnamon rolls were eaten by the B&B guests who were here earlier in the week. If you're really hungry for cinnamon rolls, I'm sure they probably have some at the bakeshop in our area."

"I might stop by there on my way home." For several seconds, Ethan stared intently at Esther, which made her squirm. Then he finally said, "Guess I'd better let you get back to whatever it was you were doin'."

She smiled. "I do have several chores I need to get done yet this morning. Bonnie will be back later today, and I want to have everything in good shape before she arrives."

"Jah, okay then." He turned and started down the stairs. When he reached the bottom step, he turned and said, "The next time I go to Hopkinsville, I'll let ya know."

Esther gave a forced smile and quickly stepped into the house. She had a hunch that Ethan's interest in her had more to do with her cooking skills than him enjoying her company. If there was one thing everyone in their community knew, it was that Ethan Zook liked to eat.

Nashville, Tennessee

"How was your flight?" Allen asked as he put Bonnie's luggage in the back of his truck.

"It went well. We didn't have much turbulence, and all my connections were on time." She smiled at him. "I really appreciate your coming to get me. I could have driven my own car here when I flew out to Portland, but not knowing how long I'd be gone, I didn't want to pay a huge parking fee if I ended up staying very long, which is exactly what happened."

"Picking you up was no problem at all. In fact, I was glad to do it," he said as she stepped into the passenger's side of his truck.

"So how's your dad doing?" he asked as he slid in behind the steering wheel.

"Much better. He's able to manage on his own now and will soon be back at work, I expect."

"I'm not sure if you ever said what he does for a living."

"He's the manager of a bank in Portland."

"Ah, I see. A big-shot, huh?"

She shook her head. "He's a pretty common guy. He's always had a good business head though. Kind of like you."

"What makes you think I've got a head for business?"

"I doubt you'd be a successful general contractor if you didn't."

Allen smiled and turned on the ignition. "Well, I do my best."

When they headed down the road a few minutes later, Allen looked over at Bonnie and smiled. "It's sure good to have you back. We've all missed you."

"I missed everyone, too." Bonnie fiddled with the handles on her purse, feeling suddenly uncomfortable. The tender expression she saw on Allen's face made her wonder if he might have missed her more than she knew. Had he come to care for her in a special way? A part of her wanted him to care, but there was the cautious part that said she must remember to keep her feelings to herself and put a safe distance between her and Allen so she wouldn't become emotionally attached to him. She'd allowed herself to fall in love once and had paid a huge price for it. Since then, she'd consoled herself with the fact that marriage wasn't what it was cracked up to be anyhow. Most married couples she knew argued all the time, the way her parents had done. Bonnie's friend Shirley, with whom she'd gone to high school, had recently been through a nasty divorce after a stormy marriage with a man who had promised to love and cherish her all the days of his life. So much for happily ever after!

When Bonnie lived in Portland, she'd focused on her job. Now she had the bed-and-breakfast to keep her occupied, so she hoped Allen didn't have any ideas of taking their friendship to the next level. She'd have to keep a handle on things—that was for sure.

Chapter 42

Pembroke, Kentucky

It's nice to have you back," Esther said to Bonnie as they sat at the supper table with Allen, Samuel, and the children.

"It's sure good to be home." Bonnie smiled. "And I really do think of this as my home now."

"It must have been hard for you to leave your dad," Samuel said.

"Yes, it was, but he understands now that I'd rather live here, and he's promised to come visit me sometime—maybe this Christmas."

"I'm happy to hear that," Esther said. "I've been praying your dad would change his mind about coming to visit you."

"Dad and I talked about a lot of things while I was there, and I think everything will be better between us from now on."

"That's good to hear." Esther was anxious to hear more about Bonnie's visit with her dad but figured now wasn't the time to discuss it—not with Allen, Samuel, and his children sitting here.

"This fried chicken is sure good," Samuel said as he took another drumstick.

Esther smiled. "Danki, Samuel."

"This ain't one of them green-egg layin' chickens is it?" Leon asked with a wide-eyed expression.

Esther shook her head. "There's no need to worry. The chicken I fixed is a fresh fryer I bought from one of our neighbors."

Leon's face relaxed. "That's good to know. Wouldn't feel right 'bout eatin' one of your hens."

"The chickens out there in the coop aren't mine," Esther said. "They belong to Bonnie."

"I knew that. Just seems like they're yours since you've been takin' care of Bonnie's place all these weeks."

Samuel tapped Leon's arm. "Why don't you eat now and quit talking so much?"

"Okay." Leon spooned some potato salad onto his plate and took a big bite. "Umm. . . This is sure tasty, Esther. You're a real good cook."

She smiled. "Danki, Leon. I'm glad you're enjoying the meal."

"I think we're all enjoying it," Allen said, wiping his mouth with a napkin. "Eating a home-cooked meal like this makes a man wish he had a wife." He glanced over at Bonnie, but she seemed intent on eating the biscuit she'd just picked up, and Esther couldn't help but notice that Bonnie's cheeks had turned a bright pink color.

"How's Cody doin'?" Marla asked, looking at Esther.

"He's getting along pretty well with his cast," Esther replied. She looked at Bonnie. "I'm glad you took it so well when I told you about his broken leg."

Bonnie shrugged. "I knew it was an accident, and it wouldn't have happened if the little troublemaker hadn't been bothering Samuel's horse. Hopefully, Cody learned a good lesson and won't chase after anyone's horse again."

"Some horses spook easier than others, especially when they're around dogs," Samuel said. "I'm afraid Socks is one of those horses that don't care much for dogs. He gets spooky around Lucky, too. Has ever since the dog was a pup and started barkin' at him."

"You're not gonna get rid of Lucky, are ya, Daadi?" Penny spoke up.

" 'Course not," Samuel said. "Like it or not, the mutt's part of our family, so he's here to stay."

The children looked relieved and went back to eating without another word.

"Did you hear that my brother's getting married in October?" Samuel asked Allen.

"Yes, Titus told me the other day when I stopped by the woodshop to see if they could make the cabinets and doors for a new house I'll be starting to work on soon."

"Will you attend Titus and Suzanne's wedding?" Esther asked.

Allen nodded eagerly. "It'll be my first Amish wedding, and I wouldn't miss it for the world." He looked at Bonnie and smiled. "I'll make sure you get an invitation, too, because I'm sure you'd enjoy seeing what an Amish wedding is like as much as I would."

"That would be interesting, all right," Bonnie said. "I hear it's a lot different from our English weddings."

"An Amish wedding is similar to the regular church services we hold every other week," Esther said. "Of course, in our wedding services, the bride and groom say their vows in front of the bishop, and the message that's preached is about marriage."

"How long does the service usually last?" Bonnie questioned.

"About three hours," Esther replied.

Allen's eyes widened as he released a shrill whistle. "Wow, that's a really long service. Most English weddings and church services don't last much more than an hour, and even then, some people complain about having to sit that long."

"You're right about that," Bonnie agreed. "It seems that some folks only want to give one hour of their time every week."

Esther thought about that for a while. She couldn't imagine anyone complaining about how long they had to be in church. She saw going to church as a privilege, and it was a Christian's duty. She'd never minded their three-hour services one bit.

They continued to visit about other things until the meal was over, and then the children scampered from the room and rushed outside to play.

"Why don't you and Esther go out and sit on the porch?" Allen said to Samuel. "Think I'll stay in here and help Bonnie with the dishes."

"Oh no, I should help her do the dishes," Esther was quick to say. "Allen, why don't you and Samuel go outside and visit?"

"No, Esther, I insist that you go outside," Bonnie said. "After all, you cooked this wonderful meal for us."

"But you just got home from a long flight," Esther argued.

"Well, I don't care who goes outside." Allen's chair scraped the floor as he pushed it away from the table and stood. "I'm going to be the one to help with the dishes." He grabbed his plate and silverware and quickly put them in the sink.

Samuel looked at Esther and said, "It's probably much cooler outside. Should we go sit on the porch swing?"

The thought of sitting on the swing beside Samuel was inviting, so Esther smiled and said, "That'd be real nice." After she'd cleared her own dishes, she followed Samuel out the door.

—~—

"Did Esther tell you that she and Samuel have started courting?" Allen asked Bonnie as he filled the sink with warm water.

Bonnie's mouth opened in surprise. "She never said a word; although I haven't been home long enough for her to say a whole lot to me yet. When did they start courting?"

"A few weeks ago. Samuel took Esther out for supper with him and the kids one evening, and I understand they all went fishing and also on a picnic together."

Bonnie handed Allen several dirty plates. "I'd hardly call them going somewhere with Samuel's kids courting."

"Well, it's a start." Allen set the plates in the sink and snapped his fingers. "Say, I've got an idea!"

"What's that?"

"Why don't the two of us go on a double date with Samuel and Esther?"

Bonnie's hands became sweaty, and she quickly set the two glasses she'd picked up off the table onto the counter, fearful they might slip from her hands. "Wh–what kind of a double date?"

"How about if we four go to the Jefferson Davis Monument this Saturday? You haven't seen it yet, have you?"

Bonnie shook her head. "No, but. . ."

"Maybe Suzanne or even her mother would watch Samuel's kids for a few hours while we're on our double date."

Bonnie shifted uneasily. "Oh, I don't know. . ."

"Come on, Bonnie, please say you'll go. I'm sure Samuel wouldn't think to take Esther there by himself, and it'll be a lot of fun for all of us."

Bonnie was tempted to use the B&B as an excuse not to go, but she didn't have any guests scheduled to come in until the middle of next week. And since this was a double date and she wouldn't be alone with Allen, she guessed it would be okay.

"Oh, all right," she finally agreed. Secretly, she wished more than anything that she could allow herself to have some fun and not feel like she had to protect herself from more hurt. After all, it was just one date, and she was only going for Esther's sake.

Chapter 43

Fairview, Kentucky

Wow, would you look at that!" Samuel said in amazement as Allen pulled his truck into the parking lot at the Jefferson Davis Monument. "It looks even bigger up close than it does from a distance."

Allen grinned. "Wait until you go up inside and see the view from there. It's just amazing."

Esther's heart started to pound. She remembered how she'd come here with Titus shortly after he'd moved to Kentucky and had refused to go up in the monument with him because of her fear of heights. Titus had been nice about it, but she'd seen the look of disappointment on his face, and it had made her feel guilty.

What had she been thinking, agreeing to come here today? Surely Samuel, and probably the others, would expect her to go up in the monument, too.

I climbed up the ladder to rescue Penny when she was stuck in that tree awhile back, she reminded herself. *At least this time I'll be inside the safety of a building. Maybe if I don't look down I'll be okay.*

"What's wrong, Esther? You look upset," Bonnie said after they'd climbed out of the truck.

"I. . .uh. . . It's nothing. I'm fine," Esther said with a shake of her head, not wanting to reveal how bad her phobia was.

"Are you sure you want to do this?" Allen asked. "I remember the last time we came here you stayed below."

"I know I did, but I—I think I can do it this time." Esther really wasn't sure she could do it, but she had to try.

"Let's get our tickets bought and go up inside right away." Allen pointed to the visitor's center, which was where they'd need to go for tickets. "I can't wait to show everyone the great view from up there."

"This is going to be fun," Samuel said as he walked beside Esther. "Don't think I've ever been in a building that tall."

Esther shivered. Was it too late to say no? Would Samuel be terribly disappointed if she waited on a bench below while he and the others went up? She didn't want to do anything that might ruin her chances with Samuel, so she wouldn't let on how fearful she felt and was determined this time to go up in that building.

—∞—

"How high did you say this building is?" Samuel asked their guide as they entered the elevator that would take them to the viewing area.

"The structure is 351 feet tall, and it was made from solid Kentucky limestone," the young man said.

"It was built in 1917. Isn't that right?" Allen asked.

"That's when it was started—built in honor of Jefferson Davis, the famous Kentuckian born June 3, 1808, right here on this site," the guide said with a nod. "But it wasn't completed right away. You see, steam was the principle source of power back then, and so the workers used steam engines to power their equipment, including steam-powered drills. A quarry was dug on the south end of the park site, and the stone was crushed in mixing cement. By the fall of 1918, the monument had reached a height of 175 feet. But then construction had to be stopped, due to rationing of building materials during World War I. Work on the monument resumed in January 1922, and it was completed in 1924. Of course, the monument has undergone major renovations since then," the guide added.

Samuel felt like his head was swimming with all that historical information. It was interesting to hear how the monument came about though.

When they stepped off the elevator and moved toward the viewing windows, Samuel noticed that Esther held back.

"Come on," he coaxed. "Shall we take a look?"

When she didn't budge, he took her hand. "Don't you want to see the view below?"

"Umm. . .sure. I guess so."

Looking none too thrilled about the idea, Esther let Samuel lead her to one of the viewing windows, where Allen and Bonnie already stood with their guide.

"The view from up here is breathtaking," Bonnie said. "I've been in plenty of tall buildings in downtown Portland, but to me, none of them had a view as nice as this. Just look at all those pretty trees!"

Esther clung so tightly to Samuel's hand that her fingernails dug into his skin. She was clearly not comfortable being up here.

"Are you okay?" he asked, leaning close to her ear.

"I–I'm fine. Just a little dizzy is all." She edged away from the window and leaned tightly against the back wall.

"I think we ought to go down now," Samuel said to their

guide. "Esther's not feeling well."

The guide looked at Allen and Bonnie. "If you two aren't done looking yet, you can ride down in the elevator with us, and then I'll bring you back up. It's against the rules for me to leave you up here alone."

"No, that's okay. I've seen enough." Allen looked at Bonnie. "How about you?"

"I don't need to come back either," she said, as though sensing Esther's anxiety.

When they stepped into the elevator and started their descent, Samuel couldn't help but notice the look of relief on Esther's pale-looking face.

"Are you okay?" he asked when they stepped off the elevator.

She gave a quick nod. "I'm fine now. Just needed some fresh air."

"It was kind of stuffy up there," Bonnie said. "Of course, we're having another hot, humid day."

"Should we go to the gift shop and get an ice-cream bar?" Allen suggested. "Maybe something cold and sweet would perk us all up."

"That sounds nice," Esther said. She'd let go of Samuel's hand and was walking with a relaxed stride toward the gift shop.

Samuel smiled to himself. He enjoyed being with Esther and hoped they could do something fun like this again soon.

CHAPTER 44

Pembroke, Kentucky

As Esther sat on a blanket near the pond, holding Jared in her lap, a feeling of contentment came over her, like a warm, cozy quilt. She glanced at Suzanne, who sat beside her, and smiled. "It's a beautiful day, isn't it? Not so hot for a change."

Suzanne smiled. "Jah. It's a reminder that fall's not far off. You can really feel and see the beauty of God's creation on a day like this." She motioned to Samuel and Titus, sitting on the ground not far away with their fishing lines cast into the pond. "It's good that they both have this Saturday off and can spend some time together doing something they both like."

"You're right about them both liking to fish," Esther agreed. "From the eager expression I saw on Leon's face when his daed baited his hook, I'd say he likes to fish equally well."

"Everyone seems quite happy today." Suzanne motioned to Marla and Penny, who were giggling and taking turns throwing a stick for Lucky to fetch.

Esther leaned back on her elbows and sighed. "I can't believe Samuel and I are actually courting."

"Speaking of courting, how was your visit to the Jefferson Davis Monument a couple of weeks ago?"

"It was okay. I forced myself to go up inside, but I got dizzy and was glad that we didn't stay there long."

"Does Samuel know about your fear of heights?" Suzanne questioned.

"I think he does because Marla mentioned it to him that day when I rescued Penny from the tree. I made myself go up in the monument because I didn't want Samuel to think I'm afraid of every little thing, or he might stop courting me the way Titus did."

Suzanne's brows puckered. "I thought when you and Titus stopped courting it was a mutual agreement. You said you weren't seriously interested in him."

Feeling the need to reassure her friend, Esther shook her head and said, "I knew after we'd gone a few places together that we weren't meant for each other, but I think Titus knew it the day I wouldn't go up into the monument with him."

"Well, if Samuel really cares for you, I don't think he'll stop courting you because you're afraid of heights."

Esther shrugged. "Maybe not, but I didn't want to disappoint him by waiting below on a bench."

Suzanne squeezed Esther's arm. "I think it was good for you to meet your fear head-on. Maybe each time you force yourself to go somewhere that's up high, your fear will lessen."

"Maybe so, but I hope I'm not faced with challenges like the monument too often." Esther placed Jared on the blanket. The little guy had fallen asleep and was getting heavy in her lap. "Are you excited about your wedding?" she asked Suzanne.

Suzanne bobbed her head. "I can't believe it's only two months away. Summer has gone by so quickly, and there's so much to do yet before the wedding."

"You've finished sewing your dress though, haven't you?"

"Jah, but lots of other things need to be done—especially during the weeks right before the wedding."

"I'll be happy to help with anything you need," Esther offered.

"That's nice of you, but between watching Samuel's kinner and helping Bonnie at the B&B, you've got your hands full."

"I don't work at the B&B when we don't have guests, and most Saturdays, Samuel doesn't work, so that gives me some time to do other things."

"But don't you want to keep your Saturdays free for times like this, when you can be with Samuel doing something fun?"

"I do enjoy being with him, but we're not together every Saturday, and since you're my good friend and I'm going to be one of your attendants, I want to help with the wedding preparations."

The sunlight glistened in Suzanne's auburn hair as she smiled and said, "I appreciate that, and when it's time to start cleaning before our guests arrive, your help will be needed and appreciated."

"Do you know how many of Titus's family members will be coming?"

"I'm not sure, but I know his folks and his twin brother will be coming, because Titus talked to them both earlier this week. While Titus wants all his brothers and sisters and their families to come, he's a little worried about where they'll stay, because his place only has three bedrooms."

"Some of them will no doubt stay with Samuel. My folks' house is big enough to put up several people."

"Even so, if everyone who receives an invitation comes, we'll need to look for more places for them to stay."

"What about the B&B? I'm sure Bonnie would give them

a discount on any of her rooms. Would you like me to speak to her about it?"

"That's a good idea. Let us know what she says, and then Titus can talk to his folks about it so they can spread the word." Suzanne nudged Esther and motioned toward the pond. "Looks like Samuel's heading this way. Maybe he's caught his limit of fish for the day."

—∞—

"Think I've done enough fishing for today," Samuel said, kneeling on the grass in front of Esther. "How would you like to go for a walk in the woods with me? If we're lucky, we might see some interesting wildlife along the way."

Esther motioned toward sleeping Jared. "If we all go for a walk, we'll have to disturb this little guy."

"I wasn't figuring on taking the kinner," Samuel said. "Thought it could be just you and me."

"Oh, I see." A blotch of red erupted on Esther's cheeks, but he was glad when she rose to her feet and didn't say no.

"Would you mind keeping an eye on the kinner for me?" he asked Suzanne. "I don't think we'll be gone too long."

"I don't mind one bit. After all, in just two more months, these sweet kinner will be my nieces and nephews." Suzanne smiled up at Samuel. "You and Esther enjoy your walk, and don't feel like you have to hurry back. Take your time, because we'll be fine here."

"I appreciate that. Oh, and make sure Lucky doesn't follow us. I don't want him scaring off any wildlife we might see." Samuel bent down and grabbed a bottle of water and a bag of pretzels from the box of snacks they'd brought along. "In case we get hungry or thirsty," he said, smiling at Esther.

She returned his smile and gave a little nod.

The birds chirped happily in the trees overhead as Samuel and Esther started walking along the trail near the water.

When they stepped into a clearing a short time later, Samuel pointed to a tall wooden structure that had been built for hunters to sit and watch for deer. "I'll bet if we climbed up there, we'd have a good vantage point and could keep an eye out for deer or any other critters, and they won't even know we're here."

Esther's eyes widened as she halted her steps. "You. . .you want me to climb up there?"

He gave a nod.

"How do you know that ladder's safe to climb? It looks pretty old."

"Esther, are you scared?"

"A little," she admitted.

"You climbed the ladder at the B&B to get Penny down from a tree."

"That was different. Penny's life was at stake, and the ladder I used was in good shape."

"I really don't think the tree stand's that old," Samuel said, "but I'll go up first and test the ladder. If I don't fall and break my neck, I'll come back and get you."

She swatted his arm playfully. "That's nothing to kid about, Samuel."

"Sorry." Samuel gave Esther's arm a reassuring squeeze and handed her the bag of pretzels and bottle of water. "I'll be fine. You'll see."

Slowly and carefully, Samuel ascended the ladder until he was standing inside the tree stand. He glanced down and saw Esther looking up at him. "The ladder's sturdy," he called, "and the view from here is really good. I'm coming back down to get you."

Samuel climbed down the ladder, took the water and pretzels from Esther, and tucked them both under one arm. "You go first, and I'll be right behind you," he said.

She hesitated but finally started up the ladder. Samuel followed, guiding her verbally with each step. When she reached the top, she drew in a sharp breath. "Ach, my! It's higher than I thought it would be."

"It's not that high," Samuel said, joining her on the wooden platform. "Compared to the Jefferson Davis Monument, this is nothing."

She inched away from the edge and closer to Samuel. "It is to me. I'm afraid of anyplace that's high up and have been since I was a kinner."

Samuel set the pretzels and water on the wooden floor and slipped his arms around Esther's waist. "You're safe with me, so don't be afraid," he murmured, leaning his head close to her ear. He felt her relax against him and was confident that her fear was abating.

They stood like that for several minutes, until Samuel spotted two doe nibbling on the leaves of some brush. "Look there," he whispered. "Do you see the deer?"

"Jah. They're beautiful, aren't they?"

"They sure are." *But not near as beautiful as you,* he thought.

Samuel kept his arms around Esther's waist as they continued to watch the deer. Then, when he was sure Esther was fully relaxed, he turned her to face him. "If you're afraid of heights, how come you went to the top of the monument with us that day?"

"I thought it would be good for me to face my fear, and I didn't want to disappoint you."

"It wouldn't have, Esther. I would have understood." He gave her a reassuring squeeze. "Are you afraid right now?"

"I was at first, but not anymore."

As Samuel enjoyed the quiet of the moment, he felt that with Esther by his side, he was right where he wanted to be. Giving in to his impulse to kiss her, he slowly lowered his head. Their lips were almost touching when—*Woof! Woof! Woof!*—Lucky bounded out of the woods and chased away the deer.

"Stupid hund," Samuel muttered. "I shoulda left him at home. Guess I'd better go get him or he'll be running through the woods chasin' some poor animal for the rest of the day."

With a feeling of regret, Samuel climbed down the ladder, guiding Esther's footsteps as she followed. Maybe it was too soon for him to be kissing her anyway. He didn't want her to think he was too forward. If he could resist the temptation, he'd wait until they'd been courting longer to try and kiss her again. Until that day came, he thought it might be best if he made sure they were never alone.

Chapter 45

Paradise, Pennsylvania

"You'd better hurry and start packing if we're gonna be ready to leave on time in the morning," Timothy said to Hannah after he'd put his own clothes into a suitcase. They'd hired four drivers with big, fifteen-passenger vans to transport the more than fifty relatives that would be going to Kentucky for Titus and Suzanne's wedding. Anxious to see Titus and Samuel, as well as the lay of the land in Kentucky, Timothy could hardly wait to get there.

"I've decided not to go," Hannah said, as she removed the pins from her hair and picked up the brush from her dresser.

Timothy whirled around to face her. "Just when did you decide that?"

"This morning when I found out that my mamm hurt her ankle."

"I'm sorry about that, but it's only a sprain, so I don't see why that should keep you from going to the wedding."

"My mamm's in a lot of pain, and she can barely put any

weight on her leg, so she's going to need some help for the next several days."

Timothy ground his teeth together. Not this again. Was Hannah looking for an excuse not to go to the wedding, or had she once more latched on to her mother's apron strings?

"Look," Timothy said, trying to keep from raising his voice, "it's not like you're the only person who can help your mamm. She can call on one of her daughters-in-law if she really needs some help."

Hannah shook her long, silky brown tresses. "My brother's wives are all busy caring for their kinner. As you well know, Mahon and Betsy have five kinner, all under the age of ten, and my brother Paul and his wife, Sarah, have four kinner, two of them still in diapers. And of course my other brothers, Stephen and Clarence, live in New York, so their wives aren't available to help."

"Okay, so none of them are free to give your mamm a hand, but she has friends in our community. I'm sure she could ask one of them to help out."

Hannah shrugged. "Maybe they could, but Mom wants me. We do many things alike, so she'll know whatever I do for her is done right."

Timothy grunted. "If you want my opinion, your mamm's too picky about things, and she shouldn't expect you to stay home from my bruder's wedding to take care of her when she could ask one of her friends."

Hannah frowned as she set her brush down and turned to face him directly. "Are you forbidding me to stay here and help my mamm? Are you going to force me to go to the wedding with you, even though you know I won't have a good time because I'd be worried about Mom the whole time we're gone?"

Timothy shook his head. "I'm not saying that at all. I just

think. . ." He lifted his hands in defeat. "All right then, you can stay home and take care of your mamm, and I'll take our *dochder* to Kentucky with me."

Hannah shook her head vigorously. "Mindy needs to be here with me."

"But you'll be busy helping your mamm, and Mindy will be underfoot."

"No she won't. I'll take plenty of things to keep her busy while I'm at Mom and Dad's house." Hannah's face softened as she placed her hand on Timothy's shoulder. "You know how frustrated you become whenever Mindy cries and you can't get her to settle down. I'm usually the only one who can make her stop crying and go to sleep."

"That's true." Timothy hated to give in, but Hannah was right—it would be hard for him to handle Mindy on his own. She'd probably wake up during the night, realize that her mother wasn't there, and start howling. Most likely, he'd be up all night trying to settle her down.

"Okay," he finally conceded. "You and Mindy can stay home, and I'll go to the wedding alone, but I really feel like you will be hurting Titus and Suzanne's feelings by not showing up at their wedding."

"You won't be alone," Hannah said sweetly. "You'll have your mamm, your daed, and all the rest of your family there with you, and I doubt Suzanne and Titus will even miss me."

"I think they will, and it sure won't be the same for me without my fraa and dochder," he muttered as he closed the lid on his suitcase and placed it on the floor.

Hannah wrapped her arms around his waist and rested her head on his shoulder. "Mindy and I will miss you, too, but you'll only be gone a few days, and then we'll be together again."

That's right. We'll be together until your mamm needs you for something else, Timothy thought with regret. *And just when I began to believe things were going better between us.*

—⁓—

Pembroke, Kentucky

"I'm glad it's working out that some of Titus's family can stay here at the bed-and-breakfast," Esther said to Bonnie as they sat in the living room, enjoying warm apple cider before they went to bed.

Bonnie smiled. "Since I knew in plenty of time how many were coming and needed a place to stay, I was able to make sure I didn't schedule any other guests during the time Titus's family will be here."

Esther finished her cider and set the cup on the coffee table in front of the sofa. "When I spoke to Suzanne the other day, she said Titus is really excited about seeing all his family again, and of course, Suzanne is, too. She met his parents when they came to Kentucky once, but the rest of his family she only met briefly when she went with Titus to attend the funeral for Samuel's wife. So hopefully, she'll get to know them all a little better while they're here."

"Allen told me about Samuel and Titus's brother Zach having been kidnapped when Samuel was a child," Bonnie said. "That was such an incredible story."

Esther nodded soberly. "Since Zach wasn't reunited with his family until he was twenty-one, they all suffered a good deal during those years he was missing."

Bonnie stared at the flickering flames in the fireplace across the room. Reflecting on Samuel's family being reunited with their long-lost son made her think of the baby girl she'd given birth to and never gotten to know. Where was her daughter now? Was she happy? Had she grown up in a good home? On more than one occasion, Bonnie had been tempted to search for the child, but she'd never followed through with the idea. She didn't want to come between the child and her adoptive parents, and she wasn't sure she could face her daughter and explain the circumstances of her conception or the reason she'd put the child up for adoption. No, she'd decided sometime ago to leave the matter alone. It was best for her and the child, who would now be a teenager.

Bonnie yawned and rose from her seat. "I don't know about you, but I'm tired and ready for bed."

"Guess I should head on out to the guest house." Esther stood, too. "It's been nice sitting here in the quiet, because in the next few days this old house will be filled with people who will probably be chattering away."

Bonnie patted Esther's arm. "I'm sure you're looking forward to meeting all of Samuel's family, because with the way things are going between you and Samuel, I'd say by this time next year, they may be your family, too."

Esther's eyes twinkled as she gave Bonnie a hopeful-looking smile. "I don't want to hope too hard for something that might never happen, but marrying Samuel would surely be an answer to my prayers."

Chapter 46

"It's so good to see you," Titus's mother said when she stepped out of the first van that had pulled in and hugged her son.

"It's good to see you, too, Mom." Titus hugged his father next and then went down the line, hugging his sister, Abby; her husband, Matthew; and their seven children. Last, but not least, he grabbed his twin brother and gave him a big bear hug.

"Where's your family?" Titus asked Timothy. "Did Hannah and Mindy ride in one of the other vans?"

Timothy's eyes darkened as he shook his head. "Hannah's mamm sprained her ankle, so Hannah thought she had to stay behind and take care of her."

"Oh, that's too bad." Titus had a hunch Hannah's mother could have managed on her own, and from the look of irritation he saw on Timothy's face, he was pretty sure Hannah may have used her mother's sprained ankle as an excuse not to come. But why? What was so terrible about Kentucky that she didn't want to come here? Didn't Hannah want to get better acquainted with her new sister-in-law, or was she afraid that if she came to Kentucky, Timothy might decide he liked it here well enough to move? Poor Timothy must feel like a part of him was missing with his wife and daughter back in Pennsylvania rather than here with him, which is where they belonged.

The other three vans pulled in, so Titus pushed his thoughts aside and went to greet the rest of his family. All his brothers and sisters and their children had come for the wedding. If Hannah and Mindy had come, their whole family would be here, and it would be like a big family reunion.

"So now that we're all here, tell us where we're going to stay," Titus's mother said.

He motioned to his double-wide manufactured home. "Well, you and Dad are welcome to stay here with me, but I thought you might rather stay with Samuel, since I'm sure you're anxious to spend some time with your *kinskinner*."

"I would enjoy being close to the grandchildren," Mom said with a nod. "Maybe Mary Ann, Abner, and their four kinner can stay here with you. Then your daed, me, Naomi, Caleb, and their kinner can stay with Samuel."

"That's fine, and if Timothy doesn't mind sleeping on the sofa, I've got room for him to stay here, too," Titus said. "The house Samuel's renting is big, so I'm pretty sure he'll be able to put up several of our family members there. Some of the cousins can share a room with Samuel's girls and some with the boys."

"Where will the rest of us stay?" Titus's sister Nancy asked after she'd given Titus a hug.

"We're friends with a young woman who runs a bed-and-breakfast nearby, and she has six bedrooms, so some of you can stay there. Oh, and Suzanne's mamm wants some of you to stay with them because they have a few extra rooms as well."

"Sounds like you've got it all figured out," Dad said, clasping Titus's shoulder. "So why don't you ride in the van with us and show us the way to Samuel's place?"

"That's what I figured on doing." Titus smiled at Mary Ann. "If you and your family want to get settled in here, just go on in and look for the two bedrooms that have a pot of mums on the dresser. Suzanne's family grows 'em, and she gave me a couple of plants the other day."

Mary Ann smiled, and the depth of her love could be seen in her pretty brown eyes. "It's sure good to see you and finally know where you live, little brother."

"It's good to see you, too," Titus replied, giving his sister another hug.

"Mama Fannie. . .Dad. . .everyone. . . It's so great to see all of you." Samuel could hardly speak around the lump in his throat. He hadn't realized just how much he'd missed his family until seeing them right now.

Naomi gave him a hug. "You look good, Samuel. You've put on a few pounds, which you really needed, and I see a look of contentment and peace on your face."

He smiled. "Jah, I think moving here has been good for me. The kinner, too," he said, motioning to his four children, who were eagerly greeting their cousins.

She gave his arm a squeeze. "I'm so glad."

"Same goes for me," Naomi's husband, Caleb, put in. "We miss you and Titus, but we're glad you've begun new lives for yourselves and have found happiness here in Kentucky."

"I agree with that," Dad said, clasping Samuel's shoulder.

Samuel looked at Mama Fannie, hoping she would add her affirmations, but she merely smiled and said, "In the nine months you've been gone, the kinner have sure grown."

Samuel glanced across the yard to where his children and their cousins were playing with Lucky. "You're right about that. I can hardly keep 'em in shoes anymore 'cause their feet are growing so fast."

Titus motioned to the suitcases that had been unloaded from the van. "Why don't we take all the luggage inside, and then we can ride over to the B&B with those who'll be staying there? Mom and Dad are probably tired from the trip, so they can get settled in while we're gone, and all the kinner can stay here, too, if they like."

"I'd like to go along," Mama Fannie said. "Samuel's told us so much about the B&B, and I'm anxious to see what it's like."

"Sure, that's a good idea," Samuel said. "It'll give me a chance to introduce you to both Bonnie and Esther."

"I see a couple of vans pulling into the yard," Bonnie said, peering out her living room window. "I'll bet it's Samuel's family."

Esther's mouth went dry, and her palms grew sweaty. What if his family didn't like her? What if they disapproved of Samuel starting to court again?

"Come on, let's go outside and greet them." Bonnie hurried out the door, and although a bit hesitant, Esther followed.

Esther did a double-take when she saw two men who looked very much alike standing together on the lawn. It didn't take long for her to realize that one of them was Titus and the other was his twin brother, because the twin wore a beard, indicating that he was married.

"This is my brother Timothy," Titus said, motioning to the young man on his left.

Esther smiled. "It's nice to meet you, Timothy."

"Wow," Bonnie said, "you and Titus look so much alike. If Timothy wasn't wearing a beard, I probably couldn't tell you apart."

Titus chuckled and thumped his brother's back. "We've been hearin' that for most of our lives."

Timothy nodded with a grin. "We used to play tricks on our teacher when we were in school. Kept her guessin' many times as to who was who."

"That's not funny," said the older woman standing beside a tall man with gray hair and a matching beard. "I think you and Titus are the reason your daed and I have so many gray hairs today."

Samuel stepped forward and motioned to Bonnie. "Mama Fannie, Dad, this is Bonnie Taylor. She owns the bed-and-breakfast." He smiled at Bonnie. "These are my folks, Fannie and Abraham Fisher."

Bonnie extended her hand. "It's nice to meet you both."

Abraham smiled warmly, but Fannie barely gave Bonnie a nod.

If Samuel's stepmother is this unfriendly to Bonnie, Esther thought, *I wonder how she'll be with me.*

Samuel, red-faced and looking a bit uncomfortable, introduced Esther next.

Esther shook his parents' hands and was relieved when Fannie smiled and said, "It's nice meeting you, Esther."

After Samuel had introduced Esther and Bonnie to the rest of his family, everyone went inside.

"This house is so cozy," Samuel's sister Nancy said as Bonnie showed them around the B&B. "You've made it nice with so many special touches."

"Thanks, but Samuel gets the credit for a good deal of

it," Bonnie said. "He worked really hard painting and fixing things that were broken, as well as remodeling most of the rooms before I was able to open for business."

"So we heard." Fannie's forehead wrinkled as she glanced at Samuel. Esther wondered what the woman's deep frown meant. Did Samuel's mother feel that Bonnie had worked Samuel too hard, or was she displeased because Samuel had moved his family to Kentucky? Esther had heard him mention a few times that his mother had tried to talk him out of moving, so maybe that was the reason for her apparent displeasure.

Samuel moved to stand beside Esther. "Uh—Mama Fannie, Dad, I've been wanting to tell you something."

"What's that?" Fannie asked.

"Not long ago, Esther and I began courting."

Esther held her breath and waited to hear their response. After several agonizing moments of silence, Fannie smiled and said, "I'm glad to hear that."

Abraham bobbed his head in agreement. "Jah, and I'd say that's a real good thing."

Esther released her breath in a sigh of relief. If Samuel should ever decide to marry her, maybe his folks would be pleased about that, too.

Chapter 47

"Well, this is the big day," Suzanne's mother said when Suzanne entered the kitchen. Mom poured a cup of coffee and handed it to her. "Are you *naerfich*?"

Suzanne nodded. "I am a bit nervous, but I'm sure I'll feel better once the wedding service starts." She glanced around. "I'm surprised none of Titus's family are out of bed yet."

"Oh, they're up," Mom said. "The men are outside helping Nelson and Chad with their chores, and the women and children went out to the barn to see the kittens that were born a week ago."

Suzanne smiled. "Kittens are always fun to watch—especially once they begin to move around and start wanting to cuddle." She moved toward the stove. "What do you need my help with this morning?"

Mom shook her head. "This is your special day, so I think you should just eat your breakfast and then go back to your room and get ready to become Titus's wife."

With a sigh, Suzanne dropped into a chair at the table.

"Do you think I'm really ready for marriage, Mom?"

"Are you concerned about your cooking skills? Because if you are, I don't think you need to worry at all. Esther taught you well, and your new husband should have no complaints. Besides, as I understand it, Titus likes to cook, too."

"I wasn't thinking so much about my ability to cook. I'm more worried about how well Titus and I will get along once we're living in the same house."

Mom poured herself some coffee and took a seat beside Suzanne. "You get along well enough now, so I don't think it'll be any different after you're married."

"But I have my own opinion on things, and I know a wife is supposed to be submissive."

Mom gave a nod. "Being submissive doesn't mean you don't have a right to your opinion. When your daed was alive, we sometimes disagreed on how things should be done, but he always listened to my opinion. If we couldn't reach an agreement, then I respected his wishes and went along with whatever he decided." Mom patted Suzanne's arm. "Just remember what the Bible says in 1 Peter 3:1 about marriage: 'Likewise, ye wives, be in subjection to your own husbands.' I'm sure the ministers will be talking about that in the wedding service today."

"Danki for the advice." Suzanne smiled and clasped Mom's hand. "I hope that by next fall, Esther and Samuel will be the ones getting married."

—∞—

Walking beside his father, Timothy headed to the Yoders' barn, where Titus and Suzanne's wedding service would be held, since the Yoders' house wasn't large enough to accommodate all the guests. He spotted the bride and groom waiting to be seated, and his thoughts went to Hannah. He could still remember how beautiful she'd looked on the day of their wedding, and how nervous and excited he'd felt sitting across from her, listening to their bishop's message on marriage and waiting to say their vows. He and Hannah had been so happy that day, and he'd been certain that was how it would always be.

But things were different now; it seemed like all they did anymore was argue. If only he could get Hannah away from her mother, he was sure things would be better between them. If Hannah had just agreed to come here for the wedding, maybe seeing the love Suzanne and Titus felt for each other would have caused her to remember that she'd promised to love and be faithful to her husband. Not that she'd been unfaithful, but Timothy was still convinced that his wife cared more about her mother's needs than his, and that had caused him to feel as if he didn't hold first place in Hannah's heart anymore. He felt cheated and hurt every time she wasn't at home when he needed or wanted her to be.

"Are you okay?" Dad whispered in Timothy's ear. "You look umgerrent."

Timothy shook his head. "I'm not upset. Just thinking about Hannah right now."

Dad gave him an understanding nod. "It's a shame she's not with you today."

Maybe things will be better when I go home, Timothy thought. *I've heard it said that absence makes the heart grow fonder. Since my birthday's next week, maybe Hannah will plan something special for me, but if not, it would just be enough knowing she truly missed me.*

—ꕥ—

As Esther sat in a straight-backed, wooden chair next to

Suzanne, tears pricked the back of her eyes. Her best friend would be standing in front of the bishop soon, saying her vows to her groom. She was happy that Suzanne was marrying the man she loved but wondered if things might change between her and Suzanne now that Suzanne was about to become a married woman. She'd be moving into Titus's house, and her responsibilities would increase. Once children came along, she'd be busier than ever. Would Suzanne continue working at the woodshop with Titus and Nelson, or would she give that up and become a full-time housewife?

I wish it was me getting married today, Esther thought as the bishop began to preach about the importance of communication in marriage. She glanced across the room and spotted Samuel, with Leon sitting on one side of him and Samuel's older brother Norman on the other side. Little Jared had fallen asleep and lay in a relaxed position across Samuel's lap. Esther noticed that Samuel's expression was nearly as sober as the groom's. It made her wonder what he was thinking right now. Her guess was he was probably remembering his own wedding day.

As the service continued, Esther's thoughts drifted back to the day she and Samuel had climbed up into the tree stand. She grinned, thinking to herself, *Did I actually climb that old thing?* But she knew at that point that no matter where their relationship was going, she would have climbed any height just to be with Samuel. Without any doubt—even high up in that tree stand—being next to Samuel was right where she'd wanted to be.

Whenever I'm with Samuel, I feel such joy and peace, Esther thought dreamily as she visualized Samuel lovingly stroking her face. *Does he feel it, too? Will he ever ask me to be his wife, or will today stir up memories of all that he had and lost?* She knew the next step would have to be up to him.

—m—

Despite the chilly fall day, the Yoders' barn was hot and stuffy. It was probably from so many bodies being crammed together in one room, but Samuel figured it would have been worse if the wedding had been held in the house, because it wasn't nearly as big as the barn. Since Titus had such a large family, and most of them had come to see Titus and Suzanne get married, this was a bigger wedding than most that took place in this small Amish community.

Samuel glanced across the room at Esther, wearing a dark blue dress with a white cape and apron and looking as sweet and pretty as ever. He could no longer deny his feelings; he'd fallen in love with Esther and wanted to make her his wife. The question was, how long should he wait to propose marriage to her?

As Bishop King stood and called Suzanne and Titus to stand before him to say their vows, Jared stirred. Fearing the child might wake and start crying, Samuel began gently patting Jared's back. It seemed to help, for the boy relaxed and continued to sleep.

The bishop looked at Titus. "Can you confess, brother, that you accept this, our sister, as your wife, and that you will not leave her until death separates you? And do you believe that this is from the Lord, and that you have come thus far by your faith and prayers?"

"Jah," Titus answered with no hesitation.

The bishop turned to Suzanne then. "Can you confess, sister, that you accept this, our brother, as your husband, and that you will not leave him until death separates you? And do you believe that this is from the Lord and that you have come thus far by your faith and prayers?"

Suzanne answered affirmatively as well.

Bishop King looked at Titus again. "Because you have confessed that you want to take Suzanne for your wife, do you promise to be loyal to her and. . ."

The bishop's words faded as Samuel's mind took him back to the moment he and Elsie had become man and wife. He'd promised to be loyal to her—on the day of their wedding, and many other times when they'd been courting. He remembered one day in particular, when they'd gone for a ride in his open buggy. He'd pulled off to the side of the road to let several cars pass. Unable to resist the temptation, he'd leaned over and given Elsie a kiss. Following the kiss, he'd whispered, "I promise, I'll never love anyone but you." She'd smiled and said, "The same goes for me, Samuel."

"So go forth in the name of the Lord. You are now husband and wife."

Samuel's thoughts halted and he snapped his attention to the front of the room. Suzanne and Titus seemed to radiate a blissful glow as they returned to their seats.

Samuel looked at Esther and his heart sank all the way to his toes. Guilt invaded his thoughts, where moments earlier he'd felt free to hope. He couldn't break the promise he'd made to Elsie that day. He could not allow himself to love Esther. Their courting days must end. Maybe it would be best if he found someone else to watch the kids, because with Esther around so much it would be hard to keep his promise to Elsie.

Chapter 48

As Samuel took a seat at a table in preparation for the wedding meal, his gaze came to rest on Esther, sitting at the corner table with the bride and groom and their other attendants. She looked so happy today—almost bubbly, in fact. She was no doubt sharing in her best friend's joy over having just gotten married.

Esther's a wonderful woman, Samuel thought. *She deserves to be happy, and I hope she finds someone who will love her as much as I loved Elsie. She's good with children and will make a fine mother, so I hope she's blessed with lots of kinner someday.*

Samuel flinched, feeling as if his heart was being torn in two. His children loved Esther, and he was sure they'd be disappointed when they found out she would no longer be taking care of them. Of course, he had to find someone to replace her first. He sure couldn't go off to work every day and leave the two younger ones alone while Marla and Leon were in school.

Samuel felt a nudge on his arm. "Hey, aren't you gonna

take this bowl of potato salad?" his older brother Jake asked.

"Oh, sorry. Didn't realize they were being passed yet." Samuel scooped some of the potato salad onto his plate and passed it along to his brother Matthew, who sat on the other side of him. Truth was, he didn't have much appetite. It was hard to think of eating when his stomach felt like it was tied up in knots.

I've got to stop thinking about Esther, he told himself. *I need to concentrate on something else.*

He glanced across the room to where his folks sat with his four children on either side of them. *Should I move back to Pennsylvania and let Mom take care of the kinner? That would make her happy, I'm sure. But if I moved, I'd miss Kentucky and the friends I've made here.*

He felt another jab on his arm and realized that Jake wanted to pass him something else. "This chicken looks pretty good, doesn't it?" Jake already had one piece on his plate, but he quickly forked another one before passing the platter to Samuel.

Samuel took the smallest piece he could find and then passed the plate on to Matthew.

"You're sure quiet today," Jake said. "Did it make you sad to see your little bruder get married?"

Samuel shook his head. "I'm happy for Titus and Suzanne."

"Jah. They make a nice couple. I'm sure they'll be very happy together." Jake passed a bowl of creamed celery to Samuel. "I've never cared much for this stuff, but you can have some if you like."

"Think I'll pass on it, too." Samuel handed the bowl to Matthew.

Matthew looked at Samuel's plate and squinted. "You're sure not eating much today."

"I'm just not that hungry, I guess."

Matthew spooned some creamed celery onto his plate. "With all this good-smelling food, I don't see how anyone could not be hungry."

"I think Samuel's saving up for the desserts," Jake said with a chuckle.

Samuel merely shrugged in reply. This wasn't the time or the place to tell his brothers that he was sick to his stomach because of the decision he'd felt forced to make. He'd have to tell everyone soon enough though. Sure couldn't let them think he and Esther might eventually get married.

"So what'd you think of the wedding?" Allen asked Bonnie as he passed her the platter of chicken.

"It was different. A lot different than any wedding I've ever attended."

He gave a nod. "That's for sure. Nothing at all like our traditional English weddings." He spooned some mashed potatoes onto his plate. "The thing I had the hardest time with was sitting on that backless wooden bench. Had to get up a couple of times and go outside so I could walk around and stretch my legs and back."

"I know what you mean." Bonnie lifted her water glass and took a drink. "Sitting there for three hours made me wonder how the Amish are able to continually do that during their weddings and biweekly church services."

"Guess they're used to it, since they've been doing it since they were kids."

She slowly shook her head. "I don't think I could ever get used to it. I think if I attended church with the Amish on a regular basis, I'd have to take a pillow to sit on, or maybe bring myself a comfortable chair."

"Yeah, me, too." Allen poured some gravy over his potatoes and took a bite. "Umm. . . The food they serve at their wedding meals is sure good."

"You're right, and can you imagine how many cooks and how much food it takes to serve so many people?"

"I couldn't even begin to guess."

They passed a few more dishes down the line, and then Allen concentrated on eating. He figured by the end of the day he'd have to loosen his belt a few notches.

"So what'd you think about the wedding service itself?" he asked, looking over at Bonnie.

"It was hard to understand, since almost all of it was in German."

"Yeah. Made me wish I'd taken German when I was in school instead of Spanish." Allen waited until the young Amish waiter pouring coffee handed him a cup, and then he turned to Bonnie again and said, "Did you notice there was no ring exchange or kiss between the bride and groom?"

"I did notice that," she said with a nod. "I also noticed that the father of the bride didn't walk his daughter down the aisle. Suzanne and Titus just walked to their seats with their attendants."

"Speaking of walking down the aisle, now that things are better between you and your dad, do you think he'd be willing to walk you down the aisle if you got married?" Allen asked.

"I suppose he would," Bonnie replied, "but that's not going to happen, since I have no plans to get married."

Allen wasn't sure how to respond. Did Bonnie feel that way because she hadn't had a proposal, or did she have something against marriage?

"You know, I've been thinking," he said.

"What's that?"

"I was wondering if you'd like to go out to dinner with me some evening next week. There's a new restaurant that just opened in Hopkinsville, and—"

"I appreciate the offer," Bonnie said, cutting him off, "but I'll be busy all of next week. The day after Samuel's family leaves, I have three couples checking into the B&B."

"How about the following week?"

She shook her head. "I'll be busy then, too."

"Oh, I see." Allen couldn't help but feel disappointed, and he wondered if Bonnie was giving him the brush-off. He'd thought the two of them were getting closer and that Bonnie might have come to care for him as much as he did her. Now he wondered if he'd been wrong about that. Maybe Bonnie only saw him as a friend and would never see him as anything more.

Allen thought about Connie, whom he'd gone out with a few times last year. The only similarity between her and Bonnie was their names, which rhymed. Connie was nothing like Bonnie, and he was glad he'd broken things off with her before either of them had gotten serious. Connie didn't want anything to do with religion and had made that quite clear whenever he'd brought the subject up. Allen knew what the Bible said in 2 Corinthians 6:14 about not being unequally yoked with an unbeliever. After he'd quit seeing Connie, he'd decided that if he ever found another woman he wanted to date, she would have to be a Christian. Bonnie was a Christian—he had no doubt of that—but she seemed to be holding him at a distance. For a while, he'd thought Samuel might be interested in Bonnie, but that idea vanished as soon as Samuel started courting Esther.

Allen glanced over at Samuel and noticed that he wasn't

smiling. He looked like he might be upset about something. If he had a chance to talk with Samuel after the meal, he'd try to find out what it was.

Feeling the need for a bit of fresh air as soon as the noon meal was over, Esther stepped outside. She spotted Bonnie sitting in one of the chairs under a maple tree in the Yoders' backyard.

"Looks like I'm not the only one out here on this chilly afternoon," Esther said, stepping up to Bonnie.

Bonnie looked up and smiled. "It was getting stuffy and warm in there, and after eating all that good food, I was afraid if I didn't get up and go outside I might fall asleep."

Esther laughed. "I know what you mean. I get drowsy after eating a big meal, too."

"It was a nice wedding," Bonnie said. "Quite a bit different than the weddings we Englishers are used to, but nice, nonetheless." Bonnie gave Esther's arm a little squeeze. "From the way things have been going between you and Samuel lately, I wouldn't be surprised if you two aren't the next Amish couple to get married."

Esther smiled but shook her head. "There are a few more Amish weddings in our community that will take place next month, but even if Samuel were to propose to me tomorrow, there wouldn't be enough time to plan a wedding for this year."

"Well, I'm sure you'll be a married woman by sometime next year," Bonnie said.

"I hope you're right about that."

Bonnie motioned to her left. "There's Samuel now, talking to Allen. Since you've had other obligations today, I don't imagine you've had much time to spend with Samuel."

"I haven't had any time at all," Esther said. "But since I'm not busy with anything right now, I think I'll walk over there and say hello. Would you like to come along?"

"No thanks. Think I'll sit here a few more minutes, and then I'll probably head for home."

"Okay. I'll see you back at the B&B later." Esther walked away, but before she got close enough to speak with Samuel, she was stopped by Ethan, who'd just stepped out of the barn.

"Wie geht's, Esther?" he asked.

She smiled. "I'm fine. And you?"

"Doin' pretty good." He gave her a wide grin. "Sure was a lot of good food served at the wedding meal, wasn't there?"

"There certainly was."

"That's why I came out here. . .to walk some of it off. I'll be back for the evening young people's supper, and I need to make sure I'm plenty hungry by then."

"I think everyone will be full by the end of the day," she said.

"Yep." Ethan gave Esther another big grin, and then he headed for a group of young Amish men who were gathered across the yard.

Esther started walking toward Samuel again, but by the time she got there, he and Allen had stepped around the corner of the buggy shed.

As she approached the shed, she heard Allen mention her name, so she stopped and listened. She knew it wasn't right to eavesdrop, but the men couldn't see her, and she was curious to know what was being said.

"How are things with you and Esther these days?" she heard Allen say.

"Umm. . . Well, okay, I guess."

"I had a lot of fun the day the four of us went to visit the monument," Allen said. "I was thinking if I can get Bonnie to un-busy herself soon, it would be fun for the four of us to go on another outing before the weather turns cold. Maybe we could go to the pond some Saturday afternoon and either do some fishing or just have a picnic lunch."

Esther heard Samuel's boots scrape across the gravel where he stood. "Well. . .uh. . .the thing is. . . I've decided not to see Esther socially anymore."

Esther pressed her weight against the side of the buggy shed, reeling with the shock of what she'd just heard. The sounds of activity, which moments ago were all around her, were drowned out by her own question. *How can this be?* Just a few days ago, Samuel had told his folks that he and Esther were courting, and now he didn't want to see her anymore? What could have happened between then and now to make him change his mind about her?

She no longer heard the children playing as they squealed with delight, chasing each other in a game of tag. She tried to focus on the women she'd seen earlier, relaxing under the shade trees and exchanging recipes, but their voices turned into murmurs and she no longer heard their words. She looked toward the buggies parked off to the side, with horses dozing as they stood waiting in the pasture. Even as tranquil as that scene was, it became a blur with tears she tried her best to hold in.

Esther covered her mouth with her hand in order to keep from sobbing out loud. Things had been going so well, and now, all of a sudden, they're not? She scolded herself for being so hopeful and believing in the happily-ever-after. She wasn't prepared to have her dreams evaporate right before her eyes. Fearing the truth, was there no chance of them ever getting married?

Chapter 49

When Esther woke up the following morning, she felt like she'd been kicked in the stomach by an unruly horse. Was it a bad dream, or had she really heard Samuel tell Allen that he'd decided not to court her anymore? No, it was true. She'd felt the pain of it all the way to her toes. She just didn't understand it at all. She'd been so sure Samuel had come to care for her.

Esther pushed the covers aside, climbed out of bed, and padded over to the window in her bare feet. Several of Samuel's relatives were in Bonnie's yard, loading their luggage into the van that was parked there. Those who had stayed at the B&B would be leaving today, and it was her understanding that a few, like Samuel's parents, would head back to Pennsylvania tomorrow. No doubt they wanted to spend a little more time with Samuel and Titus, as well as with Samuel's children.

Tears welled in Esther's eyes. From the short time she'd spent with Samuel's family, she'd concluded that they were a loving, caring group of people. It made her heart ache to think that if she and Samuel would no longer be courting, there was no chance of her ever being a part of his wonderful family.

Should I go to Samuel and talk to him? she wondered. *Should I tell him what I overheard him say to Allen yesterday?* Tears dripped onto her cheeks as she leaned against the window, *Guess I should wait until after Samuel's folks leave before I talk to him. When I go to watch the kinner the day after they leave, that's when I'll approach him about this.*

Esther wiped her eyes and turned away from the window, knowing she needed to get dressed and go up to the main house so she could help Bonnie with breakfast. But her heart just wasn't in it today. She wanted to crawl back in bed and shut out the world.

"Good morning, Mrs. Fisher," Titus said, standing beside Suzanne as she stood in front of the dresser, pinning up her hair.

She leaned into him, liking the sound of that. "Good morning, husband."

He nuzzled her neck with his nose. "Are you as tired as I am this morning?"

"Jah. Yesterday was a long day, and according to tradition, since we've spent our first night in my parents' home, we now have to help with the cleanup from the wedding, so we'll be even more tired by tonight, I expect." She set her head covering in place. "So I guess we ought to go downstairs and see if my mamm has breakfast started, and then we'll get busy cleaning the barn."

"We'll need to say good-bye to those in my family who'll be leaving today, too, and I think we ought to do that first," Titus said. "I know they want to get an early start."

She smiled. "It was nice having most of your family here for the wedding."

"It sure was, but I wish my twin brother's wife would have come with him." Titus's brows puckered. "I'm worried about Timothy. From some of the things he's told me, I think he's unhappy in his marriage."

"That's a shame. We'll have to remember to pray for Hannah and Timothy."

"You're right. Unless things change between them soon, they're going to need a lot of prayer."

"Now that you're here, I'll get breakfast started," Mama Fannie said when Samuel entered the kitchen after doing his chores.

"That's okay. I'm not hungry this morning."

"What happened? Did you eat too much at the wedding meal yesterday?" Dad asked as he shuffled into the room.

Samuel merely shrugged in reply.

"Is there something troubling you?" Mama Fannie questioned. "You've been acting kind of strange ever since we came home from the wedding last night."

"It's nothing," Samuel mumbled. He grabbed a mug from the cupboard, moved over to the stove, and poured himself a cup of coffee.

"I wish we didn't have to go home tomorrow," Mama Fannie said. "I'd like to spend more time with you and the kinner." She glanced over at Dad. "Couldn't we stay until next week? It would be nice if we could be here for Leon's birthday."

Dad shook his head. "We need to get back so Timothy and I can finish harvesting the fields. Besides, next week is also Timothy's birthday, and he'll want to be home with his wife and daughter."

"It's Titus's birthday, too, you know," she reminded.

"That's right, and I'm sure he'll be perfectly happy celebrating it with his new bride."

"Maybe we could stay here and celebrate Leon's birthday, and Timothy can go home without us."

"Nope," Dad said. "We need to get back for the harvest."

Deep wrinkles formed across Mama Fannie's forehead. "Sometimes I wish you'd give up farming. It ties you down too much."

"Farming is what I do." Dad took a seat at the table. "Wouldn't know what to do if I wasn't farming."

Mama Fannie sighed. "There are times when I wish you were still running the general store and I was managing the quilt shop. We saw more of each other then than we do now, that's for sure."

"Things change, Fannie," Dad said. "Naomi and Caleb are doing a fine job with the store, and Abby enjoys running the quilt shop."

Mama Fannie handed him a cup of coffee. "You're right, and I wouldn't take that away from them. I just wish—"

"Daadi, do something, quick! Lucky's chasin' Esther's katz!" Penny hollered as she raced into the room.

Samuel's heartbeat picked up speed. "Is Esther here?" Surely she wouldn't have come to watch the kids today. She knew Samuel's folks wouldn't be leaving until tomorrow.

Penny shook her head. "Esther's not here, Daadi. The katz I'm talkin' about is the one she gave us awhile back. Said it would help keep the mice down. Remember?"

"Oh, that's right," Samuel said with a nod. His brain felt so fuzzy this morning—probably because he hadn't slept well last night. He'd tossed and turned most of the night, his thoughts going from Elsie to Esther.

Penny stood on tiptoes and tugged on Samuel's shirtsleeve. "Are you gonna make Lucky stop chasin' the katz?"

He grunted. "There's no need for that. If the cat doesn't like being chased, he'll either climb the nearest tree or find a safe place to hide in the barn." Samuel pointed at Penny. "And if the cat does go up a tree, don't you get any ideas about trying to rescue him."

"I won't, Daadi. I know better than that now."

"Good."

Mama Fannie pulled Penny into her arms. "I'm going to miss you, sweet girl." She looked over at Dad. "Are you sure we can't stay a few days longer?"

Dad shook his head. "Nope. But we'll come back and visit again sometime next year."

Mama Fannie's shoulders slumped as she turned toward the stove. Seeing how much she missed his children made Samuel wonder if he'd made a mistake moving away. Maybe it would be better if they moved back to Pennsylvania. At least then he wouldn't have to see Esther and be reminded of what he could never have. He'd have to think on that awhile; he didn't want to make another mistake. The kids had settled in here quite well, and they might not want to leave Kentucky. For that matter, he didn't want to leave either. He just wasn't sure how he could continue living here without seeing Esther all the time.

No matter what he decided about moving or staying, tomorrow when Esther came to watch the kids, he'd have to tell her that he wouldn't be courting her anymore and that he planned to look for someone else to take care of the kids. He just wished there was an easy way to say it. Better yet, he wished more than ever that he didn't have to say anything at all. Since his family had seemed so pleased about him courting

Esther, he decided it would be best not to tell them about his decision until after they'd gone home. He didn't want to spoil the last of their visit with a bunch of questions, or worse yet, deal with Mama Fannie offering her opinion on things.

Chapter 50

When Esther arrived at Samuel's the following day to watch the children, she was surprised to see that his folks were still there. She'd figured they would have wanted to get an early start on their return trip to Pennsylvania and would have already left.

Do Titus's parents know he won't be courting me anymore? Esther halted her footsteps as a sickening thought popped into her head. *What if Samuel's parents are the reason he's decided to stop courting me? Maybe one or both of them told Samuel they didn't approve of him seeing me.*

She swallowed hard and drew in a deep breath, her feet feeling like lead with each step she took. *If I just knew why he'd made this decision, maybe I could do something about it.*

Esther stepped onto the porch and knocked on the door. It felt strange knocking on her own door, but with Samuel's folks still visiting, she didn't feel right about walking right in.

Marla opened the door and gave her a hug. "Sure am glad to see ya, Esther. Wish I didn't have to go to school today so we could do somethin' fun."

Esther gave the girl's head a pat. "We'll do something fun when you get home this afternoon."

When Esther stepped into the living room, she saw Fannie sitting on the sofa, holding Jared in her lap. Leon and Penny sat on either side of her.

"It's nice to see you again, Esther," Fannie said, offering Esther a friendly smile. "The kinner and I were just talking about how much they like having you care for them."

Relief flooded Esther's soul. *If Fannie was being so friendly and had said such a nice thing, surely she couldn't have influenced Samuel to stop courting me. Maybe Fannie doesn't even know about the decision he's made.*

Esther smiled at Fannie and said, "I enjoy being with the children, too."

Fannie stroked the top of Jared's head and bent her head to kiss his pudgy cheek. "It's been nice being with them these past few days, but I wish we could stay longer. I really miss Samuel and the kinner."

Esther nodded with understanding. She missed her folks, too, but since Samuel and his children had come into her life, she'd been less lonely and had found a new purpose.

"I also wish we'd had more time to get to know you better," Fannie said. "Maybe when Samuel and the kinner come to Pennsylvania to visit us, you can join them."

Esther had to force a smile this time. If she and Samuel wouldn't be courting anymore, he sure wouldn't invite her to go with them to Pennsylvania.

"Abraham and I are very happy with Titus's choice for a wife," Fannie added.

"Jah. I think Suzanne and Titus will be very happy together." Esther removed her shawl and outer bonnet and hung them on a wall peg near the door. She was about to take a seat in the chair across from Fannie, when Samuel stepped into the room. He halted, and his face turned red when he looked at Esther.

"Oh, I. . .uh. . .didn't realize you were here," he said, dropping his gaze to the floor.

"I just came in a few minutes ago." It made Esther unhappy seeing his reaction, as if they'd just met.

He gave a nod and looked at his mother. "Dad and the others are bringing all the suitcases downstairs."

Fannie set Jared on the floor and stood. "As much as I hate to say it, I guess it's time for me to say good-bye."

—~—

When Bonnie stepped into the kitchen after feeding the chickens, she heard the phone ringing. She hurried across the room and picked up the receiver. "Bonnie's Bed-and-Breakfast."

"Hi, Bonnie. It's Allen. Thought I'd better check up on you this morning."

She shifted the phone to her other ear. "Why would you need to check up on me?"

"You looked awful tired when I saw you at the wedding, and after you said how busy you were, I wondered if there was anything I could do to help out."

"In what way?" she asked.

"I have a few hours free this afternoon, so I thought if you had some chores you needed to have done, I could swing over there right after lunch and do 'em for you." Before Bonnie could reply, he added, "On second thought, maybe I could pick up some deli sandwiches and we could eat lunch together before I do the chores."

Bonnie leaned against the kitchen counter and closed her eyes. As appealing as the thought of having lunch with Allen was, she wouldn't feel comfortable having him here today—especially when she'd decided not to spend any time with him alone.

"You still there, Bonnie?"

Her eyes snapped open. "Yes, I'm here. I. . .uh. . .appreciate your offer to bring lunch, but I really don't have time for that today."

"Oh, okay. How about if I just drop by later then and do whatever chores you need to have done?"

"That won't work either."

"Why not?"

"The types of chores I need to have done are things only I can do." Bonnie paused and waited for his response, and when he said nothing, she added, "I do appreciate your offer though."

"Sure. Any time you have something you need to have done, just let me know."

"Okay, thanks."

"Take care, Bonnie, and I hope you have a good day."

"You, too. Bye, Allen."

When Bonnie hung up the phone she went to the sink, turned on the cold water, and splashed some onto her face. She didn't know if she felt so hot and sweaty from her trek outside or from trying to get out of seeing Allen today. She'd allowed herself to care for him and knew the only remedy was to put a safe distance between them.

—⁂—

Samuel stood on the porch with his children, watching as the vans transporting his family disappeared from sight. He and the kids had come outside to say their good-byes, leaving Esther in the basement to wash a load of clothes she'd volunteered to do. Now Samuel had to go back in the house and tell Esther what he'd decided about them. But he wouldn't do it until after Marla and Leon left for school. He didn't want them to hear what he had to say. The kids had come to care for Esther, and he knew they'd be disappointed to learn that she wouldn't be watching them while he was at work anymore. On second thought, maybe he'd wait to tell them until after he found a replacement for Esther. No point in upsetting them until he had to, at least.

"Well," Samuel said, squeezing Leon's shoulder, "you and your sister had better get your lunch pails and head for school. You don't want to be late."

"Are you gonna give us a ride today?" Marla asked.

Samuel shook his head. "It's a nice day with no rain in sight, and it'll do you both good to walk."

At first, Marla looked like she might argue the point, but then she obediently went into the house.

A short time later, Marla and Leon headed down the road with their schoolbooks and lunch pails. Since Esther was still in the basement, Samuel gave Penny and Jared a couple of picture books to look at and instructed them to stay in the living room. Then, with a feeling of dread, he headed to the basement.

He found Esther bent over the washing machine, feeding one of his shirts into the wringer. Not wishing to startle her, he waited until the shirt had come through the other end and she'd placed it in the basin of cold water to rinse.

"Ah-hem." He cleared his throat.

She whirled around. "*Ach*, Samuel! I didn't hear you come down the stairs."

"Sorry. Didn't mean to frighten you."

She straightened and reached around to rub her lower back. "Did you need me to come upstairs and keep an eye on the little ones while you take Marla and Leon to school?"

"No. They're walking today, and Penny and Jared are in the living room, looking at some picture books my folks gave them."

"Oh, I see." Esther looked up at him and blinked a couple of times. "Samuel, I was wondering—"

"Esther, I need to speak with you about something," he said.

She gave a nod. "You go ahead with what you were going to say."

He cleared his throat again and popped the knuckles on his left hand. This was even more difficult that he'd thought it would be. "I've decided it's best if you and I don't see each other socially anymore."

"Why, Samuel? Have I done something wrong?"

Samuel winced. He could see the hurt on Esther's face, and it was almost his undoing.

"You haven't done anything wrong. I just think it's best for me and the kinner if I don't get romantically involved with anyone." He shifted his weight and leaned against the wooden beam behind him, needing it for support. "You see, I'm still in love with my wife, and so—"

"I understand that there will always be a place in your heart for her, but I was hoping there might be a place in your heart for me, too."

There is, but I can't let it happen. I can't break the promise I made to Elsie.

"Samuel? Can we talk about this?"

He shook his head. "I've made my decision, and I think it's for the best."

Tears welled in Esther's eyes, and it was all Samuel could do to keep from pulling her into his arms. *How could I have been foolish enough to let myself fall in love with her?* he berated himself. *If I keep seeing Esther, I'll be breaking my promise to Elsie, and I can't live with that.*

"There's something else," Samuel said.

"What's that?" Esther's words came out in a whisper.

"I think it's best if I find someone else to watch the kinner."

Her eyes widened. "Why?"

"The more you're around them, the more attached they're becoming. Pretty soon, they'll start to think of you as their mamm."

"I'll make sure they don't," Esther was quick to say. "I'll make sure they never forget their mother."

"I've made my decision," Samuel said, drawing on all the strength he could muster. "You have plenty to do helping Bonnie at the B&B, so in the long run it'll be better if you don't have my kinner to watch."

"Oh, but Samuel, I—"

"I'll let you know as soon as I've found someone to take your place." Samuel turned and hurried up the stairs. If he stayed a minute longer, he might weaken and change his mind.

Chapter 51

Esther spent the next two days in a daze. It had been hard to go to Samuel's this week and watch the children, knowing it would all be over once Samuel found a replacement for her. What made it even worse was learning that next Saturday was Leon's birthday, and she was sure she wouldn't be included in the celebration.

"You look so tired this morning," Bonnie said, as she and Esther sat at the table in her kitchen for breakfast early Saturday morning.

"I am tired," Esther admitted. "I haven't been sleeping well lately."

"Since tomorrow will be an off-Sunday from your church, maybe you can sleep in."

"Maybe so." Esther was glad there would be no church tomorrow. She couldn't stand the thought of going to church and seeing Samuel sitting across the room with his boys beside him. It was bad enough to think about not watching the children anymore, but knowing Samuel didn't love her was breaking her heart.

"Esther, are you okay?" Bonnie touched Esther's shoulder.

Esther jerked her head. "I. . .uh. . .Actually, no. I'm not okay."

Bonnie's brows furrowed. "What's wrong?"

"I haven't said anything to you or even Suzanne because I've been too upset to talk about it, but Samuel and I won't be courting anymore."

"How come?"

"He still loves his wife, and apparently he doesn't love me." Esther gulped on the sob rising in her throat. "To make matters worse, he's looking for someone else to watch his children, so I'll soon be losing them as well."

"I'm so sorry, Esther, but maybe it's for the best."

Tears slipped from Esther's eyes and splashed onto the table. "H–how can it be for the best?"

"Think about it. If Samuel's still in love with his wife, then the memory of her would probably come between you. He might even compare everything you did to the way his late wife did things."

"I don't expect him to forget her. I just. . ." Esther's voice trailed off as she struggled not to break down.

Bonnie patted Esther's back. "I'm sorry Samuel led you on like he did. It wasn't right for him to start courting you and then drop you flat."

Esther looked at Bonnie's pinched expression, and for the first time since she'd met Bonnie, she saw a look of bitterness on her face. Could someone Bonnie once loved have hurt her real bad? Might she have suffered from a broken relationship that had left her with emotional scars? Esther was on the verge of asking when the telephone rang.

"I'd better get that." Bonnie stood and moved quickly across the room.

Esther pushed away from the table, too. It was time to get busy doing the dishes and quit feeling sorry for herself.

Paradise, Pennsylvania

"Suzanne and Titus said to tell you they were sorry you couldn't make it to their wedding," Timothy said as he and Hannah sat at the breakfast table, with Mindy in her high chair between them.

"Didn't you tell them my mamm had sprained her ankle?"

"Of course I did, but they still missed seeing you." Timothy reached across Mindy and touched Hannah's arm. "I missed you, too."

She smiled. "Well, you're home now, and just in time for your birthday next week."

"You mean you didn't forget?"

"Of course not. How could I forget my husband's birthday?"

He reached for a piece of toast and slathered it with strawberry jam. "You've been so busy helping your mamm, I wasn't sure you'd remember."

"Well, I did, and I'm planning to invite your folks and my folks over for supper that night."

"What about my brothers and sisters?"

Hannah frowned. "Our house isn't big enough for that many people. We'd have to go out to a restaurant for that."

He clapped his hands. "That's a good idea. Why don't we see if we can reserve a room at the Plain and Fancy Restaurant, and then everyone can be invited?"

Hannah handed Mindy a plastic cup filled with orange juice. "I don't think they have a room at any of the restaurants around here that would be big enough to accommodate all of your family."

"You may be right." Timothy took a bite of his scrambled egg and washed it down with a swallow of coffee. "I could clean out the barn and have my birthday supper in there."

Hannah shook her head. "That's too much work—not to mention that it would be a lot of trouble to haul all the food out there from the house. I think we should just stick with inviting your folks and mine and have a nice quiet supper here at the house."

"Okay, whatever." Timothy stared into his cup of coffee. Just like always, he was giving in to Hannah's wishes. One of these days, he was going to have something go his way, and she'd just have to deal with it.

Hopkinsville, Kentucky

"Looks like you're making good progress on that house," Allen said when he showed up at the jobsite where Samuel had been working all morning.

Samuel gave a nod and kept on painting. "I'm hopin' to get done early today so I can have my driver drop me off at the Zooks' place on my way home."

"Are you talking about Ethan Zook?"

"Uh-huh. His younger brothers and sisters are friends with my kids, and I'm hoping that Ethan's mother might be willing to start watching my kids."

Allen tipped his head. "Why would you need Mrs. Zook to watch them when you have Esther? She's watching them today, right?"

"Nope. Since the woodshop's not open today, I left them

with Suzanne." Samuel glanced at Allen then back at the house he was painting. "I need to find a replacement for Esther before next week if possible."

"How come?"

Samuel bent down and dipped his paintbrush into the bucket beside him. "Esther's got enough on her hands helping Bonnie at the B&B."

"They're only busy whenever Bonnie has guests, and with winter coming, things will probably slow down at the B&B."

Samuel shrugged and continued painting.

Allen moved closer to Samuel and looked him in the eye. "What's going on, Samuel? Is there a problem between you and Esther?"

"It's not a problem exactly," Samuel said. "We're just not going to be seeing each other anymore."

"Are you kidding me?"

Samuel shook his head and continued to paint. "I've decided it's the best thing to do."

"Best for who—you or Esther?"

"Both of us. Esther deserves someone who can love her with all their heart. I can't do that."

"Why not?"

Samuel stopped painting and turned to face Allen. "I made a promise to my wife, and I can't let myself forget what we had when she was alive."

Allen put his hand on Samuel's shoulder and gave it a gentle squeeze. "I think I understand a bit of what you're feeling. When I lived in Washington, I had a girlfriend whom I loved very much. In fact, I was hoping to marry her, but then she got hit by a car and died." Deep wrinkles formed across Allen's forehead. "A part of me died that day, too, and I was sure I would never fall in love again. But you know what, Samuel?"

"What?"

"I met Bonnie, and she's captured my heart." He frowned. "Now if I could only get her to see that."

"I'm happy for you, Allen, and I hope Bonnie loves you as much as you love her, but it's different for me."

"How so?"

"I promised Elsie that I'd never love anyone but her. I said that to her many times when we were courting and on our wedding day, too." Samuel drew in a deep breath and released it with a groan. "So I will not break my promise to Elsie."

Chapter 52

Pembroke, Kentucky

Daadi, why can't Esther come out to supper with us tomorrow tonight?" Leon asked on the morning before his birthday.

"Because tonight's just for our family," Samuel replied as they headed down the road toward the Zooks' house in his horse and buggy.

"But you said Aunt Suzanne and Uncle Titus are goin' with us," Marla put in.

"That's right. They're part of our family, and besides, this will be Uncle Titus's birthday celebration, too." Samuel glanced over his shoulder at Penny and Jared, sitting in the backseat, huddled together. It was a chilly fall morning, and he should have thought to bring a blanket along to keep the kids warm.

"I miss Esther," Marla said. "I wish she could be with us forever."

"Mama didn't stay with us forever," Leon said. "She ain't never comin' back neither."

Samuel winced. He didn't need that reminder this

morning. Just when he'd begun to deal with Elsie's death and had been trying to move on with his life, all the old feelings had surfaced again. Now the kids were missing Esther, and so was he. If only he could let go of the promise he'd made to Elsie; but no, that wouldn't be right. Why had he even made such a promise, and why couldn't he let it go?

When they arrived at the Zooks' a short time later, Penny started crying, and Jared quickly followed suit. "I don't wanna stay here," Penny wailed. "I want Esther to take care of us like she did before."

Samuel picked Jared up and patted Penny's back, hoping to calm them down, but it was useless. They both continued to cry as he ushered them to the door.

"They'll be all right once you're gone," Mavis Zook said. "I'll find something fun for them to do."

Samuel gave a nod. "Marla and Leon will come here after school. I'll be back to pick the kinner up late this afternoon." He bent down and gave Jared and Penny a hug then hurried out the door before he felt any worse.

Samuel was almost to his horse and buggy when Ethan Zook stepped out of the barn. "I heard some hollering a few minutes ago. What was that all about?" he asked.

"My two youngest aren't happy with me right now."

"What's wrong? Did ya give them a bletsching?"

"No, I didn't give either of them a spanking," Samuel said with a shake of his head. "They're upset because Esther won't be taking care of them anymore."

"I wondered why you'd asked my mamm to watch 'em today." Ethan eyeballed Samuel with a curious expression. "I heard someone saying the other day that you won't be courtin' Esther anymore. Is it true?"

Samuel gave a nod. "You heard right."

"So then I don't suppose you'd have any objections if I courted her?"

Samuel hesitated but finally said, "You're free to do as you like."

A slow smile spread across Ethan's lips. "I hope ya know what you're doin'. Esther's a real fine cook, and she'd make a good fraa."

"I'm doing what I have to do," Samuel mumbled. Quickly, he untied his horse, stepped into the buggy, and directed Socks toward the schoolhouse.

He knew he had no claim on Esther, yet it irritated him to think that Ethan was interested in Esther—especially since it was obviously for her cooking. Didn't the pudgy-looking fellow realize what a wonderful woman Esther was? She deserved better than Ethan, but it was her right to go out with him if she chose to. Maybe she'd even end up marrying the hungry fellow. Oh, but Samuel hoped not.

I just need to stay busy and keep my focus on other things, he told himself. *My business is staying true to Elsie and providing for my kids.* But could he do that if he remained in Kentucky? Could he deal with seeing Esther being courted by Ethan—or anyone else, for that matter?

When Samuel pulled the horse and buggy into the schoolyard, he turned to face Marla and Leon. "How would you two feel about moving back to Pennsylvania?"

"No way! I like it here," Leon said.

Marla bobbed her head in agreement. "Me, too."

"Why would ya wanna move, Daadi?" Leon questioned.

"I just think we might all be happier there, but I haven't made a decision yet, so we can talk about it more tonight." He motioned to the schoolhouse. "I think you may be late, so you'd better grab your schoolbooks and get inside."

The children did as they were told, and as they scampered across the grass to the schoolhouse, Samuel turned his horse and buggy around and headed for home. His driver would be there to take him to the jobsite soon, and he didn't want to be late.

—∞—

Esther had just taken a loaf of zucchini bread out of the oven when she heard the rumble of a vehicle coming into the yard. When she peeked out the kitchen window and saw Allen getting out of his truck, she set the bread on a cooling rack and went to answer the door.

"Hi, Esther, how are you?" Allen asked as he stepped onto the porch.

She gave a little shrug. "Okay, I guess."

"I heard about you and Samuel, and I'm real sorry things didn't work out."

"Me, too. Samuel's change of heart really knocked the wind out of me, but I guess it wasn't meant to be."

"Maybe Samuel will change his mind."

Esther sighed deeply. "I'd like to believe that, but he seemed pretty sure of his decision, and now he has someone else watching his children, too."

Allen's sympathetic look was almost Esther's undoing. "Is there something I can help you with?" she asked, needing to change the subject.

"I was hoping to talk to Bonnie. Is she here?"

"No, she went to Hopkinsville to run some errands."

"Oh, I see." Allen leaned against the porch railing and folded his arms. "Does Bonnie confide in you much?"

"What do you mean?"

"Does she share her innermost feelings with you?"

"Sometimes. She's told me some things about her childhood

and how hard it was when she lost her mother."

"Does she ever talk about me?"

Esther wasn't sure what Allen was getting at, but she smiled and said, "She's mentioned you a few times."

"Do you think she cares for me?"

"Well. . .uh. . . I guess so. Why are you asking me this?"

"Because I care for her, and I thought we were getting close, but then all of a sudden she pulled away." He frowned. "I've asked her out several times, but she always says she's too busy. Makes me wonder if she's using it as an excuse."

"Bonnie does keep pretty busy here at the B&B. Seems like there's always something that needs to be done."

"I realize that, and I'm busy, too, but I'd make time for her if she'd let me."

Esther didn't know what to say, and she was relieved when the phone rang and she had to excuse herself to answer it.

"Okay, I'll let you go," Allen said. "When Bonnie gets home tell her I stopped by, okay?"

Esther gave a nod and hurried away.

She'd no more than finished her phone call, when she heard a horse and buggy pull into the yard. Her heartbeat picked up speed. Could it be Samuel? Had he come to tell her that he'd changed his mind about courting her? She didn't want to be hopeful, but her heart betrayed her.

She hurried to the door, and when she stepped onto the porch, disappointment flooded her soul. It wasn't Samuel; it was Ethan Zook. She watched as he climbed out of his buggy and secured his horse, wondering why he'd be coming here.

"Wie geht's?" Ethan called as he strode across the yard toward the B&B.

"I'm okay. How are you?" Esther asked when he stepped onto the porch.

He grinned at her. "Doin' real good. I was on my way to the lumber mill to get some wood we need for our new greenhouse and thought I'd stop by here first and say hello."

She gave a brief smile.

Bonnie's cat scampered across the grass and rubbed against Ethan's leg. He bent down and rubbed the cat's head then turned his attention to Esther again. "I talked to Samuel Fisher awhile ago, and he said the two of you aren't courtin' anymore."

"That's true." Esther swallowed hard, barely able to get the words out.

"So since you won't be seein' Samuel anymore, I was wonderin' if you'd like to come over to our house for supper this Saturday night. My mamm's fixin' stromboli, and I know it's gonna be good."

Esther contemplated his offer a few seconds. While Ethan was a nice enough fellow, he really wasn't her type, so it wouldn't be right to lead him on. Still, going to supper at the Zooks' house might be better than sitting in the guest house feeling sorry for herself because she hadn't been invited to Leon's birthday supper. Yet if she agreed to go to the Zooks', Ethan might get the idea that she was interested in him and keep pursuing her.

"So what do you say?" he asked. "Would you be free to come over to our place for supper?"

Esther smiled and slowly shook her head. "I appreciate the invitation, but not this time, Ethan." Even though she knew she had no chance with Samuel, she wasn't ready to begin a relationship with anyone else right now—maybe never, truth be told.

"Would ya be willing to come some other time?" he asked with a hopeful expression.

She gave a quick nod and grabbed the broom that was propped in one corner of the porch, hoping to appear busy.

Ethan stood silently for a few seconds. Then he smiled and said, "See you at church on Sunday, Esther."

Esther returned to the house to finish her baking and clean all the downstairs rooms. By three thirty, Bonnie still wasn't home, so Esther peeled some potatoes and carrots to add to the pot roast she had simmering on the stove. She'd just put the last potato in when she heard a knock on the door.

This must be my day for visitors, she thought as she dried her hands on a towel. When she opened the back door she was surprised to see Marla and Leon on the porch, holding their backpacks and lunch pails.

"What are you two doing here?" she asked.

"Came to see you." Marla grabbed Esther's hand and gave it a squeeze. "We miss you, Esther."

"That's right," Leon said. "And we'll miss ya even more when we move back to Pennsylvania."

The shock of Leon's words made Esther feel lightheaded. She leaned against the doorway for support. Samuel must really want to get away from her if he was planning to move back to Pennsylvania. But why? What had she done to turn him away? "I—I had no idea you were moving back," she stammered. "When will you leave?"

Marla turned her hands palm up. "Don't know. Daadi just told us this mornin' that he thought we oughta move back."

"We told him we don't want to go, but Daadi probably won't listen to us." Leon looked up at Esther with imploring eyes. "Can't ya talk to him, Esther? Can't ya do somethin' to get Daadi to change his mind?"

Esther knelt down and pulled both children into her arms. "I don't want you to move either. You've come to mean so much to me, but I don't think there's anything I can do to make your daed change his mind."

The children looked up at her with tears glistening in their eyes, which only made her feel worse. If Samuel moved back to Pennsylvania, there would be no chance of them ever getting back together.

Chapter 53

"Are my kinner ready to go?" Samuel asked Mavis when he stopped by her house that afternoon to pick up his kids.

"Penny and Jared are," she said, "but Marla and Leon aren't here."

"What?" Samuel's spine stiffened. "Where are they?"

"When my Daniel and Eva got home from school, they said Marla and Leon had told them they were going over to Bonnie's Bed-and-Breakfast."

"What'd they go there for?"

Mavis shrugged. "You'll have to ask them, because since they never showed up here, I assume they're still there."

Samuel ground his teeth together. He did not need one more stop to make. After his driver had dropped him off at home, he'd hitched his horse to the buggy and come over here. He'd worked hard all day and was anxious to get back home and take a shower. Besides, if he went to the B&B, he was likely to see Esther, and he wasn't sure he could deal with that.

"Guess we'd better get going," Samuel said, knowing he had

no other choice but to go get Marla and Leon. He motioned for Penny and Jared to follow him out the door.

After they were settled into his buggy and headed down the road, he glanced over his shoulder and said, "Did you two behave yourselves today?"

Penny nodded soberly. "Mavis said she'd give us a bletsching if we wasn't good."

Samuel grimaced. When he'd asked Mavis to watch the kids, he hadn't expected her to threaten his kids with a spanking. If they'd been bad, would she have made good on her threat? As far as he knew, Esther had never been harsh with the kids, and they'd never mentioned her threatening them with a spanking either.

Samuel shook the reins to get Socks moving faster. He'd be glad when this day was over.

When he pulled his horse and buggy onto the driveway of the B&B a short time later, he spotted Esther hanging clothes on the line. Marla and Leon were nearby, playing in a pile of leaves.

"I want you and Jared to stay in the buggy and wait for me," Samuel told Penny. "I'm going to get Marla and Leon, and it shouldn't take me long."

"Can't we get out?" Penny asked. "I wanna say hi to Esther."

Samuel shook his head. He knew if he let Penny and Jared out of the buggy he'd have a hard time getting them back in. They would either hang onto Esther, run around the yard, or play with Bonnie's cat or the dog.

Samuel turned to Penny and said, "Remember now, stay right here."

As he headed across the yard, dry leaves crunched beneath his feet. He was almost to the clothesline where Esther was hanging a lace tablecloth when she turned and looked at him.

"Samuel."

He swallowed hard. Why'd she have to be so beautiful and sweet? Why couldn't he stop thinking about her all the time? And there she went again, being so cute when her cheeks flushed that light shade of pink.

He pulled his gaze away from Esther and pointed at Marla. "What are you and your bruder doin' here? You know you were supposed to go to the Zooks' after school."

"We wanted to see Esther," Leon said before Marla could reply. "We miss her, Daadi."

I miss her, too. Samuel resisted the urge to say the words. Instead, he marched over to Leon and pulled him to his feet. "Let's go. It's getting late, and we need to get home now."

"I'm sorry if they bothered you," Samuel said, glancing at Esther and then looking quickly away. "It won't happen again."

"Oh, they were no bother," she was quick to answer. "I enjoyed spending a little time with them."

"Didn't they tell you they were supposed to be at the Zooks'?"

"Yes, and I was going to take them over there as soon as I finished hanging these things on the line."

"It's kind of late to be doin' laundry, isn't it?" Samuel didn't know why he was being so irritable, but he couldn't seem to help himself. Was it the fact that the kids had come over here when they should have gone to the Zooks', or was it because he'd been forced to see Esther?

"I was busy doing so many other things today," Esther said, "and since there's such a nice wind blowing this afternoon, I figured they'd be dry before it gets dark."

"Oh." Samuel jerked his attention back to the kids. "Say good-bye to Esther, and let's go."

Marla ran to Esther first and gave her a hug, and Leon

did the same. Then they both turned and walked slowly to the buggy, heads down and shoulders slumped.

Samuel glanced at Esther once more and mumbled, "Have a good rest of the day."

"You too, Samuel." She smiled, but her expression appeared to be strained. Was she having as hard a time looking at him as he was at her?

Samuel whirled around, and as he sprinted to the buggy, he made a decision. He was glad his house in Pennsylvania still hadn't sold, because whether the kids were in agreement or not, he was moving back home.

CHAPTER 54

On Saturday morning when Samuel woke up, he lay in bed, unable to decide when he should tell the kids about his decision to move. He didn't want to spoil Leon and Titus's birthday supper this evening, so he'd wait until Sunday to give them the news. The kids wouldn't like it of course; they'd already made it clear that they didn't want to move. But once they got back to Pennsylvania, where they could enjoy both sets of grandparents and all their cousins, he was sure they'd be fine.

I wonder how Titus will feel about us moving, Samuel thought as he crawled out of bed and stepped into his trousers. *Will he try to convince me to stay, or will he be understanding and give me his best wishes? I'm sure he'd like to have some of his family around, but he's married now, and he and Suzanne will be starting a family of their own.*

Samuel ambled over to the window and stared into the yard, where Lucky ran back and forth through the scattered leaves, chasing a fluffy gray cat. *Once we move, Esther can have her house back, and she won't have to live in that little guest house at Bonnie's anymore.*

He moved away from the window and sank to the edge of the bed. Why couldn't life be simple? Why'd there have to be so many hurts and frustrations? If only Elsie hadn't died, they'd still be living in Pennsylvania, and he would never have met Esther.

Samuel's gaze came to rest on the cardboard box pushed against the wall on the other side of the room. It was the box full of Elsie's things that he still hadn't completely gone through. Samuel didn't know why, but he felt compelled to do that right now.

He rose from the bed and knelt in front of the box. When he opened it, the first thing he saw was one of Elsie's white head coverings. He'd give that to Marla when she was older. Next, he found some of Elsie's handkerchiefs. Maybe Penny would like those. Then he discovered the yellow blanket Elsie had bought for the baby they'd lost when she'd died. That would go to Jared.

Under the hankies was Elsie's Bible. Maybe he could give it to Leon. A lump rose in Samuel's throat as he lifted it out and opened the first page. Elsie's name had been written there, along with Samuel's name and their children's names. There was also a place to write in the date of Elsie's birth and her death. Elsie's birth date had been filled in, but her date of death was still blank.

Samuel picked up the Bible and carried it across the room to the dresser, where he kept a notebook and pen to keep track of his paint jobs. Tears blurred his vision as he wrote the date of Elsie's death. She'd died just a week before Thanksgiving. It was hard to believe it had been eleven months already.

Samuel stood staring at the Bible for several seconds; then he opened it to a page she'd marked with a yellow ribbon. He noticed that Psalm 147:3 had been underlined, and he read it out loud: " 'He healeth the broken in heart, and bindeth up their wounds.' "

Samuel had thought his heart was healing, but when he'd reminded himself of the promise he'd made to Elsie, the pain of her death had become real again, like a wound that never completely heals.

Oh Lord, he silently prayed. *Please give me a sense of peace. Help me to keep my focus on my kinner and not on Elsie or Esther. Elsie's gone, and she's never coming back. Esther's here but can never be a part of my life. I just want to be free of this pain.*

When Samuel's prayer ended, he made his way back to the box. He'd go through the rest of Elsie's things and be done with it, once and for all.

He pulled out a few more items—an apron, Elsie's reading glasses, and a poem Marla had written and given to Elsie on the last Mother's Day she'd still been alive.

The next thing he removed from the box was a leather journal. Inside, he saw that Elsie had posted entries about once or twice a month. Strange. He hadn't even realized she'd been keeping a journal.

He turned several pages, reading with interest as Elsie described some of the events that had happened that last month she'd been alive. When he heard the patter of feet coming down the stairs and realized the kids were up, he quickly turned to the last page Elsie had written, curious to know what her final entry said. The lump in his throat became thicker as he read her words silently.

I don't know the reason, but this pregnancy is different than my other four were. I feel so tired all the time and have been terribly sick to my stomach. Sometimes I feel dizzy, too, and I have a horrible feeling that something might be wrong with me or the boppli. Am I going to die? Or maybe the boppli will die or be born with some kind of birth defect. I need to speak to Samuel about this—need to tell him what's on my heart. Samuel has promised me many times that he'll never love anyone but me, but that's not fair to him. I need him to know that should I die before he does, he's free to love again. I want my beloved husband to find another wife—someone who will love him and our kinner as much as I do.

I must close now, as Jared is awake from his nap and crying. I'll talk to Samuel about what I've written when he gets home from work tonight.

The words on the page blurred as Samuel sat in stunned silence. Elsie had sensed there was something wrong with her or the baby. Would one or both of them have died even if Elsie hadn't fallen down the stairs?

He drew in a shaky breath and swiped at the tears running down his cheeks. Elsie had released him from his promise. She'd actually wanted him to find someone else if she died.

Tap! Tap! Tap!

"Daadi, are you in there?" Leon called through Samuel's closed door.

"Jah." Samuel could barely get the word out, his throat felt so clogged with emotion.

"We're hungerich. Are you comin' out to fix us some breakfast?"

"I–I'll be right there." Samuel pulled a hanky from his pants' pocket and blew his nose. He knew he needed to fix the kids their breakfast first, but then he was going over to Bonnie's Bed-and-Breakfast to see Esther.

—∞—

"I want you to get your teeth brushed, put on a jacket, and meet me outside," Samuel told his children after they'd finished eating breakfast.

"How come?" Marla asked.

"I'm going to see if Suzanne and Titus will keep you for a few hours, because I have an important errand to run." Samuel figured he could take the kids with him, but he wanted to be alone with Esther when he told her how he felt.

"Will ya be back in time for my birthday supper?" Leon questioned.

Samuel ruffled the boy's hair. "Don't you worry about that. I'll be back in plenty of time for us to go to supper."

"I'm glad to see you're smilin' today," Marla said. "You looked so sad yesterday."

"If things go well today, like I hope, I'll be doing a lot more smiling from now on." Samuel tweaked the end of her nose. "Now hurry and get ready to go."

The children scampered out of the kitchen, and Samuel put all the dirty dishes in the sink. He'd wash them later. Right now he had something more important to do.

—∞—

Paradise, Pennsylvania

"There's something I need to talk to you about," Timothy said to Hannah after they'd finished eating their breakfast.

"What's that?" she asked as she turned the water on at the sink to do the dishes.

"I stopped by Naomi and Caleb's store yesterday afternoon, and Naomi was pretty upset."

"How come?"

"She said she'd heard about my birthday supper tonight and wondered why she and her family weren't invited."

Hannah turned to look at him. "Why are you bringing this up now?"

"Because when I got home yesterday, you were at your mamm's, and then Mindy was fussy all evening and you kept busy tending to her. By the time you came to bed, I was sleeping."

She shook her head. "I wasn't asking why you didn't tell me sooner. I wonder why are you bringing this up when it's already been decided. When we had this discussion a week ago, we agreed that only your folks and my folks would be invited here for supper tonight."

"We didn't actually agree on it." Timothy tapped his fingers on the table. "More to the point, you pretty much said how it was going to be, and I just went along with it so we wouldn't end up in another argument."

"Then why are you bringing it up now?" She turned back to the sink.

"Because Naomi was upset about not being included."

"If we had invited her family, we would have had to include your other brothers and sisters and their families, and you know our place isn't big enough for that."

"We could have used the barn like I'd wanted to do."

Her head snapped around, and she glared at him, crossing her arms. "I told you before—that would be too much work."

He stiffened. "Anything that has to do with me is too much work, but if your mamm wants something, you don't seem to mind."

"You don't have to bring my mamm into this. She has nothing to do with it."

"Jah, she does, Hannah. You two thinking you have to be together all the time has been a source of trouble between you and me for a long time. I'm so tired of it!"

Hannah grabbed a towel, dried her hands, and hurried across the room. "Let's not argue," she said, placing her hands on his shoulders. "Mindy's in the living room playing, and I don't want her to hear us shouting at each other."

"I don't want that either."

Hannah stood silently and started rubbing his shoulders. Normally, it would have felt good, but right now, Timothy was too irritated to feel good about anything.

"We'll have a nice time tonight; you'll see."

"I'm glad you think so." He pushed away from the table and headed for the door.

"Where are you going?"

"Outside. I need some fresh air!" The door banged shut behind him.

Chapter 55

Pembroke, Kentucky

What would you like to do today?" Bonnie asked Esther after they'd cleaned up the kitchen. "I think we could both use a break from the usual cleaning we do on Saturdays."

"But if you have guests coming, we'll need to clean the rest of the house," Esther said.

Bonnie shook her head. "No guests scheduled until next Tuesday, so we'll have Monday to clean." She poured two cups of tea and handed one to Esther. "Should we take this into the living room or would you rather put a jacket on and sit outside on the porch?"

"Let's go outside," Esther said. "It's a bit chilly, but the sun's out. We may as well enjoy it now, because it won't be long before winter is here with its cold weather and probably some snow."

They slipped into their jackets, picked up their cups of tea, and went out to the porch.

"Let's sit over there so we can look out into the yard." Bonnie motioned to the wicker table and chairs on the far end of the porch.

After they were seated, Esther said, "I should have brought out some of that gingerbread I made last night. Do you want me to go get it?"

Bonnie shook her head. "I'm fine with just the tea, but if you want some, go ahead."

"Maybe later." Esther took a sip of tea and let it roll around on her tongue before swallowing. "This is so good. Peppermint is my favorite kind of tea."

Bonnie took a drink, too. "It is quite flavorful."

They sat in companionable silence for a while; then Bonnie looked over at Esther, and with a most serious expression she said, "There's something weighing heavily on my mind, and I'd like to share it with you, but only if you promise not to repeat what I've said to anyone."

"I won't say anything."

Bonnie took another sip of tea and set her cup down. "I—I hardly know where to begin."

Esther waited, figuring Bonnie needed time to think about what she wanted to say.

"As you know, Allen's asked me out several times lately, and I've said no."

"Because you're not ready for a serious relationship, right?"

Bonnie nodded. "But I'd like you to know why." She paused and stared into the yard, watching the shadows appear as a cloud drifted over the sun. After several seconds, she looked back at Esther with furrowed brows. "When I was a teenager I did something I'll always regret."

"What was it?" Esther dared to ask.

"I had a boyfriend, Darin, who said he loved me and insisted that if I loved him too, I'd be willing to. . ." Bonnie stopped talking and drew in a sharp breath. "Before my mother died, she'd talked to me about keeping myself pure and waiting for marriage to be intimate with a man, but Darin kept insisting that if I loved him, I'd do what he asked."

Esther reached over and touched Bonnie's arm. She was almost sure what Bonnie was about to say and wanted to offer her some reassurance.

Tears welled in Bonnie's eyes. "I weakened, Esther. I gave in to my feelings, and several weeks later, when I realized I was pregnant, I told him about it."

"What'd he say?"

"He laughed and said it wasn't his problem—that I'd have to deal with it on my own because he was moving to a different state and didn't care if he ever saw me again." Bonnie reached into her pocket for a tissue and blew her nose.

"What did your dad say about your situation?" Esther asked.

Bonnie swiped at the tears running down her cheeks. "Dad blew like Mt. St. Helens and said in no uncertain terms that I'd have to give the baby up for adoption."

"Did you?"

Bonnie gave a slow nod. "I felt that I had no other choice. I was only sixteen, still living at home, and with no job or money of my own."

"Could you have come here to live with your grandparents?" Esther asked.

"I suppose, but since I was still underage, I'm sure Dad would have come and got me. Besides, I didn't want Grandma and Grandpa to be disappointed in me, so they never knew about the pregnancy." She gulped on a sob. "It was hard enough to live with myself."

"Was the baby a boy or a girl?" Esther dared to ask.

"A girl. I only got to see her for a little bit, and then they whisked her away."

"Do you know who adopted her or where she is today?"

Bonnie shook her head. "Dad made sure it was a closed adoption."

"I'm so sorry," Esther said. "I'm sure it must have been difficult for you to give up your baby."

"It was, and I grieved for my little girl, like I had when my mother died." Bonnie sniffed deeply. "I can't tell you how good it feels to be talking about this with you. I've kept my feelings bottled up all these years, and it's affected me in so many ways."

"When you returned from Oregon, you said things were better between you and your dad. Did he apologize for making you give up your baby?"

"Yes, and I think I do understand his reasons. Dad was still dealing with the grief of losing my mother, and between that and the stress of his job at the bank, there was no way he could help me take care of a baby." Bonnie reached for her cup and took a drink, although Esther was sure the tea had gotten cold.

"I'm a Christian now, and I know I should have forgiven myself, as God forgave me," Bonnie said, "but I still struggle with the guilt for having gotten pregnant, not to mention giving my own flesh-and-blood child away." She paused and drew in a quick breath. "I'll never let my emotions carry me away again, and I don't think I could ever trust another man not to hurt me the way Darin did."

"Is that why you haven't gotten serious about Allen?"

Bonnie gave a nod. "I don't think the scars from my past will ever heal."

A verse of scripture Esther had read a few days earlier crossed her mind. "Psalm 147:3 says, 'He healeth the broken in heart, and bindeth up their wounds.' " Esther placed her hand on Bonnie's arm and patted it gently. "God will heal your heart, if you let Him."

"I–I've tried."

"But you have to put your faith and trust in Him and become willing to forgive yourself for the things you've done in the past, just as He forgives us."

More tears sprang to Bonnie's eyes. "Funny, but that's pretty much what I told my dad when he opened up and told me how he felt about his parents. Isn't it amazing that we humans can dole out advice, but when it comes to ourselves, we need someone else to make us see the truth?" She squeezed Esther's hand. "Thank you for helping me see the light."

"It wasn't me who opened your eyes to the truth," Esther said. "It was God's Word. That's how He speaks to us."

"I know, but God often uses others to show the truth of His Word."

Their conversation was interrupted by a horse and buggy coming up the driveway.

"It's Ethan Zook," Bonnie said. "I wonder what he wants."

Esther grimaced. "He probably came to see me."

"What makes you so sure?"

"He asked me to have supper with him tonight, and I said no. He probably came by to ask me again." Esther rose from her seat. "Guess I'd better go out and talk to him."

She hurried across the yard and joined Ethan at the hitching rail, where he'd just tied his horse.

"It's good to see you, Esther," he said with a nod. "I came by to see if I could talk you into havin' supper at our place tonight."

Esther shook her head, trying not to let her irritation show. Didn't Ethan know when to take no for an answer? "I'm really busy, so if you'll excuse me. . ."

He motioned to the porch, where Bonnie still sat. "When

I pulled in just now, I saw you sittin' up there with Bonnie. Didn't look like you were busy to me."

"We were taking a break," she explained.

Ethan leaned close to Esther—so close she could feel his warm breath against her face. "Isn't there any chance you might change your mind? I'd really like the opportunity to court you, Esther."

Esther didn't want to hurt Ethan's feelings, but she didn't want to be courted by him either. Without knowing it, he'd managed to irritate her more times than not, and she couldn't get close to someone like that. So she forced a smile and said, "I'm sorry, Ethan, but I don't think we're meant to be together."

When Samuel pulled his horse and buggy into Bonnie's yard, the first thing he saw was a horse and buggy parked in front of the hitching rail. As he drew closer, he spotted Ethan standing real close to Esther.

Oh, no. Am I too late? he wondered. *Has Ethan already begun to court Esther?*

Samuel debated whether he should turn around and head out, but when he saw Ethan climb into his buggy and pull away from the rail, he changed his mind. He was here now, and he had to speak to Esther, even if she turned him down.

Samuel held his horse steady until Ethan had pulled out of the yard; then he eased his horse up to the hitching rail and climbed down from the buggy. When he approached Esther, she looked at him strangely.

"I'm surprised to see you here, Samuel. Where are the kinner?"

"I left them with Suzanne and Titus." He took a nervous step toward her. "I wanted to talk to you alone."

"What about?"

Samuel swallowed a couple of times. "I. . .uh. . .was wondering if we could start over."

Esther stared at him with a curious expression.

He took another step toward her. "I made a mistake saying I didn't want to court you anymore, and I almost made the mistake of moving back to Pennsylvania."

"The kinner mentioned that yesterday. I was afraid you might move and wished you wouldn't," she said in a voice barely above a whisper, never taking her eyes off his face. "What made you change your mind?"

"It was something I read in Elsie's journal this morning. She wrote that she wanted me to love you, Esther."

Esther's eyebrows lifted high. "But your wife didn't even know me."

"You're right, but she was afraid she was going to die, and she wrote in her journal that if she did, she wanted me to find someone to love again. She wanted me to find someone who would love me as much as she did and who'd love our kinner, too." He touched Esther's arm gently. "I think that woman is you. Fact is, I never thought I could fall in love again until I met you."

Tears sprang to Esther's eyes and dribbled onto her cheeks. "Oh Samuel, I love you, too—and your kinner as well."

Samuel glanced around, worried that someone might be watching them. When he was sure no one was, he took Esther's hand, and they stepped around the corner of the shed, where he pulled her into his arms and kissed her sweet lips. She fit perfectly into his embrace, and he knew at that moment he would never let her go. "I don't think we should rush into anything, but after a proper time of courting, do you think you might consider marrying me?" Samuel murmured against her ear. His heart pounded, awaiting her answer.

Esther nodded and rested her head against his chest. "I know that Elsie will always have a special place in your heart, and I'd never try to take her place, but I promise to love you and the kinner with my whole heart."

They stood that way for several minutes; then Samuel tipped her head up so he could look at her pretty face. "The kinner and I are going to supper tonight to celebrate Leon and Titus's birthday. It would make the evening more special if you could be there, too."

She smiled. "I'd be happy to join you."

Samuel closed his eyes and said a silent prayer. *Thank You, Lord, for helping my heart to heal and for giving me this special woman to love.*

Epilogue

One week later

"There's something I want to share with you," Samuel said to Esther as they sat on his front porch one evening, visiting as they drank some coffee.

"What is it?" she asked.

"It's a letter I got from my brother Timothy today." Samuel pulled an envelope from his pocket and took out the letter. "Listen to what it says:

Dear Samuel:

Things still aren't going well between me and Hannah, and I've decided it's time for a change. I had a talk with Dad the other day and asked if he thought he could find someone else to help him farm his place. He was agreeable and has asked Norman's two boys, Harley and John, to take over for me, because I've decided to sell my place and move to Kentucky. I'll be in touch soon to discuss the details with you.

As ever,
Timothy

Samuel looked over at Esther and squinted. "What do you think about that?"

She sat for several seconds, letting the words from Timothy's letter sink in. "This is a surprise. I had no idea Timothy was thinking of moving here."

"When he came for Titus and Suzanne's wedding, I could tell that he liked it here, but I never expected he would move. With the way Hannah's tied to her mamm's apron strings, I'm surprised he talked her into it."

"Are you sure she's in agreement with this? Timothy didn't say so in his letter."

Samuel stroked his beard thoughtfully. "You're right about that, but I don't think he'd up and move unless she'd agreed. Timothy's always done pretty much whatever Hannah wanted."

Esther placed her hand on Samuel's arm. "I hope it works out for them as well as it has for you."

He nodded and clasped her hand. "I came here and found healing for my broken heart when I met you. I wonder what Timothy and Hannah will find."

Esther's Recipe for Boyfriend Cookies

Ingredients:

1 cup butter, softened
¾ cup granulated sugar
¾ cup brown sugar, packed
3 eggs
1 teaspoon vanilla
¼ cup whole wheat flour
¼ cup soy flour
3½ cups quick-cooking oatmeal
1½ cups salted peanuts, coarsely chopped
1 cup carob chips

Preheat oven to 350 degrees. Cream butter and sugars. Add eggs and vanilla, beating until fluffy. Sift flours and add to creamed mixture. Fold in oatmeal, peanuts, and carob chips. Drop by teaspoon 2 inches apart on greased baking sheet and bake 8 to 10 minutes. Yield: 7 to 8 dozen cookies.

the Stuggle

Dedication/Acknowledgment

To Richard and Betty Miller, our dear Amish friends who know what it's like to deal with the adjustment of having family members move away.

If ye forgive men their trespasses,
your heavenly Father will also forgive you.
Matthew 6:14

Chapter 1

Paradise, Pennsylvania

Timothy Fisher approached his parents' home with a feeling of dread. Good-byes never came easy, and knowing Mom disapproved of his decision to move to Kentucky made this good-bye even harder.

He stepped onto his parents' porch and turned, trying to memorize the scene before him. He liked the rolling hills and rich, fertile land here in Pennsylvania. As much as he hated to admit it, he did have a few misgivings about this move. He would miss working with Dad in the fields. And just thinking about the aroma of Mom's sticky buns made his mouth water. But it was time for a change, and Christian County, Kentucky, seemed like the place to go. After all, his twin brother, Titus, and half brother Samuel were doing quite well in Kentucky. He just hoped things would work out for him, too.

Shrugging his thoughts aside, Timothy opened the back door and stepped inside. Mom and Dad were sitting at the kitchen table, drinking coffee and eating sticky buns.

"Guder Mariye," he said with a smile, trying to ignore his throbbing headache.

"Mornin'." Dad motioned to the coffeepot on the stove. "Help yourself to a cup of coffee. Oh, and don't forget some of these," he added, pushing the plate of sticky buns to the end of the table.

"I'll get the coffee for you." Mom started to rise from her seat, but Timothy shook his head.

"I can get the coffee, Mom, but I can't stay long because I have some last-minute packing to do. Just wanted to see if there's anything either of you needs me to do before I leave."

Tears welled in Mom's brown eyes. "Oh Timothy, I really wish you weren't going. Isn't there anything we can do to make you stay?"

Timothy poured himself a cup of coffee and took a seat at the table. "I've made up my mind about this, Mom. Samuel's gotten really busy working for Allen Walters, and he's finding a lot of paint jobs on his own, so he has enough work to hire me."

"But you had work right here, helping your *daed* and painting for Zach."

"I realize that, but Dad's already hired someone else to work the fields, and Zach has other people working for him." Timothy blew on his coffee and took a sip. "Besides, I'm not moving to Kentucky because I need a job. I'm moving to save my marriage."

"Save your marriage?" Mom's eyebrows furrowed. "If you ask me, taking Hannah away from her *mamm* is more likely to ruin your marriage than save it! Hannah and Sally are very close, and Hannah's bound to resent you for separating them."

"Calm down, Fannie." Dad's thick gray eyebrows pulled together as he placed his hand on Mom's arm. "You're gettin' yourself all worked up, and it's not good for your health."

Her face flamed. "There's nothing wrong with my health, Abraham."

"*Jah*, well, you may be healthy right now, but with you gettin' so riled about Timothy moving, your blood pressure's likely to go up." He gave her arm a little pat. "Besides, if he thinks it's best for them to move to Kentucky, then we should accept that and give him our blessing."

Mom's chin quivered. "B–but we've already lost two sons to Kentucky, and if Timothy goes, too, you never can tell who might be next. At the rate things are going, our whole family will be living in Kentucky, and we'll be here all alone."

Timothy's gaze went to the ceiling. "You're exaggerating, Mom. No one else has even mentioned moving to Kentucky."

"That's right," Dad agreed. "They're all involved in their businesses, most have their own homes, and everyone seems pretty well settled right here."

"I thought Titus and Samuel were settled, too, but they ran off to Kentucky, and now they've talked Timothy into moving." Mom sniffed, and Timothy knew she was struggling not to cry.

"They didn't talk me into moving," Timothy said, rubbing his forehead. "I made the decision myself because I'm sick of Hannah clinging to her mamm and ignoring me." He huffed. "I'm hoping things will be better between us once we get moved and settled into a place of our own. Hannah will need a bit of time to adjust, of course, but once she does, I'm sure she'll see that the move was a good thing." He smiled at Mom, hoping to reassure her. "After we get a place of our own, you and Dad can come visit us. Please, Mom, it would mean a lot to know you understand my need to do this."

Mom sighed. "If you're determined to go, I guess I can't stop you, but I don't have to like it."

Timothy smiled when Dad gave him a wink. Mom would eventually come to grips with the move—especially when she saw how much happier he and Hannah would be. He just hoped Hannah would see that, too.

—ꙍ—

Hannah stood at the kitchen sink, hands shaking and eyes brimming with tears. She could hardly believe her husband was making them move to Kentucky. She couldn't stand the thought of leaving her family—especially Mom. Hannah and her mother had always been close, but Timothy was jealous of the time they spent together. He wanted her all to himself—that's why he'd decided they should move to Kentucky. She wished she could convince Timothy to change his mind, but he wouldn't budge.

She sniffed and swiped at the tears running down her cheeks. "It's not fair! I shouldn't be forced to move from my home that I love to a place I'm sure I will hate! I can't believe my own husband is putting me through this!"

Hannah jumped when the back door banged shut. She grabbed a dish towel and quickly dried her tears. If it was Timothy, she couldn't let him know she'd been crying. It would only cause another disagreement like the one they'd had earlier this morning, and they sure didn't need any more of those. Timothy didn't like it when she cried and had often accused her of using her tears to get what she wanted.

When Hannah was sure all traces of tears were gone, she turned and was surprised to see her mother standing near the kitchen table. Hannah breathed a sigh of relief. "Oh Mom, it's you. I'm so glad it's not Timothy."

"Are you okay? Your eyes look red and puffy." Mom's pale blue eyes revealed the depth of her concern.

Hannah swallowed a couple of times, unsure of her voice.

"I. . .I don't want to move. Just the thought of it makes me feel ill. I want to stay right here in Lancaster County."

Mom stepped up to Hannah and gathered her into her arms. "I wish you didn't have to move, either, but Timothy's your husband, which means your place is with him." She gently patted Hannah's back. "Your daed and I will miss you, but we'll come to visit as soon as you get settled in."

"But that probably won't be for some time." Hannah nearly choked on the sob rising in her throat. "We'll be staying with Timothy's brother Samuel until we get a place of our own, and I–I'm not sure how that's going to work out."

"I understand your concerns. From what you've told me, Samuel has a lot on his hands, having four *kinner* to raise and all. He'll no doubt appreciate your help."

Hannah stiffened. "Do you think Samuel will expect me to watch the children while he's at work?"

"Maybe. It would mean he wouldn't have to pay anyone else to watch them—unless, of course, he decides to pay you."

"It's my understanding that Esther Beiler's been watching them, but I suppose that could change with me living there."

Mom pulled out a chair at the table and took a seat. "You'll just have to wait and see, but hopefully it'll all work out."

Hannah wasn't sure about that. She hadn't planned on taking care of four more children. "Moving to a strange place and being around people she isn't used to seeing will be difficult for Mindy. My little girl is going to need my attention more than ever."

"That's true. It will be an adjustment. But Mindy's young, and I'm sure she'll quickly adapt to her new surroundings," Mom said.

Hannah sighed. She didn't think anything about their

move to Kentucky would work, and to be honest, she hoped it wouldn't, because if things went badly, Timothy might see the light and move back to Pennsylvania where they belonged.

Chapter 2

Lexington, Kentucky

Hannah shifted on the seat, trying to find a comfortable position. After tearful good-byes to their families last night, she, Timothy, and Mindy had left home at four this morning and spent the last ten hours on the road. The few hours of sleep Hannah had managed to get while riding in Charles Thomas's van had done little to relieve her fatigue and nothing to soften the pain of leaving Pennsylvania.

Why couldn't Timothy understand the closeness she and Mom felt? Didn't he care about anyone's needs but his own? When they'd first gotten married, he'd said he loved her and wanted to spend the rest of his life making her happy. Apparently he'd lied about that. Maybe he'd told her what she wanted to hear so she would agree to marry him. He probably only wanted a wife to cook, clean, and give him children, because he sure didn't seem to care about her wants or needs—or for that matter, what was important to her. Hannah's inner voice told her this wasn't true, but somehow it just felt better to think so.

She glanced at her precious daughter sleeping peacefully in the car seat beside her. Mindy resembled Hannah's mother in some ways. She had the same blond hair and pale blue eyes, but she had her daddy's nose and her mama's mouth. If they had more children, Hannah wondered what they would look like. Oh, how she wished for another baby. A little brother or sister for Mindy would be so nice. She thought about the miscarriage she'd had last year and wished once more that the baby had lived.

Seems like I never get what I want, Hannah thought bitterly. *Makes me wonder why I even bother to pray.*

Hannah's inner voice told her again that she shouldn't feel this way. Looking at Mindy, she knew how blessed she was to have such a special little girl.

She glanced toward the front of the van where Timothy sat talking to their driver. It made her feel sick to hear the excitement in Timothy's voice as he told Charles about the phone call he'd had with his twin brother, Titus, last night. Titus was married to Suzanne now, and Samuel and Esther would probably be married soon, as well. Both Samuel and Titus were happy living in Kentucky, but Hannah was certain she would never be happy there.

Hannah leaned her head against the window and closed her eyes as the need for sleep overtook her. She wished she could wake up and discover that this was all just a bad dream and find herself home in her own bed. But of course, that was just wishful thinking. At least for now, sleep was her only means to escape the dread that kept mounting the closer they got to their destination.

Timothy glanced at the backseat and was pleased to see that his wife and daughter were both sound asleep. They'd pushed hard all day, only stopping to get gas, eat, and take bathroom breaks. If all went well, they should be in Pembroke by this evening.

A sense of excitement welled in Timothy's soul. It would be good to see his brothers again, and he could hardly wait to start a new life in Kentucky, where he'd been told that land was cheaper and more abundant. Since their house in Pennsylvania had already sold, he had the money to begin building a home. The problem would be finding the time to build it, since he'd only be able to work on it when he wasn't painting with Samuel. Of course, it might be better if he could find a home that had already been built—maybe a place that needed some work and he could fix up in his spare time. Well, he'd decide about that once he'd had a chance to look around.

"How are you holding up?" Charles asked, running his fingers through his slightly thinning gray hair, while glancing over at Timothy. "Do you need to take a break?"

"Naw, I'm fine. Just anxious to get there is all."

Charles nodded. "I'm sure. It's been a long day, but we're making good time. According to my GPS, we should be in Pembroke by six-thirty or so, barring anything unforeseen."

"That sounds good. If I can borrow your cell phone, I'll call and leave a message for Samuel so he knows what time to expect us."

"Sure, no problem." Charles handed Timothy his phone.

Timothy dialed Samuel's number and was surprised when a young boy answered the phone. He hadn't expected anyone to be in the phone shanty.

"Hello. Who's this?" he asked.

"It's Leon. Who's this, and who are ya callin' for?"

"It's your uncle Timothy, and I'm calling to let your daed know that we're in Kentucky and should be at your place around six thirty."

"Oh, good. Should I tell Esther to have supper ready then?"

"Is Esther there now?"

"Jah. *Daadi*'s still at work, and Esther's here with me, Marla, Penny, and Jared."

"Okay, will you let your daed know when he gets home from work what time to expect us? Oh, and if Esther doesn't mind holding supper till we get there, we'd surely appreciate it. It'll save us some time if we don't have to stop and eat somewhere."

"Sure, no problem. I'll tell 'em both what you said."

"*Danki*, Leon. See you soon." Timothy hung up and put the phone back in the tray. "I think Esther will have supper waiting for us when we get there," he said to Charles. "So we shouldn't have to stop again except if you need gas or someone needs a bathroom break."

"Sounds good. Nothing like a good home-cooked meal to look forward to. Would you mind letting the other drivers know?"

"Don't mind a'tall." Timothy called each of their drivers, who were transporting his family's belongings, then settled back and closed his eyes. If he slept awhile, the time would pass more quickly.

Just think, he told himself, *in a few more hours, I'll be sitting in my brother's kitchen, sharing a meal and catching up on all his news. Sure hope I get to see Titus and Suzanne this evening, too. I can't wait to find out how they're doing.*

Chapter 3

Pembroke, Kentucky

We're here, Hannah! Better wake Mindy up so we can greet Samuel and his family."

Hannah's eyes snapped open, and she bolted upright in her seat. The moment she'd been dreading was finally here. She could see by his expression that Timothy was excited. Too bad she didn't share his enthusiasm.

Hannah fiddled with her head covering to be sure it was on straight then gently nudged her rosy-cheeked daughter's arm. "Wake up, Mindy," she said softly, so as not to frighten the child. Ever since Mindy had been a baby, she'd been a hard sleeper, and if she was awakened too abruptly, she either cried or became grumpy. It was better if she was allowed the freedom to wake up on her own, but right now that wasn't possible.

"Let's get out and stretch our legs before we go inside." Timothy had the van door open before Hannah could even unbuckle the seat belt holding Mindy in her car seat. They'd no more than stepped out of the van when Samuel rushed out the door to greet them. "It's mighty good to see you, brother!" he said, giving Timothy a big bear hug.

"It's good to see you, too." Timothy's smile stretched ear to ear as he pounded Samuel's back.

"It's nice to see you, as well," Samuel said, turning to Hannah and giving her a quick hug. "How was your trip?"

"It was long, and I'm stiff and tired." Hannah knew her voice sounded strained, and probably a bit testy, but she couldn't help it. She didn't want to be here, and there was no point in pretending she did. Life was perfect back home in Pennsylvania—at least, she thought so.

Samuel nodded with a look of understanding. "I remember how tired the Kinner and I felt when we got here last year." He smiled at Mindy and reached his hand out to her, but she quickly hid behind Hannah.

"She's a little shy—especially since she hasn't seen you in a while," Timothy said. "I think she just needs some time to get reacquainted."

Woof! Woof! A black lab bounded out of the barn and headed straight for Mindy. When Mindy screamed, Timothy quickly scooped her into his arms.

"Sorry about that." Samuel grabbed the dog's collar. "Lucky gets excited when he sees someone new to play with," he said.

Hannah frowned. "Mindy's too little to play with a dog that big. She's obviously afraid of it."

"I'll put the dog away. Come on, boy." Samuel led the dog back to the barn.

I don't think our daughter wants to be here any more than I do, Hannah thought. *Why can't you see that, Timothy? Why couldn't we have stayed in Pennsylvania? How can you expect Mindy or me to like it here? I'll never consider Kentucky my home.*

Samuel had just returned from the barn when his four

children rushed out of the house, followed by a pretty, young Amish woman with dark hair and milk-chocolate-brown eyes.

"Esther, you remember Timothy when he came for Titus and Suzanne's wedding, and I'd like you to meet his wife, Hannah, and their daughter, Mindy," Samuel said. It was obvious from his smiling face that he loved her deeply.

Esther smiled warmly and gave Hannah a hug.

"It's nice to meet you," Hannah said, forcing a smile.

"It's real good to see you again," Timothy said, shaking Esther's hand.

Samuel smiled down at his children. "So what do you think, Timothy? Have the kinner grown much since you last saw 'em?"

Timothy nodded. "They sure have. I hardly recognize Leon, he's gotten so tall, and when I called earlier, I didn't realize at first it was him on the phone. And would you look at Marla, Penny, and Jared? They've all grown a lot, too!"

Charles stepped out of the van, and Timothy introduced him to Samuel and Esther.

"The trucks with all of Timothy and Hannah's things aren't far behind," Charles said. "Should we start unloading as soon as they get here?"

"Maybe we could eat supper first," Esther said. "It's almost ready, and it won't be good if it gets cold. Believe me, there's plenty of food for everyone, even the drivers, so make sure you tell them to stay and eat with us."

"That sounds good to me." Timothy patted his stomach. "With all the work we have ahead of us yet tonight, I'll need some nourishment to give me the strength to do it."

"I'd suggest that we wait till tomorrow, but since it'll be Sunday, that won't work," Samuel said.

Sunday. Hannah groaned inwardly. If this was the week

Samuel's church district had church, she'd be forced to go and try to put on a happy face when she met a bunch of people she didn't want to know.

"Where are we going to put everything?" Timothy asked his brother. "Will there be room enough in your barn?"

"I think so," Samuel said with a nod. "And if there isn't, we can always put some of your things in Titus's barn."

"Speaking of my twin, where is he?" Timothy questioned, looking back toward the house. "I figured he might be here waiting for us."

"He and Suzanne are coming, and I'm sure they'll be here soon. Titus probably had to work a little later than usual this evening."

Esther touched Hannah's arm. "You look tired. Why don't you come inside and rest while I get supper on the table?"

Resting sounded good, but Hannah didn't want to appear impolite, so she forced another smile and said, "I appreciate the offer, but I should help you with supper."

"There really isn't that much left to do. Marla set the table awhile ago, and the chicken's staying warm in the oven. But if you really want to help, you can cut up the veggies for a tossed salad while I mash the potatoes."

"Sure, I can do that."

Hannah reached for Mindy, and when Timothy handed the child over, Hannah followed Esther into the house.

While Mindy played with her cousins in the living room, Hannah helped Esther in the kitchen.

"How long have you and Samuel been courting?" Hannah asked, feeling the need to find something to talk about.

"We started courting this past summer, but then Samuel broke things off for a while because he was afraid of being untrue to his wife's memory. Since he'd promised Elsie before she died that he'd always love her, he felt as if he was betraying her memory when he fell in love with me. But something miraculously changed his mind, and Samuel renewed his relationship with me." Esther smiled brightly. "We hope to be married sometime next year."

I wonder if Timothy would find someone else if something happened to me, Hannah mused as she washed and patted the lettuce dry. *With the way things have been between us lately, he might be glad if I was gone. He might find another wife right away.*

Hannah knew she couldn't continue with these negative thoughts, so she watched out the window as the two big trucks pulled into the yard. Timothy greeted the drivers and unloaded their two horses, Dusty and Lilly, from the trailer that had been pulled behind one of the trucks. All their furniture and household items were in those trucks, along with the buggy they used for transportation and all of Timothy's tools and farming equipment. Nothing had been left in Pennsylvania except their empty house, which would soon have new owners living in it. Everything seemed so final, and it was hard to even think about someone else living in their house.

"It's so nice that you and Timothy are here," Esther said. "I know Samuel's pleased that Timothy has made the move. And of course, Titus will be happy to have his twin brother living nearby. He's often mentioned all the fun times he and Timothy had growing up together."

Hannah was about to comment when she spotted a horse and buggy pull into the yard. A few minutes later, Titus and Suzanne climbed down, and Timothy and his twin brother embraced. When they pulled apart, Titus snatched Timothy's straw hat and tossed it into the air. When the two brothers started whooping and hollering, Hannah wondered if they would ever settle down. They acted like a couple of kids—the way they had during their running-around years. Timothy and Titus looked so much alike, and they'd always been very close. They had the same thick, dark brown hair and brown eyes; although Titus's left eye was slightly larger than his right eye. That was the only way some folks were able to tell them apart. They were obviously happy to be together again.

But I'm not happy, and nobody seems to care. Hannah fought the urge to give in to the tears stinging the backs of her eyes. They'd been in Pembroke less than an hour, and already she hated it. Pennsylvania was where her heart remained, and Kentucky would never replace it. No matter how long they lived here, Pennsylvania was the only place she'd ever call home.

Chapter 4

As Timothy sat in church on Sunday morning, he looked across the room and noticed that Hannah wasn't paying attention to the message being preached by one of the ministers. Ever since they'd taken their seats on the backless wooden benches inside Suzanne's mother's home almost three hours ago, she'd either stared out the window or fussed with Mindy, whom she held on her lap. Fortunately, Mindy had recently fallen asleep, so Hannah should have been paying attention, but she seemed completely bored, as though her mind was elsewhere. When they lived in Pennsylvania, Hannah had always appeared interested during church. Was her disinterest now because she hadn't enjoyed any of the messages, or was it simply because she didn't want to be here at all? Timothy guessed the latter, because so far, Hannah had made it clear that she didn't like anything about moving to Kentucky. He'd hoped that once she accepted the idea that this was their new home, she would learn to fit in and end up actually liking the area.

When Timothy realized that he, too, wasn't paying attention to the message, he pulled his thoughts aside and, for the rest of the service, concentrated on what was being said.

When church was over, the men and women ate the noon meal in shifts, so Timothy wasn't sure how Hannah was doing or if she'd met any of the women. Once everyone had eaten, a few people went home, but most gathered in groups to visit.

Timothy meandered around the yard for a bit then stopped for a spell to lean against the fence. Behind him he could hear cows mooing in the distance, but he preferred to watch the activities around him. He glanced at the big maple tree nearby, now barren with the approach of winter, and noticed his wife sitting on a chair with Mindy in her lap, looking more forlorn than ever. He'd seen some of the women try to talk to Hannah, but then a short time later, they would leave and join the others who were visiting on the opposite side of the yard. This caused him even more concern, wondering if his wife may have given these women the cold shoulder.

Hannah had been quiet and moody ever since they'd left Pennsylvania, and even during the time they'd spent with family last night, she'd remained aloof—as if her thoughts were someplace else. *Probably back in Pennsylvania with her mamm*, Timothy thought with regret. Keeping to herself so much was not a good thing. Worse yet, she was hovering over Mindy again, not letting her play with the other children. Timothy had hoped that by coming to Kentucky, Hannah would want to make some friends. But if she continued to remain aloof, making new friends probably wouldn't happen. He worried that people might get the impression that his wife was standoffish. But then how could they think otherwise with the way she'd acted so far?

Maybe she just needs a bit more time, Timothy told himself. *Once Hannah gets better acquainted with Suzanne and Esther, she'll fit right in. At least, I hope that's the case, because I sure wouldn't want her to mope around all the time. It could have a negative effect on Mindy, and it won't do any good for our marriage either. I'm probably rushing things and need to be more patient.*

"You look like you're somewhere far-off. What are you thinkin' about, brother?" Titus asked, bumping Timothy's arm as he joined him at the fence.

"Oh, nothing much."

"Come on now." Titus nudged Timothy's arm a second time. "This is your twin *bruder* you're talkin' to, so you may as well say what's on your mind."

Timothy smiled, knowing how it had always been between him and his twin. They could sense things about each other, good or bad. It was as if they knew what the other one was thinking. "I'm worried about Hannah," he admitted. "I'm afraid she may never adjust to living so far away from her mamm."

"I wouldn't worry too much. I'm sure she'll get used to it. But if you're really concerned, I'll speak to Suzanne and ask her to make sure Hannah feels welcome. Maybe they can hire a driver and go shopping in Hopkinsville soon or just get together for lunch or something."

"Danki. I'd appreciate that. At this point, anything's worth a try."

"You know, Timothy, you might be rushing things a bit. Maybe you just need to relax and let Hannah work through it all," Titus added. "You've only been here for one day."

"I was just thinking the same thing. You and I always did think alike."

"Jah. So changing the subject," Titus said, "have you had a chance to talk to Samuel about working with him?"

Timothy nodded. "He said he's been really busy lately, doing a lot of jobs for Allen, plus some he's lined up on his own. Starting tomorrow, I'll be working with both Allen and Samuel on a job in Crittenden County." He shifted, feeling uncomfortable all of a sudden. "You know, with this being the Lord's Day and all, guess we really shouldn't be talkin' about work."

Titus gave a nod. "You're right, so why don't we go find Samuel and some of the other men here and see if we can get a game of horseshoes started?"

Timothy smiled. "Sounds good to me. Let's go!"

—∞—

"Everything looks so different here," Hannah said after they left the Yoders' place and were heading down the tree-lined road in their horse and buggy toward Samuel's house. "The grass in the fields is an ugly brown, and from what I can tell, there aren't many houses or places of business nearby. Christian County is nothing like Lancaster County at all."

"That's true," Timothy agreed, "but it's peaceful and much quieter here, and there aren't nearly so many cars or tourists."

"I've gotten used to the tourists. In fact, if it weren't for the tourists, my daed's bulk food store wouldn't do nearly as well as it does."

"Guess you're right about that, but I still think it's nice to be here where the pace is slower."

Hannah grimaced when Mindy, who was asleep in her lap, stirred restlessly as their buggy bounced over the numerous ruts in the road. She turned in her seat a bit to look at Timothy and frowned. "The pace may be slower here, but the roads in Christian County need some work, don't you think?"

"I suppose, but there are some rough roads around Lancaster, too."

Hannah knew her husband was trying to look on the positive side of things, but so far she didn't like one thing about being here. In fact, Timothy's bright outlook actually irritated her. Every time she complained, he had some way of twisting things around to make it all sound good.

"See that driveway over there?" Timothy pointed to the right. "It leads to the bed-and-breakfast I told you about. It's run by a young English woman, Bonnie Taylor." He gave Hannah a dimpled smile. "I met Bonnie when I came here for Titus and Suzanne's wedding, and she seemed very nice. Samuel and Allen did some work on her house before she opened the B&B, and Esther's been working for her part-time ever since. She helps Bonnie in the mornings before heading to Samuel's to keep house and watch the kinner. Then she goes back to help at the B&B again in the evenings after Samuel gets home from work."

Hannah grunted in response. She wasn't interested in hearing about the B&B or the woman who owned it. She wished Timothy hadn't gone to his brother's wedding, because it wasn't long after that he'd come up with the crazy notion to move here.

Maybe I should have gone with him to the wedding, she thought. *Then I could have discouraged him from the very beginning.*

"So what did you think of the church service today?" he asked, moving their conversation in a different direction.

She sighed. "It was okay, I guess."

"Did you hear what the bishop said in his message about remembering to count our blessings and learning to be content?"

"I. . .I don't really remember."

"Well, he said contentment helps to keep one's heart free from worry. It also teaches us to live simply and think of others more than ourselves. I think his message was a good reminder for us, don't you?"

Hannah stiffened. "What are you trying to say, Timothy? Do you think I'm supposed to be thankful and content that you forced me to leave the home I loved and come here to a place I already hate? How can you even accept that someone else will be living in our house in Pennsylvania?"

Timothy gripped the reins a bit tighter. "You only think you hate it here because you didn't want to move, but if you'll give it half a chance, I think you might change your mind. Besides, the house in Pennsylvania is not ours anymore, remember?"

"Jah, you made sure of that, didn't you? And I doubt I'll ever like it here. I mean, what's to like? We're stuck living with Samuel and his kinner, and—"

"We won't be living with him forever," Timothy interrupted. "As soon as we find some suitable property, I can start building a house."

"But it's the middle of November, Timothy. Even if we could find the perfect property right away, you'd never get a house built for us before winter sets in."

"You're right, but spring will come sooner than we think."

"I can't imagine us being cooped up with Samuel and his rowdy kinner throughout the winter months." Hannah frowned. "If we have to live here, I'd really like to have a place of our own."

"And we will—just as soon as I can get one built."

"Can't we see about buying a house that's already built? We could move in quicker, and our stay with Samuel would be brief."

He shrugged. "Samuel said there's not much for sale in this area right now. He feels fortunate to be renting the house owned by Esther's folks."

"What's going to happen after he and Esther are married?" Hannah asked. "Will they continue renting the place from her folks, or will they end up buying it?'

"I'm not sure. Samuel hasn't said anything about that. And as far as I know, he and Esther aren't officially engaged yet."

"I'll bet they will be soon. Samuel needs a *mudder* for his kinner, and it's pretty obvious that he's smitten with Esther."

"I don't think *smitten* is the right word for what my bruder feels for Esther," Timothy said. "All ya have to do is watch how they interact to see that they're obviously in love with each other."

Hannah looked down at Mindy and stroked her soft cheek. *Well, at least I have you,* she thought. *That's something to be thankful for. Mindy, you are my one constant blessing.*

Chapter 5

"Wake up, sleepyhead." Timothy shook his wife's shoulder.

"I'm tired. It can't be time to get up already." Hannah moaned and pulled the quilt over her head.

Timothy nudged her arm through the covers. "It's Monday morning, and Samuel and I need to get an early start because we'll be working out of the area today. Allen will be coming by to pick us up soon."

Hannah just lay there, unmoving.

"Hannah, please get up. I was hoping you'd fix us some breakfast and pack lunches for us to take to the job."

She pulled the covers aside and yawned noisily as she sat up. "Oh, all right." Her long, tawny-brown hair hung around her shoulders in an array of tangled curls. Hannah's thick hair had always been naturally curly—which meant she had to work hard at getting it parted down the middle, twisted on the sides, and pulled back into a bun. When she took it down at night, she spent several minutes brushing it out. During the first year of their marriage Timothy had often brushed Hannah's hair. That had been a special time for him, when he felt really close to her. He hoped they could bring those days back again now that they were making a new start.

Timothy leaned down and kissed Hannah's cheek. It was warm and soft, and he was tempted to forget about going to work with Samuel and stay here with Hannah. But he knew he couldn't do that. He had to earn a living and provide for them.

"I'll see you downstairs in the kitchen," he said, before giving her another quick kiss. Then he moved away from the bed and stopped for a minute to gaze at Mindy, sleeping peacefully on a cot across the room, her golden curls fanned out across the pillow. She looked like an angel, lying there so sweet. Mindy could have shared a room with Penny, of course, but Hannah had insisted that their daughter needed to be close to them—at least until she felt more familiar with this new place. Timothy figured it was just an excuse. Hannah, following in her mother's footsteps, was too clingy and overprotective where their little girl was concerned.

Mindy's so sweet and innocent, he thought. *She's always smiling and full of curiosity.* Timothy hoped in the years ahead that he and Hannah would have a few more children, whom he was sure would be equally special. His stomach clenched as he thought about the baby Hannah had lost last year and how hard she'd grieved after the miscarriage. It had taken some time for her to pull out of her depression, but with the help and encouragement of several family members, she'd finally come to accept the baby's death, although he didn't think she had ever fully understood why God had allowed it.

Of course, God's ways aren't our ways. Sometimes it's better if we don't try and figure things out—just accept life's disappointments and trust God to help us through them, because He's in control of every situation anyhow, Timothy reminded himself as he slipped quietly out of the room.

~

After fixing breakfast for Timothy and Samuel and packing them both a lunch, Hannah, still feeling tired, was tempted to go back to bed. But she knew she couldn't do that because Samuel's children would be up soon, and then she'd have to fix them breakfast and see that the two oldest were off to school. Esther had been caring for Samuel's children, but since Samuel hadn't mentioned Esther coming over, Hannah assumed she'd be watching them. She'd been worried that it might be expected of her, but now that she was here, she'd changed her mind. Truth was, she thought she could do a better job with the kids than Esther, not to mention with keeping the house running smoother. Good habits began at an early age, and as far as Hannah was concerned, Samuel's children needed more structure.

After Leon and Marla left for school, she would find something for the little ones to do while she unpacked some of her and Timothy's clothes and got things organized in the bedroom they shared with Mindy. Hannah had suggested that Mindy sleep in the bed with her and Timothy for a few nights, but he'd put his foot down and insisted that she sleep on the cot. Didn't he care that Mindy was being forced to adjust to new surroundings and needed the comfort of her mother?

With determination, Hannah forced her thoughts aside, knowing if she didn't keep busy she would feel even more depressed. "Maybe I should organize around here today," she muttered as she put away the bread. The whole house, while clean enough, seemed quite cluttered—not nearly as tidy as she'd kept their home in Pennsylvania.

"Who ya talkin' to?" a small voice asked.

Startled, Hannah whirled around. Seven-year-old Leon,

still in his pajamas and barefoot, stared up at her, blinking his brown eyes rapidly.

"No one. I mean, I was talking to myself." She suppressed a yawn.

"Are ya bored? Is that why you were talkin' to yourself?"

"No, I'm not bored, I was just. . . . Oh, never mind." Hannah motioned to the table, where the box of cold cereal she'd served the men for breakfast still sat. "Would you like some cereal?"

He shook his head.

"Would you rather have eggs?"

"Don't want no *oier*. I was hopin' for some *pannekuche*."

"I don't have time to make pancakes this morning."

"Esther fixes us pannekuche whenever we want 'em." Leon, who had his father's light brown hair, made a sweeping glance of the entire room. "Where is Esther, anyways? She's usually here before we get up."

"I don't think she'll be here today."

He tipped his head and looked at her curiously. "How come?"

"Because I'm here, and I'll be fixing your breakfast this morning."

Leon studied her a few more seconds then shrugged. "So can we have pannekuche?"

Hannah shook her head. "I said no. I don't have time for that this morning." *This child is certainly persistent*, she thought.

He pointed to the battery-operated clock on the far wall. "It's still early. Marla, Penny, and Jared ain't even outa bed yet."

"The correct word is *aren't*, and I'm not going to fix pancakes this morning, so you may as well go back upstairs and get dressed. By the time you come down, I'll have a bowl of cereal and a hard-boiled egg ready for you to eat."

"Don't want an *oi*," Leon mumbled, shuffling toward the door leading to the stairs.

"Make sure you wake Marla," Hannah called after him. "I don't want either of you to be late for school."

Leon tromped up the stairs.

Hannah cringed. She hoped he didn't wake Mindy. Like Hannah, Mindy wasn't a morning person, and if she got woken out of a sound sleep, she was bound to be cranky.

She listened for a few minutes, and when she didn't hear her daughter, she went to the refrigerator and took out a carton of eggs. She'd just gotten them boiling on the stove when both Leon and Marla showed up.

"Leon said Esther's not comin' today. Is that true?" Blond-haired, nine-year-old Marla, asked, casting curious brown eyes on Hannah.

Hannah nodded. "I'm sure that's the case, because if she was coming, she would have been here by now." She motioned to the table. "Have a seat. You can eat your cereal while the eggs are boiling."

"I told ya before—I don't want no boiled oi," Leon said. "It'll get stuck in my throat."

Hannah grimaced. Was there no pleasing this child?

"Just eat your cereal, then," she said, placing two bowls on the table.

The kids took a seat and bowed their heads for silent prayer. Hannah waited quietly until they were finished; then she poured cereal into the bowls and gave them each a glass of milk. She'd just turned off the stove when she heard Mindy crying upstairs. "I'll be right back," she said to Marla before hurrying up the stairs.

Hannah was about to enter the bedroom she and Timothy shared with Mindy when three-year-old Jared and Penny, who was five, padded down the hall.

"*Wu is* Daadi?" Penny asked. Her long, sandy-brown hair hung down her back in gentle waves, and she blinked her brown eyes as she looked up at Hannah curiously.

"Your daddy went to work," Hannah said. "Now go downstairs to the kitchen. I'll be there as soon as I get Mindy."

"*Kumme*, Jared," Penny said, taking her blond-haired little brother's hand.

As the children plodded down the stairs, Hannah went to see about Mindy. She found the child curled up on the cot sobbing. No doubt she was confused by her surroundings. After all, they'd only been here two nights, and waking up and finding herself alone in the room probably frightened her.

"It's okay, my precious little girl. Mama's here." Hannah bent down and gathered Mindy into her arms. Truth was, she felt like crying, too. Only there was no time to give in to her tears right now. She had to feed the little ones and get Marla and Leon off to school.

—∞—

When Esther stepped into Samuel's kitchen, she was surprised to see Marla and Leon at the table eating cereal.

"Where's your daed?" she asked, looking at Marla.

"He and Uncle Timothy went to work."

Esther glanced at the clock. She knew she was running a little behind but didn't think she was that late.

"Daadi left early this mornin'," Leon explained. "Had a paint job to do up in Marion."

"Oh, I see." Esther smiled. "So did you two fix your own breakfast?"

Marla shook her head. "Aunt Hannah fixed it for us."

"I guess that makes sense. Where is Hannah?"

"Went upstairs 'cause Mindy was cryin'," Leon answered around a mouthful of cereal.

Just then, Jared and Penny entered the kitchen, both wearing their nightclothes. As soon as Penny caught sight of Esther, she grinned and held up her arms.

Esther bent down and scooped the little girl up, giving her a kiss on the cheek. Penny was such a sweet child—easygoing and so compliant. Her little brother, on the other hand, could be a handful at times, but he was still a dear. Esther loved him, as well as all of Samuel's children, as if they were her own. After she and Samuel got married, these little ones would be hers to help raise, and she could hardly wait. It would be wonderful to leave the guesthouse where she'd been staying on Bonnie's property and move back here to the home where she used to live with her parents. The best part of moving back would be that she would finally be Samuel's wife.

Esther had missed her folks dearly after they'd moved to Pennsylvania to help care for her brother, Dan, who had multiple sclerosis. Her family was never far from her thoughts.

Esther removed her shawl and black outer bonnet, placing them on a wall peg near the back door. Then she returned to the kitchen to fix Jared and Penny's breakfast. She'd just gotten them situated at the table when Hannah, carrying Mindy, stepped into the room.

Hannah blinked her eyes rapidly. "*Ach*, you scared me, Esther! I didn't expect to see you here."

"I come over every morning to watch the kinner while Samuel's at work. I assumed you knew."

"I did hear that, but since we'll be living here until we have a home of our own, I figured I would be watching the children." Hannah shifted Mindy to the other hip. "It only makes sense, don't you think?"

Esther couldn't think clearly enough to say anything. It probably didn't make sense for them both to care for the children, but Samuel had been paying her to watch them, and she enjoyed being here. Besides, some of the money Esther earned went toward her brother's medical expenses, so it was important that she keep working right now. Should she speak up and say so, or let Hannah take over? Maybe it would be best to wait until Samuel got home and let him decide who would watch the children. In the meantime, she was here now, and she planned to stay.

Chapter 6

Marion, Kentucky

This is my first time in Marion," Samuel said as he, Allen, and Timothy worked on a storefront Allen had been contracted to remodel. "It's really a nice little town."

"Yep, and there's a lot of interesting history here," Allen said while sanding around one of the large window casings.

Timothy listened with interest as Allen talked about the Crittenden County Historical Museum, which had been built in 1881 and was originally a church. "It's the oldest church building in Marion, and the interior includes original wood floors, pulpit, balcony, and stained-glass windows," Allen said, pushing his dark brown hair under his baseball cap. "The church held on for over 120 years, until it was finally forced to close its doors due to a lack of membership. Soon after that, the building was donated to the historical society. Now it houses a really nice collection of memorabilia, pictures, and many other things related to the history of Marion and the surrounding communities that make up Crittenden County." Allen looked over at Timothy and grinned. "Guess that's probably a bit more than you wanted to know, huh?"

Timothy smiled as he opened a fresh bucket of paint. "Actually, I thought it was quite interesting. Anything that has to do with history captures my attention."

"My brother's not kidding about that," Samuel chimed in. "I'm anxious to show him the Jefferson Davis Monument, because I'm sure he'll be interested in that."

"Titus told me all about it," Timothy said. "He said the view from inside the monument is really something to see."

"He's right about that," Samuel said with a nod. "Maybe in the spring, we can go there and take our kids. I think they'd get a kick out of riding the elevator and being up so high."

"I'd sure like to go," Timothy said, "but I don't know about Mindy. She's pretty young to enjoy something like that, and Hannah might not go for the idea either." He paused long enough to grab a paint stick and stir the paint in the can. "As you probably know, my *fraa* tends to be pretty protective of our daughter."

"*Fraa* means *wife*, right?" Allen questioned.

Timothy nodded. "How'd you know that?"

Allen motioned to Samuel. "Between him and Esther, they've taught me several Pennsylvania-Dutch words." His face sobered. "There was a time when Samuel thought I was interested in Esther because I talked to her so much."

"But you set me straight on that real quick," Samuel said, winking at Allen. "And now everyone knows Bonnie's the love of your life."

Allen's face reddened. "I hope it's not that obvious, because I haven't actually told Bonnie the way I feel about her yet."

Samuel snickered. "Well, you'd better do it quick, 'cause if you don't, someone else is likely to snatch her away."

Allen's dark eyebrows furrowed. "You really think so?"

Samuel shrugged. "You never can tell, but I sure wouldn't chance it if I were you."

Timothy grinned as he continued to paint while listening to Samuel and Allen kibitzing back and forth. The two men had obviously become really good friends.

I like working with both of them, he decided. In fact, so far, Timothy liked everything about being in Kentucky. The countryside where Samuel lived, as well as here in Crittenden County, was nice, and the land was fertile—just right for farming. *Now if Hannah will just catch on to the idea, we might make a good life for ourselves here,* he thought.

"How does Zach feel about you moving to the Bluegrass State?" Allen asked, looking at Timothy. "I know you used to work for him."

"Zach's fine with it. Since I only painted part-time and mostly farmed with my dad, I don't think Zach will miss having me work for him that much. Besides, he's employed several Amish men."

Allen smiled. "Zach's been my good friend since we were kids. I was hoping he might move his family here, too, but I guess that's not likely to happen."

"I'd be surprised if he ever did move," Samuel said. "After being taken from our family when he was a baby and then spending the next twenty years living in Washington State without even knowing his real name or who his Amish family was, once Zach got back to Pennsylvania, he vowed he'd never leave."

"I can't blame him for that," Allen agreed.

"I know our folks are glad Zach's staying put," Timothy said, "because Mom hasn't taken it well that three of their other sons have moved out of state."

the STRUGGLE

Paradise, Pennsylvania

Fannie had just entered Naomi and Caleb's general store when she spotted Hannah's mother, Sally, looking at some new rubber stamps.

"*Wie gehtś?*" Fannie asked, noticing the dark circles under Sally's pale blue eyes.

Sally sighed and pushed a wisp of her graying blond hair back under her white head covering. "I wish I could say that I'm doing well, but to tell you the truth, I'm really tired."

"That's too bad. Haven't you been sleeping well?"

Sally shook her head. "Not since Hannah and Timothy left. I'm concerned about how my daughter is doing."

"How come? Is Hannah *grank*?"

"She's not physically sick, but when I spoke to her on the phone Saturday evening, she said she already doesn't like Kentucky and wishes she could come home. I'm not sure that's ever going to change."

Fannie wasn't sure what to say. She wasn't any happier about Timothy leaving Pennsylvania, but it was what her son wanted, and if getting Hannah away from her mother strengthened their marriage, then it probably was for the best. Hannah and her mother were too close, and Fannie knew from some of the things Timothy had shared with her that Hannah's unhealthy relationship with her mother had put a wedge between the young couple. It was a shame, too, because Timothy really loved his wife and wanted her to put him first, the way a loving wife should.

"Don't you miss your son?" Sally asked. "Don't you wish he would have stayed in Pennsylvania?"

Fannie glanced at her stepdaughter, Naomi, who stood behind the counter, and wondered if she was listening to this conversation. She had to be careful what she said, because if Naomi repeated it to her father, he'd probably lecture Fannie about letting their children live their own lives and tell her not to discuss Timothy and Hannah with Sally.

Sally touched Fannie's arm. "Is everything okay? You look *umgerrent*."

"I'm not upset." Fannie lowered her voice to a near whisper. "You know, Sally, I haven't lost just one son to Kentucky; I've lost three. And if I can deal with it, then I think you can, too."

Sally's forehead wrinkled. "Are you saying you're okay with the fact that three of your boys live two states away?"

"I'm not saying that at all. I've just learned to accept it because it's a fact, and short of a miracle, none of my sons will ever move back to Pennsylvania."

Sally tapped her chin, looking deep in thought. "Then I guess we ought to pray for a miracle, because I really want Hannah to come home."

Chapter 7

Pembroke, Kentucky

"How would you like to go over to the B&B and meet Bonnie?" Esther asked Hannah after Leon and Marla had left for school.

Hannah shrugged. "I suppose that would be okay." Truth be told, she didn't really care about meeting Bonnie but guessed it would be better than sitting around Samuel's house all day, trying to keep Mindy occupied and making idle conversation with Esther, whom she barely knew. *Of course, I don't know Bonnie either,* she reasoned. *But it'll be good to get out of the house and go for a buggy ride.*

"We can take my horse and buggy," Hannah said. "After being confined in the trailer with Timothy's horse on the trip here, Lilly's probably ready for a good ride."

Esther hesitated a minute then finally nodded. "I'll get the kinner ready to go while you hitch your horse to the buggy."

Hannah wasn't sure she wanted Esther to do anything with Mindy, so she quickly said, "On second thought, maybe we should take your horse and buggy, because I'm not used to the roads here yet, and neither is Lilly."

"If that's what you'd prefer." Esther went over to Jared and Penny, who sat beside Mindy playing with some pots and pans, and explained that Hannah would help them wash up and get their jackets on because they were all going to Bonnie's.

Samuel's children leaped to their feet and started jumping up and down. Following suit, Mindy did the same.

"*Ruhich,* Mindy," Hannah said, putting her fingers to her lips. "You need to calm down." She looked sternly at Penny and Jared. "You need to be quiet, too."

The children looked at Hannah and blinked several times as tears welled in their eyes.

"Now don't start crying," Hannah said.

"They're just excited." Esther spoke in a defensive tone. "They love going over to Bonnie's and playing with her dog, Cody."

"Well, they're getting Mindy all worked up, and it's hard for me to get her settled down once that happens."

"Be still now," Esther said, placing her hands on Penny and Jared's heads. "Listen to Hannah and do what she says while I go out and hitch Ginger to my buggy."

The children calmed down right away, and so did Mindy. Then as Esther went out the door, Hannah led the three of them down the hallway to the bathroom to wash up. When that was done, she took their jackets down from the wall pegs in the utility room and helped the children put them on.

By the time they stepped onto the back porch, Esther had her horse hitched to the buggy. When she motioned for them to come, Hannah ushered the children across the yard. Once they were seated in the back of the buggy, she took her seat up front on the passenger's side.

"Everyone, stay in your seats now," Hannah called over her

shoulder as Esther directed the horse and buggy down the driveway. "This road is bumpy."

"You're right, the driveway is full of ruts right now," Esther said, looking over at Hannah. "That's because we've had so much rain this fall."

Hannah grimaced. She knew the damage too much rain could cause. A few years ago, they'd had so much rain in Lancaster County that many of the roads had flooded. She wondered if that ever happened here.

After they turned onto the main road and had traveled a ways, Esther pointed out various church members' homes. "Oh, and there's the store my folks used to own before they moved to Strasburg to help care for my brother, Dan."

"Who owns the store now?" Hannah asked.

"Aaron and Nettie Martin. They're a Mennonite couple, and they're fairly new to the area."

"I see. Is that where you do most of your shopping?"

"Jah, but when we're able to go into Hopkinsville, I shop at Walmart."

They rode silently for a while; then Hannah turned to Esther and said, "I understand that your brother has MS."

Esther nodded. "The disease has progressed to the point that he has to use a wheelchair most of the time."

"That's too bad. I can't imagine how I would feel if something like that happened to Timothy."

"It's been hard on his wife, Sarah, because she has a lot more responsibility now, but with my mamm and daed there to help, it makes things a bit easier."

"Easier? How could anything be easy if you have someone in your family in a wheelchair or with a severe disability?"

"Mom and Dad don't see it as a burden, and neither does Sarah. They love Dan very much, and there isn't anything they wouldn't do for him."

Hannah nodded. Some people might be able to sacrifice that much, but she wasn't sure she could. And she hoped she'd never have to find out.

Someone tapped Hannah's shoulder, and she turned around to see Penny. "What is it?" she asked, trying to keep the edge out of her voice.

Penny pointed at Mindy and said, "*Schuck.*"

Hannah looked at Mindy and noticed that she'd taken one of her shoes off. "It's fine. Don't be a *retschbeddi,*" she said, frowning at Penny.

"I don't think she means to be a tattletale," Esther said, jumping to Penny's defense. "She was probably concerned that Mindy might lose her shoe."

"Well, it's not her place to worry about Mindy—especially when she wasn't doing anything wrong."

Hannah couldn't help but notice Esther's icy stare. *She obviously doesn't like me, but I don't care. I don't care if anyone here in Christian County likes me.* She swallowed around the lump in her throat. *But if nobody likes me, I'll never fit in. Maybe I should try a little harder to be nice.*

"Just look at those maple trees," Esther said, bringing Hannah's thoughts to a halt. "It's hard to believe that just a few short weeks ago they were a brilliant reddish gold, and now they've lost most of their leaves." She sniffed the air. "That pungent odor tells me that someone in the area is burning leaves."

"It sure is chilly today," Hannah said. "I wonder if we'll have a cold winter."

"I wouldn't be surprised. A few years ago we had a terrible ice storm that left many Englishers without power. A lot of us Amish pitched in to help out wherever we could."

"I'm sure everyone needed help during that time," Hannah said.

Esther nodded. "They sure did."

They rode a little farther, and then Esther guided the horse and buggy up a long, graveled driveway. "See that big house at the end of the drive?" she said, pointing out the front buggy window. "That's Bonnie's bed-and-breakfast."

Hannah studied the stately old home. On one end of the long front porch was a swing, and two wicker chairs sat on the other end. A small table was positioned between them, holding a pot of yellow mums. The place looked warm and inviting. Even the yard was neat, with bushes well trimmed and weed-free flower beds in front of the house. "The outside of the home looks quite nice," Hannah said. "Where's the guesthouse you stay in?"

"Over there." Esther pointed to a smaller building that was set back from the house. It didn't look like it had more than a couple of rooms, but Hannah figured it was probably big enough for Esther's needs. Since she spent most of her time helping out at the B&B or watching Samuel's kids, she really only needed a place to sleep.

Just then a little brown-and-white mixed terrier bounded up to the buggy, barking and leaping into the air like it had springs on its legs.

"That's Bonnie's dog, Cody," Esther said. "He gets excited as soon as he sees my horse and buggy."

"*Hundli!* Hundli!" Mindy shouted from the backseat.

"No, Mindy," Esther said. "Cody's a full-grown dog, not a puppy."

"All dogs are puppies to her," Hannah said in Mindy's defense.

Esther silently guided her horse up to the hitching rail and climbed down from the buggy. After securing the horse, she came around to help Penny and Jared down, while Hannah put Mindy's shoe back on and lifted her out of the buggy.

Then, with the dog barking and running beside them, they made their way up to the house.

When they stepped inside, Hannah sniffed at the scent of apples and cinnamon. She figured Bonnie must have been baking. A few seconds later, a young woman with dark, curly hair and brown eyes stepped into the hallway. "Oh Esther, it's you," she said with a look of surprise. "I didn't expect to see you again until this evening."

"I came by because I wanted you to meet Samuel's sister-in-law, Hannah. They've moved here from Pennsylvania." Esther motioned to Mindy, who clung to Hannah's hand. "This is their daughter, Mindy; she's three."

"It's nice to meet you, Hannah. I'm Bonnie Taylor." Bonnie shook Hannah's hand; then she bent down so she was eye level with Mindy and said, "*Brauchscht kichlin?*"

"Why would you ask if my daughter needed cookies?" Hannah questioned.

"Oh my!" Bonnie's cheeks flamed as she straightened to her full height. "I've learned a few Pennsylvania-Dutch words from Esther and Samuel and thought I knew what I was saying. What I meant to ask was if Mindy would *like* some cookies." She looked down at Jared and Penny, who were smiling up at her with eager expressions, then motioned for them to follow her into the kitchen.

"What's that delicious smell?" Hannah asked, sniffing the air.

"Oh, you must smell my new apple-pie fragrance candle." Bonnie pointed to the candle on the table. "I bought it the other day at Walmart in Hopkinsville."

"I hope I'll get to go there soon," Hannah said. "I could use a few things that I probably can't find at the Mennonite store in this area."

"I'd be happy to drive you to Hopkinsville whenever you want to go." Bonnie motioned to the table. "If you'd all like to take a seat, I'll give the children a glass of milk and some of the peanut butter cookies I made yesterday, and we ladies can enjoy a cup of tea."

"Can we have a few cookies, too?" Esther asked, wiggling her eyebrows playfully while smiling at Bonnie. It was obvious that the two women were good friends, and Hannah felt a bit envious.

After the children finished their cookies and milk, Penny asked if she and Jared could take Mindy outside to play with the dog and see Bonnie's chickens.

"I don't think so," Hannah was quick to say. "Mindy's never been here before, and she might wander off. I'd feel better if she stayed inside with me."

Esther instructed Penny to keep an eye on her little brother and told Jared to stay close to his sister and remain in the yard. The children nodded, and after being helped into their jackets, they skipped happily out the back door.

Hannah gathered Mindy into her arms. She couldn't believe Esther would send two small children into the yard to play by themselves. She wondered what Samuel would think if he knew how careless Esther was with his children.

Bonnie took a seat at the table, and as she visited with Hannah and Esther, she couldn't help but notice the look of sadness on Hannah's face. The young woman was polite enough and appeared to be interested in hearing how Bonnie had acquired the bed-and-breakfast, but her voice seemed flat, almost forced, like she was making herself join in the conversation. Bonnie remembered when Timothy had come for Titus and Suzanne's wedding, she'd been surprised that his wife hadn't been with him. He'd said Hannah stayed home to take care of her mother, who'd sprained her ankle, but Bonnie had a feeling it was more than that. She was pretty intuitive and had a hunch that Hannah didn't like it here. Probably hadn't wanted to leave Pennsylvania at all.

"It's so nice to just sit and visit like this, with a warm cup of tea and some delicious cookies," Esther said. "I enjoy such simple pleasures."

Bonnie nodded. "I remember when I was a girl visiting my grandparents here, Grandma once said to me, 'Whatever your simple pleasures may be, enjoy them and share them with someone else.' She also said that we sometimes take for granted the everyday things that give us a sense of joy and well-being. These simple things are often forgotten when problems occur in our lives." She lifted her cup of tea and smiled. "Since I've moved here I've been trying to savor all the down-to-earth pleasures I possibly can."

Hannah smiled and nodded. At least she was responding a bit more.

Bonnie was about to ask if either Esther or Hannah would like another cookie when the back door bounced open and Penny and Jared rushed in.

Penny dashed across the room and clutched Bonnie's hand. "Eloise is *dot*!"

"Eloise is dead?" Bonnie looked over at Esther for confirmation. "Is that what she said?"

"I'm afraid so," Esther said with a nod.

"Oh my! I'd better go see about this!" Bonnie jumped up and hurried out the door.

Chapter 8

Hannah shuddered at the thought of someone lying dead in Bonnie's yard. "Wh–who is Eloise?" she asked in a shaky voice.

"She's one of Bonnie's laying hens," Esther replied. "If you don't mind keeping the kinner in here with you, I think I'll go outside and have a look myself."

"No, I don't mind." Hannah said with a shake of her head. Truth was, she had no desire to see a dead chicken, and she didn't think the children needed to be staring at it either.

Esther leaned down and gave Jared a kiss on the cheek. "Be a good boy now."

After Esther went out the door, Hannah seated the children at the table and gave them each a piece of paper and some crayons she had brought along in her oversized purse.

While they colored, she studied her surroundings some more. The kitchen was cozy, with pretty yellow curtains at the window. There was a mix of modern appliances—a microwave, portable dishwasher, and electric coffeemaker, along with an older-looking stove and refrigerator on one side of the room. Several older items—a butter churn, a metal bread box, some antique canning jars, and an old pie cupboard that looked like it had been restored—added character to the room. Everything in the kitchen looked neat and orderly, much the way Hannah had kept her kitchen back home. It was nice that Bonnie had been able to use her grandparents' place as a bed-and-breakfast so others could enjoy it. Hannah hoped when Bonnie came in that she might show her the rest of the house.

Being here, in this place so warm and inviting, made Hannah miss her home all the more. She felt like a bird without a tree to land in, and it just wasn't right. She knew, according to the Bible, that she needed to be in subjection to her husband, but it was hard when she felt he'd been wrong in insisting they move to Kentucky.

I mustn't dwell on this, Hannah told herself. *It's not going to change the fact that I'm stuck in a place I don't want to be, so I need to try and make the best of my situation—at least until Timothy wakes up and realizes we were better off in Pennsylvania.*

"What do you think killed Eloise?" Bonnie asked after she and Esther had dug a hole and buried the chicken.

"I'm pretty sure she died from old age, because her neck wasn't broken and there were no tears in her skin or any feathers missing. You can be glad it wasn't a fox, because they can really wreak havoc in a chicken coop. In fact, a fox probably would have killed every one of your chickens," Esther said.

Bonnie breathed a sigh of relief. Taking care of chickens kept her busy enough; she sure didn't need the worry of keeping some predator away.

"Shall we go back inside and give Hannah a tour of the B&B?" Esther asked once they were done.

Bonnie shrugged as she jammed the shovel into the ground

and leaned on it. "Do you think she'd be interested? She seems kind of distant."

"I believe so. She did comment on the outside of your house when we first pulled into your yard. In fact, she seemed impressed by what she saw."

"Well, she wouldn't have been if she'd seen the way it looked before Samuel and Allen did all the repairs on this place."

"It just goes to show that there's hope for almost any home, even those that are really run down," Esther said with a chuckle.

Bonnie laughed, too. "This old house was definitely run-down. I think if my grandparents were still alive, they'd be pleased with the way it looks now. And I know they'd appreciate their home being put to good use."

"I believe you're right, and I'm glad your business is doing well."

"You get the credit for some of that, because if you hadn't taught me how to cook, I couldn't offer my patrons a decent breakfast as part of their stay."

Esther smiled. "I'm glad I was able to help, and I'm appreciative for the job you've given me."

"You'll have it for as long as you like, because I have no plans to go anywhere." Bonnie gave Esther's arm a gentle squeeze. "You, on the other hand, might have other plans that don't include the B&B."

Esther tipped her head. "What other plans?"

"Marrying Samuel, of course. Once you two are married, I'm sure you'll want to be a full-time mother to his children and any other children you may have in the future."

Esther's cheeks flushed to a deep pink. "Samuel and I haven't set a date to be married yet, but I hope it'll be soon."

"Well, whenever it happens, once you're married, your first obligation will be to him and his children."

Esther smiled. "What about you and Allen?"

"What about us?"

"Has he hinted at marriage yet?"

"No, but if he had, I would have avoided the subject."

"How come?"

"You know why, Esther."

"So you haven't told him yet about the baby you had when you were sixteen?"

Bonnie shook her head. "No, and I'm not sure I ever will. I'm afraid it might ruin our relationship."

"You can't have an honest relationship if you're not truthful with him about your past." Esther's sincere expression was enough to make Bonnie tear up.

"I know I should tell him, but I need to be sure our bond is strong enough before I do."

"How long do you think that will be?"

Bonnie shrugged. "I don't know. I'll have to play it by ear." She started walking toward the house. "Now changing the subject, after I give Hannah a tour of my house, would you all like to stay for lunch?"

"That'd be nice, but we wouldn't want to impose."

"It wouldn't be any trouble, and I'd enjoy not having to eat alone."

"If it's okay with Hannah, then it's fine with me," Esther said.

When they stepped back into the house, they found Hannah watching as the children colored pictures while seated at the table.

"I was wondering if you'd like to stay for lunch," Bonnie said.

Hannah looked at Esther, as though seeking her approval.

When Esther nodded, Hannah smiled and said, "That'd be nice."

"Before we eat, though, would you like a tour of my bed-and-breakfast?"

"Yes, I would," Hannah replied. "I've been admiring some of the things you have here in the kitchen, and I'd enjoy seeing what the rest of the house looks like."

Bonnie found a game for the kids to play and situated them on the living-room floor; then she motioned for Esther and Hannah to follow her upstairs.

"I've seen all the rooms many times, so I think I'll stay down here with the children," Esther said.

"That's fine. Since you're up there cleaning every morning, you probably get tired of looking at the rooms."

Esther shook her head. "Not really. I enjoy my work, but I think it's best if I stay with the children."

"I agree," Hannah spoke up. "They might end up coloring everything in Bonnie's kitchen." A hint of a smile crossed her face, and Bonnie was pleased. It was the first time Hannah had seemed this relaxed. Maybe as Bonnie got to know Hannah better, they might even become friends.

Chapter 9

When Hannah and Esther returned from Bonnie's that afternoon, the first thing they did was put the kids down for their naps. All three of them were tired and cranky. Jared and Mindy had screamed and fussed so much on the way home that Hannah thought she would go insane. She'd figured the ride home would lull them to sleep, but it apparently had the opposite effect. They were probably full of sugar from the cookies they'd eaten. Hannah would have to watch Mindy a little closer from now on and make sure she ate properly. She didn't like it when her daughter became hyper.

"I'm going out to the phone shanty to make a call," Hannah told Esther after she'd put Mindy down and made sure she was asleep.

"That's fine." Esther smiled. "While you're doing that, I'll start cutting up the vegetables for the stew I'm going to make for supper this evening."

Hannah frowned. "Actually, I was planning to fix a meat loaf for supper. I saw some ground beef in the refrigerator and thought I'd use it for that."

"Oh, well, Samuel really likes stew, and that's what I told

him I'd make for supper tonight."

Hannah's jaw clenched. Esther and Samuel weren't even married, but she acted like she was in charge of his kitchen. For that matter, she acted like she was in charge of everything in this house, including Samuel's children.

"Will you be staying here to eat supper with us?" Hannah asked.

Esther nodded. "I usually eat supper and then do the dishes before I head back to Bonnie's."

"Now that I'm living here, you won't need to stay."

"Oh, but I want to. I enjoy eating supper with Samuel and the kinner." Esther's cheeks colored. "Unless you'd rather that I didn't join you for supper. If that's the case, I can just fix the meal and be on my way."

Hannah folded her arms. "It's not that I don't want you to stay. I just don't see the need for you to fix supper when I'm perfectly capable of doing it."

"I'm sure you are, but. . ." Esther's voice trailed off. "If you'd prefer to fix meat loaf, that's fine with me."

Hannah nodded in reply then scooted out the back door. She was anxious to call Mom and tell her about Bonnie's B&B. Seeing the antiques there had given her an idea about how she might earn some money. She was eager to tell Timothy about it as well.

When Hannah stepped into the phone shanty, she was pleased to discover a message from her mother. But as Hannah listened to Mom talk about going shopping at Naomi and Caleb's store in Paradise and then eating at Bird-in-Hand Family Restaurant, a wave of homesickness rolled over her. She sat for several minutes, fighting the urge to cry, then finally laid her head on the table and gave in to her tears.

When the tears finally subsided, Hannah dried her face on her apron and headed back to the house, not bothering to return Mom's call. When she stepped inside, she was surprised to see Esther standing in front of the kitchen sink. "Oh, you're still here?"

Esther nodded. "I'll leave as soon as Marla and Leon get home from school."

"Since I'm here to greet them, there's really no need for you to wait."

Esther, looking more than a bit hurt, nodded. "I'll see you tomorrow then."

Not if Samuel agrees to let me watch the kinner, Hannah thought.

~

Bonnie had just taken a pan of cinnamon rolls from the oven, when she heard the distinctive *clip-clop* of horse's hooves. She set the pan on the cooling rack and looked out the kitchen window, surprised to see Esther's horse and buggy coming up the driveway.

"I wonder what she's doing here at this time of the day. I hope nothing's wrong."

Bonnie slipped into a sweater and hurried outside, just as Esther was tying her horse to the hitching rail. "I didn't expect to see you until later this evening. Is something wrong?" she asked.

"Yes, I'm afraid so."

Bonnie felt immediate concern. "What is it?"

Esther's chin trembled as tears welled in her brown eyes. "Hannah doesn't like me, Bonnie. I'm sure of it."

"Did you two have a disagreement?"

"Not exactly. She pretty much told me how it's going to be."

"What do you mean?"

"Hannah let it be known that she'd rather I not stay for supper, and she didn't want me to fix the stew I'd promised Samuel I would make." Esther stroked Ginger's velvety nose, as though needing the horse's comfort. "She thinks my services aren't needed now that she and Timothy are living in Samuel's house."

"That's ridiculous! Samuel hired you to watch the kids, cook meals, clean the house, and do the laundry."

"I know, but now that Hannah's there, I feel like I'm in the way. I'm sure she's quite capable of doing everything I've been doing, and it would save Samuel some money if he didn't have to pay me."

"Have you talked to him about this?" Bonnie questioned.

"Not yet. I was hoping to speak with him this evening, but that was before Hannah practically pushed me out the door."

Bonnie put her arm around Esther and gave her a hug. "Now, don't you give in so easily. You need to talk to him soon, because Hannah has no right to just come in and take over like that."

Esther sniffed and slowly nodded. "I'll go over there a little early tomorrow morning. Hopefully, I can discuss things with him before he leaves for work."

"That's a good idea. In the meantime, you can come up to the house and have supper with me."

Esther smiled. "Thank you, Bonnie. I don't know what I'd do without your friendship."

"You've been a good friend to me, as well." Bonnie shivered, feeling a sudden chill. She hoped Hannah wouldn't do anything to mess things up between Esther and Samuel. They'd already had their share of struggles, and if anyone deserved some peace and happiness, it was them.

Chapter 10

"Where's Esther?" Marla asked when she and Leon arrived home from school.

"She went home." Hannah motioned to the stairs. "You'd better go up to your rooms and change out of your school clothes so you can get your chores done before it's time to eat supper. Oh, and go quietly, please, because the little ones are napping."

Leon looked up at Hannah with a wide-eyed expression. "Esther went home?"

"That's what I said." Didn't the child believe her, or was he hard of hearing?

"But Esther never goes home till after supper." Leon's brows furrowed; he looked downright perplexed.

"That's right," Marla put in. "And after supper, Esther and I always do the dishes together before she goes back to Bonnie's."

Hannah looked directly at Marla. "From now on, I'll be fixing supper, and you can help *me* do the dishes."

Marla opened her mouth as if to say something more, but Leon spoke first. "But what about Esther?"

Hannah sighed. "I just told you. Esther won't be here for supper."

Leon's forehead wrinkled. "But she'll still be comin' in the morning to fix our breakfast and take care of Penny and Jared while we're in school, right?"

"That hasn't been decided yet. I'll be talking to your daed about it when he gets home from work," Hannah said, her irritation mounting. "Since your uncle Timothy and I will be living here until we get our own home, there's no reason I can't watch your brother and sister during the day while you're at school and your daed's at work."

"But Jared and Penny like Esther, and so do we." Marla looked over at Leon, who agreeably bobbed his head.

"I'm sure you do, and you'll have plenty of time to spend with her once she and your daed get married."

Leon's mouth opened wide. "Daadi and Esther are gettin' married? How come nobody told us about it?"

Hannah flinched. *Oh great. Now I've said something I shouldn't have said.* "What I meant to say was that if your daed keeps courting Esther, then I'm sure in time he'll ask her to marry him."

A smile stretched across Leon's face as he hopped up and down and clapped his hands. "That's really good news! I'm gonna ask Daadi to marry Esther right away!"

"That's not a good idea," Hannah was quick to say. "I'm sure your daed will let everyone know once he and Esther have set a date."

"But he might do it quicker if we ask him to." Marla grabbed Leon's hand and gave it a squeeze. "Won't it be *wunderbaar* when Esther's our mamm?"

He nodded vigorously.

"Well, it hasn't happened yet, so you need to keep quiet

about it." Hannah wished she'd never brought the subject up. And she certainly hoped that by the time Samuel married Esther, she and Timothy would be living in their own place, because two women in the same house, each trying to do things her own way, would never work.

—∞—

Hannah had just finished making a tossed green salad when she heard the rumble of a truck coming up the driveway. Looking out the window and seeing Timothy and Samuel climb out of Allen's truck, she hurried to set the table.

A few minutes later, Samuel and Timothy entered the kitchen.

"Mmm. . .it smells good in here, but it doesn't smell like stew," Samuel said, sniffing in the air. "Esther said she'd fix my favorite stew for supper this evening." He glanced around. "Where is Esther anyway? Is she in the living room?"

"No, uh. . .Esther went home, and we're having meat loaf."

Samuel's eyebrows furrowed, and even Timothy shot Hannah a questioning look. "Why'd she go home? Was she feeling grank?" Samuel asked.

"No, she's not sick. I just told her that since I was here she wouldn't need to help with supper and could go home."

"You sent Esther home?" Samuel's eyebrows lifted high, and his voice raised nearly an octave.

Hannah looked at Timothy, hoping he would come to her rescue, but he just stared at her as though in disbelief.

"Well. . .uh, I didn't send her home exactly. I just told her that I could fix supper and that her help wasn't needed."

"What gives you the right to be tellin' Esther that?" A vein on the side of Samuel's neck bulged just a bit.

"That ain't all, Daadi," Leon said, rushing into the room.

"Aunt Hannah said she didn't think Esther would be comin' here in the mornings no more. Least not till the two of you get married."

"Is that so?" Samuel's sharp intake of breath and his pinched expression let Hannah know he was quite upset.

"I. . .I didn't actually say Esther wouldn't be coming over. I just said I'd need to talk to you about it, because I really don't see a need for her to be here when I'm perfectly capable of taking care of your kinner, cleaning the house, and cooking the meals." Hannah's cheeks warmed. "And I mistakenly mentioned that you might marry Esther."

"I do plan to marry her," Samuel said. "But it's not official yet, and I haven't talked to her about a wedding date." He leveled Hannah with a look that could have stopped a runaway horse. "I'd appreciate it if from now on you don't tell my kinner anything they should be hearin' directly from me." Samuel turned and started for the door.

"Where are you going?" Timothy called to him.

"Over to the B&B to speak with Esther!" Samuel let the door slam behind him.

"We need to talk about this," Timothy said, taking hold of Hannah's arm and leading her toward the door.

"What about supper?" She motioned to the stove. "The meat loaf's ready, and I really think we should eat."

"The meal can wait awhile. Let's go out on the porch where we can speak in private."

Before Hannah could offer a word of protest, he grabbed her jacket from the wall peg, slung it across her shoulders, and ushered her out the door.

"Now what gives you the right to send Esther away when you know she's been watching Samuel's kinner?" Timothy asked, guiding her to one end of the porch. "Do I need to remind you that this is Samuel's home, and he's been kind enough to let us live here?"

"You don't need to talk to me so harshly." Hannah's voice whined with the threat of tears.

"I'm sorry, but surely you could see how upset Samuel was. He loves Esther very much and wants her to care for his kinner when he's not at home." Timothy's voice softened some but remained unyielding. "Things shouldn't have to change just because we're living here right now."

Hannah stiffened and started to snivel. "Well, they've changed for me! But I guess you don't care about that."

"I do care, and I hope we can either build or find a place of our own really soon so we can feel settled here in Kentucky," Timothy said. "And Hannah, please turn off the waterworks. There's no reason for you to be whimpering about this. There's no question that what you said to Esther was wrong—especially when those arrangements had been worked out between Samuel and Esther long before we moved here."

"I didn't suggest that Esther leave because I was trying to change anything. I just thought it wasn't necessary for both of us to take care of the house and kinner, and I figured Samuel would appreciate me helping out." Hannah folded her arms and glared at him, wiping tears of frustration away. "And I doubt that I'll ever feel settled living here, because my home is in Pennsylvania, not Kentucky!"

"You've said that before, Hannah, and it's gettin' kind of old." He placed his hand on her shoulder. "Life is what we make it, and unless you're willing to at least try to accept this change and make the best of it, you'll never be happy. I'm tired of our constant bickering, and I'm worn-out from trying to keep the peace between us. You need to focus on something positive for a change."

Hannah stared at the wooden floorboards on the porch; then she lifted her gaze to meet his. "I think I know something that might make me happy—or at least, it would give me something meaningful to do."

"What's that?"

"Esther and I took the little ones over to see Bonnie Taylor this morning, and while we were there, I was impressed with all the antiques Bonnie has."

His forehead wrinkled. "I'm confused. What's that got to do with anything?"

"I was thinking maybe I could start my own business, buying and selling antiques. It would help our finances, and—"

He held up his hand. "You can stop right there, Hannah, because your idea won't work."

"Why not?"

"For one thing, Samuel's barn is full of our furniture, so you wouldn't even have a place to store any antiques. Second, most antiques can be quite expensive, and we don't have any extra money to spend on something that might not sell. Third, I seriously doubt that antiques would sell very well around here."

"What makes you say that?"

"There are no tourists here—at least not like we had in Lancaster County, and there aren't nearly as many people living in this area." Timothy slowly shook his head. "You need to find something else to keep yourself busy, because selling antiques is definitely out—at least for right now. It would be too big of a risk. Now let's get inside and eat supper."

Resentment welled in Hannah's soul. She was getting tired of Timothy telling her what to do all the time, and it didn't surprise her that he'd been against her idea right from the start. He didn't even want to consider it. Was there anything they could agree on, or was this a warning of how things were going to be from now on?

—∞—

Samuel fumed all the way to Bonnie's. *Just who does Hannah think she is, sending Esther home when she should have been taking care of the kinner and sharing supper with us? Hannah has a lot of nerve coming into my house and trying to take things over!* Samuel wondered how his brother put up with a wife like that. Of course, Hannah, being the youngest child and only girl in her family, had always been a bit spoiled. Even back when she was a girl growing up in their community, he'd noticed it. And it didn't help that she was under her mother's thumb, which he knew was why she'd been opposed to the idea of moving to Kentucky in the first place.

I wonder what made Timothy decide to marry Hannah, Samuel thought as he gripped the horse's reins a bit tighter. *It must have been her pretty face and the fact that she could cook fairly well, because Timothy was sure blinded to the reality that Hannah's tied to her mamm's apron strings.*

Samuel drew in a couple of deep breaths, knowing he needed to calm down before he spoke to Esther. He sent up a quick prayer, asking God for wisdom.

By the time he pulled up to the hitching rail in Bonnie's yard, he felt a bit more relaxed. He climbed down from the buggy, secured his horse, and sprinted across the lawn to the guesthouse, where he rapped on the door and called, "Esther, are you there?"

No response.

He knocked again, but when Esther didn't answer, he figured she might be up at the main house with Bonnie.

Hurrying across the lawn, he took the steps two at a time

and knocked on Bonnie's door. Several seconds went by before Bonnie answered the door. "I came to see Esther. Is she here?" Samuel asked.

Bonnie nodded. "We were about to have supper."

"I'm sorry to interrupt, but I need to talk to Esther for a few minutes, if you don't mind."

Bonnie smiled. "Come in. I'll wait in the living room while you two visit."

"Thanks, I appreciate that."

Bonnie turned toward the living room, and Samuel headed for the kitchen.

"Samuel, I'm surprised to see you here. I figured you'd be at home having supper with your family," Esther said when Samuel stepped into the room.

He frowned. "I figured that's where you'd be, too, but when Timothy and I got home, Hannah said you'd come here."

Esther nodded. "I think my being there made her feel uncomfortable. I sensed a bit of tension between us all day."

Samuel pulled out a chair and joined her at the table. "When I go back home, I plan to tell Hannah in no uncertain terms that I want you to keep watching the kinner, and that includes bein' there for supper."

"But Samuel, if it's going to cause trouble with Hannah, maybe it might be best if—"

Samuel shook his head. "It won't be best for the kinner, and it sure won't be best for me." He reached for Esther's hand. "I know it won't be easy for you to deal with Hannah, but I'm asking you to keep working for me and to try and get along with Hannah." He smiled and gently squeezed her fingers. "I'd set a date to marry you right now so you could be with us all the time, but I think we'd better wait till Timothy and Hannah find a place of their own. We have to keep reminding ourselves that these arrangements are only temporary."

Esther's eyes sparkled with unshed tears. "Oh Samuel, let's pray it won't be too long."

—∾—

Timothy stepped outside after the evening meal was finished, while Hannah cleaned up and occupied the children. It felt good to breathe in the fresh air, especially when things had gone downhill after arriving home. He didn't blame Samuel for being upset with Hannah, and he hoped it didn't put a further strain on their living arrangements until they had a place of their own.

Timothy thought about Hannah's desire to sell antiques. He had to admit her eyes had been shining when she'd shared her thoughts with him about it. It was the first time since they'd arrived in Kentucky that Hannah had showed any kind of enthusiasm.

Was I wrong to discourage her? he wondered. *Maybe something like that would help Hannah adjust to her new surroundings. Guess I was wrong for not listening more to what she had to say. I'll think about it more once we're able to get a place of our own. By then, I'll have a better idea of what our expenses will be like.*

For now, though, he should go out to the barn to make sure everything was secured for the evening. He'd wait for his brother and hope he could smooth things over with him, because the last thing he needed was for Samuel to ask them to leave. If he did, where would they go? They sure couldn't move in with Titus and Suzanne in their small place.

Now, don't borrow any trouble, he told himself. *Things will work out. They have to.*

CHAPTER 11

Leaves swirled around the yard, and the wind howled eerily under the eaves of the porch as Hannah stood waiting for Bonnie to pick her and Mindy up. She gazed at the gray-blue sky and the empty fields next to Samuel's place and wished it was spring instead of fall. They were going into Hopkinsville today to do some shopping, so maybe that would lift her spirits. Hannah looked forward to the outing because it had rained every day last week and she was tired of being cooped up in the house with Esther and the children. She'd had to learn how to deal with Esther coming over every day to watch Samuel's children, but it wasn't easy. Esther did things a lot differently than Hannah, but she found if she kept busy writing letters to Mom and cleaning house, the days were bearable. It wasn't that Esther didn't keep the house clean—she just wasn't as structured and organized as Hannah had always been. Many times Esther had tried to engage Hannah in conversation, but since they really didn't have much in common, there wasn't a lot to talk about. They'd worked out an agreement to take turns fixing supper, so at least that gave Hannah a chance to do some cooking, which she enjoyed.

Hannah watched as Esther hung some clothes on the line, using the pulley that ran from the porch to the barn. Mindy must have seen her, too, because she left Hannah's side, darted across the porch, and tugged on Esther's skirt. Esther stopped what she was doing, bent down, picked Mindy up, and swung her around. Hannah cringed as Mindy squealed with delight. It really bothered Hannah to see how Mindy had warmed up to Esther. It seemed like she was always hanging on Esther, wanting to crawl up into her lap to listen to a story, or just sitting beside Esther at the table. This was one more reason Hannah hoped she and Timothy could find a place of their own soon, where she and Mindy could spend more quality time together without Esther's influence. Everyone seemed to love Esther.

Hannah looked away, her thoughts going to Timothy. He'd been keeping very busy helping Samuel. They'd had several indoor paint jobs, which was a good thing on account of the rain. The downside was that most of the jobs were out of town, and by the time the men came home each evening, Timothy was tired and didn't want to talk with Hannah or even spend a few minutes playing with Mindy before she was put to bed. He often went to bed early and was asleep by the time Hannah got Mindy down and crawled into bed herself. Where had the closeness they'd once felt for each other gone? What had happened to Timothy's promise that everything would be better once they had moved? So many things had gotten in the way of what had brought them together in the first place.

When Esther went back inside, Hannah glanced at Mindy, now frolicking back and forth across the porch, amusing herself as she pretended to be a horse. *Your daadi hardly spends any time with you anymore, either. Will we ever be like a real family again?*

Hannah's musings were halted when Bonnie's car pulled into the yard and she tooted her horn. Grabbing Mindy's car seat from the porch, Hannah took Mindy's hand and hurried out to the car.

"Where's Esther?" Bonnie asked when Hannah opened the car door. "Aren't she and Samuel's little ones coming with us today?"

Hannah shook her head. "Jared and Penny have the beginning of a cold, and she thought it'd be best if she kept them in today."

"I guess that makes sense. Is everyone else well?"

"So far, and I hope it stays that way, because I sure don't want Mindy coming down with a cold." Hannah put Mindy's car seat in the back and lifted Mindy into it, making sure her seat belt was securely buckled. Then she stepped into the front seat and buckled her own seat belt.

Bonnie smiled. "I appreciate the fact that you use the seat belts without me having to ask. I know that the Amish don't have seat belts in their buggies, so I sometimes have to remind my passengers to use them when they're riding in my car."

"I've sometimes wished we did have seat belts," Hannah said, "because when someone's in a buggy accident, they're often seriously injured."

Bonnie nodded with a look of understanding. "Getting to know my Amish neighbors has been one of the biggest blessings in my life, and I don't like hearing about accidents of any kind. I pray often for my Amish and English friends, asking God to keep everyone safe."

"Esther mentioned that you're a Christian and that you go

to a small church in Fairview," Hannah said.

"Yes, that's right." Bonnie pulled out of Samuel's yard and headed down the road in the direction of Hopkinsville. "It's a very nice church, and I enjoy attending the services. When my grandma was alive, she and Grandpa used to go to that church."

"Have you ever attended an Amish church service?" Hannah asked.

"Not a Sunday service, but I did go to Titus and Suzanne's wedding, which I understand was similar to one of your regular preaching services."

Hannah nodded. "So what did you think of the wedding?"

"It was nice. Quite a bit different from the weddings we Englishers have, though."

"When you and Allen get married, will it be at the church in Fairview?"

Bonnie's mouth dropped open. "Where did you get the idea that Allen and I will be getting married?"

"Samuel said so. I heard him talking to Timothy about it during supper a few nights ago."

"What did he say?"

"Just that he knew Allen was planning to marry you, and he hoped it'd be soon."

Bonnie gave the steering wheel a sharp rap. "That's interesting—especially since Allen hasn't even asked me to marry him."

"He hasn't?"

"No, but he has dropped a couple of hints along the way."

"Maybe he's waiting for just the right time."

Bonnie kept her focus on the road.

Did I do it again and say something I shouldn't have? Hannah wondered. *Maybe Bonnie doesn't love Allen enough to marry him.*

Oak Grove, Kentucky

"Samuel, I wanted to tell you again how much I appreciate your understanding after we had our little talk concerning Hannah and Esther," Timothy said before hauling one of their paint cans across the living room of the older home they were painting.

"Hey, it's okay. I'm glad we had the chance to talk things out." Samuel smiled. "We're family, and it's important that we all get along, for our sake, as well as the kinners'. It's not good having unspoken tension between us."

"I don't want that either," Timothy said. "Hannah has seemed a little more content this past week, now that she and Esther are taking turns with the cooking. I'm hoping maybe with Hannah getting into some sort of a routine while getting better acquainted with life in Kentucky she'll learn to like it here as much as I do."

"I hope so, too," Samuel said, "because I'm really glad you're here."

"How are things going for you two?" Allen asked Samuel when he entered the house, interrupting their conversation.

"Real well," Samuel replied. "We should have it done before the week is out." He motioned to Timothy, who was kneeling on the floor, painting the baseboard an oyster shell white. "With all the work we've had lately, it's sure good to have my brother's help. Even though Timothy only worked part-time for Zach, he learned some pretty good painting skills."

"I can see that he's doing a fine job." Allen moved closer to where Samuel stood on a ladder. "I'm sure the folks who live here will be glad to hear that all the painting will be finished before Thanksgiving."

"Speaking of Thanksgiving, what are you doing for the holiday?" Samuel asked.

"I'm going over to Bonnie's."

"That's good to hear. I was going to invite you to join us at Titus's house if you didn't have plans."

"I appreciate the offer," Allen said, "but I'm really looking forward to spending the day with Bonnie. We've both been keeping so busy and haven't seen much of each other lately."

Samuel chuckled. "You'll never get her to agree to marry you if you don't spend some time with her."

"I know. That's why I accepted her invitation for Thanksgiving dinner. And if everything goes well, I'll ask her to marry me before the day is out."

Samuel grinned. "Well now, isn't that something? Be sure and let me know how it goes."

"I'd like to hear that news myself," Timothy called from across the room.

Allen nodded. "You two will be the first ones I tell—after my folks, of course. Oh, and I'll also tell your brother Zach, because I'm sure he'll be happy to hear I'm finally willing to give up the single life and have found a woman I want to marry."

Paradise, Pennsylvania

"Johnny, are you sure you don't need my help at the store today?" Sally asked her husband as they sat at the kitchen table eating breakfast. "Since Hannah's been gone, I've been bored and really need something to occupy my time and thoughts."

"Our niece, Anna, and her friend, Phoebe Stoltzfus, are working out really well. I'm not needed there all the time, so you wouldn't find much to do either." Johnny pulled his fingers through the ends of his nearly gray beard. "Makes me wonder if I ought to retire and buy a little place for us in Sarasota. We could live in the community of Pinecraft, where so many Plain folks retire or vacation."

Sally frowned as she shook her head. "Then we'd be living even farther from Hannah. Unless Timothy brought his family down to Florida for a vacation, which I doubt, we'd rarely see them."

He patted her arm. "Now don't look so worried. It was only wishful thinking on my part. I'm not really ready to retire just yet, but when the time comes for me to sell the store, I'd like to move to a place where it's warm and sunny all year."

Sally felt a huge sense of relief. At least she didn't have to worry about that for a while. She picked up her cup of tea and took a drink. "I've been wondering about something."

"What's that?"

"Thanksgiving's just a week away, and I was hoping we could go to Kentucky for the holiday. It would be nice to see Hannah and find out for ourselves how she, Timothy, and Mindy are doing."

Johnny shook his head. "I don't think so."

"Why not?"

"It's too soon for us to pay them a visit. Hannah needs to adjust to living in Kentucky, and seeing us right now might make it harder on her."

"But Johnny, our daughter's miserable. Every time she calls, I can hear by the tone of her voice how distressed she is. And the letter I got from her the other day made me feel so sad, reading how much she misses us and wishes she could come home."

"Just give her more time. She'll get over her homesickness after a while." Johnny gulped down the rest of his coffee, scooted his chair away from the table, and stood.

"I'm not so sure about that. Hannah liked it here in Pennsylvania, and she doesn't like much of anything about living in Kentucky."

"I don't have time to debate this with you right now. I need to get my horse and buggy ready so I can get to the store."

"But you said you weren't needed there."

"I said I wasn't needed as much as before, but there are still some things I need to do. I may have some boxes to unpack and move if the newest shipment came in yesterday afternoon when I left Anna in charge." Johnny grabbed his straw hat, slipped into his jacket, and hurried out the door like he couldn't get out of there soon enough.

Tears welled in Sally's eyes. *I don't think he cares how miserable our daughter is or even how much I miss her. If I thought for one minute that Johnny wouldn't get angry with me, I'd catch a bus to Kentucky and go there for Thanksgiving myself!*

Chapter 12

Fresno, California

Trisha Chandler sat at the head of her small dining-room table, hands folded in her lap, and lips pursed with determination. She'd just shared a delicious noon Thanksgiving meal with her two closest friends, Shirley and Margo, whom she'd met at a widow's support group after her husband died of a heart attack two years ago. As soon as they'd finished eating, she'd given them some news that hadn't been well received. But she wasn't going to let them talk her into changing her mind. No, she'd waited a long time to do something fun and adventurous, and their negative comments were not going to stop her from fulfilling a dream she'd had for several years.

"I've always wanted to travel, and now that the restaurant where I've worked since Dave passed away has closed its doors, I think it's time for me and my trusty little car to go out on the road," Trisha said.

"But it's not safe for a woman your age to be out on her own," Margo argued. "What if something happened to you?"

Trisha grunted. "Nothing's going to happen, and I'm

not that old. I just turned fifty-eight last month, remember? Besides, it doesn't matter how old I am. In this crazy world, there's no guarantee that any of us are ever really safe."

Tears welled in Shirley's blue eyes. Always tenderhearted, Shirley had joined their widow's group six months ago when her husband lost his battle with colon cancer. "After thinking it through a bit more, maybe it's not such a bad idea after all. Truthfully, I wish I could be brave enough to venture out on my own," she said. "We're going to miss you, Trisha, that's for sure."

Trisha gave Shirley's hand a gentle squeeze. "Why don't you come with me? Just think of all the wonderful things we can see."

Shirley shook her head. "I can't be gone for six months, the way you plan to do; my children would never allow it. Besides, I really don't like being too far from home."

Trisha nodded in understanding. "Since I don't have any children, there's really nothing to keep me here."

"Does that mean you plan to sell your condo and be gone for good?" Margo asked, her dark eyes widening.

"Oh no. I'm sure I'll be back."

"You know this really isn't a good time of the year to be driving across the United States," Margo pointed out. "You could run into all kinds of foul weather."

"I've thought about that, but I'll start out in the southern states, and then as the weather warms up in the spring, I'll head up the East Coast and see some of the historical sights."

Shirley took a drink of water. "What about the expense? A trip like that could cost plenty. I don't mean to pry, but can you afford the gas and hotels you'll need along the way?"

"Dave had a pretty good-sized life insurance policy, and I'm sure it'll be more than enough to provide for my needs on this trip I've always dreamed about taking."

Margo leaned forward and leveled Trisha with one of her most serious looks. "And there's nothing we can do to talk you out of it?"

Trisha shook her head determinedly. "I've made up my mind, and I'm confident that God will be with me as I venture out to see some of the beautiful country He created."

Pembroke, Kentucky

"Let's see now. . . . The turkey is in the oven, green beans and potatoes are staying warm on the stove, a pumpkin and an apple pie are in the refrigerator, and the table is set." Bonnie smiled as she surveyed her dining-room table. She'd used a lace tablecloth her grandmother had made many years ago, set the table with Grandma's best china, and placed a pot of yellow mums from Suzanne's garden in the center of the table with pale orange taper candles on either side. Everything was perfect and looked very festive. Now all she had to do was wait patiently for Allen to arrive.

Bonnie moved over to the window and pulled the lace curtains aside. The morning had started out with some fog, but then the fog had lifted and revealed a beautiful day with blue skies and white, puffy clouds, with no rain in sight. It was quite a contrast from the last few weeks when they'd had nothing but gray skies and too many rainy days.

She stepped into the hall to look in the mirror and check her appearance. She'd chosen a pretty green dress to wear today, and her dark, naturally curly hair framed her oval face. Bonnie also wore a cameo pin, one of the few pieces of jewelry that had belonged to her grandmother. She kept the brooch safely tucked away in her jewelry box except for special occasions such as this. A touch of lipstick, a little blush, and some pale green eye shadow completed her look. She'd always been told that she was attractive and didn't need makeup, so she'd never worn much. But it wasn't her natural beauty she hoped Allen was attracted to. She wanted him to see and appreciate her inner beauty as well.

Should I share my past with him today? Bonnie wondered. *Or would it be best to wait for another time? I wish I could just tell him right out, but I'm so afraid of his reaction.* Since she didn't know how he would deal with hearing she'd once had a child, she didn't want to chance spoiling the day—or worse, their relationship.

The closer Bonnie and Allen had become, the more she struggled with her insecurities and fears. Her thoughts and reality seemed to be at odds with each other these days. It was unnerving at times. She would talk herself into telling him, but then her fears got in the way and she'd chicken out.

The sound of a vehicle rumbling up the driveway put an end to Bonnie's musings. She looked through the peephole in the front door and saw Allen's truck pull up to her garage. With a sense of excitement, she waited until Allen stepped onto the porch before she opened the door.

"Happy Thanksgiving!" they said at the same time.

He grinned. "Wow, you look absolutely beautiful!"

"Thanks. You look pretty good yourself," Bonnie said, admiring his neatly pressed gray slacks, light blue shirt, and black leather jacket.

Allen followed her into the house and paused in the hall to sniff the air. "Mmm... Something sure smells good."

She smiled. "Everything's ready, so it's just a matter of putting the turkey on the platter, carving it, and serving things up. Then we can eat."

He handed her his jacket. "I'm starving! If you'll hang this up for me, I'd be happy to cut the bird for you."

"That would be great. I don't know about you, but I've always loved seeing the Thanksgiving turkey sitting in the center of the table. You know, like one of those Norman Rockwell paintings." Bonnie hung Allen's jacket on the coat tree in the hall and followed him to the kitchen. While he carved the turkey, she put the potatoes and green beans into bowls and took them out to the dining-room table, along with some olives, pickles, and the whole-wheat rolls Esther had made for her the day before. She laid a serving spoon next to the spot for the turkey platter. That way they could scoop the hot stuffing right out of the bird and onto their plates.

Oops! Guess I'd better make more room for the turkey, Bonnie thought, as she moved the yellow mums to the far end of the table. Then she returned to the kitchen to make the gravy while Allen finished up with the turkey.

"I think we're all set," Allen said, rubbing his hands briskly together. "For now, I think I've carved off enough meat for the both of us."

"Yes, it looks wonderful, and I'm right behind you with the gravy," Bonnie replied as they started for the dining room.

Once they were seated, Allen took hold of her hand. Bowing his head, he prayed, "Heavenly Father, I thank You for this wonderful meal that's set before us. Bless it to the needs of our bodies, and bless the hands that prepared it. Be with our family and friends on this special Thanksgiving Day, and keep them all safe. Thank You for the many blessings You've given to us. Amen."

Allen opened his eyes, looked at Bonnie, and winked. "As our Amish friends often say, 'Now, let's eat ourselves full!'"

"You carved the turkey, and you're my guest, so you go first," she said, pointing to the golden brown bird. "If you want some stuffing, you can use the large spoon to scoop some onto your plate."

Allen forked a few pieces of turkey onto his plate and got some stuffing as well. Then they served themselves the side dishes. As they ate, they visited about various things that had happened in the area lately. Bonnie noticed that one minute Allen seemed very relaxed and the next minute he seemed kind of nervous and fidgety and would lose his train of thought. She knew he'd been working long hours lately and figured he might be tired or uptight. Hopefully, after he finished eating, he'd feel more relaxed.

"I'm surprised you didn't go to Washington to spend Thanksgiving with your folks," Bonnie said when the conversation began to lag.

"I'd thought about it, but Mom and Dad aren't home right now. Their thirty-fifth wedding anniversary is tomorrow, so they're on a two-week vacation in Kauai."

"I'm sure they must be having a good time." Bonnie sighed. "I've always wanted to visit one of the Hawaiian islands, but I guess it's not likely to happen. At least not anytime soon."

"How do you know?"

"I'm too busy running the B&B. Besides, I'm sure a trip like that would be expensive."

"You never know. You might make it there someday. Maybe sooner than you think." Allen fiddled with his spoon. "What about you? How come you didn't go to Oregon to spend the holiday with your dad?"

"For one thing, I have some guests checking into the B&B on Saturday. Besides, my dad is coming to Kentucky for Christmas, so it's only a month before I get to see him."

Allen smiled, seeming to relax a bit. "That's good to hear. I'm anxious to meet your dad."

"I'm eager for you to meet him, and I'm sure he'll enjoy getting to know you as well."

They sat in companionable silence awhile, finishing the last of their meal. Then Bonnie pushed back her chair and stood. "As much as I hate to say it, I think it's time to clear the table and do the dishes." She motioned to the adjoining room. "If you'd like to make yourself comfortable in the living room, I'll join you for pie and coffee as soon as my kitchen chores are done."

Allen shook his head. "I wouldn't think of letting you do all the work while I kick back and let my dinner settle." He stood. "If we both clear the table and do the dishes together, we'll be done in half the time. Then we can spend the rest of the day relaxing."

"That sounds nice, and I'll appreciate your help in the kitchen."

An hour later, when the food had all been put away and the dishes were done, Bonnie gave Allen a cup of coffee and told him to go relax in the living room while she got out the pies.

"This time I won't argue," he said, offering her a tender smile. He really was a very nice man, and as hard as Bonnie had fought it, she'd fallen hopelessly in love with him.

Allen took the cup of coffee, gave her a kiss on the cheek, and headed for the living room.

Bonnie went to the refrigerator and took out the pumpkin pie and whipped cream. She was on her way to the dining room when she heard Cody barking outside.

"Would you mind checking to see what Cody's yapping about?" she called to Allen. "Sounds like he's in the backyard."

"Sure, no problem." Allen went through the kitchen and opened the back door.

Woof! Woof! Cody rushed in and darted right in front of Bonnie, causing her to stumble. The pie slipped out of her hands and landed on the floor with a *splat*, and the can of whipped cream went rolling across the room, stopping at Allen's feet.

Cody didn't hesitate to lick up the pie, and Bonnie didn't know whether to laugh or cry.

When Allen started laughing, she gave in to the urge, too. "I hope you like apple pie," she said, "because that's the only kind I have left."

"Apple's my favorite anyway, and since the whipped cream came right to me, I can just spray some on," he added, leaning over to pick up the can.

Bonnie didn't know if apple really was Allen's favorite or if he was just trying to make her feel better, but the easygoing way he'd handled the situation helped a lot. Gazing at the pie splattered all over the floor, they both gave in to hysterical giggles.

At last, Bonnie put the dog outside and, with Allen's help, cleaned up the mess on the floor.

"This might not be the most romantic place to say it," Allen said, taking Bonnie into his arms, "but I'd like to spend the rest of my life with you—cooking, cleaning, and getting after the dog."

Bonnie tipped her head and looked up him. "Wh–what exactly do you mean?"

"I mean that I love you very much, and if you'll have me, I want to make you my wife."

Bonnie felt like all the air had been squeezed out of her lungs, and she leaned against Allen for support.

"Can I take that as a yes?" he asked, kissing the top of her head.

"No. Yes. I mean, maybe." She pulled away. "What I really mean is I'd like to think about it a few weeks, if you don't mind."

Allen's forehead wrinkled. "In all honesty, I was hoping you'd say you love me, too, and that you'd be happy to be my wife."

"I. . .I do love you, Allen, but marriage is a lifelong commitment, and I—well, I don't want to make a hasty decision. I'd really like a little time to think and pray about it before I give you my answer."

He nodded slowly. "I guess that makes sense. When do you think you'll have an answer?"

Noticing his disappointment, she searched for the right words as she moistened her lips with the tip of her tongue. "Umm. . . How about Christmas Eve? Would that be soon enough?"

"That's only a month away, so I guess I can hold out that long." Allen lowered his head and kissed her gently.

Dear Lord, Bonnie prayed when the kiss ended. *Help me to have the courage to tell Allen about my past. I'm just not ready to do it today.*

Chapter 13

Paradise, Pennsylvania

"What can I do to help?" Fannie asked when she entered her daughter-in-law Leona's kitchen on Thanksgiving Day.

Leona, red-faced and looking a bit anxious, smiled and said, "I appreciate the offer, because you and Abraham are the first ones here, and I really could use some help." Her metal-framed glasses had slipped to the middle of her nose, and she quickly pushed them back in place. "Would you mind basting the turkey while I peel and cut the potatoes?"

"I don't mind at all." Fannie grabbed a pot holder and opened the oven door of the propane stove, releasing the delicious aroma of the Thanksgiving turkey that was nicely browning. "Mmm. . . Just the smell of this big bird makes me *hungerich*," she said, while reaching for the basting brush lying on the counter to her right.

Leona nodded. "I know what you mean. The smell of turkey has been driving me crazy ever since it started roasting."

"Where are the kinner?" Fannie asked after she'd covered the turkey again and shut the oven door.

"James is out in the barn helping Zach clean out a few of the stalls so the rest of our guests will have a place to put their horses if they'd rather not use the corral."

"That's where Abraham went, too, so he'll probably end up helping them," Fannie said. "Now, where are the girls hiding themselves? I didn't see any sign of them when I came into the house."

Leona pointed to the door leading upstairs. "They're tidying up their rooms so their cousins won't see how messy they can be."

Fannie chuckled. "I guess that's what you can expect with most kinner. Of course, my Abby wasn't like that at all. Even when she was little, she kept her room neat."

"Maybe I should ask her to have a little talk with Lucy and Jean. They might be more inclined to listen to their aunt than they are to me."

"I know what you mean. Someone else usually has a better chance of getting through to our kinner than we do ourselves. And that doesn't change, even when they're grown with families of their own." Fannie motioned to the variety of vegetables on the table. "Would you like me to make a salad from those?"

"I'd appreciate that." Leona placed the cut-up potatoes in a kettle of water and set it on the stove. "Now that I've finished that chore, I can help you cut up the vegetables. Have you heard anything from Timothy lately? I was wondering what he and Hannah will be doing for Thanksgiving."

"I talked to him a few days ago," Fannie replied, reaching for a head of lettuce. "He said they'd be having dinner at Titus and Suzanne's place today."

"Who else will be there?"

"Samuel and his kinner and Esther, as well as Suzanne's

mother, grandfather, brothers, and sisters."

"None of Suzanne's siblings are married yet, right?"

Fannie shook her head. "Nelson's the oldest, and from what Titus has said, Nelson used to court a young woman from their community, but they broke up some time ago because they weren't compatible."

Leona reached for a tomato and cubed it into several small pieces. "If he was thinking about marriage at all, then it's good that he realized before it was too late that she wasn't the right girl for him."

Fannie sighed deeply. "I worry about Timothy, because I don't think he and Hannah are compatible. They've struggled in their marriage almost from the beginning."

"A lot of that has to do with Hannah's mamm, don't you think?"

"I'm afraid so. Sally King is a very possessive woman, and she's clung to Hannah ever since she was born. Hannah's always turned to her mamm when she should've been turning to her husband."

"Moving to Kentucky has put some distance between mother and daughter, so maybe things will improve for Hannah and Timothy with Sally out of the picture."

"I certainly hope so." Fannie stopped talking long enough to shred some purple cabbage. "I saw Sally at the health food store the other day, and she was really depressed because Johnny said they couldn't go to Kentucky for Thanksgiving."

"Did he give a reason?"

"Said he thought it was too soon—that they needed to give Hannah and Timothy some time to adjust to their new surroundings before making a trip there."

"Did Sally accept his decision?" Leona asked.

"I guess so. She said they'd be having Thanksgiving at one

of their son's homes, but I could see that she was pining for Hannah."

Leona reached for a stalk of celery. "I hope I never interfere in my girls' lives once they get married. I wouldn't want my future son-in-law to move away because he felt that I was coming between him and his wife."

Fannie shook her head. "I doubt that would ever happen, Leona. You and Zach are raising your kinner well, and you're not clingy with them the way Sally is to Hannah."

Leona smiled. "Danki. I appreciate hearing that."

The sounds of horses' hooves and buggy wheels crunching on the gravel interrupted their conversation.

"Looks like more of the family has arrived," Leona said, looking out the window. "I see Naomi and Caleb's buggy pulling in, and behind them is Nancy and Mark's rig."

Fannie smiled. It would be good to spend the holiday with some of their family. The only thing that would make it any better would be if Samuel, Titus, Timothy, and their families could join them.

Maybe next year we can all be together, she thought. *And when Esther and Samuel get married, I'm sure most of us will go for the wedding, so that's something to look forward to.*

—ѡ—

Pembroke, Kentucky

"If everything tastes as good as it smells, I think we're in for a real treat," Timothy said as he and the rest of the family gathered around the two tables that had been set up in Suzanne and Titus's living room. Even though their double-wide manufactured home was short on space, Suzanne had wanted to host the meal, and it was kind of cozy being together in such a crowded room. Fortunately, it was a crisp but sunny fall day, and the kids could go outside to play after the meal. That would leave enough room for the adults to sit around visiting or playing board games.

"You're right about everything smelling good," Titus said. "I think the women who prepared all this food should be thanked in advance."

All the men bobbed their heads in agreement.

"And now, let us thank the Lord for this food so we can eat," Suzanne's grandfather said.

The room became quiet as everyone bowed their heads for silent prayer. Timothy recited the Lord's Prayer; then he thanked God for the meal they were about to eat and for all his family in Kentucky, as well as in Pennsylvania.

When the prayers were finished and all of the food had been passed, everyone dug in.

"Yum. This turkey is so moist and flavorful," Suzanne's mother, Verna, said. She smiled at Esther. "You did a good job teaching my daughter to cook, and we all thank you for it."

Suzanne's cheeks colored, and Titus chuckled as he nudged her arm. "That's right, and my fraa feeds me so well I have to work twice as hard in the woodshop to keep from getting fat."

Everyone laughed—everyone but Hannah. She sat staring at the food on her plate with a placid look on her face. Timothy was tempted to say something to her but decided it would be best not to draw attention to his wife's sullen mood. No doubt she was upset that her folks didn't come for Thanksgiving, but she should have put on a happy face today, if only for the sake of appearances. It embarrassed Timothy to have Hannah pouting so much of the time. Just when he thought she might begin to adjust, something would happen, and she'd be fretful again. He worried that some people might think he wasn't a good husband because he couldn't make his wife happy. Well, it wasn't because he hadn't tried, but nothing he did ever seemed to be good enough for Hannah. He worried that it never would. What if he'd made a mistake forcing her to move? What if she never adjusted to living in Kentucky and remained angry and out of sorts? Was moving back to Pennsylvania the only way to make his wife happy?

But if we did that, we'd be right back where we were before we left. Hannah would be over at her mamm's all the time, and I'd be fending for myself. If we could just find a place of our own, maybe that would make a difference. Hannah might be happier if we weren't living at Samuel's, and if we weren't taking up space in Samuel's house, he and Esther could get married and start a life of their own.

"Hey, brother, did ya hear what I said?"

Timothy jumped at the sound of Titus's voice. "Huh? What was that?"

"I asked you to pass me the gravy."

"Oh, sure." Timothy took a little gravy for himself and then handed it over to Titus.

"I thought about inviting Bonnie to join us for dinner," Suzanne spoke up, "but Esther said Bonnie had invited Allen to eat at her place today."

"Allen could have joined us here, too," Titus said. "He knows he's always welcome in our home."

Samuel cleared his throat. "Well, I probably shouldn't be broadcasting this, but I happen to know that Allen had plans to propose to Bonnie today."

"Oh, that's wunderbaar," Esther said. "I can hardly wait until I see Bonnie tomorrow morning and find out what she said."

"She'll say yes, of course." Titus grinned. "I mean, why

wouldn't she want to marry a nice guy like Allen?"

"Speaking of Allen," Samuel said, looking at Timothy, "did he say anything to you about the house that's for sale over in Trigg County, near Cadiz?"

Timothy shook his head. "What house is that?"

"It's a small one, but I think it could be added on to. Allen went over to look at it the other day because the owners were thinking of remodeling the kitchen before they put it up for sale, and they wanted him to give them a bid."

Timothy looked at Hannah. "What do you think? Should we talk to Allen about this and see if he can arrange for us to look at the place?"

Hannah shrugged, although he did notice a glimmer of interest in her eyes. Maybe this was God's answer to his prayers. While he wasn't particularly fond of the idea of living thirty-seven miles from his brothers, he was anxious for them to find a place they could call home.

"All right, then," Timothy said. "Tomorrow morning I'll talk to Allen about showing us the house."

Hannah said nothing, but she did pick up her fork and eat a piece of meat, and that made Timothy feel much better about the day.

Chapter 14

Esther woke up early on Friday morning and hurried to get dressed so she could get up to the main house and speak to Bonnie. She found her friend sitting at the kitchen table with a cup of tea.

"I wasn't sure if I'd see you this morning," Bonnie said, looking up at Esther. "Since I don't have any guests checking into the B&B until tomorrow, I figured I wouldn't see you until this evening."

"I wanted to find out how your Thanksgiving dinner with Allen went."

Bonnie smiled. "It was nice. At least I didn't burn anything."

"I didn't think you would. You've gotten pretty efficient in the kitchen."

"Yes, but I'll probably never be as good a cook as you." Bonnie's face sobered. "The pumpkin pie I made got ruined."

"Oh no! What happened?"

"Cody was outside barking, and when Allen opened the door to see what the dog was yapping about, Cody came running in." Bonnie chuckled. "After that, it was like watching a comedy act. I tripped, the pie went flying, and the can of whipped cream rolled across the room and landed at Allen's feet. Afterward, we just stood there, laughing like fools. Fortunately, I'd also made an apple pie, or we wouldn't have had any dessert at all."

"Oh my. I can almost picture it." Esther laughed. "That sounds terrible and funny at the same time."

Bonnie nodded. "But the day ended on a good note, because Allen asked me to marry him."

Esther clapped her hands. "Oh, that's such good news. I hope you said yes."

Bonnie shook her head. "I told him I needed to think about it for a few weeks."

"What's there to think about? You love Allen, and he loves you. I think you'll be very happy together."

"I still haven't told him about my past, and I'm not sure I can do it."

"Of course you can. Allen's a good man; he'll understand."

"Maybe, but I'm afraid to take the chance."

"What are you going to do?"

"I'm not sure. I told Allen I'd have an answer for him by Christmas Eve, so if I'm going to tell him about the baby I adopted out when I was a teenager, I'll need to do it before I agree to marry him." She groaned. "It wouldn't be right to wait until after we're married and then spring the truth on him."

"No, and it wouldn't be right to keep the truth from him indefinitely either."

"Guess I need to pray a little more about this and ask the Lord to give me the courage to tell Allen the truth," Bonnie said, while warming her hands on the teacup.

Esther smiled. "I'll be praying for you, too."

"Thanks, I appreciate that." Bonnie motioned to the teapot.

"I don't know where my manners are. Would you like to have a cup of tea?"

"That sounds nice. Since we don't have to do any baking this morning, there's plenty of time for me to sit and visit awhile."

"How was your Thanksgiving?" Bonnie asked after Esther had poured herself a cup of tea and taken a seat.

"The food was delicious." Esther frowned. "But Hannah was in a sullen mood most of the day, and that made us all a bit uncomfortable."

"I'm not surprised," Bonnie said. "With this being the first holiday she's spent away from her family, she probably felt sad."

"I suppose so, but I dread going over to Samuel's today, because Hannah might still be in a bad mood. I realize that she misses her family in Pennsylvania, but I wonder if the family she has right here will ever be good enough for her."

"I'm sure she'll adjust eventually," Bonnie said. "Time heals all wounds, and it will help if we all try to make her feel welcome. Right now I think what Hannah needs most is friends."

Esther nodded. "That's what I think, too, and I've been trying, but I don't think Hannah likes me. Even though she seems to have accepted the idea of me coming over every day to watch Samuel's children and cook supper every other evening, I think she still resents me. It's like she's turned this into some sort of competition or something."

"Just give her a bit more time, Esther. Once Hannah gets to know you better, she'll come to love you and treasure your friendship as much as I do."

Esther forced a smile. "I hope you're right, because if we're going to be sisters-in-law, I wouldn't want any hard feelings between us."

Hannah glanced at the battery-operated clock on the far kitchen wall and frowned. The men had left early this morning for a job in Elkton, which meant she'd had to get up early in order to fix breakfast and pack their lunches. In a few minutes, the children would be getting up, and then she'd have to fix their breakfast as well. Why was it that Esther always seemed to be late on the days she was needed the most?

Not that I really want her to be here, Hannah thought as she reached for her cup of coffee and took a sip. *It's just not fair that I should have to be responsible for two men and five children—four who aren't even my own.*

She tapped her fingers along the edge of the table. *If I wasn't here right now, and Esther was late, I wonder what Samuel would think about that. Was she ever late before we came to live here? Should he really be thinking of making her his wife?*

"For goodness' sake," she said aloud. "I don't even know what I think anymore. It wasn't long ago that I didn't want Esther here at all. Now I'm complaining that she's not here to help me."

Hannah got up from the table and moved over to the window, letting her thoughts focus on yesterday and the close friendship she'd noticed between Suzanne and Esther. It seemed like they had their heads together, laughing and talking, most of the day. Again, she found herself wishing for a friend—someone with whom she could share her deepest feelings and who wouldn't criticize her for the things she said or did—someone she could be close to the way she had been with Mom.

Oh, how she wished her folks could have joined them for Thanksgiving, but maybe they could come for Christmas. She hoped she, Timothy, and Mindy would be living in their own place by then. The house Allen had mentioned to Timothy might be the one. Hannah hoped they could look at it soon, because she really wanted to be moved out of Samuel's house before Christmas.

Chapter 15

What time will Allen be here?" Hannah asked as she, Timothy, and Samuel sat at the kitchen table drinking coffee on Saturday morning.

"Said he'd be here by nine o'clock." Timothy glanced at the clock. "So we have about ten more minutes to wait."

Hannah rose from her chair. "I'd better get Mindy's coat on so we can be ready to go as soon as he arrives."

Timothy shook his head. "I don't think taking Mindy with us to look at the house is a good idea."

Hannah quirked an eyebrow. "Why not?"

"We need to concentrate on checking out the house that Allen's found, and having Mindy along would be a distraction. You know how active she can be sometimes."

Hannah pursed her lips. "We can't expect Samuel to watch her. He'll have enough on his hands watching his own kinner today."

"I don't mind," Samuel spoke up. "Penny and Marla will keep Mindy entertained, and she shouldn't be a problem at all. The kids are all playing upstairs right now, so they'll probably keep right on playing till they're called down for lunch."

Hannah tapped her foot as she contemplated what Samuel

had said. He was pretty good with his children, so maybe Mindy would be okay left in his care. "Well, if you're sure you don't mind. . ."

Samuel shook his head. "Don't mind a bit."

"Okay, we'll leave Mindy here." Hannah glanced at the clock again. It was almost nine, and still no Allen. She really wished he'd show up so they could be on their way. And oh how she hoped the house he'd be taking them to see was the right one for them.

"Take a seat and have some more coffee," Timothy said, motioning to her empty chair. "Allen's probably running a little late this morning. I'm sure he'll be here soon."

With a sigh, Hannah reluctantly sat down. She'd only taken a few sips of coffee when she heard Allen's truck pull in. "Oh good, he's here," she said, jumping up and peeking out the kitchen window. "I'll get my shawl."

"Guess I'd better wear a jacket," Timothy said, rising from his seat. "When I went out before breakfast to help Samuel and Leon with the chores, I realized just how cold it is out there."

"Jah," Samuel said with a nod. "Wouldn't surprise me if we got some snow pretty soon."

Hannah wrinkled her nose. "I hope not. I'm not ready for snow."

"Well, the kinner might not agree with you on that." Samuel chuckled. "I think they'd be happy if we had snow on the ground all year long."

Hannah wrapped her shawl around her shoulders, set her black outer bonnet on her head, and hurried outside without saying another word. She had thought about going upstairs to tell Mindy good-bye but decided it would be best if she snuck out the back door. If she'd gone upstairs and Mindy started crying, she would have felt compelled to take her with them, which, of course, might have caused dissension between her and Timothy.

"Are you sure you don't mind driving us all the way to Cadiz?" Timothy asked Allen after they'd gotten into his truck.

Allen shook his head. "I don't mind a bit, and it's really not that far. Maybe when we're done looking at the house we can stop in Hopkinsville for some lunch."

"That sounds nice," Hannah was quick to say, "but Samuel might need some help fixing lunch for the kinner, and since today is Esther's day off, he'd probably appreciate me being there to help." Truth was, Hannah doubted Samuel's ability to fix a nutritious lunch for the children. He'd probably give them whatever they asked for instead of what they needed.

"Eating lunch at a restaurant sounds good to me," Timothy spoke up, looking straight at Hannah. "And I'm sure Samuel can manage to fix something for the kinner just fine."

Hannah was tempted to argue the point but didn't want to make a scene in front of Allen. "Okay, whatever," she said with a nod. She supposed it wouldn't hurt Mindy to have an unhealthy lunch once in a while. Forcing herself to relax, Hannah focused on the passing scenery as they headed for Trigg County.

Sometime later, Allen turned off the main road and onto a dirt road—more of a path, really. "The house is just up ahead," he said, pointing in that direction.

A few minutes later, a small house came into view. *It's too small for our needs,* Hannah thought at first glance, *but I suppose it could be added on to. Well, I'll give it the benefit of the doubt—at least until we've seen the inside of the place.*

As Tom Donnelson, the real estate agent, showed them through each room of the house, all Timothy could think was, *This place is way too small.* The kitchen, while it had been recently remodeled, didn't have a lot of cupboard space. He didn't see any sign of a pantry, either, which would have helped, since the cabinet area was so sparse. The living room and dining room were both small, too, and there were only three bedrooms. If he and Hannah had more children, which he hoped they would someday, a three-bedroom house wouldn't be large enough—especially if any overnight guests came to visit. They would definitely have to add more bedrooms to the house, as well as enlarge the living room and kitchen. And of course, since this was an Englisher's home, they would have to take out all the electrical connections.

The other thing that bothered Timothy was the distance between Trigg and Christian Counties. If they moved here, they'd have to hire a driver every time they wanted to see Samuel, Titus, and their families. And how would that work with him working with Samuel? It would be inconvenient and costly to hire a driver every day for such a distance, not to mention the miles his brothers would have to travel if they helped him with renovations on the small house. It would be expensive for Titus and Samuel to get someone to bring them here whenever they came to visit, too, and he wouldn't feel right about putting that burden on his brothers.

Timothy glanced at Hannah, hoping to gauge her reaction to the place. She'd commented on how nice it was to see new cupboards in the kitchen and bathroom and even said how convenient it would be to have everything on one floor. If she liked it here, it would be hard to say no to buying it, because keeping Hannah happy in Kentucky would mean she'd be less likely to hound him about moving back to Pennsylvania. *Is this a sacrifice I'd be willing to make?* he asked himself.

"The owners are motivated to sell," Tom said. "So I'm sure

they'd be willing to consider any reasonable offer."

Timothy looked at Hannah, but she said nothing. It wasn't like her not to give her opinion—especially on something as important as buying a house.

Timothy cleared his throat, searching for the right words. "I. . .uh. . .think my wife and I need to talk about this, but we appreciate you taking the time to show us the place."

Tom rubbed the top of his bald head. "Sure, no problem. Just don't take too much time making a decision, because as nice as this place is, I don't think it'll be on the market very long."

"We'll get back to you as soon as we can." Timothy ushered Hannah out the door and into Allen's truck, where he'd been waiting for them.

"That didn't take too long," Allen said. "So, what'd you think of the house?"

Timothy glanced at Hannah, but she didn't say a word—just sat with her hands folded in her lap, looking straight ahead.

"Well, uh. . . It's a nice little house, but I'm not sure it's the right one for us," Timothy said. "I can see we'd be sinking a lot of money into the place just to enlarge it for our needs."

Hannah released a lingering sigh. "Oh, Timothy, I totally agree."

"You do?"

She nodded vigorously. "The place is way too small, and it's so isolated out here. I wouldn't think you'd want to be this far from your brothers either."

A sense of relief flooded over Timothy. She was as disappointed in the place as he was. Even so, she was probably unhappy that they would have to continue living with Samuel for who knew how much longer.

"It's okay," he said, whispering in Hannah's ear. "I'm sure

some other place will come up for sale, and hopefully it'll be closer to home."

"Home?" She tipped her head and looked at him curiously.

"What I meant to say was, closer to Samuel and Titus's homes."

"It'll need to be a much larger house and not so isolated." Her lips compressed, and tiny wrinkles formed across her forehead. "I think I'd go crazy if we moved way out here."

"Not to worry," he said, resting his hand on her arm. "We'll wait till we find just the right place. Anyway, we can consider this as a practice run in knowing what we need to look for. Live and learn, right?"

Hannah gave a quick nod; then she leaned her head against the seat and closed her eyes. Was she still hoping he'd give up on the idea of living in Kentucky and move back to Pennsylvania? Well, if she was, she could forget that notion.

Chapter 16

Hannah glanced out the kitchen window and grimaced. It had started snowing last night and hadn't let up at all. Christmas was just two weeks away, and if the weather turned bad, it could affect her folks' plan to come for the holiday. Timothy's parents were planning to come, too. In fact, their folks planned to hire a driver and travel together. Andy Paulsen, the driver they'd asked, was single, owned a nice-sized van, and had some friends who lived in Hopkinsville, so it was the perfect arrangement.

Hannah wondered if Timothy was as anxious to see his folks as she was hers. It was different for Timothy; he had family here. She didn't. He never talked about home the way she did either, so maybe he was happy just being here, where he could see his twin brother and Samuel whenever he wanted. Despite a bit of competition between Timothy and Titus, they'd always been very close. Hannah remembered one evening when she and Timothy were courting that Titus, who liked to play pranks, had taken her home from a singing, pretending to be Timothy. Since it was dark and she couldn't see his face well, he'd managed to fool her until they got to her house and one of the barn cats had rubbed against his leg when he was helping Hannah out of the buggy. He'd hollered at the cat and called it a stupid *katz,* something Timothy would never have done. Hannah knew right away that she'd ridden home with the wrong brother.

She chuckled as she thought about how she'd decided to play along with the joke awhile and had picked up the cat and thrust it into Titus's arms. When the cat stuck its claws into Titus's chest, the joke ended.

"What's so funny?"

Hannah whirled around. "Ach, Esther, you shouldn't sneak up on me like that."

"I didn't mean to frighten you," Esther said apologetically. "I just came into the kitchen to check on the soup I've got cooking and saw you standing in front of the window laughing. I thought something amusing must be going on outside."

Hannah shook her head. "The only thing going on out there is a lot of snow coming down."

Esther stepped up to the window. "It doesn't seem to be letting up, does it?"

"Do you get much snow in this part of Kentucky?" Hannah asked.

"Some years we do. Other times we hardly get any at all." Esther motioned to the window. "If this is an indication of what's to come, we might be in for a bad winter this year."

Hannah frowned. "I hope not. The weather needs to be nice so Timothy's folks and mine can get here for Christmas."

Esther smiled. "From what Samuel's told me, his folks are really excited about coming, so it would probably have to be something bad like a blizzard to keep them at home. Maybe the snow will stick around, if it stays cold enough, and give us a white Christmas."

"My parents are looking forward to coming here, too, and

I guess if this is the only snow we get until they arrive, it would be nice to have it around for Christmas."

"Can we go outside and play in the *schnee*?" Penny asked as she, Jared, and Mindy raced into the kitchen.

"That sounds like fun," Esther said. "And when you're done playing in the snow, you can come inside for a warm bowl of chicken noodle soup."

Jared and Penny squealed, jumping eagerly up and down.

"Schnee! Schnee!" Mindy hollered, joining her cousins in their eagerness to play in the snow.

Hannah put her finger to her lips. "Calm down." She looked at Esther. "I'm sure it's frigid out there, and I don't think any of them should go outside to play."

"They'll come in if they get too cold," Esther said.

Hannah shook her head. "I don't want my daughter getting cold and wet."

"I understand that, but I don't think a few minutes in the snow will hurt her any. I'm sure when you were little you loved the snow. Didn't you?"

"Jah, but I was never allowed to play in it very long because my mamm always worried about me getting chilled."

"Please. . .please. . .can Mindy go outside with us to play?" Penny pleaded.

All three children continued to jump up and down, hollering so loudly that Hannah had to cover her ears. "Oh, all right," she finally agreed. "But I'm going outside with you, because I want to make sure Mindy doesn't wander off or slip in the wet snow and get hurt."

"I think I'll turn down the stove and join you," Esther said. "It's been awhile since I frolicked in the snow."

—ꝏ—

After all the fuss, Esther was surprised to actually see Hannah laughing and romping around in the snow like a schoolgirl.

She even showed the children how she liked to open her mouth and catch snowflakes on the end of her tongue.

"This is *schpass*!" Penny shouted as she raced past Esther, slipping and sliding in the snow.

"Jah, it's a lot of fun!" Esther tweaked the end of Penny's cold nose. "Should we see if there's enough snow on the ground to make a snowman?"

All three children nodded enthusiastically, and even Hannah said it sounded like fun.

Hannah helped Mindy form a snowball, and they began rolling it across the lawn while Esther helped Jared roll another snowball. Since Penny was a bit older, she was able to get a snowball started on her own.

As the children worked, they giggled, caught more snowflakes on their tongues, and huffed and puffed as their snowballs grew bigger. Esther was pleased to see Hannah actually enjoying herself. It was the first time she'd seen this side of Hannah. Maybe she was warming up to the idea of living here. There might even be a possibility that the two of them could become friends. It wasn't that Esther needed more friends; she had Suzanne and Bonnie. But Hannah needed a friend, and if she could act happy and carefree like she was doing now, she'd probably make a lot of friends in this community. Unfortunately, though, since Hannah had arrived in Kentucky, her actions had made her appear standoffish.

After they finished building the snowman, Esther suggested they look for some small rocks to use for the snowman's eyes and buttons for his chest.

The children squatted down in an area where some dirt was showing and started looking for rocks, and Esther joined them.

"Maybe I should run inside and check on the soup,"

Hannah said. "Just to be sure it's not boiling over."

"I turned the stove down, so I'm sure it's fine." Esther reached for a small stone she thought would be perfect for one of the snowman's eyes. "And Hannah, I just thought of something."

"What's that?"

"I was wondering what your thoughts are on the two desserts I'm hoping to make for Christmas."

"What did you have in mind?" Hannah asked.

"One of the things I wanted to make is pumpkin cookies, because I know Samuel and the kinner like them. I also found a recipe for Kentucky chocolate chip pie, and I was thinking of trying that, too. I've never made it before, but it sounds really good."

"I could make the pie if you like," Hannah said. "I'm always looking for new recipes to try."

"That'd be great." Esther was glad Hannah had made the offer. It was what she'd been hoping for. Maybe baking together would bridge the gap that still seemed to be between them.

Hannah smiled. "Timothy loves anything with chocolate chips in it, so I know at least one person who'll be eager to try out the pie. That is, if it turns out okay."

"You're a good cook, so I'm sure it'll turn out fine." Esther felt hopeful. She was glad today had been going so well.

"I can only hope so. Now, I think somebody ought to check on that soup," Hannah said. "So, if you'll keep a close eye on Mindy, I'll go do that."

"Sure, no problem." Esther glanced up at Hannah to make sure she'd heard her, and when Hannah turned and headed into the house, she continued to look for more rocks.

Esther was only vaguely aware that Jared and Mindy had

begun chasing each other around the yard, until she heard a bloodcurdling scream.

Dropping the rock she'd just found, she hurried across the yard, where Mindy stood holding her nose. Blood oozed between Mindy's gloved fingers and trickled down the sleeve of her jacket. The children had obviously collided. So much for fun in the snow!

Just then, Hannah rushed out of the house. Seeing Mindy's bloody nose, she glared at Esther. "What happened?"

"The children were running, and I think Jared and Mindy collided with each other," Esther said.

Hannah knelt down to take a look at her daughter's nose. "I thought you promised to keep an eye on Mindy for me," she said, taking a tissue from her jacket pocket and holding it against Mindy's nose. "If you'd been watching her, Esther, this wouldn't have happened!"

"I'm sorry," Esther said above Mindy's sobbing.

Hannah grabbed Mindy's hand and ushered her into the house.

That's just great, Esther thought. *Things were going so well between Hannah and me. Now this is one more thing for Hannah to complain to Samuel about when he gets home from work tonight. If Hannah and Timothy don't move into a place of their own soon, Hannah will probably have Samuel convinced that I'm not fit to be his wife or the kinner's stepmother.*

Chapter 17

Branson, Missouri

"Is this your first time here?" an elderly woman with silver-gray hair asked Trisha as she took her seat in one of the most elaborate theaters in Branson. She'd gone to the women's restroom before entering the theater and was surprised to see that even it was ornately decorated.

Trisha nodded, feeling rather self-conscious. "Does it show?"

The woman chuckled. "Just a little. I couldn't help but notice the look of awe on your face as you surveyed your surroundings. It is quite beautiful, isn't it?"

"It is a magnificent theater," Trisha said. "I've never seen anything quite like this before."

"You know the old saying, 'You ain't seen nothin' yet'? Well, you just wait until you see this show. The star attraction is a violinist, and his Christmas show is absolutely incredible. I've seen him perform before, and I guarantee you won't be disappointed."

Trisha smiled in anticipation. "I'm looking forward to it."

"So, are you here alone?"

Trisha nodded. "I'm from California, and I'm making a trip across the country to take in some sights I've always wanted to see. After I spend a few days here, I'll be heading to Nashville. From there, I'm going to Bowling Green, Kentucky, to see an old friend."

Just then the show started, ending their conversation. As the curtain went up, Trisha turned her attention to the stage, listening with rapt attention to the beautiful violin music that began the show. So far this trip was turning out well, and she looked forward to spending Christmas with her friend Carla.

Hopkinsville, Kentucky

"I'm so glad the weather's improved and there's no snow on the ground," Hannah said as she and Suzanne pushed their carts into Walmart's produce section. Since it was Saturday, and Samuel and Timothy had volunteered to watch the children, Hannah and Suzanne had hired a driver to take them to town so they could do some grocery shopping and buy a few Christmas gifts.

"It would be nice to have a white Christmas," Suzanne said wistfully, "like the ones I remember from my childhood."

"Esther said the same thing about having a white Christmas. Maybe so, but snowy weather makes it harder to travel, and I don't want anything to stand in the way of my folks coming for Christmas."

"I'm sure their driver will have either snow tires or chains for his van, so driving in the snow shouldn't be a problem. Unless, of course, it became a blizzard."

Hannah nodded. "That's what worries me. I'd be so

disappointed if my folks couldn't come, and I'm sure Timothy and his brothers would feel bad if their folks couldn't make it either."

Suzanne patted Hannah's arm. "Not to worry. I'm sure everything will be fine and we'll all have a really nice Christmas, with or without the snow."

Pembroke, Kentucky

"I've got some good news and some bad news," Timothy said when he returned to the house after checking the messages in Samuel's phone shanty.

"Let's have the good news first," Samuel said, placing his coffee cup on the kitchen table.

"Mom and Dad's message said they're still planning to come for Christmas and they can stay until New Year's."

Samuel grinned. "That is good news. It'll be great to see our folks again, and we'll have plenty of time to visit and catch up on things." He picked up his cup and took a drink. "So, what's the bad news?"

"Hannah's mother left a message saying she and Johnny won't be coming after all." Timothy groaned. "I sure dread telling Hannah about it, because I know she's gonna be very upset. She's been looking forward to her parents' visit for weeks now."

"Why can't Sally and Johnny come?" Samuel asked.

"Johnny injured his back picking up a heavy box at the store. He's flat in bed, taking pain pills and muscle relaxers. Sally has to wait on him hand and foot because he can't do much of anything right now and was advised by his doctor to stay in bed for the time being."

"That's too bad. I remember last year when Allen hurt his back after falling down some stairs. He was cranky as a bear with sore paws and none too happy about his mom coming to take care of him."

"Doesn't he get along well with her?" Timothy asked, taking a seat beside Samuel.

"They get along okay, but from what I could tell, his mom tried to baby him, and Allen didn't go for that at all."

"I guess most men don't like to be babied. We want to know that our women love us, but we don't want 'em treatin' us like we're little boys."

"That's for sure." Samuel reached for one of the cinnamon rolls Esther had baked the day before and took a bite. "So how are you gonna break the news to Hannah?"

"Guess I'll just have to tell her the facts, but I'm sure not looking forward to it." Timothy grimaced. "Hannah's been in a better mood here of late, but I'm afraid that'll change once she hears about her folks."

~

Later that night after Hannah had put Mindy to bed, she and Timothy retired to their room, and she told him what a good time she'd had shopping. "Suzanne and I found all of the Christmas gifts we had on our lists." Hannah smiled, realizing how good it felt to tell Timothy the events of her day. The outing with Suzanne had been just what she needed to vanish some of the tension she'd felt since arriving in Kentucky.

"Oh Timothy, I'm so excited about my folks coming for Christmas. It will be wunderbaar to have all of our parents here for the holidays. I think I actually feel some of that special holiday spirit." Hannah plumped up their pillows, feeling a sense of lightheartedness she hadn't experienced in some time.

But then she noticed a strange look on her husband's face.

"Hannah, I'm really glad you had such a nice day with Suzanne," Timothy said, "but there's something I need to tell you."

"What is it?"

"I wanted us to be alone when I told you this, and there's no easy way to soften the blow, so I may as well just come right out and say it. Your parents won't be able to make it for Christmas."

She hoped she'd heard him wrong. "What do you mean? Why aren't they coming?"

"Your daed hurt his back and won't be able to travel for a while."

"Oh no." She groaned, plopping down on the bed. "I just can't believe it."

"I'm sorry," Timothy said. "I know how disappointed you must be."

Hannah sniffed, trying to hold back the tears that threatened to spill over. "Jah." Her hands shook as she stood and pulled the covers back on the bed. Changing into her nightgown and climbing under the covers, she could almost feel Timothy watching her. Yet he remained quiet as he slid into bed next to her. After a few minutes, she heard his steady, even breathing and figured he must have fallen asleep.

Hannah knew it had probably been hard for Timothy to break the news about her folks not coming, and she was grateful he'd waited until they were alone to do it. But couldn't he have at least given her a hug instead of turning his back on her and falling asleep? Staring at the ceiling and feeling worse by the minute, Hannah realized there was nothing she could do but accept the fact that her folks weren't coming, but that didn't make it any easier.

Poor Dad, she thought as tears slipped from her eyes. *He must be in terrible pain, and both he and Mom are probably just as disappointed as I am that they can't come here for Christmas.*

Hannah rolled over and punched her pillow. *I'll accept it, but I don't have to like it! If I wasn't so far from home, I'd be able to help Mom and Dad right now. If. . . If. . . If. . .* She buried her face in the pillow, trying to muffle her sobs. *Why do things like this always happen to me?*

Chapter 18

"Just look at all that snow coming down. I think it's safe to say that we're gonna have a white Christmas," Timothy said as he and Samuel headed out to the barn to do their morning chores on Christmas Eve. "Sure hope Mom and Dad make it before this weather gets any worse."

"I hope so, too." Samuel's boots crunched through the snow. "This could mean we're in for a bad winter."

"If the snow and wind keep up like this, it could also mean Mom and Dad might have to stay longer than they planned." Timothy glanced toward the road. "I wonder if the snowplows will come out our way today."

"It's hard to say. Guess it all depends on how busy they are in other places."

When Samuel opened the barn door, the pungent aroma of horse manure hit Timothy full in the face. "Phew! There's no denying that the horses' stalls need a good cleaning."

"You're right about that. Guess we should have done them last night, but since we got home so late from that paint job in Hopkinsville, I was too tired to tackle it."

"Same here."

As they stepped into the first stall, Samuel asked, "Do you think Hannah and Esther are getting along any better these days?"

Timothy shrugged. "I don't know. Why do you ask?"

"I was thinking if they were, maybe Esther and I could get married sometime after the first of the year, even if you and Hannah haven't found a house by then."

"I have no objections to that, but I think it's something you and Esther will need to decide." Timothy reached for a shovel. "I know I've said this before, but I really do appreciate you letting us stay with you and giving me a job. You've helped to make things a lot easier for us, which has given me a few less things to worry about."

Samuel thumped Timothy's back. "That's what families are for. I'm sure if the tables were turned, you'd do the same for me."

Timothy gave a nod, although he wasn't sure his wife would be so agreeable about Samuel and his kids staying with them. Hannah was more desperate to find a place of their own than he was, and he figured it was because she wanted to have the run of the house and didn't want to answer to Esther. Of course, if they'd been living with Hannah's folks all this time, Hannah wouldn't have a problem with her mother telling her what to do. And if Sally and Johnny needed a place to live, Hannah would welcome them with open arms.

Ever since he'd given her the news that her folks wouldn't be coming for Christmas, she'd gone around looking depressed and had even refused to do any baking with Esther, saying she wasn't in the mood. Timothy was fairly certain that Hannah didn't know that he'd lain awake for at least an hour after she'd cried herself to sleep that night, not knowing what to say that would make her feel better. He felt even worse because, before he'd given her the news about her folks, she'd seemed upbeat about her day with Suzanne. Had it not been for the bad news, Hannah's day of Christmas shopping might have been a turning point in helping her to be more comfortable with living in Kentucky. Instead, her Christmas spirit had disappeared.

Sure hope Hannah's able to put on a happy face while my folks are here, Timothy thought, gripping the shovel a little tighter. *I don't need to hear any disapproving comments about my wife from Mom. And Hannah's negative attitude won't help Mom any, since she is already none too thrilled about any of her sons living here.*

The whole idea of moving had been to improve their marriage, and if Timothy's mother didn't see any sign of that, he'd probably have more explaining to do. Instead of getting easier, things seemed to be getting harder.

Timothy directed his thoughts back to the job at hand, and after he and Samuel finished cleaning the stalls, they left the barn.

"We must have gotten at least another two inches of snow since we started shoveling the manure," Samuel mentioned as they tromped back to the house.

"I'll say!" Timothy jumped back when a snowball hit him square on the forehead. "Hey! Who did that?" he asked, looking around as he wiped the snow off his head.

"There's your culprit!" Samuel pointed to Leon, sprinting for the back porch. "Come on. Let's get him!"

Leon squealed as Timothy and Samuel pelted him with snowballs.

"That ain't fair! It's two against one!" Leon jumped off the porch, scooped some snow into a ball, and slung it hard. This one landed on Samuel's back.

In response, Samuel turned and pitched a snowball at

Timothy. Pretty soon snowballs were flying every which way, and no one seemed to care who they were throwing them at.

"This has been a lot of fun," Samuel finally said, "but we'd better go into the house and get warmed up."

Timothy, gasping for breath, nodded, but he was grinning as he headed for the house. He felt like a kid again and was sure from the look on his brother's face that Samuel did, too. It had been good to set his worries aside for a few minutes and do something fun. He'd forgotten that playing in the snow could be such a good stress reliever. He'd also forgotten the enjoyment he and Hannah had in the earlier years of their marriage when the first big snowstorm hit Lancaster County. It had only been a few years, yet it seemed so long ago.

Peeking into the oven at the pumpkin cookies, Esther was pleased to see that they were almost done. She planned to serve them this evening, along with hot apple cider. Since Hannah hadn't made the Kentucky chocolate chip pie like she'd planned, Esther had also baked an apple and a pumpkin pie to serve for dessert on Christmas Day.

Esther looked forward to spending Christmas Eve with Samuel and his family, and was glad she could be here at Samuel's all day to help with the cooking and cleaning. She felt sorry for Hannah, though, knowing how disappointed she was over her folks not being able to come. Yet despite Hannah's sullen mood, she was upstairs right now, putting clean sheets on the bed in the guest room. Fannie and Abraham would stay here for a few nights, and since they didn't plan to return home until New Year's Day, they would spend a few nights with Titus and Suzanne. Esther knew Titus, Timothy, and Samuel were looking forward to seeing their folks. She'd hoped her own folks might be able to come for Christmas, but they'd decided it was best to stay in Pennsylvania to be with Sarah and Dan. Esther hoped they'd be able to come for her wedding—whenever that would take place. At the rate things were going, she was beginning to wonder if she'd ever become Samuel's wife.

Esther had been relieved that Hannah hadn't said anything to Samuel about Jared causing Mindy's nose to bleed the other day. If Hannah had mentioned it, then Samuel hadn't brought it up to Esther, which probably meant he either didn't know or didn't blame her. She hoped that was the case, because she didn't want anything to come between her and Samuel.

Esther had just taken the last batch of pumpkin cookies from the oven when Samuel, Timothy, and Leon entered the kitchen laughing and kidding each other.

"Brr. . . It's mighty cold out there," Samuel said, rubbing his hands briskly together.

"And it's snowing even harder now." Timothy rubbed a wet spot on the bridge of his nose. "Sure hope our folks make it here soon, 'cause I can't help but be concerned about them."

"Worrying won't change a thing," Samuel said.

"Your brother's right," Esther agreed. "Whenever I find myself worrying, I just get busy doing something, and that seems to help. It makes the time go by faster, too."

"Guess you're right. While we were out in the snow chasing each other with snowballs, I didn't even think about my worries. But now that I'm back inside, I have a nagging feeling that the weather is going to cause some problems on the roads."

"Well, I don't think it'll bother Mom and Dad," Samuel said with an air of confidence. "They've hired an experienced driver with a reliable van, and I'm trusting God to keep them all safe."

"I need to trust Him, too." Timothy moved across the room toward Esther. "Any chance I might have one of those Kichlin?"

"The cookies are really for this evening, but since I baked plenty, it's fine if you have a few. I'm sure you guys must have worked up an appetite playing out there in the snow. You can let me know if they're any good."

"If they taste as good as they smell, you don't need to worry." Timothy grabbed two cookies. "So, where's my Fraa and *dochder*?"

"Hannah's upstairs making the bed in the guest room," Esther replied. "And Mindy's playing with Samuel's kinner up in Penny's room. I think I heard Leon running up the stairs to join them. No doubt he wants to tell them about that snowball fight you all had."

"Think I'll go up and see how Hannah's doing," Timothy said, holding up one of the cookies. "I know she's feeling pretty down today, so maybe I can cheer her up with one of these." He ate the other cookie he'd taken. "Mmm. . . This is really good, Esther. Think I may need to have a couple more when I come back downstairs."

Esther chuckled. "Just don't eat too many or you'll spoil your appetite for supper."

He wiggled his eyebrows playfully. "After that snowball battle, not a chance."

When Timothy left the room, Esther turned to Samuel and said, "I doubt that one of my cookies will help Hannah. I think she'll be down in the dumps tonight and tomorrow as well."

"You're probably right." Samuel, his hair still wet from the snow, moved to stand beside Esther. "I've been thinking about something," he said, slipping his arm around her waist.

"What's that?" Esther asked as Samuel wiped a drip of water that had splashed from his hair onto her cheek.

"I was wondering how you'd feel about us getting married right after the first of the year."

Esther drew in a sharp breath. The thought of marrying Samuel so soon made her feel giddy. "Oh Samuel, I'd love to marry you as soon as possible, but Timothy and Hannah haven't found a home of their own yet."

"I realize that, but I was hoping we could get married anyway."

"You mean two families living under the same roof?"

He nodded.

"I don't think it would work, Samuel. Hannah and I do things so differently—especially concerning the kinner. It's been hard enough for us to get along with me here just a few hours each day. If I was here all the time, I'm afraid Hannah would resent me even more than she does already. Sometimes things are fine, and other times I can feel the tension between us. It's uncomfortable being constantly on edge."

Samuel nuzzled her cheek with his nose, where the drip of snow had just been. "So would you prefer to wait to get married till after Timothy and Hannah find a place of their own?"

Esther's heart fluttered at his touch. "Jah. As difficult as it will be to wait even longer, I think that would be best."

—∞—

Hannah had just finished putting the quilt back on the guest bed when Timothy entered the room. "What's that you have behind your back?" she asked, blowing a strand of hair out of her eyes.

Timothy held up the cookie. "Thought you'd like to try one of Esther's pumpkin kichlin. They're sure good." He smacked his lips and handed her the treat.

As much as Hannah disliked hearing her husband rave about Esther's cookies, her stomach growled at the prospect of eating one. The whole house smelled like pumpkin, and she had to admit when she bit into the cookie that it was really good.

"You should have seen the snowball battle Samuel and I just had with Leon. Foolin' around in the snow like that made me feel like a kid again." Timothy grinned and kicked off his boots. "Remember when we first got married, how we enjoyed doing things like that?"

"I did see you three down there in the yard," she said, ignoring his comment. "I was watching out the window and thinking how nice it would be if you spent more time with Mindy and played games with her like you did with Leon." Hannah tromped across the room and picked up Timothy's boots. "You should have taken these off downstairs. I hope you didn't track water all the way up the stairs," she grumbled. "Now please take them over to our room and put them on the throw rug. I just got this room all nice and clean for your parents, and now you're dripping water all over the floor."

Hannah watched as Timothy picked up his boots and did as she asked, not saying a word as he walked across the hall to their room. She knew his good mood had evaporated once she'd started lecturing him. But it irritated her to see Timothy have fun with Samuel's son instead of their own daughter. And couldn't he see that the room for his parents was all nice and clean?

"I guess not," Hannah muttered. "Timothy and I just don't see things the same way anymore. Maybe we never did, but it seems like it's gotten worse since we moved to Kentucky."

—w—

Nashville, Tennessee

"It sure is good to see you," Bonnie said as she and her dad left the airport terminal and headed for her car.

He grinned and squeezed her hand. "It's good to see you, too, and I appreciate you coming all this way to pick me up."

"It's not that far, Dad. Besides, this is the closest airport to where I live. I just wish you could stay longer than a few days," she said, opening her trunk so he could put his suitcase inside.

"I do, too, but I need to be back at work by next Monday."

"I'd hoped you might have put in for a few more days' vacation than that."

"Maybe I can come and stay longer sometime this spring or summer." He climbed into the passenger's side and buckled his seat belt.

As they drove toward Kentucky, they got caught up with one another's lives. "I'm really anxious to show you all the changes that have been made to your folks' old house," Bonnie said. "I think Grandma and Grandpa's place makes the perfect bed-and-breakfast."

He smiled. "I'm looking forward to seeing it, too."

As they neared Clarksville, it began to snow, so Bonnie turned on the windshield wipers and slowed down a bit. "It started snowing in Pembroke last night," she said. "And when I left to come to the airport, it was still snowing, but as I got closer to Nashville, it quit."

"I sure didn't expect to see snow on this trip," Dad said. "We haven't had any in Oregon yet."

Bonnie frowned as she stared out the front window. If

the snow kept coming down like it was right now, by this evening it could be a lot worse. She hoped Samuel's folks would make it safely and said a mental prayer for everyone who might be driving in the snow throughout the day.

Chapter 19

Out of politeness, Hannah stood on the front porch, watching as Timothy and Samuel greeted their parents. From the joyous expressions on the brothers' faces, she knew they were happy to see their folks. Fannie and Abraham were equally delighted to be here.

Hannah couldn't deny them that pleasure, but it was hard to be joyful when she missed her own parents so much. Her chin quivered just thinking that at this very moment she could have been greeting her parents as well. She looked away, trying to regain her composure and knowing she'd have to put on a happy face. She'd make every attempt to do it, if for no other reason than for Mindy's sake, because she wanted her daughter to have a nice Christmas with at least one set of grandparents. But she'd only be going through the motions, because inside she was absolutely miserable.

When Fannie finished greeting her sons, she turned to Hannah and gave her a hug. "Wie geht's?" she asked.

"I'm doing okay. How about you?"

Fannie smiled. "I'm real good now that we're here safe and sound."

"That's right," Abraham said, nodding. "The roads on this side of Kentucky are terrible, and we saw several accidents. Fortunately, none of 'em appeared to be serious."

"Let's go inside where it's warmer." Samuel opened the door for his parents. Everyone followed, including Fannie and Abraham's driver, who said he could really use a cup of coffee before heading to his friend's house on the other side of Hopkinsville.

Esther greeted Fannie and Abraham as soon as they entered the kitchen; then she and Hannah served everyone steaming cups of coffee.

"I made plenty of cookies for our dessert tonight, so we may as well have some of them now." Esther smiled as she placed a plate of pumpkin cookies on the table.

"Those look *appenditlich,*" Fannie said, reaching for one.

"You're gonna enjoy 'em." Timothy grinned at his mother. "I already sampled a few, and they are delicious."

"I can vouch for that," Samuel agreed. " 'Course, everything Esther bakes is really good." He smiled at Esther, and the look of adoration on his face put a lump in Hannah's throat. It had been such a long time since Timothy had looked at her that way or complimented her on her baking.

Maybe he doesn't love me anymore, she thought. *If he did, then why'd he force me to move here?* Hannah's mood couldn't get much lower. *Just listen to them. Everybody loves Esther's cookies.* It made her want to escape upstairs to her room. They'd probably be enjoying that Kentucky chocolate chip pie she'd volunteered to make if she hadn't changed her mind about it. But her heart just wasn't in it. Without her parents coming to celebrate Christmas with them, Hannah wasn't in the mood for much of anything. She might try making the pie some other time. Maybe after she and Timothy had a place of their own. If she baked something Timothy really liked, he might compliment her for a change.

Hannah's thoughts were quickly pushed aside when five young children darted into the room. With smiling faces, Fannie and Abraham set their coffee cups down and gathered the children into their arms.

"Ach, my!" said Fannie, eyes glistening. "We've missed you all so much."

"We've missed you, too," Marla said, hugging her grandma around the neck. The other children nodded in agreement.

After all the hugs and kisses had been given out, the children found seats at the table, and Esther gave them each a glass of milk and two cookies.

"That's plenty for Mindy," Hannah said. "If she eats too many kichlin, it'll spoil her supper."

"We won't be eating the evening meal for a few hours yet," Timothy said. "So I don't think a couple more cookies will hurt her any."

Hannah, though irritated, said nothing, preferring not to argue with her husband in front of his parents.

"I'm sorry your folks weren't able to make it." Fannie offered Hannah a sympathetic smile. "We stopped by their place before we left town to pick up the gifts they asked us to bring, and your daed seemed to be in a lot of pain."

"That's what Mom said when I spoke with her on the phone this morning." Hannah blinked against the tears pricking the back of her eyes. Not only was she sad about her folks being unable to come, but she still felt bad that Dad had injured his back, and she wished she could be there to help Mom take care of him.

"I know your mamm was really looking forward to coming here," Fannie said, "but I'm sure they'll make the trip as soon as your daed is feeling better."

"It probably won't be until spring," Hannah said, her mood plummeting even lower. "I'm sure they won't travel when the roads are bad, and I wouldn't want them to."

"Speaking of the roads," their driver, Andy, spoke up, "I'd better head to my friend's house now, before this weather gets any worse."

Timothy and Samuel both jumped up from the table. "We'll get Mom and Dad's stuff out of your van so you can be on your way," Timothy said.

"I'll come with you." Abraham pushed his chair aside and stood.

After the men went outside, the children headed back upstairs to play. "I think I'll go out to the phone shanty and call Bonnie," Esther said. "Her dad is supposed to arrive today, so I want to see if he made it okay." She slipped on her jacket and hurried out the door.

Thinking this might be the only time she'd have to speak with Fannie alone, as soon as everyone else had left, Hannah moved over to sit next to her mother-in-law.

"I know how close you've always been to your twins," she said, carefully choosing her words, "and I'm sure having them both move to Kentucky has been really hard for you."

Fannie nodded slowly. "I never thought any of our kinner would leave Pennsylvania."

"I didn't think they would either—especially not Timothy. I thought he enjoyed painting for Zach and farming with his daed."

"I believe he did," Fannie said, "but Timothy wanted a new start, as did Samuel and Titus."

"I don't like it here," Hannah blurted out, wanting to get her point across. "I want to go back to Pennsylvania, and I was hoping you might talk Timothy into moving back home."

Fannie sat quietly, staring at her cup of coffee. With tears shimmering in her eyes, she said, "I can't do that, Hannah. I've already expressed the way I feel to Timothy, and if I say anything more, it would probably make him even more determined to stay in Kentucky. It could drive a wedge between us that might never be repaired."

Hannah lowered her gaze, struggling not to cry. "Then I guess I'll have to spend the rest of my life being miserable."

Fannie placed her hand on Hannah's arm. "Happiness is not about the place you live. It's about being with your family—the people you love."

"That's right, and my family lives in Pennsylvania."

Fannie shook her head. "When you married my son, you agreed to leave your mother and father and cleave to your husband. You must let go of your life in Pennsylvania and make a new life here with your husband and daughter."

Hannah knew Fannie was right. When she'd said her vows to Timothy on their wedding day, she'd agreed to cleave only unto him. But she'd never expected that would mean moving away from her mother and father and coming to a place where she didn't even have her own home. Maybe if they could find a house to buy soon, she would feel differently, but that remained to be seen.

—w—

"It's nice to meet you, Ken," Allen said when Bonnie introduced him to her father.

"Nice to meet you, too. Bonnie's told me a lot about you." Ken grinned at Bonnie and gave her a wink.

"I hope it was all good," Allen said, taking a seat in the living room next to the Christmas tree.

"Of course it was all good," Bonnie said before her father could reply. She looked over at Ken and added, "Allen's never been anything but kind to me."

Allen smiled. Hearing her say that made him think she might be ready to accept his marriage proposal. The only problem was, he couldn't bring it up in front of her dad. He'd have to wait and hope he had the chance to speak with Bonnie alone at some point this evening. He had even gone over in his mind what he wanted to say when he finally did pop the question.

His gaze went to the stately tree he'd helped her pick out a week ago. It looked so beautiful with all the old-fashioned decorations and even a few bubble lights mixed in with the other colored lights. He wished he'd brought the subject of marriage up to her that day when they'd been alone and in festive moods. But since he'd promised to wait until Christmas Eve, he hadn't said anything.

Tonight Bonnie seemed a bit tense. Maybe she was nervous about her dad being here. It was the first time he'd come to visit since Bonnie had left Oregon and turned her grandparents' home into a bed-and-breakfast. Allen knew from what Bonnie had told him that her dad had lived here with his folks during his teenage years but had hated it. It wasn't the house or even the area he hated, though; it was the fact that he'd been forced to leave his girlfriend in Oregon. When she'd broken up with Ken, he'd blamed his folks for forcing him to move, and once he graduated from high school, he'd joined the army and never returned to Kentucky.

"I have some open-faced sandwiches and tomato soup heating on the stove, so if you're ready to eat, why don't we go into the dining room?" Bonnie suggested.

"Sounds good to me." Allen rose from his chair, and her

dad did the same.

After they were seated at the dining-room table, Bonnie led in prayer and then dished them each a bowl of soup, while Allen helped himself to an open-faced egg-salad sandwich. "These really look good," he said, passing the platter to Ken.

"They sure do. When Bonnie's mother was alive, she used to make sandwiches like these every Christmas Eve. It was part of her Norwegian heritage to make the sandwiches open-faced and garnish them with tomatoes, pickles, and olives."

Bonnie smiled. "And don't forget the fancy squiggles of mustard and mayonnaise Mom always put on the sandwiches."

Allen took a bite. "Boy, this tastes as good as it looks."

"The soup's good, too," Ken said, after he'd eaten his first spoonful. "Bonnie, you've turned into a real good cook."

"I owe it all to Esther," she said. "She's an excellent cook and taught me well. Without her help, I'd never have been able to come up with decent breakfast foods to serve my B&B guests."

"Esther's your Amish friend, right?" Ken asked.

Bonnie nodded. "I'm anxious for you to meet her, but she's with Samuel's family this evening, so you won't get the chance until tomorrow morning."

"Will she join us for breakfast?" Ken asked.

"I think so. Then she'll be going back to Samuel's to spend Christmas Day."

"I hope you intend to join us tomorrow for Christmas dinner," Ken said, looking at Allen.

"Most definitely." Allen grinned at Bonnie. "I wouldn't miss the chance to eat some of that delicious turkey you're planning to roast. The meal you fixed on Thanksgiving was great, so I'm sure Christmas dinner will be as well."

Bonnie smiled. "Thank you, Allen."

As they continued their meal, Allen got better acquainted with Ken. When he wasn't talking, he was thinking about whether he'd get the chance to speak with Bonnie alone. It made him a little nervous, hoping he'd remember what he'd practiced saying all week. Allen thought he was about to get that chance when Bonnie excused herself to get their dessert.

"Would you like some help?" he offered.

"That's okay. Just sit and relax while you visit with Dad." Bonnie disappeared into the kitchen. Allen hoped he'd get a chance to speak to her before the evening was out.

"I hear you're in the construction business," Ken said after he'd taken a drink of coffee.

"Yes, that's right." Allen glanced at the kitchen door, wishing he could be in there with Bonnie. Not that he didn't enjoy her dad's company; he just really wanted to know if she'd made a decision about marrying him.

"How do you like what Bonnie's done with the house?" Allen asked, looking back at Ken. "She's really turned this place into a nice bed-and-breakfast, don't you think?"

"Yes, it's amazing the transformation that's taken place," Ken agreed. "Not that I didn't have faith in my daughter's abilities, but to tell you the truth, this house was pretty run-down, even when I lived here, so I really didn't know what to expect."

Allen smiled. "Your daughter's pretty remarkable."

"Bonnie says you want to marry her," Ken blurted out.

Allen nearly choked. "Well, uh. . .yes, but I didn't realize she'd mentioned it to you."

Ken gave a nod. "Yep. Said she's supposed to have an answer for you soon."

"That's right. Tonight, to be exact."

"Are you planning to start a family right away?"

"I don't know. That's something Bonnie and I will have to discuss—if she agrees to marry me, that is."

"She'll make a good mother, I think. She's older and ready for that now. Not like when she was an immature sixteen-year-old and had to give her baby up."

"Wh–what was that?" Allen thought he must have misunderstood what Ken just said. *Baby? What baby?*

"She was too young to raise a child back then, and with my job at the bank and trying to raise Bonnie alone, I sure couldn't help take care of a baby. So I insisted that she give the child up for adoption."

Allen's spine went rigid. Bonnie had given birth to a baby when she was sixteen, and she hadn't said a word to him about it? What other secrets did she have?

He leaned forward and rubbed his head, trying to come to grips with this news.

"Are you okay?" Ken asked.

"Uh—no. I have a sudden headache." Allen pushed his chair aside. "And I think I'd better go before the weather gets any worse." He rushed into the hall, grabbed his jacket from the coat tree, and hurried out the door. He couldn't get out of there fast enough.

Chapter 20

Bonnie had just placed some slices of chocolate cheesecake on a platter, when she heard the rumble of a vehicle starting up. She went to the window and peered out. It was snowing pretty hard, but under the light on the end of her garage she could see Allen's truck pulling out of the yard.

Now where in the world is he going?

Bonnie hurried into the dining room. Dad sat at the table, head down and shoulders slumped. "I just saw Allen's truck pull out of the yard. Did he say where he was going?"

Dad looked up at her and gave a slow nod. "He's going home."

Bonnie frowned. "Why? What happened?"

"Said he had a headache, but I think it had more to do with me and my big mouth."

"What are you talking about, Dad? Did you say something to upset Allen?"

Dad rubbed the bridge of his nose. "I'm afraid so."

"What'd you say?"

"We were talking about his desire to marry you, and I asked if he wanted children." Dad paused and took a sip of water. "Then I. . .uh. . .mentioned the child you'd given up for adoption."

Bonnie gasped and sank into a chair with a moan. "Oh Dad, you didn't! How could you have told Allen that? It was my place to tell him about my past, not yours."

"I know that, but I figured it was something you had already told him. I mean, if you're thinking of marrying the guy, then you should have told him about the baby."

"I was planning to, but I couldn't work up the nerve, and there just never seemed to be the right time. I would have told him before I'd given an answer to his proposal though."

"Good grief, Bonnie, you can't wait to spring something like that on a man right before you agree to become his wife. What in the world were you thinking?"

Bonnie stiffened. She didn't like the way Dad was talking to her right now—as though she was still a little girl in need of a lecture.

"I'm sorry, honey," Dad said before she could offer a retort. "I wasn't thinking when I blabbed to Allen. I was wrong in assuming you had already told him. I'm sure when he comes here for dinner tomorrow you'll be able to talk things out."

Tears welled in Bonnie's eyes, and she blinked to keep them from spilling over. "I hope so, Dad, because I really want things to work out for us. I love Allen so much."

"Does that mean you're going to accept his proposal?"

She gave a slow nod. "If he'll have me now that he knows the truth about my past."

"I'm sure he just needs some time to process all of this. He loves you, Bonnie. I'm certain of it." Dad pushed his chair aside and stood. "You know, I'm really bushed, so if you don't mind, I think I'll head upstairs to bed."

"That's fine. I'll just clear things up in here, and then I'll probably go to bed, too."

"Things will work out for you and Allen. Just pray about it, honey." Dad gave her a hug. Before he headed up the stairs, he turned and looked back at her. "As I said before, I'm really sorry I blurted all that out to Allen."

Noticing her dad's remorseful expression, Bonnie said, "What's done is done, Dad. I should have told Allen sooner, and it's too late now for regrets."

"It'll work out, honey. You'll see. Allen probably just needs some time to think about it."

"I hope so. Good night, Dad. Sleep well."

"You, too."

After Dad went upstairs, Bonnie remained in her chair, staring at the lights on the Christmas tree. It had helped to hear Dad's reassuring words. Now if she could only believe them. *Does Allen really have a headache, and if so, why didn't he come to the kitchen and tell me himself? Did he leave because he couldn't deal with the truth about my past? Will he be back for Christmas dinner tomorrow? Should I give him a call or just wait and find out?*

—∞—

Trisha squinted as she tried to keep her focus on the road. With the snow coming down so hard, it was difficult to see where she was. This was so nerve-wracking, especially since she didn't have a lot of experience driving in the snow. She figured she should be getting close to Hopkinsville though, where she could get a hotel room and call her friend in Bowling Green to let her know she wouldn't arrive tonight after all but would try to get there tomorrow. At the rate the wind was blowing the snow all around, she began to question where she was. She'd lost service on her GPS and wasn't sure if she was supposed to go straight ahead or turn at the next crossroad.

Maybe Margo was right, she thought. *It might have been a mistake to venture out on my own.*

When a truck swooshed past Trisha's car, throwing snow all over the windshield, she swerved to the right and nearly hit a telephone pole. Heart pounding and hands so sweaty she could barely hold on to the steering wheel, Trisha sent up a prayer as she made a right turn. *Please, Lord, let this be the way to Hopkinsville.*

Driving slowly, with her windshield wipers going at full speed, she proceeded up the road. There were no streetlights on this stretch of road, and she had a sinking feeling she'd taken a wrong turn.

Should I turn around and head back to the road I was on or keep going? she asked herself. *Maybe I'll go just a little farther.*

Trisha saw a pair of red blinking lights up ahead. She slowed her car even more as she strained to see out the window. Then, as she approached the blinking lights, she realized the vehicle in front of her was an Amish buggy. While doing some online research of the area before making this trip, Trisha had learned that there were Amish and Mennonite families living in Christian County, Kentucky. Apparently the Amish in this buggy had been out somewhere on Christmas Eve and were probably on their way home.

Afraid to pass for fear of frightening the horse, Trisha followed the buggy until it turned onto a graveled driveway. It was then that she noticed a sign that read: BONNIE'S BED-AND-BREAKFAST.

Maybe there's a vacancy and I can spend the night, she thought, hope welling in her soul. *Then in the morning, I'll ask for directions to Bowling Green and be on my way.*

Trisha turned in the driveway and stopped her car several

feet from where the horse and buggy had pulled up to a hitching rail. When a young Amish woman climbed down from the buggy, Trisha got out of her car.

"Excuse me," she hollered against the howling wind, "but are you the owner of this bed-and-breakfast?"

The woman shook her head. "I just work here part-time, and I live over there in the guesthouse." She pointed across the yard, but due to the swirling snow, Trisha could barely make out the small building. She could, however, see the large house in front of her, which was well lit and looked very inviting right now. It was obviously the B&B.

"Is the owner of the bed-and-breakfast here right now?" Trisha asked, pulling her scarf tighter around her neck to block out the cold wet flakes that were now blowing sideways from the storm.

"I'm sure she is, but—"

"Thanks." Being careful with each step she took, Trisha made her way across the slippery, snowy yard and up the stairs leading to a massive front porch. As she lifted her hand to knock on the door, a sense of peace settled over her. She had a feeling God had directed her to this place tonight, and for that she was grateful. She just hoped she wouldn't be turned away.

Bonnie had just put away the last of the dishes she'd washed when she heard a knock on the front door. Hoping Allen might have come back or that maybe it was Esther returning from Samuel's, she hurried to the foyer. When she opened the door, she was surprised to see a middle-aged English woman with snow-covered, faded blond hair on the porch.

"May I help you?" Bonnie asked.

"My name is Mrs. Chandler, and I was wondering if you

might have a room available for the night." The woman pushed a lock of damp hair away from her face. The poor thing looked exhausted.

"The B&B isn't open during Christmas," Bonnie said.

"Oh, I see." The woman's pale blue eyes revealed her obvious disappointment, and she turned to go.

Bonnie's conscience pricked her. Like the innkeeper on the first Christmas Eve, could she really fail to offer this person a room? Thankfully, she could provide something much better than a lowly stable.

"Don't go; I've changed my mind," Bonnie called as the woman walked toward the stairs. "I have a room you can rent. This weather isn't fit for anyone to be out there—especially if you aren't familiar with the area. Come on in and warm up."

The woman turned back, and a look of relief spread across her face as she shook the snow out of her hair and entered the house. "Oh, thank you. I appreciate it so much. You're right. The roads are horrible, and I didn't want to get stuck. I could hardly see where I was going with all the snow coming down. I hate to keep rambling on about this, but this storm is a bit scary, and I had no idea where I was."

"It's not a problem." *After all,* Bonnie thought, *it's Christmas Eve, and I can't send a stranger out into the cold.*

Chapter 21

Bonnie awoke early on Christmas morning and, seeing that Mrs. Chandler was still in her room, made her way quietly into the kitchen. Once she had a pot of coffee going, she slipped into her coat and went out the back door. She was glad it wasn't snowing at the moment, even though there was more than a foot of the powdery stuff on the ground. From the way the sky looked, Bonnie figured more snow was probably on the way.

She paused on the porch to breathe in the wintry fresh air. The sight before her looked like a beautiful Christmas card, and she couldn't take her eyes off the wintry scene. Except for a few bird tracks under the feeders, the snow was untouched. Nothing had escaped the blanket of snow. In every direction was a sea of white. The mums that had long lost their autumn color were covered with snow, forming a pretty design. The pine branches were decorated with fluffs of powder, and the pinecones were like nature's ornaments.

Bonnie stepped off the porch, turned, and looked up. The rooftop on the house was covered with heavy snow, giving it an almost whimsical look. Bonnie was glad for a white Christmas.

It was what all kids, young and old, dreamed of having.

Glancing at the place where Allen's truck had been parked the night before, she noticed that the snow was so deep that it had erased all signs his vehicle had ever been there. Her heart was heavy after what had happened last night, but the beautiful white snow helped to lighten her spirits a bit. Besides, it was Christmas—a time for joy, hope, love, and a miracle. Bonnie felt it would take a miracle for Allen to understand why she hadn't told him about her past and to forgive her for holding out on that important part of her life.

Forcing her thoughts aside, she carefully made her way out to the guesthouse, knowing Esther was usually up by now. She rapped on the door, and a few seconds later, Esther, bundled in her shawl and black outer bonnet, opened the door.

"I was just on my way up to the house to see you," Esther said. "I wanted to wish you a merry Christmas and let you know that I'm heading over to Samuel's to watch the children open their gifts."

"So you won't be joining us for breakfast?" Bonnie asked, feeling a bit disappointed. "I was hoping you could meet my dad."

"How about if I stop by this evening after I get back from Samuel's?"

"That's fine. Your place is with Samuel and his children this morning." She nodded toward the road, which hadn't been plowed. "I'm a little concerned about the weather and the road conditions, though. Do you think you can make it to Samuel's okay?"

Esther nodded. "Ginger's always been good in the snow, and it's much easier for our buggies to get around in this kind of weather than it is for a car. Since I'm leaving early, there shouldn't be many vehicles on the road yet."

"You're probably right." Bonnie hesitated a moment, wondering if she should tell Esther what had happened last night between her dad and Allen.

"You look as if you might be troubled about something," Esther said, as though reading Bonnie's mind. "Is everything all right?"

"I don't know."

Esther opened the door wider. "Come inside where it's warm, and tell me what's wrong."

"Are you sure you have the time? I don't want you to be late getting to Samuel's."

"It's okay. I'm sure they won't start opening presents until I get there."

"All right, thanks. I really do need to talk."

Esther removed her shawl and outer bonnet as she led the way to her small kitchen. "Let's take a seat at the table and have a cup of tea," she said, placing her garments over the back of a chair.

"I really don't need any tea, but if we could just spend a few minutes talking, it might help me sort out my feelings."

Bonnie told Esther all that had transpired between her dad and Allen, and how Allen had told Dad he had a headache and gone home without even saying good-bye.

"But I thought you were planning to tell Allen about your past," Esther said.

"I was, and I would have done it before I gave him an answer to his proposal, but I had no idea Dad would blurt it out like that before I had a chance to explain things to Allen." Tears welled in Bonnie's eyes. "I'm afraid the reason Allen left is because he's upset with me for not telling him the truth before this. He probably thinks I'm a terrible person for what I did when I was sixteen. I doubt that he'd want to marry me now."

"Even if Allen was upset about it, I'm sure that after you talk to him, he'll understand why it was hard for you to share this part of your past with him. You can explain things when he comes over for dinner this afternoon," Esther said, placing her hand gently on Bonnie's arm.

"*If* he comes for dinner." Bonnie fought back tears of frustration. "I'm afraid the special relationship Allen and I had might be spoiled now."

"I'm sure it's not, Bonnie, and I'm almost positive he'll come for dinner. Allen's too polite not to show up when he's been invited to someone's house for a meal. I'm equally sure he'll want to talk with you about all of this."

"I hope you're right, because we really do need to talk, although if he does come for dinner, we won't be able to say much in front of my dad or Mrs. Chandler."

"Mrs. Chandler?"

"My B&B guest."

"Oh, that must be the woman I met last night when I got back from Samuel's."

"You did?"

"Yes, and she asked if I was the owner of the bed-and-breakfast. When I told her I work for you part-time and that you were probably at home, she took off for the house before I could explain that you weren't open for business on Christmas. The poor woman looked pretty desperate."

"It's okay," Bonnie said. "After Mrs. Chandler explained her need for a room, I didn't have the heart to say no. There was no way I could have made her go back out in that blizzard last night."

Esther smiled. "I figured that might be the case." She got up and gave Bonnie a hug. "You're always so kind to others. No wonder you've become such a good friend."

Bonnie smiled. "You've been a good friend to me, as well."

"I do hope everything will work out for you and Allen."

"Me, too," Bonnie murmured. "I've waited a long time for love to come my way, and if things don't work out, I'll never allow myself to fall in love again."

—∞—

"*Guder mariye. En hallicher Grischtdaag*," Timothy said, joining Hannah at the bedroom window, where she stared out at the snow.

"Good morning, and Merry Christmas to you, too," she said, in a less than enthusiastic tone.

Timothy's heart went out to her. This was the first Christmas she'd spent away from her parents, and he knew she was hurting. *I hope the gift I made for Hannah will make her feel a little happier.*

"I have something for you," he said, reaching under the bed and pulling out a cardboard box.

She tipped her head and stared at it curiously. "What's in there?"

"Open it and see."

Hannah set the box on the bed and opened the flaps. As she withdrew the bird feeder he'd made, tears welled in her eyes. "Oh Timothy, you made it to look like the covered bridge not far from our home in Pennsylvania."

"That's right. Do you like it, Hannah?" he asked.

"Jah, very much."

"I know how much you enjoy feeding the birds, so I decided to make you a different kind of feeder. See here," he said, lifting the roof on the bridge. "The food goes in there, and then it falls out the ends and underneath the bridge, where the birds sit and eat."

Hannah smiled. "Danki, Timothy. As soon as we find a house of our own, I'll put the feeder to good use."

"You don't have to wait till then," he said. "I can put the feeder up for you in Samuel's backyard. With all this snow, I'm sure the birds, and even the squirrels, will appreciate the unexpected treat."

She shook her head. "I don't want to put it here at Samuel's place."

"Why not?"

"I just don't, that's all." Hannah hurried across the room and opened the bottom dresser drawer. "I have a Christmas present for you, too," she said, handing him a box wrapped in white tissue paper.

Timothy took a seat on the bed and opened the gift. He was a little hurt that Hannah didn't want to use the bird feeder right away, but he hid his feelings, not wanting anything to ruin the day. Inside the package he found a pale blue shirt and a pair of black suspenders.

"Danki," he said. "These are both items I can surely use."

Excited voices coming from outside drew Timothy back over to the window. "Looks like Esther just arrived, so Samuel will soon present his kinner with the new pony he bought them for Christmas," he said. "Let's get Mindy up and go outside and join them."

"You go ahead," Hannah said. "Mindy needs her sleep. Besides, I don't want her getting all excited over the pony. She might think she should have one, too."

"In a few years, maybe we ought to get her one," Timothy said.

Hannah shook her head vigorously. "Ponies are a lot of work, and I don't want our daughter thinking she can take a pony cart out on the road. That would be too dangerous."

She frowned. "If you want my opinion, Samuel shouldn't be giving his kinner a pony, either. They're all too young and irresponsible."

"What Samuel does for his kinner is none of our business, and since Mindy's too young for a pony right now, there's no point in talking about this anymore." Timothy turned toward the bedroom door. "You can stay here if you want to, but I'm going outside to see the look of joy on my nieces' and nephews' faces when they see that new pony for the first time." Timothy hurried out the door.

Arguing with Hannah was not a good way to begin the day—especially when it was Christmas. But he wasn't going to let her ruin his good mood. Why couldn't things stay positive between them, the way they had been when he'd given her the bird feeder? Would they ever see eye to eye on anything that concerned raising Mindy? Was he foolish to hope that at least Christmas would be a tension-free day?

Allen sat at his kitchen table drinking coffee and stewing over what Bonnie's dad had told him last night. Now he wasn't sure what to do. Should he go over to Bonnie's for dinner this afternoon or call her and say he'd decided to stay home? He could probably use the weather as an excuse. The roads had been terrible last night, and from the looks of the weather outside, they most likely weren't any better today. Besides, with it being Christmas, the state and county road workers were probably stretched pretty thin, with only a skeleton crew filling in on the holiday. But blaming the weather for his absence would be the coward's way out, and running from a problem wasn't how he handled things. Of course, he'd never asked a woman to marry him, only to find out from her father that she'd given birth to a baby and given it up for adoption. It might not have been such a shock if Bonnie had told him herself. But the fact that she'd kept it from him made Allen feel as if she didn't love or trust him enough to share her past. Was she afraid he would judge her? Did she think he would condemn her for something that had taken place when she was young and impressionable?

How do I really feel about the fact that the woman I love had a baby out of wedlock? Allen set his cup down and made little circles across his forehead with his fingers, hoping to stave off another headache. *Is that what really bothers me, or is it the fact that she didn't tell me about the baby? If we'd gotten married, would she ever have told me the truth? Do I really want to marry her now?* There were so many questions, yet no answers would come.

Allen sat for several minutes thinking, praying, and meditating on things. The words of Matthew 6:14 popped into his head: *"If ye forgive men their trespasses, your heavenly Father will also forgive you."*

He groaned. *I know I'm not perfect, and I've done things I shouldn't have in the past. It's not my place to judge Bonnie or anyone else. The least I can do is give her a call and talk about this—let her explain why she didn't tell me about the baby.*

Allen was about to reach for the phone, when the lights flickered and then went out. "Oh great, now the power's down. Someone must have hit a pole, or it's due to the weather. Guess I'll have to use my cell phone."

Allen went to the counter where he usually placed the cell phone to be charged and discovered that it wasn't there. "Now what'd I do with the stupid thing?" he mumbled.

He checked each room, looking in all the usual places. He also searched the jacket he'd worn last night, but there was no sign of his cell phone.

Maybe I left it at Bonnie's, he thought. *If I could use the phone and call her, I could find out. Guess I'd better drive over there now and hope she has power at her place, because if I stay here with no heat and no way to cook anything, I'll not only be cold, but hungry besides.*

Allen grabbed his jacket and headed out the door. When he stepped into his truck and tried to start it, he got no response. Either he'd left the lights on last night, or the cold weather had zapped the battery, because it was dead.

"This day just keeps getting better and better. That settles that," he muttered as he tromped through the snow and back to the house. "Looks like I'll be spending my Christmas alone in a cold, dark house and nothing will be resolved with Bonnie today."

Chapter 22

"That's a mighty cute pony Samuel bought for the kinner, isn't it?" Fannie said as she, Hannah, and Esther worked in the kitchen to get dinner ready.

"Jah, it certainly is." Esther smiled. "And I think the name Shadow is perfect for the pony, because it sure likes to follow the kinner around."

"Looks like they all took to the pony rather quickly, too," Fannie added.

Hannah rolled her eyes. "If you ask me, Samuel's kinner are too young for a pony. They can barely take care of their dog."

"They're not too young," Fannie said with a shake of her head. "Marla and Leon are plenty old enough to take care of the pony."

"I agree with Fannie," Esther said, reaching for a bowl to put the potatoes in. "Having a pony to care for will teach the children responsibility."

Hannah made no comment. Obviously her opinion didn't matter to either of these women. She picked up a stack of plates and was about to take them to the dining room when

Esther said to Fannie, "When Suzanne and Titus were here last night, she mentioned that she's been feeling sick to her stomach for the last several weeks. I was wondering if she said anything to you about that."

"No, but it sounds like she might be expecting my next *kinskind.*" Fannie grinned. "And if that's the case, I think it would be wunderbaar, because Abraham and I would surely welcome a new grandchild."

Hannah swallowed hard. She couldn't help but feel a bit envious—not only because she wanted to have another baby and hadn't been able to get pregnant again, but because she saw a closeness developing between Esther and Fannie.

It's not right that Fannie's nicer to Esther than she is to me. I'm her daughter-in-law, after all. Esther isn't even part of this family yet. Hannah wished, yet again, that her parents could have been here for Christmas. It would help so much if she and Mom could sit down and have a good long talk. Hannah's mother had always been there for her and would surely understand how she felt about things.

Trisha yawned, stretched, and pulled the covers aside. She couldn't remember when she'd slept so well. "Oh my, it's so late," she murmured after looking at her watch and realizing it was almost noon.

She sat up and swung her legs over the edge of the bed, just as her cell phone rang. "Hello," she said, suppressing a yawn.

"Trisha, this is Carla."

"It's good to hear from you! Merry Christmas."

"I wish it was a merry Christmas. Jason and I just received some bad news."

"I'm sorry to hear that. What's wrong?"

"Jason's mother was taken to the hospital this morning, so we'll be heading to Ohio right away."

"That's too bad. I hope it's nothing serious."

"They think she had a stroke."

"I'll be praying for her, and for you and Jason as you travel."

"Thanks, we appreciate that." There was a pause. "I'm sorry we won't be here to have Christmas dinner with you."

"That's okay. I understand. Now be safe, and I'll talk to you again soon."

When Trisha hung up, she hurried to take a shower and get dressed. She probably should have checked out by now and might even be holding things up for the owner of the bed-and-breakfast if she had Christmas plans, which she probably did. Most everyone had plans for Christmas—everyone but her, that is.

Maybe I should have stayed in Fresno instead of taking off on this trip, she thought. *At least there I could have spent Christmas with Margo and Shirley. Well, it's too late to cry about that now. I'm not in Fresno, and I need to get back on the road. With any luck, I may be able to find a restaurant in Hopkinsville that's open on Christmas Day. That is, if I can even find Hopkinsville.*

Trisha picked up her suitcase and went downstairs, where a tantalizing aroma drew her into the kitchen.

"I apologize for sleeping so late," she said to Bonnie, who stood in front of the oven, checking on a luscious-looking turkey. "I was snuggled down under that quilt, feeling so toasty and warm, and I didn't want to wake up."

Bonnie closed the oven door, turned to Trisha, and smiled. "That's okay. I'm glad you slept well. I figured you must be tired after your drive here last night. I know from experience that driving in such bad conditions can really exhaust a person, especially when they are unfamiliar with the roads." She motioned to a tray of cinnamon rolls on the counter. "Would you like a cup of coffee and some of those?"

Trisha's mouth watered. "That sounds so good. I'll just eat one and be on my way."

"Do you have any plans for today?" Bonnie asked.

"Not anymore." Trisha told Bonnie about the call she'd had from Carla. "So, if you'll be kind enough to tell me how to get to Hopkinsville, I'll see if any restaurants are open there. After I eat, I'll probably head on down the road."

"I doubt that any restaurants will be open today. And if you did find a restaurant, what fun would it be to eat alone?"

"It's never fun to eat alone," Trisha admitted, "but I've gotten used to it since my husband passed away."

"Why don't you stay here and join me and my dad for Christmas dinner?" Bonnie offered.

"It's kind of you to offer, but I wouldn't want to impose."

"It's not an imposition. There's plenty of food, and if you'd like to spend another night here, that's fine, too."

"Really? You wouldn't mind?"

"Not at all."

"Thanks, I think I'll take you up on that." Truth was, this charming B&B had captivated Trisha—not to mention that it would be much nicer to have a home-cooked meal in the company of Bonnie and her dad than to sit alone in some restaurant to eat.

Trisha glanced around the room. "Is there anything I can do to help you with dinner?"

"I appreciate the offer, but there's nothing that needs to be done until closer to dinnertime. So why don't you just relax for now?"

"Maybe I'll take my coffee and cinnamon roll upstairs. I really should call a few of my friends from California and wish them a merry Christmas."

—ꝏ—

A few minutes after Trisha left the kitchen, Bonnie's dad came in.

"Did you meet my B&B guest out in the hall?" Bonnie asked. During breakfast she'd told him about Mrs. Chandler.

"Nope. I came from the living room, but I did hear footsteps on the stairs, so I guess that must have been her."

"I hope you don't mind, but I invited Mrs. Chandler to join us for dinner today. Oh, and she'll be staying one more night, too."

Dad smiled. "You're sure accommodating, Bonnie. Most people running a business that is supposed to be closed for the holiday wouldn't have welcomed a guest at the last minute the way you did."

"I couldn't very well send her out into the cold. Besides, the poor woman looked tired and lonely. And she's not from around here."

"How do you know?"

"When she was filling out the paperwork to check into the B&B last night she said she was from California."

"She's a long ways from home then."

"Yes, and she could have easily gotten lost in that blinding snow."

"Have you heard anything from Allen today?" Dad asked.

Bonnie shook her head. "I tried calling him at home awhile ago, but the phone just rang and rang."

"Maybe he's on his way here. Did you try his cell phone?"

"No, I didn't. Even if he was coming for dinner, I didn't think he would have left already, so I only called his home phone."

"Why don't you give his cell phone a try?" Dad suggested.

"Good idea." Bonnie picked up the phone and dialed Allen's cell number. She was surprised when she heard a phone ringing somewhere else in the house. It sounded like it was coming from the dining room.

"What in the world?" Moving quickly into the dining room, she discovered Allen's cell phone lying in the chair where he'd been sitting last evening.

"It must have fallen out of his pocket," Bonnie told Dad when he followed her into the dining room. "I guess now all we can do is wait and see if Allen shows up for dinner."

"I hope he does," Dad said with a nod. "I owe him an apology for what I blurted out last night, and I know you're anxious to talk to him, too."

"Yes, I am, although I'm feeling nervous about it." Hearing the wind howling outside, Bonnie glanced out the window and saw that it was snowing again. "I hope if Allen is on his way over that he'll be safe. Whatever roads have been plowed will probably drift shut again since the wind has picked up."

"Try not to worry; I'm sure he'll be fine," Dad said.

"You're right. Worry won't change a thing, so I'll pray and trust God to bring Allen here safely today."

"Good idea." Dad moved toward the living room. "If you don't need me for anything, I think I'll go relax in front of the fire for a while. Since I don't have a fireplace in my house, I'd forgotten how nice one can be."

Bonnie noticed a faraway look in his eyes. He'd obviously had some good memories from living in this place.

"I remember how my mom used to sit in front of the fireplace humming while she knitted," Dad continued. "I can still almost hear the click of her knitting needles, as though keeping time to her music."

"Yes, I recall her doing that when I came here to visit

sometimes." Bonnie patted Dad's arm. "You go ahead and relax. I'll call you when dinner's ready."

"Thanks, honey."

When Dad left the room, Bonnie said a prayer for Allen; then she picked up his cell phone and returned to the kitchen to check on the meal. By the time she had everything on the dining-room table, it was two o'clock, and still no Allen. She was sure he wasn't coming.

Bonnie was about to call Mrs. Chandler for dinner when the lights went out. Fortunately, she was done cooking, so at least they wouldn't have to worry about eating cold food.

While Dad added more wood to the fireplace, Bonnie lit some candles, grabbed a flashlight, and headed upstairs to the room she had rented to Mrs. Chandler.

She knocked on the door, and a few seconds later, Mrs. Chandler, looking half-asleep, answered. "Oh, I'm so sorry. After I made my phone calls, I laid down on the bed to rest and must have fallen asleep." She yawned and stretched her arms over her head. "I can't believe with all the sleep I had last night that I could still be so tired. I slept like a baby, though. It's so peaceful and quiet here, and as soon as I reclined on the bed and pulled that beautiful quilt over me, I was out like a light."

"That's okay. You must have needed the extra rest, and you know, I think there's something about being wrapped up in a quilt that makes a person feel safe and comforted."

"You're so right. I was asleep almost before my head hit the pillow. If you'll give me a minute to freshen up, I'll be right down."

Bonnie explained that the power was out and gave Mrs. Chandler the flashlight, because there were no windows in the hall. Then she carefully made her way down the stairs, where she opened all the curtains to let what little outside light there was into the house.

A short time later, Bonnie's guest came down and joined them in the dining room. Bonnie introduced Dad to Mrs. Chandler, and they all took their seats. Even though she'd opened the curtains, the room was quite dark, but the flickering candles helped. Bonnie thought the candlelight made it seem more relaxing and festive—sort of like back in the days of old.

After Bonnie prayed, giving thanks for the meal, she passed the food around.

Dad looked over at her and said, "It doesn't look like Allen's coming, does it?"

"No, I'm afraid not. Once the lights come back on, I'll try calling him again. He needs to know that his cell phone is here, because I'm sure he's going to need it when he goes to work tomorrow morning."

"You mean, *if* he goes to work," Dad said. "With the way the snow's been coming down, the roads might not be passable by morning."

The conversation changed as Bonnie asked Mrs. Chandler a few questions about herself, including her first name.

"Oh, it's Trisha. My husband and I used to live in Portland, Oregon, but we moved to Fresno, California, shortly after we got married."

"What was your maiden name?" Dad asked with a peculiar expression.

"It was Hammond."

Bonnie heard Dad's sharp intake of breath and wondered if he'd choked on something. Just then, the lights came back on, and Bonnie worried more, because Dad's face looked as white as Grandma's tablecloth.

"Dad, are you all right?"

He just sat staring at Trisha as if he'd seen a ghost.

Trisha studied him for several seconds, and then she gasped. "Kenny Taylor? Is that you?"

Dad nodded. "What are you doing here in Kentucky? Did you know I'd be here at my folks' old house?" His eyes narrowed and deep wrinkles formed across his forehead.

Trisha shook her head vigorously. "Of course not. I had no way of knowing you were here, or that this was where you used to live. How would I have known that?"

"You sent me a letter after I moved here, remember? Or did you forget about that?"

Trisha's brows furrowed as she slowly nodded. "I'd almost forgotten about that, and I sure didn't remember your address after all these years. When I pulled in here last night, I had no idea this used to be where you lived."

"So what are you saying—that it was just a twist of fate that brought you here?"

"Maybe; I don't know. The snow was really bad, and I had to get off the road. I didn't even know where I was. Thankfully, I saw the blinking lights on a horse-drawn buggy and followed it here." Trisha paused, and her voice lowered as she looked at him and said, "Maybe it was God, and not the weather, who led me here."

Dad grunted. "Yeah, right."

Bonnie, feeling as shocked as Dad obviously was, could almost feel the tension between him and Trisha. She wished there was something she could do. What a stressful Christmas this had turned out to be. It was bad enough that the man she loved was so upset with her that he didn't want to join them for Christmas dinner. Now, as fate would have it, Dad's old girlfriend had shown up out of the blue, and Dad's Christmas had been ruined, too. How much worse could it get?

Chapter 23

"I'm sorry about what happened between me and your dad yesterday. I'm sure it ruined your Christmas," Trisha said the following morning when she entered the kitchen and found Bonnie sitting at the table reading her Bible.

Bonnie looked up and smiled. "It's not your fault. Dad should be the one apologizing—and mostly to you, because you had no way of knowing he was here."

Trisha sank into a chair with a sigh. "I'm glad you realize that, but even after all these years, I believe he's still angry with me for breaking up with him. I don't understand it, though. It's not like we were engaged to be married or anything. We were just teenagers back then and thought we were in love."

"I think the reason Dad was so upset is because when you broke up with him, he believed it was due to the fact that he was moving to Kentucky. So he was upset with his parents and blamed them for the breakup."

"But I sent him a letter telling him I'd fallen in love with Dave, and that was the only reason I broke up with him shortly before he moved. After reading my letter, Kenny should have realized that our breakup had nothing to do with him moving, and most of all, that it wasn't his parents' fault."

"Bonnie shook her head. "Dad never got your letter."

"How do you know that?"

"Soon after I moved here, I found the letter stuck between some papers in an old pie cupboard in the basement. The letter was unopened," Bonnie explained. "Then later, when I went to Portland to take care of Dad after he'd been in a car accident, I showed him the letter."

"What'd he say about that?"

"He was stunned and said he'd never seen the letter before. After he read it, he regretted having blamed his parents for making him move to Kentucky and wished he could tell them how sorry he was. But since they'd both passed away, it was too late for that," Bonnie added.

"So Ken's more upset about how our breakup affected his relationship with his folks than he is with me for choosing Dave over him?"

"I think so. Although I know from the few things Dad's told me that he really did care about you. I believe it was a long time before he got over you breaking up with him." Bonnie motioned to her Bible. "Dad's a Christian now, and he needs to remember what God says about forgiveness."

"I'm a Christian, too," Trisha said. "I found the Lord soon after Dave and I moved to Fresno and started going to a neighborhood church."

"Since you and Dad are both Christians, you ought to be able to work this out." Bonnie rose from her seat and pointed out the window, where huge snowflakes swirled around the yard. "And from the looks of this weather that's set in, I'd say you're both going to be stuck here for a few more days, which should give you enough time to make peace with each other."

the STRUGGLE

—∞—

Paradise, Pennsylvania

"How's Johnny doing?" Naomi asked when Sally entered her store shortly after it had opened.

"He's still in quite a bit of pain." Sally frowned. "He's also cranky and impatient."

"A back injury can cause a person to be out of sorts. I hope it didn't ruin your Christmas."

Sally shrugged and picked up a shopping basket. "Our sons and their families came over for a while on Christmas Day, so that helped, but I wish we could have gone to Kentucky like we'd planned."

"I talked to my daed earlier this morning, and he said they're having blizzard-like conditions in Christian County right now, so maybe it's a good thing you had to stay home."

"Is everyone okay there?" Sally questioned, feeling concern.

"Dad said everyone's fine, but if the weather doesn't improve, they may end up having to stay a few days longer than they'd planned. He also mentioned that many people have been without power in the area, which is affecting quite a few of their English neighbors."

"If there's no power, how'd Abraham manage to call you this morning?"

"The power was on in Samuel's phone shanty, but Dad said with the wind blowing like crazy, there was a good chance they might lose power there, too."

"I'd better do my shopping in a hurry so I can get home and call Samuel's number. I want to check on Hannah and be sure she and the others are okay." Sally started down the notions aisle and nearly bumped into Phoebe Stoltzfus. "What are you doing here?" she asked.

"I came in to get some sewing supplies for my mamm," Phoebe replied with a smile.

"Shouldn't you be at the bulk food store right now? You can't expect Anna to handle things by herself, you know." Sally hoped Phoebe wasn't the kind of person who shirked her duties.

"I don't expect that at all." Phoebe's face turned red. "Since the store doesn't open for another half hour, I figured I'd have time to make a quick stop here before going to work."

"Oh, I see." Sally didn't know why, but she didn't quite trust Phoebe. She remembered how a few years ago the rebellious young woman had been going out with Titus Fisher but broke things off and headed for California with a friend. If Phoebe hadn't done that, Titus would still be living in Pennsylvania because the only reason he'd moved to Kentucky was to start a new life and try to forget about Phoebe.

Maybe that's why I don't care much for Phoebe, Sally thought. *Her foolish actions set the wheels in motion for three of the Fisher men to move to Kentucky. If Phoebe had stayed put in Lancaster County, she'd probably be married to Titus by now, and none of the brothers would have moved away, so Hannah would still be here, too.*

Turning her attention back to the issue at hand, Sally said to Phoebe, "Well, just see that you're not late for work today. Johnny and I don't want any of our employees sloughing off on the job."

"No, I won't be late," Phoebe mumbled before hurrying down the aisle.

~

Pembroke, Kentucky

Hannah glanced out the living-room window at the swirling snow and frowned. She hated being cooped up in the house—especially with so many people. Why couldn't Fannie and Abraham have stayed with Titus and Suzanne the whole time? Having them here was just a reminder that her folks were at home and Dad was down with a sore back. With the exception of the bird feeder Timothy had given Hannah, it had not been a very good Christmas. And now this horrible weather only made her feel worse. She knew it had upset Timothy that the bird feeder he'd given her would remain in the box until they got a place of their own. But she didn't want the feeder put up in Samuel's yard, even if temporarily. Hannah wanted the feeder in her own yard, not someone else's.

Then, to give her one more thing to fret about, this morning after breakfast, Samuel and Timothy had taken off with Samuel's horse and buggy for Hopkinsville, because they hadn't been able to get ahold of Allen and were worried about him. Hannah had tried talking Timothy out of going, reminding him that the roads were bad and it was hard to see. But he'd been determined to go, and nothing she'd said made any difference. It seemed as though whatever Hannah wanted, Timothy was determined to do just the opposite. Or at least that's how it had been since they'd moved to Kentucky.

"I think I'll go out to the phone shanty and see if there are any messages from my mamm," Hannah said to Fannie, who sat in the rocking chair by the fire with Jared and Mindy in her lap.

"It's awfully cold out there," Fannie said. "Abraham said so when he went out to help Samuel clean the barn this morning."

"I'll be fine." Hannah stepped into the hall and removed her heavy woolen shawl from a wall peg. After wrapping it snugly around her shoulders, she put on her outer bonnet, slipped into a pair of boots, and went out the door.

The snow was deeper than she'd thought it would be, and

she winced when she took her first step and ended up with icy cold snow down her boots. By the time she reached the phone shanty, her teeth had begun to chatter, and goose bumps covered her arms and legs. To make matters worse, Hannah's feet were soaking wet and fast getting numb from the snow that kept falling inside her boots.

I should have thought to put on some gloves, she told herself as she stepped inside the shanty and turned on the battery-operated light sitting on the small wooden table beside the phone. She blew on her fingers to get the feeling back in them, took a seat in the folding chair, and wiggled her toes, hoping to get some warmth in her boots before punching the button to listen to their voice-mail messages. There was one from Mom, saying she'd heard about the bad weather they were having and asking if everyone was all right. Hannah picked up the phone and dialed her folks' number, but since no one was in the phone shack, she had to leave a message. "Hi, Mom, it's Hannah. I wanted to let you know that we're all fine here, but the weather's awful, and I really miss you. I wish we could have been in Pennsylvania for Christmas instead of here."

Hannah hung up the phone, and with a feeling of hopelessness, she trudged back to the house, trying not to get more snow in her already-soaked boots.

Hopkinsville, Kentucky

Allen shivered as he pulled a blanket around his shoulders and made his way to the kitchen. He couldn't believe he'd been without power for twenty-four hours, and with no phone or battery for his truck, it looked like he would be stuck here until the power came on and he could call someone for help.

"Man, it's sure cold in here! Guess this is what I get for building my home where there are no neighbors close by," he grumbled. If he had, he could have asked one of them to give him a ride into town where he could buy a new battery for his truck.

"Let's see now, what do I want to eat?" he asked himself, peeking into the refrigerator, which had stayed plenty cold despite the loss of power. A peanut butter and jelly sandwich would be real good about now, but he knew there was no peanut butter. It was on his grocery list. There was no jelly either, but he did find a package of cheddar cheese, a bottle of orange juice, two sticks of butter, and a carton of eggs. He wasn't in the mood for raw eggs, so he took out the cheese and orange juice, got down a box of crackers from the cupboard, and took a seat at the table. "Dear Lord," he prayed, bowing his head, "bless this pitiful breakfast I'm about to eat, restore power to the area soon, and be with my family and friends everywhere. Amen."

Allen's thoughts went to Bonnie. Did she have power at her place? Was she doing okay? He wished he could just jump in the truck and head over there now—or at least call to check up on her. "I'm such a fool," he muttered. He regretted the way he'd left on Christmas Eve and knew he needed to apologize for not showing up yesterday, too, although that was completely out of his control. Things had sure changed from when he had fretted over not flubbing up his proposal to Bonnie. He wished now her answer was all he had to worry about. One thing for sure: he needed to talk to Bonnie soon.

Allen had just eaten his second cracker when a knock sounded on the front door. He jumped up and raced over to the door to see who it was. Timothy and Samuel stood on his porch dressed in heavy jackets and straw hats.

"We've been trying to call and became worried when we didn't get an answer," Samuel said, his brows furrowed. "When Esther mentioned that Bonnie said you never showed up for Christmas, we decided we'd better come and check on you."

"How'd you get here?" Allen asked, looking past their shoulders.

"Came with Samuel's horse and buggy." Timothy motioned to where they'd tied the horse to a tree near Allen's garage.

"Wow, it must have taken you awhile to get here," Allen said. "Especially in this horrible weather."

Samuel nodded. "Took us over an hour, but there weren't any cars on the road, so we moved along at a pretty good clip."

"I'm glad you're here," Allen said, "because the power's out, and to top it off, the battery in my truck is dead. Since yesterday morning, I've been stranded with no heat, and I can't find my cell phone, so I haven't been able to call anyone for help."

"You left your cell phone at Bonnie's on Christmas Eve," Samuel said. "She told Esther that, too."

"Oh, I see. I kind of figured that might be the case." Allen opened the door wider. "You two had better come inside. It's not much warmer in the house than it is outside, but at least it's not snowing in here," he added with a chuckle.

"Why don't you gather up some clothes and come home with us?" Samuel suggested after they'd entered the house.

"I appreciate the offer, but I wouldn't want to impose."

"It's not an imposition," Samuel said. "Besides, if you stay here and the power doesn't come on soon, you'll either freeze to death or die of hunger."

"You've got that right. Although, I guess I could have tromped through the snow and pulled my barbecue grill out of the garage." Allen's nose crinkled. "But I don't have much food in the house, and even if I did, I don't relish the thought of bein' out in the cold trying to cook it."

"I can't blame you there," Timothy said.

"Give me a minute to throw a few things together, and then we can head out." Allen started for his room but turned back around. "Say, I have an idea."

"What's that?" Samuel asked.

"Instead of taking me to your place, how about dropping me off at Bonnie's? That way I can get my cell phone, and if she's still speaking to me, maybe I can talk her into letting me have one of her rooms at the B&B for the night."

"Why wouldn't she be speaking to you?" Timothy questioned.

"It's a long story. I'll tell you both about it on the way."

Samuel nodded. "If it doesn't work out and you still need a place to stay, you're more than welcome to come home with us."

"Thanks. Depending on how things go with Bonnie, I may need to take you up on that offer."

Chapter 24

Pembroke, Kentucky

"It looks like Bonnie must have a guest," Allen said when Samuel pulled his horse and buggy up to the hitching rail. A small blue car, mostly covered in snow, was parked near the garage.

"That's right, she does," Samuel said. "Esther mentioned that the woman is from California and she arrived here late on Christmas Eve."

"I thought the B&B was closed for the holidays," Allen said, climbing down from the buggy.

"It was, but Bonnie made an exception because the woman couldn't find her way to Hopkinsville in the snow and needed a place to stay."

Allen smiled. That sounded like Bonnie. She was a good person, and they really did need to talk.

"Maybe you'd better come inside where it's warmer and wait until I see if Bonnie will rent me a room," Allen said, looking first at Timothy and then Samuel.

"Sure, we can do that," Samuel said, "but I doubt that

Bonnie would turn you out in the cold."

Allen wasn't so sure about that. He'd walked out Christmas Eve without a word of explanation or even telling her good-bye. No doubt, Bonnie's dad had told her about the conversation they'd had regarding Bonnie's past, so by him not showing up for dinner yesterday, she probably thought he was angry with her.

Well, I was at first, he admitted to himself as he tromped through the drifts of snow in the yard. *I was angry and hurt, but I'm going to fix things now if I can.*

After the three men stepped onto the porch, Samuel knocked on the door. A few seconds later, Bonnie opened it, and she looked at them in disbelief. Then her gaze went to the yard, where the horse and buggy stood. "I'm surprised to see you out in this horrible weather." She glanced over at Allen. "Did you come here in Samuel's buggy?"

He nodded.

"Where's your truck?"

"At home with a dead battery. I've been stranded there since Christmas morning, with no electricity, no vehicle, and no cell phone."

"Your cell phone is here. We found it on the chair you sat in on Christmas Eve." Bonnie opened the door farther and moved aside. "Come in, everyone, where it's warmer."

As they stepped into the entryway, Allen caught a glimpse of a middle-aged woman sitting in front of the fireplace in the living room to his right. He figured she must be Bonnie's unexpected guest.

"Let's go into the kitchen," Bonnie suggested. "I'll pour you some coffee, and how about a piece of pumpkin pie or some chocolate cheesecake to go with it?"

Allen's mouth watered. "Mmm. . .that sounds really good."

"Same here," Samuel and Timothy said in unison.

"Which one do you want—the cheesecake or the pie?" Bonnie asked.

"Both," Allen replied with a grin. "I've had very little to eat in the last twenty-four hours, and I'm just about starved to death."

"No problem. I have pie and plenty of leftovers from yesterday's Christmas dinner."

Allen grimaced. If he'd been there yesterday to eat with them, there wouldn't be so many leftovers, and he wouldn't feel as though he was close to starvation right now.

"Is your dad still here?" Samuel asked as he removed his jacket and took a seat at the table, along with the others. "I was hoping I'd get the opportunity to meet him."

"Yes, he's in his room right now, but I'll call him down before you leave." Bonnie poured them all coffee, and then she took a delicious-looking pumpkin pie from the refrigerator, cut three slices, and gave them each a piece. Following that, she placed a dish of chocolate cheesecake on the table and said they could help themselves.

"Dad was planning to leave today, but with the weather turning bad, he called the airlines and canceled his flight," Bonnie said. "He doesn't want to go until the weather improves, because he's concerned about me driving him to the airport on snowy roads."

"My truck has four-wheel drive, so I'd be happy to take him," Allen offered as he helped himself to a generous slice of pumpkin pie. "As soon as I get a battery for it, that is."

"I appreciate the offer, but I'm sure I can manage to get him there." Bonnie smiled, but it appeared to be forced.

She is upset with me, and I need to talk to her about my actions on Christmas Eve, but I can't very well say anything with Timothy and Samuel sitting here. Allen blew on his coffee and took a drink. "Uh. . .the reason we came over is, I was wondering if I could rent a room from you for the night."

She shook her head.

"You won't rent me a room?" He couldn't believe she would turn him out in the cold.

"No, but I will let you stay in a room free of charge." Her smile softened, reaching all the way to her eyes this time.

Allen relaxed and released a deep breath. "Thanks. I appreciate that very much."

They sat quietly for a while as the men drank their coffee and ate the pie. Then, when they were just finishing up, Bonnie excused herself and left the room. When she returned several minutes later, she had Allen's cell phone, and her father was with her.

"Dad, I'd like you to meet Samuel Fisher," she said, motioning to Samuel. "And this is his brother Timothy."

"It's nice to meet you both," Ken said, shaking their hands. "You did some real nice work on this old house," he added, looking at Samuel.

Samuel motioned to Allen. "I can't take all the credit. My good friend here did some of the work."

Ken looked at Allen and smiled. "It's good to see you again. We missed you on Christmas Day."

Allen explained his situation and why he was here right now. What he didn't admit was that even if he hadn't been stranded, he might not have come for Christmas dinner. He'd really needed the time alone to spend in thought and prayer. So at least something good had come from him being alone on Christmas Day, sad as it was.

"I'm sorry you were stranded but glad you're here now," Ken said, clasping Allen's shoulder. "I think you and my daughter need to talk."

Before Allen could respond, Samuel pushed his chair aside and stood. "Since Allen has a place to spend the night, I guess Timothy and I will be on our way. We've been gone quite awhile, and we don't want Esther, Hannah, or our mom to start worrying about us."

"Knowing Hannah, she's probably been worried since the moment we left," Timothy said.

"I'll walk you to the door," Ken offered.

Timothy and Samuel said their good-byes and started out of the kitchen.

"We'll be back to check on you tomorrow, Allen," Samuel called over his shoulder.

"Okay, thanks."

"Would you like another cup of coffee?" Bonnie asked Allen as the other men left.

He nodded. "That'd be nice. I hadn't had anything hot to drink since I lost power at my place."

"Oh, and would you like something more than just the pie to eat? I can fix you some eggs and toast."

"That does sound good, but if you don't mind, I'd like to talk to you first." He glanced toward the door to see if Ken might come back to the kitchen and was relieved when he heard footsteps clomping up the stairs.

"What did you want to talk about?" Bonnie asked, taking a seat across from him.

Allen cleared his throat a few times. "First, I need to apologize for rushing out of here on Christmas Eve without saying good-bye."

Bonnie sat staring at him.

"And second, I want you to know the reason I left."

"I think I already know," she said. "Dad told you about the baby I had when I was a teenager, and you were upset by it, so you went home." Tears welled in her eyes. "You probably think I'm a terrible person now, don't you?"

He shook his head. "We all make mistakes, Bonnie. You were just a confused teenager with no mother to guide you and a father who was struggling to raise you on his own."

She nodded slowly. "But that's still no excuse for what I did. I'd been brought up with good morals, and—" She stopped talking and reached for a napkin to wipe the tears that had dribbled onto her cheeks.

"Beating yourself up about the past won't change anything," Allen said. "And just so you know—the fact that you had a baby out of wedlock wasn't really why I left."

"It. . .it wasn't?"

"No. The main reason I left was because I couldn't deal with you having kept it from me—especially when I'd thought we'd been drawing so close."

"I was planning to tell you, Allen. I just couldn't seem to find the nerve or the right time to say it."

"How come? Did you think I wouldn't want to marry you if I knew about your past?"

"That's exactly what I thought." Bonnie blew her nose on the napkin. "I was afraid you might not want me if you knew what I'd done."

Allen left his chair and skirted around the table. Gently pulling Bonnie to her feet, he whispered, "I love you, Bonnie Taylor, and if you'll have me, I want to be your husband."

"Oh yes, Allen. I'd be honored to marry you," she said tearfully.

A wide smile spread across his face. "I was hoping you'd say that, and I'm also hoping you'll accept this." Allen reached into his jacket pocket and pulled out a small velvet box. When he opened it, Bonnie saw the beautiful diamond ring inside and gasped.

"Oh Allen, it's perfect!"

He removed it from the box and slipped it on her finger then pulled her into his arms.

They stood together for several minutes, holding each other and whispering words of endearment. Then, when Allen's stomach gurgled noisily, Bonnie laughed and pulled away. "I think I'd better give you something more to eat before you starve to death."

Allen chuckled and patted his stomach. "That might be a good idea, because I feel kind of faint. Of course," he quickly added, "it probably has more to do with the excitement I feel about you accepting my proposal than it does with my need for food. It isn't exactly how I wanted to propose; I had this big long speech I'd practiced for days that I was gonna give on Christmas Eve."

She gave him a quick kiss on the cheek. "Your proposal was perfect—simple and sweet. Now, take a seat and relax while I get some bacon and eggs cooking, and then I'll tell you about the woman who showed up here after you left on Christmas Eve."

—∞—

"The one good thing about being snowed in like this is that it's given us more time to spend with the *kinskinner*," Abraham said to Fannie as they stood in front of the window in Samuel's guest room, looking out at Marla and Leon, who were in the yard tossing snowballs at each other and giggling.

"You're right about that," she said with a nod. "And even though I miss our grandchildren at home, I've enjoyed being here with Samuel's four kinner and Timothy's little Mindy." She sighed deeply. "It's just too bad they have to live so far away, which means we can't see them very often."

Abraham grunted. "Now, don't waste time on trivial matters."

"It's not a trivial matter to me. I miss my boys and their families."

"I understand that, because so do I, but it won't do any good for you to start feeling sorry for yourself. We'll come here to visit whenever we can, and I'm sure that our boys will bring their families to Pennsylvania as often as they can, too."

"Humph!" Fannie frowned. "I doubt that'll happen too often. With Suzanne most likely expecting a *boppli*, she and Titus will probably stick close to home. And as busy as Samuel seems to be, I'll bet we won't see him before he and Esther are married—whenever that's going to be." She folded her arms. "Then there's Timothy, who might never come back to Pennsylvania to see us."

"What makes you say that?"

"Think about it, Abraham. He moved here to get his wife away from her interfering mamm. If he takes his family home for a visit, Hannah will want to stay, and then Timothy will have an even bigger problem on his hands."

Abraham quirked an eyebrow. "Bigger problem?"

She nudged his arm. "He already has a problem with a wife who does nothing but complain and doesn't want to be here. To tell you the truth, I don't think she wants us here either."

"Now, Fannie, you shouldn't be saying things like that."

"Why not? It's the truth. Hannah's just not accepting of me the way our other daughters-in-law are. She rarely makes conversation, and when she does say something to me, it's usually a negative comment or she's expressing her displeasure with something I've done."

"Now what could you possibly have done to upset Hannah?" he asked.

"For one thing, just a little while ago she became upset

when I was about to give Mindy some Christmas candy." Fannie sighed deeply. "It's not like I was going to give her the whole box or anything; it was just one piece."

"Well, Hannah is the child's Mudder, and it's her right to decide when and if Mindy should have candy."

"But it's not fair that Mindy's cousins got to have a piece of candy and she didn't." Fannie moved away from the window. "I wish Timothy had never married Hannah. She's selfish, envious, and too overprotective where Mindy's concerned. She even wanted me to convince Timothy to move back to Pennsylvania."

Abraham's brows shot up. "Really? What'd you say?"

"Told her I couldn't—that Timothy wouldn't appreciate it." Fannie sighed. "You know, Abraham, Timothy and Hannah's marriage is already strained, and it makes me wonder if things will get worse in the days ahead." She clasped Abraham's arm. "I just have this strange feeling about Timothy and Hannah. Of all our Kinner, he's the one I'm the most worried about. Timothy and Hannah certainly need a lot of prayer."

Chapter 25

For the next several days, the bad weather prevailed. But by Monday, the snow had finally stopped and the roads were clear enough to drive on, so Abraham, Fannie, and their driver left for home. Hannah felt relieved, because Fannie was beginning to get on her nerves. Not only that, but Samuel's kids had been noisier than usual with their grandparents here, always vying for their attention and begging Abraham for candy, gum, and horsey rides. Mindy had also been whiny and often begged for candy and other things Hannah didn't want her to have. If that wasn't bad enough, it had sickened Hannah to see the way Esther acted around Fannie—so sweet and catering to her every whim. Was she trying to make an impression, or did she really enjoy visiting with Fannie that much?

Maybe it's because Esther's folks live in Pennsylvania, Hannah thought as she stared out the living-room window. *Is it possible that Esther misses her Mamm as much as I do mine?*

"As much as I hate to say this," Timothy said, slipping his arm around Hannah's waist, "Samuel and I have a paint job in Oak Grove this morning, and our driver just pulled in, so I need to get going."

Hannah squinted at the black van. "That doesn't look like Allen's rig."

"You're right; it's not. We won't be working for Allen today. This house is one Samuel lined up on his own, so he called Bob Hastings for a ride because his vehicle is big enough to haul all our painting equipment."

"Oh, I see." Hannah turned to look at Timothy. "Do you have any idea how long you'll be working today?"

He shrugged. "It'll probably be seven or eight before we get back home. Since we've been hired to paint the whole interior of the house and the owners would like it done by the end of the week, we'll need to put in a long day."

Hannah sighed. "It's my turn to cook supper this evening, so would you like me to fix it a little later than usual?"

He shook his head. "You and the kids should go ahead and eat. Maybe you can keep something warm in the oven for Samuel and me, though."

"Sure, I can do that."

When Timothy went out the door, Hannah headed for the kitchen, where Esther was doing the breakfast dishes.

"Would you like me to dry?" Hannah asked.

Esther turned from the sink and smiled. "That'd be nice."

Hannah grabbed a clean dish towel and picked up one of the plates in the dish drainer. "It seems quiet in here with Fannie and Abraham gone, Samuel and Timothy off to work, and Samuel's two oldest kinner at school," she said.

"Jah, but I kind of miss all the excitement."

Hannah couldn't imagine that. She preferred peace and quiet over noise and chaos. She was actually glad Christmas was over.

They worked quietly for a while; then Hannah broke the

silence with a question that had been on her mind. "Do you miss not living close to your mamm?"

"Of course I do." Esther placed another clean plate in the drainer. "But I know Mom and Dad are needed in Pennsylvania so they can help my brother and his family. I also know that my place is here."

"How can you be sure of that?"

"Because this is where Samuel lives, and I love him very much."

"So love is what's keeping you here?"

"Jah. That, and the fact that this is my home. I mean, I like it here in Kentucky, but if Samuel wanted to move back to Pennsylvania after we got married, I'd be willing to move there, too."

"So I guess that means I should have been willing to move here because it's what Timothy wanted?" Hannah couldn't keep the sarcasm out of her voice.

"A wife's place is with her husband," Esther said. "It's as simple as that."

Hannah cringed. Maybe a wife's place was with her husband, but wasn't the husband supposed to care about his wife's needs and wishes, too?

"Are you sure you don't mind taking me to the airport this afternoon? I feel bad asking you to drive after the snowy weather we've had these last few days," Bonnie's dad said as the two of them sat in the living room enjoying the warmth of the fireplace.

"Of course I don't mind, and since the roads are pretty well cleared, I'm sure we'll be fine."

"Excuse me," Trisha said, entering the room with her

suitcase in hand. "I wanted to let you know that I'm ready to head out, so if you'll print out my bill, I'll settle up with you now."

"Where will you be going from here?" Bonnie asked, leading the way to her desk in the foyer.

"Since my friend and her husband from Bowling Green are still away, I won't be stopping there. So I'll probably head for Virginia and check out some of the sights that I've read about."

"This sure isn't a good time of year to be traveling anywhere by car," Dad called from the other room. "Maybe you should head back to California."

Trisha looked at Bonnie and rolled her eyes. "He always did like to tell me what to do," she whispered.

Bonnie smiled. That didn't surprise her one bit, because Dad was a take-charge kind of guy.

Once Trisha's bill had been taken care of, she stepped into the living room and said good-bye to Dad.

"Have a safe trip," he mumbled.

Trisha hesitated a minute. Then she moved closer to him and said, "It was nice seeing you again, Kenny, and I'm truly sorry for whatever hurt I may have caused you in the past."

"It's Ken, not Kenny," Dad mumbled.

Trisha stood a few seconds, as if waiting for some other response, but when Dad said nothing more, she picked up her suitcase and opened the front door.

"It's been nice meeting you. Feel free to stop by if you're ever in this area again," Bonnie said, stepping onto the porch with Trisha.

Trisha turned and smiled. "I appreciate the offer, but if I do come back this way, I'll be sure and call first. I wouldn't want to be here if your dad's visiting, because it's obvious that

I make him feel uncomfortable."

"Well, he needs to get over it and leave the past in the past—forgive and forget. Life's too short to carry grudges, and I plan to talk to him more about that. You just call, no matter what, if you should ever come by this way again."

Trisha gave Bonnie a quick hug then started down the stairs. She was almost to the bottom when her foot slipped on a still-frozen step and down she went.

"What did I go and do now?" Trisha wailed. She tried to get up but was unsuccessful. "Oh, my ankle. . . It hurts so much!"

Bonnie, being careful not to slip herself, made her way down the porch stairs and knelt beside Trisha. After a quick look at Trisha's already swollen ankle, she determined that it could very well be broken. "Stay right where you are," Bonnie said when Trisha once more tried to stand. "I'll get Dad's help, and we'll carry you into the house."

CHAPTER 26

I can't begin to tell you how much I appreciate you letting me stay here while my ankle heals," Trisha said to Bonnie as she hobbled into the kitchen with the aid of her crutches.

"It's not a problem," Bonnie said. "Since you broke it after falling on my slippery steps, the least I can do is offer you a room free of charge." She motioned to the table. "Now if you'll take a seat, I'll fix you some breakfast."

Trisha still felt bad about imposing on Bonnie like this, but she really did appreciate all she had done for her since she'd fallen two days ago. Bonnie had even gone so far as to call her fiancé, Allen, and ask that he take her dad to the airport so she'd be free to take Trisha to the hospital to have her ankle x-rayed. And when they'd learned that it was broken, Bonnie had stayed with Trisha at the hospital and brought her back here to care for her. It was definitely more than she had expected.

Being with Bonnie was a taste of what it might have been like if Trisha had been able to have children. She'd always longed to be a mother and had wanted to adopt, but Dave wouldn't even discuss that option. He'd said on more than one occasion that if they couldn't have children of their own, then he didn't want any at all. Trisha thought it was selfish of him to feel that way—especially when there were children out there who needed a home. But out of respect for her husband, she'd never pushed the issue. Besides, she'd always felt that a child needed love from both parents.

"Would you like a bowl of oatmeal and some toast this morning?" Bonnie asked, breaking into Trisha's thoughts.

"Yes, thank you; that would be fine." Trisha seated herself at the table and watched helplessly as Bonnie made her breakfast. "I feel like I ought to be doing something to earn my keep," she said.

Bonnie shook her head. "It's no bother, really. I have to fix breakfast for myself, anyway."

"But you've done so much for me already—even giving up your room downstairs and moving into one of your upstairs guest rooms.

"I'm happy to do that. After all, you can't be expected to navigate the stairs with your leg in a cast and having to use crutches."

"I'm just not used to being waited on or pampered," Trisha said. "I've always been pretty independent, and after Dave died, I really had to learn how to fend for myself."

"I understand. Dad was the same way after Mom passed away from a brain tumor."

"How old were you when she died?"

"Thirteen."

"That must have been hard for both you and your dad."

"It was." Bonnie went to the cupboard and took out a box of brown sugar, which she placed on the table. "Mom was a very good cook, and she didn't like anyone in her kitchen, so I never learned to cook well. After she died, Dad and I just kind of muddled by."

"But you obviously learned how to cook somewhere along the line, because that Christmas dinner you fixed was delicious."

Bonnie smiled. "I had a good teacher."

"Who was that?"

"Esther Beiler. When I moved into Grandma and Grandpa's house and decided to open the B&B, Esther came to work for me. At first she did most of the cooking, but then she took the time to teach me." Bonnie moved back to the stove to check on the oatmeal. "Of course, I'll probably never be as good a cook as Esther, because she just has a talent for it."

"Guess everyone has something they're really good at," Trisha said, reaching for two napkins from the basket on the table. She folded them and set them out for the meal.

"That's true. Where do you feel your talents lie?" Bonnie questioned.

"I don't know if I'm as good a cook as Esther, but I used to be the head chef for a restaurant in Fresno, and the customers often raved about some of the dishes I created. So I guess if I have a talent, it's cooking."

"Oh my!" Bonnie's cheeks turned pink. "I had no idea there was a chef who could no doubt cook circles around me sitting at my table on Christmas Day. If I'd known that, I probably would have been a complete wreck."

Trisha laughed. "I've never considered myself anything more than someone who likes to cook, so you really don't need to worry about whether anything you fix measures up."

"That's good to know, because the oatmeal's a little too dry. I probably didn't put enough water in the kettle."

Trisha waved her hand. "Don't worry about that. It's funny, but whenever someone else does the cooking, no matter what it is, the food always tastes so much better. I used to tell my husband that his toast was the best-tasting toast I'd ever eaten. Anyway, a pat of butter and some milk poured over the top, and I'm sure the oatmeal will be plenty moist."

"I know exactly what you mean about someone else's cooking. It's kind of like eating outdoors. When does the food taste any better than that?" Bonnie set two bowls on the table and took a seat. "No wonder my dad fell so hard for you when you were teenagers. You're a very nice woman, Trisha Chandler."

Trisha smiled. "Thanks. I think you're pretty nice, too."

—⁂—

When breakfast was over and Trisha was resting comfortably on the living-room sofa, Bonnie did the dishes. She'd just finished and was about to mop the kitchen floor when Esther showed up.

"I'm surprised to see you," Bonnie said. "I figured you'd be over at Samuel's by now."

"I told Hannah last night that I'd be coming over late because I had some errands to run," Esther said. "To tell you the truth, I think she was glad."

"Are things still strained between you two?"

"A bit, although I believe they are somewhat better. We've been talking more lately, and I think that's helped."

Bonnie smiled. "I'm glad. You should bring Hannah and the little ones over to see me again. Maybe Suzanne would like to come, too."

"That sounds like fun. And speaking of Suzanne, I found out yesterday that she and Titus are expecting a baby. She's due sometime in August."

Bonnie squealed. "Now that is good news! I'm sure everyone in Suzanne's family must be very excited."

"They are, and so are Titus's parents. We suspected it when they were here for Christmas, and when Titus called his folks and told them the official news, they were delighted."

"I'm sorry I didn't get to see Abraham and Fannie while they were here this time," Bonnie said. "I enjoyed meeting them when they came for Titus and Suzanne's wedding. They seem like a very nice couple."

"They are, and I look forward to having them as in-laws."

"How soon will that be?" Bonnie asked, taking a seat at the table and motioning for Esther to do the same.

Esther lowered herself into a chair. "I don't know. Samuel would get married tomorrow if it was possible, but I really think we should wait until Hannah and Timothy have found a place of their own."

"I understand, but what if it's a long time before they find a place? Will you change your mind and marry Samuel anyway?"

Esther shrugged. "I don't know. Guess I'll have to wait and see how it all goes." She reached over and touched Bonnie's arm. "Speaking of weddings, have you and Allen set a date for your wedding yet?"

"Not a definite one, but we're hoping sometime in the spring."

"I've never been to an English wedding before, so I hope I'll get an invitation."

"Would you be allowed to go? I mean, it's not against your church rules or anything, is it?"

Esther emitted a small laugh. "No, it's not."

"Then you'll definitely get an invitation. In fact, I'm sure Allen will want to invite all our Amish friends."

"Will Allen sell his house and move here to the bed-and-breakfast, or will you sell this place and move into his house with him?"

"We haven't actually discussed that. And you know, until

this minute, I hadn't even given it a thought." Bonnie's forehead wrinkled as she mulled things over. "I sure would hate to give up this place, and I do hope Allen doesn't ask me to."

"I don't think he will. He knows how much you enjoy running the B&B."

"That may be so, but some men expect their wives to do things they don't really want to do. Take Hannah, for instance. She didn't want to move to Kentucky, but Timothy insisted."

"And with good reason," Esther said. "He had to get Hannah away from her mother in order to make her see that her first priority was to him."

Bonnie's lips compressed. "Hmm. . . I wonder if Allen will make me choose between him and the bed-and-breakfast."

Hannah had just sent Marla and Leon off to school when she looked out the kitchen window and spotted Suzanne's horse and buggy pull into the yard. A few minutes later, there was a knock on the door.

"Brr. . . It's cold out there," Suzanne said after Hannah opened the door and let her in.

"Do you think it's going to snow again?" Hannah asked.

"I don't believe so. The sky's clear with no clouds in sight, so that's a good thing."

"After that blizzard we had, I don't care if I ever see another snowflake," Hannah said.

Suzanne laughed. "I'm with you, but I think the kinner might not agree."

"So what brings you by here this morning?"

"I need to go to the store to pick up a few things, and since Samuel's place is right on the way, I decided to stop by and see how you're doing."

Hannah could hardly believe Suzanne would ask how she was doing. No one else seemed to care—least of all Timothy. "I'm okay," she murmured. "How about you? I heard you've been having some morning sickness."

"That's true, and I felt nauseous when I first got up today, but after I ate something and had a cup of mint tea, it got better." Suzanne removed her shawl and black outer bonnet then placed them on an empty chair before taking a seat.

"Would you like something to drink?" Hannah asked. "There's some coffee on the stove, or I could brew a pot of tea."

"No thanks. I'm fine."

Hannah was tempted to start washing the dishes but figured that could wait. The idea of visiting with Suzanne a few minutes seemed appealing, so she also took a seat. "I remember when I was expecting Mindy, for the first three months I felt nauseous most of the day. After a while, it got better though."

"Speaking of Mindy, where is she right now? She's so sweet. I was hoping I'd get to see her today."

"She's still sleeping, and so are Jared and Penny."

"Now, that's a surprise. I figured they'd all be up, running all over the house by now."

Hannah frowned. "Those kids of Samuel's are just too active."

"They do have a lot of energy," Suzanne agreed. "But then I guess most kinner do." She placed her hand against her stomach. "I know I have seven more months until the boppli is born, but Titus and I can hardly wait for our little one to get here."

"Are you hoping for a *bu* or a *maedel*?"

"I think Titus would like a boy, but I don't really care what we have; I just want the baby to be healthy."

Hannah cringed, remembering the miscarriage she'd had last year. *I wish the baby we lost would have gone to full-term and been healthy. I wish I was pregnant right now.*

Chapter 27

Get your coat; there's something I want to show you," Timothy said to Hannah one Saturday morning toward the end of January, when he entered the kitchen and found her doing the dishes.

"What is it?" she asked, turning to look at him.

"It's a house I want you to look at."

"Is it for sale?"

He nodded. "Samuel and I spotted the For Sale sign yesterday on our way home from work."

"How come you didn't mention it last night?"

"Because I knew we couldn't look at it until this morning, and I didn't want you bombarding me with a bunch of questions I couldn't answer till I knew more about the house."

She flicked some water at him. "I wouldn't have bombarded you with questions."

"Jah, you would." He dipped his fingers into the soapy water and flicked some water back in her direction, enjoying the playful moment—especially since things were so up and down between him and Hannah.

She moved quickly aside. "Hey! Stop that!"

He chuckled. "I figured if you wanted me to have a second shower of the day, then you'd probably want one, too."

"I don't think either of us needs another shower, but I do want to see that house. So let me finish up here, and we can be on our way." She paused, and tiny wrinkles formed across her forehead. "Will Samuel be able to watch Mindy, or do we need to take her along?"

"I've already talked to him about it, and he said he's fine with watching her, since he'll be here with his kinner anyway."

"Okay, great. I'll just be a few more minutes."

Timothy leaned over and kissed Hannah's cheek. She'd been so sullen since their move. It was good to see her get excited about something. He just hoped she wouldn't lose her enthusiasm once she saw the house he was interested in buying.

—∞—

Bonnie had just finished feeding the chickens when she spotted Allen's truck coming up the driveway. She'd spoken to him on the phone several times but hadn't seen him for a while because he'd been so busy with work and bidding new jobs. It was amazing that he'd have so much work to do at this time of the year, but she was glad for him, as she knew many others were out of work.

"It's good to see you," she said when he stepped out of the truck and joined her near the chicken coop.

He leaned down and gave her a kiss. "It's good to see you, too. Are you busy right now? I'd like to talk to you about something."

"I've got the time, but let's go inside where it's warmer."

He smiled and took her hand. "That sounds like a plan, but I'd like to talk to you in private, and I know Trisha's still with you right now, so I thought maybe we could go for a ride."

"Trisha came down with a cold and is in her room resting."

"Sorry to hear she's not feeling well." Allen flashed Bonnie a look of concern. "I hope you don't get sick, too. You've been doing extra duty taking care of her since she broke her ankle, so your resistance might be low right now."

"I'm fine," she said as they strode hand in hand toward the house. "I take vitamins, eat healthy foods, and try to get at least eight hours of sleep every night."

He squeezed her fingers gently. "That's good to hear."

When they entered the house, the smell of something burning greeted them.

"Oh, no. . .my cookies!" Bonnie raced into the kitchen and opened the oven door. The entire batch of oatmeal cookies looked like lumps of charcoal. "That's what I get for thinking I could multitask," she muttered. "I figured I'd be finished feeding the chickens in plenty of time before the cookies were done."

Allen stepped up behind Bonnie and put his arms around her waist. "It's my fault for keeping you out there so long."

"It's okay. I have more cookie dough in the refrigerator, but I'll wait until after our talk before I make any more." Bonnie turned off the oven and took the burned cookies out. "I think I'll set these on the back porch so they don't smell up the house more than they already have. I can crumble them up later for the birds. I'm sure they'll eat them."

"Here, let me do that." Allen picked up another pot holder, took the cookie sheet from her, and went out the back door. When he returned, Bonnie had a cup of coffee waiting for him, and they both took seats at the table.

"So what'd you want to talk to me about?" she asked.

He reached for her hand. "Now that we're officially engaged,

I think it's time we decide on a wedding date, don't you?"

She smiled. "Yes, I do."

"So how about Valentine's Day?"

Her eyebrows shot up. "Oh Allen, I could never prepare for a wedding that soon. Valentine's Day is just a couple of weeks away."

His shoulders drooped. "I figured you'd say that, but I'm anxious to marry you, and you can't blame a guy for trying."

She giggled. "I'd really like to have a church wedding and invite all our friends—Amish and English alike. Of course, my dad and your folks will also be invited, and we'll need to give them enough time to plan for the trip."

"That's true. So how long do you think it'll take for us to plan this wedding?"

"How about if we get married in the middle of May? The weather should be pretty nice by then, and we could have the reception here—maybe outside in the yard."

"That would mean a lot of work for you, making sure everything looks just the way you want it."

"I'm sure some of our Amish friends will help me spruce up the yard, and I'll ask Esther to make the cake and help with all the other food we decide to have."

He leaned closer and kissed the end of her nose. "Sounds like you've got it all figured out."

"Not really, but I'm sure it'll all come together as the planning begins." She paused and moistened her lips, searching for the right words to ask him a question. "There's something else we haven't talked about, Allen."

"What's that?"

"Where we're going to live once we're married."

"Oh, that." He raked his fingers through the ends of his thick, dark hair. "I'm guessing you don't want to give up the B&B?"

She shook her head. "This place has come to mean a lot to me. But I suppose if you don't want to live here—"

He put his finger against her lips. "I have no objections to living in this wonderful old house with you. After all, I did have a little something to do with making it as nice as it is." He winked at her.

"Yes, you sure did." Bonnie tapped her fingers along the edge of the table. "But what about your house? I know you built it to your own specifications, and—"

"It's just a house, Bonnie. I can be happy living anywhere as long as I'm with you."

She gently stroked his cheek, not even caring that it felt a bit stubbly. "I'm a lucky woman to be engaged to such a wonderful man."

"No, I'm the lucky one," he said before giving her a heart-melting kiss.

—∞—

"How far away is this place?" Hannah asked when she stepped outside and found Timothy standing beside their horse and buggy. "I figured we'd have to hire a driver to take us there."

"Nope. It's just a few miles from here."

"That's good to hear." Hannah wasn't thrilled with the idea of living too far from Timothy's brothers and their families. She figured Timothy would be excited to hear that from her, but for some reason she wasn't ready to share those new feelings just yet. She had to admit, if only to herself, that since she'd gotten to know Esther and Suzanne better, she wanted to be close enough so they could visit whenever they wanted to.

"We'd better get going," Timothy said, helping her into the buggy. "I told the real estate agent we'd meet him there at nine o'clock."

With a renewed sense of excitement, Hannah leaned back in her seat and tried to relax. If they could get this house, they might be able to move out of Samuel's place within the next few weeks.

As they traveled down the road, Timothy talked about how much he was enjoying painting with his brother, and then he told Hannah that the place they'd be looking at had fifty acres, which meant he could do some farming if he had a mind to.

Hannah knew he'd enjoyed farming with his dad in Pennsylvania, but if he was going to keep working full-time for Samuel, she didn't see how he'd have time to do any farming. Maybe they could lease some of the land and only farm a few acres for themselves. She kept her thoughts to herself though. No point in bringing that up when they didn't even know if they'd be buying the house.

A short time later, Timothy guided the horse and buggy down a long dirt driveway with a wooden fence on either side. A rambling old house came into view. It looked like it hadn't been painted in a good many years, but Hannah knew Timothy could take care of that. What concerned her was that the shutters hung loose, the front porch sagged, the roof had missing shingles, and several of the windows were broken. If that wasn't bad enough, the whole yard was overgrown with weeds.

"Ach, my!" she gasped. "This place is an absolute dump! Surely you don't expect us to live here!"

Chapter 28

Timothy's mind whirled as he groped for something positive to say about the house before Hannah insisted that they turn around and head back to Samuel's place.

"Listen, Hannah," he said, clasping her arm, "I think we need to wait till we've seen the inside of the house before drawing any conclusions. Let's try to keep an open mind—at least for now."

She wrinkled her nose. "If the inside looks even half as bad as the outside does, then I'm not moving here."

"Well, let's go inside and take a look. I see the agent's car over there, so he's probably in the house waiting for us."

Hannah sighed. "Okay, but where are you going to tie the horse? I don't see a hitching rail, which probably means this house belongs to an Englisher."

"That may be, but if we buy the place, we can put up a hitching post, and of course we'll have to remove the electrical connections." He directed Dusty over to a tree. "I'll tie my horse here, and he should be fine for the short time we'll be inside the house."

When they stepped onto the porch a few minutes later,

Timothy cringed and took hold of Hannah's hand. There were several loose boards—the kind that looked like if you stepped on them the wrong way, they'd fly up and hit you on the back of the head. The porch railing was broken in a couple of places, too.

"I know this porch looks really bad right now, but imagine if the boards and railing were replaced and it was freshly painted," Timothy said with as much enthusiasm as he could muster. "And look, the front of the house faces east. Think of all the beautiful sunrises we can watch from here on warm summer mornings."

"I guess that's one way of looking at it," Hannah said in a guarded tone.

Timothy was about to knock on the door when it swung open. Tom Donnelson greeted them with a smile. "It's good to see you both again. Come on in; I'm anxious to show you around."

As they entered the living room, where faded blue curtains hung at the window, Tom explained that the elderly man who'd owned the house had recently passed away, and his children, who lived in another state, had just put the place on the market. He then took them upstairs, through all five bedrooms, each needing a coat of fresh paint, and pointed out that there was an attic above the second story that would give them plenty of storage. The wide woodwork around the floor base, as well as the frames around the doors, were impressive, but they were badly scratched and needed to be sanded and restained.

When they got to the kitchen, Hannah's mouth dropped open. Timothy was sure she was going to flee from the house in horror. Not only did it need to be painted, but the sink was rusty from where the faucet had been leaking, the linoleum was torn in several places, the counter had multiple dings, and some of the hinges on the cabinet doors were broken. An old electric stove and refrigerator sat side-by-side and would need to be replaced. Most of the rooms had been wallpapered with several layers that had been put on over the years. So before any painting could be done, the walls would have to be stripped clean.

"I think this old house has some potential," Tom said. "It just needs a bit of a face-lift."

"A bit of a face-lift?" Hannah exclaimed with raised brows. "If you want my opinion, I'd say it needs to be condemned." She turned to Timothy and frowned. "Don't you agree?"

He shrugged his shoulders. "I know it's hard to see, but if you could just look past the way the house looks right now and imagine how it could look with some remodeling—"

"But that would take a lot of time, and probably a lot of money, too," she argued.

"I'll bet with the help of Samuel and Titus we could have this place fixed up and ready to move into by spring."

"The beginning of spring or the end of spring?" she questioned.

He turned his hands palms up. "I don't know. Guess we'd have to wait and see how it all goes."

Hannah's dubious expression made Timothy think she was going to refuse to even consider buying the house, but to his surprise, she turned to him and said, "If you really think you can make this place livable, then let's put an offer on it."

"Are you sure?"

She nodded.

"All right then." Timothy looked at Tom. "Can we do that right now?"

Tom gave a nod. "There's no time like the present. Let's head over to Samuel's house, and we can discuss a fair offer, and then you can sign the papers."

—~~—

That afternoon after Timothy and Hannah got back to Samuel's house and shared the news that they hoped to buy the house they'd looked at, Samuel decided to head over to the B&B and tell Esther. This was not only good news for Timothy and Hannah, but for him and Esther, as well, because it meant they could be married soon.

"Can we go with you, Daadi?" Leon asked as Samuel took his horse out of the barn. "We haven't gone over to play with Cody in a long time."

"And since Esther didn't come over here today, she's probably busy bakin' cookies," Marla added as she joined her younger brother. She licked her lips. "Sure would like some of those."

"I suppose you can go along, but Jared and Penny will probably want to go, too, and if they both go, then Mindy will want to be included, and I'm not sure Hannah will go for that."

"Can we at least ask?" Leon looked up at Samuel with pleading eyes. "If Aunt Hannah says Mindy can't go, then just the four of us will go with ya, okay?"

"Jah, and then Mindy will cry. You know she will." Marla frowned. "She's a whiny baby, and besides that she's spoiled."

Samuel reached under the brim of his hat and scratched his head. "You think so?"

"Sure do," Marla said with a nod.

"Hmm. . . Seems to me that Hannah's always telling Mindy no about something or other," Samuel said. "So I wouldn't call that spoiled."

"Mindy may not get everything she wants, but she's a big mama's baby, and Aunt Hannah's always fussin' over her," Leon interjected.

For fear that whatever he said might get repeated, Samuel didn't agree with the children, but he didn't disagree either. Truth was, he got tired of watching the way Hannah doted on Mindy, but if Timothy didn't say anything to his wife about it, then it wasn't Samuel's place to comment. He'd watched Esther with his children many times and was glad she didn't smother them with too much attention. He knew she loved them very much and felt sure that she'd make a good wife and mother.

"I'll tell you what," Samuel said, looking at Leon. "You run into the house and tell Aunt Hannah that you, Marla, Penny, and Jared are going over to see Esther with me, and if she doesn't mind, Mindy is welcome to come along."

"Okay. I'll be back soon!" Leon raced across the yard and into the house.

Samuel bent and gave Marla a hug. "You can get in the buggy if you want to."

"Okay, Daadi." Without waiting for Samuel's assistance, Marla climbed into the buggy and took a seat in the back.

He smiled. His oldest daughter was such a sweet little girl. In many ways she reminded him of Elsie. How glad he was that Marla and Leon had both been old enough when their mother died so they would have some memories of her as they grew up. Penny might remember some, too, but little Jared would only know whatever he was told about his mother. At least the children had Esther, and in fact, Jared and Penny often called her "Mama." Samuel had no problem with that.

Hearing the sound of laughter, Samuel glanced toward the house. Leon, Penny, and Jared, wearing straw hats, jackets, and scarves, pranced like three little ponies across the lawn. When they reached the buggy, they grabbed hold of Samuel's legs and squeezed.

"We can head out now, Daadi," Leon said. "Hannah said Mindy can't go."

"I figured as much," Samuel mumbled before lifting Penny and Jared into the buggy. *It's a shame Mindy couldn't join us,* he fumed. *Hannah is way too protective of that child.*

Leon climbed in last and took a seat up front on the passenger's side. "Hold the reins steady now while I untie my horse from the hitching rail," Samuel told the boy.

When Samuel took his seat on the driver's side, Leon handed him the reins and smiled. "Sure can't wait to play with Cody!"

Paradise, Pennsylvania

As Sally meandered up their driveway after getting the mail, she decided to stop at the phone shack and see if there were any new messages. She'd just stepped inside when she heard the phone ring, so she quickly grabbed the receiver. "Hello."

"Hi, Mom. This is a pleasant surprise. I wasn't expecting anyone to pick up the phone."

"Hannah, it's so good to hear your voice! How are you? How are Mindy and Timothy doing?"

"We're all fine. Mindy's taking a nap, and Timothy's in the house with our real estate agent, going over the paperwork we need to sign."

"Paperwork?"

"Jah. We found a house today, and we're going to put an offer on it."

"Wow, that was quick."

"Jah, quick as dew."

"I guess that means you'll be staying in Kentucky?" Sally

couldn't keep the disappointment she felt out of her voice.

"That's what Timothy wants, so I suppose we are."

Sally had expected Hannah to say she didn't want to stay in Kentucky, like she had so many other times when they'd talked. Maybe she'd resigned herself to the idea, knowing it was the only way to keep her husband happy.

"So tell me about the house. Is it close to where Timothy's brothers live?" Sally asked.

"It's just a few miles down the road from Samuel's place and not far from Titus's home either."

"Is it nice and big?"

"It's big, but. . .well, not so nice. In fact, it needs a whole lot of work."

Sally grimaced. "If it needs a lot of work, then why are you buying the place?"

"Because it's reasonably priced, and Timothy thinks he can have it fixed up enough so we can move in sometime this spring. With him and his brothers doing most of the work, it will save us a lot of money, too."

"I see."

"You and Dad will have to visit us after we get moved in. There are five bedrooms, so there's plenty of room for us to have company."

"Jah, we'll have to do that."

"How's Dad's back? Is he doing a lot better now?"

"He's working a few days a week at the store again but still has to be careful not to overdo. He had quite a siege with his back this time."

"I'm glad he's doing better." Hannah paused. "It's been good talking to you, Mom, but I'd better hang up now. I need to check on Mindy and see if the paperwork is ready to sign."

"Okay. Take care, Hannah, and please keep in touch."

"I will. Bye, Mom."

When Sally hung up the phone, a sick feeling came over her. Now that Timothy and Hannah were buying a house, she was almost certain they would never move back to Pennsylvania. If only there was something she could do to bring her daughter back home where she belonged. But what would it be?

With the mail in her hand and a heavy heart weighing her down, Sally trudged wearily toward the house. When she stepped inside, she found Johnny sitting in the recliner with a fat gray cat in his lap.

"You know I don't like that critter in the house," Sally snapped. "She gets hair everywhere!"

"I'm not letting her run all over the place, Sally. As you can see, I'm holding Fluffy in my lap."

Sally ground her teeth together, not even bothering to mention that there was cat hair clinging to her husband's pants, and tossed the mail onto the coffee table in front of the sofa. "I just spoke with Hannah on the phone, and guess what?"

"I have no idea." Johnny stroked the cat behind its ears and stared up at Sally with a smug expression. It only fueled her anger, watching more cat hair fly each time Johnny petted the feline.

"Hannah and Timothy are buying a house."

"That's good to hear. Samuel's been nice in letting them stay with him, but they really do need a place of their own."

Sally stepped directly in front of Johnny, her hands on her hips. "Don't you realize what this means?"

"Jah. It means they'll have a place of their own where we can stay when we go to visit."

She clenched her teeth so hard her jaw started to ache. "It

means they aren't moving back to Pennsylvania. They wouldn't be buying a house unless they planned to put down roots and stay in Kentucky."

"I think you're right about that, and it's probably for the best."

"What's that supposed to mean?"

"It means Timothy moving his family to Kentucky was the best thing he could have done for his marriage." Johnny stared at Sally over the top of his glasses, as if daring her to argue with him. "We've been through all this before, but I'm going to remind you once more that the Good Book says when a couple gets married, they are to leave their parents." Johnny let go of the cat and spread his arms wide. "And they are to cleave to each other. Leave and cleave!" He brought his hands together quickly and made a tight fist. "And that's the end of that, no matter what you may think."

CHAPTER 29

Pembroke, Kentucky

As soon as Samuel pulled his horse and buggy into Bonnie's yard, Cody leaped off the porch and darted into the yard to greet them. The children were barely out of the buggy when the dog was upon them, yapping excitedly and leaping into the air.

"Calm down, Cody," Samuel scolded, snapping his fingers at the dog. He remembered how once last year Cody had gotten his horse riled up and the critter ended up getting kicked pretty bad. The end result was a broken leg for the dog. Samuel sure didn't want anything like that to happen again.

"Take the dog over there to play," Samuel told Marla as he pointed to the other side of the yard. "That way he won't get kicked by the horse like he did last year."

She bent down and grabbed Cody's collar then led him across the yard. The other children quickly followed.

Samuel secured his horse to the hitching rail and hurried up to the house. He was about to knock when the door opened and Bonnie stepped out.

"Oh, it's you and the children. I heard Cody barking and wondered what all the commotion was about."

Samuel chuckled. "Yeah, that critter can get pretty worked up sometimes—especially when my kids come around."

Bonnie smiled. "Maybe the kids would like to come in for some cookies and hot chocolate."

"I don't know about the kids, but I'd like some." Samuel jiggled his eyebrows playfully, which was easy to do because of his good mood. "I'd like to talk to Esther first, though. Is she here or at the guesthouse?"

"She's upstairs right now, cleaning one of the rooms. I have some guests checking in later today." Bonnie motioned to the stairs. "Feel free to go on up if you'd like to talk to her, and then when you're done, you can join me and the kids in the kitchen for a snack."

"Sounds good to me." Samuel hung his jacket and hat on the coat tree in the entryway and sprinted up the stairs, hearing his kids squealing with delight as Bonnie called them in for a snack. He found Esther in one of the guest rooms sweeping the floor.

"Guder mariye," he said, stepping into the room.

Esther jumped. "Ach, Samuel, you startled me! I didn't realize you were here."

"Sorry about that. I'm surprised you didn't hear my noisy boots clomping up the stairs," he said.

"Well, I did, but I thought it was Bonnie."

"Bonnie has loud-clomping boots?"

Esther giggled, and her cheeks turned a pretty pink. "Her snow boots are a bit loud, but since we don't have any snow right now, I guess she wouldn't have been wearing any boots."

Samuel grinned. Esther looked so sweet when she looked up at him, almost like an innocent little schoolgirl. His heart ached to marry her, but he was trying to be patient.

"So what are you doing here?" she asked, setting her broom aside.

"Came to see you, of course." He took a few steps toward Esther. "I wanted to share some *gut noochricht.*"

"What's the good news?"

"Timothy and Hannah are buying a house. Their real estate agent's at my place right now, and they're signing papers to make an offer on the place. If their offer's accepted, they hope to be moved in by spring." He moved closer and took Esther's hand. "So you know what that means?"

"I guess it means Hannah will be happy to be living in a place of her own, where she won't have to share a kitchen or worry about anyone giving Mindy too much candy."

"That's probably true, but what it means for us is that once they're moved into their own home, we can get married."

"But what if their offer's not accepted?"

"I think it will be. It's a fair offer, and Tom Donnelson told Timothy that the owner of the house has passed on, and his adult children are anxious to sell the place."

"If they're so anxious to sell, then why would it take until spring before Timothy and Hannah can move in?" Esther questioned.

"The place is pretty run-down, and it's going to take a few months to get it fixed up so it's livable." Samuel gave Esther's fingers a gentle squeeze. "But if Titus and I help with the renovations, I think we can have it done in record time."

"I believe you could. It didn't take long for you and Allen to fix this old place up, so I'm sure with three very capable brothers working on Timothy's place, it could be done in no time at all." Esther's eyes sparkled as she smiled widely. "Oh Samuel, after all these months of waiting to become your wife, I can hardly believe we could actually be married in just a few months." Her face sobered. "I think it's best if we don't set a definite date yet, though—just in case the owners of the house don't accept Timothy and Hannah's offer."

Samuel pulled Esther into his arms and gave her a hug. "I'm sure it'll all work out, but we can wait to set a date until we know something definite. Now, why don't you take a break from working and come downstairs with me? Bonnie's promised to serve hot chocolate and cookies to me and the kids, and I'd like you to join us."

"I'm almost done here. Just let me finish sweeping the floor, and I'll come right down."

"Okay, but you might want to hurry. The kinner are in the kitchen with Bonnie, already enjoying those kichlin, and I'm going down now and make sure there are some left for us." Smiling, and feeling like a kid himself, Samuel gave her a quick kiss and hurried from the room.

~

Esther smiled as she finished sweeping the floor. Did she dare hope that she and Samuel could be married in a few months—or at least by early summer? Of course, she'd need a few months to make her wedding dress and plan for the wedding. Since Samuel was a widower, they wouldn't have nearly as large a wedding as younger couples who'd never been married. But there would still be some planning to do.

Oh, I wish Mom could be here to help me prepare for the wedding, Esther thought wistfully. *But it wouldn't be fair to ask her to come when she's needed to help Sarah care for Dan.*

Esther knew she could probably count on Suzanne to help with wedding details, but with Suzanne being pregnant and possibly not feeling well by then, she might not be able to help that much.

I could ask Bonnie, but then she has her own wedding to plan for, and I'm sure that's going to take up a lot of her time. Then there's Hannah, but I'm not sure she'd even want to help—especially now that they may be buying a house that needs a lot of work.

Even though Hannah had been a bit friendlier to Esther lately, she still kept a little wall around her—like she didn't want anyone to get really close. Esther hoped that wall would come down someday, because she still wanted to be Hannah's friend.

I'd better wait and see first if Hannah and Timothy get that house. Then I can begin planning my wedding and decide who to ask for help.

Once Esther finished sweeping, she emptied the dustpan into the garbage can she'd placed in the hall and went downstairs to join everyone for a snack. She didn't realize how hungry she'd gotten.

She'd just stepped into the kitchen, where Samuel and his children sat at the table, when the telephone rang.

"Hello. Bonnie's Bed-and-Breakfast," Bonnie said after she'd picked up the receiver. There was a pause; then she said, "As a matter of fact, Esther is right here. Would you like to speak with her?" She handed Esther the phone. "It's your mother."

With a sense of excitement, Esther took the phone. "Mom, I was just thinking about you. I wanted to tell you that—"

"Esther, your daed's in the hospital." Mom's voice quavered. "They've been treating him for a ruptured appendix, and now he's in surgery."

Esther gasped. "Ach, Mom, that's *baremlich*! I'll either hire a driver or catch the bus, but I'll be there as soon as I can."

"What's terrible?" Samuel asked when Esther hung up the phone.

She relayed all that her mother had said and then asked Bonnie if she could have some time off.

"Of course you can," Bonnie was quick to say. "Other than the guests coming in later today, I have no one else booked until Valentine's Day."

Esther looked at Samuel. "Do you think Hannah would be willing to take over full responsibility of your kinner and all the household chores until I get back from Pennsylvania?"

"I'm sure she will," Samuel said. "And if she's not, then I'll find someone else to help out. Your place is with your family right now."

Esther smiled, appreciating the understanding of both Samuel and Bonnie. She felt sick hearing about Dad's ruptured appendix, knowing how serious something like that could be. She closed her eyes and sent up a quick prayer. *Lord, please help my daed to be okay.*

Chapter 30

A ray of sunlight beckoned Hannah to the window in Marla's bedroom, where she'd been cleaning. Esther had only been gone a week, and already Hannah was exhausted. Samuel's children were a handful—especially Jared, who was a lot more active than Mindy. Hannah never knew what the little stinker might get into, and she had to stay on her toes to keep up with him. Jared was also a picky eater, often refusing to eat whatever she'd fixed for meals. Esther had usually made him something he liked, but Hannah felt that Jared could either eat what was on his plate or do without. She figured in time he'd learn to eat what the others ate, even if he didn't particularly like it.

Then there was all the extra cleaning she had to do. It seemed that no matter how many times she got after the children to pick up in their rooms, they just ignored her. Penny and Jared were the worst, often scattering toys all over the place. It was either nag them to clean up or do it herself, which was what she was doing today. She was glad Marla and Leon were both in school, and she'd put the three younger ones down for a nap. It was easier to get things done when they weren't underfoot. Hannah often found herself wishing

Esther hadn't gone to Pennsylvania, because she now realized that it had been much easier to share the work.

Hannah sighed and bent to pick up one of Marla's soiled dresses that should have been put in the laundry basket. The only good thing that had happened this week was that the offer she and Timothy had made on the old house had been accepted. So she could now look forward to the day when they'd be able to move in. As soon as the deal closed, which should happen in a few weeks, Timothy would begin working on the interior. He and his brothers would take care of exterior work as well, but most of those renovations could be done once they were moved in.

Samuel had heard from Esther a few days ago, giving him an update on her dad's condition. Even though he'd made it through surgery okay, there'd been a lot of infection in his body, and he was still in the hospital being carefully watched and getting heavy doses of antibiotics. The family had been told that he'd probably be there at least another week. After that, he would need a good four to eight weeks for a full recovery. So Esther had decided that she would stay and take over the stands her dad had been managing at two of the farmers' markets in the area. The stands really belonged to Esther's brother, but with Dan's MS symptoms getting worse, he certainly couldn't manage them anymore. Esther's mother probably could have taken over the stands, but she felt Dan's wife needed her help to care for their home and two children, as well as Dan.

As Hannah moved across the room to make Marla's bed, her thoughts went to Bonnie. *I wonder how she's managing without Esther's help.*

Hannah knew the woman from California was still at the B&B because her ankle wasn't completely healed. No doubt, having her there created more work for Bonnie. She probably felt as overwhelmed as Hannah did right now.

—~~—

"I was wondering if you've heard anything from Esther," Trisha said when Bonnie joined her in the living room in front of the fireplace.

"Her father is still quite sick, and Esther plans to stay in Pennsylvania and take care of the stands he's been running. It could be up to eight weeks before she returns to Kentucky," Bonnie said.

"So who will take her place helping you here at the bed-and-breakfast?"

Bonnie shrugged. "I don't know. If things get too busy, I'll probably have to place a help-wanted ad in the local newspaper."

"I could help. I'm getting tired of sitting around so much, so it would give me something meaningful to do."

Bonnie's eyes widened. "But your leg's still in the cast, and once you get it off, you'll need physical therapy. I sure can't expect you to climb the stairs and service the guest rooms."

"I could do some of the cooking. I'm pretty good at that, even if I do say so myself."

Bonnie folded her arms and leaned against the bookcase behind her. "That's right. Since you used to work as a chef, I'll bet you could create some pretty tasty dishes for my B&B guests."

Trisha nodded. "I could make them as fancy or simple as you like. I'd even be happy to work for my room and board."

Bonnie shook her head. "If you're going to work for me, then I insist on paying you a fair wage, as well as giving you room and board. I was doing that for Esther, you know."

Trisha smiled as a sense of excitement welled in her chest.

Maybe God had sent her here on Christmas Eve for a reason. She might even end up staying in Kentucky permanently. Of course if she did, she'd no doubt be seeing Bonnie's dad again.

Would I mind that? she asked herself. *Maybe not.*

Chapter 31

By the middle of February, Timothy and his brothers had done a lot of work on the house. If things went well, they hoped to have it fixed up enough so that Timothy, Hannah, and Mindy could move in by the middle of March, even if some things still needed to be done. Hannah thought she could live with that—as long as it didn't take too much time to finish the house after the move. She was so anxious to have her own place.

On this Saturday, Timothy and Titus were working at the house while Samuel went to Hopkinsville to run some errands. Hannah, tired of being cooped up in Samuel's house with five active children, decided to bundle the kids up and go over to her house to see how things were progressing. She'd also made the men some sandwiches because they'd left early this morning before she'd had a chance to fix them anything for lunch.

"You're the oldest, so I want you to keep an eye on the other children and wait here in the house while I get the horse and buggy ready," Hannah told Marla.

Marla looked up at her with a dimpled grin. "Okay, Aunt

Hannah. I'll watch 'em real good."

Hannah patted Marla's shoulder. Of all Samuel's children, Marla was the easiest to deal with. She was usually quite agreeable and seemed eager to please. She was also the calmest child, which Hannah appreciated, because Samuel's other three could think of more things to get into than a batch of curious kittens. She did notice, though, that Marla had a funny habit. Every so often, the child put her hand inside the opposite sleeve of her dress, as if hiding it or maybe trying to warm it up. No one else mentioned this or seemed to take notice, and Hannah didn't spend much time wondering about it herself. *After all, I used to chew my fingernails when I was a girl.* Fortunately, she gave up the habit before she reached her teen years, so she figured Marla would probably do the same.

"I shouldn't be too long, but give me a holler if you need anything," Hannah said before going out the back door.

Since the buggy was already parked in the yard, all she had to do was get her horse. When Hannah entered Lilly's stall, the horse flicked her ears and swished her tail.

"Would you like to go for a ride, girl?" Hannah patted the horse's flanks. "You need the exercise, or you'll get fat and end up in lazy land." She smiled to herself, remembering how Mom had often used that term to describe someone who didn't want to work.

Lilly whinnied in response and nuzzled Hannah's hand. She was glad they had been able to bring both of their horses when they'd moved. Having them here was a like a touch from home. Hannah glanced at the other side of the barn where all their furniture had been stacked under some canvas tarps. Once they could bring their belongings to the new house, she hoped it would help her feel closer to the home she used to know and love in Pennsylvania. Starting over was difficult, but it would be a bit easier when they could use their own things again. While Samuel's house was comfortable enough, nothing in it belonged to Hannah, and she still felt out of place—like a stranger at times.

Hannah was about to put the harness on Lilly when a little gray mouse darted out of the hay and zipped across her foot. Startled, she screamed and jumped back. There were a few critters she really didn't like, and mice were near the top of her list.

Hearing Hannah's scream must have frightened Lilly, for she reared up and then bolted out of the stall. Hannah chased after the horse, and realized too late that she'd left the barn door open.

"Come back here, Lilly!" Hannah shouted as she raced into the yard after the horse.

Around and around the yard they went, until Hannah was panting for breath. She knew she had to get Lilly back in the barn or she'd never get her harnessed and ready to go. And if the crazy horse kept running like that, she might end up out on the road, where she'd be in jeopardy of getting hit by a car.

"Whoa! Whoa, now!" Hannah waved her hands frantically, but it did no good. Lilly was in a frenzy and wouldn't pay any attention to her at all.

Hannah heard someone shout, and when she turned her head, she was surprised to see Leon running out of the house, waving his arms and hollering at Lilly. While the boy might be young, he must have known exactly what he was doing, because it wasn't long before he had Hannah's horse under control and running straight for the barn.

Hannah hurried in behind them and quickly shut the door. "Whew! Lilly gave me quite a workout! Danki for coming to my rescue, Leon."

The boy looked up at her and grinned. "I've helped Daadi chase after his horse before, so I knew just what to do. And if our pony ever gets outa the barn, bet I can get him back in, too." Leon's face sobered. "Marla said I wasn't supposed to go outside, but when I saw your horse runnin' all over the place, I had to come out and help. Sure hope that's okay."

She smiled and gave his shoulder a gentle squeeze. "I'm glad you did. Would you like to help me put the harness on Lilly?"

"Jah, sure."

A short time later, Hannah's horse was hitched and ready to go. Now all she needed to do was load the children into the buggy, and they could be on their way.

"Could you give me a hand with this drop cloth?" Timothy called to Titus, who was on the other side of the living room, removing some old baseboard that needed to be replaced.

"Sure thing." Titus stopped what he was doing and picked up one of the drop cloths. "Do you want to cover the whole floor or just this section for now?"

"If you're about ready to paint your side of the room, we may as well cover the entire floor," Timothy said.

"I will be as soon as I put the new baseboard up."

"Okay then, let's just cover the floor on my side for now. Sure am glad we both know how to paint," Timothy said as they spread out the drop cloth.

"Jah, but you've done more painting than I ever have, so your side of the room will probably look better than mine. Think I'm better at carpentry than painting."

"You are good with wood," Timothy agreed, "but your painting skills are just fine. I think you sell yourself short sometimes."

Titus shrugged. "That's what Suzanne says, too."

"Speaking of Suzanne, how's she feeling these days?"

"She's still havin' some morning sickness, but at least it doesn't last all day like it did at first." Titus's forehead wrinkled. "Since we've only been married a few months, we weren't expecting a boppli this soon. But then God knows what we need and when we need it, so we've come to think of it as a blessing."

Timothy thought about his brother's remark. He'd always felt that God knew what he needed and when he needed it, but he wasn't so sure Hannah shared that belief. Sometimes her faith in God seemed weak, and she usually had little to say about the sermons they heard at church. He felt that this move to Kentucky had been God's will, but he didn't think Hannah had come to accept it just yet. They still quarreled a lot, and Hannah often nagged him about little things. But since they'd bought this house, her outlook seemed a bit more positive. He hoped after they moved in and she arranged things to her liking she'd feel more like Kentucky was her home.

The brothers worked quietly for a while, until Timothy heard a horse and buggy pull in. Thinking it was probably Samuel coming to help, he didn't bother to look out the window.

A few minutes later, the front door opened, and Hannah stepped into the room carrying a wicker basket. Marla, Leon, Penny, Jared, and Mindy traipsed in behind her.

That's just great, Timothy thought. *The last thing we need is the kinner here getting in the way.* He was about to ask Hannah what they were doing when Mindy rushed over to Titus, who was crouched down with his back to them, and threw her little arms around his neck. "Daadi!"

With a look of surprise, Titus whirled around, nearly knocking the child off her feet. Mindy took one look at Titus's face and started howling. She'd obviously mistaken him for her daddy, but after seeing his beard, which was much shorter than Timothy's because he hadn't been married as long, she'd realized her mistake.

Hannah placed the basket on the floor, hurried across the room, and swooped Mindy into her arms. "It's all right, little one. That's your uncle Titus. Don't cry. Look, daadi's right over there." She pointed to Timothy.

Hannah set Mindy down, and the child, still crying, darted across the room toward Timothy. In the process, she hit the bucket of paint with her foot and knocked it over. Some of the white paint spilled out, but at least the drop cloth was there to protect the floor. When Mindy saw what she'd done, she started to howl even louder—like a wounded heifer.

Timothy, grabbing for the paint can and more than a bit annoyed, glared at Hannah and said, "What are you doing here, and why'd you bring the kinner? This is not a place for them to be when we're tryin' to get some work done!"

Hannah pointed to the basket she'd set on the floor. "You left so early this morning that I didn't get a chance to make your lunch, so I decided to bring it over to you." She motioned to the children, who stood wide-eyed and huddled together near the door. "I could hardly leave them at home by themselves, now, could I?"

"Of course not, but—"

"And I wanted to see how you're doing and ask if there's anything I can do to help," she quickly added.

"Jah, there is," Timothy shouted. "You can just leave the lunch basket and head back home with the kinner while I clean up the paint that got spilled!"

Hannah's chin quivered, and even from across the room he could see her tears. "Fine then," she said, bending to pick up Mindy. "I guess that's what I get for trying to be nice!" She ushered the kids quickly out the door, slamming it behind her.

"Hey, Timothy, you need to calm down. You caught the paint before too much damage was done, so did you have to yell at Hannah like that?" Titus asked, moving over to the basket. "I'm hungerich, and I'm glad she brought us some lunch."

"It was a nice gesture," Timothy agreed, "but she should have left the kinner in the buggy while she brought the lunch basket in here. She ought to know better than to turn five little ones loose in a room that's being painted." He shrugged his shoulders. "But what can I say? Sometimes my fraa just doesn't think."

"No one is perfect, Timothy. Maybe you're just too hard on Hannah. It might help if you appreciated the good things she does, rather than scolding her for all the things she does that irritate you."

A feeling of remorse came over Timothy. He didn't know why he'd been short on patience lately. Maybe it was because he wanted so badly to get this house presentable enough so they could move in. Even so, that was no excuse for him losing his temper—especially in front of the children.

"You're right, and I appreciate the reminder. I should have handled it better," Timothy said, watching out the window as the buggy headed down the road. "Guess it's too late now, but as soon as I get home, I'll apologize to Hannah and try to make things right." He dropped his gaze to the floor. "Guess I'd better say I'm sorry to the kinner, too—especially my sweet little girl, who probably thinks her daadi's angry with her."

Chapter 32

Trisha had just taken a loaf of banana bread from the oven when the telephone rang. Knowing Bonnie was outside emptying the garbage, Trisha picked up the receiver. "Hello. Bonnie's Bed-and-Breakfast."

"Bonnie, is that you?"

"No, this is Trisha." Then, recognizing the voice on the other end, she said, "How are you, Kenny?"

"I'm okay, and if you don't mind, it's Ken, not Kenny." There was a pause. "How's your ankle doing?"

"It's better. I got the cast off a week ago, but now I'm doing physical therapy."

"How much longer will you be staying at Bonnie's?" he asked.

"I don't know. I guess that all depends on when Esther returns from Pennsylvania."

"What's she doing in Pennsylvania, and what's that got to do with you?"

Trisha explained about Esther's dad and then told Ken that she'd been doing the cooking for Bonnie and that Bonnie was taking care of servicing the rooms. "I thought Bonnie would have told you that," she added.

"Nope. She never said a word."

Hmm. . .that's strange, Trisha thought. *I know Bonnie's talked to her dad since Esther left. I wonder why she didn't mention any of this to him.*

"She probably didn't mention it because she thought I wouldn't approve," Ken said, as though anticipating the question on the tip of her tongue.

"And would you?" she dared to ask.

"The B&B is Bonnie's to do with as she likes, so whomever she hires to work there is her business, not mine."

"So you're okay with me working here?"

"I didn't say that. Just said—"

The back door opened suddenly, and Bonnie stepped in. "It's your dad." Trisha held the receiver out to Bonnie. "I'm sure he'd rather talk to you than me."

After Bonnie took the phone, Trisha left the room, wondering once again if things would ever be better between her and Ken. She hoped they would, because over these last several weeks, she and Bonnie had become good friends. She'd gotten to know Allen, too, and appreciated the way he always included her in the conversation whenever he came to see Bonnie, although Trisha usually tried to make herself scarce so he and Bonnie could have some time alone.

I wish I could be here for Bonnie and Allen's wedding, Trisha thought as she entered the living room and took a seat in the rocker. *Maybe when Esther comes back I can find another job somewhere in the area and rent an apartment in Hopkinsville—at least until after Bonnie and Allen are married.*

If she and Ken hadn't broken up when they were teenagers, would she have visited him at this house? What if she had married Ken instead of Dave? Would they have ended up living in Kentucky instead of Oregon?

"Shoulda, woulda, coulda," she murmured, leaning her head back and closing her eyes. "There's always more than one direction a person can take. I guess there's no point in pondering the 'what if's.' "

It had taken Hannah awhile to get the children settled down after they'd gone back to Samuel's. They'd clearly been upset by Timothy's outburst. After they'd had silent prayer before lunch, Leon looked up at Hannah and said, "How come Uncle Timothy's mad at us?"

"I don't think he's mad at you," Hannah assured him. "He was just upset because we went over to the house when he was really busy, and when the can of paint got spilled, he was left with a mess to clean up. I think he was more upset with me than anyone," she added.

"When we first moved to Kentucky, Daadi used to yell at us like that," Marla spoke up, putting her hand inside the sleeve of her dress.

"He did?"

"Jah. Esther said it was because he missed our mamm so much, but we thought he didn't love us."

"But you know now that he loves you, right?" Hannah questioned.

Leon bobbed his head. "Daadi got better after I ran away from home. Maybe you oughta run away, too, Aunt Hannah. Then when ya come back, Uncle Timothy might be nicer to ya."

Hannah smiled despite her sour mood. "Sometimes I do feel like running away, but it probably wouldn't be the answer to our problems."

"What is the answer?" Marla asked.

Hannah shrugged. "I'm not sure. I guess I just need to let your uncle Timothy work on the house and not bother him when he's there." She reached over and wiped away a blob of peanut butter Mindy had managed to get on her chin.

Truth was, when Timothy snapped at her like he had today, it made her long to be back in Pennsylvania, where she'd have Mom's love and support. That wasn't likely to happen, though—especially now that they'd bought a house. Hannah figured she'd better make the best of things and try to stay out of Timothy's way when he was busy working on the house. That would be easier than quarreling all the time or being hurt when he said something harsh to her, which seemed to be happening a lot lately. She knew Timothy didn't like to argue either, but they seemed to do it frequently.

Maybe he thinks I'm hard to live with, Hannah thought.

The children had just finished their lunch, when Hannah heard the sound of horse's hooves coming up the driveway. When she went to the window, she was surprised to see Timothy's horse and buggy pull up to the hitching rail. *I wonder what he's doing back so early. Maybe he forgot a tool. Or maybe he came to lecture me some more.*

Fearful that Timothy might say something to upset the children, Hannah told them to go upstairs to their rooms.

"What about our *schissel*?" Marla asked. "Don't you want us to clear them first?"

Hannah shook her head. "That's okay. I'll take care of the dishes." She lifted Mindy from her stool and told her to go upstairs to play with Marla and the others.

When the children left the room, Hannah started clearing the table. She'd just put the last dish in the sink when Timothy entered the kitchen.

"What are you doing here?" she asked over her shoulder. "I thought you planned to work at the house all day."

"I do, but I had to come home for a few minutes." He stepped up to Hannah and placed his hands on her shoulders. "*Es dutt mir leed.*"

"You're sorry?"

"That's right. I shouldn't have gotten so angry about the spilled paint and spouted off like I did. Will you forgive me, Hannah?"

She nodded, feeling her throat tighten. "I'm sorry, too," she murmured. Hannah couldn't believe he'd come all the way home just to say he was sorry, but it softened her heart. She felt more love for her husband than she had in a long time. Did she dare hope that things would be better between them from now on?

Chapter 33

By the middle of March, Timothy and Hannah were able to move into their home. Not everything had been fixed, but at least it was livable. Since Esther was still in Pennsylvania, Hannah had agreed to watch Samuel's children at her house, which meant he had to bring them over every morning, but he seemed to be okay with that.

One sunny Monday, Hannah decided to take advantage of the unusually warm weather and hang her laundry outdoors, rather than in the basement. As she carried a basket of freshly washed clothes out to the clothesline, she wondered if they'd made a mistake in buying this old house. So much remained to be done. Several upstairs windows needed new screens. Some screens were broken, and some were missing altogether. The barn needed work, too, which was important because it not only housed their horses, but also Timothy's farming tools, painting supplies, and many other things, including hay and food for the animals. Then there was the yard. Hannah didn't know if she'd ever get the weeds cleared out in time to plant a garden this spring. The fields behind the house looked like they hadn't been cultivated in a good many years, and they'd need to be plowed and tilled before Timothy could plant corn. It was all a bit overwhelming, and having to take care of Samuel's children during Esther's absence only made it worse for Hannah. However, she'd agreed to do it, and the money Samuel insisted on paying her was nice for extra expenses.

Hannah shifted the laundry basket in her arms. On a brighter note, soon after they'd moved in, Timothy had mounted the covered-bridge bird feeder he'd given her for Christmas on a post in their backyard. Hannah glanced at the feeder and smiled when she saw several redheaded house finches eating some of the thistle seed she'd put out. She found herself humming and enjoying the joy spring fever always brought.

Redirecting her thoughts, she set the laundry basket on the ground and turned to check on the children. Penny, Jared, and Mindy sat on the porch steps, petting the pathetic little gray-and-white cat that had wandered onto their place the day they'd moved in. The kids had named the cat Bobbin because he bobbed his head whenever he walked. The poor critter had trouble with his balance and sometimes fell over when he tried to run. Hannah figured he'd either been injured or been born with some kind of a palsy disorder. One thing for sure, the cat had been neglected and was looking for a new home. While Hannah wasn't particularly fond of cats, she couldn't help feeling sorry for Bobbin, so she'd begun feeding him, which of course meant the cat had claimed this as his new home. For the sake of Mindy, who'd latched on to the cat right away, Hannah had allowed Bobbin to stay. But she'd made it clear that he was not to be in the house. She didn't want to deal with cat hair everywhere, not to mention the possibility of fleas.

As Hannah hung a pair of Timothy's trousers on the line, she thought about how hard he and his brothers had worked on the house. Looking around, she had to admit they really had accomplished a lot in a short amount of time.

She giggled to herself, thinking back to the day when their new propane stove had been delivered. When they were moving the appliance into place, part of the floor gave way, and the stove became wedged halfway between the kitchen floor and the basement ceiling. Everyone stood with looks of shock until someone had the good sense to suggest that they secure the stove before it fell any farther through the floor. Then they worked together to get the stove hoisted back up in place. Apparently, the wood floor had weakened in that area from a leaky pipe, because originally the sink was located there. It wasn't funny at the time, and it set them back a few days, but Timothy, Samuel, and Titus managed to get the floorboards replaced and a nice square area inlayed with brick for the stove to set on. Except for a few scratches on her new stove, which Hannah wasn't happy about, it had all worked out.

"*Frosch schpringe net.*"

Hannah looked down, surprised to see Jared standing beside her, and wondered what he meant about a frog not jumping. She was about to ask when he pointed to her laundry basket. A fat little frog sat looking up at her.

Hannah screamed. She hated frogs. Even the sight of one sent chills up her spine. "Get that frosch out of there!"

Jared looked up at her like she was a horse with two heads as he picked up the frog.

"Put it over there," she said, pointing to a clump of weeds near the barn. She would have told him to take it all the way out to the field, but she didn't want him going that far from the house.

As Jared walked off, Hannah shook her head and continued to hang up the laundry. *That boy is really something,* she thought with a click of her tongue. *I hope Esther knows what she's getting herself into by marrying Samuel.*

She'd just finished hanging the last of the towels when she spotted a car coming up the driveway. When it pulled up next to the barn, she realized it belonged to Bonnie.

"Guder mariye," Bonnie said as she joined Hannah by the clothesline. "That is how you say *good morning*, isn't it?"

Hannah nodded, surprised that Bonnie knew some Pennsylvania-Dutch words.

"It's so nice out today, and I decided to take a ride and come by to see your new house. Oh, and I brought you a few housewarming gifts." Bonnie motioned to her car. "They're in there."

"I'd be happy to show you the house, but you didn't have to bring me anything," Hannah said.

Bonnie smiled. "I wanted to welcome you to the neighborhood. You know, my B&B isn't too far from here, so feel free to drop by any time you like."

"Thanks." Hannah bent to pick up the empty laundry basket. "Let's go inside, and I'll show you around."

"Sounds good. I'll get your gifts from the car and follow you up to the house."

Hannah skirted around the weeds and stepped onto the porch. "You all need to come inside now," she said to the children.

"Can't we stay out here?" Penny asked in a whiny voice. "We want to pet the katz."

"You can pet the cat later. I need you inside where I can keep an eye on you."

Penny's lower lip jutted out, and when Mindy started

to howl, Jared did, too. Their screams were so loud Hannah feared their nearest neighbor might call the police, thinking something horrible had happened. She held the laundry basket under one arm and against her hip then put her finger to her lips. "Hush now, and come inside, *schnell.*"

But the children didn't come quickly, as she'd asked them to do. Instead, they sat on the porch step, with Mindy still holding the cat, and all three of them crying.

Just then, Bonnie showed up carrying a wicker basket. She placed it on the little wooden table on the porch, reached inside, and handed each of the children a chocolate bar. Even though Hannah didn't normally allow Mindy to have candy—especially so close to lunchtime—she offered no objections, because Bonnie's gift to the children was all it took to stop their crying.

"You can eat the candy, but only if you come inside," Hannah said, opening the door. The children put the cat down, and as he bobbled off to chase after a bug, they followed Bonnie and Hannah inside.

Once inside, Hannah instructed them to go to the kitchen to eat their candy bars, while she gave Bonnie a tour of the house.

"This is a nice-sized home," Bonnie said when they stepped into one of the bedrooms upstairs. "Plenty of room for a growing family and extra room for any company you may have."

"Our family's not growing at the moment," Hannah said. "Unless you count Bobbin, the cat."

"I assume you and Timothy will want other children?" Bonnie asked.

Hannah nodded. "I had a miscarriage last year, but I haven't been able to conceive since then. Timothy says it's because

I'm always stressed out, but I think my womb might be closed up."

Bonnie gave Hannah's arm a gentle squeeze. "I'll pray for you."

"Thanks, I appreciate that." Hannah was surprised to see such compassion on Bonnie's face. It made her think maybe Bonnie might want children, too.

"The men did a good job painting all the rooms," Bonnie said, as they moved on to another bedroom.

"Yes, they did. It took them awhile to strip off the wallpaper, but it turned out nice. There's still some work that needs to be done up here, though." Hannah motioned to the windows. "Some of the screens are missing, and some are old and loose, so they'll all need to be replaced. But considering the repairs that have been done since we bought this place, we're fortunate that we could move in so quickly."

"There were a few missing screens at the B&B when I first moved in," Bonnie said. "But between Samuel and Allen, those were taken care of before the warm weather arrived last year."

"Hopefully, Timothy will get all the screens replaced here soon. With nicer weather on the way, it will be good to have fresh air circulating through the house."

Hannah left the room and stepped into the hall. "I think we should go downstairs now and see what the kids are up to in the kitchen."

"Oh yes, and I want to give you my housewarming gifts, too."

When they entered the kitchen, the children were gone. Hannah checked the living room and found them sitting on the floor with a stack of books. "Go to the bathroom and wash up," she instructed. "You probably have chocolate on your hands, and I don't want that getting on any of Mindy's books."

The children did as she asked, but they didn't look happy about it.

Hannah turned to Bonnie and said, "Those kids of Samuel's can sure be stubborn."

Bonnie chuckled. "I guess all kids can be that way at times."

The two women continued on into the kitchen, and Bonnie removed a carton of eggs, a cookbook, several dish towels, and a loaf of homemade bread from the wicker basket she'd set on the table. "The eggs are from my layers," she said. "Oh, and Trisha made the bread, I made the dish towels, and the cookbook was put together by some of the women at my church. I have one, too, and all the recipes I've tried so far have been very good."

"Thank you for everything," Hannah said as they both took a seat at the table.

Hannah thumbed through the cookbook and stopped when she came to a recipe for Kentucky chocolate chip pie. "You know, I was planning to make this pie for Christmas, but I didn't feel like doing any baking. I really do need to try it sometime though. Timothy likes anything with chocolate chips in it, and I bet he'd enjoy the pie."

"It does sound tasty," Bonnie agreed. "If you try it, let me know how it turns out. I could even be your guinea pig," she added with a gleam in her eyes.

"I might just do that." Hannah laughed. "Would you like a cup of tea?" She offered, feeling cheerful. "It won't take long to get the water heated."

"That sounds nice, but I really should get going. I need to drive Trisha to her physical therapy appointment this afternoon, and if we get an early start, I may try to get some shopping done while we're in Hopkinsville."

Bonnie was just starting for the door when a fat, little frog hopped out of the sink onto the counter, then leaped onto the floor by Hannah's feet. She screamed and jumped up. "Jared Fisher, did you bring that frosch into the house?"

Wearing a sheepish expression, Jared shuffled into the kitchen. Hannah pointed at the frog. "Take it outside, right now!"

Hannah was relieved when the child did as she asked but embarrassed that she'd made a fool of herself in front of Bonnie. "I've had a fear of frogs ever since my oldest brother put one in my bed when I was a little girl," she explained. "And I sure never expected to see a frog this early in the year."

"It must be the warm weather that brought it out." Bonnie smiled. "And believe me, I understand about your fear. I think we all have a fear of something."

"Not Timothy. I don't think he's afraid of anything."

"Most men won't admit to being afraid because they want us to think they're fearless." Bonnie chuckled and moved toward the door. "It was nice seeing you, Hannah, and thanks for giving me a tour of your new home."

"Thank you for stopping by and for all these nice things."

Hannah stood at the door and watched as Bonnie walked out to her car. It had been nice to have an adult to visit with for a while. Even though Hannah kept busy watching the children, she often felt lonely and isolated. Oh, what she wouldn't give for a good visit with Mom.

Chapter 34

As Esther's driver, Pat Summers, turned onto the road leading to Pembroke, Esther's excitement mounted. Here it was the first Saturday in April, and she could hardly believe she'd been gone two months. But her help had been needed in Pennsylvania, and she'd stayed until Dad was well enough to take over working the stands at both farmers' markets. It had been good to spend time with her family, but as hard as it was to leave, she knew her place was here in Kentucky with Samuel and his children. She would stop by the B&B first to drop off her luggage and let Bonnie know she was back, and then she would head over to see Samuel and the children.

"I hope the woman you work for at the bed-and-breakfast will have a room available for me to spend the night," Pat said as they neared Bonnie's place. "If there are no vacancies, I'll have to look for a hotel in Hopkinsville. I've done enough traveling for one day and need to rest up."

Esther smiled at her. "When I spoke to Bonnie on the phone a few days ago, she said she didn't have any guests coming until next weekend. So unless things have changed, I'm sure she'll have a room for you."

"I'm anxious to see the B&B," Pat said. "From what you've told me, it sounds like a real nice place."

Esther nodded. "It is now, but you should have seen the house before Samuel and Allen fixed it up. Both men are good carpenters, and Samuel's an expert painter, so Bonnie was very pleased with how it turned out." Esther motioned to the B&B sign on her right. "Here we are. Turn right there."

Pat drove up the driveway and parked her van on the side of Bonnie's garage. When they got out of the van, Cody leaped off the porch and ran out to greet them.

"Oh, I hope he doesn't bite," Pat said when the dog jumped up on Esther.

"No, he's just excited to see me." Esther told Cody to get down; then she bent over and stroked his head. "Good boy, Cody. Have you missed me?"

Woof! Woof! Cody wagged his tail.

"I've missed you, too," Esther said with a chuckle. "Now be a good dog and go lie down."

Cody darted over to Pat and sniffed her shoes before making a beeline for the porch, where he flopped down near the door.

Esther found the front door open, so she didn't bother to knock. They'd just entered the foyer when Bonnie stepped out of the kitchen. "Oh, it's so good to see you!" she said, giving Esther a hug. "I knew you were coming back today, but I wasn't sure what time you'd get here."

"We spent last night in a hotel in Louisville and got an early start this morning," Esther explained. She turned to Pat and introduced her to Bonnie.

"I was wondering if I might be able to rent a room for the night," Pat said after shaking Bonnie's hand.

Bonnie nodded. "I have no other guests right now, so you

can take your pick from any of the rooms. Shall we go upstairs and take a look right now?"

"Sure, that'd be great."

While Bonnie took Pat upstairs, Esther meandered into the kitchen. She found Trisha baking cookies. "Ah, so that's the source of the wonderful aroma," she said, motioning to the cookies cooling on racks.

"It's nice to see you, Esther," Trisha said. "I'm sure you're glad to be back."

Esther nodded. "Yes, I am. I've missed seeing all of my friends here."

"How soon will you want to start working at the B&B again?" Trisha asked.

"I'm not sure. I'll need to talk to Bonnie about that." Esther motioned to the cookies. "If those taste as good as they smell, I'd say any B&B guests who might get to eat them are in for a real treat."

"I hope so."

"I hope you'll stay here for a while," Esther said. "At least until I know what my plans are going to be."

Trisha quirked an eyebrow. "What do you mean? Are you saying you might not continue to work for Bonnie?"

"I'm not sure. It'll depend on how soon Samuel and I get married, and whether he wants me to keep working or not." Esther leaned on the edge of the counter. "I probably shouldn't have said anything until I've talked to Samuel, so I'd appreciate it if you didn't mention this to Bonnie."

"I won't say anything."

"If I should decide to quit, would you stay to help Bonnie?" Esther asked.

Trisha shrugged. "Maybe. I do like it here, and Bonnie and I have become quite close. In fact, I've begun to feel like she's the daughter I never had."

Esther smiled. "I'm glad."

Just then Bonnie and Pat entered the kitchen. "You were right. This place is wonderful," Pat said, looking at Esther.

"Which room did you choose?" Esther asked.

"The one with the Amish theme. I love that Log Cabin quilt on the bed."

"It is nice," Esther agreed. "But then I like most Amish quilt patterns."

"Why don't we all take a seat?" Bonnie motioned to the table. "We can have some of Trisha's delicious cookies and a cup of hot tea."

—∞—

A crisp afternoon breeze brushed Hannah's face, and she shivered. It might be officially spring, but the chilly weather said otherwise.

I wish Timothy didn't have to spend the day plowing the fields, Hannah thought as she hitched Timothy's horse to the buggy. She'd wanted to spend the day as a family—maybe hire a driver and do some shopping in Hopkinsville—but Timothy said he didn't have time. It seemed like whenever he wasn't painting with Samuel, he had work to do here. Hannah kept busy during the week, taking care of Samuel's kids and keeping up with things around the house, but when the weekend came, she was ready to do something besides work. Since Timothy wasn't available today, she'd decided to take Mindy and go over to see Bonnie for a while. Hannah's horse, Lilly, had thrown a shoe, so Hannah knew if she wanted to go anywhere, she'd have to take Dusty. She hoped he would cooperate with her and take it nice and easy, because there had been times when she'd ridden with Timothy that he'd had to work hard to keep the horse under control. Since Dusty had been let loose in the pasture this morning and had a good run, Hannah figured he might be ready for a slower pace.

As she guided the horse and buggy down the lane, Hannah saw Timothy out in the field. He must have seen her, too, for he lifted his hand in a wave. Hannah waved back and stopped the horse at the end of the lane to check for traffic. Seeing no cars coming, she directed the horse onto the road. They'd only gone a short ways when Dusty started to trot, but it quickly turned into a gallop. Hannah tightened her grip on the reins and pulled hard, but that didn't hold the horse back. "Whoa!" she hollered, using her legs to brace the reins. "Whoa, Dusty! Whoa!"

Dusty kept running, and the foam from his sweat flew back on Hannah, but she was concentrating so hard, she barely took notice. As the horse continued to gallop, the buggy rocked from side to side. If she didn't get Dusty under control soon, the buggy might tip over.

The sound of the horse's hooves moving so fast against the pavement was almost deafening as Hannah struggled to gain control. Dusty clearly had a mind of his own.

This is what I get for taking a horse I really don't know how to handle, Hannah fumed. *Guess I should have stayed home today and found something else to do.*

The buggy swayed, taking them frighteningly close to a telephone pole, and Mindy, sitting in the seat behind Hannah, began to cry.

"It's gonna be okay, Mindy," Hannah called over her shoulder. "Hang on tight to your seat, and don't let go!"

Chapter 35

Hannah's fingers ached as she gripped Dusty's reins and pulled with all her strength. Why wouldn't the crazy horse listen to her and slow down? If she wasn't able to get control of him soon, she didn't know what would happen.

Another buggy was coming from the opposite direction. As it drew closer, she realized it belonged to Titus and Suzanne. They must have known she was in trouble, for as soon as they passed, Titus whipped his rig around and came up behind Hannah's buggy. A few minutes later, his horse came alongside hers. Grateful for the help, but fearful a car might come and hit Titus's buggy, all Hannah could do was cling to the reins and pray.

Titus's horse was moving fast, and he managed to pass and move directly in front of Hannah's horse and buggy. Hannah knew if Dusty kept running he'd smack into the back of Titus's rig, but thankfully, the horse slowed down. When Titus pulled over to the side of the road, she was able to pull in behind him. Titus then handed Suzanne the reins, hopped out of his rig, and came around to Hannah's buggy. "Are you okay?" he asked with a worried expression.

Out of breath and barely able to speak, she nodded and said, "Dusty got away from me, and I couldn't slow him down."

"Well, slide on over and let me take the reins," Titus said. "I'll drive your horse and buggy, and Suzanne can follow us in my rig."

"Danki. I appreciate your help so much," Hannah said, blinking back tears and grateful that nothing serious had happened—especially since she had Mindy with her.

"Where were you heading?"

"I was going to visit Bonnie, but I've changed my mind. I just want to go home."

Titus climbed into the buggy and took a seat beside Hannah. Then glancing into the backseat, where Mindy was still crying, he said, "It's okay, Mindy. Everything's gonna be fine."

Hannah was so relieved that Titus had come along and taken control of Timothy's horse. One thing she knew for sure: she'd never take Dusty out again by herself!

—∞—

Esther's heart raced as she neared Samuel's house. Rather than taking the time to hitch her horse to the buggy, she'd ridden over on her scooter. Since Samuel's place wasn't far from Bonnie's, it hadn't taken her long to get there.

Esther parked the scooter near the porch and hurried up the steps. Just then the door opened and Samuel, as well as all four of his children, rushed out to greet her.

Samuel gave Esther a hug. "It sure is good to see you!"

She smiled. "It's good to see all of you, too."

The children began talking at once, asking Esther questions and vying for her attention.

"All right now," Samuel finally said, "you can visit more

with Esther later on. Right now I'd like some time to visit with her alone. Why don't you all go to the kitchen and eat a snack? There's some cheese and apple slices in the refrigerator."

"I'm not hungerich." Penny pointed to her stomach. "My silo's still full from lunch."

"So your silo's still full, is it? Didn't know my little maedel had a silo right there." Samuel gave Penny's stomach a couple of pats; then he leaned his head back, and the sound of his laughter seemed to bounce off the porch ceiling.

Esther and the children laughed, too. It was good to be back with Samuel and his family. She'd missed them all so much. These children had become like her own, and she couldn't wait to become their stepmother.

When the laughter subsided, the children gave Esther another hug and bounded into the house.

As Esther and Samuel sat on the porch visiting, she studied the man with whom she'd fallen so hopelessly in love. Samuel's light brown hair, streaked with gold from the sun, was thick and healthy-looking. His dark brown eyes, so sincere, spoke of his love for her.

"Now that you're back," Samuel said, reaching for Esther's hand, "can we set a date for our wedding?"

She smiled. "I'd like that."

"How about next month?"

Esther shook her head. "Oh Samuel, as much as I would like that, it's just a bit too soon. I'll need some time to make my wedding dress, and with Bonnie and Allen getting married soon, and then going on a two-week honeymoon, I'll also need to help at the B&B. Could we get married the last Tuesday in June?"

"I'd sure like it to be sooner, but I guess June isn't that far off," he said.

"No, it's not, and we do need to give our folks some advance notice so they can plan for the trip." Esther's face sobered. "I hope Mom and Dad will be able to come. With my brother not doing well, they may feel that they can't leave Sarah to care for him on her own."

"I'm sure they can get someone else to help with Dan's care for a few days," Samuel said. "I don't think your parents would miss your wedding."

"I hope not. I'd really like to have them here."

"Speaking of your parents, maybe when they come for the wedding I can ask about buying this house. I've appreciated being able to rent the place from them, but I'd really like to have a house I can call my own."

Esther nodded. "It's good that you mentioned it, because that topic came up while I was in Pennsylvania. Mom and Dad said they'd be willing to sell the house to us for a reasonable price, and I'm sure Dad will discuss the details with you soon."

Samuel grinned. "Now, that's good news!"

"There's something else we need to discuss," Esther said.

"What's that?"

"I was wondering if you'd like me to quit my job at the B&B after we're married."

Samuel pulled his fingers through the ends of his beard and sat quietly as he contemplated her question. Finally, he smiled and said, "It's really your decision, but if it were left up to me, you'd quit working for Bonnie and be a full-time wife and mother."

"I feel that way, too," Esther said. "And I think Trisha might be willing to stay on and keep working for Bonnie. She seems really happy there. In fact, if she agrees, then I can quit even before we get married."

"That's good to hear. Sounds like it will all work out."

"As I said, I'll need to help out at the B&B while Bonnie and Allen are on their honeymoon. If things get busy, Trisha will need some help."

"That's fine with me." Samuel smiled widely. "I can't wait to share the news with my family that you and I will be getting married in June."

Chapter 36

"Are you getting nervous yet?" Trisha asked when Bonnie came down to breakfast two days before her wedding.

Bonnie nodded. "I'd be lying if I said I wasn't."

"I understand. My stomach was tied in knots for two full weeks before my wedding."

"I think I'll feel better once I get busy around here. Since Allen and I will be going to Nashville tomorrow to pick up my dad and his folks at the airport, I need to get as much done today as I can in preparation for the reception."

"I'll do everything I can to help, and don't forget, Esther will be coming over."

"I'm sure Dad and Allen's folks will help when they get here, too." Bonnie opened the refrigerator and took out a boiled egg. "Guess I'd better hurry and eat so I can get going."

"You'd better have something more than an egg to eat, or you'll run out of steam before you even get started." Trisha placed a plate of toast on the table and poured Bonnie a glass of orange juice and a cup of coffee.

"Thanks." Bonnie smiled. "You certainly do take good care of me."

A lump formed in Trisha's throat. "You've become very special to me, and it gives me pleasure to do things for you."

"You're special to me, too," Bonnie said as she took a seat at the table. "Are you going to join me for breakfast?"

"I already ate, but I'll have a second cup of coffee and visit while you eat."

After Trisha joined her at the table, Bonnie said a prayer, thanking God for the food and for her and Trisha's friendship. When the prayer ended, she reached for a piece of toast and spread some strawberry jam on top. "Are you sure you can manage on your own for the two weeks Allen and I will be in Hawaii?" she asked Trisha.

"Esther will be helping as much as she can, so between the two of us, we'll manage just fine."

Bonnie placed her hand on Trisha's arm. "I'm so glad you've decided to stay here permanently."

"I'm happy about it, too; although some of my friends in California weren't too thrilled when I called and gave them the news."

"I'm sure that's only because they're going to miss you and had hoped you might be returning to California soon."

"I suppose." Trisha pursed her lips. "I just hope your dad won't mind when he hears the news."

"Why would he mind?"

Trisha shrugged. "He might not like the idea of his ex-girlfriend working for his daughter."

"Dad already knows you're working for me, and he hasn't said anything negative about it."

"He may not have said anything to you, but when I spoke to him on the phone the last time, he made it pretty clear that he wasn't thrilled about me being here." Trisha's forehead wrinkled. "He probably didn't say anything to you because he assumed my working at the B&B was temporary. He may have figured by the time he came here for your wedding, I'd be long gone."

"I think you're worried for nothing. I'll bet when Dad gets here he won't say a negative thing about you working for me." Bonnie gave Trisha's arm a little pat. "Now, I'd better finish my breakfast, because this is going to be a very long day."

The slanting afternoon sun glared in Hannah's face as she gripped the hoe and chopped at the weeds threatening to overtake her garden. Weeding was no fun, but it needed to be done. She'd planted several things a few weeks ago, and already the weeds looked healthier than the plants coming up. Maybe what they needed was more water. They'd had a dry spring so far, and Hannah had to water her vegetable garden, as well as the flowers she'd planted close to the house, by hand. Oh how she wished they would get some much-needed rain.

Mo-o-o! Mo-o-o! A brown-and-white cow in their neighbor's pasture peered across the fence at Hannah with gentle-looking eyes but a forlorn expression that matched Hannah's mood. She would much rather be doing something else, but if she didn't stay on top of the weeds, she wouldn't have any homegrown food to can in the fall.

Of course, she thought ruefully, *all the homegrown food in the world won't stave off the loneliness I've often felt since we moved to Kentucky.* In Pennsylvania she'd had some friends, and Hannah's mother had always been available whenever she'd needed help. *If Mom were here right now, she'd be helping me with the weeding.*

Hannah knew she should quit dwelling on the same old thing. After all, she was making some new friends here in

Kentucky, and things had been a little better between her and Timothy since they'd moved into their new home.

Hannah's thoughts were halted when she heard buzzing to her left. Three hummingbirds fluttered around the glass feeder she'd hung on a shepherd's hook in one of her flower beds. It was always fun to watch the tiny birds skitter back and forth between the trees and the feeder. If more hummingbirds came, she'd need to put up a second feeder.

Just then the van belonging to Timothy's driver came up the lane. Hannah smiled. Timothy was home early today. Maybe he'd get those screens put in the window like he kept promising to do. Or maybe they could spend some time together this afternoon and do something fun with Mindy.

After Timothy told his driver good-bye, he joined Hannah by the garden. "Looks like you've been busy," he said.

She nodded. "It's a lot of work to keep up a garden."

"Jah, but it'll be worth it when we have fresh produce to put on the table, not to mention whatever you're able to can for our use during the winter months."

"I'm surprised to see you back so early," she said, changing the subject.

"Samuel and I finished our job in Clarksville sooner than we thought, and he figured it was too late in the day to start something else, so he said I should go home."

"I hope you won't have to work this coming Saturday," Hannah said. "It's Bonnie and Allen's wedding day, remember?"

"Don't worry. Neither Samuel nor I will be working that day, and Titus won't be working at the woodshop either, so we'll all be free to go to the wedding."

"I've never been to an English wedding," Hannah said. "I wonder what it'll be like."

"We'll find out soon enough, but right now I'm going to

get some work done around here."

"Are you going to be able to replace those screens for the windows today?" she asked.

He shook his head. "I need to get some more planting done in the fields, but I'll get to the screens as soon as I can."

"But it's hot and stuffy upstairs, and it's only going to get worse as the weather gets warmer."

"So open the windows awhile."

"Flies and other nasty insects will get in."

"If you can't stand the flies, just keep the doors and windows downstairs open during the day, and that should help."

"It seems like you never finish anything when I ask," Hannah mumbled. "At least not since we moved here."

"I'll get the screens done as soon as I can. Right now, though, I'm going into the house to get something to eat before I head out to the field."

"Don't eat too much," she admonished, "or you'll spoil your supper."

"Well what can I say?" he said with a sheepish grin. "I'm a hardworking man, and I need to eat a lot in order to keep up my strength. You wouldn't want me to waste away to nothing, would you?"

"No, of course not."

He started to walk away, but she called out to him, "Don't make a bunch of noise when you go inside. Mindy's taking a nap. Oh, and please don't make a mess in the kitchen. I just cleaned the floor this morning."

He grunted and strode quickly up to the house.

Hannah sighed. Since Timothy seemed in a hurry to get out to the fields, she hadn't even bothered to mention them doing anything fun together this afternoon. What was the point? She was sure he would have said no. Between Timothy's paint jobs and his work in the fields, they rarely spent any quality time together anymore. And what time they did spend, Timothy either had work on his mind or ended up talking about Samuel and Titus. With the exception of church every other Sunday, they hardly went anywhere as a family. They'd talked about going to see the Jefferson Davis Monument, which wasn't far from where they lived, but they hadn't even done that. Hannah was beginning to wonder if all Timothy wanted to do was work. Maybe he thought she would be happy working all the time, too. As it was, she kept busy doing things she didn't really enjoy in order to keep from being bored. She'd all but given up on the idea of buying and selling antiques. The last time she'd mentioned it to Timothy, he'd repeated his objections.

Timothy has his brothers and Allen for companionship, Hannah thought. *But who do I have? Just Mindy most of the time, and of course that dopey little cat who likes to lie on the porch with his floppy paws in the air. Bonnie and Esther are busy planning their weddings, and Suzanne only comes around once in a while.*

Hannah knew she was giving in to self-pity, but she couldn't seem to help herself. Her resolve to make the best of things was crumbling. *Maybe I should join Timothy for a snack. I could really use something cold to drink, and at least it would give us a few minutes to visit before he heads out to the fields.*

She set the hoe aside, stretched her aching limbs, and hurried toward the house. When she stepped into the kitchen, she halted, shocked to see Timothy sitting on a chair with Mindy over his knees, giving her a spanking.

"What do you think you're doing?" Hannah shouted over Mindy's cries.

Timothy looked at Hannah, but he didn't speak to her

until he'd finished spanking Mindy. Then he set the child on the floor and told her to go upstairs to her room.

Mindy looked at Hannah with sorrowful eyes, tears dribbling down her cheeks. Hannah reached out her arms, but Timothy shook his head. "She's a *nixnutzich* little girl and deserved that *bletsching*." He pointed to the door leading to the stairs. "Go on now, Mindy, schnell!"

Alternating between sniffling and hiccupping, Mindy ran out of the room.

Hannah placed her hands on her hips and glared at Timothy. "Now what's this all about, and why do you think Mindy is naughty and deserved to be spanked?"

"When I came in to get a snack, I figured Mindy was still taking a nap," Timothy said. "But what I found instead was our daughter with a jar of petroleum jelly, and she was spreadin' it all over the sofa. When I told her to come with me to the kitchen, she wouldn't budge—she just looked up at me defiantly. So I picked her up and carried her to the kitchen. After she started kicking and screaming, I'd had enough, so I put her across my knees and gave her a well-deserved spanking."

"She shouldn't have been playing with the petroleum jelly," Hannah said, "but she's only a little girl, and I think you were too harsh with her." Irritation put an edge to Hannah's voice, but she didn't care. As far as she was concerned, Timothy had punished their daughter in anger, and that was wrong.

"I may have been angry, but I didn't spank her that hard. I just wanted Mindy to learn that it's wrong to get into things and make a mess, and that her disobedience will result in some kind of punishment."

"It doesn't have to be a bletsching." Hannah's tone was crisp and to the point. "There are other forms of punishment, you know."

"Sometimes a spanking's the best way to teach a child as young as Mindy that there are consequences for disobedience."

Hannah's mouth quivered as she struggled not to give in to the tears pricking the back of her eyes. *I won't let him see me cry. Not this time.*

Timothy stood and pulled her gently into his arms. "Let's not argue, Hannah. I love you, and I love Mindy, too."

"You have a funny way of showing it sometimes."

He brushed a kiss across her forehead. "I'm doing the best I can."

Hannah shrugged and turned away.

"Where are you going?" he called as she headed for the stairs.

"Upstairs to comfort Mindy!" Hannah raced from the room before he could say anything else. Timothy might think he was doing his best, but at the moment, she wasn't the least bit convinced.

Chapter 37

Hopkinsville, Kentucky

When Allen stepped out of his bedroom, he heard his parents' voices coming from the kitchen. Hearing his name mentioned, he paused and listened, even though he knew it was wrong to eavesdrop.

"I can't believe our son is finally getting married," Mom said. "I was about to give up."

Allen rolled his eyes. Mom could be so dramatic about things.

"I know," Dad agreed. "This is a very special day for him, and for us, too."

"Maybe there's some hope of us becoming grandparents."

"That would be nice. Think I'd enjoy having little ones to buy Christmas gifts and birthday presents for."

"I wonder if Allen and Bonnie are planning to start a family right away."

"Are you two talking about me behind my back and planning my future to boot?" Allen asked, stepping into the kitchen. He wasn't really irritated—just surprised by their conversation.

Mom smoothed the lapel on Allen's white tuxedo. "You and Bonnie do want children, don't you?"

Allen nodded. "Yes, Mom, we do."

She smiled. "You know, when I came here last year to help out after you'd injured your back, I had a hunch you and Bonnie would get together."

He tipped his head. "Oh, really? What made you think that?"

"I could see the gleam in your eyes whenever you spoke of her. After spending time with Bonnie yesterday when you two picked us up at the airport, I could see how well you complement each other."

"I agree with your mother," Dad said. "Bonnie's a great gal, and I do believe she was worth waiting for, son."

Allen smiled. "You're right about that. Bonnie is all I could ever ask for in a wife, and I hope we have as good a marriage as you two have had."

Fairview, Kentucky

"Dad, there's something I've been wanting to talk to you about," Bonnie said after she'd pulled into the church parking lot and turned off the car.

"What's that?" he asked, turning in the passenger's seat to face her.

"Trisha plans to make Kentucky her permanent home. She'll be working for me at the B&B full-time."

His mouth dropped open. "How come?"

"Because Esther will be getting married toward the end of June, and she won't be working for me any longer."

He folded his arms and stared straight ahead. "I see."

"I have a complaint." Bonnie readily listened to the

complaints of others, but rarely spoke of her own. Today she would make an exception.

"What's the gripe?" he asked.

"I'm not happy about the way you give Trisha the cold shoulder."

"I don't do that."

"Yes you do. I have a hunch you're still angry with her for breaking up with you when you were teenagers. You know, you shouldn't think negative thoughts about someone until you have all the facts."

Dad frowned deeply. "Facts about what? Trisha broke up with me; I blamed my parents; and I can't go back and change any of it—end of story."

"But you're still angry about it."

"So?"

"So, you need to forgive Trisha as well as yourself. And remember, what lies behind us and what lies before us are small matters compared to what lies within us."

Dad rubbed his forehead, as though mulling things over.

"Remember when you asked what I'd like for a wedding present?"

He nodded.

"Well, the one thing that would give me the greatest pleasure would be for you to make peace with Trisha. Is that too much to ask?" She sat quietly, hoping he'd take her words to heart.

He turned his head and gave her a faint smile. "I'll give it some thought."

Pembroke, Kentucky

As Samuel stood in front of the bathroom mirror combing

his hair, he smiled. Two of his good friends were getting married today, and he couldn't be happier for them. He was glad Allen and Bonnie had invited him and the kids to attend the wedding, but he was a bit nervous about going. He'd never been to an English wedding before and wasn't sure what to expect. The ceremony would be quite different from Amish weddings, and he hoped the kids wouldn't say or do anything to embarrass him.

They usually behave themselves during our church services, he reminded himself. *So, hopefully they'll be on their best behavior today.*

Setting his comb aside, Samuel opened the bathroom door and was surprised to see Penny standing in the hallway.

"I smell peppermint candy," she said when Samuel stepped out of the bathroom. "Were you eatin' candy in there, Daadi?"

Samuel chuckled and patted the top of her head. "No, silly girl. Daadi washed his hair with some new shampoo that smells like peppermint."

Penny stuck her head in the bathroom and sniffed the air. "Are ya sure 'bout that?"

"Of course I'm sure. Now go tell your brothers and sister that it's time for us to pick Esther up. We don't want to be late for Allen and Bonnie's wedding."

Penny looked up at him with a serious expression. "I wish it was you and Esther gettin' married today."

"I wish that, too, but just think. . .by the end of June, Esther will be my fraa, and your new mamm."

Penny offered him a wide grin. "I can hardly wait for that!"

Samuel smiled and nodded. "No more than I can, little one."

Chapter 38

Fairview, Kentucky

"You make a beautiful bride," Trisha said as she helped Bonnie set her veil in place. "And your dress is absolutely gorgeous!" She gestured to the hand-beaded detail on the bodice and hem of the long, full-gathered skirt made of an off-white satin material.

"You don't think it's too much, do you?"

Trisha shook her head. "Absolutely not. Your wedding gown is as lovely as the woman wearing it, and you deserve to look like a princess today."

Bonnie smiled. "You're a pretty matron of honor, too."

Tears pooled in Trisha's eyes. "I'm honored that you would ask me to stand up with you."

Bonnie gave Trisha a hug. "You've become a good friend."

"But Esther's your friend, too, and I figured you'd want her to stand up with you."

"You're right, Esther's a very special friend, but I'm fairly sure that her church wouldn't allow her to be part of my bridal party, so I only asked you." Bonnie readjusted her lacy veil just a bit. "I'm glad most of my Amish friends will be able to attend the wedding, however."

"Will you be invited to Esther and Samuel's wedding?" Trisha questioned.

"Oh yes. I went when Titus and Suzanne got married, so I'm sure I'll get an invitation to Esther and Samuel's wedding, too."

"Are Amish weddings much different than ours?"

"They definitely are." Bonnie smiled at Trisha. "Since you and Esther have gotten to know each other quite well, I'm almost sure you'll get an invitation to her wedding."

"I hope so. That would truly be an honor for me."

A knock sounded on the door of the little room in the church where Bonnie and Trisha had gone to get ready.

"Would you like me to see who that is?" Trisha asked.

Bonnie nodded. "If it's Allen, I don't want him to see me until I walk down the aisle, so please don't let him in."

"Don't worry. I won't." When Trisha opened the door, Bonnie's dad walked in. He stepped up to Bonnie and stared at her as though in disbelief.

"Doesn't your daughter look beautiful in that dress?" Trisha asked.

"Yes, she's stunning." Dad smiled and gave Bonnie a hug. Then he turned to Trisha and said, "You look very nice, too."

Trisha's cheeks flushed. "Why, thank you, Kenny—I mean, Ken. You look pretty spiffy yourself."

Bonnie smiled. For the first time, she felt the barrier between Dad and Trisha come down a wee bit. *Thank You, God, for this answered prayer.*

"I believe it's time for me to walk you down the aisle," Dad said, extending his arm to Bonnie. "Your groom is waiting for you and probably growing anxious."

"No more than I am," Bonnie said, blinking back tears.

They followed Trisha from the room, and when they reached the back of the sanctuary, Trisha turned and gave Bonnie's dress and veil a quick once-over. After offering Bonnie a reassuring smile, she made her way slowly down the aisle in time to the soft organ music.

Bonnie clung to Dad's arm as they followed Trisha down the aisle. Just as all the wedding guests stood, an explosion of sunlight spilled through the stained-glass windows. The light seemed to guide Bonnie down the aisle, where her groom waited beside his cousin, Bill, whom he'd chosen to be his best man. Every fiber of Bonnie's being wanted to be Allen's wife. He was like a magnet drawing her to him.

Bonnie glanced to her left and spotted Esther sitting with Samuel and his children. In the pew next to them sat Titus and Suzanne, along with Timothy, Hannah, and little Mindy. To the right, she saw Allen's parents, and behind them Allen's friend, Zach, with his wife, Leona. They'd come from Pennsylvania for this special occasion and would be staying at Titus's place. Others from Bonnie's church and some from the community had also come to witness the wedding. It was wonderful to know she and Allen had so many good friends.

When Bonnie and Dad joined the wedding party at the altar, Pastor Cunningham smiled and said, "Who gives this woman to be wed?"

"I do," Dad answered in a clear but steady voice. When he kissed Bonnie's cheek and hugged her before taking a seat in the first pew, Bonnie noticed tears in his eyes.

Hannah sat straight as a board as she watched this very different wedding ceremony and recalled her own wedding day. She wondered what it would have been like to wear a long white gown with a veil and walk down an aisle in a church with people sitting on both sides of the sanctuary watching her every move. At least in an Amish wedding, the bride and groom were able to sit throughout most of the service. They didn't stand before the minister until it was time to say their vows.

"Dearly beloved," the pastor said, capturing Hannah's attention, "we are gathered together in the sight of God and the presence of these witnesses to join this man and this woman in holy matrimony, which is an honorable estate instituted by God in the time of man's innocence, signifying unto us the mystical union that exists between Christ and His Church. It is, therefore, not to be entered into unadvisedly, but reverently, discreetly, and in the fear of God. Into this holy estate these persons present now come to be joined."

The pastor's expression was solemn as he continued: "Allen and Bonnie, I require and charge you both as you stand in the presence of God, to remember that the commitment to marriage means putting the needs of your mate ahead of your own. The act of giving is a vivid reminder that it's all about God and not you. Be an encourager to your mate. The more you bless each other, the more God will bless you."

Hannah cringed. She had fallen short when it came to encouraging Timothy—especially when he'd decided to move to Kentucky. She rarely put his needs ahead of her own.

"Remember, too, that it's a privilege to pray," the pastor continued. "Turn your thoughts toward God in the morning, and you'll feel His presence all day. Make each day count as if it were your last, and forget about the *if only*s, for they can only lead to self-pity. Tell yourself each morning that this day is what counts, so you may as well make the most of it. Finally, don't harbor bitterness toward God or your marriage partner."

Hannah shifted uneasily in her seat. She'd been harboring bitterness toward Timothy ever since they moved to Kentucky, and when he'd spanked Mindy the other day, it had fueled her anger.

She turned her head and smiled at Timothy and was glad when he smiled in response. Maybe they could start over. Maybe if she tried harder to be a good wife, things would go better between them.

Chapter 39

Paradise, Pennsylvania

Sally had just finished washing the supper dishes when she looked out the kitchen window and spotted a horse and buggy coming up the driveway. When the driver stopped near the barn, she recognized who it was.

"Abraham Fisher is here," she called to Johnny, who sat at the table reading the newspaper.

"He must have come to look at the hog I have for sale." Johnny left his seat and hurried out the back door.

A few minutes later, Sally saw Fannie standing near the buggy, so she opened the back door and hollered, "You're welcome to come inside if you like!"

Fannie waved and started walking toward the house.

"Let's go into the kitchen and have a glass of iced tea while the men take care of business," Sally suggested when Fannie entered the house.

Fannie smiled. "That sounds nice. It's been hot today—too hot for the first day of June, if you ask me."

"I agree. Makes me wonder what our summer's going to be like."

Sally poured them both a glass of iced tea, and they took seats at the table.

"I haven't heard from Timothy in a while," Fannie said. "Have you heard anything from Hannah?"

"No, not for a week or so."

"The last I heard from Timothy, he mentioned that he and Hannah were going to Allen Walters's wedding."

"Hannah mentioned that, too, but I haven't heard anything from her since," Sally said. "To tell you the truth, I haven't been phoning Hannah as often as before."

"How come?" Fannie took a sip of iced tea.

"Johnny pointed out that I need to give our daughter some space." Sally sighed. "I still miss Hannah something awful, and it's hard having her living so far away."

"I understand," Fannie said. "Try as I may, it's still hard to accept the fact that three of my sons have moved to Kentucky. I'd always hoped and believed that when Abraham and I reached old age we'd have all our kinner and kinskinner living close to us. But I've learned to accept that it's not meant to be."

"The problem for me," Sally said, "is that I'm not as emotionally close to our sons and their wives as I am to Hannah. That's made it doubly hard for me since she moved away."

"I understand, but you can still be close to your daughter without her living nearby." Fannie smiled. "Just be there for her, if and when she needs you. That'll count for a lot."

—∞—

Pembroke, Kentucky

Trisha couldn't believe how lonely she'd felt since Bonnie and Allen had left on their honeymoon. She'd become used to fixing supper and sharing it with Bonnie and didn't enjoy eating all her meals alone. She didn't have any guests at the B&B right now, either, so things had been unusually quiet.

"Now quit feeling sorry for yourself," Trisha mumbled as she entered the kitchen. "You've been living alone since Dave died and managed okay, so why's this any different? Besides, you should be enjoying this little rest before things start to pick up again."

Resolved to make the best of the situation, Trisha took a container of leftover soup from the refrigerator and poured the contents into a kettle. She was about to turn on the stove when the telephone rang. She quickly picked up the receiver. "Hello. Bonnie's Bed-and-Breakfast."

"Trisha, this is Ken."

"Oh, hi. How are you?"

"I'm doing okay, but I was wondering if you've heard anything from Bonnie lately. I'm worried about her and Allen."

"How come?"

"I just heard on the news that one of those tour helicopters from Kauai went down, and I know they were planning to go up in one, so I'm wondering if—"

"Did you try calling them, Ken?"

"Yes, I did, and I had to leave a message on both of their cell phones. I'm telling you, Trisha, this has me really worried."

"I'm sure they're fine. If Bonnie and Allen were involved in that crash, I'm certain you would have heard about it by now." Trisha cringed. *Oh, I hope they weren't in that helicopter. What a tragedy that would be.*

"You know, I never used to worry so much, but the older I get, the more I fret about things."

Trisha gave a small laugh, hoping to reassure him. "I know what you mean. I'm the same way."

"How are things going there?" he asked. "Have you been really busy since Bonnie and Allen left?"

"No, not really. Actually, business has been kind of slow, but I'm sure it'll pick up now that summer's almost here. I guess I should enjoy this little break before it gets busy again."

Trisha jumped as a gust of wind blew against the house, causing the windows to rattle. Rain pelted down on the roof. When the lights flickered, she said, "I hate to cut this short, Ken, but I'd better hang up. It's raining really hard, and the wind's howling so much that I'm afraid the power might go out. I need to get out some candles and battery-operated lights, just in case."

"Okay, I'll let you go. Oh, and Trisha, if you hear anything from Bonnie, would you please ask her to give me a call?"

"Yes, of course I will." The lights flickered again then went off, leaving Trisha in total darkness.

Exhausted after a hard day's work, Timothy flopped onto the sofa with a groan. He'd put in a full eight hours painting in Clarksville then come home and worked in the fields until it had started raining real hard. Every muscle in his body ached.

He leaned his head against the back of the sofa and closed his eyes, allowing his mind to wander. Things had been better between him and Hannah lately—ever since Allen and Bonnie's wedding, really. They hadn't argued even once, and Hannah seemed much sweeter and more patient with him. She hadn't nagged when he'd left his shoes in the living room the other day or complained because he'd tracked dirt into the house. Timothy didn't know the reason, but Hannah had definitely changed her attitude and actually seemed more content.

He smiled. Hannah was in the bathroom right now giving

Mindy a bath. He'd promised when she was done and had put Mindy to bed that the two of them would share a bowl of popcorn while they relaxed. He looked forward to spending time alone with his wife but wasn't sure he had the strength to stand in front of the stove and crank the lever on the corn popper. He figured Hannah would probably be awhile, so if he rested a few minutes, he might feel more like popping the corn by the time she was done bathing Mindy.

Timothy was at the point of nodding off when Mindy bounded into the room wearing her long white nightgown and fuzzy slippers. She climbed onto the sofa and put her little hands on both sides of his face. "*Gut nacht*, Daadi."

"Good night, little one." Timothy's heart swelled with love as he kissed her forehead. "Sleep tight."

Hannah smiled. "I'm taking her up to bed now, and I shouldn't be too long, so if you want to start the popcorn, I'll pour the lemonade as soon as I come down."

"Okay." How could he say no when Hannah was being so sweet?

As Hannah and Mindy headed up the stairs, Timothy pulled himself off the sofa and ambled into the kitchen. He glanced out the window. It was pitch dark, and the rain pelted the house so viciously it was almost deafening. It was hard to believe a day that had begun so sunny and warm could turn into such a stormy night.

Sure hope it'll be better by morning, he thought. *Samuel and I won't be able to finish the outside of that house we started on today if it's still raining tomorrow.*

By the time Hannah came downstairs, Timothy had made the popcorn and drizzled it with melted butter.

"That smells wunderbaar," she said, sniffing the air. "If you'll take it into the living room, I'll join you there in a few minutes with some lemonade."

"Sounds good."

A short time later, Timothy and Hannah were on the sofa with a large bowl of popcorn between them and glasses of cold lemonade.

"It sure is a stormy night," Hannah said. "A lot different than today was, that's for sure."

"You're right about that." Timothy frowned. "I'm afraid if the rain doesn't quit, I might lose my corn. It's coming down pretty fierce out there."

"I know how hard you worked planting that corn," she said. "I hope you don't lose it."

He nodded. "Working with the land reminds me that it's the Lord's creation, and it makes me feel at one with nature. We need that corn for our own use, and it would also be nice to have some to sell."

She gave him an encouraging smile. "My daed once said that disasters often bring a person back to what really matters. And if you have to replant, then there's no shame in asking your friends and family to help."

"Your daed's a wise man." Timothy's gaze came to rest on the faint smattering of freckles on Hannah's nose that had been brought out by the sun. He leaned over and nuzzled her cheek. "And as my daed always says, 'If we let God guide, He will provide.' "

The house was quiet, and the kids had gone to bed some time ago. Samuel removed his reading glasses and rubbed his eyes then put his Bible on the table. He was wide awake and had the house all to himself—a rare opportunity for him these days.

"Guess if I'm gonna be any good tomorrow, I better get

some sleep." he murmured, slowly rising from the chair in the corner of the living room. Quietly, he walked down the hall to his room, so as not to waken anyone. His body was weary from putting in long days, but he was thankful Allen had several jobs lined up for him and Timothy. It was a blessing to have steady work, especially in these hard economic times.

When Samuel entered his bedroom, he didn't bother to turn on the battery-operated light; he just got undressed and crawled into bed. Outside the wind was blowing so strong it made the window sing. The heavy rain sounded like pebbles being thrown against the side of the house. In an effort to drown out the noise, he grabbed his pillow and put it over head. But it was no use.

Samuel groaned and stretched, trying to get the kinks out of his muscles. It was going to be one of those nights where sleep would not come quickly. True, he was bone tired, but maybe he was just too tired to sleep. Normally the rain would have lulled him to sleep, but for some reason, it had the opposite effect on him tonight. Maybe he ought to go back to the living room and read more from the Bible. Or a glass of warm milk might help him become drowsy enough to fall sleep.

Stepping into the kitchen a short time later, Samuel was surprised to find Marla sitting at the table in the dark.

"What are you doin' in here, sweet girl?" he asked, turning on the gas lantern overhead.

Marla sighed. "Oh, just thinking is all. I woke up and couldn't get back to sleep."

"I couldn't sleep either. That's some storm out there, isn't it?"

She nodded.

"The wind's blowing so hard it made my windows sound like they were singing." Samuel smiled, thinking Marla might get a chuckle out of that, but then he noticed tears glistening on her cheeks. "What's wrong? Are you afraid of the storm?" he asked.

She shook her head. "Daadi, do you think Mama would mind that you're gonna marry Esther, and that Penny and Jared have already started callin' her 'Mamm'?"

Samuel studied Marla's face and was reminded again how much she was like her mother. The child was kind and always concerned about others—just the way her mother had been. His little girl seemed to have grown up right before his eyes. She seemed more like a young lady than the nine-year-old that she was.

"Is there a reason you're thinking about this, Marla?" Samuel asked. "I thought you liked Esther."

"Oh I do, Daadi. In fact, I like Esther a lot. I just hope if Mama's lookin' down from heaven that she's not upset."

Before Samuel could respond, Marla continued. "I had a dream tonight before I came down, and it got me to thinkin'."

"Was it a bad dream?" he asked.

She shook her head. "It was kind of a nice dream, but somethin' strange happened."

"What was that?"

"I was dreamin' that we were all back in Pennsylvania, like it used to be before. . ." Marla looked down as if struggling for the word.

"Before what, Marla?'

"Before Mama died. We were sittin' by this pond, havin' a picnic. All of us were eatin' and laughin' and havin' a good time. Then, just like that, we were back in Kentucky, still sittin' by a pond havin' a picnic—only Mama's face disappeared, and it was Esther's instead." Marla sniffed. "Then the dream ended, and when I woke up, it made me wonder if Mama would be sad about Esther comin' into our lives."

Samuel's heart almost broke for his daughter's concern. She was such an innocent child with grown-up feelings. He decided right then and there to be honest with her.

"You know, Marla, I used to ask myself that same question. And before I go on, let me say that it's important for you to know that Esther is in no way replacing your mamm. No one could ever do that. You also need to know that I was torn about letting Esther into my heart when we started to have feelings for each other. I prayed about it and almost moved us back to Pennsylvania because I thought it was wrong." Samuel noticed that Marla seemed to be hanging on his every word.

"Then, while I was struggling with what to do, your mamm spoke to me in a very special way," he continued.

"She did? How'd she do that, Daadi?" Marla questioned.

Samuel didn't want to reveal just yet about Elsie's journal, because one day when Marla was an adult, he planned to give her the diary on a special occasion. He would know when the time was right.

"Well, it's kind of personal to me right now, and one day I'll share with you how I know." Samuel smiled and tousled his daughter's hair. "Believe me when I tell you that your mamm did let me know that it was okay for me to love Esther."

Marla grinned, and Samuel was glad to see her relax. They sat together in silence awhile, until he noticed that Marla was holding something and kept wrapping it through her fingers.

"What have you got there?" he asked.

"It's one of Mama's hankies." Marla's voice grew shaky. "I. . .I hope you don't mind, Daadi, but last year on my birthday when you gave me Mama's teacup and it broke, I knew you went out to the barn. So I left my room and was gonna ask Esther if you were okay, but when I walked past your room,

I saw a box sittin' on the floor. I knew it was wrong, but I went into your room to see what was in the box. When I saw Mama's hankie with the butterfly on it all folded up nice and neat with all the other things, I took it." Tears gathered in the corners of Marla's eyes. "I'm real sorry, Daadi. I shouldn't have done that, but I've taken good care of the hankie. Ever since that night, I keep it with me under the sleeve of my dress. Then at night, I put it under my pillow to keep it close. It makes me feel like Mama's right here with me. When I'm hurtin', I can just reach my hand into my sleeve and hold the hankie, and it's like Mama's holdin' my hand and makin' me feel better."

Samuel was so choked up it took a moment before he could speak. "Ach, Marla," he whispered, taking her into the comfort of his arms and rocking her as he'd done when she was a baby. "It's okay; don't you worry now. Keep your mamm's hankie close and never let it go, and do whatever you have to so that you won't forget her."

Samuel paused a minute, trying to keep his emotions under control. "Your mamm left wonderful memories behind for me, you, and your brothers and sister. They were so young at the time, but someday when Penny and Jared are older, they'll be coming to you and Leon and wanting to hear all that you remember about their mamm. Never be afraid to talk about her, even to Esther. That's what keeps her memory alive—remembering our time with her."

Samuel sat with his arm around Marla a few more minutes, enjoying this tender moment. Then, when she said good night and headed to her room, he remained at the table and bowed his head. *Thank You, Lord, for special moments like this and a memory that will be with me forever.*

Chapter 40

When Timothy came in from doing his chores the following morning, he wore a sorrowful look. "Sometimes I just want to give up." He flopped into a chair at the table with a groan. "Why is it that a person can feel so good about things one day, and a day later everything just comes tumbling down?"

"What's wrong?" Hannah asked, feeling concern as she handed him a cup of coffee.

"It's the corn crop," he said with a slow shake of his head. "Almost all of it's ruined, and of course after all that rain we had, it's hot and muggy now."

"I'm sorry," she said. "Did the rain cause the damage, or was it the high winds that came up last night?"

"I think it was mostly the wind, because much of the corn is lying flat. I'll either have to forget about having a corn crop this year or replant and hope the warm weather stays long enough for all the corn to grow and mature." Timothy groaned. "It's a shame, too. The corn was looking so good before the storm blew in and ruined it."

"What are you going to do now?" Hannah asked, joining him at the table.

"I don't know. What do you think about all of this?"

Hannah blew on her coffee as she contemplated the situation. She was tempted to tell Timothy that this might be a sign that they shouldn't have moved to Kentucky but knew that would probably make him all the more determined to stay. Besides, after hearing what the pastor had said during Bonnie and Allen's wedding, Hannah had resolved to be a more supportive wife. And lately she'd been thinking that living here might not be so bad after all.

"Well," she said, "since you're so busy painting right now and really don't have the time to replant, maybe you ought to forget about trying to grow corn this year. We could plant some in the garden for our own personal use and see how that does. We could always lease some of the land and keep a few acres for our own use. That way it won't be so much for you to handle."

He offered her a weak smile and reached for her hand. "I think you might be right about that."

Hannah smiled, too. It felt good to be making a decision together.

The phone rang, and Trisha hurried into the foyer to answer it. "Hello. Bonnie's Bed-and-Breakfast."

"Hi, Trisha, it's Ken."

"Oh, I'm surprised you're calling so early." She glanced at the clock on the mantel in the living room. "It's eight o'clock here, so it must only be six in Oregon."

"Yeah, it's early yet, but I had a hard time sleeping last night and got up at the crack of dawn."

"How come? Are you still worried about Bonnie and Allen?"

"Yes, I am, but I'm also worried about you."

Now that's a surprise. "Why are you worried about me?" she asked.

"When we talked last night, you said the weather was bad and you might lose power."

"The electricity was out for several hours, and we had pounding rain with harsh winds most of the night. But the weather looks much better this morning. The sun's out now, and it's warming up fast, so I think things will dry fairly quickly this morning."

"That's good to hear. I'm glad you're okay. But I don't think it's good for you to be in that big house all alone."

Trisha smiled. She could hear the concern in Ken's voice, and it made her feel good that he might care more for her than he was willing to admit. Or maybe it was just wishful thinking. Even if he did feel something for her, with him living in Oregon and her in Kentucky, it wasn't likely that they'd ever begin a relationship.

They talked awhile longer, until Ken said, "I'd better let you go. I'm going to keep trying to get ahold of Bonnie, and I'd appreciate it if you'd let me know if you hear anything from her or Allen."

"I certainly will. You take care and try not to worry. Good-bye, Ken." Trisha hung up the phone and leaned against the doorjamb with a sigh. She knew it was silly, but talking to Ken on the phone reminded her of when they were teenagers and used to spend hours talking to each other. Part of her missed those carefree days, yet she really wouldn't want to go back to being a teenager again.

"It's time to get some breakfast and begin my day," she told herself as she headed for the kitchen.

—∞—

"You look kind of down in the dumps this morning," Samuel said when Timothy showed up at his house. "Did you and Hannah have a disagreement?"

"Nope. We've been gettin' along much better lately," Timothy said. "But that nasty weather we had last night completely ruined my corn crop."

"I'm sorry to hear that. It's supposed to be dry the rest of this week, and there's even going to be a full moon. Would you like me to help you plant more corn?"

Timothy shook his head. "You're busy enough, and so am I. After talking things over with Hannah, I've decided to forget about trying to grow more corn this year. Might even consider leasing some of the land next year so I don't have so much to take care of. For now, though, I think I'll just concentrate on our jobs and on getting the rest of the things done at my house that still need to be taken care of."

"Are you sure? I'd be happy to help if you want me to."

"No, that's all right. You and Esther will be getting married in a few weeks, and you're gonna be busy preparing for that."

"I can't believe it's finally going to happen." Samuel grinned and thumped Timothy's back. "Won't it be great to have most of our family here for the wedding?"

Timothy nodded. "It'll be good to see everyone again."

"Esther talked with her folks the other day, and they're planning to be here, too. It's going to be a great time."

—∞—

Hannah swatted at a pesky fly. She'd been working in the garden all morning while keeping an eye on Mindy, who was squatted in the grass nearby, picking dandelions. It was hot and humid, but the rustle of grass gave Hannah some hope that the wind might bring relief from the muggy weather. She guessed this kind of weather was better than the awful storm they'd had last night. As much as they'd needed some rain, they hadn't wanted that much. Hannah knew how hard Timothy had worked planting the corn, and she felt bad when he'd told her that it had been ruined. Well, some things couldn't be helped. They'd just have to try again next year or think about leasing some of the acreage out like they'd discussed.

Maybe this afternoon I'll bake that Kentucky chocolate chip pie I've been wanting to try, she decided. *It might cheer Timothy up when he comes home to a dessert that I'm almost sure he'll enjoy.*

Hannah glanced at Mindy, who had moved closer to the house. *My little girl is growing so much, and she's so full of curiosity. I hope Mom and Dad can come for a visit soon. They're missing so much by not being able to see all the little things Mindy does.*

Hannah leaned her hoe against the fence and headed for the house. Like it or not, it was time to start lunch. Her bare feet burned as she hobbled across the gravel but found relief as soon as she stepped onto the cool grass.

"It's time to go in for lunch," Hannah said to Mindy. "After that, Mama's going to bake a pie."

Mindy looked up with a sweet expression and extended her hand, revealing one of the dandelions she'd picked earlier. *"Der bliehe."* Apparently she didn't care about pie today.

"Jah, I see the flower. Leave it on the porch and come into the house with me now." Hannah opened the door and held it for Mindy. The child, still clutching the dandelion, trotted into the house.

Hannah washed her hands at the kitchen sink and took out a loaf of bread for sandwiches. While she was spreading peanut butter, a fly buzzed noisily overhead. It was hot in the kitchen, and Hannah fanned her face with one hand while swatting at the bothersome insect with the other. Would she spend the whole summer killing bugs and trying to find a way to stay cool? Of course, the reason there were flies in the house was because she'd opened the upstairs windows this morning, trying to get some ventilation.

Mindy tromped into the kitchen and tugged on Hannah's apron. "Der bliehe," she said, showing Hannah the dandelion she still held in her hand.

Hannah, feeling a bit annoyed, said, "Mindy, I want you to go to the living room and play until I call you for lunch."

Mindy gave Hannah's apron another tug. "Der bliehe."

"Not now, Mindy! Just do as I say and go to the living room."

Mindy's lower lip protruded as she turned and left the room.

Bzz. . .bzz. . . Hannah gritted her teeth as the irksome fly kept buzzing around her head. Finally, in exasperation, she grabbed the newspaper Timothy had left on the counter last night, waited until the fly landed on the table, and gave it a good whack.

"That's one less thing I have to deal with right now," she said, scooping the fly up with the paper and tossing it in the garbage can.

Hannah went to the sink and wet a sponge. Then she quickly wiped the table where the fly had landed and went back to finishing the sandwiches she'd started.

When their lunch was ready, Hannah went to the living room to get Mindy. The child wasn't there. She opened the front door and looked into the yard but saw no sign of Mindy there either.

I wonder if she went upstairs to her room.

Hannah hurried up the stairs, and when she entered Mindy's bedroom, she spotted the child's favorite doll lying on the floor under the window. Then her gaze went to the open window. Now, the once-broken screen was no longer there.

With her heart pounding, Hannah moved slowly forward, while her brain told her to stop. She felt cold as ice as she approached the window. She held her breath as her gaze moved from the horizon, down to the yard below. She already knew what she would see but prayed it wouldn't be so. Mindy lay on the ground in a contorted position. She wasn't moving.

Hannah dashed down the stairs and out the front door, her fear mounting and making it hard to breathe. When she reached Mindy, she noticed that her daughter still held the shriveled-up dandelion she'd tried to give Hannah only a short time ago.

Hannah dropped onto the grass and checked for a pulse, but there was none. Stricken with fear such as she'd never known, Hannah raced for the phone shanty to call for help, while whispering a desperate prayer, *"Please, God, don't let our precious Mindy be dead."*

Chapter 41

Trisha had just started baking some bread when the telephone rang. She wiped her floury hands on a clean towel and picked up the receiver. "Hello. Bonnie's Bed-and-Breakfast."

"Hey, Trisha. It's Bonnie."

"Oh, it's so good to hear from you!" Trisha sighed with relief. "Your dad and I have both tried calling you and Allen, but all we ever got was your voice mail. We've been worried about you two ever since we heard about a helicopter crash on Kauai. Your dad was afraid you might have been on that 'copter, but thank goodness, you obviously weren't, and I'm so relieved."

"Yes, it's been all over the news, and it was a terrible tragedy. Allen and I might have been on the helicopter had we not decided to go on a boat cruise instead. I'm so sorry we made you worry. I lost my cell phone on the beach, and the battery in Allen's phone was dead and wouldn't recharge. So he got a new battery this morning. And I never did find my cell phone but decided to wait until we get home to buy a new one."

"Oh, that's too bad. Have you called your dad yet to let him know you're all right?"

"Yes, I did, and he was thankful to hear from me."

"The last time Ken and I talked, I told him that I was sure we'd have heard if something tragic had happened to you and Allen." Trisha took a seat at the desk that held the phone. "Speaking of tragedies, we had one in this community three days ago."

"What happened?" Bonnie asked.

Even though she'd only known the people in this community for a short time, Trisha struggled to convey the news and explain about Mindy's death without breaking down.

"Oh no, that's terrible! I can't imagine how Timothy and Hannah must feel." Bonnie paused before continuing. "Have they had the funeral yet? I wish we could be there for it."

"Her funeral is today, but I'm not going because I don't know the family that well and wasn't sure if I'd be welcome."

Trisha could hear Bonnie sniffling.

"I hope this hasn't ruined your honeymoon," Trisha said. "I thought you should know so you can be praying for Mindy's family."

"Yes, we'll definitely do that."

"Oh, and some of Timothy's relatives are staying here at the B&B since there wasn't enough room at all the brothers' homes for everyone who came."

"I'm glad you had the rooms available. Oh, and Trisha, please let them know that there will be no charge for the rooms. It's the least I can do to help out during this difficult time."

"That's very generous of you. I'll let them know." Trisha paused then quickly added, "Try to relax and have a good time during the rest of your honeymoon, okay?"

"Yes, we will, though it won't be easy. It's so hard to believe Mindy is dead, but thank you so much for letting us know."

—ꝏ—

Hannah, dressed in black mourning clothes, stood in front of a small wooden coffin in shock and disbelief. The body of the little girl inside that box just couldn't be her precious daughter. It wasn't possible that they were saying their final good-byes. Hannah's eyes burned like hot coals. She wished this was just a horrible nightmare. But as hard as she tried to deny it, she knew Mindy was gone.

Over and over, Hannah had replayed the horrible event that had taken place three days ago. Looking out Mindy's bedroom window and seeing her daughter's body on the ground below had nearly been Hannah's undoing. After she'd gone to the phone shanty to call for help, she'd returned to Mindy and stayed there until the paramedics came. Hannah, though clinging to the hope that it might not be true, had known even before help arrived that Mindy was gone. Yet in her desperation, she'd continued to pray for a miracle—asking the Lord to bring Mindy back to life the way He had the little girl whose death was recorded in Matthew 9.

If God could do miracles back then, why not now? Hannah asked herself as she gazed at Mindy's lifeless body. But Hannah's pleas were for nothing. Mindy was dead, and God could have prevented it from happening—and so could Timothy. *If only he had put in those screens when I asked him to.* A deep sense of bitterness welled in Hannah's soul. *If Mindy hadn't fallen through that broken screen, she would still be alive—running, laughing, playing, picking dandelions.*

Her stomach tightened as she thought about the comment their bishop's wife had made when she and the bishop had come to their house for the viewing. "I guess our dear Lord must have needed another angel."

He shouldn't have taken my angel! I needed Mindy more than He did. Hannah lowered her head into the palms of her hands and wept.

"It's time for us to go the cemetery now," Timothy said, touching Hannah's arm.

Hannah didn't budge. *I don't want to go. I don't want to watch as my only child is put in the cold, hard ground.*

Hannah's mother stepped between them and slipped her arm around Hannah's waist. "Everyone's waiting outside for us, Hannah. We need to go now."

Hannah, not trusting her voice, could only nod and be led away on shaky legs. How thankful she was for Mom's support. Without it, she would have collapsed.

Outside, a sea of faces swam before Hannah's blurry eyes—her brothers and their families, Timothy's parents and most of his family, as well as many from their community. Most were already seated in their horse-drawn buggies, preparing to follow the hearse that would take Mindy's body to the cemetery. A few people remained outside their buggies waiting to go.

Hannah shuddered. She'd attended several funerals, but none had been for a close family member. To lose anyone was horrible, but to lose her own child was unbearable—the worst possible pain. Hannah feared she might die from a broken heart and actually wished that she could. It would be better than going through the rest of her life without Mindy. Yes, Hannah would welcome the Angel of Death right now if he came knocking at her door.

Once Hannah's parents had taken seats in the back of the buggy, Hannah numbly took her place up front beside Timothy. She blinked, trying to clear the film of tears clouding her vision, and leaned heavily against the seat. Oh, how her arms ached to hold her beloved daughter and make everything right. If only there was some way she could undo the past.

As the buggy headed down the road toward the cemetery, the hooves of the horse were little more than a plodding walk. Even Dusty, who was usually quite spirited, must have sensed this was a solemn occasion.

When they arrived at the cemetery, Hannah sat in the buggy until the pallbearers removed Mindy's casket from the hearse and carried it to the grave site. Then she and all the others followed.

After everyone had gathered around the grave, the bishop read a hymn while the coffin was lowered and the grave filled in by the pallbearers. With each shovelful of dirt, Hannah sank deeper into despair, until her heart felt as if it were frozen.

Even though Hannah hadn't actually spoken the words, Timothy knew she blamed him for Mindy's death. Truth was, he blamed himself, too. If only he'd taken the time to replace the screens, the horrible accident that had taken their child's life would not have happened. If he could just go back and change the past, they wouldn't be standing in the cemetery right now saying their final good-byes.

A lump formed in Timothy's throat as he tried to focus on the words of the hymn their bishop was reading: "*'Ah, good night to those I love so; Good night to my heart's desire; Good night to those hearts full of woe; Out of love they weep distressed. Tho' I from you pass away; In the grave you lay my clay; I will rise again securely, Greet you in eternity.'*"

Timothy glanced at his parents and saw Mom's shoulders shake as she struggled with her emotions. Dad looked pale as he put his arm around her.

Timothy looked at Hannah's parents and saw Sally sniffing as she swiped at the tears running down her cheeks. Johnny stood beside her with a pained expression.

Nearly everyone from Timothy and Hannah's families had come for the funeral, and each of their somber faces revealed the depth of their compassion and regret over the loss of Mindy. *Do they all think I'm responsible for Mindy's death?* he wondered. *I wouldn't blame them if they did.*

Timothy's gaze came to rest on Hannah. Her face looked drawn, with dark circles beneath her eyes. She hadn't slept much in the last three days, and when she had gone to bed, she had slept in Mindy's room—probably out of a need to somehow feel closer to her. Timothy missed having Hannah beside him at night, for he desperately needed her comfort. If she could just find it in her heart to forgive him, perhaps he might be able to forgive himself.

The bishop's reading finally ended, and everyone bowed their heads to silently pray the Lord's Prayer. Timothy noticed how the veins on Hannah's hands protruded as she clasped her hands tightly together and bowed her head. He suspected she was only going through the motions of praying, because that's what he was doing. What he really wanted to do was look up at the sky and shout, "Dear God: How could You have taken our only child? Don't You care how much we miss her?"

When the prayer ended, most of the mourners moved away from the grave site, but Hannah remained, hands clasped, rocking back and forth on her heels.

"Hannah, it's time for us to go now. We must return to the house and spend time with our guests," Timothy said, gently touching her shoulder.

Hannah wouldn't even look at him. Finally, Hannah's mother and father led her slowly away.

Timothy stayed at the grave site a few more minutes, fighting to gain control of his emotions. He knew he had to find a way through the difficult days ahead, but he didn't know how. Worse yet, he feared that his wife, who'd been so close to their daughter, might never be the same.

Chapter 42

Paradise, Pennsylvania

"I'm worried about Timothy and Hannah," Fannie told Abraham as they ate breakfast a week after they'd returned from Kentucky.

"I know you are, Fannie, but worrying won't change a thing." Abraham rested his hand on her arm. "We're told in 1 Peter 5:7 to cast all our cares on Him."

"I realize that, but it's hard when you see a loved one hurting and know there's nothing you can do to ease their pain."

"There most certainly is. We can pray for them, offer encouraging words, and listen and be there when they want to talk."

"You're right." Fannie sighed. "I just wish we could have stayed in Kentucky longer. I really think Timothy and Hannah need us right now."

"But remember, Fannie, Hannah's folks are still there, and I think it might have been too much if we'd stayed, too."

"But we could have stayed with Samuel," she argued.

"There's plenty of room in that big house of his, and we would have been able to go over often and check on Timothy and Hannah."

Abraham stroked Fannie's hand. "We'll be going back in a few weeks for Samuel and Esther's wedding. I'm sure Hannah's folks will be gone by then, and it'll give us a chance to spend more time with Hannah and Timothy."

"That's true, but how can we celebrate what should be a joyous occasion when our son and his wife are in such deep grief?"

"While there will be some sadness, it'll be good for everyone to focus on something positive," he said. "Samuel went through a lot when he lost Elsie, and he deserves to be happy with Esther."

Fannie nodded. "You're right. And since I've come to know Esther fairly well, I believe she's the right woman for Samuel and his kinner."

"I agree, and I hope Timothy and Hannah are able to be at the wedding, too, because I'm sure Samuel would be disappointed if they didn't come."

"Do you really think Hannah will be up to going? You know how upset she's been since Mindy died." Fannie paused, feeling the pain of it all herself. "Abraham, it about broke my heart to see the way she shut Timothy out. She barely looked at him the day of Mindy's funeral."

"I know."

"Timothy thinks she blames him for Mindy's death." Fannie's forehead wrinkled. "Do you think our son is responsible for the tragedy?"

Abraham shrugged. "Guess there's a little blame on everyone's shoulders. Timothy for not putting in new screens; Hannah for not keeping a closer watch on Mindy; and even little Mindy, who shouldn't have been playing near the window." He sighed. "But as I told Timothy when I spoke to him on the phone last night, blaming himself or anyone else will not bring Mindy back."

Fannie nodded slowly. "You're right, of course, but it's a hard fact to swallow."

"I also reminded our son that in order to find the strength to press on, he needs to spend time alone with God."

"That was very good advice," Fannie said. "I just hope Timothy will heed what you said."

Pembroke, Kentucky

"You really need to eat something," Sally said, offering Hannah a piece of toast.

Hannah shook her head. "I'm not hungry."

Sally frowned. She was worried sick about her daughter. Over the last week, a number of women from the community had brought food, but Hannah wouldn't eat anything unless she was forced to. She simply sat quietly in the rocking chair, holding Mindy's doll.

If all I can do is offer comfort and sit beside Hannah, then that's what I'll do, Sally thought, taking a seat beside Hannah. "You can take comfort in knowing that Mindy is in a better place," she said, placing her hand on Hannah's arm.

"Better place? What could be better for my little girl than to be right here with me?" Hannah's eyes narrowed into tiny slits. "It's Timothy's fault Mindy is dead! If he'd just put new screens in the windows like I asked—"

"Kannscht ihn verge ware?" Johnny asked as he entered the room.

Hannah slowly shook her head. "No, I don't think I can ever forgive him."

Johnny stood beside Hannah and placed his hand on her shoulder. "If there's one thing I've learned over the years, it's that we don't get to choose our fate. We can only learn how to live through it."

Hannah just continued to rock, staring straight ahead.

"God doesn't spare us trials," Sally said. "But He does help us overcome them."

Hannah made no reply.

"Maybe we should leave her alone for a while." Johnny nudged Sally's arm and motioned to the kitchen. "Let's go eat breakfast. Timothy's finishing his chores in the barn, and I'm sure he'll be hungry when he comes in."

Sally hesitated. She really wished Hannah would join them for breakfast but didn't want to force the issue. Maybe Johnny was right about Hannah needing some time alone; she had been hovering over her quite a bit this week. With a heavy sigh, Sally stood and followed Johnny to the kitchen.

When Timothy joined them a few minutes later, Sally couldn't help but notice the tears in his eyes. He was obviously as distressed about Mindy's death as Hannah was, but at least he continued to eat and do his chores. Yet Timothy spoke very little about his feelings. Maybe he thought not talking about it would lessen the pain. Sally knew otherwise.

The three of them took seats at the table, and after their silent prayer, Sally passed a platter of scrambled eggs and ham to Timothy. He took a piece of the ham and a spoonful of eggs; then after handing the platter to Johnny, he said, "I appreciate all that you both have done, but you've been here almost two weeks now, and I think it's time for you to go home."

"But Hannah's not doing well, and she needs me," Sally argued. She couldn't believe Timothy would suggest that they return to Pennsylvania right now.

With a look of determination, Timothy shook his head. "Hannah and I need each other in order to deal with our grief. As long as you're here, she'll never respond to me."

Sally winced, feeling as if he'd slapped her face. Did Timothy honestly believe that Hannah, who hadn't said more than a few words to him since Mindy's death, needed him more than she did her own mother? She was about to tell him what she thought about that when Johnny spoke up.

"I believe you're right, Timothy. Sally and I will leave in the morning."

Chapter 43

Timothy leaned against Dusty's stall and groaned. It had been three weeks since Mindy's death, and things seemed to be getting worse between him and Hannah. He'd figured once Hannah's parents went home, Hannah would return to their own room at night, but she'd continued to sleep in Mindy's bedroom. To make matters worse, whenever Timothy spoke to Hannah, she barely acknowledged his presence. Didn't she realize how horrible he felt about Mindy's death? Didn't she know that he missed their daughter, too?

Despite his grief, Timothy knew he needed to get back to work or they wouldn't have money to pay their bills and buy groceries. Yet he couldn't leave Hannah by herself all day—not in the state she was in. So he'd called and left a message for Suzanne last night, asking if she'd be willing to come and sit with Hannah. He hoped that either she or Titus had checked their voice mail, because Samuel and his driver would be coming by in an hour to pick him up. If Suzanne didn't come over by then, there was no way Timothy could go off to work. He couldn't ask Esther to stay with Hannah. Between taking care of Samuel's kids and doing last-minute things for her upcoming wedding, she had her hands full. Thankfully, Bonnie and Allen had returned from their honeymoon a few days ago, so Esther's help wasn't needed at the B&B anymore.

Forcing his thoughts aside, Timothy finished feeding Dusty and Lilly then went back to the house. Hannah was sitting in the rocking chair with Mindy's doll in her lap.

"We need to talk," he said, kneeling on the floor in front of her.

Hannah kept rocking, staring straight ahead, with no acknowledgment of his presence. If her pale face and sunken eyes were any indication of how tired she felt, she hadn't slept much since the accident, but then, neither had he. How could he get any quality sleep when his wife stayed two rooms away and wouldn't even speak to him? He longed to offer Hannah comfort and reassurance, but it wouldn't be appreciated. Hannah had shut him out, and he wasn't sure she would ever let him into her world again. Her brown eyes looked so sorrowful behind her tears, yet she wouldn't express her feelings.

Timothy was even more worried because he'd noticed that Hannah had lost a lot of weight since the accident. She ate so little, and then only when someone practically forced her to do so. Did she think that not eating would dull her pain, or was she trying to starve herself to death? He hoped she wasn't so depressed that she wanted to end her own life. He couldn't deal with another tragedy—especially one of that magnitude. He'd just have to try harder to get through to her.

"I love you, Hannah. Please talk to me." Timothy's fingers curved under her trembling chin.

She winced and pulled away as if she couldn't stand the sight of him. Her reluctance to look at him or even speak his name was so strong he could feel it to the core of his being. Even his gentle touch seemed to make her cringe. If only there was something he could do to bridge the awful gap between them.

"Why are you shutting me out?" he asked, trying once again. "Don't you think I miss Mindy, too?"

Hannah turned in her chair, refusing to make eye contact with him.

Timothy swallowed around the lump in his throat. It hurt to know she didn't love him anymore.

A knock sounded on the back door, and he went to answer it.

"I got your message," Suzanne said when he found her standing on the porch. "I'd be happy to stay with Hannah while you go to work today."

Timothy breathed a sigh of relief, trying to stay composed. "Let's go into the kitchen so we can talk," he said.

When they entered the kitchen, Timothy shared his concerns about Hannah. "I know it's only been a few weeks since Mindy died, but Hannah's still grieving so hard it scares me. What if she doesn't snap out of it? What if—"

"I'll try talking to her," Suzanne said. "Maybe she'll open up to me."

"You might be right. Since she doesn't blame you for our daughter's death, she probably won't give you the cold shoulder the way she does me. I can't get her to respond to me at all."

Suzanne offered Timothy a sympathetic smile and patted his arm. "Things will get better in time; you'll see."

Timothy sighed. "I hope so, because the guilt I feel for not putting in new window screens is bad enough, but having my wife shut me out the way she has is the worst kind of pain."

"I can only imagine."

A horn honked, and Timothy looked out the window.

"Samuel and his driver are here, so I'd better go. Thanks again for coming, Suzanne."

"You're welcome."

—✿—

As Hannah continued to rock, her shoulders sagged with the weight of her depression. She almost felt paralyzed with grief and was sure that her life would never be normal again.

When she'd refused to talk to Timothy, she'd seen the pained expression on his face, but she didn't care. Because of him, she was miserable. Because of him, she'd never see her precious little girl again.

Hannah stopped rocking, lifted Mindy's doll, and studied its face. *If Mindy had lived and been crippled, that would have been better than her dying,* she thought. Then she remembered a conversation she'd had with Esther some time ago about her brother, Dan, who was struggling with MS. Hannah had mentioned that she didn't think she could take care of someone like that. If she could have Mindy back, she'd gladly make the sacrifice of caring for her, even if she was disabled.

Suzanne stepped into the living room, disrupting Hannah's thoughts. "I'm here to spend the day with you," she said, handing Hannah a cup of hot tea.

Hannah shook her head. "I don't want anything to drink, and I don't need you to babysit me."

Suzanne set the teacup on the small table near the rocking chair and took a seat on the sofa across from Hannah. "Timothy is really worried about you."

Hannah said nothing.

"We're all worried, Hannah."

Hannah started the rocker moving again. *Creak... Creak... Creak...* It moved in rhythmic motion.

"I know you're going through a hard time, but if you ask God for strength, He will give it to you. When you're hurting, He will give you comfort in ways that no one else can."

Hannah's throat constricted, and a tight sob threatened to escape. "God doesn't care about me."

"He most certainly does. God loves and cares about all His people."

"Then why'd He take Mindy?"

"I don't know the answer to that, but I do know that accidents happen, and—"

Hannah's face contorted. "It was an accident that shouldn't have happened! God could have prevented it, and so could Timothy. He should have put new screens on the windows when I asked him to. Now our daughter is gone, and she's never coming back!"

—∞—

Hopkinsville, Kentucky

"Are you sure you're ready to begin working again?" Samuel asked Timothy as he set a ladder in place inside the doctor's office they'd been hired to paint.

"Whether I'm ready or not is beside the point. I have to work. We need the money, and I need to keep busy so I don't think too much," Timothy said after he'd opened a bucket of paint.

"It's good to be busy, but I'm concerned that you might not have given yourself enough time to heal before returning to work," Samuel said. "You look like you haven't been sleeping well."

"I haven't. It's kind of hard to sleep when I know it's my fault that my daughter is dead. And knowing Hannah blames me for the accident makes it even worse." Timothy clenched his fingers tightly together. "When I look in the mirror these days, I don't like what I see."

"That's *narrish*. Blaming yourself will only wear you down."

"It might seem foolish to you, but that's the way I feel." Timothy dropped his gaze as he continued. "I keep hearing Hannah that day, asking me to fix the window screens upstairs. But I was too worried about planting the field. I kept putting it off and finding other things to do. Now in hindsight, I keep asking myself, *What was I thinking?* Replacing those screens, especially in my daughter's room, was far more important than the corn crop that ended up getting destroyed. Same goes for the rest of the projects I did instead of taking care of the screens. Mindy's life was at stake, and now I'm paying the price for being so stupid."

Samuel moved across the room and clasped Timothy's shoulder. "It takes a strong person to deal with hard times, and you're a strong person. So with God's help, you can choose to forgive yourself and go on with your life. And never forget that you have a family who loves and cares about you. We're all here to support you through this difficult time. Remember, Timothy, I was in a similar situation over a year ago when I lost Elsie. I know it's not exactly the same, but the pain is just as strong. In time, good things will happen again in your lives. I never would have believed it myself, but good things have happened for me."

"I appreciate hearing that, and I know as time passes it might get easier. I couldn't get through this without my family's support, but I sure wish I had Hannah's. She won't even speak to me. In fact, she avoids looking at me." Timothy groaned. "I really don't know what to do about it."

"Would you like me to talk to her? With all I went through

after Elsie died, I might be able to help Hannah through her grief."

"You can try if you like. Suzanne said she'll attempt to get through to Hannah, too, but I doubt it'll do any good." Timothy picked up his paintbrush. "Guess we'd better get to work, or this job will never get done."

Samuel nodded. "Just remember one thing: I'm here for you, day or night."

Chapter 44

Pembroke, Kentucky

"Mom, Dad, it's so good you could be here for my wedding today," Esther said as she sat with her folks eating breakfast at Bonnie's dining-room table. Mom and Dad had arrived yesterday afternoon and would be staying for a few days after the wedding. Esther's brother James and his family, who lived in Lykens, Pennsylvania, had also come. But due to Dan's failing health, he and his family had remained in Pennsylvania.

"We're glad we could be here, too," Mom said, smiling at Esther. "There's no way we could miss our only daughter's wedding."

Dad bobbed his head. "Your mamm's right about that."

Esther glanced across the table at Samuel's sister Naomi. She and her husband, Caleb, as well as some other members of Samuel's family, were also staying at the bed-and-breakfast. Esther appreciated the fact that Bonnie had graciously agreed to let them all have their rooms at no cost. They'd set up a cot for Trisha in the guesthouse, and she'd slept there last night, since they needed all the extra rooms for their guests. Trisha would be living in the guesthouse full-time after Esther was married.

"I can't believe this day is finally here," Esther murmured. "I just feel a bit guilty getting married when Timothy and Hannah are still grieving for Mindy. Samuel and I had thought about postponing the wedding for another month or two, but Timothy wouldn't hear of it."

"One thing I've always thought was special about you is that you can't look the other way when someone you know is hurting," Mom said, smiling at Esther. "But postponing your wedding won't bring Timothy and Hannah's little girl back, and I'm sure they would want you to go ahead with your plans."

Esther nodded. "That's exactly what Timothy told Samuel."

"Life goes on even when people are hurting. Maybe going to the wedding will help them focus on something else, if only for a little while," Naomi spoke up. "I remember when my little brother Zach was kidnapped. Nothing seemed right. But we forced ourselves to keep on with the business of living despite the pain we felt over losing him."

"That's right," Naomi's sister Nancy said. "It was hard going on without our little brother all those years, but God helped us get through it."

"And He will help Timothy and Hannah, too," Allen said. "They just need to stay close to Him and rely on others for comfort and support."

"Do you think they'll attend the wedding?" Bonnie asked, turning to look at him.

"Well, Timothy's back working with Samuel again, and when I spoke to him yesterday, he said he was planning to go and that he hoped Hannah would feel up to it."

~

When Timothy entered the kitchen, Hannah was standing in front of the stove making a pot of coffee. That was a good sign, because ever since Mindy died he'd had to make his own coffee in the mornings.

"I'm just going to have a bowl of cereal, and then I'll need to get ready for the wedding," he said, stepping up beside her.

No reply. Not even a nod.

"Hannah, are you planning to go Esther and Samuel's wedding with me?"

She slowly shook her head.

"Maybe I shouldn't go either, because I don't want to leave you here alone."

"Just go on without me; I'll be fine," she mumbled. Well, at least she was talking to him again.

"Are you sure you won't go? It might do you some good to get out of the house for a few hours."

She whirled around and glared at him. "You can't expect me to put on a happy face and go to the wedding when I feel so dead inside!"

Normally, Timothy preferred to listen rather than talk, but something needed to be said, and he planned to say it. "You know, when we first made plans to move to Kentucky—"

Her eyes narrowed. "Your plans, don't you mean? You never considered whether I wanted to move. All you thought about was yourself!"

"I wasn't just thinking of me. I was thinking of us and our marriage."

She folded her arms. "Humph!"

"We can make this work, Hannah, but it's going to take both of us to do it."

"It's never going to work, and I don't see how you can expect it to," she said. "If we were still in Pennsylvania, none of this would have happened. Don't you realize that the day our daughter died, a part of me died, too? You took her from me, Timothy. You took our precious little girl, and she's never coming back!" Hannah turned and rushed out of the room, leaving him staring after her, eyes wet with tears.

—᧐—

It had been hard for Timothy to hitch his horse to the buggy and go over to Samuel's for the wedding, but out of love and respect for his brother, he'd made himself do it. Now, after turning his horse loose in the corral and starting in the direction of the house, he was having second thoughts. Maybe he should have stayed home with Hannah. She was terribly upset when he left. But if he couldn't get through to her in the kitchen this morning, it probably wouldn't have mattered if he'd stayed there all day and talked to Hannah. Suzanne had tried, Samuel had tried, and Esther had tried, but no one could get through to her. Hannah blamed Timothy for Mindy's death, and she obviously wasn't going to forgive him. Short of a miracle, nothing he could say or do would change the fact that she no longer loved him. He feared that for the rest of their married life they'd be living in the same house, sleeping in separate bedrooms, with Hannah barely acknowledging his presence. That wasn't the way God intended marriage to be, but Timothy didn't know what he could do about it.

As he neared the house, he spotted Bonnie and Allen on the front porch talking to Trisha. He wasn't surprised that they'd been invited, since Allen and Samuel were good friends and so were Bonnie and Esther. And since Trisha and Esther had been working at the B&B together for the last several weeks, it was understandable that she'd received an invitation to the wedding as well.

"It's good to see you," Allen said, clasping Timothy's shoulder as soon as he stepped onto the porch.

"Thanks. It's good to see you, too."

"How's Hannah doing?" Bonnie asked. "I was hoping she might be here today."

Timothy shook his head. "Hannah's still not doing well. She didn't feel up to coming."

"That's too bad. I've been meaning to drop by your place and see her," Bonnie said. "I was busy getting ready for the out-of-town wedding guests, and I'm sorry I didn't take the time to check on her. I'll try to do that within the next day or so."

Timothy forced a smile. "I appreciate that, and hopefully Hannah will, too." He motioned to the house. "Guess the service will be starting soon, so I'd better get inside."

When Timothy took a seat beside his dad, he noticed that Samuel and Esther had already taken their seats, facing each other. They fidgeted a bit, an indication that they were nervous, but their eager smiles let him know how happy they were. They'd both been through a lot, so they deserved all the happiness of this special day.

Timothy glanced to his right and saw his other five brothers sitting beyond his dad. On the benches behind them were his three brothers-in-law. His sisters sat together on the women's side of the room with his sisters-in-law. Many of his nieces and nephews had also come to the wedding, making quite a large group from Pennsylvania. They'd hired several drivers with vans to make the trip.

As the first song began, Timothy thought about how this was the second of his brothers' weddings he'd attended alone. Last October, Timothy had left Hannah and Mindy in Pennsylvania when he'd come to Kentucky to attend Titus and Suzanne's wedding. Hannah had used the excuse that her mother needed help because she'd sprained her ankle, so she'd insisted on staying home. Now Timothy was at Samuel and Esther's wedding, and he was alone once again. This time he understood why Hannah hadn't wanted to come. It had been difficult for him to come, but he was happy Samuel had found love again, and Timothy wanted to witness his brother's marriage.

As the service continued, Timothy thought about his own wedding. He'd loved Hannah so much back then—and still did, for that matter. But things had changed for Hannah. Even before Mindy's death, she'd often been cool toward him. He'd shrugged it off, figuring she was still upset with him for making them move to Kentucky. But there had been times, like the week before Mindy died, when he thought Hannah was beginning to adjust to the move and had actually warmed up to him. Just when he'd felt there was some hope for their marriage, Mindy's tragic death had shattered their world. Timothy was convinced that Hannah's love for him was dead. Their tragedy was so huge, nothing short of a miracle could mend their relationship.

Timothy's thoughts were halted when Bishop King called Esther and Samuel to stand before him. Their faces fairly glowed as they each answered affirmatively to the bishop's questions. When the vows had been spoken, the bishop took Esther and Samuel's hands and said, "So go forth in the name of the Lord. You are now husband and wife."

I hope they will always be as happy as they are right now, Timothy thought. *And may nothing ever drive them apart.*

—∞—

As Hannah entered the cemetery to visit Mindy's grave, she spotted a lone sheep rubbing its nose on one of the headstones. At least she thought it was a sheep. Due to the tears clouding her vision, she wondered if she might be seeing something that wasn't actually there.

Hannah moved forward and stopped when she heard a loud *baa*. There really was a sheep by that headstone. But why would the creature be in the cemetery, and who did it belong to?

Hannah heard another *baa* and glanced to her left. Several sheep grazed in the field on the other side of the cemetery. Apparently one had found a way out and ended up over here. Well, the sheep could stay right where it was, for all she cared.

Hannah ambled slowly through the cemetery until she came to the place where Mindy's body had been buried. The simple granite headstone inscribed with Mindy's name, date of birth, and date of death had been set in place, making the tragedy even more final. Tears welled in Hannah's eyes, and she swayed unsteadily. The anguish that engulfed her was so great she felt overcome by it. She dropped to the ground and sobbed. "Oh Mindy, my precious little girl. . . How can I go on without you?"

Chapter 45

After Hannah returned home from the cemetery, she sat on the porch awhile, holding Bobbin and hoping the cat would offer her some comfort. He didn't. She just felt worse because she was reminded of how Mindy had enjoyed playing with the animal. One time Bobbin had lost his balance and rolled down the stairs like a sack of potatoes. Mindy had been so concerned and looked so relieved when she'd seen that the cat wasn't hurt.

Even with the memories she had left of Mindy, Hannah didn't think anything would ever bring her the comfort she so badly needed. She barely noticed the birds singing in the trees and refused to look at the flowers she'd planted in the spring. She thought about the dandelions Mindy had picked on the morning of her death and winced. It was such a bittersweet memory.

Bobbin rubbed his nose against Hannah's hand and purred, as though sensing her mood; yet Hannah felt no comfort.

When the sun became unbearably hot, Hannah set the cat on the porch and went inside for a glass of water. She took a seat at the table and sat staring at the stool Mindy used to perch on during their meals. This house was way too quiet without the patter of Mindy's little feet and the sound of her childish laughter bouncing off the walls. She'd been such a happy girl—curious, full of energy, so cute and cuddly. Hannah's arms ached to hold her and stroke her soft, pink skin.

Giving in to her tears, Hannah leaned forward and rested her head on the table. She'd been on the brink of tears every day since Mindy died, and often let herself weep, as she was doing now.

"Oh how I wish I'd had the chance to say good-bye, kiss my precious girl, and tell her how much I love her," Hannah sobbed. Overcome with fatigue and grief, she closed her eyes and drifted off.

Sometime later, Hannah was awakened when Timothy entered the kitchen, touched her shoulder, and said, "How come you're sitting here in the dark?"

Hannah sat up straight and rubbed her eyes. "I must have dozed off."

Timothy lit the gas lamp above the kitchen table. "Sorry I'm so late. There were lots of people from my family at the wedding, and I wanted to visit with them."

Hannah glanced at the clock on the far wall. It was almost seven o'clock. Had she really been asleep nearly two hours?

"Mom and Dad said to tell you hello. They'll be over to visit in the next day or so. I think tomorrow they're going to help Esther and Samuel with the cleanup from the wedding."

Hannah shrugged. She didn't care whether Fannie and Abraham came over to see her. She wasn't good company and really had nothing to say to either of them.

"Have you eaten supper yet?" Timothy asked.

She shook her head. "I'm not hungry."

"Hannah, you need to eat. I'm worried because you've lost so much weight, and it's not good for your health to skip meals like you do."

"Why'd the Lord bring us here, only to forsake us?" she wailed.

"God hasn't forsaken us, Hannah. He knows the pain we both feel." Timothy rested his hands on her trembling shoulders, and for just a minute, Hannah's pain lessened a bit.

"Why don't the two of us go for a ride?" he suggested. "It'll give us a chance to enjoy the cool evening breeze that's come up, and I think it would be good for you to get out of the house for a while."

She shrugged his hands away. "I don't want to go for a ride. I just want to be left alone."

"Not this time, Hannah. You need me right now, and I. . .I need you, too."

Hannah just stared at the table, fighting back tears of frustration.

"Don't you love me anymore?" he asked, taking a seat beside her.

His question burned deep in her heart, and she shifted in her seat, unsure of how to respond.

He leaned close and moaned as he brushed his lips across her forehead. "I love you, Hannah, and I always will."

Overcome with emotion, she took a deep breath and forced herself to look at him. His eyes held no sparkle, revealing the depth of his sadness. When he pulled her into his arms, she felt weak, unable to resist.

As Timothy's lips touched Hannah's, a niggling little voice in her head said she shouldn't let this happen, yet her heart said otherwise, and she seemed powerless to stop it.

Finding comfort in her husband's embrace, Hannah closed

her eyes and allowed his kisses to drive all negative, hurtful thoughts from her mind.

—∞—

When Timothy awoke the following morning, he glanced over at his sleeping wife and smiled. She looked so peaceful with her long hair fanned out on the pillow and her cheeks rosy from a good night's sleep. He decided not to wake her. After all, he'd been fixing his own breakfast for the last few weeks, so he could do it again this morning.

He grabbed his work clothes, bent to kiss Hannah's forehead, and slipped quietly out of the room. There was extra pep to his step because, for the first time in weeks, he actually felt hopeful.

As Timothy fixed a pot of coffee in the kitchen, he thought about last night and thanked God that he and Hannah had found comfort in each other's arms. Timothy was certain her response to him had been the first step in helping them deal with the pain of losing Mindy. He felt hopeful that they could now face the loss of their daughter together and find the strength they both needed to go on.

When Timothy walked out the door to wait for his driver, he leaned against the porch railing. Watching the sunrise, he thought it had never looked more beautiful.

—∞—

Hannah yawned and stretched her arms over her head. Her brain felt fuzzy—like it was full of thick cobwebs. She must have slept long and hard.

When Hannah sat up in bed and looked around, she felt as if a jolt of electricity had been shot through her. She was in her own bedroom, not Mindy's! *How in the world did I end up here?*

Hannah rubbed her forehead. Then she remembered Timothy's kisses and words of love. She'd needed his comfort and let her emotions carry her away.

"What was I thinking?" Hannah moaned. She hadn't forgiven Timothy for causing Mindy's death and didn't think she ever could. One night of being held in his arms wouldn't bring Mindy back to them, and it may have given Timothy false hope.

Hannah pushed the covers aside and crawled out of bed. With tears blinding her vision, she stumbled across the room. She couldn't stay here anymore. She had to get away.

As Hannah packed her bags in readiness to leave, pain clutched her heart. If they hadn't moved to Kentucky, none of this would have happened. Mindy would still be with them, and they'd be living happily in Pennsylvania.

After Hannah got dressed, she opened the bedroom door, set her suitcase in the hallway, and headed for Mindy's room. When she stepped inside, she stared at her daughter's empty bed. She hadn't even changed Mindy's sheets since the tragic day of her death. A deep sense of sadness washed over Hannah as she sat on the bed and buried her face in Mindy's pillow. She took a deep breath, trying to keep her daughter's essence within her. But sadly, she was reminded once again that Mindy was never coming back. Hannah wouldn't see her little girl's sweet face again—not in this life, anyhow. The only way she could deal with this unrelenting pain was to leave this place, where painful memories plagued her night and day, and return to Pennsylvania. At least there she would have Mom and Dad's love and support. Yes, that's what she needed right now.

With one last glance, Hannah spotted Mindy's favorite doll. She picked it up and carried it, along with her suitcase, down the stairs. Upon entering the kitchen, she found a notepad and pen and quickly scrawled a note for Timothy, which she left on the table.

Hannah pushed the screen door open and stepped onto the porch. A blast of warm, humid air hit her full in the face, yet she still felt chilled. She heard a pathetic *meow.* Looking down, she saw Bobbin lying on his back on the porch, paws in the air. Did the poor cat know she was leaving? Did he even care?

Shoulders slumped and head down, Hannah stepped off the porch and made her way down the lane, where she would stop at the phone shanty to call her driver for a ride to the bus station in Clarksville.

As she ambled slowly past the fence dividing the lane from the pasture, Mindy's doll slipped from her hand, unnoticed. Squinting against the morning sun, blazing like a fiery furnace, Hannah kept walking and didn't look back. It was best to leave all the painful memories behind.

When Timothy's driver dropped him at the end of their lane that evening, Timothy winced with each step he took. He hurt all over—even the soles of his feet. He and Samuel had worked on a three-story house in Hopkinsville today, and he'd been up and down the ladder so many times he'd lost count. It had been easier to work, however, knowing things were better between him and Hannah and that she'd be waiting for him when he got home. He hoped she'd have supper ready and that they could sit outside on the back porch after they ate and visit while they watched the sun go down and listened to the crickets sing their nightly chorus.

As Timothy continued his walk up the lane, he kicked

something with the toe of his boot. He looked and was surprised to see Mindy's doll lying facedown in the dirt.

"Now what's that doing here?" he murmured. Could Hannah have gone out to get the mail today and taken the doll along? She'd had it with her almost constantly since Mindy died and often rocked the doll as though it were a baby. Hannah had probably dropped it on the way back from the mailbox and just hadn't noticed.

Timothy picked up the doll and carried it under one arm. When he entered the house, all was quiet, and he didn't smell any food. It was a disappointment, but he was used to it because Hannah hadn't done any of the cooking since Mindy died. Timothy stepped into the utility room and put the doll on a shelf then went to the kitchen. Hannah wasn't there, and he was about to call for her when he spotted a note on the table. He picked it up and read it silently.

Timothy,

I'm sure you'll be disappointed when I tell you this, but I can't stay here any longer. Every time I look at you, I remember that you could have prevented our daughter's death, and it's too painful for me to deal with. I'm returning to Pennsylvania to be with Mom and Dad. Please don't come after me, because I won't come back to Kentucky, and I can no longer live with you. It's better this way, for both of us.

—Hannah

Timothy sank into a chair and groaned. He couldn't believe it. After last night, he was sure things were better between them. Why had she let him kiss her and then slept in their room if she hadn't forgiven him for being the cause of Mindy's death?

He shuddered and swallowed against the sob rising in his throat. He'd not only lost his daughter, but now his wife was gone, too. He didn't know if he'd ever see Hannah again. She hadn't even signed the note with love. Should he go after her—insist that she come home? Or would it be better to give her some time and hope she'd come back on her own? After so many weeks of trying to remain strong, Timothy could no longer hold in his grief. He leaned forward and sobbed so hard it almost made him ill. He didn't care anymore. He was exhausted from trying to be strong for Hannah, and now he had nothing left. How much more could a man take?

Chapter 46

Paradise, Pennsylvania

Sally had just entered the phone shack to make a call when the telephone rang. She quickly picked up the receiver. "Hello."

"Sally, is that you?" a male voice asked.

"Yes, it's me. Who's this?"

"It. . .it's Timothy."

"Is everything all right? You sound *umgerennt*."

"I am upset. I came home from work today and found a note from Hannah." There was a pause. "She said she was leaving me and returning to Pennsylvania."

Sally drew in a sharp breath. "Hannah's on her way here?"

"Jah. I'm not sure if she hired a driver or caught a bus." Another pause. "I thought maybe you would have heard from her."

"No, but then maybe she didn't call because she was afraid we would have told her she shouldn't come."

"Would you have?"

Sally sank into the folding chair, unsure how to respond. If Hannah had told her that she was coming, it would have been hard to dissuade her. But she was fairly sure if Hannah had talked to Johnny about this, he would have told her to stay put—that her place was in Kentucky with her husband.

"Sally, are you still there?"

"Jah, I'm here."

"What are you gonna do when Hannah gets there?" Timothy asked.

Sally was glad he hadn't forced her to answer his previous question. She shifted the phone to her other ear.

"We'll make her feel welcome, of course."

Timothy grunted. "Figured as much."

"Hannah's obviously in great distress or she wouldn't have felt the need to leave Kentucky. Seriously, we can hardly ask her to go as soon as she gets here."

"No, I suppose not, but Hannah's place is with me."

"Maybe she needs some time away—time to think and allow her broken heart to heal."

"You might be right, but I'm hurting, too, and I think I should be the one to help Hannah through her grief."

"You may not realize this now, but a time of separation might be what you both need."

"It's not what I need, Sally. When Hannah gets there, will you please ask her to come home?"

"Pennsylvania has been Hannah's home since she was a baby."

"Not anymore," Timothy said forcefully. "Her home's here with me!"

"I can't talk anymore," Sally said. "I need to fix supper for Johnny. One of us will call and let you know when Hannah arrives so you won't worry about her. Good-bye, Timothy. Take care." Sally hung up the phone quickly, before he could respond.

She sat for several minutes, mulling things over. *So Hannah's coming home. I wonder what Johnny will have to say about this?*

—∞—

Pembroke, Kentucky

When Timothy hung up the phone, he sat in disbelief. After his conversation with Sally, he was convinced that she had no intention of trying to persuade Hannah to return to Kentucky.

Needing some fresh air, he stepped out of the hot, stuffy phone shanty. He needed to talk to his brothers about this, and he'd start with Titus, since he lived the closest.

Timothy sprinted up to the barn to get his horse and buggy, and a short time later he was on the road. He let Dusty run, and as the horse trotted down the road, Timothy's thoughts ran wild. He remembered the day he'd told Hannah he wanted to move to Kentucky. She'd argued with him and begged him to change his mind. When she'd asked if he would be sad to leave Pennsylvania, he'd replied, "As long as I have you and Mindy, I'll never be sad." Little did he know then that less than a year later, he'd be sadder than he ever thought possible.

"Maybe Hannah was right about my decision to move here," he mumbled. "But if we'd stayed in Pennsylvania, Hannah would have continued to put her mamm's needs ahead of mine, and she'd have spent more time with her than she did me."

Who am I kidding? My marriage to Hannah is in more trouble now than it's ever been. I'd thought things were better last night, but I was wrong. Hannah obviously doesn't love me. She probably had a moment of weakness and, when she woke up this morning, realized her mistake and wanted to get as far away from me as possible. No doubt she'd rather be with her Mamm right now.

By the time Timothy pulled into Titus's place, he felt even more confused and stressed out. He really did need to talk to someone who'd understand the way he felt about things.

"What brings you by here this evening?" Titus asked, stepping out of the barn. "Is everything okay?"

"No, it's not," Timothy said, climbing out of the buggy. "Hannah's gone!"

"What do you mean?"

Timothy explained about the note he'd found and told Titus about the conversation he'd had with Hannah's mother.

"Would you like my opinion?" Titus asked.

"Jah, that's why I came over here. I'd also like Suzanne's opinion. Is she in the house?"

"No, she's feeding the cats in the barn. You want me to call her, or should we go in there?"

"Let me secure my horse, and then we can go in the barn."

When they entered the barn a few minutes later, Timothy spotted Suzanne sitting on a bale of hay with Titus's cat, Callie, in her lap. Seeing Suzanne so large in her pregnancy reminded him of Hannah when she was carrying Mindy. How long ago that now seemed.

"Oh hi, Timothy," she said, smiling up at him. "Is Hannah with you?"

He shook his head then quickly explained the situation. "I can't believe she would just up and leave me like that," he said.

"She's been an emotional wreck ever since Mindy died, and people like that don't think things through before they act," Suzanne said. "If you want my opinion, I think you should give her some time."

"So you don't think I should go after her?"

Suzanne shook her head. "That might make matters even worse."

Timothy looked at Titus. "What are your thoughts?"

"I agree with my wife. If you try to force Hannah to come back to Kentucky, she might resent you more than she already does. It could drive a wedge between you that will never break down."

"What if Hannah never gets over Mindy's death? She blames me for the accident, and I'm afraid—" Timothy stopped talking and drew in a shaky breath. "You don't think Hannah will divorce me, do you?"

Suzanne gasped. "That would be baremlich, and it goes against our beliefs."

"Jah, it would be terrible," Titus said, "but I really don't think Hannah would do such a thing."

"How do you know?" Timothy questioned.

"If she got a divorce, she'd have to leave the Amish faith. Can you really see Hannah doing something that would take her away from her family—especially her mamm—and in such a tragic way?"

"I hope not, but in Hannah's current state of mind, she might do anything." Timothy sank to a bale of hay and let his head fall forward into his hands. All he could do was wait and pray for a miracle.

Chapter 47

Paradise, Pennsylvania

Hannah sat in a wicker rocking chair on her parents' front porch, watching two of Dad's cats leaping through the grass, chasing grasshoppers. It made her think of Mindy and how she'd loved playing with Bobbin. Mindy had also liked playing with her doll, but a few days after she'd arrived at her folks', Hannah had realized that Mindy's doll must still be in Kentucky. She'd had it with her when she was walking down the lane to call for a driver, so she assumed in her grief, she must have dropped it along the way. It was probably just as well. Seeing it all the time would be a constant reminder of what Hannah had lost.

Tears sprang to her eyes. She remembered the time she'd entered the living room and spotted Mindy leaning against the wall, wearing Timothy's sunglasses and a grin that stretched from ear to ear. She'd been such a happy child—so spontaneous and curious about things.

"Mind if I join you?" Mom asked, joining Hannah on the porch.

"No." Hannah motioned to the chair beside her.

"Are you doing okay?" Mom asked, taking a seat. "You look like you're deep in thought."

"I was thinking about Mindy and how much fun she used to have playing with the cat." Hannah sniffed. "Thanks to us moving to Kentucky, you and Dad missed so many of the cute little things Mindy said and did. I wish. . . ." Her voice trailed off, and she stared down at her hands, clasped firmly in her lap.

Mom reached over and took Hannah's hand. "It's all right, Hannah."

"Would you like to hear about some of the things Mindy did?"

"Of course."

"One day Mindy and I were walking on the path leading from our house to the mailbox. She stopped all of a sudden and looked up at me with a huge smile. Then she said, 'I love you Mama.'"

Hannah stopped talking and drew in a shaky breath, hoping to gain control of her swirling emotions. "Another time, Mindy was picking dandelions and kept calling them 'pretty flowers.' She had a dandelion in her hand when she died, Mom." Hannah paused again, barely able to get the words out. "I. . .I will never forget the shock of seeing my precious little girl lying there so still, with a withered dandelion in her hand." Hannah nearly choked on the sob rising in her throat. "I don't think I can ever forgive Timothy for causing Mindy's death."

—∞—

Pembroke, Kentucky

"Not long ago, Trisha and I were talking about how food always tastes so much better when it's eaten outside," Bonnie said as she and Allen sat on the front porch of the B&B eating supper. They'd invited Trisha to join them, but she'd declined, saying she wanted to give the newlyweds some time alone and would fix something for herself in the guesthouse.

"You're right about the food tasting good," Allen agreed, after taking a bite of fried chicken. "The only problem with eating outside is this hot July weather. Whew! It makes me glad for air-conditioning! I don't know how our Amish friends manage without it."

Bonnie smiled. "I guess one never misses what one's never had."

"That's true."

"By the way," she asked, "have you seen Timothy since he ate supper with us last week? I've been wondering how he's doing."

"Not very well. I saw him yesterday, and he's so despondent. It's a miracle he's been able to keep going at all."

"I wish Hannah hadn't walked out on him. She may not realize it, but she needs her husband as much as he needs her."

"I agree." Allen reached for Bonnie's hand. "If we ever had to go through anything like that, I'd want you right by my side."

She nodded. "I'd want you near me as well, but I hope we're never faced with anything like what Hannah and Timothy are going through right now."

—∞—

In the two weeks Hannah had been gone, it had been all Timothy could do to cope. He missed his wife so much and longed to speak with her. He'd called her folks several times and left voice messages for Hannah, but she never responded. He'd gotten one message from Sally the day Hannah got there, but it was brief and to the point. She didn't think Timothy should try to contact Hannah and said Hannah would contact him, if and when she felt ready.

"What a slap in the face," Timothy mumbled as he made himself a sandwich for supper. Since he wasn't much of a cook, he'd been eating sandwiches for supper every evening unless he ate at one of his brothers' homes. Both Esther and Suzanne were good cooks, so he appreciated getting a home-cooked meal. He'd eaten supper at Bonnie and Allen's one night last week, and that meal had been good, too.

If I could just talk to Hannah, he thought, *I might be able to convince her to come home.*

Timothy wanted to go to Pennsylvania and speak to her face-to-face, but Samuel and Titus had both advised him to stay put and give Hannah all the time she needed. Trisha, who had lost her husband a few years ago, had reminded Timothy that everyone was different and that it took some people longer than others to deal with their grief. Timothy understood that because he was still grieving for Mindy. He really believed he and Hannah needed each other during this time of mourning. He also feared that the longer they were apart, the harder it would be to bridge the gap between them.

Through prayer and Bible reading, Timothy had been trying to forgive himself, but it was difficult knowing Hannah might never forgive him or come back to Kentucky. How could he go on without her? Nothing would ever be the same if they weren't together as husband and wife.

Timothy set his knife down and made a decision. He would call his mother and ask her to speak to Hannah on his behalf. He just hoped Hannah would listen.

Chapter 48

On Monday morning, during the second week of August, Titus showed up at Samuel and Esther's house with a big grin. "Suzanne had the baby last night, and it's a boy!" he announced, after he'd entered the kitchen, where they sat with the children having breakfast.

Samuel jumped up and hugged Titus. "That's really good news! Congratulations!"

"How are Suzanne and the baby doing?" Esther asked.

"Real well, all things considered. Her labor was hard, but then I guess that's often the case with first babies. The boppli is healthy and has a good set of lungs. Oh, and he weighs nine and a half pounds, and he's almost twenty-two inches long."

"That's a pretty good-sized baby," Samuel said with a low whistle. "Much bigger than any of my kinner when they were born. I think Leon was the biggest; he weighed seven pounds, eleven ounces. The other three were all six and seven pounds."

"What'd ya name the boppli?" Marla asked.

Titus's grin, which had never left his face, widened. "Named him Abraham, after my daed. 'Course we'll probably call him Abe for short."

"I like that name," Leon spoke up. "It'll be nice to have another boy cousin."

"I'm sure Dad will be happy to hear you named the baby after him." Samuel motioned to the table. "If you haven't had breakfast yet, you're welcome to join us."

"I appreciate the offer, but I'm too excited to eat anything right now. I've gotta call the folks and leave 'em a message. And I want to stop and tell Timothy the news. Then I'll be heading back to the hospital to see how my fraa and boppli are doing."

"What about Suzanne's family?" Esther questioned. "Do they know about the baby?"

Titus bobbed his head. "Suzanne's mamm went with us to the hospital last night, so she was there when the boppli came."

"I'll bet she was excited," Esther said. "Especially since this is her first grandchild."

"Jah. Since Nelson seems to be in no hurry to find himself a wife, our little Abe will probably be the only grandchild for Suzanne's mamm to dote on for some time." Titus rolled his eyes. "Which means he'll probably end up bein' spoiled."

"We're really happy for you," Samuel said. "There's nothing quite like becoming a parent." He patted the top of Jared's head.

Esther smiled. She knew how much Samuel loved his children and hoped it wouldn't be long before they could have a child of their own to add to this happy family.

—∞—

Paradise, Pennsylvania

Fannie had just finished making french toast for breakfast when Abraham ambled into the kitchen with a smug-looking smile. "I've got some good news," he said, clasping Fannie's arm.

"Glad to hear it, because it'll be nice to get some good news for a change. Seems like there's too much bad going on in our world these days."

"I just came from the phone shack, and there was a message from Titus."

"Oh? What'd it say?"

"Suzanne had her boppli last night, and they named him after me."

Fannie smiled widely. "They had a boy?"

"Jah. A big, healthy boy, at that."

"That's wunderbaar! Just think, Abraham, this gives us forty-eight kinskinner, not counting dear little, departed Mindy. Oh, I wish we could go to Kentucky right now so we could see the new boppli."

"We'll go soon, Fannie—unless Titus and Suzanne decide to come here first."

She shook her head. "That's not likely to happen. From what Titus said the last time we talked, things are really busy in the woodshop right now, so I doubt he'll be taking time off for a trip anytime soon. Besides, it's a whole lot easier for us to travel than it would be for a young couple with a new baby."

"You're probably right, so we'll go there soon. But I think we should give 'em some time to adjust to being parents before we barge in, don't you?"

She nodded slowly. "I suppose you're right, and when we do go, it'll be nice to see Samuel and his family, as well as Timothy."

Abraham took a seat. "Speaking of Timothy, have you been able to talk to Hannah yet? You did promise him you'd try to talk her into going back to Kentucky, right?"

"Jah, I did, but every time I've gone over to the Kings' place, I've only seen Sally." Fannie sighed deeply. "She always gives me the excuse that Hannah's resting or isn't feeling up to company. Makes me wonder if I'll ever get the chance to speak to Hannah face-to-face."

"Well, don't give up. One of these days when you stop over there, Sally's bound to be gone, and then she won't be able to run interference for Hannah." Abraham grunted. "Wouldn't surprise me one bit if she doesn't do it just so she can keep Hannah all to herself. You and I both know that Hannah's mamm had such a tight hold on Hannah before Timothy moved them to Kentucky that it was choking the life out of their marriage. Now that Hannah's back home and livin' under her folks' roof again, Sally will probably do most anything to keep Hannah there."

"Oh, I hope that's not the case." Fannie set the platter of french toast on the table and took a seat beside Abraham. "As soon as we're done with breakfast, I'm going over to see Hannah again. Since I promised Timothy I would talk to her, I need to keep trying."

Hannah had just entered the kitchen when a wave of nausea ran through her. She clutched her stomach and groaned. This was the third day in a row that she'd felt sick to her stomach soon after she'd gotten out of bed. *Could I be pregnant?* she wondered. *Oh, surely not. I don't see how. . . .*

Hannah's thoughts took her to the last night she'd spent in Kentucky. She remembered how she'd allowed herself to find comfort in Timothy's arms and had awakened the next morning fearful that because of her willingness to be with him, he'd gotten the wrong idea. Had Timothy believed she'd forgiven him and that things were better between them? Well, he ought to know that just wasn't possible! Even if Hannah was carrying Timothy's child, she could never return to Kentucky and be the wife Timothy wanted and expected her to be. The only way Hannah could cope with Mindy's death was to stay right here in the safety of her parents' home.

Hannah had just put the teakettle on the stove when her mother entered the kitchen. "I'm going shopping as soon as we're done with breakfast, and I was hoping you'd come with me," Mom said.

Hannah shook her head. "I don't feel like it, Mom. I just want to stay here."

"Oh, but Hannah, you've been cooped up in this house ever since you came home, and I think it would be good for you to get out for a few hours."

"I can't. I might see someone from Timothy's family, and then they'd probably tell me I was wrong to leave Timothy and that my place is in Kentucky with him." Hannah leaned against the counter as another wave of nausea rolled through her stomach.

"Are you feeling all right? You look pale," Mom said with a worried frown. "Are you grank?"

"I'm fine. Just tired, is all."

"That's because you're not sleeping well. I think you should let me take you to the doctor and see if he'll prescribe some sleeping pills."

Hannah shook her head vigorously. "I don't want any sleeping pills. I sleep when I need to—sometimes during the day. I'm sure I'll feel better once I've had some breakfast."

Mom pulled Hannah into her arms for a hug. "I can't help but worry about you. Maybe I should wait until tomorrow to do my shopping."

"I'll be fine. Go ahead with your plans."

"All right, then. Is there anything you'd like me to pick up for you while I'm out and about?"

Hannah shook her head. "There's nothing I need." *Except a sense of peace I may never feel,* she added to herself.

—∞—

Soon after Mom left, Hannah decided to sit on the porch for a while because it was so hot and stuffy in the house. With a cup of peppermint tea in one hand, she took a seat on the porch swing and tried to relax. Besides the nausea that still plagued her, the muscles in her back and neck were tense. She leaned heavily against the back of the swing and concentrated on the noisy buzz of the cicadas coming from the many trees in her parents' yard.

Hannah had only been sitting a few minutes when a horse and buggy pulled into the yard. Her first impulse was to dash into the house, but curious to see who it was, she stayed. When she saw Fannie Fisher climb down from the buggy, Hannah felt her heart pound. *Oh no! Not her! I can't deal with the questions I'm sure she's likely to ask.*

Hannah jumped up and was about to run into the house when Fannie called, "Stay right there, Hannah! I need to speak to you!"

Feeling like a defenseless fly trapped in the web of a spider, Hannah collapsed onto the swing. She supposed she couldn't avoid Timothy's mother forever, so she might as well get it over with. Maybe after she explained how she felt about things, Hannah wouldn't be bothered by Fannie again.

"Wie geht's?" Fannie asked as she joined Hannah on the porch.

"I'm surprised to see you," Hannah mumbled, avoiding

Fannie's question about how she was doing.

"I've come by several times to see you, but your mamm's always said you weren't up to company."

Hannah didn't say anything—just waited for the barrage of questions she figured was forthcoming.

Fannie shifted from one foot to the other; then without invitation, she took a seat in one of the wicker chairs. "I understand that you're hurting, Hannah. Losing Mindy was a horrible tragedy, and we all miss her."

Just hearing Mindy's name and seeing the look of compassion on Fannie's face made Hannah feel like crying.

"I also understand why you may have felt that you needed to get away from Kentucky for a while," Fannie continued. "But have you considered how much this is hurting Timothy? He's grieving for Mindy, too, you know."

Hannah's jaw clenched. "I'm sure he is, but it doesn't change the fact that it's his fault our little girl is dead."

A pained expression crossed Fannie's face. "Timothy blames himself, too, but all the blame in the world won't bring Mindy back."

"Don't you think I know that? When I discovered Mindy lying on the ground so still, I begged God for a miracle, but He chose not to give me one. Instead, He snatched my only child away when He could have stopped it from happening in the first place." Hannah couldn't keep the bitterness out of her voice, and it was a struggle not to give in to the tears pricking the back of her eyes.

"You know, even with a brand-new screen on a window, someone could still fall through if they ran into it too hard or leaned heavily against it. Screens are only meant to keep bugs out, not prevent people from falling out of windows."

Hannah offered no response. She was sure Mindy had

fallen out the window because the screen was broken, and nothing Fannie could say would change her mind.

"You're right that God could have prevented Mindy's death," Fannie said with tears in her eyes. "He could let us go through life protected from every horrible thing that could hurt us."

"Then why doesn't He?"

"I don't know all of God's ways, but I do know that whenever He allows bad things to happen to His people, He can take those things and use them for good." Fannie slipped her arm around Hannah's shoulder. "But we have to decide to let it work for our good and not allow bitterness and resentment to take over. We can choose to let God help us with the hurts and disappointments we must face."

Hannah's throat felt so clogged, she couldn't speak. What Fannie said, she'd heard before from one of the ministers in their church. But letting go of her hurt wouldn't bring Mindy back, and besides, she didn't think she could do it. Hannah felt the need to hold on to something—even if it was the hurt and bitterness she harbored against Timothy.

As though sensing Hannah's confusion and inability to let go of her pain, Fannie said, "The only way you'll ever rise above your grief is to forgive my son. Bitterness and resentment will hurt you more in the long run, and when you do the right thing, Hannah, God will give you His peace. Won't you please return to Kentucky and try to work things out with Timothy?"

Hannah looked away, tears clouding her vision. "I just can't."

Fannie sat for several minutes; then she finally rose to her feet. "I pray that you'll change your mind about that, for your sake, as well as my son's." She moved toward the porch steps but halted and turned to look at Hannah. "Oh, before I go,

I thought you might like to know that Suzanne had a baby boy last night. They named him Abraham, and I guess they're planning to call him Abe for short."

It took all that Hannah had within her, but she forced herself to say she was glad for Suzanne and Titus. Inside, however, just hearing about Suzanne's baby made her hurt even more. It was one more painful reminder that Hannah no longer had any children to hold and to love.

"We'll be going to Kentucky to see the boppli in a month or so. Maybe you'd like to go along," Fannie said.

Hannah shook her head. A wave of nausea came over her, and she thought she might lose her breakfast. "I don't mean to be rude, but I'm not feeling so well, and I need to lie down." Before Fannie could respond, Hannah jumped up and rushed into the house.

Pembroke, Kentucky

When Timothy arrived home from work that day, the first thing he did was head to the phone shanty to check for messages. He found only one—it was from Mom, and it wasn't good news. She'd spoken to Hannah but couldn't get her to change her mind about coming back to Kentucky.

With a heavy heart, Timothy dialed his folks' number to leave a message in return. He was surprised when Mom answered the phone.

"It's Timothy, Mom. I just listened to your message about seeing Hannah today. Is there anything else you can tell me about your visit with her?" he asked.

"Hannah isn't the same woman you married, Timothy,"

Mom said. "Losing Mindy has changed her. She's bitter and almost like an empty vessel inside. I fear she may never be the same."

"Does she still blame me for Mindy's death?"

"Jah, and she's not willing to return to Kentucky."

Sweat beaded on Timothy's forehead, and he reached up to wipe it away. "She didn't mention divorce, did she?"

"No."

"Well, that's a relief. Maybe it's for the best that she's not with me right now. Seeing her every day and knowing how she feels about me would only add to the guilt I already feel for causing Mindy's death."

"I think maybe Hannah needs more time, Timothy. We're all praying for her, and for you as well. You've got to stop blaming yourself, son, because all the blame in the world won't bring Mindy back, and it's not helping your emotional state, either."

"I know, Mom, but if I could, I'd give my life in exchange for my daughter's."

"That's not an option, and you need to find a way to work through all of this. You need to get on with the business of living."

"How can I do that when my wife hates me and won't come back to our home?"

"I don't think Hannah hates you, Timothy. I just think she's so caught up in her grief that she needs someone to blame. I also believe in the power of prayer, so let's keep praying and believing that someone or something will help Hannah see that her place is with you. I don't think you should try to force her to come back."

"I would never do that, Mom. If Hannah decides to return

to Kentucky, it has to be her decision of her own free will."

Timothy blinked as a trickle of sweat rolled into his eyes. "And I. . .I want more than anything for Hannah to say that she's forgiven me and can love me again."

Chapter 49

There's something I need to tell you," Bonnie said to Allen as they shared breakfast together one Saturday morning in mid-September.

Allen set his cup of coffee down. "You look so somber. I hope it's not bad news."

She shook her head. "It's good news. At least it is to me. I'm hoping you'll think it's good news, too."

He wiggled his eyebrows. "Then tell me now, because I can't stand the suspense."

Smiling and taking in a deep breath, Bonnie said, "I'm pregnant."

Allen stared at her like he couldn't believe what she'd just said. "Are. . .are you sure?" he asked in a near whisper.

"I took a pregnancy test earlier this week, and I saw the doctor yesterday afternoon. It's official, Allen. The baby's due the first week of April."

"How come you waited till now to tell me?" Allen's furrowed brows let Bonnie know he was a bit disappointed. Was it because she hadn't told him sooner, or was he upset about her being pregnant?

"I know we've only been married four months, and I'm sorry if you're disappointed because we didn't expect to start a family so soon, but—"

Allen placed his finger against her lips. "I'm not the least bit disappointed. I'm thrilled to hear such good news. You just took me by surprise, that's all." He smiled widely then leaned over and gave her a kiss. "Wow, I can't wait to tell my folks this news. Mom will be so excited when she hears that she's gonna be a grandma. Have you told your dad yet?"

"No, you're the first one I've told, and I would have given you the news last night, but you fell asleep soon after we ate supper."

"I don't usually conk out like that," Allen said, "but I've been working such long hours lately, and I can't seem to get enough sleep."

She smiled. "I understand. Things have been busier around the B&B recently, too, and it's keeping me and Trisha hopping."

"You should probably slow down now that you're expecting a baby. Maybe you ought to consider hiring someone else to help Trisha so you can take it easy and get plenty of rest."

"I promise I won't overdo it, but I can't sit around doing nothing. It's not in my nature."

He nodded. "Okay. I guess you know what you're capable of doing."

Bonnie finished eating her scrambled eggs then pushed away from the table. "I think I'll call my dad right now. After that, I'm going to share our good news with Trisha."

"Sounds like a plan. While you're calling your dad, I'll use my cell phone and give my folks a call." Allen grinned. "Something tells me that once the baby comes, they'll be making a lot more trips to Kentucky."

Bonnie nodded. "I'll bet Dad comes to visit us more often, too."

—∞—

"You look like you're in a good mood this morning," Trisha said when she found Bonnie humming as she did the breakfast dishes.

Bonnie turned from the sink and smiled. "I sure am. In fact, I'm feeling very blessed and happy."

"Would you like to share some of that happiness with me?"

"That's exactly what I was planning to do." Bonnie motioned to the table. "Let's have a seat, and I'll tell you about it."

Leaning her elbows on the table, Bonnie smiled and said, "Allen and I are going to have a baby. I'm due the first part of April."

Trisha grinned and reached for Bonnie's hand. "Oh, that is good news! I'm so happy for you, Bonnie."

"I appreciate God giving me a second chance at motherhood since I was forced to give up my baby when I was sixteen."

"I know you'll make a good mom. I've seen how patient and kind you are with Samuel's kids. And Allen will make a good daddy, too."

"Yes, I believe he will." Bonnie tapped her fingers along the edge of the table.

"Is there a problem?" Trisha asked.

"Well, no, not for me, but you might not see it that way."

"What is it?"

"When I called Dad to give him the good news, he was very pleased."

"I imagine he would be."

"Well, the thing is. . ." Bonnie paused and moistened her lips. "He said something about quitting his job at the bank and moving here so he can be closer to me and the baby."

"I can understand him wanting to do that."

"How would you feel about it if Dad decides to move?"

Trisha shrugged. "Whatever Ken does is his business."

"I know there has been some tension between you two, and if he moves here, you'll be seeing him fairly often, so I thought—"

"It's not a problem, Bonnie. When your dad came to your wedding in May, things were better between us, so I don't anticipate any issues if he should decide to move here."

"That's a relief. I want having this baby to be a positive experience, and I was a little concerned that you might decide to leave if Dad moves to Kentucky."

Trisha shook her head. "As long as you want me to help at the B&B, I'm here for you."

"I'm glad to hear that, because my business has picked up since you came to work for me. Besides, you and I have become good friends, and I'd miss not having you around."

Trisha smiled. "I'll stay as long as you want me to."

—∾—

Paradise, Pennsylvania

Hannah sat in the rocking chair inside her parents' living room and placed both hands against her stomach. It hadn't taken very long for her to realize that she was definitely pregnant. Due to the morning sickness, Mom had figured it out, too. Hannah was okay with her folks knowing, but she didn't want anyone else to know—especially not anyone from Timothy's family. If they knew she was expecting a baby, they'd tell Timothy. And if he knew, Hannah was sure he would come to Pennsylvania and insist she go back to

Kentucky with him. So Hannah had asked her folks not to tell anyone, and they'd agreed to keep her secret. But Dad had made it clear that he wasn't happy about it. He'd said several times that he thought Hannah's place was with her husband, no matter how she felt about him. "Marriage is for keeps, and divorce is not an option," Dad had said the other night.

Hannah grimaced. She'd never said she was going to get a divorce, but one thing she did know: she couldn't be with Timothy right now.

A tear trickled down her cheek as she thought about the baby she carried. She wasn't ready to be a mother again—wasn't ready to have another baby. She wasn't even sure she could provide for this child and wondered whether Mom and Dad would be willing to help her raise it.

—∞—

Pembroke, Kentucky

"As time goes on, I become more worried about Timothy," Samuel said as he dried the breakfast dishes while Esther washed. "When Hannah left three months ago, Timothy hoped she would change her mind and come back to him, but the longer she's gone, the more depressed he's become. I really don't know how much longer he can go on like this."

Esther nodded. "It's sad to think of him living all alone in that big old house, feeling guilty for causing Mindy's death and longing for Hannah to come home."

"I've tried everything I know to encourage him, but nothing I've said has made any difference." Samuel reached for another plate. "My mamm tried talking to Hannah several weeks ago, but it was all for nothing. Mom told Timothy that Hannah wasn't very cordial and she isn't willing to forgive him or come back to Kentucky."

Esther slowly shook her head. "I've said this before, Samuel, and I'll say it again. All we can do for Timothy is pray for him and offer our love and support. What Hannah decides to do is in God's hands, and we must continue to pray for her, too."

Chapter 50

Paradise, Pennsylvania

Fannie had just entered her daughter's quilt shop when she spotted Phoebe Stoltzfus's mother, Arie, on the other side of the room by the thread and other notions. Fannie and Arie had been close friends when Titus and Phoebe had been courting, but after the couple broke up, the two women saw less of each other. Of late, Fannie hadn't seen much of Arie at all. She figured that was probably because Arie had been busy helping Phoebe plan her wedding, which would take place in a few weeks.

"It's good to see you," Fannie said when Arie joined her at the fabric table. "It's been awhile."

Arie nodded. "I've been really busy helping Phoebe get ready for her wedding, this is the first opportunity I've had to do some shopping that doesn't have anything to do with the wedding."

Fannie smiled. "I know how that can be. When Abby was planning her wedding, I helped as much as I could. Of course, the twins were still little then, so I couldn't do as much as I would have liked. But then, Naomi and Nancy helped Abby a lot, so that took some of the pressure off me."

"Speaking of your twins, I saw Timothy's wife the other day," Arie said.

"Oh, really? Did you pay her a visit?" Fannie was anxious to hear about it, because she wondered if Hannah had been more receptive to Arie than she had to her.

"I saw Hannah coming out of the doctor's office in Lancaster," Arie said.

"Has she been grank?"

"I don't know if she's sick or not. I didn't say anything to Hannah, because as soon as I approached her, she hurried away." Arie's forehead wrinkled. "That young woman, whom I remember as always being so slender, has either put on a lot of weight or else she's pregnant."

Fannie's mouth dropped open. "Are you sure it was Hannah?"

"Of course I'm sure. Her belly was way out here." Arie held her hands several inches away from her stomach.

Fannie frowned. "Hmm. . ."

"Have you seen Hannah lately?" Arie questioned. "Do you know if she's pregnant?"

"I saw her some time ago but not recently. She's been staying with her folks for nearly five months, so I don't see how she could be pregnant. Unless maybe. . ." Fannie set her material aside. "I've got to go. It was nice seeing you, Arie."

"Where are you off to?"

"I'm going to pay a call on Hannah," Fannie said before hurrying toward the door.

—∞—

When Fannie arrived at the Kings' place a short time later, she found Sally on the porch hanging laundry on the line that had been connected by a pulley up to the barn.

"Is Hannah here?" Fannie asked, joining her.

"Jah, but she's not up to visiting with anyone right now," Sally said, barely looking at Fannie.

"She never is. At least not when I or anyone from my family has come by. What's going on, Sally?"

"Nothing. Hannah's just not accepting visitors right now."

"Why not?" Fannie's patience was waning.

"Well, you know how sad Hannah feels about losing Mindy, and she doesn't want anyone bombarding her with a bunch of questions. I thought you understood that she needs to be alone."

"Wanting to be left alone for a few weeks or even a month after losing a loved one might be normal, but this has gone on far too long, and it doesn't make sense."

Sally's eyes narrowed. "What are you saying, Fannie?"

"I'm saying that it isn't normal for a wife to leave her husband the way Hannah did and then stay cooped up in her parents' house and refuse to see anyone but them."

"Everyone grieves differently."

"That may be so, but most people know when they're going through a rough time that they need the love and support of their family and friends. That should include Hannah's husband's family, too, don't you think?"

Sally said nothing. She picked up a wet towel and hung it on the line. Then she bent down to pick up another one.

"Is Hannah expecting a boppli?" Fannie blurted out.

Sally dropped the towel and whirled around to face her. "What made you ask such a question?"

"Someone saw Hannah coming out of the doctor's office in Lancaster the other day, and they said she looked like she was pregnant." Fannie took a step closer to Sally. "Is it true? Is Hannah pregnant?"

Sally lowered her gaze. "Hannah's asked me not to discuss

anything about her with anyone."

Fannie tapped her foot impatiently. "I'm not just anyone, Sally. I'm Hannah's mother-in-law, and if she's carrying my grandchild, I have the right to know."

Sally lifted her gaze, and tears filled her eyes. "I really can't talk about this right now."

Fannie stood several more seconds then hurried away. Even without Sally admitting it, she was quite sure Hannah was expecting a baby. It wasn't right that she was keeping it a secret. Timothy deserved to know, and Fannie planned to call him as soon as she got home.

Chapter 51

If Fannie suspects I'm pregnant and tells Timothy, I don't know what I'll do if he shows up here," Hannah said after her mother told her about Fannie's most recent visit.

"Now, you need to calm down and relax," Mom said, handing Hannah a cup of herbal tea. "Since I didn't admit anything to Fannie, she would only be guessing if she told Timothy you were expecting a boppli."

Hannah got the rocking chair she was sitting in moving harder and grimaced when the baby kicked inside her womb. This baby was a lot more active than Mindy had been when she was carrying her. It seemed like the little one was always kicking. Sometimes it felt as if the baby was kicking with both feet and both hands at the same time. When that happened at bedtime, it was hard for Hannah to find a comfortable position so she could sleep.

"Was that Fannie Fisher's rig I saw pulling out when I came in?" Dad asked, stepping into the living room.

Mom nodded. "She wanted to speak to Hannah, but I wouldn't let her."

"Any idea what she wanted to talk to her about?" he asked.

"Fannie suspects that I'm pregnant," Hannah said. "I. . .I'm afraid she may tell Timothy."

Dad crossed his arms. "That might be the best thing for everyone concerned. I never did think Timothy should be kept in the dark. I've been tempted to tell him myself, but I knew if I did, I'd have you and your mamm to answer to."

"You've got that right," Mom said with a huff. "If Hannah doesn't want Timothy to know, we need to respect her wishes."

"That's kind of hard to do when I think she's wrong." Dad's forehead wrinkled as he narrowed his eyes and looked right at Hannah. "I think you should forgive that husband of yours and go on back to Kentucky."

"I just can't." Hannah placed her hands on her swollen stomach, and even though she knew the next words were ridiculous, she couldn't seem to stop them. "Even if I could forgive him for causing Mindy's death, how could I trust him not to do something that could hurt this boppli, too?"

Pembroke, Kentucky

"How'd things go for you today?" Esther asked when Samuel came in the door around six o'clock.

"Okay. Timothy and I are almost done with the house we've been painting in Herndon. If all goes well, we should be able to start on another house in Trenton by the end of this week." Samuel slipped his arm around Esther's waist. "How was your day?"

"Good. Trisha and Bonnie picked me up, and the three of us went to see Suzanne and the boppli." Esther smiled. "Little Abe is so cute, and I really enjoyed holding him. Even Jared and Penny were taken with the little guy."

Samuel chuckled. "I'll bet those two would like to have a baby brother or sister of their own to play with."

Esther sighed. "Are you disappointed that I haven't gotten pregnant yet?"

" 'Course not," Samuel said with a shake of his head. "We haven't been married half a year yet, so there's plenty of time for you to get pregnant."

"But what if I don't? Maybe I won't be able to have any children."

Samuel gave Esther's arm a tender squeeze. "Try not to worry. It'll happen in God's time, and if it doesn't, then we'll accept it as God's will."

Esther smiled. She appreciated her husband's encouraging words. She was about to tell him that supper was almost ready when she heard several bumps followed by a piercing scream.

Esther and Samuel raced into the hall, where they found Penny lying at the foot of the stairs, red-faced and sobbing. Leon, Marla, and Jared stood nearby, eyes wide and mouths hanging open; they looked scared to death.

Samuel dropped to his knees. "Are you hurt, Penny?" he asked, checking her over real good.

"I. . .I'm okay, Daadi." Penny sniffed and sat up.

"What happened?" Esther asked. "Did you trip on the stairs?"

Penny turned and pointed to a small wooden horse.

Samuel's face flushed. "How many times have I told you kids not to leave your toys on the stairs? Now I hope you see how dangerous that can be!"

The children nodded soberly.

Esther knew Samuel's first wife had died after falling down the stairs, so she could understand why he would be upset, but she thought he was being a little too hard on the children.

"I'm sorry, Samuel," she said. "I should have kept a closer watch to make sure that nothing was left on the stairs."

"It's not about things getting left on the stairs," Samuel said, shaking his head. "The toy horse shouldn't have been there in the first place."

"You're right." Tears welled in Esther's eyes. "I guess I'm not doing a very good job with the kinner these days."

"That's not true," Marla spoke up. "You take real good care of us."

All heads bobbed in agreement, including Samuel's. "Marla's right, Esther. You've done well with the kinner ever since you started taking care of them, but you can't be expected to watch their every move." He gave each of the children a stern look while shaking his finger. "It's your job to watch out for each other, too, and that includes keeping the stairs and other places free of clutter so you'll all be safe." He smiled at Esther. "And I want you to be safe, as well."

"I talked to my dad today," Bonnie told Allen as they sat at the dining-room table, eating supper that evening.

"What's new with him?"

"He'll be moving here next week."

Allen's eyebrows shot up. "Here, at the B&B?"

"Only for a little while—until he finds a place of his own. If it's okay with you, that is."

"Sure, I have no problem with that."

"He got word that he'll be managing one of the banks in Hopkinsville."

"That's all good news." Allen grinned. "Does Trisha know about this?"

Bonnie nodded. "To tell you the truth, I think she was rather pleased."

"Well, who knows? There might be a budding romance ahead for those two."

Her eyebrows arched. "You really think so?"

"Would you be okay with it?"

Bonnie smiled. "Most definitely. I think Dad and Trisha would be perfect for each other."

"Hmm. . .you might be right about that." Allen reached for his glass of water and took a sip. "So tell me about your day. Did you get some rest?"

"I didn't work, if that's what you mean. Trisha and I took Esther over to see Suzanne's baby, and holding little Abe made me even more excited about having our own baby."

Allen grinned. "I'm looking forward to that, too."

Bonnie handed him the bowl of tossed salad. "And how was your day?"

"Busy. I bid two jobs in Hopkinsville and then stopped at the house Samuel and Timothy have been working on this week."

"How's Timothy doing?" she asked, reaching for her glass of water.

"Not very well, I'm afraid. He doesn't look good at all, and he's pushing himself way too hard. He probably believes working long hours will help him not think about Hannah so much." Deep wrinkles formed across Allen's forehead. "If Timothy's not careful, though, he'll work himself to death."

Chapter 52

On Friday afternoon after Timothy got home from work, he fixed himself a sandwich. Then he headed for the barn to feed the horses, muck out their stalls, and replace a broken hinge on one of the stall doors.

Ever since Hannah had left, he'd worked on some unfinished projects—including new screens for all of the windows in the house. His most recent project was the barn. So far, he'd reinforced the hayloft, replaced a couple of beams, and fixed a broken door. Tomorrow, with the help of Samuel, Titus, and Allen, he planned to re-roof the barn. It felt good to keep busy and get some of the projects done that he'd previously kept saying he would do later. It was the only way he could keep from thinking too much about Hannah and the guilt he felt for causing Mindy's death.

It was dark by the time Timothy finished up in the barn, and he was so tired he could barely stay on his feet. He shook the grit and dust from his hair and headed for the house, not caring that he hadn't gone to the phone shanty to check for messages. Stepping onto the porch, he barely noticed the hoot of an owl calling from one of the trees.

When Timothy entered the house, he trudged wearily up

the stairs, holding on to the banister with each step he took. After a quick shower, he headed down the hall toward his room. But as he neared Mindy's bedroom, he halted. Other than the day he'd replaced the screen in her window, he hadn't stepped foot in this room. For some reason, he felt compelled to go in there now.

Timothy opened the door, and a soft light from the moon cast shadows on the wall.

"Oh Mindy girl, I sure do miss you," he murmured. "Wish now I'd spent more time with you when you were still with us. If I could start over again, I'd do things differently." Tears coursed down Timothy's cheeks as a deep sense of regret washed over him. "If I'd just put a screen on your window when your mamm asked me to, you'd be here right now, sleeping peacefully in your bed, and your mamm would not have left me."

Timothy moaned as he flopped onto Mindy's bed and curled up on his side. With his head resting on her pillow, he could smell the lingering sweetness of his precious little girl. After Hannah had left, he'd thought about changing Mindy's sheets but hadn't gotten around to it. Right now he was glad.

Mindy. . .Mindy. . .Mindy. . . Timothy closed his eyes and succumbed to much-needed sleep.

—∞—

"Daadi. . .Daadi. . .I love you, Daadi."

Timothy sat up and looked around. Had someone called his name? The voice he'd heard sounded like Mindy's, but that was impossible—she was dead.

"Daad–i."

Timothy blinked, shocked to see Mindy standing on the other side of her bedroom. Her clothes glowed—illuminating the entire room.

"I…I must be seeing things!" Timothy rubbed his eyes and blinked again. Mindy was still there, moving closer to him. Her golden hair hung loosely across her shoulders, and her cherubic face glowed radiantly.

"I'm sorry, Daadi," she whispered, extending her hand to him.

"Sorry for what, Mindy?"

"I shouldn't have been playin' near the window that day. Don't be sad, Daadi. It's not your fault. You work so hard and just got busy and forgot about the screens."

Timothy drew in a shaky breath, struggling to hold back the tears stinging his eyes. He reached out his hand until his fingers were almost touching hers. Mindy looked like a child, but she sounded so grown-up. "Mindy, my precious little girl. Oh, I've missed you so much."

"Don't cry, Daadi. I'm happy with Jesus, and someday you and Mama will be with us in heaven."

Timothy nearly choked on a sob as he lifted his hand to stroke her soft cheek. Then she was gone, and the room lost its glow.

"Mindy, don't go! Come back! Come back!"

—∞—

Feeling as though he were in a haze, Timothy pried his eyes open and sat up. Sunlight streamed in through the bare window, and he knew it was morning.

Timothy glanced down at himself and realized he must have fallen asleep on Mindy's bed. He sat for several minutes, rubbing his temples and trying to clear the cobwebs from his brain. He'd seen a vision last night. Or was it a dream? Mindy had spoken to him and said he shouldn't blame himself for the accident. She was happy in heaven, as he knew she must be, and that gave him a sense of peace.

Timothy rose to his feet and ambled over to the window. "Thank You, God," he murmured with a feeling of new hope. "I believe You gave me that dream last night so I would stop blaming myself. Now if Hannah would only forgive me, too."

—∞—

Paradise, Pennsylvania

"Mama. I love you, Mama."

"Mindy, is that you?" Hannah sat up in bed with a start, rubbing her eyes in disbelief.

"I'm over here, Mama."

A bright light illuminated the room, and Hannah gasped. Mindy stood by the window, dressed all in white with golden flecks of sunlight glistening in her long hair.

"Mindy! Oh, my precious little girl!" Hannah gulped on a sob, grasping the quilt that still covered her.

"Don't cry, Mama. Don't be sad. I'm happy livin' in heaven with Jesus. Someday you and Daadi will be with us, too."

Hannah couldn't speak around the lump in her throat. All she could do was hold out her hands.

"Don't blame Daadi anymore, Mama. He just got busy and forgot about the screens. Daadi needs you, Mama. Go back to him, please."

Hannah sniffed deeply as tears trickled down her cheeks. She was unable to take her eyes off her precious angel.

"Go soon, Mama. Tell Daadi you love him."

Hannah blinked. Then Mindy was gone.

—∞—

Hannah's eyes snapped open when she heard the clock ticking beside her bed. It was early—not quite five o'clock. She'd had a restless night, trying to turn off her thoughts and find a comfortable position for her sore back. "I had a dream about Mindy," she murmured. The dream had been so real, Hannah wondered if it hadn't been a dream at all. If it was a dream, could it have been God's way of getting her attention—making her realize that she needed to forgive Timothy and return to Kentucky?

Hannah swung her legs over the side of the bed and ambled across the room. Then she lowered herself into the rocking chair near the window. *You must forgive Timothy,* a voice in her head seemed to say. *Mindy wants you to.*

Hannah thought about a Bible verse she'd learned as a child and quoted it out loud: " 'If ye forgive men their trespasses, your heavenly Father will also forgive you,' Matthew 6:14."

A sob tore from Hannah's throat, and in the dimness of the room, she bowed her head and closed her eyes. "I forgive him, Father," she prayed. "Forgive me for feeling such resentment and anger toward my husband all these months."

Hannah opened her eyes and gently touched her stomach. "Timothy and I can be one again. Together we can welcome this miracle into the world," she whispered.

Bracing her hands on the arms of the chair, Hannah stood and gazed out the window, watching the light of dawn as it slowly appeared in the horizon. It was almost December, and mornings were chilly in Pennsylvania this time of the year, but feeling the need for a breath of fresh air, she opened the window. Taking in a few deep breaths, Hannah felt as if a heavy weight had been lifted from her shoulders. "I need to return to Kentucky. I need to go now."

CHAPTER 53

Sally had just starting making breakfast when Hannah came into the room, looking bright-eyed and almost bubbly. It was the first time since her daughter had been home that Sally had seen a genuine smile on her face.

"You look like you're in a good mood this morning," Sally said. "Did you sleep well last night?"

Hannah nodded. "I had a dream, Mom. It was a dream about Mindy."

"Oh? Was it a good dream?"

"Jah, it was a very good dream. Mindy said I shouldn't blame her daed for the accident. She also said she was happy in heaven." Hannah took a seat at the table. "Mindy was right, Mom. My unwillingness to forgive Timothy was wrong."

Mom touched Hannah's shoulder. "Perhaps God gave you that dream so you would realize the importance of forgiveness."

"I need to return to Kentucky," Hannah said. "Timothy needs to know that I've forgiven him. I also want to tell him about the boppli I'm carrying."

Sally was quiet for a few minutes as she processed all of

this. She knew Hannah's place was with her husband, but she would miss her daughter. *I can't say or do anything to prevent her from going,* she told herself. *Timothy wishes to make his home in Kentucky, and even though I'm going to miss her, I know that's where my daughter belongs.*

Sally was about to voice her thoughts when Johnny entered the room. "Is breakfast ready yet?" he asked. "I need to get to the store and open it, 'cause neither of my helpers can come in till ten this morning."

"I think I ought to start working in the store again, and then we can let those two young women go," Sally said. "Once Phoebe gets married, she'll probably want to stay home and start raising a family, anyway."

"You're welcome to work in the store if you want to," Johnny said, "but I thought you liked staying at home."

"I do, but now that Hannah's going back to Kentucky, I'll be alone and will need something meaningful to do."

Johnny's eyebrows shot up. "Hannah's returning to Kentucky?"

"That's right, Dad." Hannah repeated the dream she'd had and told him about the decision she'd made to be reunited with her husband.

"Well all I've got to say is it's about time you saw the light." Johnny shook his head. "I never did think you should have left Timothy, and not telling him about the boppli wasn't right, either."

"Hannah doesn't need any lectures this morning," Sally was quick to say. "What she needs is our love and support."

Johnny bobbed his head and smiled at Sally, obviously happy to hear her say that. "She definitely has my support, and I think I know a way she can head for Kentucky today."

"How's that, Dad?" Hannah asked.

"Abraham Fisher came by my store yesterday, right before

closing time. He mentioned that he'd hired a driver to take him and Fannie to Kentucky to see Titus and Suzanne's baby. He said he'd arranged it without Fannie knowing, and that he was going to surprise her with the news this morning. Guess the plan is for them to leave sometime this afternoon, and they'll get to Titus's place tomorrow." He grinned at Hannah. "I'm sure their driver would have room for one more if you'd like to go along."

Hannah's eyes brightened. "I definitely would! It's like this was meant to be."

"Great! I'll stop by Abraham's place on my way to work and set it all up." Johnny clapped his hands together. "Now I think we'd better have some breakfast so I can get going and you can pack."

—∞—

Pembroke, Kentucky

"This roof is even worse than I thought," Timothy called to Samuel, who stood on the ground below picking up the shingles his brother had already thrown down to him.

Samuel cupped his hands around his mouth and shouted, "When Titus and Allen get here, one of 'em can go up there and help you!"

"Okay, whatever!" Timothy gave a quick wave and continued to almost frantically tear off more of the shingles.

Samuel was still worried about his brother. Timothy had been driving himself too hard. Truth was, he probably shouldn't be working on the barn roof at all today. But the weather had been nicer than usual for this time of year, and Timothy had insisted on getting the roof done before bad weather set in. Samuel had suggested that Timothy rest awhile and let him take over the job of removing shingles, but Timothy wouldn't hear of it. Samuel was afraid if Timothy didn't slow down soon, he'd keel over from exhaustion. Maybe when Allen and Titus showed up, one of them could talk some sense into him.

—∞—

As Hannah rode in Herb Nelson's van, along with Fannie and Abraham, all she could think about was her dream. She'd shared the details of the dream with Fannie and Abraham and thanked them for allowing her to travel to Kentucky with them. Now, as they neared Pembroke, Hannah felt compelled to tell Fannie something she hadn't shared with anyone yet.

"All this time, I've been blaming Timothy for Mindy's accident, but I really think I'm the one to blame," Hannah said.

Fannie's eyes widened. "Wh–what do you mean?"

"When Mindy came into the kitchen that day, she held a dandelion in her little hand that she wanted to give me. But I sent her away—told her to go out of the room and play." Hannah swallowed hard. Just thinking about it made her feel sad. "If I hadn't done that, she wouldn't have gone upstairs to her room, and if I'd kept her in the kitchen with me, she'd still be alive."

Fannie reached across the seat and took Hannah's hand. "It was an accident—perhaps one that could have been avoided—but if it was Mindy's time to go, then she could have died some other way."

Hannah nodded slowly. "One thing I do know is that Mindy's happier in heaven than she ever could be here on earth, and the dream I had gave me a sense of peace about things."

Fannie smiled. "I'm glad, and I'm also pleased that you're going back to Timothy. I know he will be so happy to see you."

"He'll also be glad about the boppli you're expecting, just as we are," Abraham said from the front passenger's seat.

Hannah looked down at her growing stomach. "I'm grateful God's given us another chance to be happy, and I pray that we'll do a good job raising this baby."

"You'll do fine, Hannah," Fannie said. "I just wish we'd known about the boppli sooner."

"I didn't feel like I could tell anyone. I was afraid if Timothy found out, he'd insist that I go back to Kentucky. Until I had that dream about Mindy, I just wasn't ready to go back. Now this van we're riding in can't seem to get me there fast enough."

As they turned onto the road near her house, Hannah leaned toward their driver and said, "Would you mind dropping me off by the mailbox? Then I can walk up to the house and surprise Timothy. I'd like a few minutes alone with him before you all join us," she added, looking at Fannie.

"I have a better idea," Abraham said. "How about if after we drop you off, we head over to Suzanne and Titus's place to see their new boppli? Then in a few hours, we'll go over to your house and surprise Timothy, because he has no idea we're coming."

"That'll be fine," Hannah said with a nod. "After I've greeted Timothy and we spend some time together catching up, I plan to make him something special. It seems like ages ago now, but I've been wanting to bake Timothy a Kentucky chocolate chip pie. We can all have some when you come over later on."

Abraham grinned. "Sounds good to me. Never have been known to turn down a piece of pie. Isn't that right, Fannie?"

"Absolutely!" Fannie reached over the seat and gave his shoulder a pat.

When their driver pulled over by the mailbox a few minutes later, Hannah got out of the van, took her suitcase, and said, "I'll see you in a few hours." Then she turned and headed down the lane with a sense of confidence, letting her hand bounce between the boards on the fence. Her heart picked up speed as the path curved, taking her closer to the house. She could hardly wait to see Timothy.

Just as Hannah stepped into a clearing, she spotted a red-and-blue ambulance with its lights flashing. She tensed. Something terrible must have happened. Clutching her stomach, she let the suitcase drop to the ground. Her breath came hard as she ran the rest of the way. *Please, God, I pray that nothing's happened to Timothy.*

When Hannah got closer to the house, she spotted Samuel, Titus, and Allen near the ambulance. "Wh–what happened?" she panted. "Where's Timothy?"

"Hannah?" Titus looked stunned. "What are you doing here?"

"I'll explain later. Please tell me what's going on. Has someone been hurt? Is. . .is it Timothy?"

Samuel clasped Hannah's shoulders. "Jah. Timothy was working on the barn roof, and he slipped and fell."

Hannah swayed unsteadily, and Titus reached out to give her support. "Oh, dear Lord, no!" she cried, looking toward the sky. "Please, don't take my husband from me now, too!"

Chapter 54

"Would you mind if I skip out on you for an hour or so while I run a few errands?" Bonnie asked Trisha as she finished putting some bread dough into two pans.

"Of course not. I've never minded when you run errands without me," Trisha said.

"Well, since my dad will be arriving sometime later today, I don't want you to worry that I might not make it back before he gets here. He's driving instead of flying this time, so there's no way I can be sure what time he'll arrive. When I spoke to Dad on the phone last night, he said he thought it would probably be later this afternoon, so I'm sure I have plenty of time."

Trisha put the loaves of bread in the oven and closed the door. "If for some reason you're not, I'll show him which of the guest rooms you have reserved for him."

Bonnie smiled. "What would I ever do without you, Trisha?"

"You'd be fine. Just like you were before I showed up at your door last Christmas."

"I was managing okay," Bonnie said, "but things have gone

even smoother since you started working here. I never thought anyone could cook better than Esther, but I think you're a pro."

Trisha's face heated with embarrassment. "I appreciate the compliment, but the only reason I cook as well as I do is because I've had a few more years' experience than Esther. For a young woman in her twenties, she's not only a good cook, but a very capable wife and mother to Samuel's four lively children."

"That's true, and I don't know how she does it all." Bonnie patted her protruding stomach. "When this little one makes his or her appearance, I hope I can be even half as good a mother as Esther is to those kids."

"I'm sure you will be."

Bonnie slipped into her jacket and grabbed her purse. "I'd better get going, or Dad will definitely be here before I get home." She hugged Trisha and hurried out the door.

For the next two hours, Trisha kept busy cleaning the kitchen, mixing cookie dough, and answering the phone. She'd just taken a reservation from a couple who would be staying at the B&B in a few weeks when she heard a car pull into the yard. She figured it must be Bonnie but was surprised when she glanced out the kitchen window and saw Ken getting out of a black SUV. Her heart skipped a beat. Even in his late fifties, he was as handsome as he had been in his teens.

Now stop these silly schoolgirl thoughts, she reprimanded herself. *I'm sure Ken doesn't feel all giddy inside every time he sees me.*

Drawing in a deep breath to compose herself, Trisha wiped her hands on a paper towel and went to answer the door.

"It's good to see you," she said cheerfully when Ken entered the house. "How was your trip?"

"Long and tiring, but at least there were no problems along the way."

"That's good to hear. Bonnie's out running errands at the moment, but I can show you to your room if you'd like to rest awhile," Trisha offered.

He shook his head. "If I lie down, I'll probably conk out and won't wake up till tomorrow morning. Think I'll just sit in the living room and wait for Bonnie to get home. I'm anxious to find out how she's feeling."

"She's doing real well," Trisha said. "Not much morning sickness and not as tired as I figured she'd be."

"That's because she comes from hardy stock," he said with a chuckle.

Trisha laughed, too, and felt herself begin to relax. "Would you like a cup of coffee, Ken?"

"Sure, that'd be great."

"I was just making some cookies when you pulled in," she said. "If I put a batch in the oven now, you can have some of those to go with the coffee."

He smacked his lips. "Sounds good. I'm always up for cookies."

Ken followed Trisha into the kitchen, and after he'd taken a seat at the table, she handed him a cup of coffee.

"Why don't you join me?" he asked. "The cookies can wait a few minutes, can't they?"

"Sure." Trisha was pleased that he wanted her to sit with him. "So when will you be starting your new job?" she asked after she'd poured herself some coffee.

"Monday morning. I'll need to start looking for a house pretty soon, too, because I don't want to take up a room here that Bonnie could be renting to a paying customer."

"I'm sure Bonnie won't mind you staying here for however long it takes to find a place."

"That may be so, but I'm not going to take advantage of

my daughter's good nature."

Trisha smiled. "Oh, I have something I'd like to show you."

"What is it?"

Trisha went to the desk and removed a manila envelope from the bottom drawer. "Bonnie found this in the attic a few days ago. It's full of pictures—some of you and me when we were teenagers." She handed Ken the envelope and sat down across from him.

Ken pulled out the pictures and smiled. "We made a pretty cute couple, didn't we?"

Trisha nodded, looking at the photos again. "We had a lot of fun together back then."

"Have you ever wondered how things would have turned out if you'd married me instead of Dave?" he asked, surprising her.

"Yes, I have," she answered truthfully. "But if you'd married me, you wouldn't have Bonnie for a daughter."

"You're right. We would have had some other child, or maybe we'd have several."

Trisha slowly shook her head. "No, Ken. We wouldn't have any children."

"How do you know?"

"Because I'm not able to have children of my own." Tears welled in Trisha's eyes, blurring her vision. "I wanted to adopt, but Dave wouldn't hear of it. Since I'm an only child, and so was Dave, I don't even have any nieces or nephews to nurture and enjoy. So to help fill the void in my life and because I love kids, I taught the preschool Sunday school class at our church for several years, and I volunteered once a month for nursery duty during worship services."

"Trisha, I'm so sorry," he said sincerely. "I know not having children or being able to adopt must have been hard for you."

She nodded, swallowing around the lump in her throat.

Ken left his chair, and taking the seat beside Trisha, he pulled her into his arms.

His kindness was her undoing, and she dissolved into a puddle of tears.

—∞—

When Bonnie drove into her yard, she was surprised to see Dad's SUV parked alongside the garage. She really hadn't expected him this soon.

After she turned off the engine and gathered up her packages, she quickly headed for the house, anxious to greet him. When she stepped into the kitchen, she halted, surprised to see Dad sitting at the table hugging Trisha. She stood in disbelief, and when she cleared her throat, they both quickly pulled away.

"Sorry," Bonnie apologized. "I didn't mean to startle you." Seeing the tears in Trisha's eyes, she said, "Is everything all right? You look upset, Trisha."

Trisha reached for a napkin and dried her eyes. "It's nothing to worry about. I was just telling your dad about my inability to have children, and I got kind of emotional."

"I. . .I was comforting her." Dad's cheeks were bright red, and Bonnie was sure he was more than a little embarrassed. Could something be happening between Dad and Trisha? Maybe some sparks from their teenage years had been reignited. She hoped it was true, because they both deserved a second chance at happiness.

"Come here and give your old man a hug." Dad stood and held his arms out to Bonnie.

"It's so good to see you," she said after she'd set down her packages and given him a hug. "I didn't expect you so soon, though. How was your trip?"

"I made good time, so I can't complain, and the trip was fine." He gave her stomach a gentle pat. "How's that little grandson of mine doing?"

Bonnie shook her head. "Dad, that's wishful thinking on your part. We don't know if it's a boy or a girl."

"Well you ought to find out. I thought most pregnant women were doing that these days."

"Not me. Allen and I want to be surprised when the baby comes."

Dad grunted. "But if I knew for sure it was a boy, I could start buying things for the little fellow."

"You can decide what to buy after the baby gets here, and it might end up being girl toys and pretty pink dresses."

He nodded. "Guess you're right about that. I'll try to be patient, and I want you to know, I'll be just as happy if the baby's a girl."

Bonnie smiled. Like Dad had ever been patient about anything.

"Why don't you sit down and visit with your dad while I bake some cookies?" Trisha suggested. "I was getting ready to do that when he arrived."

"Thanks. I'm kind of tired, so I think I will take a seat."

Bonnie talked with Dad about his trip until he changed the subject. "So where's that son-in-law of mine?" he asked. "Is Allen working today?"

"Not his usual job, but he is helping Timothy re-roof his barn. Samuel and Titus are supposed to be there helping, too."

Dad smiled. "I've said this before, and I'll say it again: that man of yours is a keeper."

Bonnie nodded vigorously. "You're right about that, and I love him very much."

Just as Trisha took the first batch of cookies from the oven, Allen showed up.

"Look who's here," Bonnie said, motioning to Dad. "He arrived earlier than expected."

Allen smiled and shook Dad's hand. "I'm glad you made it safely." Then he turned to Bonnie and said, "I have some bad news."

"Oh dear. What is it?"

"Timothy fell off the roof of his barn, and he's in the hospital."

Bonnie gasped. "Oh no. Was he hurt badly? Is he going to be okay?"

"I don't know yet. After the ambulance came, I drove Hannah, Titus, and Samuel to the hospital, and then—"

"Hannah was there?"

Allen nodded. "She showed up unexpectedly, and you know what else?"

"What?"

"She's pregnant."

"Wow! Now that is a surprise!" Bonnie hardly knew what to say. She'd never expected Hannah to return to Kentucky, although she had been praying for that. And the fact that Hannah was expecting a baby was an even bigger surprise.

"I can't stay long," Allen said. "Timothy's folks are over at Titus and Suzanne's place, and I need to let them know what's happened. They'll no doubt want a ride to the hospital." He touched Bonnie's arm. "Do you want to go along?"

"Definitely," she said with a nod.

—∞—

Hannah felt as if everyone in the waiting room was staring at her as she paced back and forth in front of the windows.

She was just too nervous and worried to sit still. Before Allen, Bonnie, Fannie, and Abraham got there, she'd explained to Titus and Samuel what made her decide to return to Kentucky. Then when the others arrived, she'd told Bonnie and Allen.

After that, Hannah hadn't said much because all she could think about was Timothy. What could be causing them to take so long in finding out the extent of his injuries? What would she do if Timothy didn't make it? How would she find the strength to go on? She'd exhausted her storehouse of endurance.

"Lord, we need Your help," Hannah whispered tearfully. "Please be with Timothy, and let us hear something soon."

"Why don't you come and sit with us?" Bonnie said, gently touching Hannah's shoulder. "You look worn-out, and you're not doing yourself any good by pacing."

Hannah couldn't deny her fatigue, but just sitting and doing nothing made her feel so helpless. "I wish we'd hear something," she said, fighting tears of frustration. "It's so hard to wait and not know how Timothy is doing. I. . .I'm so afraid he won't make it."

"I understand, but I'm sure you'll hear something soon." Bonnie took hold of Hannah's arm. "You must never give up hope. Just put your trust in the Lord, Hannah."

Trust. It was hard to trust when her future was so uncertain, but Hannah knew that she must. Reluctantly, she allowed Bonnie to lead her to a chair.

"Is it all right if I say a prayer out loud for you and Timothy right now?" Allen asked.

Hannah nodded and bowed her head. She knew they needed all the prayers they could get.

"Heavenly Father," Allen prayed, "we come to You now, asking that You'll be with the doctors and nurses as they examine and care for Timothy. Give them wisdom in knowing what to do for him, and if it be Your will, we ask that Timothy's injuries are not serious. Be with Hannah, and give her a sense of peace as she waits to hear how her husband is doing. We thank You in advance for hearing our prayers. In Jesus' name we ask it, amen."

Hannah had just opened her eyes when a middle-aged man entered the room and walked over to her. "Mrs. Fisher?"

Hannah nodded and swallowed hard. She didn't know if she could stand hearing bad news. *Help me, Lord. Please help me to trust You.*

"I'm Dr. Higgins," he said, offering Hannah a reassuring smile. "I wanted you to know that your husband has suffered a mild concussion. He also has several nasty bruises, a few broken ribs, and a broken arm. But as bad as that might sound, he's not in serious condition and should be able to go home in a day or so."

Hannah breathed a sigh, almost fainting with relief. "Oh, I'm so thankful. Can I please see him now?"

The doctor nodded. "Certainly. Follow me."

Hannah looked at Timothy's family members. "Would you mind if I go in alone and speak to him first?"

"Of course not," Fannie spoke up. "You're his wife, after all."

Hannah smiled and gave Fannie a hug. Then, sending up a prayer of thanks, she followed the doctor down the hall.

When she entered Timothy's room, she found him lying in the hospital bed with his eyes closed. Quietly, she took a seat in the chair beside his bed. It scared Hannah to see her husband all bandaged up and his arm in a cast, but she knew it could have been so much worse. She'd only been sitting there a few seconds when Timothy opened his eyes and turned his head toward her.

"Am I seeing things, or am I dreaming? Is that really you,

Hannah?" he asked, blinking as he gazed at her with disbelief.

Hannah's eyes burned as she thought of how close she'd come to losing him. Jumping up and reaching for his hand, she blinked against the tears that sprang to her eyes. "Yes, Timothy, it's really me—you're not dreaming. The doctor said you're going to be all right, and it's the answer to my prayers."

"But how'd you get here? When did you arrive? Wh–what made you come?"

Hannah explained everything to Timothy, including the dream of Mindy that she'd had.

"That's really strange," he said, "because I had a dream about Mindy, too." Hannah placed her hand gently on Timothy's arm. "I want you to know that I've forgiven you, and I. . .I need to ask your forgiveness, too. It was wrong of me to leave the way I did, and I'm sorry for putting all the blame on you for Mindy's death. I've had a long time to think about things, and I know now that I'm also at fault for what happened to our daughter."

"Wh–what do you mean?"

"I should have been watching her closer that day, and I never should have sent her out of the kitchen because I thought I was too busy and couldn't be bothered."

Tears pooled in Timothy's eyes. "It's okay, Hannah. I forgive you, and I'm grateful that you've found it in your heart to forgive me. Now we both need to forgive ourselves."

She nodded solemnly. "There's. . .uh. . .something else you should know."

"What's that?"

Hannah pulled her coat aside.

Timothy's eyes widened as he stared at her stomach. "You. . .you're expecting a boppli?"

"Jah." She seated herself in the chair again, feeling suddenly quite weary. "It'll be born next spring."

"Oh Hannah, what an unexpected blessing! Even in our grief, God has been so good to us."

"And He was watching out for you today," she said. "Falling off the barn roof could have ended in tragedy. How grateful I am that your injuries aren't life-threatening."

"I'm thankful for that, too, and from now on, whenever I'm working up high, I'll be a lot more careful than I was today."

"I don't know what I would have done if something had happened to you." Hannah leaned close to him, and despite her best efforts, she couldn't hold back the tears.

"I love you, Hannah," Timothy said as he reached out his hand and wiped away the tears trickling down her cheeks. "Oh, how I've prayed for this moment!"

"And I love you," she murmured. "Forever and always."

Epilogue

Six months later

Hannah hummed as she placed one hand on each of her twins' cradles in order to rock the babies to sleep. Little Priscilla Joy was the first to doze off, but Peter John wasn't far behind.

Hannah sighed. God had surely blessed them with these two precious bundles, and she was ever so grateful—not just for the privilege of raising these special babies, but for the opportunity to be Timothy's wife. She loved him so much and knew with assurance that he loved her, too.

Once Hannah was sure the babies were asleep, she stopped rocking their cradles and moved to the living-room window to look out at the beautiful spring day. The birds were singing so loud she could hear them from inside the house. To her, they'd never sounded more beautiful. A multitude of flowers had popped up in the garden, and the grass, which had recently been mowed, was lush and green. Their home looked beautiful. *Yes, our home,* she thought. It had been a long time in coming, but Hannah knew without a doubt that this was where she belonged.

Hannah's gaze went to the field where Timothy had been working all morning. She didn't see any sign of the horses or plow, so she figured he must have stopped to take a break. She glanced toward the kitchen and chuckled. Even the scratches on her new stove made her smile, remembering how it had happened all those months ago. She'd been upset about it at the time. Now Hannah couldn't believe she had let something so trivial bother her. She saw the mishap with the stove as a reminder of how hard her husband and his brothers had worked to turn this house into a real home. It had also become a good conversation topic when friends or family came to visit. The story of how the stove fell halfway through the floor always gave everyone a good laugh.

Hannah's thoughts took her back to the day they'd brought Timothy home from the hospital, two days after he'd fallen from the roof of their barn. Hannah had seen that he was settled comfortably on the sofa and then gone to the kitchen to prepare something for supper. Going into the utility room to get a clean apron, she'd been surprised to discover Mindy's doll on a shelf. When she'd asked Timothy about it, he'd explained that he had found the doll lying on the path leading to the mailbox. Hannah couldn't have been more relieved. After that, she'd taken the doll and tucked it safely away. One day she would give it to Priscilla Joy and let her, as well as Peter John, know all about their sister, Mindy.

Hannah had struggled with discontentment and bitterness when they'd first moved to Kentucky, but now she saw the Bluegrass State for its beauty and peacefulness and was happy to call it her home. She was thankful for English friends like Bonnie, whose baby girl, Cheryl, had been born two weeks before the twins. Things were going well for Trisha, too.

She'd sold her condo in California and was planning to marry Bonnie's dad in June. Hannah had also established a closer bond with Suzanne and Esther. Suzanne's baby, Abe, was growing like a weed, and Esther had told her the other day that she and Samuel were expecting a baby in October. The Fisher family in Christian County, Kentucky, was definitely growing, and Hannah was happy to be part of their clan.

Hannah sighed contently. Everything seemed right with the world.

"Are you wishin' you were outside working in the garden on this nice spring day?"

Hannah smiled at the sound of her husband's deep voice as he came up behind her. "I guess you are taking a break. I didn't think I'd see you until suppertime."

"The horses needed a break more than I did, but I used it as an excuse to come up to the house."

Hannah heard the laughter in Timothy's voice and knew even before she turned around that there must be a smile tugging on his lips. "I'm glad you came in."

"Me, too. I decided while the team rested I'd spend a few minutes with my fraa and bopplin, which is where I'd rather be, anyway."

Hannah gently squeezed his arm. "The babies are sleeping right now, but you're just in time to have a piece of the Kentucky chocolate chip pie I baked this morning."

"Mmm. . .that sounds good." He wiggled his eyebrows playfully. "But aren't you worried that it'll spoil my appetite for supper?"

She shook her head. "Supper won't be ready for a few hours yet. By then, I'm sure you will have worked off that piece of pie and will be good and hungry."

He grinned and nuzzled her cheek with his nose. "You

know me so well, Hannah."

"That's right, I do. I know and love you, Timothy Fisher. And you know what else?" she asked, tipping her head to look up at him.

"What's that?"

"Despite any struggles we may encounter, I know in my heart that we can make it through them because we'll have each other." She stepped into her husband's embrace. "And most importantly, we'll have the Lord."

"That's right," he agreed, brushing his lips across her forehead. "For as we are reminded in Psalm 71, He is our rock and our fortress."

Hannah's Kentucky Chocolate Chip Pie

Ingredients:
1 stick butter or margarine, melted
2 eggs, beaten
1 cup sugar
1 teaspoon vanilla
1 cup chocolate chips
1 cup nuts, chopped
1 (9 inch) unbaked pie shell

Preheat oven to 325 degrees. In small kettle, melt the margarine and set aside. In bowl, beat eggs, sugar, and vanilla. Add chocolate chips and nuts and stir. Add margarine and beat well. Put in unbaked pie shell. Bake for 50 minutes or until done.

About the Author

New York Times bestselling author, Wanda E. Brunstetter became fascinated with the Amish way of life when she first visited her husband's Mennonite relatives living in Pennsylvania. Wanda and her husband, Richard, live in Washington State but take every opportunity to visit Amish settlements throughout the States, where they have several Amish friends. Wanda and her husband have two grown children and six grandchildren. In her spare time, Wanda enjoys photography, ventriloquism, gardening, beachcombing, stamping, and having fun with her family.

To contact Wanda and to learn about her other books, visit Wanda's website at www.wandabrunstetter.com.

Other Books by Wanda E. Brunstetter

KENTUCKY BROTHERS SERIES
The Journey
The Healing
The Struggle

INDIANA COUSINS SERIES
A Cousin's Promise
A Cousin's Prayer
A Cousin's Challenge

BRIDES OF LEHIGH CANAL SERIES
Kelly's Chance
Betsy's Return
Sarah's Choice

DAUGHTERS OF LANCASTER COUNTY SERIES
The Storekeeper's Daughter
The Quilter's Daughter
The Bishop's Daughter

BRIDES OF LANCASTER COUNTY SERIES
A Merry Heart
Looking for a Miracle
Plain and Fancy
The Hope Chest

SISTERS OF HOLMES COUNTY SERIES
A Sister's Secret
A Sister's Test
A Sister's Hope

Brides of Webster County Series

Going Home

On Her Own

Dear to Me

Allison's Journey

Amish White Christmas Pie

Lydia's Charm

The Half-Stitched Amish Quilting Club

Nonfiction

The Simple Life

A Celebration of the Simple Life

Wanda E. Brunstetter's Amish Friends Cookbook

Wanda E. Brunstetter's Amish Friends Cookbook, Vol. 2

Wanda E. Brunstetter's Amish Friends Cookbook: Desserts

Children's Books

Double Trouble Series—Mattie & Mark Miller

The Wisdom of Solomon

Rachel Yoder—Always Trouble Somewhere 8-book Series

A *Lancaster County* SAGA

DON'T MISS A SINGLE BOOK

The Discovery: Part 1 – Goodbye to Yesterday

Instead of experiencing newlywed bliss, Meredith and Luke Stoltzfus are faced with the hardest challenge of their young lives. Financial struggles. Arguments. A confirmed pregnancy. A last-minute trip to South Bend, Indiana. A drug addict on the run. A deadly encounter at a Philadelphia bus station... is only the beginning of the story.

THE STORY OF THE DISCOVERY CONTINUES WITH...

The Discovery: Part 2 – *The Silence of Winter*

The Discovery: Part 3 – *The Hope of Spring*

The Discovery: Part 4 – *The Pieces of Summer*

The Discovery: Part 5 – *A Revelation in Autumn*

The Discovery: Part 6 – *A Vow for Always*

AVAILABLE AT YOUR FAVORITE BOOKSTORE

Go to www.facebook.com/TheDiscoverySaga to learn more!